ABBY

AND THE

OLD GUY

Robert Quinn

ISBN: 9781730913365

*I have been blessed throughout my life
with good health, good fortune and good people.
I am especially thankful
For my wife Barbara
For my sons Rob and Andy
For Mom and Dad
For all the girls who made life interesting
For seven decades of best buddies
For my friends at Bill Gray's Restaurant in
Penfield where I wrote many pages of Abby
For my editor Beth "Huck" Quinn
And for Scottie, Molly, Dooley, Jennie and Nicky
- my baby dogs - for their unwavering
loyalty and devotion.*

– Bob Quinn
October 2018

Part One
Matt

I saw Abigail McKay for the first time in one of my favorite coffee spots, Kitty's Korner at Gibbs and East, on a dismal Monday morning, November 12, 2007. It was the day after Veterans Day, so government offices and schools were closed, but *my* office was open. It was the kind of morning when the only thing better than a good cup of coffee would be to bag the office and go back to bed.

I was sixty-one, a part-time attorney and part-time financial guy—investments, insurance, retirement plans—and not enjoying either profession as much as I used to. But I relished good coffee more than ever. I always have a mug with me: in my Jeep, on my desk at the office and in just about every room in the house. My favorites are my Scottie puppies mug, my blue Yellowstone mug (which looks like one of those old-fashioned tin cups), my Yankees travel mug and the mug with the picture of my son Matt carrying my son Danny—dressed in his tux—stretched horizontal in his arms on the night of Danny's senior prom.

Abigail McKay was standing behind Kitty's counter, in her black and white uniform, looking much brighter and cheerier than the gray Rochester day. I glanced at her name tag and said, "Abigail, I'm Matt, and how is your coffee today?"

She smiled. "Better than the weather. What can I get you?"

"A regular roast, medium decaf."

"Cream and sugar?"

"Just two of the yellow stuff, or pink or blue, whatever you have."

"One seventy-nine plus tax, one ninety-three." There was no one else in line, and Abigail McKay had the kind of deep green eyes and strawberry blond hair that made you want to hang around, so I gave her a five and asked her if everybody called her "Abby." Pretty *lame*, right? But she didn't blow me off; she gave me my change and started talking.

"Mom and Dad and my whole family call me Abby—except for Nannie, my mom's mother, who calls me Abigail Elizabeth because I got my middle name from her. After I graduated from grammar school to Fatima High, all my girlfriends called me Abigail."

It was the same, she said, when she went off to Newton College in Boston, "where *Abigail* is a popular name because of Abigail Adams." The one boyfriend from Boston College who lasted for a few months also called her Abigail, but then he unapologetically left her in her sophomore year for a socialite from Wellesley named Courtney.

"Abigail, I hope you won't hold it against me, but *I* went to Boston College, and *John* Adams is one of my heroes. I'm a regular customer and I have never seen you in here before. How have you come from Newton College to work for Kitty?"

"I'm in graduate school at RIT, and this is my work-study semester. I have a twenty-hour-a-week internship in graphic design at Mangrums but I *have* to make some money on the side, so here I am. I could save the money if I went back home with my parents in Brighton, but at age twenty-six I think I need my own apartment."

"Where do you live?"

"I rent half a house on Meigs Street, near Clinton."

"That's a good spot—close to everywhere. On a nice summer day you could *walk* from home to Kitty's. Speaking of Clinton, I would like to stay here, have more coffee and a cheese Danish and keep talking with you, Abigail, but I have this *office* at Main and Clinton and this new *client* coming in at nine, so I gotta go. What days do you work here?"

"Only Monday and Tuesday. Can you come in *tomorrow*? We open at seven."

"Okay. I'll see you tomorrow. Have a good day . . . and *save* me a Danish."

She laughed as I went out the door.

Snow was starting to fall. I *hate* November snow. November is the worst month of the year. It was a very short drive from Kitty's shop to my office, but time enough for a bushel basket of questions to flash through my brain, questions that would involve very *long* answers: What was so different about Abigail McKay? Was I *actually* thinking that at age sixty-one and widowed for ten years I might find *romance* with Abigail McKay? I had ordered a *thousand* cups of good and bad coffee in a *thousand* coffee shops from a *thousand* uniforms behind a *thousand* counters; and many of the waitresses, young and old,

3

were *just* as pretty as Abigail McKay, and *many* more sensuous. She *did* have her own special aura, though, which was almost indescribable: strawberry blond hair, creamy vanilla skin, playful and musical—which made me think of the mischievous Amy Adams in some of her movies and the luminous Rachel McAdams in some of hers—with a freckle on the left side of her nose that moved when she smiled, which was often, and all with an overlay of honey.

And why did *she* invite *me* back tomorrow? Was she just being polite? What questions did *she* have? Did we have *time* for long answers? Even if the only conclusion was another great cup of coffee, I knew I would be there at seven the next morning.

Tuesday morning was buried in snow. Penfield schools were closed, and so were the city schools. It was the kind of morning where many people *did* bag the office and go back to bed. I had an e-mail telling me that my office was closed, and I had no clients for the day. Would Kitty's Korner be open? What was I *thinking* anyway?

Penfield is an eastern suburb of Rochester, and the seven-mile drive downtown usually takes about fifteen minutes. It took me *thirty-five* minutes on Tuesday morning, and there was almost no traffic; but every street was a big rut, and I was distracted enough that I didn't run my usual number of yellow lights.

Kitty's was open, and Abigail had made it in. At seven-twenty there was only one customer at a table and none in line. Abigail met me with a smile at the counter. "I'm glad you made it in."

"Well, Abigail, as good as Kitty's coffee is, I only drove through the ruts and the slush to keep talking with *you*."

"So you don't 'have this office . . . and this client' this morning?"

"Nope and nope. *You* are the reason I didn't go back to bed."

"Same decaf as yesterday?"

"No, give me the *good* stuff today. How about the Italian roast?"

"You're not going to get *crazy* on me, are you?"

"Nah, I'm half Italian and I need a fix once in a while."

"Kitty said I can sit at a table for a few minutes, as long as there's not a line. So you're half *Italian*? I didn't even get your *name* yesterday—Matt *what*?"

"Flynn. My dad's German-Irish, but my mother, Angie Fiorino, is full Italian. Both of my Italian grandparents came from Sicily around 1900. How about *you*, Irish on both sides?"

"Almost. My dad, Gerald McKay, is one hundred percent Irish, and his mother, Grandma Mary, was a Sullivan; the McKays and Sullivans came from Kilkenny in the late 1800s. But my *mom*, Peggy Dolan, is another story. Her mother, my Nannie, Elizabeth Connor-Jones, is from Swansea in Wales. My Gramps, Patrick Dolan, was an American GI stationed in Wales in the summer of 1944, after D-Day. He went into combat— almost into Germany—a month before the Battle of the Bulge in December. But during his five months of training in Wales, he met a pretty shop clerk named Betsy, my Nannie. Is this too much? Am I boring you?"

"*No, no*! We could talk about this *forever*. My dad might have been in Wales at the same time as your grandfather. But that's another cup of coffee."

"Well, lots of the local girls had American boyfriends. Some girls got married, and some had babies. My Nannie and Gramps just dated, although they dated *every* day. Movies, rainy walks, the USO, fish and chips. And then, when Gramps went off to the front, Nannie wrote him letters *every* day. I have most of them."

"And I have most of the letters between my mom and dad from 1943 to 1945. Do you know what unit your grandfather was in? My dad was in the 99th Infantry Division."

"I don't remember, but there is a bag in Mom and Dad's attic with all of Grandpa's wartime stuff. And I can ask him when I see him. He and Nannie live in Stockbridge, Mass. In the late summer of 1945, when the war was over in Europe, and after we dropped the bombs on Japan, Gramps was shipped back to the states and sent home from Fort Dix. One year on his birthday, when I was at Fatima and pestered him all the time, Gramps told me the story of how he proposed to Nannie.

"'Abigail,' he said, 'I came home in the second week of September, and my mother and father—your Great Grandma and Grandpa Dolan—and my brother Tommy were there to meet me at the train station on Central Avenue. Ma couldn't stop crying. Pa kept slapping me on the back. Tommy carried my duffel bag, and we rode home in his 1942 Chevy. My sister Connie was waiting for us, and so was Dooley, our Scottie dog, and there was hot beef stew on the table. And you know what *else* was waiting? In the two weeks since I'd told your Nannie when I would be getting home, she had mailed *eight* letters to Ma and Pa's. So the next morning, right after breakfast, I took the

Highland streetcar to the county airport and bought a one-way plane ticket to Cardiff, Wales, by way of New York and Dublin. I didn't even tell your Nannie I was coming. I was too scared.

'Two days later, I walked into her mother and father's dry goods store in my Eisenhower jacket with five stripes—Tech. Sgt. Dolan. I caught Betsy's eye behind the cash register, knelt down in the middle of the store, held out a tiny diamond ring and asked her to marry me. She made the loudest noise I *ever* heard her make in her *life*, almost knocked the cash register off the counter, knocked *me* on my behind, knocked my garrison cap out the doorway, knocked the ring on the floor and cried on my chest for what seemed like an hour. Somewhere in there she said Yes! You ask your Nannie if I missed anything,' he said with a grin."

"That's a *beautiful* story. I love all the stories about war brides. I'm a Vietnam veteran, and I know a few guys from my local chapter, and one cousin, who brought brides back from Vietnam. And I'm also in a VFW post—Veterans of Foreign Wars—mostly with World War II vets, and two or three of them brought back brides from England, and one from Italy. And you know the best thing about all those wartime romances? They almost all last forever. All of my Vietnam vet friends are still married to their war brides after *forty* years; and the World War II old-timers who are *still* around are *still* with their British girls—after almost *sixty-five* years! It's a special treat to be able to sit with them over a beer or a cup of coffee at the annual picnic and get them to tell the stories of how they met; and how all the girls wrote and agonized and prayed until the end of the war; and how the deliriously happy GIs and sailors and airmen made their way back to England, and were lucky enough to find their girls leaping into their arms, or even knocking them down on the floor. Usually the old soldiers have tears in their eyes while they tell their stories. Has your grandmother ever told you *her* side of the story?"

"I have asked Nannie many times, and the most she ever told me was, 'Your grandfather has it down pretty well, except for the part about the tiny ring. That was the biggest and most beautiful ring I had ever seen. The band finally wore so thin that it simply fell apart so we put the diamond into the necklace we had made for you when you graduated from Fatima.' You're right, though, about the emotions. Nannie did have tears in her eyes when she told me even that little bit. I'm going to have to have a girl-to-girl conversation with her on my next trip to Stockbridge and coax her into telling me more."

"The only instance I know of personally when a wartime marriage didn't pan out was my late father-in-law, Dave Martin."

"Are you married?"

"No. Not now. My wife Sarah died ten years ago."

"I'm sorry."

"Thanks. Her father was in the Army artillery in North Africa and met a French woman in the USO in Casablanca. She was a black-haired beauty—my wife had one picture of her—he fell madly in love, and she said *yes*. Who *wouldn't* fall in love in Casablanca, right? But it turned out to be a one-sided romance. She wanted to go to America and get a mink coat, and once she made it to New York City with Dave and he bought her the mink coat, she left him for a trumpet player. Dave came back to Rochester, and a year later he met my future mother-in-law, Helen Long. Kitty's waving to you."

"I'll be right back."

Abigail was back in a couple of minutes, with a slight frown that hid her freckle. "Kitty wants to close up. There hasn't been another customer since you came in forty-five minutes ago."

"I could buy another cup of coffee and a doughnut."

"Well, in order to make up for our usual seven o'clock to eight o'clock business, you'd have to buy about *thirty* more cups of coffee and about the same number of doughnuts, bagels, muffins and pieces of coffee cake. Anyhow, Kitty says we can stay as long as we want to keep talking. She'll lock up the front door and flip the *CLOSED* sign, and we just have to lock up the back on our way out. She trusts me and she knows you, so refills and doughnuts are free. You can help me put things away, right?"

"Sure."

And we talked for another hour, over two more cups of Italian roast, while the wind on Gibbs Street whipped the snow almost up to the *CLOSED* sign. We talked about our families: her older brother Jack and younger brother Patrick, and my sons Matt and Danny. We talked about our memories of Boston, her four years at Newton College, and my seven at Boston College and B.C. Law. There were a lot of intersecting lines separated by decades. We were attempting to inhale each other's lives on a single, snowy morning in November. It was impossible, of course, and we both grinned at the same time when we realized how hard we were trying. *Why* were we doing that?

Abigail started cleaning up. "Can you give me a ride to my apartment?"

"Sure. How did you get here this morning?"

"The guy who lives downstairs, who owns the house, works at the Appellate Division library right over there across Gibbs, and he drives me in on days when I don't walk."

"Do you have a car?"

"I do, but I leave it at my mom and dad's most of the time and drive it on weekends. I have everything turned off and buttoned up. Do you want one more hit of Italian before we go?"

"No, I'm *way* revved up. Let's go brave the blizzard in my Jeep."

After we crawled through the empty streets to Meigs, Abigail pointed, "It's the double yellow house, number 647, right next to the old church parking lot. Will you come up for a minute?"

"Sure. Where should I park?"

"The church parking lot is probably the best idea. We have alternate-side parking, and today is *my* side, but with all this snow the plows will be out and cars have to be off the street. Watch your step going up the old wooden steps. This porch is very slippery when it's wet. I have my own door up to the second floor. Don't mind the clutter. My apartment is pretty crowded, so I kind of store stuff on the stairs. I don't have many people visiting. You might be the first person I've asked up since my brother Patrick helped me move in. You can hang your jacket on one of the pegs there in the kitchen. I don't have any coffee—I get my fill at the shop, I guess—but I can make you some tea."

"Okay, that would be nice."

"I have Irish Breakfast or Earl Grey."

"Earl Grey is my favorite."

"Matt, please feel free to take off your boots and put them on the floor grate in the kitchen— especially upside down—and they'll be warm and dry when you're ready to leave. That's one of the features that make these old houses loveable."

"There's a floor register in the kitchen at Mom and Dad's old house in Irondequoit. Every winter day growing up, when my brothers and I came home from school, we would go right to the floor register and wait for the heat to kick on and climb up inside our pant legs. The only thing better on those cold days was when Mom was also making meatballs and spaghetti."

"Do you like lemon in your tea?"

8

"I do, but not just lemon *juice*. You know how I like it? When I was at B.C. I had a girlfriend from Bermuda—*very* British and proper—and her mother sliced her lemons thin and straight across and floated the slices on top of the tea. Then you *smelled* it as much as you tasted it. Ellen and her mother didn't last long, but I still slice my lemons that way. Limes, too."

"Well, here you go. Get it while it's still floating. Why don't you go in the living room and put your feet up. I would like to get out of this starchy uniform and into some relaxing clothes. How long can you stay?"

"I don't have anything scheduled. As full as this morning has already been, it's still only ten-fifteen. Jock and Maggie, my Scottish terriers, will need me by the early afternoon. They will be the *only* ones to have fun in this snow. How about you?"

Abigail came into the living room in a dark green peasant skirt and a very-cozy-looking beige sweatshirt, smiled and said, "This is *much* better. I needed to warm myself up. I have to be at Mangrums on Hawkes Avenue by two o'clock. That's my Tuesday and Thursday schedule, two o'clock to eight o'clock."

"How do you get there and back?"

"My brother Patrick takes me over on the way to his internship at the airport. He wants to be an air traffic controller. And my friend Grace, who is also a Mangrums intern—in their personnel resources program—brings me home on the way to her apartment on Harvard Street. You can *see* that I have it all figured out. I wouldn't be surprised, though, to get a call from Mangrums telling me that they're closing the offices early and sending everybody home. That would be just *peachy* with me; I wouldn't mind an afternoon nap today."

Abigail curled up at the other end of the sofa, in the way that only girls can do, with her arms and legs tucked under both her skirt and her sweatshirt. All you could see were her red socks.

"Matt, I don't want to push my luck, because I don't know . . . well, there's something I need to find out first . . . but I have this overwhelming desire to *know* you. As much as we have talked already, I want to know you *faster*. Does that make sense? I remember when I was still smoking there were times when I wanted a cigarette *so* much it had to be *now*—not tomorrow and not even an *hour* from now. But you can't know a person as fast as you can satisfy a craving. So I have to slow myself down. I'm not a silly sixteen-year-old, and it won't matter anyway unless you want to know *me* just as much. What

9

would your mother and father, or your two sons, say if they were listening to me talking like this?"

"Let's leave Matt and Danny for another cup of coffee or tea, but if *Dad* were watching right now he'd say, 'Why is that girl sitting at *one* end of the davenport'—Dad's 1930s word for sofa— 'and *you* at the other end?' And if *Mom* knew you were twenty-six she would probably be thinking about how cute *I* was when *she* was twenty-six."

"Well, *I* think you're *still* cute, so why don't you come over here on the *davenport*?"

As I slid closer but not quite close enough to touch, I said, "Abigail, you were a *big* surprise yesterday, and you are *still* a surprise today. I keep wanting to ask you what you think is going to happen, or what you *want* to happen. My first instinct is to be careful and pull back. You have probably guessed by now about how *old* I am, and I'm not sure that I want you to bring me back to life. I haven't felt like this—I haven't felt an urge for *any* woman—since my wife died. *Hell*, I don't think I've felt that urge since I *met* my wife. Do you know what I mean by *urge*?"

"Passion, desire?"

"No, not exactly. And it's not romance or lust or love or want either; although it can change into *all* of those things at any time. It's . . . it's like there's no other place I'd rather be than right here, where I can absorb you with all my senses, and that's how I can know *you* faster. But *I* was a smoker too, so my second instinct is to beware of magnifying a craving into an urge—which I have done *way* too many times in my former life—*talked* about it too much, *thought* about it too much and killed the possibility. So my years say *caution*, but my senses say *surprise*. You must have walked along some ocean beaches, right?"

"Sure, many times. New England, New Jersey, Florida. I like New England the best."

"Well, I like the *big* beaches: Gloucester, the Cape, the Jersey Shore, the Carolinas. I haven't been to the Jersey Shore since my wife died, but we used to go three or four times a year. When you walk down the beach when the tide is coming in, the seagulls are lurching through the wind and along the waves, and the sandpipers are scurrying over the sand. When the waves roll in, the sandpipers scurry to higher, dry sand, but as soon as the waves recede, they scurry back down to the wet sand looking for

10

snacks. And while you're watching them play the ebb and flow on the sand, the seagulls all hurtle into the air at the same time, and you have to hang on to your hat. And while you're ducking the crazy gulls and admiring the busy sandpipers, a surprise wave crashes around your knees and soaks you to the crotch. All your senses are surprised. There is no power on earth that can match the impact of sensuous surprise on a man or a woman. It hasn't happened to *me* in more than *twenty* years. Has it happened to *you*?"

"I don't think so; not with any *boyfriend*, for sure, even when we had sex. I don't remember ever getting *lost* in sex: I always knew where I was; I was always in control of my body. Maybe it happened when Patrick almost died in a car accident, and I spent the night alone with him in the emergency room at Rochester General. I actually went to sleep with my head on his shoulder in the hospital bed, and when I woke up in the morning, he was looking at me and stroking my cheek. I cried so hard I couldn't see. After a few weeks he was as good as new, but I have never looked at him the same way since. Is *that* what you mean?"

"Maybe. I think it's different for everybody. It's a blessing when it happens to you, and it *can* be life-changing, but only if you *recognize* it when it comes. Too many people don't."

"How did you recognize *me*?"

"I think it was the freckle," I said, touching the left side of her nose.

"So, what *are* you, old guy, fifty-eight, fifty-nine?" she teased.

"I was sixty-one in July."

"Too old for a surprise like *me*?"

"I don't know; we haven't *tasted* each other yet."

"How do I compare to the seagulls and sandpipers?"

"Well, you're quieter than the seagulls; and you haven't knocked my *hat* off yet; and none of those beach birds have red feet."

"Would you like more tea, old guy?"

"No, Abby, right now I need you to be *close*. I need *me* to be close."

"Matt, will you kiss me?"

"Yes."

"A *real* kiss, like in the movies?"

I stood up and took both her hands. "Come here," and I lifted her off the sofa. I tangled my fingers in her hair behind her ears and kissed her lightly on the lips, tasting her. Abigail took a deep breath. Then I kissed her around her mouth, and the freckle on her nose, and her eyes, which were closed. And I rubbed my face on her cheeks, feeling her, and kissed her ears.

I heard her say, "*My God!*" She had her arms clasped tightly around the middle of my back, as if she were trying to pull herself right through me.

"*Oh, God, Matt!*"

I kissed her forehead tenderly and stirred my nose in her strawberry blond hair all around her ears, smelling her. I was stunned by her *softness*. Abigail's hair and her skin were like a little girl's, like my granddaughter's.

She tilted her face down to my neck, and I heard her whispering breathlessly, "I found out . . . I found out what I needed to know. *My God*, I don't believe it!"

I stroked her hair with both of my hands, and the back of her neck with my fingers; and then I raised her head and pressed her lips to mine in an urgent kiss.

Abigail murmured, "*My God!*" and held me *ferociously*, as if she were afraid to fall.

I caressed her back, through the folds of her sweatshirt, down to the slope of her hips. I felt her breathing so *fast* . . . I couldn't tell if she was gasping or sobbing.

Then Abigail became calmer, with her face against my chest and her arms still squeezing me hard. I held her with my right hand in the hollow of her back and lifted up her chin with my left hand. She had tears covering her face. I kissed her and tasted her tears.

"I had an orgasm," she said. "You gave me an orgasm with just a kiss. That's never happened to me. *Please* don't let go. I don't think I can stand up."

"Abby, you are *so* beautiful."

"With all my boyfriends—not that many, really—one in high school, three in Boston, one at RIT, it seemed as if I always had to try too *hard* for my orgasms. Nobody carried me away in *rapture*, like in the movies. I didn't think it could happen in real life. And now it's happened. When you started kissing me, I was lost. I couldn't think. I could hardly breathe. Matt, I need to lie down. Can I lie down on the sofa? And put my head in your lap?"

Abigail stretched out, with her head in my lap. I stroked and twirled her hair, and she closed her eyes. I thought she might fall asleep, but then she took my hand and said, "Matt, have I gone *way* overboard? I don't know what to do next. Isn't it bad for me to be so honest? Shouldn't I *care* that you're not twenty-something or thirty-something? My mother would undoubtedly tell me to 'slow down, Abigail, be careful and think about the long-term consequences.' That was Mom's favorite word with my brothers and me growing up: *consequences*. But I don't *care* about consequences. I want *you*. I *need* you inside me." She looked up at me, into my eyes, upside down. "When can I have you *inside* me? I know it won't be today. Mangrums hasn't called, and Patrick will be here in about an hour. But *soon*, please? I found out what I needed to know about you, Matt, and I don't want to slow down."

"Abby, beautiful girl, what did you find out about me?"

"I found out that you are gentle, but full of *fire*. That you are not afraid to let your feelings take over. And I found out that *I* am willing to risk everything because my senses tell me that *you* are too."

I touched her freckle again. "Tell me again about your Mangrums and RIT schedule for the rest of the week."

"Today and Thursday at Mangrums, two to eight in the advertising department. Friday is my office day, a regular eight to four in the sales department. My RIT classes are all on Monday and Wednesday: three classes both days—print media, visual marketing and ergonomics—running from eleven to three-thirty. If I keep on liking you, I'm going to have to get my old car out of Mom and Dad's garage. I don't think I'll be able to fit you into Patrick's schedule, and he just might want to protect me from you."

"He just *might*. I would do the same for *my* sister, if I had one. How about if I pick you up at Mangrums tonight? You can bring your books and do your homework at *my* house, and then I'll get you to RIT tomorrow, unless they call it off because of the snow."

"*Homework*? Will *you* be my homework for tonight? I never do any schoolwork on my two Mangrums nights. A glass of wine, maybe a good book, maybe a movie on cable, maybe early to bed, especially in the wintertime. It makes me more tired when it gets dark so *early*. Can we light some candles and curl up together inside a big quilt?"

"Sounds like a famous poem: *A giant quilt, and candlelight,*

13

and thou."

"I know that one. *Omar Khayyam*, right?"

"That's right. Pretty girl, remind me to add to the list of a million things to ask you, what you studied at Newton. But for now, I'll go. *Mmm*, you were right—these boots are toasty. Where do I pick you up?"

"At the biggest door of the biggest building at 1500 Hawkes. I'll be the girl who looks as if she's waiting for her date to the senior prom."

"If I need to call you because of the weather or anything . . ."

"You can call me at 722-1972. That's the intern desk, and I'm not usually very far away. Drive *carefully* in your tough-guy Wrangler."

Then Abigail put one soft hand on each of my cheeks and gave me a laughing kiss for the road.

2

The weather had not improved, so it was slow going out to Penfield. Four-wheel drive doesn't get you there any faster when the cars in front of you *don't* have it. Jock and Maggie were happy to see me, and literally jumping for joy when I asked them if they wanted to "go outside." Those are magic words for my dogs, ranking right up there with "do you want some supper?"

We usually do a twenty-minute walk around my street, which is a half-mile circle. Jock and Maggie want to either jump in or sniff *every* snow pile, especially where there's yellow snow. By the time we get back home, their skirts are heavy with hanging snowballs, which usually have to be pulled off one by one. When it's *really* bad I carry them both into the bathtub, where they can—at their own pace—chew off the snowballs themselves.

It was two o'clock, and it was hard to think about anything except *eight* o'clock, but I forced myself to check my home and office e-mails and phone messages; and I called a couple of clients who had annuity and long-term care applications being processed. I lined up some files for my next trip to the office, which would probably be late Wednesday morning, weather permitting, after I drove Abigail to RIT. *After I drove Abigail to RIT? After I picked up Abigail at the Mangrums office at eight o'clock tonight?* I had to look at myself in the mirror to make sure I was the same guy who left his house yesterday morning and decided to stop at Kitty's for coffee on his way to an early client at the office.

And then I sat with Jock and Maggie on the sofa in the TV room and told them about Abigail.

My wife Sarah and I had two Scotties, Herbie and Lucy, before she died. After Herbie died, I got Jock to be Lucy's friend. When Lucy died a few years ago, I got Maggie to be *Jock's* friend. I have always talked with my dogs—consulted even—all the time when I'm at home, and I work at home now *much* more than in the office. There's almost nothing you can't do at the computer except actually meet with clients.

So I told Jock and Maggie that we were having a special guest tonight. They have a way of cocking their heads to one side and tilting their noses up to make you feel that they are *really* trying to understand what you're saying. They are supposed to be among the brightest of dog breeds. I remember one TV commentator at the annual AKC dog show saying that Scotties were *so* smart that about the only thing that separated them from humans was opposable thumbs. Jock and Maggie were looking at me as if they had *two* questions on their minds: 1) Is Daddy talking about supper? and, 2) Will this Abigail person upset their sleeping arrangements? And then we all took a little nap on the sofa to dream about such things.

At four o'clock I gave the dogs their supper and then walked them around the circle again. It had stopped snowing. I believe my dogs sensed my excitement because they kept biting their leashes and jumping up at me. I was trying to remember the other days in my life when I had been *this* excited with anticipation: my wedding day, for *sure*, in July 1977; the day I flew to Bermuda in July 1968 to spend a week with Ellen, the girl I met in college in Boston; the day I came home from Vietnam in June 1971—the same day my brother Tom graduated from Dominic Savio; the day I flew out to Oshkosh, Wisconsin, to surprise Melissa—Missy—the baby sister of my best Army buddy, Joe Steger, in July 1972. They were all *summer* days. Would *November* make a difference? Ellen, Missy and my wife Sarah—three of the five great loves of my life. Would Abigail be number six? Did I even *want* a number six?

From Catherine, my steady sweetheart from Fatima High School, who did *not* invite me to her senior prom and *broke* my heart; to Bonnie, the country girl I met at the beach in the summer after Dominic Savio; to Ellen, to Missy, to Sarah— forty-four years of hopes, dreams, anticipation and heartache. Did I want to listen to that music, to reach for that brass ring, *again*? The answer, of course, is that life offers nothing more wondrous or sensuous than the love of a woman. At eight o'clock tonight I would most likely be as crazy and excited as I was when I pinned on Catherine's corsage for my Savio senior ball; when I touched Bonnie under her plaid blanket on that hill in August; when I looked into Ellen's *incredible* cobalt blue eyes; when Missy fell asleep on my shoulder in the car; and when I kissed Sarah on the bridge over the Genesee. I may be sixty-one, but I have never outrun the joy of my youth.

Abigail was waiting promptly at eight, outlined by the glittering front doors of Mangrums, with a tan bag on her left shoulder. Her strawberry blond hair fell in a wavy, layered flip and barely spilled over the collar of her dark chocolate wool coat. I couldn't see what she had on under her coat, but she was wearing cream-colored leather gloves and matching high boots.

"You look *delicious*," I said as I opened the navy blue door of my Jeep. "The running board is wet, so be careful in those pretty boots."

Abigail reached her right hand around the back of my neck, kissed me straight on, grinned and said, "*You* look delicious, too," grabbed my shoulder for support and hopped in.

"Abigail, there's some Irish breakfast tea with honey in the travel mug for you."

"Thanks, Matt. You are *so* nice, and I *am* a little cold." She took off her leather gloves, put her hands on top of mine as I shifted gears through the next traffic light, and then rested them on my leg when we got on the expressway. "So tell me, old guy, after an afternoon to talk it over with your two Scotties, do you still want to *play* with me?" She hugged my right arm with both hands, like a body pillow, and rested her face on my shoulder.

"Pretty girl, here I am, a veteran guy, and I am as excited as if this were my high school junior prom. I should have brought you a *corsage*."

"Well," she squeezed with both hands, "that might have given you a better chance of getting to second base." I could almost *feel* her freckle dancing on her nose.

"Abigail, you are loving and dazzling, and there are no words I know to express the thrill of the breathtaking idea that you *want* me. All words fall *way* short. '*It*'—whatever *it* is between us— it has to play out. It could be true love eternal, or a little less than that. It could last *forever*, or it could only last until Christmas, or spring, or summer. That would still be wonderful for *me*. What do *I* have to lose? But *you*, beauty, you who smell so good, what about *you*? You are twenty-six, bright and beautiful, and you should be looking for someone twenty-six, bright and handsome, to spend your life with, to grow with, to have three happy children with."

Abigail still had her head on my shoulder as I pulled into my driveway, and I felt her start to cry as I opened the garage door and drove the Jeep in.

"Abby, why are you *crying*? I didn't mean to say anything to hurt you."

"Matt, it's nothing you said; it's not you." And then we were interrupted by Jock and Maggie rushing to the door to greet their new guest. Jock displayed his excitement and affection by jumping and barking, and Maggie displayed hers by jumping and trying to lick Abigail—who squatted down and hugged and kissed both dogs. "Matt, they're *beautiful*!" she said. "I love them *already*!" But she was still crying. She stood up and touched my cheeks with her fingers.

"Matt, I probably can't have children. I had the mumps when I was eleven, and my mom said . . . listen, Matt, I know we have a *lot* to talk about: my family, your sons, your wife; but not now, okay? I need you inside me first; I want the candles and the quilt tonight. There are *way* too many answers I don't know, and *way* too many questions I haven't thought of yet. But most of them won't matter if you don't want me more in the morning than you do now."

"*Want* you, Abby? I want to touch you and kiss you, all over, and love you, but . . ."

"No '*buts*' tonight, Matt. Maybe tomorrow, but *not* tonight. I know you're concerned about the age thing, but I haven't met any guy *my* age—from my first boyfriend at Fatima—interesting enough either mentally or physically to hold my attention long, even when we had good sex; so I don't want to talk about 'someone twenty-six' tonight. I don't want to talk any more."

While Abigail sat on the landing going upstairs, I turned off the outside lights, hung up our coats, put Maggie in her crate in the kitchen and covered her up, grabbed a bottle of *Chianti* and two wine glasses, and turned off the rest of the downstairs lights. Jock sensed that tonight was different and went to his bed in the living room without protest. Usually he followed me up the stairs. Abigail reached around my waist and tucked her right hand in my belt as we quietly went up to my bedroom.

When we walked into the bedroom, Abigail sat facing the door on the edge of the blue-and-white quilt on the bed, while I put the wine and glasses on the long dresser and lighted two tall bayberry candles.

"Matt, don't pour me a whole glass. I'll just have a sip of yours."

"Okay, I only wanted a few sips myself," I replied as I poured half a glass, and then flopped down behind her on the bed.

"Abby, this is a special quilt that I got out *just* for you."

"Are these supposed to be little clouds in a blue sky?"

"Cartoon clouds in a cartoon sky."

"They look like small kernels of popcorn, all the same size, in neat rows."

"Turn the quilt over, beauty, and you'll see why."

"*Winnie-the-Pooh* and *Piglet* holding hands and walking on a sunny day, with popcorn clouds in a blue sky! It *can't* be you and me."

"No, all the animals in *Pooh* are boys—except Kanga. But it *is* me. I'm not a winter guy; I'm a summer boy: shorts, a T-shirt, bare feet. In the summer, I don't have to be grown up."

We both had our sips of the dark red wine. Abigail turned the slim glass all the way around once in her hands, watching the reflection of the candles in the crystal. Then she set it on the nightstand, took my hands in hers and kissed them.

"Matt, will you undress me?"

"Yes." I knelt by the side of the bed and tugged off her soft vanilla boots and kissed both her feet. She stood up, letting her fingernails play with the hair on top of my head, as I unzipped her creamy wool skirt and slipped it slowly over her hips, with all my fingers spread wide to touch as much as I could, to learn the shape of her. Abigail stepped out of the skirt. Then I slid down her sheer pantyhose, which was like electricity in my finger tips. I wrapped both of my arms around the back of her hips and pressed my cheek against her pale green panties. Abigail shivered. I tightened my arms and inhaled her deep fragrance, and I felt her fingers tremble in my hair.

I stood up and met her wide, glistening, dark green eyes. Abigail leaned her forehead into my left shoulder while I unbuttoned her white blouse and unhooked her bra. I kissed her nipples, which were the color of new pennies. She had many matching freckles falling from her neck to the down-slope of her breasts, all sparkling against her vanilla skin. She flipped the quilt to the side with *Pooh* and *Piglet*, lay with her head on the pillow in the middle of the bed, pulled my hands down to her panties and rocked gently back and forth while I slid them off her hips.

"Come on, Matt, show me the summer boy with the bare feet."

I undressed and lay down at her left side.

"Before I go *crazy*, Matt, just for a minute, just *hold* me, okay?" We measured up well: toe to toe, my arms around her back, hers around mine, our noses and lips together.

"*Abby*, do you *know* what it *is* to touch you and breathe you in!"

"I know what it is for *me*. Tell me how *pretty* I am, Matt. Tell me with your hands and your kisses. Love me the way you would if we were all alone on your surprise seashore."

There was *no* part of Abigail—from the delicate, fuzzy hair on the nape of her neck, to her closed eyelids, to the inside of her elbows, to her pink knees, to the freckles trickling from her navel down her belly to her curly strawberry hair, which was a little more *red* than her wavy flip—that I wouldn't have wanted to touch and kiss for hours. For *me*, it *was* a blanket on an ocean beach with Abigail. The sounds she was making, her murmuring and whispering—all I could make out was, "*Mmm*, Matt, *mmm*"—could have been the surf rushing up and down the sand. Her fingers everywhere—twirling my hair, brushing my gray sideburns, playing on my stomach, tracing my mouth, exploring the inside of my thighs—could have been balmy sea breezes. I was a summer boy again, and Abigail was the promise of a summer mood forever.

She wrapped her legs around my waist, reached down between us, took hold of me and guided me inside her. I felt her exhale into my chest. "Oh, *Matt!*" She tangled her fingers in my hair, pulled my head down to her breasts and started rolling and squeezing with her arms and her legs and her belly. Abigail's murmurs and whispers turned into sharp breaths and exclamations. Her fingers and her lips were all around my face and my chest and my neck. My lips were in her hair and down her cheeks and her arms. My hands caressed her neck, and down to the small of her back, and over her round buttocks to the wondrous top of her thighs.

It had been so long for me that it might just as well have been my *first* time. Every fresh, new, sensuous discovery of Abigail—every touch, every sound, every taste of her—could have been a memory of the most intimate moments of my life. I wanted to pay attention, to listen, to meet the urges of her body without losing my own, but I could *not* do it. Once I was inside Abigail, I did not know . . . I could not feel where *she* left off and *I* began. We were lost together in a single swirl of heat and tears and sweat. I don't even remember that the swirling stopped, or how fast it became almost quiet. Abigail was taking *quick* breaths—maybe sobs—and continuing to hold me tightly with her arms and legs. I was still inside her, and I remember pulling the quilt over the top of us. Several minutes passed, and I felt her breathing slower against my chest.

"Matt, are you sleeping?"

"No, but I'm dreaming of *you*."

"Matt, I don't know how long—five minutes, an hour?—we were making love, but whatever it was, they were the most *wonderful* minutes of my life, maybe even better than the morning I woke up in emergency, and Patrick was okay." Just then, Abigail felt me slipping out of her, and she reached down and touched me. "Matt, he's so *little* and soft now. Remind me to give him some kisses later and thank him for showing a girl a good time. Do you know what happened when you were inside me? I was *outside* of myself, looking down on us making love. I was somewhere above—in the sky, maybe, or on the ceiling—looking down, watching us, listening to us. I wanted to reach down and touch us, but I couldn't. We were so *small* and so far *away*. It was like when you look through a telescope from the fat end to the little end, everything is so far away and tiny. Do you know what I *mean*?"

"That's happened to me before, but not this time. This time, I felt like I was *completely* inside you—not just my penis but my *whole* body. My *mind* too. I disappeared. I didn't know where I was. All I knew was your skin, your hair, your aroma, your tears, your little cries. That's never happened to me before. I've had wonderful sex with a handful of women, and I was always able to tell my excitement and pleasure from theirs—even when we came at the same time. This time, Abby," I stroked her hair back around her ears and kissed her, "this time I didn't feel *my* orgasm, I felt *yours*. I was *lost* in the middle of yours. Do you know what *I* mean?"

"I'm not sure, Matt. I'm so *tired* all of a sudden, I don't want to *think* any more."

"Abby, just let me blow out the candles."

"Matt, I do know *one* thing. You told me with your hands and your kisses that I'm pretty."

"Abby, you're *way* at the top of pretty. You're *so* beautiful!"

"If you think I'm beautiful *now*, Matt, wait'll you see me in the *morning*. I'm going to wake you up early. Tonight you gave me something I've never had before, and I want more."

With that, she curled her right leg over mine, stretched her

21

arm across my stomach and laid her head on my chest. I could feel her falling asleep in less than a minute.

I don't think there can be a better feeling in life than the soft, rhythmic breathing of the woman you love asleep in your arms. I tried to recall everything that had happened in the past two days, but my thoughts were lost in the touch of Abigail's skin on mine, the movements of her fingers in sleep, her warm breath on my chest, and the fragrance of her hair under my chin. I didn't even hear the storm outside. With every breath, Abigail took me deep with her into the night.

3

The trick with dogs in the morning—except for the nights they spend in bed *with* you—is to be *very* quiet, until you are actually ready to get up; *then* get them up, give them their breakfast and take them outside to do their business. They hear a lot better than we do, so if you try to deviate from that sequence and sneak in any other activity, they will literally *hound* you until you get back on *their* schedule.

I woke up first. The digital clock on the nightstand read *7:05*. Abigail was sleeping on her back, with her lips open just a little, her right hand under her pillow, and her left arm on my leg. I got up as gently as I could. I didn't want to wake her. I raised a couple of the shades to bring in the daylight, and "what to my wondering eyes should appear" but a deep blanket of new snow covering my back yard, and a blustery wind whipping up drifts against the windows of my back porch. *We won't be going anywhere soon this morning*, I thought.

And then I lifted back *Pooh* and *Piglet* to look at Abigail in the morning light. It had been a long time, for sure, but I couldn't remember ever seeing *such* beauty that close to me. She was sleeping *very* softly. I could see the rising and falling of her stomach, but I couldn't hear her breathing until I lay back down next to her on the bed, propped on one elbow, and heard a faint whistle between her lips. It was almost like those nights when my granddaughter and grandson stayed over, and I would go in to check on them after they went to bed. I had to get really close to Matthew's bed and Emily's crib to see them moving in sleep and listen to their breathing. It was always a special moment.

It was *just* as special now, watching Abigail. She was absolutely right last night when she said, *"If you think I'm beautiful now, Matt . . . "*

I put my hand on her belly, below her navel, and felt the rhythm of her breathing. In the morning light her creamy skin glowed from her forehead to her feet as if her whole body was illuminated from inside. Abigail's freckles—all tiny and the same

23

color of new pennies—flowed down her chest and arms, to her belly and her fingers, to her thighs and her knees. They were lightly scattered, so they didn't dominate her skin. But they sparkled as if they were *also* glowing from within. They made me think of the glitter that young women spray on their cheeks or hair, shoulders or necklines when they're going out on a date or to a party.

I turned the radio on low to the local news station to listen for closings due to the storm. And then I wondered how long it would take me to touch and kiss all of Abigail's freckles, so I started to find out. After about twenty or thirty, mostly on her arms and her belly, Abigail began to stretch and purr. I stretched with her and put my right arm under her neck; and then she rolled off her pillow, rolled on top of me, and opened her dark green eyes.

"*Mmm*! Good morning, Matt. I *love* you."

"Good morning, beauty. I love you, too." I put my finger on her lips. "*Shh*! If we're quiet, Jock and Maggie will leave us alone for a while." I kissed her, with my fingers playing on her ears, as if it were the only way I could breathe.

"Matt, what time is it?"

"Seven-twenty. We had a big snowstorm overnight. RIT has canceled all classes."

Abigail's eyes lit up as she jumped out of bed to the window.

"*Wow*! Look at that! The snowdrifts are almost covering your back porch windows. And the wind is *wild*! Do you have to *go* anywhere?" she said, with a pretend scowl.

"No, beauty. No clients, no meetings. Just you."

"Matt, can we stay in bed all day?" She jumped back into bed and pulled *Pooh* and *Piglet* over both of us.

"Abigail, I would say . . . until you get hungry . . . *yes*, except . . ."

"Except *what*?"

"Except for Jock and Maggie."

"Okay, we'll take turns making love and playing with Jock and Maggie. But all kidding aside, Matt, I have *never* been this happy in my *life*. Are you sorry about anything that's happened in the last two days?"

"Not a thing, Abby. I know I love you. But I told you, I'm cautious and I *think* about things. If you change your mind about me because you meet someone else, or I get to be too old, I know I will be able to handle it. You are a wonderful gift to

24

me, but I have loved and lost three or four times in my life. I'm more worried about *you*. What if something happens to me, or I fall for a twenty-six-year-old waitress in an Italian restaurant?" I smiled.

"Matt, I know you've been a gentleman. I already told you that—tender *and* gentle. But you're full of fire, too. Don't sell yourself short, or sell my instincts short. These last two days haven't just been a special surprise for *you*, you know. I'm not so *young*, and you're not so *old*, that we can't dream together. I've had boyfriends from age sixteen to thirty-six, from high school to last month, and they all behaved the way they thought I *expected* them to behave. You don't do that. You behave like yourself. I don't get the feeling that you're trying to prove anything to *me* or anybody else."

And then Abigail stretched her body the full length of mine, as if she were trying to touch all of me at once.

"Abby, what do you say we make some coffee, feed the dogs and take them out? Then they will spend the rest of the morning licking the snow off themselves and napping; and you and I will spend the rest of the morning—uninterrupted, I promise—right *here*, touching each other and sleeping and dreaming."

"I didn't bring my walk-the-dogs parka."

"I have a warm jacket with a hood, some thermal sweats and duck boots that will fit you. I think you will look extremely cute in my Cleveland Browns bench warmer."

"Let's go do that coffee and see if Maggie and Jock remember me from last night."

It was not easy to stop touching Abigail and leave the bed, which was now filled with her flavor. When we got downstairs, Jock and Maggie pretty much ignored *me* and went crazy for Abby. They jumped up again and again, trying to lick her face, until she finally gave up and squatted on her knees, hugging one dog with each arm, with her cheeks against their cold noses.

"Matt, they are so *sweet*! Maggie's hair is softer than Jock's, but her tail doesn't stand up like his. They both have so many *colors* in their hair! How old are they?"

"Jock is eight, and Maggie is four. They're brindled. That's why they have all the colors, all the same colors since they were puppies. Jock generally barks more often at more things, and Maggie likes to lick everybody. Here's their food. They get one cup each. You can also fill their water bowls while I get the coffee going. Would you like anything else before we go out?"

"I just want you back in bed, summer boy."

Jock and Maggie never took very long to gobble their food, and then they usually wiped their faces on the living room rug. I hooked their leashes on, and Abigail and I bundled up. She *did* look extremely cute in my Cleveland Browns jacket. I put some "puppy cookies" in *my* jacket pocket—to reward Jock and Maggie for doing their business—and we all ventured out into the winter. There was about eighteen inches of fresh snow in the driveway, and the icy wind was whipping up drifts twice as high all over the yard and down the street.

Jock and Maggie were in their glory, leaping like deer from one drift to the next and poking their noses down into the snow all along the street in search of mythical squirrels or chipmunks, or places other dogs had marked earlier in the morning. Abigail was like a little kid watching the dogs frolic. She started making snowballs for them to try to catch and bite. And to throw at me when she thought I wasn't looking. It was like a high school date. We would have flopped on our backs and made snow angels, but the doggies were bounding ahead up to their ears, and the blowing snow might have covered us over in thirty seconds, anyway.

I live on a circle, and it's about half a mile around. By the time we plodded all the way back to the house, Jock and Maggie were completely white, and our footprints down the driveway had vanished. We got a couple of big towels and dried off the dogs—in between their repeated efforts to shake all the snow off themselves—and pulled most of the snowballs from their skirts. The rest would be resolved by licking and drip-drying. Abigail hung up our wet snow outfits on the enclosed back porch while I poured two mugs of fresh coffee.

"What do you like in your coffee?" I yelled.

"Just the yellow stuff, or pink or blue, whatever you have." I could hear the smile in her voice as she came up the steps from the porch to the kitchen and grabbed her coffee. As we walked upstairs, Abby put her free hand in my back pocket and said, "Matt, this time I want to undress *you*."

In the bedroom I sipped my coffee. "*Mmm*, that's good! Where do you want to start, beauty?"

"Let's start at the top, old guy," and she slipped my sweatshirt and T-shirt over my head. "The hair on your tummy is very soft," she said as she brushed it with her fingers. "And I don't see any gray—just blond and brown. Are you *sure* you're not forty-something?" she teased.

"I'm not sure of *anything* after last night."

Abigail pulled my jeans and long johns down and walked around me.

"You have nice legs, you know . . . and a *great* butt."

"Abby, isn't that what *I'm* supposed to say about *you*?"

"I think you're supposed to say *ass*—I have a nice ass."

"How about *tail*? Did you ever read *Lady Chatterley's Lover* by D.H. Lawrence?"

"No, but I read *Women in Love*."

"They're all terrific. D.H. Lawrence was my favorite in college. Remind me later to tell you a funny story about that. Anyway, Connie Chatterley's lover, the gamekeeper Mellors, tells her fondly while he's caressing her fanny—just like this— that she has a *nice tail*."

"I can go with *tail*. I can go with whatever you say, Matt, as long as you keep touching me like that. Come here," she whispered as she pulled me into bed.

Abigail was soft all over me—her fingers, her hair, her lips, her thighs. She moved up and down my body, while the white and windy light from outside flashed over her creamy skin. Once I was inside her again all sounds stopped. Her fragrance, lilies-of-the-valley, the taste of her, the feel of her skin everywhere and the vision in my mind—though my eyes were closed and buried in her hair falling over her ears—of all the colors of Abigail . . . it was all so vivid and sensuous— except there was no sound. No thoughts. No time. We fell asleep tightly wrapped together.

When I began to wake up, slowly, I didn't know whether I was waking from a dream or into one. A soft and beautiful woman was wrapped in my arms, breathing on my chest, and my face was in her hair, tasting her. Her name wouldn't even come to me at first. The winter sounds were there again: the west wind blowing the snow against the windows, and the empty black branches whipping across the roof and the siding. But wasn't it a hot summer day just a few minutes ago? I was walking with a beautiful girl up Mom and Dad's driveway to their front porch. Dad opened the screen door. They had the radio on, listening to the Yankee game. My father was holding a can of Bud, and Mom was sipping a Tom Collins.

"Where have you been, stranger?" Mom said. "You haven't called all week!"

27

"Sorry, Mom. Matt and Claire were out of town for two days so I had Matthew and Emily. It made for a crowded week."

"Good to see you, son!" Dad said.

"Mom, Dad, I'd like you to meet"—and then her name came to me—"Abigail McKay."

"Hi, Mr. Flynn, Mrs. Flynn. It's very nice to meet you both."

"Matt, call me Matt," Dad said. "Sit down and join us."

We both sat on the glider at the end of the porch.

"Would you kids like something to drink?" Mom asked.

I stood up, with my hand on Abigail's shoulder. "What would you like, miss?"

"Pop? I'll have half of whatever you have." She smiled.

"I'll come with you," Mom said. "I need more ice, and your father will have another beer."

"Abby, don't believe half of what my dad tells you."

In the kitchen, Mom looked up at me and smiled.

"Matt, Abigail is adorable! Where did you meet her?"

"In a coffee shop downtown where I stop on my way into the office in the morning. She works part-time as a waitress while she's getting her masters degree at RIT."

"She's very pretty, but isn't she a little young for you? You have two grandchildren."

"She doesn't think so. I don't know yet, Mom."

4

The sounds of the snowstorm brought me back to the bedroom. That was a very unusual dream for me. In the twenty-five years since my mother had almost died from a stroke, I had not dreamed about her more than three or four times. And she was very *old* in those dreams. In this dream on the porch, both Mom and Dad looked as if they were in their late forties, when I was in college. Was it possible for *this* dream girl lying beside me in bed to change the time line of my life? The more I thought about it the more I realized that I wasn't puzzled as much as I was peaceful. Abigail had brought peace back into my world.

My life had been okay since Sarah died. My sons and their wives were doing pretty well. My two young grandchildren were beautiful, healthy and smart, and—just as important—they lived only five minutes away. I had many good friends from high school, college, the Army, law school and all my years in Rochester. I took good care of my financial clients, and most of them were now retiring with enough money to live comfortably. I occasionally dated interesting women. I enjoyed traveling to visit friends and family around the country. I liked my home, which was in good shape, and I loved Jock and Maggie, my devoted and constant companions. On many days I talked to Jock and Maggie more than to *any* humans in my world, and they often made more sense.

But Sarah had been my center. Sarah was where I found peace. The rest of my life was usually centrifugal, but Sarah held it together. She gave it balance, rhythm and perspective. She kept me from collision courses and brought me back home, again and again. In the ten years after she died, I lived from cliche to cliche: *I coped, I did the best I could, I kept a lot of balls in the air, I dealt with things, I hung in there, I compensated.* But what I really did was *spin.* I spun around people, I spun around problems, I spun through years. I was good at it. I was a good father, grandfather and friend. I don't think anybody knew how much I missed my center. Most of my nights were restless and full of thoughts. Sleep was elusive. My mornings were not optimistic, even though Jock and Maggie (and Lucy before them) were full of cheer every day. I went through the motions at the office. I did what I needed to do. Like I said, a life of cliches. I learned to live *without* peace. I stopped looking for it in other people, other women. I figured Sarah was it, and that I already had been blessed with more peace than most people ever have.

So it was incredible to me to fall asleep, not once, but *twice* in half a day, with Abigail in my arms and *no* thoughts in my head. And to sleep like a *two*-year-old, to hug and nuzzle this girl the way my grandson hugs and nuzzles his blue blanket. And to wake up with *no* thoughts beyond the warmth of her skin, the smell of her hair and the peace of her breathing.

The digital clock read *10:30*. I needed to get back to her freckles, where I left off below her bellybutton. With each kiss, I took a deep breath and ran my hands down the outside of her hips. Abigail started to stretch and murmur. I kissed her between her legs, on the inside of her thighs, all around her curly hair. Now both of her hands were on the top of my head, with her fingernails pressing into my scalp. All she whispered was, "*Oh . . . Matt!*" softer and faster. I buried my face between her legs. My hands were touching that magical fold where the back of her thighs met the curve of her "tail." Abigail pressed deeper with her nails. And then my tongue was inside her.

Abigail *gasped*, and her whole body stiffened. "*Oh . . . Matt*, nobody's ever done that before!"

"I'm sorry, Abby, sorry you had to wait so long, but don't think about it. Your body will go with it. Just let yourself go." I caressed her again inside. I reached her warm and deep center. I felt her womb squeeze and let go, squeeze and let go. Abigail's fingers pressed harder into my scalp. Her little cries became fervent, craving and breathless. Her thighs pushed into my cheeks, and her heels dug into the small of my back, as she rolled her hips left and right. My hands moved over her belly to touch her breasts and touch her lips. And then Abigail crashed. She let go, with a *huge* sigh. Her arms and legs fell away from me. Her cries stopped. My head was still between her legs, and I could feel the even rise and fall of her belly. My beauty, my dream girl, was *very* deep in sleep.

I sat up and looked at Abigail. I remembered again what she said last night: "*If you think I'm beautiful now, Matt . . .*" I laid the palms of my hands between her breasts so that I could feel her heart beating. I listened to the whispers of her breath between her parted lips. I watched the rapid movement of her eyes under her eyelids. I brushed her strawberry blonde hair off her forehead and tucked it around her ears. Abigail was *perfect*. I closed my eyes and said a short prayer thanking God for bringing this *unimaginable* girl into my life. And then I laid my cheek on her belly, curled up on my right side, wrapped both of my arms around her left thigh, and fell asleep.

When I woke up, neither Abigail nor I had moved an inch. I couldn't see a thing outside because the windows were covered with snow. I thanked God again for snowing us in. The evening we had, and the morning we had, and the day we were still having—they all would have strained credibility even in a novel or a movie. I heard Jock and Maggie whining downstairs and looked at the clock: it read *1:15*. I had been sleeping for more than two hours; Abigail was *still* sleeping. I needed to take the dogs out. I found a Post-it note in the drawer of the night stand and wrote: "I love you, beauty. I'll be right back. I have to take the dogs out." I put the note gently below her navel, covered her with *Pooh* and *Piglet* and went downstairs to bundle up.

The snow had stopped, but not the driving wind; the drifts were twice as high as they were at eight o'clock. My driveway had been plowed, which amazed me because I never heard the guy come. Ed always made a lot of noise scraping the snow down to the foot of the driveway and piling it up. *That* was how soundly I had been sleeping with Abigail. The town plows had done the circle, so both sides of the road were flanked by four-foot banks. It wasn't easy for Jock and Maggie to do their business, so this was a quick, "number-one" run. The dogs don't like the wind, and the banks kept them from playing in the snow, so they were just as pleased as I to be back in the house. I spread their blankets out on the living room floor and put biscuits covered with peanut butter inside each of their favorite rubber chew-toys—their Kongs—to keep them busy for a good while. Then I brought two cups of hot coffee upstairs.

I found Abigail standing in the front bedroom, which doubled as my office, wrapped in *Pooh* and *Piglet*, looking out the window at the driveway and the street. "I saw you come back down the street with Maggie and Jock. Not much of a day for a summer boy, huh?"

"Abby, this is the most beautiful snow I've ever seen because it's keeping you here with me."

"I got your sweet note. It's a very funny thing: As soon as you weren't there touching me in bed I woke up. Otherwise, I think I might have slept forever next to you. Let's go back to bed."

"I brought you some coffee."

"Thank you."

"Is there anybody you need to call? Will anybody be worried about you?"

"I'll call Patrick tonight. Mom and Dad don't call me every day, and I don't usually answer the phone when I'm home. They probably know that RIT is closed and they'll just figure I'm sleeping in or studying. I can call them tomorrow."

We sat in the middle of the bed, wrapped together in the flip side of the quilt—the popcorn clouds in a royal blue sky—sipping our coffee. Abigail touched my face and kissed me on the cheek. "Matt, what you did this morning . . . it wasn't just an orgasm. It was wave after wave of them—an ocean of orgasms—washing over me and rolling through my whole body. When you started, I tried to not think about it, and let myself go—just like you said; but then my mind was empty, and my body far away from me, rising and falling in the waves without me. And then I completely crashed. How long was I out?"

"About two hours."

"*Wow*. How did you feel . . . I mean, while I was being swept away?" She touched my lips with her fingers.

"Abby, this may sound strange, but believe me, it's true: I was so caught up in the rhythm of your body . . . the power of the woman in you . . . your wild cries . . . that my only sensations, my only pleasures, were yours. This has only happened to me a couple of times before, and my feeling was the same: *awe*. People use the word *awesome* too much and don't know what it really means, but I do. I am in awe of your physical and emotional power as a woman. I don't think men can ever get to that level of sensuality. *I* never have. I'm sure many women never do either. But *you*, beauty, you did this morning, and it was wonderful and *awesome* to be in your body and in your senses with you. Nothing could ever be better than that. Do I sound crazy?"

"You sound like a poet who loves me, Matt. Can you sweep me away like that again? Will it be the same as this morning?"

"I don't know. This morning I took you by surprise. Next

time, there won't be surprise, but anticipation can be even more exciting than surprise. I hope it will be better *every* time." I took a sip of coffee and grinned. "Which side of this fancy quilt do you like the most?"

"I like 'the most' being inside both sides with you. Why aren't there any girls in *Winnie-the-Pooh*? Are you hungry? I'm hungry. I would *love* a cheeseburger and fries."

"A lot of places will be closed because of the weather, but Phil Green's might be open. Our Penfield Phil Green's is only three minutes away. Do you like Phil Green's?"

"I *love* Phil Green's, and they have hot chocolate too. Can we go right now, Matt?"

"Let me just change out of this quilt, beauty, and I'll start the Jeep." We kissed one more time among the popcorn clouds and then headed downstairs to put our dog-walking outfits back on.

Phil Green's was open, though the parking lot was almost empty. Todd, the assistant manager, was at the counter. "Hey, Matt, *hooray* for making it in here! Who is your *very* pretty friend?"

"Abigail, meet Todd. Watch out: Todd thinks he's the best-looking guy at Phil Green's and he hits on *all* the prettiest customers. What would you like on your cheeseburger, beauty?"

"Mustard, lettuce and tomato. I usually get onions too, but not today." She smiled. "And a hot chocolate and regular fries, please."

"So, Todd, we'll have two cheeseburgers, mine plain on a whole wheat roll with a side of mayo, one order of fries and two hot chocolates."

Todd repeated our order back to us. "That will be $12.96, including tax; hot chocolates are on the house," and he handed our buzzer to Abigail with a flourish. We picked out a booth away from the cold doorway; and while we were waiting for our buzzer to light up and vibrate, I kidded with Abby, "You know, beauty, I've been taking girls to Phil Green's after dates ever since high school—right up until Sarah died. You might be number one hundred."

"Well, old guy, I'll bet you didn't bring any of the other ninety-nine here after making love three times in half a day by candlelight in a blizzard."

"You're right about that. I was pretty much scared to death

of touching a girl in high school; and Dominic Savio was all boys then, which didn't help to speed up my development. How about you, miss? I think you said you had one serious boyfriend when you were at Fatima. Where did he go to school?"

"Cardinal O'Haran. Lots of Fatima girls dated O'Haran guys. They had joint mixers once or twice a year. Jeff and I met at a spring mixer at Fatima when we were sophomores, and we dated steadily for the next two years. He was handsome, the star of the basketball team and a nice guy, but he was always more interested in the way I looked than in what I had to say. He asked me to both his junior prom and senior ball at O'Haran, and I invited him to both of mine at Fatima. Jeff won scholarships to B.C. *and* Georgetown; but when I chose *Newton* right after Christmas and he chose *Georgetown*, I should have known that he didn't feel I was the love of his life. We kept in touch by e-mail for about a month after we left for college, but then his e-mails stopped, and Jeff didn't call me when he came home for Thanksgiving or Christmas. I never saw him again, but I didn't miss him either. *Hey*, there's our buzzer!"

After lunch, Abigail and I shared vanilla ice cream and lime sherbet, over several more cups of hot chocolate. We sat on the same side of the booth; it was impossible not to keep touching her.

"Matt, how many refills of hot chocolate can we *have* before they shut us off and kick us out?"

"Abigail, I am a very loyal customer, and my guess is that Mr. Phil Green would let me drink hot chocolate until I turned brown."

"Matt, what do we do now?"

"I say we go home, make love and take a nap. When we wake up, we feed the dogs, make love and think about what we want for dinner. After dinner, we walk Jock and Maggie, make love and fall asleep watching one of my favorite movies. That's a good plan, right?"

"Best plan I ever heard . . . for a Wednesday. But seriously, Matt, what about *tomorrow*? What about Friday and the next day and . . . you know what I mean." She faked a scowl.

I reached my arm around her neck, nibbled on her ear and whispered, "I know what you mean, Abby. Jock and Maggie asked me to tell you that they want you to stay. Will you stay with us?"

"Matt, I love you, and Maggie and Jock too, but are you sure you want me to move in after we've only known each other for *three* days?"

"Well, beauty, I could wait until tomorrow to ask you, and then it would be *four* days." I smiled and sipped my hot chocolate.

"Of course I want to be with you! How could I give up a handsome summer boy who loves hot chocolate and Scottie dogs, and can carry me away into ecstasy three times in *half* a day? But it's going to get messy, isn't it, Matt? Real life, I mean? Not the simple stuff like my old car and my apartment, and RIT and Mangrums; but Mom and Dad and my brothers; and *your* mom and dad and your sons. How hard is it going to be?"

"Well, I have a two-car garage and a basement for your apartment stuff," I teased. "What kind of car do you have, anyway?"

"Mom and Dad's 1998 Taurus, but stop *teasing* me, Matt. I haven't thought this far ahead yet. I meant to when I woke up this morning, but then you were kissing my belly, and all my thoughts ran away, and here we are. There's so *much* we still don't know about each other. Can we ever catch up? What do you think your sons are going to say? When do we tell our families? *What* do we tell our families?"

"Abigail, we don't have to catch up. We *can't ever* do that—not the way you want. We can't spend the past five years together. We shouldn't even *try* to catch up. Sure, there are ten million things we don't know about each other, but most of them are not so important compared to what we already *do* know. Not important enough for me to start an Abigail checklist, or turn your life into a connect-the-dots challenge. I'll be happy to discover something new about you every day."

"Yes, Matt." Her eyes were laughing.

"Yes? Yes, what?"

"Yes, I want to move in with you and Maggie and Jock. Is today too soon?"

"Today is perfect. We can bring your apartment stuff over one Jeep-ful at a time—whenever you need it."

"I'll get my car from Mom and Dad's on Saturday. I'll tell Patrick that I will get a ride from friends tomorrow and Friday. What are we going to tell everybody? *When* are we going to tell everybody? Thanksgiving is next week. What are they going to say?"

"Abigail, we don't need to force anything or push anything. We don't want to do that. Let the days and the family come naturally. I don't know your family yet, so I don't have any idea what they're going to think or say. With Matt and Danny, when I tell them I have a woman friend I want them to meet, they will be happy for me. They think about their mother every day, and we talk about her all the time, but they have both been telling me for years that I should find someone new—that it will be okay with them. What happens when they meet you and find out you're about the same age as they are—*that* I don't know. My guess is they will be even happier for me and welcome you with open arms. They're *my* sons, after all; how could they *not* like you? Mom and Dad will love you; no doubt there. What about *your* mom and dad and your brothers?"

"I don't know. Mom and Dad will like you for sure. Under normal circumstances, you all would hit it off famously. But these are not normal circumstances, huh? Whether they like you *for me* is another story. My older brother Jack and I have never been really close, and he is usually all business, so I have trouble reading him. He might be suspicious and think that you're just taking me for a ride." Here Abigail poked me playfully with her elbow. "You would never do that to a trusting girl like me, right?"

"Beauty," I whispered, "Jeep and I will only take you for rides to places you want to go."

"My kid brother Pat will see right away that you're cool—because *he* is—and that you make me happy, and that will be all he needs to know."

"What does your family do for Thanksgiving?"

"We all go to Mom and Dad's: Patrick and his girlfriend Laurie, and Jack and his wife Catherine and their daughter Betsy—usually in the middle of the afternoon, with dinner around five o'clock. How about your family?"

"Since Sarah died I've been going almost every year to Tommy and Diane's—my youngest brother and his wife—in Webster. I pick up Mom and Dad, who still live in our old house in Irondequoit. My middle brother Alan and his wife Lisa live in North Carolina, so I don't see them much."

"So you're the oldest brother?"

"Yep, three boys, no girls. I always missed not having a sister. It would have helped me learn about girls a *lot* faster—and better. *My* two boys—who are also deprived of a sister—are usually not in town for Thanksgiving. My younger son Danny, who is a doctor, lives in Boston with his wife Emma. She's from Long Island, so that's where they usually go for Thanksgiving. My older son Matt and his wife Claire and my two grandchildren live right here in Penfield—thank God-- but they go to Claire's family home in Saratoga for Thanksgiving. At Christmas everybody will be here. I think I would like you to meet Matt and Claire and the kids before they leave for Saratoga next Wednesday. Does that sound okay?"

"*Sure*, I would like that. What about your son Danny? Do we have to wait until Christmas to surprise him and his wife?"

"Well, Danny and I call each other every couple of days, so the next time, I'm gonna tell him that I got a *girlfriend*," I said with a big grin. "You can talk with him, too. But maybe we can fit in a weekend drive to Boston after Thanksgiving."

"Yeah, getting back to Thanksgiving, Matt, will you come to Mom and Dad's?"

"Am I *invited*?"

"Here I am whispering your invitation in your ear."

"*Mmm* . . . Abigail, I'll be wherever *you* are. But would you like to take me by to meet your mom and dad *before* Thanksgiving? Just to cut down on the shock a little, and have a chance for a quiet conversation without the crowd and the buzz at Thanksgiving?"

"Good plan. Can we do dinner on Saturday, and then I'll tell Mom and Dad that I got a *boyfriend* I'm bringing over for dessert?" she said with a grin.

"Dinner and dessert it is. Speaking of which, it's almost three-thirty. Would you like to go to your apartment right now and pick up some things? Then we won't be too late getting home and giving the doggies their supper. They're smart dogs, and this time of year when it gets so dark so early, they start looking for their supper sooner."

"Okay. I can get my school stuff . . . my cosmetics . . . clothes for tomorrow and Friday . . . and my favorite pillow. Matt, you said '*getting home.*' Do I really have a new home? I've never had a home except Mom and Dad's."

"Complete with wine, candles, a fancy quilt and two loving doggies."

"And *you*, Matt . . . my summer boy that I've known for all of *three* days. Tomorrow is another two-to-eight day at Mangrums. You'll be able to take me and pick me up, right?"

"Right. In the morning, weather permitting, I have a breakfast meeting with a client at Joe's Diner on University; and then I'll stop in to the office to submit some paperwork, make a few copies and pick up my mail. You won't mind being home for a couple of hours by yourself with the dogs, will you?"

"*Mind*? Are you *kidding*? Being home with the dogs . . . what a wonderful thought. No, Matt, I usually do course work on Tuesday and Thursday mornings, and I have a marketing presentation to fine-tune for Mangrums. And I get to explore *home*. Let me know if there are any places you don't want me to snoop."

"Zip up that Browns jacket, and let me fix the hood. It stopped snowing, but the wind still looks mean," I said as we headed out to my Jeep and into the city to Meigs Street.

The roads were not too bad, and we were back from Abigail's apartment at four-thirty. Jock and Maggie were very glad to see us and get their supper. Then we took them for a walk before it became completely dark. I stoked up the fireplace in the living room, and Abigail and I cut up a couple of McIntosh apples, opened two bottles of my son's home-brewed stout and made fat roast beef sandwiches on Mangrums whole wheat bread. We spread out on the rug in front of the fireplace, kept Jock and Maggie happy with some apple chunks, and pretended to have a picnic in November. I called my son Matt and told him I had a new friend I wanted to bring over to meet him, Claire and the kids; and we settled on Sunday evening for pizza.

Abigail gestured for the phone, so I passed it to her. "Hello, is this Matt? I'm Abigail McKay, and your dad picked me up in a coffee shop, and now we're washing down rare roast beef with your delicious brown beer." Then she laughed. "Say that again . . . your son says that the stout is strong, and I should watch out for you. Matt, do you think your father might be trying to take advantage of me? Uh-huh. Your son wants to know if we're sitting in front of the fireplace. Uh-huh. He says it wouldn't be the first time." She smiled and ran her fingertips over my cheek.

"Thanks for the heads-up, Matt. I can't wait to meet you and your wife and your children on Sunday. Do you want to talk with your dad again? Okay, good night. See you soon."

We watched the fire settle for a while into smaller flames and glowing ashes until Abigail started to doze in my lap. Maggie noticed Abigail's little snore and came right over and licked her face and woke her up. Some of the logs in the fire crumbled at the same time, which made Jock bark, and we all laughed. Abby sat up and yawned.

"This is *way* comfortable, Matt, but before I get *too* comfortable, or just want to take you back to bed, is there a desk or some place where I can set up my school and Mangrums stuff?"

"Sure. Let's take your stuff up to the other front bedroom— not the office where you were looking out the window." We carried up her books, laptop and printer, backpack, briefcase and notebooks. "This was Matt's room when we first moved into the house twenty-five years ago; and then when Matt went off to college in 1997, Sarah turned it into her office and computer room. She died later that year. That's a nice desk where Sarah's old computer used to be. My Uncle Vinny—my mother's brother and my godfather—he made that for me when I was about ten years old."

"This will be perfect, Matt, especially with the desk right in front of the window. I love to work with the natural light. How did your wife die? She had to be pretty young."

"Forty-seven. Abby, I will tell you all about Sarah . . . soon, but not tonight, okay? I don't want to keep any secrets, but this is your first day in your new home—*our* home—and that's enough for me for one day."

"Me too, Matt. Come over here and give me a hug. *Mmm*, thanks."

We looked out through the crystals on the front windows to the snowdrifts and the shadows from the empty trees. Half a moon was coming up over the golf course to the east.

"Sometimes, when I'm alone in my apartment, these long, dark evenings get me down. But you, summer boy, brighten everything up. Can we take *Pooh* and *Piglet* downstairs, split a glass of red wine and cuddle for a little while in front of the fire before we go to bed?"

Jock and Maggie, who had followed us upstairs, followed us back down and settled on their beds to watch us in front of the glimmering fire. Their "beds" were actually large fleece blankets folded a couple of times. Jock's was navy blue with the interlocking white *NY* of the New York Yankees; Maggie's was burgundy with the curly white *P* of the Philadelphia Phillies. Both were souvenirs of my baseball trips with Matt and Danny.

"Matt, do Maggie and Jock ever sleep with you?"

"Sometimes. I always leave the bedroom door open, and

39

they surprise me. Sometimes *both* of them—which can make even a king-size bed very cozy—and sometimes they both sleep down here. I sleep mostly on the door side of the bed, so when they come up they either jump over me—which is a *real* wake-up—or go around to the window side. Jock usually stretches out near the foot of the bed, and Maggie likes to curl up with her head against the pillows. We'll need to have a family meeting in the next few days to discuss the new sleeping arrangements," I grinned.

"Maybe if I sleep close enough to you, old guy, there will still be enough room for Maggie and Jock. I don't want them to think that I'm coming between them and their Daddy." Now *she* grinned.

"Maybe. Abby, I'm getting the feeling that with you *everything* is possible. By the way, miss, do you have a side?"

"A *side*? Of what?"

"A favorite side of the bed."

"No, only the side next to you." She laid her head in my lap.

"So when the baby dogs come up, you'll be in between them and me."

"Sounds too good to be true. Why do you call them 'baby dogs,' Matt?"

"When Sarah and I got our first Scottish terrier the year we moved into this house—Matt and Danny named him 'Herbie' from the *Love Bug* movie—he just looked so *little* compared to all the other dogs on the street that I started calling him 'baby dog.' I used to do that with my old Volkswagen *Beetle* too. I called it my 'baby car' for 100,000 miles."

"When did you have a Bug?"

"I bought it in 1971 when I was in the Army, when I came home from Vietnam and was stationed at Fort Sam Houston, near San Antonio. It was my first car."

"*Army, Vietnam, San Antonio*—you owe me a lot of stories, Matt."

"A *lot* of stories, Abby, I promise." I stroked her cheek with the back of my fingers. "By the way, getting back to the doggies for a second, don't be surprised when they want to snuggle on the bed *in between* you and me. They're smart dogs; they know the best places to be."

"I'll have a talk with Maggie and Jock tomorrow." She yawned. "I think maybe it's time for me to warm up my side of the bed. What time do you have to get up?"

"Six-thirty. My breakfast meeting is at eight o'clock, but I'm slow in the morning, and I need enough time to shave and shower and feed Jock and Maggie and take them for a walk. I'll try really hard to not wake you up."

"Well, I hope I'm awake so I can help you with the dogs. I wouldn't mind watching you shave and shower, either," she smiled.

We turned off all the downstairs lights and put the doggie gate at the foot of the stairs, so Jock and Maggie would know that—at least for tonight—Daddy and his new friend would be sleeping without them.

We made love slowly, softly, quietly. As I kissed and held Abigail, I was recalling the last three wondrous days: her loving sounds, her shy touches, her little looks, her flavors, her copper and creme colors, her sweet and caring questions. I thought she was asleep.

"Matt, are you awake?"

"Yes, just thinking about my life since Monday."

"When's the last time I told you that I love you?"

"Once coming up the stairs and five or ten times while we were making love."

"Matt, I've never made love more than two times in one day. Actually, *made love* is a real stretch—*had sex* is more like it. So, if this sounds like a dumb question, I hope you'll forgive me; but the last three days have been too unbelievable for me to understand yet. Can we keep doing this? Can we do it every day? Can we keep doing it *forever*? Will these feelings last forever? Our love . . . will it last forever? What you call *urge*? Can they last forever, or will they run out? Will we get tired and use them up?" I felt her squeeze my arm with both hands.

"Abby, my beautiful girl, I think every time we make love— when you open your whole self to me, and I give you all I have inside me—your love fills me up all over again, and I hope my love fills you the same way. We can never run out as long as we love each other. And we can never get tired as long as we breathe energy into each other. So, sleep tight, beauty. I love you." She nestled her head on my shoulder, I kissed her forehead and I felt her drop off to sleep in seconds.

41

5

The radio alarm—tuned to our local country and western station—woke us at six-thirty to the caressing voice of Shania Twain.

> *From this moment, life has begun.*
> *From this moment, you are the one.*
> *Right beside you is where I belong,*
> *from this moment on.*
>
> *From this moment, I have been blessed.*
> *I live only for your happiness.*
> *And for your love I'd give my last breath,*
> *from this moment on.*

Abigail and I stretched . . . and listened. I couldn't believe WCWM was playing the perfect song at the perfect time. Abby was trying to squeeze her toes in between mine.

"Good morning, Matt. Did you call and request that song specially for me?"

"My beauty, I should lie and take credit, but Julie and Rick, the WCWM morning crew, must have picked it out. I could wake up to Shania every morning, but how did they know *you* would be here?" I wrapped my arms around her and smelled the morning in her hair. "You should go back to sleep. I can take care of the dogs before I go to my meeting."

"No way, old guy. I'm going to make you coffee, walk the doggies with you, and kiss you as you rush out the door to work. Just like in the movies. And then I'm going to curl up with *Pooh* and *Piglet* and go back to sleep. What time do you think you'll be back?"

"Ten-thirty. What time do you have to be at Mangrums?"

"I like to be there by one-thirty."

"Okay. Let's feed the dogs and take them out, and then I'll shave and shower. But first, a little treat for you. Stay right where you are, under the covers. I'm going to let Jock and

42

Maggie come up and say good morning."

I went downstairs. Jock and Maggie were wagging their tails at the foot of the stairs and waiting for me to move the doggie gate (originally a safety gate for the kids), so they could run up. They raced upstairs in tandem and jumped onto the bed, then hopped back and forth like bunnies over Abigail, Jock barking at her and Maggie stopping to lick her face.

Abby laughed and reached for them. Jock licked her hand and then jumped in a circle. Maggie let herself be scratched around her ears and then tried to get under the quilt with Abigail. Then the dogs started to do what I call their "figure-eights." They spin in a circle on the bed, jump into the hallway, spin again, jump back onto the bed, spin again, jump back into the hallway, run down the stairs into the living room, spin again, run back upstairs, jump back onto the bed and start all over. Abigail was laughing so hard she had tears in her eyes. After two sets of figure-eights, Jock settled on top of the quilt over Abby's thighs, and Maggie curled up under her arm on the pillow, both heaving with their tongues hanging out.

"Beauty, I think you are now officially their Mommy." I knelt on the bed and kissed Abigail slowly across her lips. "You can have this every morning; it's a package deal."

"Where do I sign up? I was out of breath just watching them. Jock is heavy."

"They both weigh about thirty pounds; they're bigger than average Scotties. They're actually cousins. Jock's mother and Maggie's father are sister and brother. I got them both from the same breeder in Holcomb. Are we ready to give them breakfast and take them out?"

"Let's go. It looks brighter outside. Maybe we'll have some sun for a change."

The sky was clear for the first time all week, and the glow from the rising sun was starting to outline the trees on the golf course. Jock and Maggie wanted to race up each plowed driveway looking for snowdrifts low enough for them to jump in and do their business. Abigail and I had our travel mugs of coffee and we laughed at the dogs' antics all around the circle.

After I shaved and stepped in the shower, Abby sat on the sink and we talked about the next couple of days.

"When are you going to talk with your son in Boston?" she asked.

"I'll call Danny and Emma tonight, tell them I have a

surprise for them, and then it'll be your turn. You did such a good job with Matt. I'll also ask them about their schedule, just in case we have a chance to get to Boston for a quickie." I heard her laugh. "And I'll call my brother Tom to let him know that I might not make it for Thanksgiving. Although, depending on the dinner times—you said five o'clock at your mom and dad's, right?—we might be able to go to Tom and Diane's *before* we go to your house. Then you could meet my mother and father too."

"That would be nice. I'll call Mom and Dad today and pin down the time for Thanksgiving. Would you like me to wash your back, old guy?"

"*That* would be nice!" I slid the shower curtain halfway along the tub. "Here's the back brush and the soap." It was amazing how comfortable we were with each other only three mornings after Monday in the coffee shop.

Abigail, with Jock and Maggie at her heels, *did* hand me my Yankee mug full of fresh coffee and kiss me goodbye as I went out the door from the family room to the garage. As she closed the door, I heard her say, "Come on, baby dogs, let's go back to bed."

Rush hour traffic was almost back to normal after two semi-official snow days, but a very nervous normal. Everybody was slowed by the brown mush on the streets, squeezed by the high snowbanks overlapping all the curbs and unable to see around corners and driveways because of the plowed piles. Some time after I left my client at Joe's Diner, while stopped for a couple of cycles at the next red light on the way downtown, I sensed that Sarah was with me in the Jeep.

What do you think about this, Sarah? It's been ten years, sweetheart, and I never thought this would ever happen to me again. I never thought I could ever love anybody after you. What do you think of Abigail? She's only twenty-six. I think you would like her. She's a lot like you in the ways she sees and hugs the sunny side of life. You know, when we first met, YOU were only twenty-six. I was thirty. Tell me again what you saw that made you love me. I can't still be the same person thirty-one years later, can I? There must be more—you made me a better man. Can Abigail see the things that you saw? Don't be upset with me, sweetheart. You know . . . if I had been the one to go ten years ago, I would wish the same chance for happiness for you. I know this looks crazy, but isn't love always the right thing to do? It sure was the summer I met you. Will you tell Matt and Danny to go easy on me? Stay with me, sweetheart.

I was in and out of the office in an hour. Some mail, some faxes, some insurance applications to process. Everybody was trying to catch up after two days at home with their kids, spouses, shovels and pets. I did call Tom and told him there was an Abigail, and also that neither Matt nor Danny would be home for Thanksgiving. He said that Diane was planning dinner for about three o'clock and that I had "damn well better" bring my new friend to meet the family. I replied that for now her mother and father had first dibs on Thanksgiving, but I'd let him know in a couple of days if we could do both.

When I come home during the day in the good-weather months—April through September—Jock and Maggie hear my Jeep pull up the driveway and meet me at the front door, Jock barking and Maggie jumping. The rest of the year, they hear my Jeep pull up *and* the garage door go up, and they meet me at the door to the family room, barking and jumping. Today was no different. I scratched them under their chins and asked them where "Mommy" was, and they scampered upstairs through the kitchen and the front hall to the upstairs landing, where they waited. When I got there, we all saw Abigail coming out of the bathroom wrapped in the Confederate flag beach towel that I had bought when I was in college.

Jock and Maggie wagged their tails, and I grinned. "That old towel never looked so good, pretty girl. How did you find it?"

"I looked through your linen closet for the most interesting big towel I could find, and this was the winner. Did *you* buy it, or did someone give it to you as a gag gift?"

"I bought it in my senior year at B.C., when I took my one-and-only spring vacation trip to Florida. I think I spent more on that towel than I did on food for the whole week in Ft. Lauderdale. It's the only souvenir of my spring fling."

"Why a towel? Why a Confederate flag?"

"I needed a big towel for girl-watching on the beach, of course, and I always liked the style of the Confederate flag. There were plenty of those to choose from in Florida. I tried to pick out the softest one, and the one with the brightest colors."

"Well, it's a cozy towel—just my size—and it's still really soft after all those years. So, does that mean you're a rebel, Matt?"

"Not an anti-Yankee rebel; the right side won the Civil War.

45

But I was never one to go along with the crowd; I never worried about standing out or being different. Remind me to tell you about the tux I wore to my Dominic Savio Senior Ball."

"I'm making a list, you know, of all the stories you promise to tell me. Do you mind if I hang up this historic towel?" Abigail grinned. "Come into bed with me for a few minutes, and I'll tell you about my phone call to Mom."

"And what would your mother say about the two of us taking off our clothes to talk about her? I called my brother Tom from the office, but you first."

I stretched out next to Abby and curled my arms and legs around her.

"I can't think while you're nibbling; *stop* for a minute and let me tell you! Maggie and Jock and I went back to bed for about an hour after you left. When Maggie woke me up with some kisses, I was hungry, so I checked out the refrigerator. I ate the last hard-boiled egg in the blue bowl, but then I cooked a half-dozen more for you."

"Just for *me*?" I tickled the freckle on her nose.

"Okay, for me too." She laughed. "Then I had some orange juice and half a banana, poured my second cup of coffee into your blue, speckled Yellowstone mug—another story, right?— and called Mom. I told her I met a great guy I really like and I was thinking of inviting him for Thanksgiving dinner, and would that be okay with her and Dad? And then she did all of her mother questions: What's his name? Where did you meet him? How old is he? What does he do? Is he divorced? Where does he live?"

"Abby, I'm guessing that you've heard those questions before."

"With just about every guy I've ever dated. Don't forget that my mother is always on the alert for *consequences*." Her eyes were mischievous. "I told Mom that you are a financial planner and a lawyer; that you live in Penfield; that I met you at Kitty's; and that your wife died ten years ago and you have two sons. And then, of course, she asked me again how old you are. I said, 'Matt's several years older than I am, Mom.' And then, of course, she asked me, 'How many is *several*?' Don't you dare laugh . . . it's your fault for being so *old!* I told her, 'More than ten and less than a hundred. I want you and Dad to meet him first, Mom, and then you can ask him all the questions you want. We thought we would come over after dinner Saturday night.

About seven o'clock.' And I asked her to make her special chocolate cake. So, how did I do?"

"You did great, Abby." I kissed her hair all around her left ear. "I'll have to get to work on my answers. My conversation with Tommy was a lot easier. I told him I had a girlfriend; that I might be going to her mom and dad's for Thanksgiving; and that Matt and Danny would both be out of town. He said that Diane was planning dinner at three o'clock and that I had 'damn well better make the time' to bring you over to meet the family. I told him I would try real hard and let him know if we could do both. How did I do?"

"You did great too, handsome. Speaking of *do*—I thought I heard you mention a 'quickie' in the shower—I'm feeling very soft and warm all of a sudden . . . do we have time for a 'quickie' before you bundle me off to Mangrums?"

Abigail was right: every part of her I touched was soft and warm; all the sounds she made were soft and warm; the sunlight on her skin was soft and warm. We were so melted together that we didn't hear the doggies come upstairs. They sensed that even though we weren't sleeping, they should wait for us quietly on the rug below the foot of the bed.

It was hard to believe how much this beautiful girl loved me.

With Jock and Maggie hopping from window to window in the back seat of Jeep, I dropped Abby off at Mangrums at one-thirty. I had packed her a peanut butter sandwich, a hard-boiled egg and a banana for dinner.

"Would you like the sofa and a movie when you get home tonight, pretty girl?"

"I would like that just fine, Matt. What movie do you have in mind?"

"Have you seen *Serendipity*?"

"No, what's it about?"

"It's a romance with a happy ending; you'll love it."

"I love *you*." She touched both my cheeks with her fingertips, kissed me gently and jumped out of the Jeep, tapped on the plastic side window where Jock and Maggie were pressing their noses, and ran through the front door of Mangrums.

I stopped on the way home for gas, and then at Mangrums for ice cream, cold cuts, Coke, bread and apples. The doggies needed a walk as soon as we got home, and then we all settled in for an afternoon of paperwork, mail and client calls. I had a little trouble concentrating because Abigail—her sounds, her colors, her fragrance, her flavor—kept flashing into the middle of each phone call and letter. How could my life have changed so much in *four* days?

She called about four o'clock. "What are you, Maggie and Jock doing?"

"We're in the family room. Jock and Maggie are warming up the sofa for you and giving me dirty looks if I try to take a break. I'm doing some letters on the computer and returning calls to clients. How about you?"

"Working with the advertising people on a new line of ready-made dinners that busy people can grab on the way home from the office and just throw in their microwaves."

"Any free samples?"

"First we need a marketing plan, silly, and next the glossy advertising materials—delicious looking photos of the fourteen different dinners—and then they will go into the stores a few at a time. This is all top-secret, you know."

"Got ya. Your lunch bag may seem dull after all the pretty pictures."

"What could be more exciting than my old guy packing a lunch for me? By the way, I had one quick bite of my peanut butter sandwich when I got here, and it has butter on it—no jelly. I've never had a peanut butter and *butter* sandwich."

"My specialty. That's what my mother made for me, and that's the way I've eaten them all my life. Never took a fancy to jelly or jam. Do you like it?"

"I *love* it! Next time you're going to have to make me two. By the way, I couldn't help it—I *had* to call Patrick and tell him about you; he can't wait to meet you, so he and Laurie are coming to Mom and Dad's Saturday night. You won't have to worry about any tough questions from Pat; he's always on my side. Oh . . . I'm getting buzzed. Gotta go. See you at eight."

"See you at eight."

Supper for me was one of my bachelor, three-course standards: a bowl of *Honey Nut Cheerios* with a banana sliced in; a peanut butter and butter sandwich on whole wheat; and, for dessert, a dish of vanilla ice cream with a handful of *Nestle Toll House Semi-Sweet Morsels* thrown in.

I always keep an old peanut butter jar filled with the morsels in the refrigerator; I like them cold. Sometimes I keep the jar in the freezer because I like them *crunchy* and cold. The dark chocolate chips have been my snack of choice ever since I used to sneak them out of the yellow bag my mother always kept on hand in the kitchen cupboard to make her delicious oatmeal chocolate chip cookies. I could never open an unopened bag because my mother would have known; but she only used half a bag for each batch, so after the first batch, when the half-full bag was back in the cupboard tightly closed with a rubber band, I could sneak a few as long as I didn't get greedy and sneak so many that she would notice the difference. I'm sure she knew anyway. Mothers *always* know anyway.

When the dogs and I don't have company, I'm always doing something else while I'm eating: reading the mail or the newspaper or a book; reviewing a client file; paying the bills; watching the news or a movie or a Yankee game; working at the computer. I'm a lazy eater. I like food I can carry around the house and eat with my fingers without getting too messy. Jock and Maggie love my diet; they are especially fond of *Cheerios*, bananas, pizza crust, peanut butter, baby carrots and oyster crackers. No matter how loud the television may be in any room of the house, or the stereo in the living room, my dogs always hear me opening the *Cheerios* bag and come running and barking for their handful.

When I put the night's dishes on the kitchen floor so the doggies could lick them clean, I said, "Puppies, how do you think Abigail is going to change our eating habits? More hot food, do you think? Less pizza?" They always cock their heads to one side as if they're trying hard to understand what I'm saying.

I got to Mangrums just before eight, and Abigail rushed out the front door right on time. In spite of her nibbling on my ear and playing with my fingers on the stick, we made it home safely in fifteen minutes. The doggies went crazy when they saw her come in from the garage.

"Did you have enough to eat, beauty? Can I fix you something?"

"I'm fine, Matt. Besides the delicious dinner you packed me, it was another intern's birthday, and she brought in an ice cream cake from Lollycup's. All I want is a mug of hot coffee and you, and to curl up on the couch and watch that movie. If you warm up the coffee, I'll go up and get *Pooh* and *Piglet*. And maybe we can split a glass of Chianti, too."

I went to the kitchen and got the bottle of Ruffino Chianti and one of the old crystal wine glasses that we found at Grandma and Grandpa Fiorino's house when my Aunt Connie had to move to a nursing home. I also brought the portable phone.

Abigail and I settled at one end of the couch, and Jock and Maggie jumped up and filled the other end. We sipped our coffee and Chianti, and Abby told me about her afternoon and evening at the office.

"Art Mangrum *himself* came by to say hello to the interns and have a piece of cake. He had his nephew with him, Chris Mangrum, who is a lawyer with Old Northeastern Life. So naturally I said that I know someone at Old Northeastern Life, Matt Flynn; and both of them know you. Chris said he has worked with you on a couple of trusts; and Art said he remembered you from your years in politics. Another story for me later, right?"

"Right. Later, but not tonight. Chris is a good man and an *excellent* trust attorney; and Art, of course, is a great and visionary man—one of the most important persons in Western New York in the last twenty or thirty years, and a wonderful benefactor of our alma mater, Dominic Savio. But you'd never know it from talking with him: he's so humble and down-to-earth."

"He's a *lovely* man. You can see in his eyes that he is *really* interested in what you have to say. This Chianti is *so* good. I never drank any before this week." Abigail grinned. "I don't think I've ever had *any* red wine, period—only some white wine in college or on a date. I never had an Italian boyfriend before; and growing up in an Irish family we learned to drink beer at an early age, but there was never any wine around the house."

"So now you have a half-Italian boyfriend and half a glass of Italian red wine. Do you like Italian food? I have ten or twenty favorite Italian restaurants in Rochester."

"Love it! When can we start?"

"How about tomorrow night? I thought that after I pick you up at work, I would take you to Palermo's ristorante on the bay, and then we can go surprise my mother and father. I can't wait to see their faces when they meet you."

"I would like that a lot, Matt."

"Will we pick up your car when we go to your mom and

dad's on Saturday?"

"That makes sense. We can't exactly go over earlier now that I told them that we would be there after dinner. Can we go get the rest of my clothes, and my books and my furniture and stuff from my apartment on Saturday morning?"

"Sure, beauty, any time you want. Shall we call Danny before we start the movie?"

"Okay, but . . . you haven't told me very much about your sons, old guy. Tell me about Danny before we call him."

"Danny is a *great* kid. He'll be twenty-six on St. Patrick's Day. He's always been at or near the top of his class—from grammar school through medical school. He's a natural athlete: fast, quick and bright. He could coach *any* sport he ever played, and he played most of them, from first grade tee-ball through his freshman year at Fordham: Little League, Pop Warner football, soccer, basketball, tennis, and varsity track and football at Penfield. Even though he's not that big, he was a starting cornerback and the best defensive player—with the most tackles—on the Penfield football team.

"I can't ever remember him doing anything bad or dumb. He got his degree in biology at Fordham in three years and then went to Syracuse Medical School. He married pretty Emma Swift last August and graduated from Syracuse this May. He started on July 1 as a resident in the urology department at the Tufts and Mather Memorial Hospital in Cambridge. The hospital is named after a famous colonial doctor, Cotton Tufts, and a famous colonial preacher, Cotton Mather. Everybody in the Boston area calls the hospital The Cottons. Emma works for a sports marketing company in downtown Boston."

"Wow! I can see the pride in your face and hear it in your voice, and with good reason. I've heard of Cotton Mather; wasn't he a 'fire-and-brimstone' guy?"

"No, Mather was more reasonable and moderate than most of the other Puritan preachers. And he is almost as well known for advocating for inoculation for smallpox—against general fear and opposition among most Puritans—in the early years of the 18th century. Dr. Cotton Tufts was also a staunch supporter of inoculation in the later years of the 18th century, which is how people get hospitals named after them. Is there anything else I can tell you about Danny before we call?"

"No, let's call. I can find out more as I go along. But I would like a warm-up on the coffee and another half a glass of

Chianti, if you don't mind, sir."

"Say 'when' on the Chianti."

"When."

"I'll be right down with the coffee. Don't let the doggies take my place."

We settled in at our end of the sofa, put our feet up on the coffee table and I dialed Danny at his apartment in Cambridge. "Hey, Daniel, it's Dad. How are you and Emma? That's good. No colds or anything? I'm good, too. Have you gotten any of this snow that clobbered us the past two days? We must have eighteen inches on the ground, plus all the drifting and huge piles from the plows. The only good thing is that it covered up all the leaves that I haven't gotten around to raking in the back yard. I'll have to pay for that later. How are things going at The Cottons for my favorite first-year resident? That's a lot of hours. There was an article in the paper last week about medical residents working too many hours. I know. Did you just get home? I don't want to hold up supper for you and Emma— maybe we can catch up more during the day tomorrow—but I have a new friend, Abigail Elizabeth McKay, and she wanted to say hello to my son the doctor, so be nice."

"Hi, Danny? . . . this is Abigail . . . call me Abby . . . I'm fine, thanks, and I hope you and your wife are also . . . not very long . . . we met in a coffee shop on Monday . . . right, only *three* days . . . it sure *is* hard to believe . . . really? . . . your brother Matt said almost the same thing when we called him last night . . . he *is* teaching me how to drink Chianti, but I still think he's a gentleman . . . I hope so . . . maybe sooner than that . . . we're going to meet Matt and his family on Sunday . . . you too . . . enjoy your late dinner . . . sounds *way* too healthy for me . . . do you want to talk with your old dad again? . . . okay, good night."

She put the phone down on the coffee table and took a sip of wine.

"So, now you've talked with both of my sons."

"And both of them said you are a wily guy and I should watch out for the Chianti and the brown beer." Abigail's green eyes sparkled. "Danny said he and Emma look forward to coming home for Christmas and meeting me. He also said that they were having some kind of exotic salad with arugula, chicken, broccoli and walnuts, and that he would call you tomorrow from the hospital."

"Danny is my health-food son—arugula, chicken and raisin bran. Matt is my comfort-food son—hot dogs and hot pizza. Come closer, beauty. It seems that you have already charmed *both* my sons, and once they meet you they will probably like you better than they like me."

"I'm getting *very* soft and comfortable here, old guy, so let's start the movie before you have to carry me up to bed. You have to get me to Mangrums at seven-thirty, remember." She rubbed her head on my shoulder and put her feet—in her red socks—on top of mine on the coffee table.

Serendipity starts at Christmas time in Bloomingdale's.

"Matt, you know I've only been to New York City once, with a bunch of girlfriends right after we graduated from Newton. It was *so* expensive; we didn't even stay overnight. I've never been to Bloomingdale's."

"Well, maybe we can get there in the spring. I love walking around New York; I love walking through all the famous and fancy stores: Macy's, Bloomingdale's, Tiffany's, Brooks Brothers, all the designer names. Whoever I'm with . . . we laugh at all the prices but we never buy anything. My favorite is FAO Schwarz."

"Oh, the famous toy store! That store is in *so* many movies. I love Tom Hanks dancing on the giant piano in *Big*."

Just then, Jonathan and Sara grabbed the same pair of black gloves in Bloomingdale's.

Abigail poked me in the ribs. "John Cusack is very cute."

"He's too old for you." I kissed her nose.

"Well, I love him anyway."

"That's okay because *I* love Kate Beckinsale."

"She's too old for *you*." She poked me again.

When Jonathan and Sara took their shared pair of gloves to the *Serendipity* patisserie for fancy, blended coffees, Abigail said, "*There* are both of my jobs: I wonder if we could redesign Kitty's coffee shop and turn it into a restaurant and general store like *Serendipity*?"

"The Eastman Theater *is* at the end of the block. If Kitty wanted to open her place on concert nights for dinner and after the shows, it might catch on."

"Matt, do you think you would like my hair darker, like Kate Beckinsale's?"

"Your hair is so alive and bright—I doubt it, but some day maybe you can try chestnut."

"Do you think chestnut would go with my freckles?"

"It just might. Speaking of freckles, watch this scene."

Jonathan and Sara were skating on a rink in Central Park, with snowflakes falling, when Sara slipped and cut her forearm. They sat down on a park bench, and Jonathan was cleaning up the cut when he noticed the freckles on Sara's arm. He traced the constellation Cassiopeia in her freckles and then showed her the same stars in the clear New York sky.

"The only constellation I know is the Big Dipper, Matt. Can you show me Cassiopeia?"

"I can do that . . . first clear night. We'll look tomorrow night. I used to have a *National Geographic* star map and I'd study the skies during the different seasons. What's your birthday?"

"May fifth."

"I think your sign is Taurus, right?"

"Right. How did you know that?"

"One of my old girlfriends was a Taurus. Have you ever seen Taurus the Bull in the sky?"

"No. Can you show me that one, too?"

"I can. It's one of my favorites."

"What's *your* sign?"

"Cancer, the Crab. Those stars are a little harder to find than Taurus."

At this point in the movie, Jonathan and Sara just barely missed each other getting off and on the elevators on the twenty-third floor of the Waldorf-Astoria. Abigail yawned and tugged on my ear lobe.

"Matt, I'm having a hard time keeping my eyes open, and I don't want to miss any of the movie. Can we stop it here and go upstairs?"

"Good idea. If you'll grab the coffee mugs, I'll bring the wine and our favorite quilt and turn everything off. Jock, Maggie, let's go upstairs, puppies."

Abigail brushed her teeth and was in bed in five minutes. Jock and Maggie settled on their fleece beds in the upstairs hallway. I stretched on my back next to Abby and put my arm under her head as she curled her arm over my chest and her leg over mine. We were both asleep before we could think about it.

6

She woke me up with her hand stroking the inside of my thigh, whispering in my ear, "Good morning, handsome. I love you."

"Abby . . . "

"*Shh*. It's six o'clock, and I turned off the alarm. Maggie and Jock are still quiet." She ran her hand across my stomach. "Don't say anything, Matt. It's Friday morning, and TGIY— Thank God it's you! Four days . . . we've been together a *whole* four days, and I already can't imagine being anywhere else. I wanted to climb all over you and make love when we came upstairs last night, but as soon as you put your arm under my head I was gone. So I'm going to make up for crashing on you. *Shh*." Abigail put two fingers on my lips. "Stay right where you are, summer boy." She rolled over on top of me and smiled. "*You* are my breakfast treat." She ran her fingers over my temples and kissed me. "I'm going to eat you up."

At six-thirty, we fed the dogs and took them for a walk, which was a challenge because the early bus was making its stops for the high school kids, and nothing gets Jock barking as much as a school bus. Then we had orange juice, hard-boiled eggs, coffee and toast (which we shared with Jock and Maggie) and jumped into the shower together. This time we *both* got our backs scrubbed, but I didn't do such a good job because I couldn't stop nibbling on the wet curls on the back of Abigail's neck. Her hair was much darker—almost red—when it was wet. Abby said she never imagined that a soapy washcloth could be so much fun. We both laughed while we were rubbing each other dry—even between our toes—and sipping from our coffee mugs on the sink. We took turns on the bathroom scale, pretending to hide our weights from each other. *A whole four days* Abby had said, but it was as natural as if we had been doing these things all our lives.

I threw on old jeans and my favorite long-sleeved T-shirt— *ARMY Black Knights*—which was a souvenir of the cold, rainy October day at West Point six years earlier—right after 9/11—

when Danny, Matt and I were chilled to our bones at the Army-TCU football game. There were at least two cadets in helmets and flak vests, armed with M-16 rifles, guarding every intersection at the Military Academy. Abigail dressed for her day at the office: tan skirt and jacket, white silk blouse, matching tan shoes—beautiful *and* professional.

"You look as if you're ready to take over for Wally Mangrum at the top," I said.

"Thanks, old guy, and you look as if . . . "

" . . . I'm ready to work through a pile of client files at the kitchen table?"

She laughed. "I was going to say the *dining* room table. Will you make me lunch, sir?"

"Coming right up, beauty."

I found Matt's old *Rocky and Bullwinkle* lunch box and packed Abigail a peanut butter sandwich, Oreos, oyster crackers and a McIntosh apple. She laughed.

"*Rocky and Bullwinkle?*"

"Another story for your list, Abby. 'Rock' was my nickname in high school."

She laughed even harder, and we headed out the door to Mangrums.

"Did I tell you, beauty, how much I enjoy packing you off to work with lunch and a kiss?"

"Getting rid of me, Matt, after only *four* days?" Abigail gave me a slow kiss. "Don't you like picking me up more?"

"I'll show you this afternoon at four o'clock. Do you think you'll want to come home first, or would you like to go right to Palermo's?"

"*Come home first* . . . do you know how good that sounds? I think I'd like to come home first, give the doggies some scratches, freshen up my lipstick, brush my hair—all that girl stuff. Should I bring anything to your mom and dad's?"

"Good thought! We can pick up a red rose for Mom and a coconut cream pie for Dad, and they will never forget the day they met Abigail Elizabeth McKay."

"One rose?"

"My trademark. I bought Mom a pewter bud vase when I was in college, and she is always happy when I bring her a long-stemmed red rose for the vase. And Dad's favorite dessert is coconut cream pie. It'll be nice to surprise them. *Hey*, get going, beauty; it's twenty to eight. See you around four. Have a

56

nice day in the office."

Back at the house, Jock and Maggie sat with me in the kitchen as I organized my files for next week. I was working on a financial plan for a retired couple when Danny called at eleven-thirty.

"Hi, Dad, how are you doing?"

"Good, Danny, how about you? Are you at the hospital?"

"Yes, but I have twenty minutes in between conferences so I thought I'd try you. Can we talk about Abigail—is it *serious*?"

"Did you enjoy talking with her last night?"

"She sounded nice but . . . Dad, how old is she?"

"Twenty-six."

"Dad, she's less than *half* your age. Why did you let this happen? She's only a year older than *I* am! Has she moved in to the house?"

"Yep, on Wednesday."

"Only *two* days after you met her? Why does she want an old guy like you?" I could imagine Danny wrinkling his face in a skeptical smile. "Seriously, Dad, since Mom died I've seen you flirt with waitresses and store clerks a hundred times. Heck, I saw you do it a hundred times *before* Mom died. You're a nice guy, and it's *fun* for you, and sometimes they flirt back; but it's always been five minutes and done. Abigail sounded like she was *way* past flirting. You could have easily made this *not* happen. Why didn't you? You're a really smart guy, so you know it can't *last*, right? Have you told Matt?"

"We called Matt last night. He doesn't know any details, but he and Abigail hit it off right away on the phone. He warned her to watch out for me. We're going over Sunday evening for pizza, so you and Emma can call Matt and Claire Sunday night for their first impressions. Listen, Danny, I appreciate your concern, and the smart thing for me might have been to stop flirting with anybody under the age of *fifty*, but I think it's too *late*—and I'm too *old*—for analysis and logic. For better or worse, I have always been a guy who makes eye contact. That's how I met your mother. The thing about 'smart' is that it's not one of the senses. 'Smart' might have worked after I first talked with Abigail on Monday morning, but we made eye contact; and what I saw made me want to go back and talk with her some more on Tuesday. You can ask her yourself what *she* saw that made her ask *me* if I could 'come in tomorrow.' I already know."

"Dad, you have many good qualities. You're smart, attractive, in pretty good shape, a charming guy—for sixty-one. But the point is that *you* were supposed to be the grownup here. What were you *thinking* in leading her on?"

"Danny, nobody *led* anybody anywhere. On Monday morning we liked each other right away, but *thinking* didn't have anything to do with it. The *real* point is that when people meet, thinking only takes them so far, and then their senses kick in. Well, ours kicked in when we started talking again on Tuesday morning. We can no more shut out our senses than Jock and Maggie can ignore the sight of squirrels scampering up a tree fifty feet away, or the scent of deer that just ran through the snow in the front yard, or the sound of thunder or another dog barking. And even though the dogs react instinctively, while we can sometimes control our senses and even decide whether they are good for us or not, we can *never* keep our senses from affecting our emotions. Once Abigail and I felt what was happening, we talked about the age thing for hours—the risks and the challenges—but what we saw in each other's eyes and what we felt when we touched each other trumped all the challenges and risks. And how do you know Abigail didn't lead *me* on? I've always been a soft touch when it comes to women."

"You're right, Dad, there's a lot I don't know; but I can't help wondering what happens next week or next year or five years from now."

"I don't know either, Danny. Look, we're not naive or stupid. We know there will be many problems, and even people close to us will be upset and critical. We're not teenagers, and this may not be love at first sight—though I *believe* in love at first sight—but it is *surely* love. What might happen next week or next year? I don't know, but I'm willing to find out. Whether I was twenty-one or *sixty*-one, I couldn't *not* fall in love with this girl. I think it will make more sense when you meet her. Which reminds me: I don't want to wait until you and Emma come home for Christmas. Can we drive up to Boston for a weekend before Christmas?"

"I think so. We'll be on Long Island for Thanksgiving weekend with Emma's family, but the first weekend in December might work. I'm not on call in December. I'll talk with Emma tonight. I didn't mean to give you a hard time, Dad. There's no reason why a sixty-one-year-old guy and a twenty-six-year-old girl can't fall in love. If she makes you happy, I can't wait to meet her."

"Okay . . . thanks, Danny. I'll call you in a couple of days. Give my best to Emma."

"Will do. 'Bye, Dad."

Abigail called at about twelve-thirty. "How are things at the kitchen table, Matt?"

"The puppies and I are doing pretty well. Danny called at eleven-thirty and slowed us down some, but we're catching up. We are sharing mozzarella cheese sticks and peanuts. Did you have your delicious lunch yet?"

"Just finishing up. The oyster crackers were a nice touch. What did Danny have to say?"

"Danny thinks you're too *old* for me." I could hear her laugh at the other end of the line. "He and Emma are anxious to meet you, and we're all looking at the first weekend in December for a drive to Boston."

"That sounds wonderful! I'll have to practice being mature between now and then."

"Don't expect me to practice *with* you. Peter Pan is still one of my heroes."

"I don't want you to *ever* grow up, summer boy. But you will have to tell me later what Emma's like, in case I need her help to win Danny over."

"What's happening in the advertising department today?"

"The project for this whole month is to brainstorm ways to double the sales of plants and flowers in all the stores. We can start by buying the red rose for your mom later."

"Well, if we want to help Wally Mangrum double his sales, we'll have to buy *two* red roses."

"Why two?"

"I want to add someone to my red rose list. What would you prefer, beauty, a crystal bud vase or a pewter one?"

"Surprise me, Matt. That's what you've been doing every day. Gotta go—floral displays and cornucopias are calling. See you at four. Love you."

As soon as I got off the phone, I remembered the milk glass bud vase from Aunt Connie and Uncle Vinny's house. Grandma and Grandpa Fiorino had bought the house on the west side in 1923. Grandma died four months before I was born in 1946, and Grandpa died in 1956. Before, during and after The War, my three bachelor uncles—Sal, Patsy and Vinny—and my maiden Aunt Connie lived in the family homestead. After Grandma died, Aunt Connie took care of Grandpa and "the boys," as she called them, until each of them passed away—Patsy in 1966, Sal in 1976 and Vinny in 1995. After Uncle Vinny died, Aunt Connie was in the house by herself for seven years. I used to visit her about once a week, and she told me lots of stories about the family. She told me that as long as she could remember, Grandpa had put a red rose in the milk glass vase for Grandma once a week until she died. After that, the vase was never used again. It was wrapped in a linen napkin in a cabinet in the dining room until Aunt Connie got it out for me fifty years later. Grandpa had brought it from Sicily when he came to America with his three sisters around the turn of the century. If you looked closely at the vase, you could see the pattern of little olive trees. Sarah had her favorite, classic, cream-colored Lenox bud vase with fine gold trim at the top and bottom, so I never used Grandpa's vase. It had been collecting dust on a bookcase in the TV room for years, but I thought it might be just right for Abigail.

When I picked her up at Mangrums at four o'clock, she had a large, colorful plant in her arms. It was all large leaves, shiny leaves, mostly green with veins, edges and highlights of red, yellow and orange.

"Hello, beauty. What kind of plant is that? I've never seen one like it."

"Hi, Matt. Do you like it?"

"It's really beautiful. I love the way all the different-colored leaves are mixed together totally at random."

"It's called a 'garden croton.' After spending most of the day in the garden department, all of us interns got to take any plant or flowers we wanted, and I thought your mom might like this one. It's supposed to get flowers, but I'm not sure what time of year that happens."

"Mom will *love* it, especially coming from you. She might never have seen one before."

"We're still going to buy the long-stemmed red rose, right?"

"*Two* red roses. Mom will be in her glory with a red rose *and* this beautiful plant; and I think I found the perfect bud vase for you."

"When do I get to see it?"

"We'll stop at the Mangrums in Penfield on the way home and buy the roses and the coconut cream pie. You can put your rose in your vase . . . as long as you like it."

"Silly boy, how could I *not* like the vase if *you* picked it out for me? Will we be able to watch the movie later?"

"I hope so, if it's not too late after Mom and Dad's."

We stopped at Mangrums, which was jammed with Friday night shoppers, went home and took care of Jock and Maggie, and Abigail freshened up. Then before we left for dinner, I gave her the milk glass bud vase, with a red ribbon that I had tied around the neck. She had tears in her eyes as she snipped off the base of the long, thorny stem and put the rose in water in the vase.

"Matt, it's *perfect*! Where did you get it?"

"It was my Grandma and Grandpa Fiorino's. This is the first rose that's been in this vase since my Grandma died a few months before I was born. That's how special *you* are. I'll tell you the whole story at dinner."

Our booth at Palermo's was tucked in a quiet nook in the northwest corner of the *ristorante*, overlooking the south end of Irondequoit Bay. Abigail insisted on carrying *her* bud vase in the Jeep to dinner, so we had our own special centerpiece. The bay was bleak. The shore was buried in snow, the water looked almost black, and there were only a few hardy geese and seagulls near the empty docks.

"Abby, have you ever been here before?"

"Only once, with a manager from Mangrums, on a double date this summer with Patrick and Laurie. We sat way up near the front. My date picked out a bottle of white wine which wasn't all that good, and I had spaghetti and meatballs because I didn't know what else to order. We never had much Italian food around our house while I was growing up. I only started to like it when I was in college. This menu is huge! Tell me what your favorites are."

Carlo, our waiter, brought us a carafe of the house Montepulciano d'Abruzzo, and over our first restaurant toast together I described the delights of the menu to Abigail: fettuccine alfredo, rigatoni Bolognese, braciola, chicken and veal parmigiana, baked ziti, penne carbonara—most of the dishes I had ordered so many times at so many excellent Italian restaurants.

"Both Grandma and Grandpa Fiorino were born in Sicily, in the hills surrounding Palermo, though they never knew each other in the Old Country. They came to America around 1900.

So my mother grew up with the traditional, thick, smooth, red tomato sauce of Sicily, and naturally that's what she made for Dad and my brothers and me, too. Mom's spaghetti sauce is still the *best*; it's so smooth that you don't even know there are tomatoes in it. I've never liked marinara sauce with chunks of tomatoes. Palermo's is one of the best southern Italian restaurants in town. In the northern Italian restaurants, which tend to be more gourmet and expensive, it's hard to find a dish on the menu with a red sauce."

"Matt, we're going to have to come here a lot so that I can try all the dishes you like. They all sound wonderful. By the way, what is this wine called again?"

"Montepulciano d'Abruzzo, from the Abruzzi region of Italy. It's one of my favorite reds. Do you like it?"

"I *love* it. It's almost as good as the Chianti. So what are we going to have for dinner, sir?"

"How about we share, Abby, so that you can taste *two* new dishes? We'll order rigatoni Bolognese and veal parmigiana. Have you ever had veal?"

"Never. Roast beef, corned beef, lamb, ham, pork—and some kind of potatoes *every* night— that's what I remember most at home."

"Well, I think you're in for a treat. And these garlic breadsticks are the best around."

We savored and shared . . . the family-style salad with house Italian dressing; the rigatoni in its thick meat sauce; the thin cutlets of veal parmigiana over penne pasta; the breadsticks dipped in olive oil, red wine vinegar, black pepper and grated Romano cheese; and the Montepulciano . . . and many McKay and Flynn stories. With just about every bite of food or sip of wine, Abigail touched the bud vase and gave it a half-turn. I told her about how Grandpa Fiorino had wrapped it up and put it away after Grandma died. And I told her about the *nine* Fiorino children: five boys and four girls. My mother was the baby.

"It's *sad* that you never knew your grandmother. She must have been a wonderful woman to raise *such* a family! I feel so blessed that all of my grandparents are still alive and living in their *own* homes and doing pretty well."

"It *is* a blessing, Abby. All of my grandparents were gone by the time I was eleven, and I don't remember much about them. I remember Grandpa Fiorino speaking Italian all the time. Even in his late eighties, he had thick white hair and a fat moustache—

kind of like the one Tom Selleck has, but white. I can't ever remember him smiling or calling me by my name. He sat in the same blue chair by the parlor door all the time. He always had his cane in his hand and he would rap me with it if I was running too fast through the room."

"The *parlor*?"

"My father always called the living room the 'parlor'—he still does—you know, as in 'davenport' instead of sofa?"

"What about your dad's parents?"

"The only thing I remember about Grandpa Flynn is going to visit him at the county hospital just before he died. He had a corner room on the first floor, and Dad boosted me in through the window because little kids were not allowed in the wards. I was only six. Grandma Flynn died the year after Grandpa Fiorino, and even though I was a *big* kid of eleven, I just can't remember anything about her. We never spent as much time with the Flynns as we did with the Fiorinos. Mom's huge Italian family has always been more fun than Dad's German-Irish family. More cousins, more parties, more weddings, more vacations, more trips—more fun. You'll see. If you stick with me for a while, you're liable to meet a *few* of them," I grinned, "and all the Fiorinos welcome everybody into the family with open arms and hugs."

"I'll practice my hugging on you." She grinned. "Even though Irish families are supposed to be *just* as big, Mom and Dad's are fairly small. Dad has one brother and one sister, Uncle Barney and Aunt Helen; and Mom *also* has one brother and one sister, Uncle Jimmy and Aunt Roberta. I only have *six* first cousins: Uncle Barney never got married; and Aunt Helen, Uncle Jimmy and Aunt Bertie each have two children. And they're all very nice people, but they're not huggers— except for Patrick and me." Abigail's green eyes sparkled as she gave the vase another half-turn.

"Beauty, we're going to need a *thousand* more dinners for all the family personalities and old stories. And then *another* thousand just for your own stories and mine, too. You haven't told me anything about your Grandma and Grandpa McKay. But as much as I would like to start another carafe of Montepulciano with you and keep talking family, we have to go. It's seven o'clock, and I told Mom and Dad we would be there between seven and seven-thirty. And my parents are a *lot* more punctual than I am."

"Mine too; I think it must be a generation thing. But I'm so *comfortable* here, Matt—it's such a cozy place on a winter night—and to tell the truth, I'm getting a little nervous about meeting your mom and dad."

"I know. I've been thinking about *my* turn tomorrow night. But we'll be okay. My guess is that our parents are probably more anxious than we are. I'm sure that Mom and Dad are going to *eat* you up," I teased, "especially after we tell them that you're fifty-one but you have always looked *really* young for your age."

Abigail poked me in the ribs as she took my arm on the way to the car.

"You're not helping, Matt. This is a *serious* moment in my young life."

"What about *me*? I haven't brought home a date in over *thirty* years! And then it gets *worse*: your mom and dad tomorrow, then Matt and Claire on Sunday, then your whole family and most of the rest of mine on Thanksgiving, and then Danny and Emma the week after that. And what about Jock and Maggie? When do *they* get to meet your family?"

"Matt, stop kidding around. What if nobody *likes* us together?"

"Impossible, Abby . . . we're *perfect* together . . . and *that* I'm not kidding about."

We pulled into Mom and Dad's driveway, and I gave Abby a hug. "We'll be fine, beauty. Don't worry. By Christmas we'll be looking back at all these *serious* moments and laughing."

The light went on in the side hallway, and Dad stepped slowly down to the door. Mom was right behind him on the landing steps. Dad was eighty-seven and Mom eighty-six, and although they still got around without walkers, they moved more cautiously even in the familiar rooms of the house where they had lived for over fifty years.

Dad opened the door and took a close look at Abigail. "Come on in! She's *real* pretty, Matt!"

"She sure is! Hi, Dad. Hi, Mom."

Mom waved from the top step. "You two must be *freezing*. Everybody, come in the kitchen and warm up."

Abigail and I stomped the snow from our feet.

"Matt, should I take off my boots?"

"Not here, Abby, up in the kitchen," and I put my hands on

her waist and nudged her up the steps and into the kitchen. "Stand on the heating grate next to the refrigerator—it's just like the one in your apartment—and it will warm you up all the way from your toes to your nose. Mom and Dad, this is Abigail McKay. Abby . . . Matt and Angie Flynn."

"It's so nice to meet you, Mr. and Mrs. Flynn!"

"Call me Matt," said Dad. "Let me take your coats."

"What have you got there?" asked Mom.

"A coconut cream pie for Mr. Flynn . . . *Matt*, and a red rose and a plant for you."

"I've never seen a plant with leaves like that . . . all those different colors. What is it?"

"It's a garden croton, Mrs. Flynn. I hope you like it. It's supposed to get flowers."

"It's beautiful. I'll try to take good care of it. And one of those red roses is also for me?"

"This one . . . for your pewter vase. Matt got one for me, too . . . and this *special* vase."

"The rose is beautiful. I always love the *red* ones the best. It was very thoughtful of both of you. Abigail, may I take a look at that vase?"

Just then Dad chimed in from the hall closet where he had taken our coats, "Did I hear something about a coconut cream pie?"

Mom was turning the vase in her delicate, wrinkled fingers. "Hold your horses a minute about the pie, honey. I think I *know* this vase. Matthew, where did you get it?"

Abigail squeezed my arm with both hands and smiled.

"You're right, Mom, you *do* know the vase. Aunt Connie gave it to me before she moved out of the house. She said . . . "

"Pa used to put a red rose in this vase *every* week for Mama—from his own rose bushes in the back yard in the spring and summer, and from Giovanetta's market down the street in the fall and winter—*every* week . . . on the little table in the front window between the statues of the Infant of Prague and the Blessed Virgin." Mom had tears on her cheeks. "And then just before you were born, Matt . . . it was a beautiful Sunday afternoon in the spring . . . Mama died. After that, Pa never cut another rose from any of his bushes, and he put this vase in a drawer in the sideboard in the dining room. Sometimes, when no one was looking, I would take it out of the sideboard and unwrap the white linen napkin and just touch it. It always made me think of that Sunday afternoon when I was pregnant and Mama died. I'm *so* glad Connie saved it and gave it to you."

Mom hugged me and Abigail, who also had tears on *her* cheeks.

"*Now*, Matthew Flynn, Sr., why don't you put some coffee on, and we can get to your coconut cream pie. I also made a batch of Aunt Theresa's Italian cookies. Abigail, I know Matt likes a glass of milk with his pie and cookies; would you like some too?"

"Yes, please, Mrs. Flynn."

Dad interjected, "The coffee is ready to go. I just pushed the button, and it will be done in *six*
minutes. These new coffee machines are *really* something. Abigail, tell us about your family— where do they live?"

We sat around the table in Mom and Dad's snug kitchen with our milk and cookies and pie and coffee, and we talked: about Abigail's mom and dad in Brighton; about her brothers; about her RIT courses and her job at Mangrums; about her upstairs apartment on Meigs Street.

"That's the neighborhood where I grew up—it used to be called Swillburg," said Dad, as we moved into the living room.

With Dad all conversations usually get around to World War II—The War—and that snowy November evening with Abigail was no exception. Once she started talking about her grand-parents and her grandfathers' service in the Army and Navy in The War, Dad wanted to know where they served, what ships, what units, when they went over and when they came home. He made Abigail promise to find out more from her grandfathers and come back and talk again.

Mom changed the subject several times; she wanted to hear about Abigail and her family: *Where do your mother and father live in Brighton? How about your brothers? How old is your brother's daughter? What is your younger brother studying at RIT? Do you like all of your courses? What does a graphic designer do? Isn't that something? Is that what you studied at Newton? When will you be done with your degree? Would either of you like more cookies or pie? More coffee, Matthew? Are you all done, Abigail? Shall we go back in the kitchen for seconds? Are any of your grandparents in town? So your mother is a Dolan? Stockbridge? Isn't that just off the Massachusetts Turnpike on the way to Boston? Matt, how many times did we drive by Stockbridge on our way to visit Matthew at*

66

Boston College? And your Grandma and Grandpa McKay?
Valley Manor? The high towers? Honey, would you please put
another log on the fire?

"Stay put, Dad, I'll do it. It was nice of you to get a fire going for us. I'm gonna have just a little bit more coffee. Abby, would you like a warm-up?"

"Just a half, Matt, and then we probably should head home. It was a long day at Mangrums, and Maggie and Jock will be jumping to go out as soon as we come in the door."

I saw Mom look at Dad at the mention of *home*, and she took Abigail's cup and walked with me into the kitchen.

As she poured the coffee, Mom whispered, "Matthew, Abigail is *adorable* . . . and *so* pretty, but isn't she too *young* for you? You have two grandchildren."

"*She* doesn't think so, Mom. I thought she was at first, but now I'm sure that Abigail is a gift I probably don't deserve— from God . . . from Sarah? I don't know, Mom."

"What are your *sons* going to say? They're about the same age as Abigail. And the rest of the family?"

"Well, Abby and I are going to Matt and Claire's on Sunday for pizza, and driving to Boston the first week in December to see Danny and Emma, so I'll let you know."

I gave her my best little boy grin.

Mom poked me in the ribs. "You've used that grin on me *way* too many times. Don't think it's always going to get you off the hook. Abigail moved in with you in less than a *week*?"

"Three days, actually." I grinned again. "But she only moved in a little bit. We still have to get all her stuff from her apartment."

This time Mom pinched me—with a twist—on the cheek. "Matthew, what am I gonna do with you? Always making everything funny."

"Ouch! That's gonna leave a mark." I gave her a hug. "Mom, Abby brings the house to life. She loves Jock and Maggie, and they love her . . . she loves *me*. Don't worry, it'll be okay."

We went back in the living room, where Abigail had joined Dad on the *davenport*, and the two of them were poring over the photographs in one of Dad's World War II scrapbooks. Dad had his arm around Abigail's shoulder as she carefully turned the brittle pages. He was in his glory as he talked about his buddies and the towns and villages in the photos.

He looked at Mom with the same little boy grin I had just used. "Angie, when can we have these kids over for dinner so that I can show this pretty girl more of my ancient history?"

With an exaggerated sigh, Mom said, "Abigail, I should have warned you about my soldier boy and his scrapbooks."

"They're *wonderful*, Mrs. Flynn! My grandfathers have never shown me any pictures from *their* World War II days. I *love* the ones of you with your curly hair—in those *short* dresses!"

"I guess we were *babes* then. We *did* love to dress up for a night on the town."

As we bundled up to leave, we settled on the Wednesday after Thanksgiving for dinner. Mom and Dad thanked us again for the rose and the plant and the coconut cream pie, and Mom asked Abigail what she would like her to make for dinner.

"Mrs. Flynn, Matt says you make the best spaghetti and meatballs in town."

"Matthew's a good boy. You take *care* of him."

"I will, Mrs. Flynn. Good night, Mr. Flynn—Matt. See you soon."

7

As Abigail had surmised, once Jock and Maggie heard our car in the garage, they jumped against the inside of the door so energetically that it was hard for us to open it. We took them out right away for a happy but icy walk around the circle—enhanced by a black and starry sky.

"Abby, look right over the top of our house . . . that's north. See the Big Dipper and the North Star? And right opposite . . . see the crooked 'W' . . . the five stars? That's Cassiopeia."

"Just like the freckles on Kate Beckinsale's arm." She squeezed *my* arm.

"Not quite as pretty. Speaking of pretty . . ." I watched her breath come out into the cold air and moved my face close enough to breathe it in. And I kissed her red cheeks.

"And usually, just to the east over the golf course, you can see Taurus, but the 'Bull' is not up yet tonight. If you wake me up at three, I'll take you out and show you." I kissed her red nose.

"Can I wait for another night when he might come up *earlier*?"

"There will be lots of nights, beauty. Let's go in and get warm."

We settled into our end of the sofa in the family room with our glasses of Chianti. Jock and Maggie curled together on the red fleece at *their* end.

"It's nine-thirty, Abby. Shall we watch a little more of *Serendipity* before we go to bed?"

"My eyes aren't closing yet, old guy, so let's see what Jonathan and Sara did after they missed each other on the elevators. *Hey*, what happened to your face?"

"My mother gave me her Sicilian pinch—with an extra twist—when we were talking about your coming to live with Jock and Maggie."

"Just Maggie and Jock? She doesn't mind my living with *you*?"

"Well, that too," I laughed. "She likes you a lot, but she

thinks you're too *mature* for a kid like me." This time, *Abby* pinched me on the cheek. "Mom'll come around; Dad's crazy about you."

"He's such a sweet guy. They're beautiful together, like Grandpa Dolan and Nannie. Matt, I had a *lovely* evening at Palermo's and your mom and dad's." She nestled against my left arm.

In the movie, John Cusack ran out of the Waldorf into the street looking for Kate Beckinsale, but she was gone. The next scenes show Jonathan and Sara a few years later: Jonathan at a dinner with his fiancée Halley three days before their wedding; and Sara agreeing to marry her rock star fiancé Lars; but both of them thinking—and seeing reminders every place they go in New York—of that magical evening a few years earlier.

"Can you stop it there, please, Matt? He was so sad when he lost her in the crowd and had to get on the subway all alone. Even on a crowded subway in New York City, he was all alone. I feel a couple of yawns coming and I don't want to keep crashing on you every night."

"Beauty, I don't mind so much if you keep waking me up like you did this morning."

"Well, hush, because I want to tell you something. It's been buzzing around in my head for a couple of days, and meeting your mom and dad made me want to tell you tonight. When I see people like your mom and dad and my Grandpa Dolan and Nannie—who have loved each other and devoted their whole lives to each other for more than *sixty* years—I realize how lucky I am that you walked into Kitty's on Monday. It could have been Wednesday, and I might have missed you forever.

"Matt, I've loved you all my life. I just never knew when I was going to *find* you. I was never even sure *if* I was going to find you, but I dreamed I would. I prayed I would. With all the guys I've met—from high school to last week—I knew, every single time, that they were *not* you. Some of them I liked, some were smart, some were hot, some were rich, some turned me on, and two of them even asked me to marry them. But none of them were *you*. That's why I'm so very happy: I'm only twenty-six and I've found you already."

She laughed, stretched on her back on the sofa with her head in my lap and lifted her feet up on the back cushions. Jock and Maggie had to shuffle their positions at the other end of the sofa and scrunch closer together. They were watching us intently.

70

Then Abigail reached up and took my face in both her hands and laughed again. "You *are* going to ask me to marry you, right, summer boy? I mean, we can't just *live* together. I'm too *old* for all that." She grinned at me, upside down, tugged on my ears and teased. "If you think my mom and dad are going to grind their teeth about the *age* thing, think again about how they're going to grind their teeth if their little girl is just *living* with an old guy."

"Abby, you've know me for less than a *week* and you want to *marry* me?"

"No, Matt, I want *you* to marry *me*. Remember, summer boy . . . I've loved you all my *life* and now I want to catch up on my dream of you."

"Let's go to bed, beauty. *I* feel a couple of yawns coming, so we might have to continue this wondrous conversation tomorrow morning. Come on, puppies, upstairs. Abby, you know I love you, so you know I will do whatever is in my power to make you happy."

"So you *will* ask me to marry you?" She tugged me up the stairs by my belt buckle, with Jock and Maggie right on my heels.

"In the morning . . . if you are nice to me . . . and if you answer one simple question."

"What's the question, Matt?"

"One knee or two, Abby?" She laughed and unbuckled my belt.

"Good night, baby dogs. You sleep on your beds in the hallway. Mommy and I are going to close the door tonight."

With no alarm because it was Saturday, Abigail and I were awakened by Jock and Maggie scratching in the hallway. It was eight o'clock, so they were already past their usual breakfast and walk time. We stretched and sighed together. We were so tangled it was hard to tell Abigail's arms and legs from mine. I was amazed after ten years of spreading out and taking up a whole king-size bed myself that I could sleep completely wrapped in a woman again.

"*Mmm* . . . good morning, Matt. I love you. *Mmm* . . . my buddy down there is *very* tall this morning."

"That happens some mornings, even when there is *no* beautiful girl in bed with me."

"Can we do that stretch again with him inside me? *Mmm* . . . he's so alive! What a way to say 'good morning' and wake me

71

up!"

We stretched our legs full length together. I could feel Abigail's taut muscles from her thighs all the way to her feet. Our bellies pushed into each other, our arms tight around our backs, our lips crushed together . . . and we rolled as one across the bed . . . and across again.

When Abigail relaxed her arms and legs, she put both her hands on my butt and tried to keep me inside her as long as she could. I was still holding her just as tightly, with my eyes closed and my lips still on hers. I could have gone right back to sleep like that—stretched into her body and breathing in her lips.

"Matt, should we let the puppies in? I still want to play with you some more this morning. It's Saturday. I know we have a lot to do, but before we go to my apartment and get into our jobs list, I want to *play* with you. And I have the answer to your question."

"What is the answer, beauty? I have to remember the question."

"One."

"One *what*?"

"One *knee*, old guy." She laughed and tickled my right ear.

"Oh, *that* question." I nibbled around her *left* ear. "Do you want me to ask you the *next* question before or after we let in the dogs, or give them breakfast and take them for their walk?"

"Let's let them in, and they can be witnesses. And if you ask me the right question, and I give you the right answer, then we can make the doggies their breakfast and take them for a walk. And *then* we can come back to bed so I can play with you some more. Isn't that a great plan?"

Abigail walked her fingertips through my hair.

"*Mmm* . . . beauty, that is a *delicious* plan."

I opened the door for Jock and Maggie, and they jumped over both of us to Abigail's side of the bed and licked her face and hair.

"Abby, you have taken over; they don't even know I'm here."

I sat up and took her left hand, and we stepped onto the floor on my side of the bed. Then I knelt on my right knee and took *both* her hands. Jock and Maggie stood on the edge of the bed, their noses almost touching my arm and Abigail's hip. It was what they used to call a 'Kodak moment' in the old days, except that Abigail and I didn't have any clothes on. Our witnesses were dressed in their blue and red neckerchiefs.

"Abigail Elizabeth McKay, my breathtaking beauty, the wonder of my second life, will you make me the happiest old guy in the world and be my wife?"

"How do you do that, Matt? How do you turn everything into a poem?"

"You are a poem, Abby. You are *way* more than that—you are a love song."

She knelt down in front of me, touched my face with all her fingers, and brushed her lips softly around my mouth.

"Matthew Howard Flynn . . . Junior, I will be your wife. I want *so* much to be your wife. I love you, and you will make me the happiest girl in the world."

Tears fell down Abigail's cheeks, and she gathered them with her fingertips and wiped them over my lips so I could taste them. Then she buried her face in my neck and wrapped her arms around my waist. She was still crying, and I could feel her trembling. Jock and Maggie—still standing on the edge of the bed—were distressed by the quiet and poked me with their cold noses to see what was wrong. As I stroked Abigail's back, I told the dogs, "Everything's okay, puppies. Mommy's okay. We'll go downstairs in a minute." At the word 'downstairs' they jumped off the bed and into the hallway.

Abigail looked up. "Matt, I love you *so* much. Sorry I'm such a crybaby; I just can't believe I'm this happy. Let's go do breakfast with the doggies and take them out. Then I still want to play with you some more—and maybe cry more too."

It was a gray morning, but not as cold as it had been all week. The snow in the street was mushy and dirty after a week of sand, salt and cinders from the town plow-trucks. We tried to keep Jock and Maggie out of the brown-sugar mush as much as possible.

When we got back, we spread the dogs' towels on the living room rug and put the gate at the bottom of the stairs so they couldn't go up while they were still wet. Then Abigail and I took our mugs of hot coffee to the bedroom and curled up under *Pooh* and *Piglet*.

"Matt, do you think Maggie and Jock understood our bedside ceremony?"

"Maybe, Abby; they are very smart dogs. But I think there are plenty of *people* we know who might not understand." I twirled some hair falling over her ear.

She rubbed her hand on my stomach. "Should we wait a little

73

while . . ."

". . . until we tell the family that we're going to get married? That's probably a good idea, my beautiful girl. Our families will have enough to get used to . . ."

". . . just seeing us together, especially through the holidays and all the family gatherings."

She wiggled her little finger in my navel. "How long can we keep it a secret?"

"Maybe until some cold, dark day in January?"

"I can do that. If I get an irresistible urge, I could just tell Patrick. He would never say a word, not even to Laurie."

We were warm by then from the coffee and the quilt. I threw *Pooh* and *Piglet* to the end of the bed and studied the beautiful woman next to me.

"Abby, I want to know every inch of your beautiful body. I may have to count your freckles; has anybody ever done that? Here's number one," and I touched the freckle on her nose.

"Nobody has ever noticed them much, except for my boyfriend at B.C. who wondered once *what you would look like without those freckles*. I'll bet his new girlfriend at Wellesley didn't have any. By the way, old guy, there's one more on my nose that I don't think you've noticed. See, here, just below the tip?"

"How about that? I'm going to have to look much closer . . . starting now," and I kissed her all around her nose.

"Matt, nobody's ever been this close to me, not even the guys I had sex with. They put their hands on me and kissed me, but mostly they just wanted to *do it*. They never looked into my eyes the way you do, and they never looked into my body at all. Never mind looking into my *heart*."

"Abby, there are no *parts* of you. You are *all* of my dreams and senses together . . . and all at the same time. The first morning in bed . . . Wednesday? . . . I woke up before you did and I was watching you sleep . . . and breathe. The sun was coming in the windows, and you were glowing, but *not* from the sun. You were glowing from inside. I could see into your body the same way I can see into your eyes right now. I can see into your heart; I can see myself reflected there."

"Matt, my old guy, my poet, the man who turns my life on in the morning and keeps me safe at night when he holds me in his arms . . . I *love* you. I love the *touch* of you. Your touch brings out the woman I want to be. I *need* that . . . I need it all the time.

Sometimes I want your touch so bad I can hardly breathe. Like now . . . can you see into my mind right now? Can you see into my belly? Touch me, Matt, kiss me . . . all over my belly, all the way down, between my legs, inside my thighs . . . and that special kiss inside me . . . and those waves. Can you take me on those waves again, Matt?"

One of the hundreds of remarkable things about the human body is that you can be completely physically engaged, so completely enveloped in your five senses without awareness of a single thought in your mind, and yet images and scenes can still flash through your consciousness like waking dreams.

Abigail was all of my senses: her flavor, her warmth, her fragrance, her glow, her cries. I felt everything and thought nothing. And yet the young boy on the hill in the bright sun floated past my closed eyes; and the sunburn on Bonnie's legs; and Missy's head on my lap in the car; and Eddie Fisher singing "Oh, My Papa"; and Mickey Mantle Day at Yankee Stadium. There was no rhyme or reason to the random pictures from corners of my past that careered with Abigail over the bed. And suddenly she was still, the pictures were all gone, and I remembered where I was.

Abigail had been so wild that all the pillows were off the bed. I picked up her favorite, softly lifted her head, and tucked the pillow under her left cheek. I tucked mine under my right cheek, kissed both of Abby's moist eyes, and pulled the popcorn-cloud side of the quilt over both of us.

"Matt?" Abigail's fingers were gently scratching my chest. "Matt?" She blew softly on my face. "It's almost eleven o'clock, summer boy. We have some *other* jobs to do."

"*Mmm* . . . jobs. This is my new favorite job, beauty: making waves." I grinned with my eyes closed. "How were the waves this time, Abby?"

"Don't you *know*, Matt? Can't you *tell* when it's happening?"

"I can't *think* when it's happening—I'm completely dissolved in you—but I sense this lovely shape pitching and rolling in perfect synch with the waves. I sense the cries and the crashing."

"Matt, you drowned me again. At the beginning, I felt your hands on my hips; I felt you inside me; I heard myself crying. And then I couldn't hear my cries any more and I was lost in the loud waves. You drowned me again, captain, sir. Can we do this every morning?" She traced my lips with one finger.

"Abby, I could touch you all day long, *every* day . . . never let go . . . never take my hands off you. At least until Jock and Maggie got jealous or hungry." We both laughed. "I hope we have a million more mornings like this one."

"Did you have mornings like this with Sarah?"

"Yes."

"When are you going to tell me about her, Matt?"

"I would start right now, but we really need to get to your apartment. How about tonight when we come home from your mom and dad's?"

"If they don't wipe us out too much, right?"

"We'll be okay, beauty. Your mom and dad will see how happy you are, and that should be enough for them. Isn't that what all mothers and fathers want for their children? And how could they not like *me*?"

"Of course they'll like you—they are *my* parents, after all—and Pat will be on your side too."

"And you know who is on *your* side, Abby? Sarah. I talked with her in the car on Thursday morning, during the slow ride from Joe's Diner to my office. She likes you; she knows you're good for me; and she wants us to be happy. She was the same age as you when I met her . . . But that's for later. Let's get over to Meigs Street."

At Abigail's apartment, we gathered up all her clothes—she still kept a lot of them at her mom and dad's—her favorite towels and pillowcases, and most of the packaged and canned food in the cupboards in her kitchen. While Abigail continued in the kitchen, cleaning out the refrigerator, I collected all her papers, books and files for RIT and Mangrums, and her CDs and DVDs.

"Abby, how about the prints and stuff on the walls?" I yelled from the living room.

"Leave those for the next time, Matt, but fold up the red-white-and-blue afghan on the back of the sofa and throw it in one of the bags with the clothes."

"This looks like the *Union Jack*."

"It *is* the *Union Jack*. It's one of my most special things. Nannie knitted it for me to take to college. I love it as much as you . . . *we* . . . love the popcorn clouds. I curled up in it on my first night in Boston—that's *eight* years ago—and almost every night since until you carried me away this week."

"Abigail Elizabeth, would you come here for a second?"

"Abigail *Elizabeth*? That's a first. That's what my mother calls me when I do something bad. Did I do something bad?" She walked into the living room and gave me a mischievous look.

I was standing in front of the sofa, holding the *Union Jack.*

"Stand right here." I wrapped the afghan around her, took her head in my hands and kissed her slowly. "This is the scene of our first kiss, beauty . . . only *four* days ago. And *how much* I love you now. *Four* days."

Abigail wrapped the afghan around both of us and pulled me close.

"And let's not forget the best part, old guy: this is the scene of my first Matt Flynn orgasm— when I knew for sure that *I* loved *you*."

I kissed her again . . . more slowly.

"If you do that one more time, Matt, I'm going to have to lie down on the sofa, and you're going to have to lie down with me. As delicious as that sounds, we have to get going. All the stuff we're loading *into* your Jeep we're going to have to load *out*." We laughed and folded up the *Union Jack.*

While Abigail packed up her bathroom and bedroom stuff and checked for loose ends, I made several wet trips up and down the narrow stairs and loaded my Wrangler until you couldn't see out the plastic windows of the rag top. And then we headed back to Penfield.

At home, Abigail set about finding the right places for all of her things, while Jock and Maggie followed her devotedly from room to room.

"Matt, the closet is empty in the front bedroom where I have Uncle Vinny's desk set up with my computer and Mangrums and RIT projects. I think I'll put all my hanging clothes in there, and my shoes and boots too."

"The dresser in there is also empty, Abby, but so is most of the long dresser in our bedroom. That was always Sarah's, and it's *yours* now. I only use the tall old dresser in the corner. Spread out your clothes and all your things wherever you find the space."

"I don't want to crowd you, old guy. Maybe squeeze you, though."

I laughed as I brought coffee upstairs for both of us. "Don't worry about that, Abby; I like being squeezed. Sarah always seemed to fill up seventy-five percent of all the closets, so I got used to the corners. And now, after ten years as a bachelor . . . well, I've never been a clothes horse. I don't need more than the corners."

I sat with my coffee on the stairs and scratched Jock and Maggie, who were starting to punch me with their noses because it was suppertime.

"I put your CDs with mine on the library table in the living room. Uncle Vinny took that out of a cubbyhole in his attic—where it had collected dust for twenty years—and repaired and refinished it for me when Sarah and I moved in to this house in 1980. It has always been a perfect spot for my CD and cassette player and my old turntable."

"You have a *turntable* . . . a *record* player? You actually play *records*?" Abigail forced a giggle. "You *are* an old guy. Hey, I like this little painting in the hallway. Is it an original?"

"Which one, love?" I shifted sideways on the top step to see where she was looking.

"It's a boy lying on a hill in the sunshine. Is it *you*, summer boy?"

"It's just a cheap print I found somewhere, but it's one of my favorites because the shirtless boy with bare feet really *could* be me. It's called *Dreamer*, and the painter is a famous old New Englander named Frank Kerrigan—F.X. Kerrigan."

"I've actually heard of him. Sort of a lesser Norman Rockwell, right?"

"Right. I think he's still alive and painting, living in one of those fishing ports—Gloucester, maybe. I met him once when he spoke at a fine arts seminar at B.C."

"I remember there were a lot of 'F. X.' guys at Newton and B.C., students *and* professors."

"Yeah, they're all named after St. Francis Xavier, the famous Jesuit missionary. During my B.C. undergrad years, the governor of Massachusetts was Francis X. Bellotti, and one of my best day-hop friends was Charles F. X. O'Brien."

"What's a *day-hop*?"

"A day student, a commuter, one who didn't live in the dorms but came from home every day. Didn't you have day-hops at Newton?"

"We just called them 'commies' or commuters."

"How are you doing with all your stuff, beauty? Can I help

you?"

"I'm getting all my things situated just fine. There's lots of room. You definitely needed a woman around here to take up space. Did you put my DVDs with yours in the family room?"

"Yep. We'll have to sit on the floor over several cups of coffee and organize them. I kind of let them sprawl everywhere over the past few years."

"I can alphabetize with the best of them, Matt."

"I could see that in you from the first minute in the coffee shop. That's the *real* reason I came back the next day to talk with you again." I gave Abigail my toothy, fake grin.

"Damn! I thought you liked my body."

"Come here, let me refresh my memory." I held her close, stroked the small of her back, and rubbed my cheek on her ear. "You're right. I can always look up the alphabet on Google. We should take a puppy break. If you will give Jock and Maggie their supper, I'll go rearrange a few things in the garage and on the back porch to make room for your car later."

After we walked the dogs, Abigail said she'd been thinking about a cheeseburger and tater tots all day, so we went to Phil Green's for a quick bite. I sensed that she was nervous about taking her old guy to meet her parents. Even though she'd seemed unconcerned about it all week, the fact that it was about to happen had her worried. It was different than with *my* mom and dad. They were as old as Abigail's grandparents, but her father was only three years older than I, and I was actually six months *older* than Abigail's mother. I knew her parents and I could be comfortable because we were contemporaries, but the idea of one of their contemporaries dating their *daughter* was a much different story.

"Should I wear anything special, Abby, maybe to make your mom and dad think I'm half my age?" I said with a shrug.

"Dad likes corduroys and sweaters this time of the year, and Mom likes Dad in his corduroys and sweaters. Mom also thinks that I look very professional in a white blouse, medium-length skirt and boots, so that's what *I'm* going to wear."

"I happen to agree with both your mom and dad. I have some light brown corduroys, and how about this blue sweater?"

"Ooh, I like that! That's what they call slate blue, and it brings out the pretty blue of your eyes. Mom will fall in love with you too." Abigail squeezed my shoulder and kissed me.

"Well, that won't make your dad happy. I'll try not to flirt with your mother too much. What does your dad do? Is he retired?"

"He works in the auditing department at the Kodak office on State Street. He got his degree in accounting from Canisius and went to Kodak right from college. He'll be sixty-five next summer and he said he's going to retire at the end of next year. Mom got her teaching degree at Brockport and has taught and substituted in Brighton on and off—in between her three children—for thirty-nine years. We have been in the same house in Brighton since my older brother Jack was born in 1975—Monteroy Road. Do you know the neighborhood?"

"Sure. Not only do I have a lawyer friend, Nick Keller, who lives on Monteroy, but I spent a year in between the Army and law school working as a mailman, and a lot of my substitute routes were out of the Twelve Corners Post Office. I know every street within a mile of the old Don and Bob's. And I was at Nick's house many times for parties and picnics, so I might have seen you playing outside over the years. Rochester is a small town."

"So now I have to add Post Office to my long list of things to learn about you? We live almost across the street from the Kellers. They're at seventy-four, and we're at sixty-seven. Their son Jimmy is my age. He went to Brighton schools all the way, and I went to Catholic schools, but we played together when we were on vacation, and he asked me to one dance at Brighton High in his freshman year. Then we decided to just be friends.

"If Mom and Dad kick us out tonight, we can go over and say hello to the Kellers."

8

Abigail's family house was a large, center-entrance colonial, so Mr. and Mrs. McKay, Patrick and Laurie all greeted us in the foyer which opened into the dining room on the right, the living room on the left, and led straight into the kitchen.

"It's nice to meet you, Mrs. McKay, Mr. McKay, Patrick, Laurie."

"Jerry and Peggy," said Mr. McKay, who was dressed in tan corduroys and a maroon sweater.

"Pat," said Patrick, who was in a sweatshirt and jeans.

Abigail and I sat on the love seat near the fireplace at the end of the living room. Patrick and Laurie shared the long sofa against the front wall with Mr. McKay, and Mrs. McKay sat in an old, formal Queen Anne chair near the opening into the family room.

"Matthew, Abigail Elizabeth, would you like something to drink?" asked Mrs. McKay.

Abigail gave me a covert elbow to my right ribs.

"My mother thinks I'm being bad," she whispered, hardly moving her lips.

"We have a couple of fine Irish brews, Matt," chimed in Mr. McKay, "Harp Lager and Murphy's Irish Red Ale."

"I like Harp, but I've never had Murphy's Irish Red, so I'll try that, thanks."

Patrick stood up. "I'll go get the drinks, Dad. Abby, how about you?"

"I'll share with Matt. Dad, Matt's a good friend of Nick Keller."

"No kidding! Nick and I have clinked many a bottle on our front stoops on a warm summer night. Abby told Peggy that you're a lawyer. Is that how you know Nick?"

"Mostly. We never worked at the same firm, but we hit it right off when we had a few real estate and business deals together, and our kids were about the same ages, so we started to do some family things together."

"So your children are about the same age as Abby?" I

thought I saw just a hint of a wink from Mr. McKay.

Abigail gripped my thigh and whispered, "Sorry, Matt, I should never have mentioned Nick."

I stroked her hand on my leg. "It's okay, Abby, it had to come up soon."

At that moment, Patrick walked over to us with our bottle of Murphy's Red and two glasses and whispered, "Dad'll be easy, but it's Mom you have to watch out for."

I poured one glass, took a full swallow and handed it to Abigail.

"This is really good ale, Mr. McKay . . . Jerry. My dad always swore—he still does—that beer is better than ale, but I can never tell the difference. I guess he's an expert because he's German *and* Irish. I'm a much better judge of wines, compliments of my Italian mother."

Mr. McKay chuckled, "Well, I sure don't know much about wine, but those of us who are *Irish* and Irish don't believe there are any better brews on this good earth than Irish beer *and* ale."

"In answer to your question . . . Jerry, I have two sons. Matt will be twenty-nine in February, and Danny twenty-six in March. Matt lives here in Penfield with his wife Claire and my two beautiful grandchildren, Matthew and Emily. He's an associate professor of history at MCC, and Claire is a full-time mom and a part-time press secretary for State Senator Mary Kelly. Danny is a urologist at the Tufts and Mather Memorial Hospital in Cambridge—near Harvard—and lives in Boston with his wife Emma."

Then it was Mrs. McKay's turn. "What do your sons think about you dating a girl *their* age?"

Patrick laughed, "Mom always gets right to the point, Matt."

"Hush, Patrick! I'm the mother, and we're talking about your sister here."

"That's a fair question, Mrs. McKay. I can't tell you what my son Matt thinks, but Abigail and Matt have talked on the phone, and we're going to their house for pizza tomorrow night, so we'll find out soon. Same for Danny. Abigail has talked with him, too, and we're going to Boston to visit Danny and Emma the week after Thanksgiving. I *can* tell you that both of my Scottie dogs, Jock and Maggie, love your daughter to death."

I gave Mrs. McKay my best smile.

"Abigail Elizabeth, I don't remember your ever liking dogs."

"Well, Maggie and Jock are very special dogs, Mom. Even

you would like them. Some day you'll have to tell me why *we* never had a dog."

"Well, putting the dogs aside for a minute, Matthew, what do *you* think about dating a girl who is the same age as your sons?"

"I will confess, Mrs. McKay, that I had serious doubts, and I shared them with Abigail. I told her it was very flattering to have a beautiful young woman interested in an older guy like me, that I didn't want to take advantage of her feelings, and that she should be looking for someone her own age, someone to build a family with and love for the rest of her life."

"That was good advice. And what did she say?"

"Hello? Mom? I'm right here! I said *forget it, Matt*. Mom, do you remember what you first said to Dad when you knew you loved him?"

Mr. McKay jumped in. "I remember, Peggy." I thought I saw another wink.

"It's not your turn, Dad," interrupted Patrick.

Abigail had fire in her eyes. "I said Matt, will you kiss me, a real kiss like in the movies? I need to find out something. And when he took me in his arms and kissed me, I said Matt, hold on to me tight because I don't think I can stand up. I said I found out what I needed to know. I said I've been looking for you all my life. I said I've dated a lot of guys my age but none of them were you. I said the age thing doesn't matter because I've been waiting for you for so long, and now I don't have to wait any more. I said I love you."

Abigail was out of breath, and her hands were trembling when she wrapped them around my arm and hugged it to her chest. The living room was suddenly so quiet that the only sound was the crackling of the fire. Laurie leaned against Patrick with tears in her eyes. Mr. McKay sipped from his Pilsener glass of Harp and looked me squarely in the eyes. Mrs. McKay seemed frozen, tightly gripping the arms of the Queen Anne chair with both hands.

Mr. McKay broke the silence: "Peggy, haven't you always told Abby to follow her heart, to do what she believes is right, and not to worry about what other people think? Isn't that what she's doing now?"

Mrs. McKay let go of the arms of the chair, clasped her hands—as if in prayer—just under her chin and looked at Abigail and me. "Matthew, I hope I didn't offend you; you seem to be a fine man. And Abby, I'm sorry I doubted your judgment.

You know *I'm* happy when *you're* happy."

"I know, Mom," Abigail sighed. "You're doing your job, as you've done so well for so many years, and I love you for it."

The worst seemed to be over, and Abigail loosened her grip on my arm, but Mrs. McKay wasn't quite finished. "As for *you*, Gerald Michael McKay, I *do* remember what I said to you thirty-five years ago: I said that I didn't want to spend another day without you, and I never have—in spite of *my* mother, who wondered what I saw in such a rascal as yourself."

Abigail laughed. "*Nannie* said that? I'm going to ask her about it the next time I see her."

As Mrs. McKay got up from her chair she said, "I think that Nannie and Grandpa Dolan might be coming for Christmas. Abby, did you tell Matthew about my famous chocolate cake?"

"You bet I did, Mom. You don't think he came here just for Dad's beer, do you? Matt would rather have a piece of chocolate cake and a glass of milk than anything else . . . except maybe a hug from me and a hot cup of coffee. Does that mean it's dessert time?"

We all got up and headed for the kitchen. It was a relief to sit around the kitchen table—with chocolate layer cake, milk and coffee—and have the conversation turn away from Abigail and me. Patrick talked about how much he was learning at the airport, and about a national air traffic controller conference at O'Hare in Chicago that RIT would be sending him to in January. Laurie was excited about her new payroll software design job at Paychex.

Mr. McKay mused about the bittersweet prospect of 2008 being his last year at Kodak. Mrs. McKay enthusiastically outlined their plans for taking that long-dreamed-of trip to Ireland "in the spring after Mr. McKay retires." And she was clearly delighted when I mentioned that I would love another piece of her delicious cake.

"Matthew, I have never seen anyone eat my chocolate cake the way you just did. You carved out all the cake on the inside, ate that first, and left the top and outside frosting standing on its side. And then you ate all the frosting. It was fun to watch."

Abigail laughed and poked me in the stomach.

"Mrs. McKay, I've been eating chocolate cake this way since I was a little boy, and that's why a layer cake is *so* much more enjoyable than a sheet cake. My mother always made her chocolate cakes the same way you do—I think because she saw how my brothers and I devoured them—and *your* Devil's food cake and buttercream frosting are as good as Mom's."

"Thank you, Matthew," she said as she lovingly placed another wedge of cake on my plate.

"I'll bet you say that to all the girls, sailor," teased Abigail.

"Abby, I may lie, smile and flatter about other things, but *not* about chocolate cake."

Mrs. McKay interrupted our banter. "More milk, Matthew?"

Mr. McKay couldn't resist jumping in. "Matt, the quickest way to Peggy's heart has always been through her cake."

"Hush, Mr. McKay! Matthew is clearly smarter and nicer than Abby let on. If I had met *him* thirty-five years ago, I might have picked him first." She gave her husband a demure smile.

Abigail couldn't resist. "Mother, Matt is too *old* for you."

Mrs. McKay laughed and changed the subject to Thanksgiving. Dinner would be at five-thirty, and Abigail and I could bring rolls, Italian bread and wine. Laurie and Pat were assigned cheese, beer and nuts. Mrs. McKay and Jack's wife Catherine would do most of the cooking.

Our surprisingly lovely evening broke up at about nine-thirty. I got hugs from Mrs. McKay and Laurie as Abigail and I went out the door from the kitchen to the garage to get her red Taurus.

We were home in about ten minutes, to a robust reception from Jock and Maggie. After we walked the dogs and warmed up some coffee, we all settled on the sofa to catch up on Sara and Jonathan in *Serendipity*.

"Matt, you were great with Mom and Dad. Dad was easier, for sure, because you're at least partly Irish and you liked his red ale, but the way you buttered up my mother for her buttercream frosting was a work of art." Abigail leaned her head on my chest. "It took you all of *two* hours to become part of the family. Even my grumpy brother Jack—who likes to criticize all the time—will be hard pressed with the rest of the family solidly behind you."

"Abby, my fearless Irish beauty, it was *you* who were dazzling in the *parlor* on Monteroy. Your mother gave it her best shot. It must be hard for any mother to eventually have to concede that her daughter is a woman on equal footing with herself. You walked into the living room as a daughter who was 'being bad'—as you said—and walked out as a woman who has fallen in love and made her choice, the same as your mother fell in love thirty-five years ago and made *her* choice. The way you told your mom about our first kiss was perfect: you weren't mean, you were gentle; but you forced your mom to forget logic and remember love and passion. And she remembered because she is clearly a loving and passionate woman. Your dad is a lucky guy."

"Matthew Flynn, I love you more every day, and my plan is to make you an even *luckier* guy. Let's see what Sara and Jonathan are doing."

We picked up *Serendipity* with Jonathan and Halley in their apartment, where Halley is going through the closets and making a pile for Jonathan to start packing for their honeymoon. In the pile he finds the Bloomingdale's Christmas bag with one of the two gloves he and Sara had grabbed at the same time on that magical evening a few years earlier. He enlists his best friend and best man Dean to help him with one final search of the city to try to either find Sara or get her out of his system. And we see Sara telling her fiancé in San Francisco that she has to get away to New York to sort some things out and clear her mind, but in reality to try to either find Jonathan or finally get him out of *her* system.

Before Sara and Jonathan lost each other in the Waldorf-Astoria, she had written her name and phone number on the blank page inside a hardcover copy of *Love in the Time of Cholera*, and Jonathan had written *his* name and phone number on a five-dollar bill. If he found the book or she found the five-dollar bill, Sara said they were meant to be together. Of course they had both been looking at every *Cholera* book and five-dollar bill since that night.

"Matt, would you have let me do that? I know it's a movie, but after we reached for the same gloves, after we had coffee in the cafe, after we went skating and I fell in Central Park and you put a bandage over the freckles on my arm, would you have let me go away without making a date or at least getting my phone number?"

"No, beauty, I sure wouldn't. And Jonathan didn't want to either. He was being a nice guy so he played along with Sara, but one step too far: getting on the elevators. I think Sara changed her mind just as her elevator door was about to close, when she flipped the Bloomingdale's bag to Jonathan and said, 'It's Sara, my name is Sara.' I think she was just as unhappy as he was when they missed each other getting off the elevators.

But it made for a great movie."

"So you won't let *me* go, old guy, even though we've only known each other for five days?"

"Never, Abby. You know what I *do* think about, though? I think about the two or three or four years between when Jonathan and Sara met and when they found each other again at the end of the movie. What would their lives have been like if they had stayed together from that first night . . . if Jonathan had gotten off the elevator on the floor where Sara was sitting and waiting for him? Would they have been happier than they ended up? Would they have stayed together? Or were they better in the long run because they missed each other and searched all those years?"

"The *what ifs* happen in so many lives. I know lots of families—I'm sure you do too—where the husbands and wives were all wrong for each other from the beginning, but they have beautiful kids, so they wouldn't want to take it back or do it over. And for every one of those families there are high school sweethearts who broke up—probably for silly reasons—but found each other thirty or forty years later and were just as much in love."

"I do, Abby, I know many of those people. And then there's always *timing*, being in the right coffee shop on the right day." I squeezed her and kissed her on the top of her head.

"I had a handful of serious girlfriends before Sarah, and each girl I thought was the love of my life, but it was either the wrong time in our lives, or she didn't feel the same way I did. With a couple of them, I think if we had met a year earlier or a year later, it might have worked. But then I would not have met Sarah, and there would be no Matt and Danny, so *why* would I ever want to go back and change anything with any of the old girlfriends? Still, I loved them all and I have wondered over the years what life would have been like with Cathy or Bonnie or Ellen or Missy."

"Four loves *before* you got married? I hope you don't mind my saying that I'm not sorry they didn't work out, because then I wouldn't be here with you on your sofa with your two beautiful dogs. You might be in Wisconsin or Virginia on a different sofa with different dogs." She looked up and smiled.

"I know, beauty. The only thing I would change, of course, is that Sarah and I only had twenty years together. *Sixty* would not have been enough."

"What happened, Matt?"

"She died when a brain aneurysm burst. We never knew there was a problem. One day she suddenly developed a bad headache, and the next day she was gone."

"I'm so sorry. You and Matt and Danny must have been devastated."

"Danny was in his sophomore year at Penfield, and Matt was a freshman at Albany. They were both very strong and helped me get through many hard months. I have always believed that everything happens for a reason, that God doesn't play tricks on us. My sons and I have been closer since Sarah died, and we all feel certain that she has been watching out for us every day of the past ten years. And now *you're* here, and that didn't just happen by chance. I think Sarah felt it was time for me to be in love again."

"Oh, Matt, how can I compare with *that* kind of love?" Abigail had tears in her eyes and was gripping both my hands tightly.

"No, Abby, *no*. Don't look at it that way. I'm not comparing, and you're not replacing. It's not like that. Sarah wasn't my one-and-only soul mate, the only love of my life, the only girl of my dreams. Those expressions have been used so much that they don't *mean* anything. Sarah has a very special place in my heart as the mother of my sons, but I didn't love her *more* than I loved Missy or Bonnie or the other girls. I didn't love her *more* than I love you."

I kissed Abigail and held her close.

"Each time, each girl was different. Each time I was a little older. Each time life around me was different. I grew from high school to college to the Army to law school to a job, and each time I learned. Each girl I appreciated more than the previous one because I knew more about love . . . and girls. So I may not love you more or less than Missy and Sarah and the others, but I hope I will love you *better*."

"I'm happy, Matt. I don't know how anybody could be better than you. *Wait* a minute, was that the five-dollar bill?"

"Yep."

"But Sara didn't see it. It sounded as if she's giving up on finding Jonathan. Look . . . she just missed him getting out of the cab in front of *Serendipity*."

I whispered in Abigail's ear, "Don't forget, it's a *movie*, beauty."

"What's he doing? After all of his searching, did Jonathan just give up too?"

"*Sort of*, and Sara *sort of* gave up and is ready to fly back to San Francisco. But don't worry, Abby, you haven't seen the last of the *Cholera* book and the five-dollar bill. Let's stop the movie here, before Jonathan's wedding rehearsal and before Sara gets on the plane. I think we're going to sleep well tonight. What a week we've had, huh?"

"Every today better than yesterday, Matt, and yesterday was the best day of my life." Abigail curled on her side with her head in my lap. Jock and Maggie snuggled around her feet.

"And I've slept like a baby in your arms every night . . . not like in my apartment, where I've been rolling around and waking up every few hours thinking about my projects for the next day. Speaking of 'the next day,' do you go to church on Sunday?"

"I do, usually to either the eight-thirty or ten-thirty Mass at Holy Innocents on Creek Street."

"I was there once for a wedding. It's different from most Catholic churches—kind of *boxy*. I would like to go with you tomorrow. I usually go to St. Gregory, which is just around the corner from my apartment."

"Most of Dad's family and friends growing up in *Swillburg* used to go to either St. Gregory or Holy Eucharist on Monroe."

"That's a beautiful old church. I walk there on some Sundays when the weather is especially nice. That would be a lovely church to get married in."

Abigail looked up from my lap and smiled.

"When we tell everybody our secret on the 'cold, dark day in January,' we can talk more about churches. Your mom and dad might push for your family church, which is . . .?"

"St. Thomas Aquinas on East Avenue."

I twirled my index finger in the hair around her left ear. Abigail began to giggle when Maggie started licking her feet at the same time.

"Are you all ganging up on me?"

"You *are* fun to play with, and I believe you have become Jock and Maggie's favorite toy."

"Can they stay in the bedroom with us tonight?"

"Sure. It'll be *very* cozy."

Abigail laughed, "I promise not to leave enough room for either of them to get between us."

"The first rule we'll have to teach them is that we sleep *under* the covers and they sleep on *top* of *Pooh* and *Piglet*."

"Let's go up, old guy. Come on, baby dogs."

In the morning we woke up with Jock lying across our feet and licking his stomach and Maggie sharing Abigail's pillow and licking her cheek. It was eight o'clock and another Kodak moment. We stretched, laughed, hugged each other and scratched the dogs—more or less at the same time.

"Morning, Matt, I *love* you. I think the doggies woke us up too late for the eight-thirty Mass."

"Morning, beauty, I love *you*. Let's throw some clothes on, give Jock and Maggie their breakfast and take them around the circle. Then we can jump in the shower and have plenty of time to get to the ten-thirty Mass. I don't need to shave today if it's okay with you."

"It's okay with me; you can be my *cowboy* today." Abigail's eyes sparkled.

When we got in the shower, she said, "I've never done this before . . . showered with a guy. The handful of times I spent the night with someone, I don't think either of us really knew what to *do* in the morning. Stay in bed, have sex again, have breakfast, *what*? It never felt natural. It felt *so* strange, as a matter of fact, that I never spent a second night with the same guy. I didn't know why at the time, but I do now. None of those guys were *you*. Here I am in your bathtub lathering up this old brush to scrub your back, and here *you* are. You washed my hair and massaged my head, and now you're smoothing soap over my breasts and down my belly. And everything feels right—without a second thought. It's the way it should be."

When Abigail was done with my back, I turned around, pulled her close and ran my soapy hands down the slope of *her* back and over her hips to the back of her thighs.

"How's my 'tail' today, Matt?" she said playfully.

"Abby, I might say this to you a thousand more times but it will always be true: I could *die* for the touch of you."

"Well, don't die, old guy, because I want to hear you *say it* a thousand more times. Why don't you rinse me off, and then we can get some coffee and hard-boiled eggs."

When we pulled back the shower curtain, there was Jock stretched out at full length on the bath mat. Abigail laughed so loud she startled him, and he stood up, looking at her.

"What are you doing there, baby dog?"

"He does that a lot, Abby. Wait'll you see what happens

next. Step onto the mat right behind his tail." She did, and Jock immediately walked out of the bathroom . . . and Maggie walked in and started licking Abigail's legs from the knees down.

"Oh, Matt, what a feeling! Does she do this to you, too?"

"Yes, she does. I started to call myself her 'Daddy Popsicle.' But I'm sure she likes licking you better."

"She's drying my legs, even around the back—she's grooming me! What fun!"

I stepped out of the tub and hugged Abigail on the bath mat.

"Let's have a little slow dance, beauty, and see what Maggie does."

We went around in a small circle, and so did Maggie, trying to lick each leg before it got away. And then we stopped for a long, wet kiss—our hair was still dripping—and Maggie left to join Jock back up on the bed.

9

At the ten-thirty Mass we sat in the center of the "boxy" church. I like to move to the middle of the pew and let people fill in from both aisles. Many of the parishioners I saw every Sunday gave me an interesting look when they noticed Abigail holding my arm.

I spotted cousin Terry a few pews in front of us and whispered to Abigail, "See the short woman with streaked chestnut hair in the beige coat in front of us? That's my first cousin, Theresa Ruggeri—Terry. Her dad, Uncle Johnny, Giovanni Fiorino, was Mom's oldest brother.

"He and his wife, Aunt Thomasina, had four daughters: Anna, Martha, Theresa and Donna, in that order. Terry's husband Salvatore died about five years ago. She has four children, two boys and two girls. We'll say hello after Mass."

I gave Abigail a squeeze and kissed her hair above her ear. "That will make Terry the first member of the family—other than Mom and Dad—to meet my new *girlfriend*."

Abigail wrapped both her hands around my arm and leaned her head on my shoulder.

"I hope they all like me," she whispered back.

I squeezed her again. "You're a sure thing, beauty."

Father Ben's sermon was about Mary's journey "to a town of Juda" to visit her cousin Elizabeth, and they were both "with child." When they greeted each other, Elizabeth's infant—John the Baptist—leapt in her womb at the presence of Mary's infant, and Elizabeth said to Mary: *"Blessed art thou among women and blessed is the fruit of thy womb! And how have I deserved that the mother of my Lord should come to me? For behold, the moment that the sound of thy greeting came to my ears, the babe in my womb leapt for joy."*

Abigail whispered, "Matt, I want to have a baby—your baby. Can we pray for a miracle?"

"We can, Abby." I brushed my cheek across her forehead.

Theresa saw us and smiled at me as we were walking back to our pew from Communion, but she didn't know Abigail was with me until we waited for her in the front entrance of the church after Mass.

"Matt! How are you? I haven't seen you here in a while." We hugged and kissed each other. "How are Aunt Angie and Uncle Matt?"

"We're all fine, Terry, and how about your family?"

"Good, everybody's good. Did you know that Gina's expecting again?"

"No, nobody told me. Congratulations, grandma! How many will that be?"

"Five. Two for Gina, two for Becca, and one for Sal."

"Well, give Gina a hug from me. Terry, I want you to meet my friend Abigail McKay. Abby, this is my cousin Theresa Ruggeri."

"Nice to meet you, Theresa." Abigail held out her hand.

Theresa ignored the hand and gave her a hearty hug. "Call me Terry, please."

"Abby, didn't I tell you that the Fiorinos are huggers." We all laughed.

"Abigail, we haven't seen Matt with a woman since Sarah died. He's just about my favorite cousin, so you be nice to him, okay?"

"I promise." Abigail warmly hugged her back.

"You two look good together and very happy."

"We are, Terry. I can't believe I thought I was happy *before* I met Matt."

"Since you weren't with Matt at Aunt Angie's birthday party last month, I'm guessing you haven't known each other very long."

"One week tomorrow. I discovered this beauty in Kitty's coffee shop downtown on Monday."

"So, Abigail, was it love at first sight?"

"I'm not sure about *that*, Terry, but it was definitely love at *second* sight when Matt came back for coffee and me the next morning."

"Have you met Aunt Angie and Uncle Matt yet? My dad was Aunt Angie's oldest brother."

"Matt told me. I met his mother and father on Friday night after dinner."

"Knowing Uncle Matt—who used to flirt with me even with Aunt Angie or my husband Sal in the room—I'll bet he liked you right away. He probably thought you were too *old* for Matt but just right for him," Theresa smiled as she crooked her index finger playfully at Abigail, "but I would not be surprised if Aunt Angie gave you the evil eye."

"You're right, Terry, my father was hooked the instant he took Abby's hand and looked into her eyes. But *I* was the one who got the evil eye from Mom. She pulled me aside in the kitchen and gave me the third degree, but she came around quickly when she realized that I wasn't nuts but in love."

"Wait'll I tell my kids, especially the girls. Abigail, my daughters Gina and Becca—Regina and Rebecca—are twins and they have been crazy about their cousin Matt since they were little girls. I hope you can meet them soon. Did Matt tell you that I used to babysit for him a lot when he was a little towhead right after The War? We called him 'Matty' when he was a little boy."

Abigail laughed. "That's really funny. I'm supposed to be the one who's too young, and yet here I am with the toddler and his first babysitter. Terry, if everybody in Matt's family is as nice as you are, I can't meet them all soon enough."

"We have been blessed with a warm, welcoming family— thanks to Grandma and Grandpa— and I can see that you will fit right in. Matt, you are such a lucky guy! My daughters and I were sure that you could never find anyone as pretty or as nice as Sarah."

"Terry, I will always settle for lucky because I wasn't even looking this time, at least not for anything except coffee." We all laughed. "I've been in that coffee shop a hundred times since Sarah died, so lucky is *way* good enough for me . . . although I like hearing 'cute' once in a while. What are you and your family doing for Thanksgiving?"

"Going to Sal and Wendy's. Wendy and the girls and I will split up the cooking, and my son won't have much to do except set the table and throw logs on the fire. Dom—that's my younger son Dominic, Abigail—says he's bringing a new girlfriend, so we'll see. How about you?"

"We'll be doing a double: early afternoon at Tom and Diane's with Mom and Dad and all the family—except that Matt, Claire and the kids will be in Saratoga with Claire's family, and Danny and Emma will be with her family on Long Island. Then at about five o'clock, we'll have dinner at Abby's mom and dad's."

"So, Abigail, you haven't met either of Matt's sons yet?"

"No, but I talked with both of them on the phone, and we're

going to Matt and Claire's house for pizza this afternoon."

"Matt and Danny are *great* kids and they will *love* you, and their wives are just about as pretty as you are, so no one should be jealous of Matthew's young *babe*." Theresa winked and squeezed Abigail's hands.

"Terry, you're the best, no matter what your sister Anna says," I whispered as I hugged her.

"You know Anna has always been jealous of my chestnut hair."

We all laughed, and Theresa put both her hands on Abigail's cheeks; it was a loving, motherly gesture. She smiled straight into Abigail's green eyes.

"Abigail, you are an *adorable* girl. I'm not sure any man *deserves* you, but Matt deserves the *best*, and you will be a Thanksgiving blessing for the whole Flynn family. Since I'm the first to meet you—and I know stories about Matt that no one else in the family knows—I expect to be your favorite Italian cousin." Theresa's eyes sparkled. "Please come and see us at Christmas."

"I'll make sure that Matt doesn't forget."

"*Ciao*, Terry! We'll call you and pick out a good time to come over. Give our love to Gina, Becca, Sal, Dom and all the family."

"*Dio la benedica*," Theresa whispered. Then we walked to our cars and waved good-bye.

As she got in the Jeep, Abigail asked, "What did Theresa just say, Matt?"

"She said 'God bless you' in Italian, Abby."

We spent Sunday afternoon catching up. Abigail worked at Uncle Vinny's desk in the front window on a paper for her ergonomics class and a homemade-Christmas-cookie presentation for Mangrums as part of her visual marketing class. I brought her coffee and massaged and kissed the back of her neck to keep her on task. Jock and Maggie, who usually followed me wherever I went in the house, chose to sit at Abigail's feet by the desk all afternoon. I had lost my doggies.

But as I looked at Abby with the low sun coming through the window, I could hear Uncle Vinny saying, "Matty, I put a lot of love into that desk for you, and I was always happy to see Sarah sitting there. Now I'm happy again for you. Ten years is a long time. I would like to still be around so I could make something nice for Abigail."

I worked on some client correspondence and annuity illustrations on my computer in the family room, read the Sunday paper and paid the bills. I had the Hallmark channel with its "countdown" of Christmas movies on the televisions in the bedroom, kitchen and family room. It was the best background atmosphere for puttering, working or playing around the house. I very seldom watched the NFL games any more because my favorite team, the Cleveland Browns, had become perennially pathetic.

At four o'clock we gave the doggies their supper and took them for a walk. Then we got ready to go to Matt and Claire's. We brought a package of Lollycup's ice cream sandwiches and a bottle of Chianti. In the Jeep on the way over, Abigail asked me to tell her about my grandchildren.

"Matthew Howard Flynn IV—Matt and Claire call him 'Matthew'—was three on October 14, and Emily Marie was one on November 3. They are bright and beautiful children. They have Claire's fair skin, and Matthew has her blonde hair, but he has *my* blue eyes, and Dad's too."

"I got a good look at your dad's blue eyes when we were talking in the kitchen. What about your son Matt, no blue eyes for him?"

"Nope, he got Mom's dark brown hair and Sarah's green eyes, same as Danny."

"Green eyes, huh?" Abigail's green eyes sparkled.

"Yep, I definitely am a pushover for green eyes," I laughed, "but yours are much darker than Sarah's were. Hers were more of a lime green, and yours are so dark they're almost Christmas tree green. Or deep ocean green . . . I know *I* sink *way* down in your eyes."

I kissed Abigail on her forehead, and she caressed my hand on the Jeep stick.

"There's my poet again." She rubbed her cheek on my shoulder. "What about Emily?"

"Emily has Claire's hazel eyes and Matt's dark brown hair. Both of the kids are happy, pushy and smart. Emily tries to imitate everything her big brother does, so she's learning how to walk and talk faster than he did. Matthew watches everything you do, so if you don't want him to do something, don't let him see *you* doing it. They both surprise me every time I see them. I'm sure it was just the same for both of my sons . . . but it was so long ago that I can't remember. When you watch Matthew or Emily quietly for a few minutes—playing with their toys, reading a book, watching a movie—you can almost *see* them learning something new."

"I've noticed the same thing with my niece Elizabeth—Betsy—Jack's daughter. You'll meet her on Thanksgiving. You can see it in her eyes."

"Has Betsy gone through her *princess* stage? Emily has already taken to most of the Disney princesses. Ariel is her favorite."

"Betsy has stayed loyal to Snow White, who was the first princess she knew. We still watch the movie or read the book together almost every time I babysit for her."

"I do the same with *The Little Mermaid*. Matthew, on the other hand, knows and throws all the balls in the sports universe. So far his favorite seems to be a baseball. He's also getting into giant yellow vehicles like school buses and dump trucks. I plan on getting him a Tonka front loader for Christmas. It's so big that he will actually be able to sit on it while he's working all the parts. But I think the kids' favorite toys are Jock and Maggie. They love to lie on them, tug on their tails and ears and chase them around the house, especially when the dogs are doing their figure eights."

"I can't wait to share Christmas with you and all your family—and mine too! It's a whole new world for me, Matt."

"Well, my beauty, even though I've been there before with Sarah and my boys when they were little, it's a blessing *and* a blast to be able to get a second fatherhood with my grandchildren, and practically a *miracle* to have another chance at love forever. Abby, you and I are going to be the talk of the family—both families—at Christmas. Are you ready, love?"

"Ready, old guy," Abigail whispered as I pulled into Matt's driveway.

Matt heard my Jeep and opened the porch door.

"Hiya, son!"

"Hey, Dad!"

"Matthew Howard Flynn III, I would like you to meet Abigail Elizabeth McKay. Abby, this is my older son Matt."

"Hi, Matt! Please call me Abby."

"Nice to meet you, Abby. Come on in."

Just then little Matthew ran up behind his father and peeked around his leg.

"Grapa, look what I got from the library!" He held up a CD case. "It's a *Matt the Builder* movie with big trucks! Can we watch it?"

"Wow, his name is *Matt*, just like you! Maybe we can watch it after dinner. Matthew, this is my friend Abby."

Abigail reached down and took my grandson's hand.

"So nice to meet you, Matthew! My brother always liked *Matt the Builder* movies too!"

"Really? Babby, did you know we're having pizza and ice cream for dinner?"

We all laughed and walked through the laundry and mud room into the kitchen where Claire was arranging paper plates and napkins on the table. She waved some plastic forks and laughed. "Hi, Dad, welcome to our pizza picnic!"

Emily was already in her high chair. When she saw me she chirped, "Beeba!"

I walked to her chair and kissed her forehead. "Hi, sweetie!"

I gave Claire a big hug and said, "Between the pizza and the fireplace, it smells great in here, Claire!" but I sensed that she was looking past me at Abigail—with a slow, head-to-toe look. She was waiting to be introduced.

"I'd like you to meet my friend Abigail. Abby, this is Matt's wife Claire."

"It's so nice to be here, Claire. You have a lovely home."

"Thank you, Abigail. I'm glad Dad brought you over. I've never seen him with a girl. I didn't meet Matt until several years after his mother died.

"Why don't you and Dad sit at this end next to Emily? Matt and Matthew, your usual spots. Everybody, sit. The pizza's hot. We have one large with mozzarella only, one large with mozzarella and pepperoni and a small one just for you, Dad, with anchovies and sauce only."

"Tonight, Claire, you are my favorite daughter-in-law. Abby, I'll bet you've never had an old-fashioned Sicilian pizza with just tomato sauce and anchovies."

"You would be right about that, old guy. Those little fish look *gross*."

"I grew up with this kind of pizza. My mother's older sister, Aunt Lucy, used to make them for the family all the time. Some with tomato sauce and anchovies, and some with just olive oil and anchovies—Mom called it 'white pizza.' Then we would sprinkle Parmigiano or Romano cheese on each piece. You should try . . ."

Claire interrupted, "Abigail, you called Dad 'old guy.' How about that, Dad?"

"I think it's a term of endearment, Claire; at least I hope so," I grinned.

"Speaking of terms of endearment, Matthew Junior, you called Matt III 'son,'" said Abby. "I've never heard any father or mother do that before. My mom and dad never called my brothers 'son' or called me 'daughter' either."

Claire agreed. "I also thought that was strange when I joined the Flynn family. But Dad," she continued to tease, "if Abigail's term of endearment for you is 'old guy,' is 'young chick' your pet term for *her*?"

"Well, Claire, without giving away too many secrets at our first family pizza picnic, Abby is 'my beauty' all the time."

Abigail smiled, squeezed my knee with one hand under the table and gave Emily a spoonful of green baby food with her other hand. Everybody was suddenly quiet except for little Matthew who was singing while he was picking the pepperoni slices off his pizza.

"Claire, thank you for my custom pizza. Matt, how about cracking that bottle of Chianti we brought? Little Matt, are you only going to eat the pepperoni, or some pizza, too? And Abby, before I was interrupted, I was going to offer you a taste of your first anchovy pizza. Here, take a bite. Be brave."

"Okay, but you owe me when I ask *you* to eat something weird. *Ooh*, this is *really* salty! May I have a glass of pop, Claire?"

"We have Sprite or Dr Pepper, Abigail."

"I *love* Dr Pepper, and please call me Abby."

Emily was finished with her Gerber peas and her bottle of chocolate milk, so Abigail wiped her face and hands, lifted her out of the high chair and nestled her on her knee at the table. Emily was delighted to be at the grownup table where she could bang her spoon on anything within her reach. She stopped banging when she remembered who was holding her and looked up at the new person in her world. She studied Abigail's face and reached up and touched the freckle on her nose. Abigail smiled and put her finger on Emily's.

"That's my freckle, Emily."

Emily smiled, pointed her freckle finger at me and said, "Beeba."

Claire said, "That's amazing, Abby. Emily is usually shy with strangers. She has never taken to anyone outside the family that fast. Who would like peanut butter swirl ice cream or one of the ice cream sandwiches that Abby and Grandpa brought?"

Little Matthew was first. "I want a scream sanwich."

"What do you say, Matthew?"

"Pease, Mommy?"

Abigail took Emily's hand in hers and waived them together at Claire. "May we share a dish of peanut butter swirl, please?"

Claire laughed. "Abby, Emily is not going to let you go for the rest of the night. Okay, one ice cream sandwich and one dish of peanut butter swirl. Dad, Matt, how about you? And who would like coffee?"

"I'll make the coffee, honey. No ice cream for me right now. Dad?"

"No ice cream for me just yet, but Abby and I both love a good cup of coffee." I grinned and pointed at Abigail and Emily. "Emmy, sweetie, Grandpa *met* Abby in her coffee shop."

"Let me show you my new Hamilton Beach coffee maker, Dad."

While Claire cleared the table and brought out the ice cream, Matt and I played with his coffee maker in the far corner of the kitchen, where he whispered, "Dad, Abby *is* a beauty and *so* nice. You haven't lost your touch after all these years. But she's so *young*! What's going to happen? Plenty of people we know are going to disapprove *big time* and think there's something wrong with you."

"I know, Matt; you're right about all of that, and Abby and I have discussed it at great length. You and I can talk about it some more this week—just the two of us—over breakfast or lunch. But what you and Claire need to know right now is that Abby and I love each other. She has moved into the house; *your* bedroom is now her office."

I gave my son an affectionate punch in the arm. "*Hell*, Jock and Maggie already love her more than they love *me*. Matt, we almost never know anything for sure, but I'm *pretty* sure this is not a passing fancy. It's hard to believe, but I think Abigail is with me to stay."

"*Hey*, you two Matts, how's that coffee coming?" Emily and Abigail were both banging their spoons on the table. "Emmy and I would like some coffee before our peanut butter swirl melts."

We all laughed except little Matthew, who was too busy mashing pieces of his ice cream sandwich into his mouth and all over his face.

After dessert, we all moved into the family room with our coffee, and Matthew IV put his *Matt the Builder* movie on. I sat on the floor with him to watch, while Emily settled into Abigail's lap at the TV end of their red sofa. Matt got himself a beer and brought in more wood from the back porch for the fire. Claire stayed busy picking up and cleaning up both the kitchen and the family room, but I noticed that from all angles and corners of both rooms—which flowed together—she was furtively observing Abigail on the sofa with Emily. It wasn't easy to read her expression, which she occasionally directed my way, but I thought it was somewhere between amazement and contentment.

Matt and Claire eventually snuggled in at the other end of the sofa, and we all watched *Matt the Builder* construct a new school before it was bedtime for Matthew and Emily.

Emily wouldn't let go of Abigail, so the three girls went upstairs together to read Emily a story and get her into her Ariel jammies, while my son and I took Matthew up for his "tubby." Matt supervised the bath while I read to Matthew from *Winnie-the-Pooh.*

Abigail and I were home by nine o'clock. We walked Jock and Maggie, made some English Breakfast tea and all settled on the sofa in the family room for a little more *Serendipity.* Abigail leaned on my shoulder and squeezed my arm.

"Matt, tomorrow is our anniversary." Her eyes glistened.

"*One* incredible week, beauty. One week ago I didn't know you and I had no idea how my life was about to change. We should go to Kitty's in the morning to celebrate." I tickled her ear.

"Silly, I'll be there from seven to nine . . . in uniform. Are you going in to your office?"

"I have some paperwork to submit, which should take me about an hour. No appointments. I could drop you at Kitty's, grab a coffee, go do my stuff at the office and pick you up at nine. Or were you planning on taking your car?"

"I'd rather go with you and have you bring me home. Mostly because I'll be with *you,* but also because it will give me a little extra time to change clothes and cross a couple of T's in my print media editorial assignment. Okay, old guy?"

"Did you like the way Claire picked up on that?"

"They're really nice, Matt . . . Matt and Claire. And Matthew and Emily are just *beautiful*. I know Claire was stunned, maybe even appalled, at first. And I noticed her studying me, practically non-stop, after dinner. But when we went upstairs and bundled Emily into her crib, Claire gave me a hug and said, 'I've never seen Dad this happy, not even when our babies were born.' So I think Claire and I are okay . . . better than okay. And Matt is a prince, but how could he *not* be."

"And *I* think you have this remarkable ability to not only make me agree with everything you *say* but also to bring out the best in everybody I *know*."

"*Mmm*, Matt, you know I always like it when you talk poetry to me. Let's watch Jonathan and Sara for a few minutes before I fall asleep. It's going to be an early morning."

Jonathan has decided that his search for Sara is over and he is destined to marry Halley, but he is distracted at his wedding rehearsal at the Waldorf. He is looking at everybody *except* Halley.

"Matt, his mind may have decided to give up the search, but his heart is still looking for Sara."

In the meantime, Sara's fiancé has traveled across the country to tell her he misses her, but in what should have been a romantic horse-and-buggy ride through Central Park Lars gets into a long cell phone call from his business manager. Sara realizes that his singing career will always be more important to him than she will. She hops out of the carriage and walks down to a bench at the ice skating rink. When she notices Cassiopeia in the black sky and breathlessly takes off her leather jacket to check her freckles, you know she's finished with Lars.

Abigail poked me in the cheek and whispered, "It's almost the same thing, Matt. Sara let her girlfriend talk her into believing that she had to stop searching for Jonathan, but her heart is still waiting for him."

And then, back at the rehearsal, Halley gives Jonathan his traditional groom's gift: a beat-up first edition of *Love in the Time of Cholera*. I could feel Abigail shiver when Jonathan unwraps the book. And then he lifts open the cover, and there is the name *Sara Thomas* with her phone number. Abigail squeezed my hand *and* my arm.

"Matt, it's hard to keep my eyes open; I don't want to miss

anything. How much longer till the end?"

I paused the movie and whispered in her ear, "Beauty, as much as I love to watch you close your eyes and to feel your body relax when you fall asleep, stay with me for two or three minutes until Sara gets on her plane to San Francisco."

Sara and her girlfriend Eve had inadvertently switched purses, so when Sara hands a $5 bill to the stewardess for a headset to watch the in-flight movie, she sees the name *Jonathan Trager* and *his* phone number written in red on the back of the bill.

Abigail sat up and poked my thigh. "Matt, she found it!"

Sara grabs the bill from the stewardess and rushes off the plane to find Jonathan. Then we see Jonathan and his friend Dean taking their seats on a later plane to San Francisco to find Sara.

"So Sara's going back to New York to find Jonathan, while he's going to San Francisco to find her," Abigail yawned.

"*Now* it's time for bed, little girl. We'll see how they find each other tomorrow night."

Jock and Maggie came upstairs with us and settled on their soft and thick, blue and red fleece blankets on the floor at the foot of the bed. I set the alarm for five-thirty, and Abigail and I were curled together under the covers in five minutes.

"What a week, huh, Matt? I still can't believe everything that's happened. First, this handsome old guy comes in from the cold—from out of nowhere—into my coffee shop; then I fall in love with him and, amazingly, he falls in love with *me*; then he makes love to me so many times that I can't even go back and remember how many; and he doesn't simply make *love* to me, he opens up my body and uncovers my deepest center; he touches the heart of the woman inside me and brings her alive; and if *that* weren't enough for a lifetime, in the very same week we meet the parents, and Pat and Laurie, and Matt and Claire and your beautiful grandchildren, and your cousin Theresa. And here I am in your house; and I love you *so much*. And Maggie and Jock have taken me in as their Mommy. Are *all* of our weeks going to be like this one?"

"I hope so, Abby. Why not? Every time I touch you and look deep into your green eyes and breathe you in is better than the time before. Your coming into my life is so unbelievable that I don't even question it anymore. I take it on faith. Why shouldn't tomorrow morning be better than yesterday morning?"

"*Mmm*, Matt, before I fall asleep there's this one thing . . ." Abigail murmured as she reached her right arm and leg across my body and rolled her belly onto mine. "This one thing . . ." as she tangled the tips of her fingers in my hair and kissed my face. "This one thing . . ." as she pressed her belly into mine and squeezed the back of my neck with both her hands as we came together. "This one thing, Matt . . ."

And then her hands fell away from my neck, and her belly let go, and her face tilted to the left, and I felt her soft breath on my chest, and then I was asleep, too.

10

Monday morning was unlike any Monday I had experienced in the past ten years. When the radio went on and Abigail stirred in my arms, I knew that all the dismal November mornings that had depressed me since Sarah had died were gone, banished by this bright woman stretching her body against mine. Even Jock and Maggie—who both jumped on Abigail's side of the bed and tried to be the first to get their ears scratched—sensed that life was better with a Mommy in Daddy's bed.

"Good morning, beauty, I love you. You make my whole body smile. If I live to be a hundred I will never be able to find the right words to tell you how delicious you smell and taste and feel in the morning. Abby . . ."

"*Mmm* . . . Matt, you feel *so* good, *so* warm."

". . . trying to describe you is like taking a photograph of a rainbow or a sunset. No matter how great the photographer and the camera are, the colors never come out the same. I could eat you up *every* day."

"My sweet poet, except for Maggie and Jock licking the back of my neck, I could stay right here in the middle of this bed with *you* all day . . . forever."

"Do you remember falling asleep on top of me last night?"

"I remember squeezing your neck and you lifting up my belly, with your hands stroking my backside, and then everything got soft, and I was gone. It's hard to make love when you're tired. I could get ferocious with you right now, but I'm guessing that we don't have any time to spare."

"Not if you want to get to Kitty's before she opens for business. But we don't have any place to go tonight, right? You can devour me for dessert if you eat all your dinner."

We both laughed and stretched together one more time under *Pooh* and *Piglet*.

"Let's shower and get dressed, beauty, and walk the dogs when there's a little more daylight."

"You shave first, and I'll go downstairs and get us some hot coffee."

I hope I never get over—or take for granted—the childlike but erotic pleasure of smoothing handfuls of soapsuds over the body of a beautiful woman, especially while she's doing the same to me. Abigail wouldn't stop the wet kisses and slippery hugs that came with the soap until Jock started barking on the bathmat for his breakfast.

Abigail impishly said, "Next time we do this, Matt, let's do it with more time and more soap, and persuade Maggie and Jock to wait for us in the big bed."

It was a clear, calm and cold morning. All the dirty, mushy snow in the streets had frozen into ruts overnight, so the drive downtown was crunchy. We got to Kitty's at ten to seven, and Abby ran in and brought me out an Italian decaf for the office. She wrote "I love you!" on my spattered side window and ran back in to the café. I could see Kitty watching inside and laughing.

At the office I finished up two long-term care insurance applications for Steve and Margaret Carroll, old lawyer friends who were the only husband-and-wife lawyers I knew who managed to stay together for more than ten years. I figured the fact that they were both divorce lawyers gave them enough insight and good sense to make the marriage work. I schmoozed with Gretchen, our receptionist, who always brought me chocolates, and was back at Kitty's promptly at nine.

Abigail ran out with two "to-go" cups of coffee which she placed in the cup holders in my Jeep and said with a grin, "Kitty wants you to come in so she can give you a hug. She's leaving today to visit her mother in Virginia, so the coffee shop will be closed for the rest of the week."

"*Nice* . . . we won't have to get up at the crack of dawn tomorrow."

Kitty was waiting in front of the counter. "Come here, Mister Matt—I never caught your last name—I understand you've been hitting on one of my best waitresses."

"It's Flynn, Kitty, and we always called it 'flirting' in my day."

"Well, Mister Flynn, I like to watch out for my girls, so give me a hug; I can always tell from a hug if a man can be trusted."

Abigail sat on the counter and laughed as I gave Kitty a slightly playful hug.

"Do that again, Matt Flynn," Kitty teased, "and I might try to take you *away* from Abigail."

"Kitty, as great as your coffee is, I think you're too *young* for me . . ."

That got *both* Abigail and Kitty laughing.

". . . but I've been waiting all week to thank you for hiring Abigail. If it weren't for you, not only would I have missed out on this magical girl and a second chance at true love, but I would still have to pay for my coffee when I come in here."

With that Abigail hopped off the counter, pinched my cheek and scolded, "Matthew Flynn, do you mean to tell me that you really love me for the *free coffee*?"

Kitty chimed in, "Because you two would be nowhere without *me*, does this mean that I will be invited to the wedding?"

"*Shh*, Kitty, Matt and I are going to try to keep all wedding thoughts secret until some frozen, dark day in January when we surprise the hell out of our families."

"Good luck with *that*, sweetie. You've got Thanksgiving and Christmas coming, and all your friends and family—unless they're *blind*—are going to see right away that you're in love."

In my Jeep on the way home, Abigail said that her best friend from Fatima—who also went with her to Newton College— Mary Kathleen Galvin, was coming home for Thanksgiving.

"Mary Kay is working at the State Department and getting her Ph.D. in foreign languages at Georgetown. Her family lives in Penfield off Embury Road. Her high school sweetheart, Josh Simpson, graduated from Penfield, and his family lives on Jackson Road. I used to spend a lot of time at both of their houses when Mary Kay and I were at Fatima.

"Anyway, Josh works as a staff photographer for the Discovery Channel in Silver Spring, Maryland, and they have an apartment together in Falls Church, Virginia. He's going to be home, too, and Mary Kay would like us all to go out to dinner together. What do you think . . . maybe Friday or Saturday night?"

"Sure. How much have you told Mary Kay about me?"

"She's been my best friend since we were six years old. We tell each other *everything*. I told her that you are a lawyer and a financial planner, that you are *way* old, that all the sex I've ever had before you—*added up*—doesn't come close to the way I feel when you touch me; and I told her I love you."

"And she *believes* you?" I kidded.

"She knows that I would never lie to her, so *don't* let me

down," Abigail kidded back.

"Never, beauty. Let's do Friday night if that's okay with them. Where would you like to go?"

"Can we take them to Palermo's? It's *our* special place, and I'm sure Mary Kay will love the food and the atmosphere as much as I do. I'll even bring Grandma and Grandpa Fiorino's vase with a red rose for a centerpiece." Her eyes were glistening when we pulled in the garage.

"I'll make reservations for seven o'clock."

We took Jock and Maggie around the circle, and then Abigail changed, packed a snack and got ready to go. As she ran downstairs to the garage to take her car, she yelled up, "I'll be home about four-thirty. Can we do Phil Green's? I think I'm going to want to put my feet up in our booth, cuddle with my date and talk and nibble."

The dogs and I had a quiet afternoon. I paid some bills, called a couple of clients to follow up on how their investments were performing, and sent a lengthy quote from George W. Bush's Second Inaugural Address to a handful of my liberal buddies from Dominic Savio and Boston College to annoy them. Then I made out Thanksgiving cards to Mom and Dad, my sons and my brothers and their families.

I also cut and pasted a special card for Abigail: photographs of Jock and Maggie and me sipping through straws from a huge mug of hot chocolate and marshmallows—with Abigail's picture on it. I wrote this caption: *We love you more than hot chocolate and marshmallows, and we are WAY thankful that you are now part of our home and the center of our lives. Love, Daddy, Jock and Maggie.*

We heard Abigail's car just after four-thirty, and Jock and Maggie were the first to rush down the stairs to the family room. Jock barked as usual, and Maggie pawed the inside of the door to the garage. I sat on the sofa with my feet on the coffee table. The dogs both jumped all over Abby when she came in, jockeying for hugs, kisses and scratches.

"Welcome home, dear!" I waved from the sofa.

"Why weren't you over here in line for a kiss?" she teased.

"Drop those bags, beauty, and come over here and sit with me."

We stretched out on the sofa and nuzzled while the dogs camped on the throw rug next to us.

"Tell me about your day on campus, love."

"Well, in ergonomics we've been analyzing the pluses and minuses of locating some product areas—such as baked goods, produce, flowers and plants—near the front of the stores, and what staffing changes that might require. That means a lot of research, both on foot and on line, as to how other supermarkets are laid out and how they are performing. We'll have a paper due after Christmas.

"In print media we're comparing competitors' ads in the daily *Times Chronicle* and in the weekly supplements and inserts, and also in the suburban town papers. We compare them for location in the paper, for layout and content, and for price. Our term assignment in print media will be to design our own twenty-two-inch-square sheet of Mangrums ads for whatever products we choose. It then gets folded twice into a standard eleven-by-eleven supplement. I might let you help me with that one," Abigail said as she squeezed closer on the sofa to make room for Jock and Maggie to jump up with us.

"Come on, babies, up on the sofa! Matt, this is so cozy that I could either fall asleep curled up here with you and the dogs, or attack you if you keep kissing my hair and playing with my ears. But I'm *hungry*! Did you feed Maggie and Jock?"

"I did and took them for a walk, too. Do you still want to go to Phil Green's?"

"I've been thinking all day about a cheeseburger, Dr Pepper, tater tots and chocolate almond ice cream with rainbow sprinkles." Abigail looked at me and grinned. "Can we please go *now*, Daddy? I'm *hungry*!"

"Okay, baby dogs, let's go upstairs. Mommy and I are going to get something to eat and then we'll be right back."

Once we settled side by side in our booth and started on our burgers and taters, I asked Abigail about her third class, visual marketing.

"I think that's the most fun, Matt: television ads, short and long, including health and diet tips; billboards along the roads and those tasty-looking pictures on the sides of our eighteen-wheelers; radio ads, too, even though they're not visual; and internet pop-ups and websites. We brainstorm new ideas and discuss location, frequency, consistency among the different visuals—the internet spots shouldn't contradict the TV ads, and so on—and cost-effectiveness among all the various types of visual marketing.

"But changing the subject, old guy, since you're on the outside of the booth, would you get me a refill of Dr Pepper and a cup of dill pickles?"

I took Abigail's cup and kissed her hair behind her ear. *"Yum . . .* be right back, beauty."

When I came back with more hot chocolate for me and pickles and Dr Pepper for Abby, she put her hand on my thigh, put a scowl on her face and said, "Mom called me at school today and told me that my brother Jack is really upset about you and me. He said that if you're going to be at Mom and Dad's for Thanksgiving, he's not coming."

"That's not good. I'm sorry, Abby. What did your mom say?"

"She told Jack that he shouldn't be judging people before he meets them and that I wasn't a little girl any more, and she said that when Dad came home from work he would be over to talk to him. Jack said that would be a big waste of time because there was *no way* his younger sister should be going out with a sixty-year-old guy. Matt, I would really like to put my feet up. If I sit sideways in the booth, will you pull off my boots and rub my feet? I can keep them under the table so no one will see. I put on clean socks before we left the house." She grinned.

"Sit sideways and give me those feet," I laughed.

Abigail leaned her back against the side wall of the booth and closed her eyes as I rubbed both her feet in between sips of hot chocolate.

"Mmm . . . that feels *so* good. If I fall asleep, wake me up in twenty minutes for my chocolate almond. *Mmm . . .* did I tell you since I came home that I love you? . . . and not just because you are massaging my feet."

Abigail *did* doze off for a few minutes while I continued to play with her feet. Her lips parted a little, and I could hear her soft snore. When she woke with a quiver she stretched her arms and legs, yawned and sighed and murmured with her eyes still closed.

"Mmm . . . Matt, this is *heaven*. When you took off my boots and started touching my feet I thought about what I was doing only *one* week ago. I was in the kitchen at Mom and Dad's having supper, and Mom asked me what I was daydreaming about. I was thinking about this nice guy I had met that morning—but I didn't let on to Mom and Dad—and wondering what would happen if he really *did* come back the next day.

Matt, will you dump out the rest of my Dr Pepper and get me some hot chocolate, too? I'll stretch my feet under the table to the other side of the booth."

When I came back, Abigail said with a frown, "My brother Jack is hot-headed and a know-it-all, but I think Dad will convince him to come for Thanksgiving. It would be terribly unfair to my sister-in-law and to Betsy if Jack kept them away from the family. He'll probably be rude and grumble for a while after he meets you—he has rarely approved much of my choices—but I hope he will come around." Abigail lifted her feet on top of mine on the other side of the booth.

"What do Jack and Cathy do, Abby?"

"Now that Betsy started kindergarten in Webster this year, Cathy is back at her job as manager of the children's book department at Barnes & Noble on Ridge Road. Jack has been with Xerox since he graduated from high school. I think he's now a supervisor of copier technicians, but I get the feeling he doesn't like being at Xerox any more."

Abigail wrapped both her arms around my chest and nibbled on my cheek.

"Is it time for ice cream now, Daddy?"

While we slowly savored our ice cream—chocolate almond for Abigail and peanut butter chunk for me—Abby asked me to tell her more about Sarah and her family.

"Sarah Post Martin—her father was David Post Martin, and her mother was Helen Constance Long. They both died a couple of years before Sarah. She had two lovely sisters, Rebeccah and Norah, who live in North Carolina and Oregon. They each have a son and daughter who are about the same ages as Matt and Danny. The last time we saw them all was at a Martin family reunion at Beccah's home in Wilmington, North Carolina, the fall after Sarah died. We still exchange e-mails and greeting cards a few times a year. Sarah wanted Danny's middle name to be 'Martin' after her family, which was more than fair after we named Matthew Howard III after me and Dad. I'm going to get some more hot chocolate, beauty girl; would you like a refill?"

"May I switch to coffee, sir? How long can we play before Phil Green kicks us out?"

"Ha! You asked me that last week when we came in here and talked all afternoon in the snowstorm. We can stay as long as we want unless you stick your feet outside the booth. We are loyal customers, remember?"

When I came back with the refills, Abigail asked me where I met Sarah.

"It wasn't in a coffee shop, was it?" she said mischievously.

"No, love, you are my one-of-a-kind coffee shop girl. I met Sarah during the summer of 1976 at a reception for Vice President Nelson Rockefeller. I was fresh out of B.C. Law; I had taken the New York State Bar Exam in Buffalo in July, and I was putting together my resume to send out to law firms. I wanted to meet as many new people as possible, and one of the first organizations I joined was the Penfield Republican Committee."

"Almost everybody in my family is a Democrat, but Pat and I have a secret liking for George Bush; Laura too. I think they have so much more class than those phony Clintons, and President Bush has done a wonderful job of protecting our country since 9/11."

"You are a gem, Abby, and every new thing I discover about you makes you sparkle brighter. Well, 1976 was the Bicentennial, and there were celebrations all over the country. Rockefeller had been New York's governor for sixteen years when he was picked by President Gerald Ford to be the new vice president after Nixon resigned. The reception in early August was at the brand new Convention Center downtown, and all of us committee members were encouraged to go. It was only fifty dollars, and I thought I might meet some *older* lawyers who might be interested in hiring some *younger* lawyers.

"Sarah was the music teacher at Penfield High, and the New York State Teachers Union sent representatives from each of the Monroe County school districts. Not many teachers are Republicans, and Sarah was active in the union so she was an easy choice. She was also easy to spot in a crowd—even for a short guy like me. In her bare feet she was five-ten, and I am five-eight, but in heels she was over six feet and stood out in every crowd with her long, dark red hair. Sometimes in the right light it almost looked chestnut.

"Needless to say, I spotted her and joined her to talk about life and Nelson Rockefeller over a few glasses of Pinot noir and some chicken fingers. We started dating the moment we walked out of the Convention Center, and the rest is history. We were married the following summer on July 9, my birthday."

"Wow . . . I love that *tall* story, Matt. And now you've come down to five-six Abby McKay," she laughed as she tickled my

112

cheek.

"The good thing about *little* girls like you," I responded with some tickles of my own, "is that I don't have to spend so much time on my toes."

"Speaking of toes, as much as I hate to put my cold boots back on, we should go home now so that I can do a little school work before we watch the end of *Serendipity*. That was a great choice for the beginning of our romance, old guy. What's our next movie going to be?"

"The next movie should be *your* choice, Abby. What are some of your favorites?"

"There are a lot; most of them are what guys always call 'chick flick' movies, like *Sleepless in Seattle* or *The Lake House*, or any of the Nicholas Sparks stories."

"I call them 'boy-meets-girl, boy-and-girl-fall-in-love and boy-and-girl-live-happily-ever-after' movies. They're my favorites. Romances with happy endings—with the occasional sad one thrown in like *The Bridges of Madison County*—and also uplifting movies like *Remember the Titans* or *A Walk to Remember*. No matter how many times I've seen them, they still bring tears to my eyes."

"I just bought *Enchanted* with Patrick Dempsey and Amy Adams. For some reason I seem to be partial to Patrick Dempsey," Abigail grinned sheepishly. "I also have *Sweet Home Alabama*. Have you ever seen *The Notebook*? I have that one, too."

"I've seen a few minutes here and there on television, but I've never sat down long enough to watch the whole movie. Who's in it?"

"The older stars are James Garner and Gena Rowlands, and the young ones are Ryan Gosling and Rachel McAdams. It's not just a beautiful love story; it's very poetic. It should be perfect for an old poet who is also a summer boy." Abigail's grin had turned from sheepish to impish.

We went home and walked Jock and Maggie, and then Abigail settled in at Uncle Vinny's desk in the front window while I went through the mail and checked the phone messages. And that reminded me to poke my head into Abby's office with a question.

"Beauty girl, have you changed your mailing address to here? Or your home phone?"

"I've been meaning to ask you about that, Matt. The address

I *have* changed, so my mail will start coming here. But is it okay to give my friends and family your home number? Will it cause any trouble? You're on the answering machine, so maybe I should just have everybody call me on my cell phone and not confuse or upset them."

"Abby, soon enough everybody in our world is going to know that you and I are together here in this house, and everywhere else, too. It's not just *my* home number any more. Tomorrow we'll change the message. You and Jock and Maggie can do all the talking and tell the world who lives here. *That* should amuse several of my clients and friends. Back to work. Would you like some tea or coffee?"

"A mug of Irish Breakfast or Earl Grey would be lovely, thanks. I'll be finished in about forty-five minutes, so you and the doggies can warm up the sofa."

When we resumed *Serendipity*, Sara had located Jonathan's apartment, but his neighbors told her that his wedding was taking place at the Waldorf at *that* minute, so she rushed to the Waldorf only to find that Jonathan had called off the wedding. She didn't know where to look next, but she started anyway. Meanwhile, Jonathan had found another couple in Sara's house in San Francisco and was flying back to New York disillusioned and not knowing what to do next.

"Matt, New York is *so* big. How could they possibly still hope to find each other?"

"Well, maybe in real life they couldn't, but after last week nobody can tell *me* that impossible miracles or chance encounters only happen in movies. Besides, I've seen this movie elebenteen times so I know the answer to your question," I teased as I paused the movie.

"*Elebenteen?*" Abigail looked up wonderingly from my lap and touched my lips. I lifted her head gently and kissed her softly. She took a deep breath and reached her fingers up to my hair.

"*Elebenteen*, Matt?"

"*Dennis the Menace* used to say that all the time. Now *I* say it a lot. I always liked *Dennis*, and *Peter Pan,* too. I still haven't grown up, you know."

"I know, summer boy." She touched my lips again. "Why do you think I'm *here?*"

"Abby, pretty girl, if you were Sara, where would you look for Jonathan in New York City?"

114

"I would probably go back to his apartment to see if he were there and at least leave a note on his door telling him that *I* had been there, that I had been to the Waldorf and knew that he had called off the wedding; that I was staying at the Waldorf myself, in room 710; and that he should call me *soon,* either at the hotel or on my cell.

"And then I would go to the places we had gone together on our one magic evening in New York. I would start with the skating rink in Central Park or maybe the Serendipity Café, and then Bloomingdale's, and end up back at the Waldorf. And if I hadn't heard from him or found him by then, I would probably cry myself to sleep. Start it up again, Matt."

In a few minutes, Jonathan and Sara *did* find each other at the skating rink—with snowflakes floating down and Cassiopeia in the sky—and, of course, they lived happily ever after. Abigail, Jock and Maggie stretched contentedly before we all went upstairs to warm each other to sleep. Abby curled her arm around my neck and whispered, "Matt, I don't have to leave for Mangrums until about one-thirty. Where do *you* have to go in the morning?"

"I need to be in the office at eleven to put together a proposal and then I have a lunch meeting with a small business owner in Greece to talk about life insurance for his buy-sell agreement."

"Some day—not now—you can tell me what a 'buy-sell' is. I just wanted to make sure I'll have plenty of time to make love to you in the morning. It's only a week, I know, but I have this warm glow all over me when I'm touching you. Maybe it will go away some day, but not if *I* can help it. You've spoiled me. I don't want to let a day go by without you touching me inside and out. I love you too much to get used to you."

"I won't let it happen, beauty, I promise. Sleep tight." I kissed her arm resting under my chin and cradled the back of her head as she fell asleep on my shoulder. I slowed my breathing down until it matched the rhythm of Abby's breath on my chest.

11

Jock and Maggie woke us with licks a little after seven. We all cuddled together until Maggie started poking my hand with her nose to let me know that she was hungry and it was time to stop playing in bed and go down to the kitchen. Abigail told me to stay put. She threw on pajamas, sweat suit and slippers and went downstairs to get the coffee and the dog food going. Naturally the dogs followed Abby and left me alone in bed for the first time since the night after I met her.

The bed suddenly seemed enormous. Through all the ten years since Sarah died I had become a reluctant and restless sleeper. I went to bed late and only out of necessity. I spent so many nights throwing my arms, legs and pillows to all four corners of the bed that even Jock and Maggie and Lucy before them thought it was too crowded. And I got up as early as my body would allow.

Now bed was fun again, and I felt really small—like a little kid making a tent under the covers—as I rolled and poked around and sniffed for traces of Abigail. I was sixty-one and exploring under the covers.

"Come on down, Matt! Maggie and Jock are done with breakfast, and your coffee is ready. I want to take the dogs for their walk and then get you back in bed."

And so we did, with only a glass of orange juice and a hard-boiled egg in between the dogs and bed. Abigail's mood this morning was not only flirtatious but mischievous, and I could tell—even though she didn't say a word—that she wanted me to linger everywhere over her body. If I didn't linger long enough, she held me tight and wouldn't let me move until I did.

"Abby, you are a bossy beauty this morning," I said, out of breath, laughing. "You're treating me like a sex object."

"*Shh*, old guy. You're good . Stay right there."

I left for the office at ten-thirty, and Abigail—back in her pajamas and sweat suit—was working on her laptop at Uncle Vinny's desk,with Jock and Maggie at her feet.

"I hope your business meeting goes well, Matt."

"I'll call you before you leave for Mangrums, love."

I called during a break in my meeting, but Abigail must have left a little earlier than usual for Mangrums. She had already changed the message on the answering machine though.

"Hi, you have reached the happy home of Matt and Abigail and Maggie and Jock (barking in the background). We are probably out playing. Please leave a message at the beep, and we will call you back as soon as we can. Have a good day!"

I can't wait to listen to some of our new messages, I thought with a big grin on my face. All of my old world was about to discover the center of my new world: Abigail Elizabeth McKay.

On my way home, I stopped at Mangrums and Target to buy two special treats for Abby: a red rose for her bud vase and a Tinker Bell travel mug for her car. I put the rose in her vase with a note From Your Old Italian Guy, and I wrapped the mug in green tissue with another note From Peter Pan. As I wrote the notes at my old butcher block table in the kitchen while the dogs and I grazed on Iams, Cheerios and peanut butter, I sensed Sarah's presence. So did the dogs. They stopped begging and lay flat on the floor looking up at me.

You haven't changed a bit, Matthew Howard Flynn. You have never grown up—ever—and you have gotten away with it for all these years because you have always been lucky. You were lucky to spot me in that huge crowd in the Convention Center thirty-one years ago. But one of your best qualities has always been that you never take your luck for granted. You test it, you play with it, you push it, you chase it, you run with it. So here you are—thirty-one years later—still not grown up but still lucky. You walk into a coffee shop on a random Monday in November, and a beautiful, bright young woman like Abigail McKay just happens to be there. But that's where the luck ends and your faith begins. You look into her eyes—as you looked into mine—you find love, and you believe. I could feel the love and see the faith thirty-one years ago; and Abigail could see it and feel it last week. You're not afraid to risk everything, and that's why I was with you for twenty-one years and Abigail is with you now. That and your baby blue eyes, you lucky rascal!

The phone rang at six-thirty. I let it ring four times until the answering machine kicked in with Abigail's new message, and then I listened to hear who our first lucky caller was. It was

Abby. I laughed and picked up the phone.

"Here I am, beauty. How do you like your message? You're the first caller. You should have seen Jock and Maggie's ears perk up when they heard your voice on the machine."

"How do you like it, Matt? Is it okay?"

"It's great. It's going to make me smile every time I hear it. How are things at Mangrums?"

"It was a regular afternoon of brainstorming sessions, small research groups and workshops with some of the retail managers—and then Wally and Maureen suddenly appeared to round up all the interns and take us to dinner in the executive dining room on the third floor. I think they're trying to get to know each of us personally so they will have a better idea next spring about which interns they might want to hire. At any rate, the food was great, and it's fun asking the president of the company to 'pass the rolls.' Wally sat right next to me."

"I'll bet he did. Wally's no dummy. Does he know about you and me?"

"I haven't told him anything, but I'm sure he suspects. He asked about you today, asked me to say hello from him, and talked about the year you were on the Madison Town Board and he and Art opened their new superstore on Hill Road. He said he packed a complimentary bag of food and gifts for you and Sarah personally."

"That was a nice day—summer of 1990, I think—and a very enjoyable tour of their state-of-the-art store with Wally, Art and Maureen. I spent most of the tour exchanging old stories with Art about our alma mater, Savio, and applauding his staunch support for Catholic schools. He loved having Sarah on his arm as we walked up and down the aisles. We also reminisced about the handful of times I caddied for him at Pine Hill. Art wasn't a good golfer but he was a great tipper. He was one of the few guys who gave me ten dollars for carrying his bag."

"Can I tell him that the next time I see him?"

"Sure, Art will get a kick out of it. I have never met a more humble great man in my life. Our doggies want to know when you're coming home?"

"Eight-thirty. And there is no school tomorrow. RIT is closed for Thanksgiving vacation. No school for five days! And the Mangrums offices are closed on Friday, too. So I'm going to jump into my pajamas, put my feet up on the sofa, have some ice cream with chocolate chips and play with my favorite doggies and old guy. Maybe start a new movie. What do you think?"

"I think that Jock and Maggie and I can hardly wait. See you soon."

While the dogs and I watched *November Christmas* on the Hallmark channel in the TV room, I lit a bayberry candle, poured two glasses of Montepulciano, brought down Abigail's green shamrock pajamas and arranged the pajamas, wine, bud vase and Tinker Bell mug on the coffee table. When we heard the garage door open and the old Taurus pull in, Jock and Maggie charged to the door. I put my feet up on the sofa and pretended to be nonchalantly reading the newspaper. Abigail hugged the dogs, poked her head into the family room, took in the scene and laughed.

"Look at you! Wine, a candle, my pajamas . . . aren't you the seductive old guy! And the red rose clinches it. I think you're going to get lucky tonight."

Abby jumped on top of me, threw the newspaper on the floor, held my face in both her hands, kissed me softly several times and said, "One look in your baby blue eyes is more than enough, you know."

Then she lay her cheek on my chest and noticed the notes and the green wrapping paper.

"Hey, what's this? From Your Old Italian Guy, From Peter Pan? You have way too many personalities for me to resist. What's in here . . . Tinker Bell? A travel mug! Thank you, Peter. Tinker Bell was trouble for Peter, you know."

"But loving and loyal. You keep lighting up the house, beauty, and I'll take my chances. Are you hungry?"

"Only for you, Matt. Wally Mangrum filled me up pretty well," she teased. "Let me take all my stuff upstairs and change into my pajamas and cozy socks, and then we can nestle, sip some wine and coffee, and you can tell me about your day. I've only been thinking about doing that since two this afternoon," she laughed as she ran upstairs with the dogs trailing her.

Abigail was quiet and seemed deep in thought when she came back down in her green pajamas and fat, fuzzy socks. She snuggled next to me on the sofa, put her feet up on the coffee table, and alternately rotated the bud vase slowly on the glass table top and turned the Tinker Bell mug over and over in her hands. She sipped both her wine and coffee.

"Matt, before you tell me about your day, let me tell you what I've been thinking about all day. First . . . you, of course—every minute, even when Wally Mangrum was flirting with me. I love you so much, and not just for the wine and roses, you know. I love you because you make love to me as if I were the most beautiful and sensuous woman in the world; and you play with me as if I were your dearest friend; and you treat me with respect as if I were Princess Abigail.

Second . . . how you have changed my life. I figured that once I graduated next spring with my MBA in retail marketing, Mangrums would offer me a job because of my energy and ability, and I would go on the road to work on their expansion from the northeast as far south as Virginia: the location, site plans, construction, internal layout and design, inventory, local marketing and advertising for all the new stores. I could do that because I was single and not attached and I didn't have anybody who was depending on me every day."

"And then I messed everything up." I put my arm around her and kissed her forehead.

Abigail tucked herself as tightly under my left arm as she could, her hand rubbing my stomach.

"And then there you were in my coffee shop, and the next day you actually came back. And you kissed me, and now you have to help me figure out my plans. Our plans, really. Whatever job I get—just as Mom said to Dad—I don't want to spend another day without you. Or without these baby dogs either." She laughed as she scratched Jock and Maggie next to her on the sofa.

"Mangrums is your first choice?"

"Mangrums would be a great opportunity. Their expansion strategy has been brilliant, and they are miles ahead of all their supermarket competition in management, efficiency and innovation. Plus, their benefits are second to none in the retail industry, and they treat their employees like family."

"It sounds perfect for you, Abby. With your passion and ideas you'll be a star at Mangrums."

"I want more than that, Matt: I want us to be a family. Do you believe in miracles?"

"After this past week, beauty, I believe that nothing is impossible." I wrapped my right arm around her, pulled her against me and kissed her hair. I felt her tears on my neck. "I know you want to have a baby, Abby."

"I want to have *your* baby, Matt. For years, I've been told it was almost impossible for me to get pregnant. I had resigned myself to the prospect of never having children. But now you're here, and I'm not resigned any more. My pediatrician way back told me that there might be treatments some day or that as I grew older and became sexually active my infertility might just go away.

"I think I'll go to my OB/GYN right after Christmas and look for some answers . . . if that's what you want, too. What do you think, old guy? I know it's a lot to throw at you. And here I was just going to put my feet up and ask you about your day."

"Abby, you are my day, but let me tell you in twenty words or less. My meeting went well. My client and his attorney will draw up a buy-sell agreement soon enough, and some day I'll explain to you what a buy-sell is, but not today."

"Matt, you are the first guy I've ever made love with for eight consecutive days who has really listened to me and let me keep talking—and still kept listening to me. Of course, you're the only guy I've ever made love with for more than two straight days, but the other guys all wanted to talk and tell me how smart they were and show me how funny and clever they were."

"Abby, beauty, I love to listen to you, I love the touch of you, I love to breathe you in, I love to watch you move and see all your colors catch the sunshine, I love to taste all your flavors. And when I listen to you, I love not just the sound of your voice—which is pure honey to my ears—but the inner voice of your mind coming through your words. Just be Abigail, by my side, and I will go where you want to go and share your dreams."

"My sweet poet. Can we have a baby, Matt?"

"I believe we can, beauty; I believe there are more miracles ahead for us. The arithmetic will be a challenge. If we get married in 2008 and if we get pregnant in 2008, we could have a baby in 2009—when I'm sixty-three. That would make me about eighty-one when our baby graduates from high school. But you, Abigail Elizabeth McKay, have the faith to move mountains, as the Bible says, and that should be enough for both of us."

"I have that much faith in you, Matt. You will be strong enough for both of us. What do you have to do tomorrow? I'd like to stop at Mom and Dad's, see if Mom needs any help with dinner on Thanksgiving and find out what happened with my brother Jack."

"I thought I'd call Matt and Danny in the late morning and see when they're hitting the road for Saratoga and Long Island;

and call Mom and Dad, let them know what time we'll pick them up on Thursday, and ask Mom about dinner at her house next week."

"That's Wednesday night, right?"

"Right. I thought it might be nice to get there a little early so that you and Mom can play and talk in the kitchen while Dad and I talk about you girls in the living room."

"You mean the 'parlor' don't you?" Abigail teased.

"I have to remember to ask your mom and dad if you have always been this saucy, or if I'm the one who brought out the smarty-pants in you. I would like to take you to Joe's for breakfast in the morning, Miss Smarty-Pants."

"And that will be a special treat, Mister Summer Boy, as long as it's not too early because an even bigger treat will be having extended playtime before we have to get out of bed."

Abigail stretched out on the sofa, laid her head in my lap and squeezed her feet in between Jock and Maggie at the other end.

"I talked with Mary Kay, and she is so excited about meeting you. Who is your best friend?"

"You mean my old best friend?" I smiled and brushed my fingers through her hair around her ears and across her cheeks. "Probably Joe Steger, my best Army buddy from the time we met at Fort Benning for our officer combat training, to our assignment at the Army Language School in Monterey, California, through our year together in Vietnam supervising and teaching officers at the English Language Center in Saigon.

"When we came back to the states and I fell in love with his sister Missy, that brought us even closer together. But I have other best friends from other compartments of my life: Kevin Flynn—no relation—and Tony Lenzi from Boston College; Jerry Brongo from B.C. Law; and Dave Connolly and Ken Bauman from Dominic Savio. I've always been blessed with a lot of good, close friends."

"It's a blessing for sure, but it's also an accomplishment to have even one close friend, and you have so many! Mary Kay and I have had to work hard over the years to keep our friendship strong and caring—and we've only known each other for twenty years. How have you done it for so many more years with so many more guys? What a dumb question! I knew the answer before I asked: you are a man who cares about other people, a man who listens, and that's why I'm here on your sofa—that and your baby blue eyes. Will I get to meet some of your old best friends?"

"I hope you'll get to meet them all, Abby. I sure want them to meet you. They were all at my wedding and couldn't believe I landed a woman as beautiful as Sarah. Thirty years later, they're going to be dumbfounded when they see a bright beauty like you with an old guy like all of us."

"Are all of them married?"

"All except Kevin Flynn from B.C. He's a confirmed bachelor in a large Irish family. All the others have two children each. Tony Lenzi has two granddaughters in Boston, and Joe Steger has two grandsons in Minnesota. Lots of places for you and me to visit, Abby."

"How about I make some fresh coffee, old guy, and we take our conversation and Maggie and Jock up to bed and watch some of *The Notebook* to remind you of how young you and your best buddies used to be," she said impishly from my lap.

It was almost eleven o'clock when we started *The Notebook*. Abigail stopped the movie when Noah and Allie lay down in the middle of the intersection on the night of their first date.

"Matt, would you do anything that crazy with me?"

"I sure will, first chance we get. I did almost the same thing with Missy Steger—except it was during a snowstorm in January in Oshkosh, Wisconsin; we lay down in the middle of the parking lot at an Albertsons supermarket and made snow angels. A bunch of cars actually formed a circle around us with their headlights on, honking their horns. Good entertainment is hard to come by in the middle of winter in Oshkosh."

"But not in the middle of this magic bed. Come here, angel, and wrap me up in your wings. I haven't thanked you properly for my red rose and Tinker Bell."

Our lovemaking was so quiet and gentle that Jock and Maggie curled together undisturbed in their corner of the bed, and were still curled in the same corner when the sound of the wind and snow against the windows wakened us all in the morning. With Abigail soft and warm against my skin, with both of us wrapped snugly under *Pooh and Piglet,* and with Jock and Maggie now stretching across our feet, I couldn't imagine a better place to be this side of heaven. It was not easy to break the spell and think of a reason to get out of bed.

When we walked in to Joe's for breakfast, I spotted Dave and Ann Connolly in a booth along the windows, caught their eye and waved.

"Abby, you're about to meet one of those old best friends sooner than I expected. That's Dave Connolly and his wife, Ann. Dave and I went to St. George's and Dominic Savio together, so we go back more than fifty years."

We joined the Connollys in their booth. I introduced Abigail, and she was the star of breakfast for the next hour. She alternated between drawing out Dave and Ann about their children, Bobby and Lynn, and highlighting her first week with me.

Bobby, who was the assistant superintendent of buildings and grounds at the University of Buffalo, was coming in for Thanksgiving with his girlfriend Amanda; and Lynn, an associate professor of languages at Skidmore, was coming with her boyfriend Jared.

"Matt and I met for the first time a week ago Monday at Kitty's cafe at Gibbs and East," Abby told them.

I had little more to do than smile and laugh inside as I watched the range of expressions on Dave and Ann's faces. Abigail told them just enough to create wide-eyed wonder in Dave but not enough to elicit skepticism or disapproval from Ann.

"Matt's house is so comfortable that it fits me like a soft old bathrobe and slippers, and Maggie and Jock and I are already best friends," Abby said.

Dave and Ann were captivated. Clearly, Abigail would have no trouble traveling anywhere in my world—though I still had doubts about making my way in hers.

We left breakfast and the Connollys with a promise to pick an evening before Christmas to get together for dinner. I also got an e-mail from Dave later in the morning. Could I meet him at Joe's at seven-thirty on Monday? I knew he wanted to find out more about Abby without Ann around. I would have done the same thing if Dave had suddenly turned up with an Abigail.

We drove home after Joe's and then split up to visit our parents and run our errands. I bought four large red mum plants at Mangrums, one each for Abigail, Mrs. McKay, Mom and Diane. I also went to Millie's Wine Rack in the Mangrums plaza for several bottles of Chianti, Moscato d'Asti and white Lambrusco—Diane's favorite—for our Thanksgiving dinners.

As soon as I walked into the family room from the garage, before I even had a chance to scratch the dogs, I heard the end of a message from Abigail on our machine. "Don't you just love our new message, Matt? Mom and I are at Mangrums to pick up some last-minute Thanksgiving stuff. Do you need anything? Breakfast with your friend was great, but I'm not sure about his wife yet. Mom said Jack is still grumbling about you, but he's coming tomorrow. I'll be home around four. Can we have pizza for dinner? I have a coupon for Frederico's—two small pizzas for the price of one. I bought you a few cans of anchovies—the flat ones. How many times have I told you today that I love you?"

There were two other messages. The first was from my brother Tom, complimenting Abigail on her message and letting us know that dinner was still at three but we could come over any time before that. The second was from Joe Steger, wanting to know "how and when the hell did you get yourself an Abigail?" and wishing us a Happy Thanksgiving today because he and Margie were going to be on the road tomorrow from Ohio to spend the weekend with their son in Minnesota. I saved them both for Abigail to hear.

When Abby got home, we ordered the two small pizzas from Frederico's, hers with mozzarella, sausage and green peppers and mine with tomato sauce and anchovies only—just the way Aunt Lucy used to make them. They were delivered in thirty minutes, and we gobbled them up—with several glasses of Chianti—just as quickly. We ate around most of the crust and cut it into bite-size chunks, which I have always mixed in with Jock and Maggie's regular dog food for several days after I have pizza. Both dogs love their "pizza cookies."

I got a fire going in the fireplace, and Abigail and I camped out with our coffee mugs and the dogs on their fleece blankets in the living room. She laughed at Joe Steger's message and asked if she could call him later. Then she told me about her afternoon with her mother.

"Mom's conversation went in as many different directions as the different aisles we turned down in Mangrums. She actually asked me if you were still going to come tomorrow! I said, 'Mom, I love him! Do you think he's going away?' Then she switched to what effect is he going to have on your masters program. I said, 'Mom, Matt loves me. He's going to be at my side and support me in whatever I want to do.'

"Then she switched to are you living together and have you talked about getting married. I said, 'I have moved in to Matt's house but, Mom, it feels like my house now.' I sort of lied and continued, 'We haven't talked about marriage yet, but don't bet against it, Mom.' Then she gave up and changed the subject to my dogenhead of a brother."

"Wow . . . I thought Dad was the only person who knows the word 'dogenhead.' Did you get that from your mom and dad?"

"Dad . . . and Grandpa McKay. Apparently my dogenhead brother Jack has decided that all of my family are dumber than Irish potatoes if they think that you and I will make it past Christmas, but he promised my father that he would keep his mouth shut and not be ornery tomorrow. Jack always intimidated my boyfriends when he was around. Maybe he thought it was his job because Dad was always nice to them. I hope he doesn't create a black cloud over dinner tomorrow."

"Here's my answer to that, Abby." I turned her face to mine and kissed her mouth, her nose, her cheeks, her eyes, her hair—and started over again. "I'll be as nice to Jack as I will to Patrick. He won't be the only person close to us who thinks we're crazy and have no future. We'll be nice to them one at a time and hope they will come around. You know . . . everybody in my family might not love you as much as cousin Terry does.

"Let me warm up our coffees and bring in the phone. I'm going to call Joe Steger and put the two of you on speakerphone so I can hear his side of the conversation. I've called Joe 'Hot Shot' ever since I met him because he's a wise guy. Don't be surprised by anything he says. What really matters is that Joe would take a bullet for me, and I'd do the same for him."

"What's he doing now?"

"He and Margie have a very successful travel agency in Columbus. VIP stuff. Professional athletes, politicians, Ohio State professors and dignitaries from universities across Ohio and most of the surrounding states. When it's time for our first getaway, we'll call Joe."

"Tell me about his family."

"German on both sides. He's the son of Gerhard Steger and Amelia Schrader. No brothers, only sister Melissa. They were all born and raised in Oshkosh where his mom and dad still live. Missy also, who married a local chiropractor the year after she dumped me."

"How could she do that?" Abigail teased.

"I used to ask myself that question every day—even when I was married to Sarah—before I met you. I never held it against

Joe. He couldn't understand it either. He once told me that Missy told him that she decided to be safe with the hometown guy who knew what he was going to do for the rest of his life and made her feel comfortable, as opposed to the soldier boy poet who didn't know what he wanted to do after he got out of the Army and scared her a little by loving her so much. It was 1972.

"She broke my heart, and I didn't go out with anybody for almost four years—all through law school—until I met Sarah. But back to Joe. He has two sons, Matthew—named after me, believe it or not—and Edward, who was named after Margie's father. Eddie is married—no children yet—and builds houses in Oshkosh. Matt is married, has two sons, and he and his wife both teach school in Little Falls, Minnesota.

"The phone is ringing, Abby. Here you go," and I handed her the phone.

"Hello? I know this number. Is that you, Flynnie?"

"Is this Joe 'Hot Shot' Steger? This is Abigail McKay."

"Matt's new Abigail? Flynnie, are you there listening?"

"Pretend I'm not, Hot Shot."

"Abigail, what have you done to my best buddy? I let a week go by without calling him, and look what happens. Matt didn't tell me he was looking for a new girlfriend. Hell! He hasn't had any girlfriend since Sarah died."

"He wasn't looking for a girlfriend, but he was looking for *me*. And I've been waiting for *him* for a long time. You've known Matt for more than thirty-five *years*, so you, more than most, know the kind of man he is. I've known the old guy for ten *days*, so I'm still learning. I'm hoping you'll be able to fill in some gaps for me."

"Ten days! It took me ten *years* to get to like him. The 'old guy' has plenty of gaps I can help you with. Where did you two meet?"

"We found each other last Monday in the coffee shop where I work two mornings a week."

"Well, Matt has always loved his coffee—so it was 'coffee at first sight,' huh? Hey, old buddy, if Abigail calls you 'old guy,' what do you call her?"

"Pretend I'm not here, Hot Shot."

"Abigail, you don't sound a day over forty-seven. Why do you want an old guy like Matt?"

"He's hot . . . and I'm not a day over twenty-seven."

"Hoo-ah! I have to meet you . . . soon! Tell Flynnie when you see him that we have to plan a weekend celebration together—maybe in Pittsburgh—right after the New Year. When Margie hears about you, she might not want to wait that long. I have to go right now. My wife expects me to have the car packed before she gets home so we can leave for Minnesota at the crack of dawn. I expect you and Flynnie will have an amusing Thanksgiving with both your families. Stay well and give the old guy a hug for me."

"Old Flynnie says tell him I love him and have a safe trip."

The fire was crumbling down to charcoal and ashes, and Jock and Maggie curled closer to us as the fire cooled. Abigail played with Jock's ears while Maggie licked my hands.

"Are you thinking about tomorrow, Matt?"

"No, beauty, actually I was thinking about Captain Joe Steger and Captain Matt Flynn during those terrible days in Saigon in 1970 when the Viet Cong repeatedly tried to attack our school on Tan Son Nhut Air Base. The first time was a mortar attack, and four of our students were killed and a dozen injured, including three teachers."

Abigail immediately took my hands away from Maggie and squeezed them hard.

"How awful that must have been, Matt. Were you hurt?"

"Not that day, but there's another day I'll tell you about at another time. The three teachers were okay after two or three days in the infirmary, but the four students who died—just kids, really—were from Joe's and my classes. After that day we carried our M-16s with two full clips of bullets in the pockets of our fatigues to our classes every day."

"So my poet is also a war hero. You are one surprise after another, Matt Flynn. There's a gap that Joe filled in without even being here. I can't wait to meet him and Margie. Can we do that Pittsburgh weekend he was talking about?"

"We will do that, Abby. Joe and I have been brothers of the heart ever since the day we met at Fort Benning.

"Are you worried about tomorrow? Do you have any things to do before we go to Tom and Diane's? I thought we could get there at about two-thirty."

"I'm all yours tomorrow, Matt. I am a little nervous. Not about my family—as long as brother Jack behaves—but I don't know what to expect from your brother and his family."

"Expect the best, love. Tom is easygoing, and so's the whole

128

family. Diane will make you feel like her sister right away, and their kids, Stephanie, Barbara and Trent—and this is the funny part because they are so close to you in age—will treat you like their sister, too. Don't worry about the Flynns. I have been the beloved but single uncle and brother for ten years. I'm pretty sure they'll all be delighted to see me walk in the door with a beautiful Abigail on my arm."

"Okay. Can we go up and get in bed? I'm so tired all of a sudden from thinking about you in Vietnam and two Thanksgiving dinners. The list of things you have to tell me about is increasing geometrically—even if I take off everything except your careers."

"Well, I had My Army Career penciled in on my list of Things to Tell Abigail in Week Three of Our Life Together," I teased, "so that would be next week, beauty."

"You are just as much of a wise guy as Joe Steger," she responded as she pinched my butt two or three times going up the stairs.

In the bedroom Abigail lit a fat bayberry candle before she curled under the quilt.

"Come closer, soldier boy," she whispered as she wrapped her arms and legs around me. "I know we have plenty of time to learn about each other, and I can wait till Week Three to hear the rest of the Army tales of Captain Flynn, but don't make me guess too much, Matt. Since you first kissed me, I have wanted to know all there is to know about you. Instantaneously would be nice, I thought, but maybe uncovering you a little at a time is better. *Mmm* . . . except in bed. I'm tired of thinking about tomorrow. Kiss my thoughts away, Matt, my old guy . . . my sweet guy . . . take me in your dreams . . . just touch me . . . touch me to sleep."

We melted together under the quilt, between Jock and Maggie, with the bayberry candle still burning on my old highboy. Just before I fell asleep, I was remembering some of the not-so-happy Thanksgivings since Sarah died, and praying.

Thank you, Lord, for giving me Abigail.

12

"*Come on*, baby dogs, let's touch Daddy awake."

I felt Abigail on my right side rubbing her belly against the small of my back and running her fingers across my chest; and Jock and Maggie walking up the edge of the bed on my left side and licking my face.

"*Mmm* . . . Abby . . . babies. Nobody in the *world* could be happier waking up this morning than *I* am. Our first Thanksgiving, beauty. I love you."

"Our first Thanksgiving, old guy. I love you *so* much. It's a beautiful morning, Matt. Look at the sun shining through the snow and ice crystals on our windows. Can you *believe* that bayberry candle is *still* burning?"

"Once you fell asleep, pretty girl, I couldn't let go of you and get out of bed to blow it out."

"I'm sorry if I was a little droopy last night. You made it all go away. This morning I don't *care* what my brother Jack does or says. When I'm with *you* I don't care what *anybody* does or says, so the secret to happiness is to always be *with* you. Don't be upset, but I think what I've been really worrying about for the past week is that you would change your mind: *Abigail is too young, too silly; her brother is a pain; I want my quiet house back; I don't want to hurt Sarah.*"

Abigail pulled my face to hers and kissed me tenderly several times.

"And talking to Joe last night reminded me how *special* you are—*both* of you, really."

"Abby, *I'm* the one who should be worried. Beauties like you don't latch on to old guys like me except in the movies. So forget it. I'm not going anywhere without you."

"Let's get the doggies going, and then I want to make you my special oatmeal before I take you back to bed," she grinned.

"Miss Abigail, may I make *you* my special omelet to go with your oatmeal?"

On our sunny walk around the circle, Jock insisted on burying his nose in every deer hoof print in the fresh snow, while Maggie repeatedly rolled on her back making *her* version of snow angels.

We greeted a handful of neighbors either walking their dogs, or with their children bundled up in strollers, or clearing their driveways—all enjoying the lovely, quiet morning. I noticed several double takes, from newer neighbors who had never seen me walking my dogs with company, and from older neighbors who remembered me walking my dogs with Sarah. It was cold, so the street
conversations were short: *Happy Thanksgiving! This is my friend Abigail. Have a good day!*

Back in the kitchen, Abby and I went to work on our specials while Jock and Maggie lounged under our feet hoping for treats. Abby cooked her oatmeal—enough for two—with chocolate milk and one heaping tablespoon of peanut butter stirred in. It was the *best* I've ever had. I made my double omelet with five eggs, diced ham, shaved carrots, milk and plain cream cheese mixed together, and provolone cheese on top. Abby said it was the best omelet *she'd* ever had. We took our mugs of coffee up to the bedroom, left the dogs on their beds in the hallway, and made love and dozed, with the sunlight streaming through the frosted windows, for the rest of the morning.

We picked up Mom and Dad at two o'clock. We switched cars to drive to Tom and Diane's because Mom and Dad can't climb into my Wrangler, so we took their old Chevy Caprice. Abigail sat in the back with Dad, and Mom sat in front with me. It was a bright afternoon with the low sun sparkling on the new blanket of snow.

Tom and Diane's house was alive with cheerful noise and the aroma of Thanksgiving. As soon as Mom and Dad stepped into the front hallway, Tom and Diane's two chocolate Labs started barking, and Trent spotted us.

"*Hey*, everybody, Grandma and Grandpa are here! And Uncle Matt and his new friend!"

All the bustling in the house stopped—except for Brownie and Oreo's barking—and the whole family surrounded us in the living room: Tom and Diane; Stephanie and her husband Warren and their children Jeff and Julie; Barbara and her husband Chuck and their daughter Amy; Trent and his girlfriend Katy; and, of course, Brownie and Oreo.

The loving and grateful hugs and kisses for Mom and Dad were slightly different from the warm but curious hugs and kisses for Abigail. The girls especially—Diane, Stephanie and Barbara—were measuring Abigail against their long-dormant expectations of the kind of woman I might one day welcome into my life. It was clear within a minute or two that the smiles and laughs among all the girls were genuine and caring. Abby was already one of the family by the time we took off our coats.

I kissed the back of her neck as I took her coat and whispered, "You're a big hit, beauty."

Trent caught my eye, grinned and gave me a thumbs-up, and my brother grabbed my arm and led me toward the kitchen where he had been mashing the potatoes. As we walked through the dining room, I heard my nieces telling Abigail, "Uncle Matt is a great guy and still a kid at heart.
Wait'll you hear about some of his famous *shenanigans*!"

Tom cracked open Coronas for both of us and kidded, "She's a *babe*, Matt! How did you *do* it? I already saw Katy pinch Trent for hugging Abigail a little *too* long. She reminds me of Amy Adams in *Junebug* or *The Wedding Date*, or maybe Rachel McAdams in *The Notebook*. What can she possibly *see* in an old fart like you? How about working on the turkey while we talk?"

As I carved the turkey while Tom went back to mashing the potatoes, I recounted some of the highlights of my ten days with Abigail since our first coffee conversation at Kitty's.

"I *like* that place. I get in there occasionally after a concert at the Eastman. But what *I* want to know is how an old guy like you—what *are* you, sixty-one?—picked up a *hot*, twenty-six-year-old waitress in a coffee shop?"

"*First* of all, Abigail is a *hot*, twenty-six-year-old *grad student* at RIT who will get her MBA in May. She's working two mornings a week at Kitty's to help pay her school bills. *Second* of all, I think *she* picked *me* up."

"*That* I find hard to believe."

"Well, I went in to Kitty's on the Monday morning after Veterans Day and made conversation with Abigail while she was getting my coffee—the same way I've done it with *hundreds* of pretty waitresses—and she seemed eager to talk. You know *me*: I always make eye contact, and she has those deep green eyes. We talked for a few minutes because there were no other customers. Then I said I would like to keep talking with her but I had to meet a client at my office, and I asked what days she worked. She said that she only worked Monday and Tuesday mornings, and asked— much to my surprise—'Can you come in tomorrow?' Probably much to *her* surprise I actually came back in the next morning; and here we are."

"Wow! So the spark was there from the first cup of coffee? This sounds serious, brother."

"That's an understatement: I still find it hard to believe, but I think Abby is in my life to stay."

Tom clapped me on the back and laughed.

"*Maybe*, unless my wife and daughters scare her away with some of their favorite stories about you! All kidding aside, hurrah for you, Matt! I couldn't be happier for you."

Then he threw the hand-masher into the sink, took off his apron and said, "We are all done here. Let's call everybody in to the table. Thanks for carving the bird; that's one of those 'man-of-the-family' jobs I wish Dad were still doing."

Dad sat at the head of the table with Mom on his right. I sat on Dad's left; then Abigail, Julie, Stephanie, Jeff, Warren, Katy, Trent (at the other end of the table), Chuck, Amy, Barbara, Diane, Tom, and back to Mom. In typical Flynn fashion, everybody around the table talked all at once and passed oval platters and deep bowls of food in both directions at the same time—which is one of the main things that makes all of our Thanksgivings memorable. The only quiet moment was when seven-year-old Jeff led us in Grace.

All the traditional Thanksgiving fare was as delicious as Diane and her girls always prepare it, especially my favorite dish, the classic giblet stuffing, which Diane magically mixes just the way Mom always did. I had my usual two helpings of stuffing, mashed potatoes, and white *and* dark meat, all swimming in gravy. I skipped the non-essentials: the fruits, rolls, breads, vegetables,
casseroles and salads, which filled the table.

Abigail tried—and enjoyed—a little of just about every dish on the table, but her favorites were Diane's stuffing and Stephanie's sweet corn-and-cheddar casserole. She had seconds on those and admitted that the stuffing was "way" better than the Ritz cracker-and-sausage stuff her mom made. She also kept looking at the mounds of food spilling over the edges of my plate, laughed and poked me in the side repeatedly.

"Hey, old *piggy*, aren't you going to save any room for dinner at the McKay's? Now I finally get to see your German-Irish side with all those piles of meat and potatoes."

"Don't worry, sweetie. I'll skip dessert here and I'll be ready for the works at your mom's; and my Italian side will be back tomorrow night for dinner at Palermo's."

Much to my surprise and delight, Abigail got into the Flynn family kidding and teasing almost immediately, something that took years for Sarah to barely tolerate, and never really appreciate. Before we had finished pouring our gravy, Abby was bantering as if she'd grown up at the Flynn dinner table. In between burps and sips of red wine, I watched with amazement and pleasure as she connected with all my family. Every time Abby was kidded or teased and she responded with grace, laughter and a smile, I stroked her thigh under the table or rubbed the back of her neck and whispered, "Beauty, you are *easily* a match for the Flynns. Welcome to the family."

We were done with dinner at about four-thirty. Abigail and I helped clear the table and set out all the desserts, which looked *way* too good to leave behind. We had enough time for coffee and catching up on the news in Tom and Diane's family. Chuck and Barbara had bought a house off Hard Road in Webster and would be moving in January. Katy and Trent, who had gotten engaged *last* Thanksgiving, had set the date for their wedding: June 14, 2008. Mom and Dad were tickled pink. Trent would be the last of their seven grandchildren to get married.

Just before Abigail and I left, Alan and Lisa called from North Carolina to wish everybody a Happy Thanksgiving, and— almost on cue—their daughter Debbie, her husband Fred and their son Billy walked in the door on their way home from dinner with Fred's family.

In the middle of all the fresh hugs and kisses for Debbie (who had not heard about Abigail) and her family, she looked me squarely in the eye and said with a grin, "Uncle Matt, you are the *best* godfather, but I think you should have asked me before you got yourself a girlfriend."

"Sorry, Debbie," I teased. "I tried to get to see you but there was too much snow all week. For my next girlfriend I'll do better, okay?"

"Well, the two of you will have to come over to our house *soon*—before Christmas for sure— so I can tell Abigail a few things about you before she gets in too deep."

Diane wrapped two pieces of coconut cream pie for us take home, gave me one more hug for the road, and said, "Matthew, Abigail is a *dream*; don't let her go."

"Thanks, Diane. That's my plan. Dinner was wonderful.

Thanks again."

Abby and I drove to Mom and Dad's to switch back to my Jeep, stopped at our house to feed and walk the dogs, and arrived at the McKay house at five-thirty. We brought our assigned rolls, Italian bread and two bottles of Chianti; and two six-packs of Harp and yellow mums for her dad and mom, who greeted us warmly at the door.

The rest of the family joined us in the kitchen. Pat and Laurie gave us both hugs. Jack, Catherine and Betsy hugged Abigail but shook my hand. Jack glared, and Catherine and Betsy scrutinized. Then Mr. McKay handed me a Harp, and the four of us "boys" moved into the living room, leaving all the "girls" to bustle between the kitchen and the dining room—no doubt talking as much about *me* as about Thanksgiving. Flames were leaping in the fire, just as they were at Tom's when we left.

Never having done two Thanksgivings before, I was surprised to notice so many differences—some subtle, some not—between the celebrations at the Flynn's and McKay's. The McKays were a lot quieter, and there was no music. The Flynns talked more and louder, and my brother always had his eclectic, famous-hit CDs playing in the background. The McKay house was dimmer—only the kitchen had an overhead light. Every room at the Flynn's had a ceiling light *and* fan—Tom learned to be a good electrician from Uncle Vinny.

This was only my second visit to the McKay house, but I had yet to see a television on. At Tom and Diane's, the televisions in both the living room and the kids' playroom were always on— with *Sponge Bob*, or *Home Alone* or *National Lampoon's Christmas Vacation*, or NFL football—even while we were all feasting in the dining room.

The McKay house was cleaner, neater—probably because there were no dogs and only one child. It smelled older, and the furniture was more dignified. The Flynn house, with two chocolate Labs and three to eight kids, depending on how many of the seven grandchildren were visiting, was chaotic and cozy, and the chairs and sofas were rumpled and comfortable.

I spent a lot of time on holidays on the living room floor at Tom's—usually with my shoes off—playing with the dogs, the kids and their toys. I could not see that happening at the McKay's. And even though turkey was traditional at both houses, the aroma from the McKay kitchen bore little resemblance to the smell of Diane's kitchen.

I had time for such musing while we were sitting in the living room waiting for the girls to call us to dinner because of the regular gaps in our conversation. Mr. McKay and Patrick did as much as they could, but every time I asked Jack about his job or his home or even his daughter Betsy,
he gave a one-syllable answer, and he *never* looked me in the eye. He clearly had not yet bought in to Matt Flynn as a lasting presence in his sister's life. After two rounds of grudging responses, Mr. McKay and Pat ignored Jack and talked with me about the chances of the Cleveland Browns
finally making the playoffs or the New England Patriots going undefeated all the way to the Super Bowl. Fortunately, the girls called us for dinner after only one beer.

It turned out that Abigail and Mrs. McKay did a much better job of selling me to Catherine and Betsy. Not only was Catherine extremely cordial and inquisitive when we sat down to dinner, but Betsy even wanted to sit between "Aunt Abby and her friend Matt." I had no doubt that Jack was grinding his teeth and—as I said to Abby later—I would have really enjoyed listening in on their conversation about me when they got home.

Mrs. McKay made a great dinner. The flavors were different from the Flynn's, but everything I had was delicious. Even the Ritz cracker-and-sausage stuffing—though not classic giblet— was tasty. And after two pieces of Mrs. McKay's chocolate layer cake, I felt as if I had broken my single-day eating record. While I was finishing the rich frosting on my second piece, Abigail reached over, grinned, rubbed my stomach and whispered to Betsy, "My friend Matt has a *very* full tummy." I don't think Jack was amused when Betsy also rubbed my stomach, and giggled. As a matter of fact, not *one* time throughout dinner did he either look at me or say a word.

Catherine, on the other hand, *was* interested. She asked about my job: *What is an annuity?* She asked about Sarah: *How long were you married?* She asked about my dogs: *Do Scotties shed?* It sounded as if she and Betsy wanted a dog, but Jack was balking.

Mrs. McKay excused us from helping to clean up because we "should get home and take care of my daughter's favorite dogs." We left at eight o'clock and did just that. Jock and Maggie were all over us after their quiet day, and when we came back from their walk, the four of us stretched out together on the living room floor in front of the fireplace. Abby said we should bring the dogs with us the next time we go to Tom and Diane's.

"I think you're right, beauty. I think Jock and Maggie and Brownie and Oreo would get along just fine. I'll mention it to Tom, and maybe we can try it around Christmas. Of course it would not have worked today because . . . "

"I know . . . we couldn't bring them to Mom and Dad's. Maybe on a nice April day—when the world outside isn't wet and dirty—we'll spring Maggie and Jock on Mom and Dad and hope for the best. Did you get the feeling that Catherine and Betsy would like to have a dog?"

"For sure, but Jack is probably saying no to that idea, right?"

"Jack says no to just about everything except golf with his buddies. It's always been hard to believe that Jack and Patrick are brothers."

Abigail rolled on her side, massaged my belly and kissed me on the cheek.

"How's that tummy of yours, summer boy? Except for Patrick, I've *never* seen anybody eat so much. Thank *God* you saved room for Mom's cake. She would have been crushed if you hadn't."

"Well, I *was* able to pace myself from dinner to dinner; but I might have to stay up an extra ten or twenty minutes and circle the family room a few times to let all that stuffing settle. Otherwise, I'll be burping too much for you to want to even *sleep* next to me, let alone make love."

"No chance of that, Matt. After this momentous two-family day, I want you *twice* as much as yesterday. I *love* your family. Stephanie and Barbara and I are already planning to go Christmas shopping together on the Saturday after we get back from visiting Danny and Emma. Diane invited me to come over some evening next week to look through two closets full of clothes that Stephanie doesn't wear any more And, last but not least, Tom gave me a *huge* hug in the kitchen while you were playing on the living room floor with Amy and Jeff, and thanked me for 'bringing my brother back to life again.' Is your other brother like you and Tom?"

"Not much. Alan is a decent guy, but he's a classic middle child. He's not as dutiful a son as I am. He's not as easygoing as Tom. And he's not as family-oriented as *either* of us. He moved to North Carolina for a teaching job at UNC-Wilmington six or seven years ago, and he and Lisa don't come home much. Debbie and Fred live in Honeoye Falls. And Alan and Lisa's son Barry lives with his wife Eileen and their daughter Jean outside of Pittsburgh."

"Will we see them at Christmas?"

"Probably not. Debbie and Barry and their families usually go to Wilmington for Christmas."

Abigail sat up, lifted my head onto her lap, and rubbed both dogs with her fuzzy slippers.

"Are you tired, old guy? I was sure *I* would be at the end of *this* day, but I think all the great family vibes have my adrenalin flowing."

"Mine too, love. I don't know whether our families think you and I are just having a fling or we're together forever, but right now they are surprisingly understanding and supportive. I think even *Catherine* liked me by the end of dinner."

"She sure did! Just before we left, she even apologized to me for Jack's behavior; and she said she'd try to talk him into having us over for dinner before Christmas."

I reached up and ran my fingers through Abby's hair behind her ears.

"So you think we have a good chance to make it to Christmas, huh, beauty?"

"Christmas what *year*, old guy? *This* year's a cinch, but *2050* may be a stretch." She laughed and traced my lips with her finger. "Let's go down to the family room and check in on Allie and Noah. You can do your laps while Maggie, Jock and I cuddle on the sofa. I need to decompress, or debrief, or deconstruct—whatever the astronauts do when they come back from space. I need to stop *thinking* for the rest of the night. Why don't you get the movie started, and I'll brew some *Earl Grey*. Do you want honey in yours? Come on, baby dogs."

I only managed two "laps" around the coffee table in the family room before I curled up on the sofa with Abigail and the dogs. We watched Allie and Noah in their summer of young love, and we must have fallen asleep just after Allie's mother and father broke them up and took her off to school up north.

When Jock heard a siren and barked, both dogs jumped off the sofa and woke us up. *The Notebook* was over and the credits were playing. We laughed, stretched and yawned, and shut down the family room and took our "decompressing" party up to bed.

Abigail made love to me twice, "once for each of our families," she whispered. Then she lay very warm and quiet on

138

top of me—soft and still from head to toe—and she fell asleep before I could say good night. *Ten days since I first kissed this beautiful girl*, I thought, as I felt Abby's light breath on my chest. *Ten days*, as I ran my hands down her back and over the curves of her buttocks.

Ten days.

If I should die before I wake, I've already been to heaven.

13

The wind and the rain on the west window woke up Jock, Maggie and me a little after eight. Most of my adult life, the day after Thanksgiving had been an anticlimax. The family hubbub and togetherness was over, the kids wanted to play with their friends rather than their cousins. When my sons were in college and came home for Thanksgiving, they wanted the *cars* to play with their friends. And the girls regularly went to the malls for those early Christmas bargains. That "black" day after Thanksgiving could be too quiet and almost lonely.

But not this time. Not with Abigail sleeping on her back at my side, with her left arm under my neck and her left leg draped over mine, her lips parted slightly, snoring gently. In spite of the dull daylight of a rainy morning, Abby's colors illumed the bed. Even the dogs were temporarily content to look at her sleeping rather than lick her awake.

I nudged Jock and Maggie to the foot of the bed and pulled back the covers to continue my freckle count. I didn't want to touch her—not yet. It was magical enough to simply watch Abby breathe, shift her leg on mine, and murmur and smile in her sleep. It was magical enough to simply absorb her warmth and her glow. *No morning will ever be gloomy with this beauty next to me*, I thought.

I kissed her breasts and then her belly and then her ears, and Abigail slowly opened her eyes and walked her fingers up my back.

"*Mmm*, Matt . . . *nice* wake-up. Is that *rain*?" She stretched. "This is the first rain in our life together. Where are the doggies?"

"We all wanted to look at you and not wake you up."

"Well, if you're done '*spectating*,' summer boy," Abby chided as she pulled me on top of her, "do you mind finishing the wake-up properly? Off the bed, baby dogs."

It was eager, hungry lovemaking. Our mouths were all over each other, and we crashed every corner of the bed before we fell asleep. *Pooh* and *Piglet* ended up on the floor with the dogs.

This time the wind and the rain woke Abby first, and she invited Jock and Maggie back on the bed to help wake *me* up. Abby nibbled on my face while the dogs nibbled on my feet.

"Matt, have you ever made love outside in the rain?"

"As opposed to making love *inside* in the rain?" I grinned.

"You know what I mean, wise guy," she responded, pinching my ear lobe. "I have never made love outside on *any* kind of day."

"Only one time for me, when I was home from college, on a hot summer day in August; but as a true summer boy, I would like to volunteer to be *your* first, beauty—rain or shine, your choice."

"Even if I'm a *middle child*, Matt? You didn't think I was going to let you *skate* on that, did you? I gave you a pass last night in the living room because we had just too many things to think about yesterday, and we were talked out. But *not* today. So tell me, old guy, are middle children better in bed? You didn't have high praise for your brother Alan, so how does little middle Abby compare? Are *you* blushing?"

"You *got* me, *little middle Abby*." I laughed and hugged her to me tightly. "I thought about it as soon as I said it last night, and I was surprised that you didn't poke or pinch me immediately in some tender spot."

"You're not off the hook yet, old guy. Tell me how I fit into the *middle child syndrome*."

"You don't—you're not like Alan at all. You're a real family person. You're not a loner. I don't think you're playing with *me* just to get attention. Sometimes you're as responsible as the oldest child, and sometimes you're as easygoing as the youngest. Middle children are also supposed to be more creative and artistic—are *you* creative and artistic? There are still lots of things we don't know about each other."

"What about Sarah and the other great loves of your life?"

"Let me think a second . . . Sarah was the oldest, Cathy and Ellen were middle children, and Bonnie and Missy were the babies of the family. Sarah, Bonnie and Missy were good lovers, but you are by far the best *ever* for me. Some of it is inclination and natural ability, for sure, but just as much is age and appreciation?"

"Appreciation?"

"The older I've grown, the more I've appreciated women. My middle girls—Cathy and Ellen—were teenagers when I was

141

in love with them. I was in high school and college. We were very romantic, but scared and clueless. I don't think the fact that they were middle children had anything to do with anything. I always wished that I had met them ten years later when I would have known how to treat them better and appreciate them more. I was a very slow learner. I once wrote in a poem to Missy after she broke up with me: *I could never have loved her more, but I could have loved her better.* That's the way it always was with me. And now, ten years after Sarah—ten years without a woman in my life—I appreciate you more than *all* of my other five great loves put together."

Abigail wrapped her arms and legs around me, squeezed everywhere, and brushed my cheek with hers. Then she took a deep breath and whispered into my neck, "I am *so* lucky to follow all of those girls because I could not possibly find a better lover than you, summer boy. I will be thankful every *day* for every *thing* they taught you." Then she grinned impishly. "I only wonder what would have happened if I had met you when *I* was eighteen?"

We finally got up, fed Jock and Maggie and took them out for their walk, but they couldn't get back inside fast enough. As much as they love snow, they hate rain. It was a good morning for all of us to catch up on real life—for checklists, homework, loose ends and hot coffee.

Abigail called her boss at Mangrums and was allowed to change her schedule for the next two weeks to add two hours to each of her Tuesdays and Thursdays—from noon to eight—so she could take off next Friday for our trip to Boston. I called Danny to let him know we'd be coming in the afternoon on Friday and leaving on Sunday after breakfast, and he said he would book a nice bed and breakfast just around the corner from their apartment in Cambridge. I also called Shelby at Happy Tails, Jock and Maggie's favorite kennel, to book them for *their* weekend visit, which would include the doggie spa package: grooming, bubble baths and peticures.

Then we went to Phil Green's for hot dogs, hot chocolate and ice cream. Our favorite counter person, Jinks, was working, and she slipped us a couple of free kiddie packs of Oreos with our order. We stretched out together on one side of our favorite booth in the corner window and made notes on the brown paper napkins: go to Abby's apartment and clean out the rest of her stuff; buy a red rose at Mangrums; bring Abby's vase with the rose to dinner tonight; rewind *The Notebook* to where Matt and Abby fell asleep *last* night; clean the house; wash Maggie and Jock's beds and towels; watch the B.C. vs. Holy Cross football game; finish Abby's ergonomics project, and put up the outdoor Christmas lights tomorrow.

Then Abigail wrote on a separate napkin: Make love at least three times before Saturday night!

Then she unfolded *another* fresh napkin and wrote: Softball, tennis, piano and charcoal.

"Napkin number *two* I understand," I said with a kiss, "but what's napkin number *three*?"

"You wanted to know if your favorite—I hope—*middle* child is artistic and creative. The answer is 'yes,' my favorite *oldest* child. And *athletic,* too. I started playing the piano when I was three or four. I played varsity softball and tennis all four senior high years at Fatima. And I've been drawing charcoal portraits and landscapes ever since my seventh grade art class with Sister Mary James at Fatima. What about *you*, old guy? Can you match *that*?" she teased.

"Miss Abigail, I already knew you were athletic from the way you throw me around the bed. I can't wait to see your drawings. I hope they're better than my poems. Maybe we can put some of my old poems and your old drawings together into a book. Better yet, we can work on *new* ones together.

"Musical and athletic, however, I am *not*. I tried out for track and golf at Dominic Savio, but I didn't have quite enough discipline to stay with track practice, and not quite enough talent to make the golf team—although I'm good enough to beat my buddies most of the time. I bought a banjo when I got out of law school because I always loved the lively sound, and I took lessons for a while. But then I married Sarah, and Matt and Danny came along, and my lawyer schedule got *way* crowded, and I had to put the banjo in its black case on a basement shelf— where it *still* sits. I mean to pick it up again some day."

"Matt, this is all going to be *great* fun: reading your poems, showing you my old drawings, dusting off your banjo, finding me a piano, teaching you to play tennis and me to play golf—all beautiful things we can do together—some old, some brand new. But right now, unfortunately, we need to take our hot chocolate on the road and go clean out my apartment. I told my landlord I'd have all my things out today, and he plans on subletting it starting next week, which will save me the last month's rent on my lease."

Abigail had rented the apartment furnished, so there wasn't much left to take: some clothes, a few items of packaged food, a tower for her Cds, and one prized possession—a cherry night stand that her Grandma McKay had given her, which was inlaid with half-inch-square, cream-colored ceramic tiles on which was painted in gold the famous *Breastplate* prayer of Saint Patrick:

Christ be with me, Christ within me,
Christ behind me, Christ before me,
Christ beside me, Christ to win me,
Christ to comfort and restore me,
Christ beneath me, Christ above me,
Christ in quiet, Christ in danger,
Christ in hearts of all that love me,
Christ in mouth of friend and stranger.
Christ in every eye that sees me,
Christ in every ear that hears me.

"This is so beautiful, Abby! I've never seen anything like it!"

"Grandma Mary—Grandma McKay—gave this to me when I turned thirteen. She said that *her* grandmother, Kathleen Sullivan, gave it to *her* when *she* was thirteen years old. That would have been in 1935. She said Grandma Sullivan, who was my great-great-grandmother and was born in 1875, was given the table on *her* thirteenth birthday by *her* mother, Nell Flaherty, my great-great-great-grandmother, who was born in 1851. I once took it to an antique furniture expert who told me it was probably made in the mid-nineteenth century, so for Nell Flaherty this might have been her brand-new bedside table."

"*Bless us and save us!* that's a lot of Irish girls—going almost all the way back to Saint Patrick *himself*! We should have taken this with us *last* week; weren't you worried about it?"

"Last week—in case you forgot already—I was falling crazy in love with you, and you made me just *slightly* discombobulated. I forgot about the table for a few days. I have already apologized in my mind and prayers to all of my great-grandmother Sullivans, and I don't plan to tell Grandma Mary a thing about it. When she comes to visit us, I will just show her how pretty it is in our bedroom."

We loaded the Jeep, took one final look around the apartment, and stopped in front of the sofa for a farewell kiss—"one for the road," said Abigail—in the very same spot where she first asked me to kiss her. She buried her face in my neck for several minutes and whispered at last, "First kiss, first orgasm, first true love."

We stopped at Mangrums on the way home for a few staples—including Popsicles, Coke and Chianti—two new puppy toys and Abigail's red rose. Jock and Maggie were excited about their new toys: stuffed, softball-size baseballs that squeak when you squeeze them, with two feet in blue sneakers on the bottom and a rope handle on top for playing tug-of-war.

We unloaded the Jeep and dressed for dinner. I wore khaki slacks and a maroon sweater; Abby wore a beautiful, sleeveless, white sheath dress, which came about four inches above her knees. It had navy blue piping along the scoop neck, around the arms, down both sides and around the hem. She also sported matching, satin, navy blue high heels. She was *breathtaking*.

"*Wow*! What a dress! Abigail, you're really a *babe*, you know. And look at those *shoes*!"

"Matt, you're going to have to drop me right at the door. I can't walk through a wet parking lot in *these* babies."

"I think I'll let Joey the valet park my Jeep tonight; I don't want to let you out of my sight for one minute in that outfit."

"I would hope you'd feel that way *every* day."

"I do, Abby. There's *no* morning any more where I would not rather stay in bed with you than get up and do *any* other thing—except play with *you* all day. But in that dress, with your hair just perfect, you are *so* movie-star gorgeous that I could easily skip Palermo's, put my hands on you and eat *you* for dinner."

"Save me for dessert, old guy. I need to show you off to Mary Kay. She has never been fond of any of my boyfriends. And you might learn a few things about me from her."

I laughed, stooped a little, wrapped both of my arms around the top of Abby's thighs, lifted her straight up over my head, and kissed her belly through the white wool.

"Sorry, beauty, I can't resist."

She *squealed*, grabbed the top of my head with all her fingers, and pressed her knees into my stomach as if she were trying to balance both of us to keep us from crashing to the kitchen floor.

"Put me *down*, Matt, you'll hurt yourself! How did you *do* that? *I'm* no lightweight. You're pretty *strong* for an old guy."

We met Mary Kay and Josh at six-thirty at Palermo's. Mary

Kay is about the same height as Abigail, but thinner. Her hair is dark brown, and she looked very pretty in a lemon yellow suit. Josh was taller and leaner than I with a dark complexion and a big smile. I was amused at both of their expressions and reactions. Josh was *dazzled* by Abigail and looked at *me* curiously. Mary Kay *gushed* over Abby's dress and shoes and stared at me in astonishment.

Dinner was delightful. Abby arranged us with a purpose at our table. She seated herself next to Josh and across from Mary Kay. I was next to Mary Kay and across from Josh. She successfully introduced Mary Kay and Josh to Chianti and, with Abby's red rose as our centerpiece, the table talk was as good as the Italian food.

Mary Kay was finishing her Ph.D. thesis on *The Influence of Latin on the Arabic Languages in the Eastern Mediterranean Countries That Were Former Provinces of the Roman Empire*. I got a laugh when I suggested that with *that* title it might not be a best seller. She thought she would be stationed in Rome after she received her degree in April, but that might depend on Josh. He was on the road regularly for the Discovery Channel.

Unlike *National Geographic* photographer Clint Eastwood in *The Bridges of Madison County*, Josh took more videos than photographs. The next Discovery special incorporating his videos was going to be about the annual upstream salmon run in Alaska. I mentioned that I had read a lot about that in James Michener's *Alaska*, and Josh said that Michener's narrative was going to be used extensively on the two-part special.

"You two are going to be all over the world pretty soon," I said. "It's a good thing Mary Kay and Abigail made this happen. A quiet dinner with best friends from Fatima and Penfield might become a *very* rare event for you."

"Well, then we might have to go visit *them* on the other side of some ocean," Abby chimed in.

By the second glass of Chianti, even though Josh remained dazzled by Abigail, Mary Kay was no longer astonished by me. Josh couldn't take his eyes off Abby, and directed his conversation almost exclusively to her. This didn't seem to bother either Abigail or Mary Kay. Abby actually winked at me furtively a few times to let me know that she was pleased with the table dynamics, as if it was part of her plan. Mary Kay seemed genuinely attracted to me and determined to figure me out. Her baby blue eyes looked straight into mine many times, and I could see the questions she hesitated to put into words: It's easy to understand why you are in love with Abby, but why is she in love with you? Are you just playing with my best friend and reveling in the pleasure of the moment, or do I see "forever" in your eyes?

I actually saw her expression soften, and a warmer smile fill her eyes, when she *did* find "forever" in mine. At that moment, Mary Kay put her hand on mine, and I saw a hint of tears. The look on her face, the touch of her hand not only said *thank you for loving my friend*, but also *I haven't found my "forever" yet*.

I doubted Josh had any idea.

I looked in her eyes and whispered, just barely moving my lips so not even Abigail would hear, "Mary Kay, you've been a wonderful friend to Abby, but now you're *my* friend, too. I hope you find your 'forever' guy soon."

She gave me an emotional hug and wiped her tears on my shoulder so Josh and Abby wouldn't see them. I rubbed her back to try to hide her shaking.

"How did you *know*?" she whispered.

Abigail sensed Mary Kay's distress and interrupted Josh.

"Mary gal, are you *okay*?"

That forced Josh to finally notice us hugging.

"*Hey*, what are you guys *doing* over there? Should we switch seats?"

I tried to lighten the moment with, "*Mary gal* was sharing some secrets about *Abby gal*."

Abigail laughed, gave me a grateful glance, got up from her chair, took Mary Kay's arm and cheerily announced, "Mary gal, it's time for us *gals* to freshen up before dessert."

As they headed arm-in-arm to the ladies room, Josh looked at me suspiciously and asked, "What was *that* all about? Was she *crying*? Did you say something to get her upset?"

"No, no, it's girl stuff: I think Mary Kay was surprised to find out that she really likes me, and she feels I'm good for Abby. Best girlfriends can get emotional about such things—at least they do in the movies. And don't they always seem to run off to the ladies room when that happens?"

"I guess I'll take your word for it. Those are not my kinds of movies."

The girls were smiling but quiet when they came back to the table. They said they decided to switch sides for dessert. As Mary Kay sat down next to Josh, she gave me a quick, wistful smile. Abigail, on the other hand, tenderly stroked my hair as she gazed into my eyes with a look I hadn't seen before and couldn't read right away. Was it love mixed with pride, surprise, wonder?

We agreed, over our shared desserts—Tiramisu, lemon ice and ricotta cheesecake—to pick a day between Christmas and New Year's to meet again for dinner or dessert and a movie. As we left the ristorante and said good night, I felt that my hug and kiss from Mary Kay were probably more sincere and heartfelt than the ones I saw Josh giving Abigail.

Abigail leaned against me and held on tight to my arm with both hands all the way home, but she didn't say a word. Even when we walked Jock and Maggie around the circle, she talked to the dogs but not to me. She gripped my hand firmly with every step, though, so I was pretty sure she wasn't upset with me. As soon as we brought the dogs in, Abby put on a fresh pot of coffee, took me downstairs to the family room and said quietly, "Sit, old guy. Take your shoes off. Get *The Notebook* set to wherever we fell asleep. I'm going to grab the popcorn clouds from the bed, and the coffee should be ready in two minutes."

She brought down the quilt and our favorite mugs, curled up next to me on the sofa with her feet tucked under her, wrapped the quilt around our shoulders, took my face in her hands, kissed me *fiercely*—straight on—then whispered tenderly:

"You are not only my *love*, Matt, but you are my *hero*. I can't believe that it's even *possible*, but I love you more than *yesterday* . . . more even than this morning. Mary Kay told me what you said to her. She was so *touched* . . . *moved*. What you did was caring . . . loving, even *brave*. But how did you *know*? Mary Kay only called and told me this morning—just before we went to Phil Green's—that she and Josh were having trouble. You have *never* met her or even *talked* with her. How did you *know*?"

"I saw it in her eyes."

Abigail gave me the same wondering look she gave me at Palermo's, stroking my cheeks and shaking her head slowly sideways, with the glimmer of a smile in her eyes.

"You are an amazing man, my sweet old guy. Mary Kay was *stunned*—and even more so when I told her I hadn't said a *word* to you about Josh. She said she was looking into *your* eyes to see if you will really be good for me. And almost at the same moment that she found her answer and was so happy for me, she said to me, 'Matt'—in her words in the ladies room—'Matt read my *heart*, Abby. *Nobody* has ever done that. Josh never came close. I am *so* happy for you that you have found a man who can read your heart, and touch your heart.'

"I told Mary Kay that not only have you *read* my heart and *touched* my heart since the second morning you came into Kitty's Korner, but you have been *inside* my heart, inside *all* of me—heart, mind and body—down to my deepest center *every* minute of every day since then. We hugged and cried for a while after that before we came out for dessert. By the way, how did you know about the 'Abby gal' thing? Mary Kay started calling me that at Fatima, so I started calling her 'Mary gal' because of her last name."

"I *didn't* know, but I heard you say 'Mary gal' so I thought I could make a joke and lighten the atmosphere, especially for Josh, who sounded a little tense."

"Well, it did the trick. I don't think Josh suspected anything. I'm going to meet Mary Kay for coffee tomorrow morning so she can tell me more about what's going on."

"Tell her I'm sorry if I upset her."

"No, she wasn't upset, she was relieved. She *wanted* to let it out and tell me. You helped her. She said you are a good friend."

Jock and Maggie joined us on the sofa, and we all nestled and watched Allie and Noah. After Allie's parents took her away in tears—up "north" where she would attend Sarah Lawrence—Noah wrote her a letter every day for 365 days, but Allie's mother intercepted *every* one of them, so Allie never knew. She and Noah were both heartbroken.

Noah enlisted in the Army after Pearl Harbor and eventually served in Europe—fighting in the Battle of the Bulge—through the end of The War. When he came home, his father helped him buy the run-down mansion he had promised to rebuild and restore for Allie. Noah went to work with a vengeance, imagining Allie in every square inch of the old plantation.

Up "north," Allie graduated from Sarah Lawrence, where she dreamed of Noah in every classroom, and then volunteered in a hospital for wounded soldiers, where she saw Noah in every GI she consoled and bandaged. Here Abby paused the movie and looked up at me.

"Matt, when I watched this movie the first time—with a date—before I knew how it came out, I was crying so much at this spot that I almost left the theater. And I never dated that guy again."

"Because of the *movie*?"

"Because the movie made me realize, *vividly*, what I suppose I knew deep down all along: that life would never make any sense until I met the man I could love *that* much, and who would love me as much as Noah loved Allie. My date was *not* that man. I know it's just a movie and a book, but movies and books make you dig deep and learn about yourself. The next time he called and asked me out, I just said, 'I'm sorry, and don't take this personally because you're a good guy, but you're not my Noah.' Allie and Noah knew right away, and I believed I would too."

Abigail was squeezing me so hard that her arms seemed to be inside my sweater. She stopped the movie when Allie—not having heard from Noah for seven years—agreed to marry the handsome and rich Army officer she had nursed back to health. Even *then* Allie saw Noah's face.

"Matt, I'm tired—emotionally exhausted. Soothing Mary Kay in the ladies room *really* got to me. Take me up to bed. I need you to recharge me. Am I asking too much from you, old guy? I don't want to burn you out. I'm gonna need you every day for the next *fifty* years."

"Up we go, beauty. Remember I told you we will *never* burn out. We will always keep filling each other up again. Come on, doggies, let's take Mommy to bed."

Abigail and I held each other so tightly that we took up less than half the bed, so Maggie and Jock had room to maneuver and shift positions before they settled against Abby's back and hips. They looked up curiously over their shoulders when we made love twice, but our loving was peaceful, almost pensive. Abby held my face softly between her hands the whole time, gazing straight up into my eyes. Then she wrapped her arms around my back and kept me on top of her.

"Stay here, Matt. You're not heavy, and it feels as if we only have one body when you're on top of me and I can look into your eyes. They look almost as green as mine in this candlelight. I guess we girls ganged up on you tonight, huh?"

"Pretty girl, watching you *any* time, and you and Mary Kay *tonight*, and trying to read your body language and the tone of your conversation—all up close—is like reading Shakespeare or listening to Beethoven. There is significance in almost every word and note, glance and touch, pause and laugh, shrug and breath. There is love, loyalty, concern, understanding.

"Poke me or flip me if I get too heavy. I believe the bond between guy friends is just as strong as between girl friends— *way* stronger, in fact, when they've been in combat like Joe and me—but they don't show it the way girls do.

"It's not that guys take such friendship for granted; but they *know* it's there and will *always* be there when needed, and that's enough for them. I'm a hugger, so I hug my best buddies more than most guys do, but usually a stranger would never see the affection or sense the bond between two buddies. You and Mary Kay, on the other hand, *radiate* care and love, and sympathy and support. I don't mean to boast—and it *sure* wasn't true when I was *twenty-six*—but I have become very good at reading women over the years, and it was a pleasure to observe you two best friends tonight in spite of the emotional turmoil."

"So you *like* Mary Kay?"

"I *love* Mary Kay. I told her she's now *my* friend too. She's a beautiful woman; and I could see from the long time I spent looking into her light blue eyes that she's just as beautiful inside. She seems a little thin to me, though, so I'm glad we got her a hearty meal tonight."

"You know, *Romeo,* Josh's eyes were up and down my body all night, so I don't think he ever noticed how you and Mary Kay were locked in to each other. But *I* was tempted a few times to throw a bread stick across the table to break up your eye contact. It was *way* more intense than most people can handle. But some inner voice told me that Mary Kay needed the long, searching look and you would be good for her. Even now, my old guy, in the candlelight I can see not only understanding but kindness in your eyes. And you're right about Mary Kay. She's lost too much weight—probably because of Josh, and finishing her thesis, and the thought of being stationed so far from home when she graduates. That's a *lot* for another troubled middle child," Abby teased.

"You're never going to let me forget that, are you?"

"Not likely."

"Well, beauty, at least you should be thankful that I'm not a 'troubled middle child' too," I whispered with a tired grin in the candlelight.

I got a poke in the ribs *and* a pinch on the butt for that, but Abby was still looking straight up into my eyes and smiling. Then she stroked my temples and kissed me.

"Where are you meeting Mary Kay in the morning?"

"She's going to pick me up here at nine-thirty. She wants to see our house, then we're going to Joe's. When she brings me home I want to help you with the Christmas lights before I get going on part two of my ergonomics paper."

"*That* will be fun. Nobody has helped me with the lights since my sons went off to college," I said with a *huge* yawn. "If I fall asleep, love, just be careful not to flip me off the bed."

Abigail kissed me and then rested my head on her shoulder and traced my lips until I fell asleep.

14

The next thing I was aware of was Maggie standing on her hind legs next to the bed with both wet front paws on my pillow, licking my face. Then Abby skipped in to the bedroom whistling our Shania Twain song.

"Rise and shine, handsome! *'From this moment'* . . . *I love you* this morning! Here's your old Yellowstone mug. It's eight-thirty, and I already fed and walked Maggie and Jock, so *don't* let them tell you anything different. If you want to say 'hi' to Mary Kay when she gets here, I *insist* that you put on some clothes. I'm sure she has a serious crush on you after last night."

"Dad used to say 'rise and shine' when we were kids. And 'up and at 'em.' And 'the early bird gets the worm,' too. I'll have to ask Mom if he still says any of that. How did you get out of bed without my noticing? *That's* a first. *Why* did you get out of bed without *playing* with me? That's *another* first."

"You looked *so* peaceful, Matt . . . beautiful even. You know, I think *your* 'tail' is prettier than mine. But as much as I wanted to touch you and nibble, I wanted even more for you to get some extra rest—and maybe dream more about *me*—after being my knight in shining armor last night, and maybe Mary Kay's too. I'll make it up to you later—the touching and the nibbling—I promise, old guy. Come on down and have some orange juice and a hard-boiled egg before Mary Kay gets here."

Mary Kay was right on time, and we both met her at the door. She hugged each of us without saying anything, then looked me squarely in the eyes and hugged me again.

"Thank you guys for a *lovely* dinner last night in spite of the drama. I can still taste the breadsticks and the tiramisu and the veal when I burp—which is often. That was a *huge* meal for me. I hope we can go back there again when I come home for Christmas, maybe without the drama."

Mary Kay squatted down to meet Maggie and Jock.

"I *love* your dogs. They are *so* beautiful! Hi babies! Which one is Maggie?"

Abigail squatted next to Mary Kay and scratched both dogs

around their ears.

"Maggie has the red neckerchief."

"So this is Jock in blue. Come, give me kisses, babies. Mommy is going to show me around your house."

I read the paper at the butcher block table in the kitchen while the girls and dogs whirled, ran, laughed and barked up and down the stairs and in and out of every room.

"You have a warm, friendly, comfortable home, Matt," Mary Kay said, "but I can see from the closets and the accessorizing that Abigail has completely taken over. I remember when she used to do exactly the same thing—on a smaller scale—in our dorm rooms and our apartment. *Good luck* ever getting your house back!"

She hugged me one more time on her way out the door, kissed me on the cheek and whispered, "Thank you for last night. I needed to find a way to move into the next chapter in my life, and you showed me. Abby is *blessed* to have you."

I finished the paper, walked the dogs, shaved and showered while the girls were at breakfast. When Mary Kay brought Abigail home, she didn't come in. She waved from her car and was gone. Abby sat me down at the kitchen table, poured two cups of coffee and recounted the gist of their conversation at Joe's.

"I'm sure we had several of Joe's regulars staring and scratching their heads because we were alternately crying and laughing all through breakfast. Mary Kay said she and Josh were up long after midnight talking about what had gone wrong. Apparently Mary Kay has been so busy with her thesis that she didn't notice how *much* Josh wasn't around. She thought it was all his work at the Discovery Channel, getting ready for his next photo expedition.

"It turns out that Josh has an assistant named Alana who has not only been working him *overtime* at the office but also went on his last photo trip with him. Josh confessed as much but said he *still* loved Mary Kay. Mary Kay said, 'No thanks. After spending all these years with you, *I* deserve better than that. And after we get back to Virginia on Sunday, *you're* moving out.'

"She told me that seeing 'the love and the fire'—her *exact* words—'between you and Matt' made her realize that she didn't *need* to make any more excuses for the hard work and passion that she was devoting to the career of her dreams. And she didn't *want* to make any more excuses for a boyfriend who either couldn't understand or wouldn't share her passion and her dreams. So Josh is all done.

"Then Mary Kay asked me if you have a younger brother—and *that's* when we started laughing hysterically. I told her they are both taken, so she said to let you know that if you ever get tired of me, she'll be waiting. By the time Hannah brought us our check, even *we* could not tell whether we were laughing or crying. I'm really going on and on here, huh? Shall we put up the Christmas lights before it starts to snow again?"

I have three strings of outdoor lights, twenty-five bulbs on each, old-fashioned glass, C-9 size. They're the ones you screw in one at a time, the ones that break when you drop them in the driveway, the ones with all the usual colors—red, orange, green, blue and white. I have held out on my street against all of my neighbors who hang those dull, opaque plastic icicles. Abby and I hung the seventy-five lights on the split-rail fence along the front steps, around the front door and over the garage doors.

"This is the first time I've ever done this, Matt. Are you turning me into a *housewife*?"

"Well, maybe a *homeowner,* beauty," I laughed. "Sarah always left the lights completely up to me, so I've never had a girl help me before. You're not too bad for a middle child," I teased. Abigail whacked me playfully on the arm with the metal staple gun we used to attach some of the lights to the split-rail fence.

"Okay, wise guy, I'm going in to work on part two of my ergonomics project."

"What exactly is 'ergonomics part two,' beauty?"

"Part *one* was studying the floor plans and layouts of stores that have moved their baked goods or garden or produce departments to the front of their stores. Part *two* is estimating or projecting the staffing changes or additional staffing needs that might result from moving those departments. And part *three* will be a cost analysis of the whole reorganization."

"How many interns from your group do you think Mangrums will hire when you graduate?"

"Wally said they usually hire two or three. My plan has been to knock his argyle socks off and be one of those two or three."

I laughed. "Wally is *famous* for his socks, but I expect that they won't help him defend himself against your plan. Let's get to work, love. While you are in your front office *ergonomicking*, Jock and Maggie and I are going to do some laundry and housecleaning before the B.C. football game. Think about where you'd like to go for a bite to eat after the game. I'm going to make a fresh pot of coffee. I'll bring you up a cup as soon as it's done."

When I went upstairs to grab the laundry basket and bring Abigail her coffee, she said, "Come *here*, summer boy. The sun is shining on my face, and it makes me want to kiss you. I think I want to eat lighter tonight after all the rigatoni and breadsticks last night at Palermo's. Where can we go for a Caesar salad and a beer?"

"Shannon's Tavern on Ridge Road. Have you ever been there? They also have *great* popcorn."

"Never. Sounds *perfect*! How dressed up do I have to be?"

"Jeans and whatever—just what you're wearing now."

Jock and Maggie and I finished our chores just in time for the annual B.C./Holy Cross football game. Historic Catholic school rivals, they played every year on the Saturday after Thanksgiving. I only saw one of those classic games. In my senior year, I stayed with my friends Tony and Maria Lenzi in Concord. I had Thanksgiving dinner with Maria's family and triple-dated with Tony and Maria, cousin Kevin Flynn from B.C. and his girlfriend Brenda, and *my* date, Cassie O'Hara, an Irish beauty from South Boston and a childhood friend of both Tony and Kevin. I was *crazy* for Cassie but that's the only date I remember with her; so I think she must have found another guy or tired of me quickly, and I just blocked out forever the end of her story.

This year's game was at Holy Cross in Worcester, and it snowed throughout the game. Boston College had had a good season and was ranked in the top twenty-five in the country, but the snow slowed down their running game and, much to my chagrin, Holy Cross beat them 17-14 on a last-minute field goal. I told the doggies, "As *Chester A. Riley* used to say, '*What a revoltin' development this is!*' eh, puppies?"

Dinner at Shannon's was fun: two Caesar salads with extra anchovies. How many old guys are lucky enough to have a girlfriend who likes *anchovies*, several pints of Killian's Red and *way* too many dishes of salty, buttery popcorn? As usual we sat on the same side of the booth and played with each other under the table. Abigail and I were *eighty-seven* years old, total, but most of the time we behaved like high school sweethearts. How could life be any better?

"Matt, can we finish watching *The Notebook* tonight? I thought next week we could do something different for our evening entertainment. I'd like to show you some of my charcoal drawings; and I'd like you to read me some of your poems. Can we do that?"

"Are you *kidding*? I would *love* to show you my poems even though you might discover *all* of my secrets from reading them."

"*First* of all, old guy, I don't *want* to know all your secrets, so you pick out the poems that will tell me what *you* want me to know. Even sweethearts should have *some* secrets from each other. *Second* of all, I don't want to *read* your poems; I want *you* to read them to *me*. I'm sure I'll enjoy them and understand them better that way."

When we got home from dinner and settled on the sofa with the dogs, we picked up the movie with Allie planning her wedding to her rich tobacco heir, Lon, and Noah finishing the renovations to his old mansion. When Allie sees Noah's photo in the paper and the story about his restoration project, she decides to go see him one more time before her wedding. Of course, she learns about Noah's *365* letters and her mother's duplicity, and both Allie and Noah rediscover their love and passion for each other. Her mother and Lon show up to intervene, but Allie chooses passion and love over security. She and Noah are inseparable until the night they die in each other's arms in a nursing home.

Abigail wiped a few tears from her eyes, looked in mine and whispered, "Old guy, does love *ever* make any *sense*? Allie's mother and her fiancé talked *sense*. And Allie's mother marrying her father instead of *her* summer boyfriend also made sense. I love you *so* much, but we don't make any *sense*, do we?"

"No, not much . . . if sense means *common* sense. But if sense means *seeing* life, *touching* life, *tasting* life, *listening* to life, *breathing* in life, *feeling* life, *living* life . . . then *love* is the only thing that *does* make sense. If *logic* were the rule of life then there is *no way* you and I should be here together. But if *love* is the way to live, there is *no way* you and I can *ever* be apart again. Just like Allie and Noah. Does *that* make sense, beauty?"

"Matt, when you turn my questions into poetry the answers *always* make sense. Let's take the baby dogs upstairs. I owe you some nibbling."

15

Sunday morning appeared gray and dismal through the bedroom windows, and the reality was worse when we got outside with Jock and Maggie. The cold drizzle blew straight into us from the west—causing both dogs to turn their tails into the wind and shake the water off several times— and by the time we got halfway and headed back home, the drizzle had changed into sleet. Jock and Maggie required substantial rubbing with the big blue living room towels before they began their figure-eights to warm each other up to their satisfaction.

We saw cousin Terry again at the eight-thirty Mass, and after church she invited us to dinner at her house on Monday, December 10. She said she would make sure that all her kids would be there to "meet their future cousin Abigail." With that, Terry winked and observed that the fact that we were back at Holy Innocents together "probably means that you two made it through your joint Thanksgiving okay." We all laughed and agreed that Christmas might be *slightly* easier.

Matt and Claire called us from their car to let us know that they were on their way to Melina's Diner in Penfield in case we wanted to join them and the kids for breakfast, and of course we did. We grown-ups ordered oatmeal and omelets, and the kids shared a Mickey Mouse chocolate-chip pancake and some of our eggs and oatmeal. Matt and Claire were having a bunch of their best friends over later for the Buffalo Bills game and pizza. The Bills were awful, as usual, but not as bad as my beloved Cleveland Browns.

Abigail wanted to go for a ride before we went back home to work on our paper projects, so we drove up the Sea Breeze Expressway to the lake. The Outlet bridge had opened for vehicles on November 1, so we parked in the boat launch lot, walked over the bridge to the Webster side and out to the end of the east pier. It was a slow walk because we were huddled together against the wind and sleet, and we had to stop periodically for cold, wet kisses. When we got to the end of the Webster pier, we took cautious baby steps around the mini-lighthouse with the *green* light, made two wishes and followed our slow tracks back to the bridge. Then we walked to the end of the longer west pier—which curls northeast around the entrance to the outlet to protect the in-and-out water traffic from the rough lake waves—made two *more* wishes at the lighthouse with the *red* light and hustled back to my Jeep. We stopped at the Sea Breeze Phil Green's to warm up with a little hot chocolate before we headed home.

After we walked Jock and Maggie, Abigail went back to her ergonomics, and I decided to skip the football games and catch up on my Winston Churchill. My sons had given me Churchill's six-volume history of *The Second World War* for my sixtieth birthday, and I was almost finished with Volume III, *The Grand Alliance*. Churchill is one of those supremely able and fascinating *giants* of history—probably in my top ten—with whom I would have loved to share a few hours of robust conversation and several pints of robust beer in a quiet pub.

For supper, I made my famous "Dad Soup" which always surprised a skeptical Sarah because it tasted better than it sounded, and which my sons *still* ask me to make for them— especially if they have a cold. It's cooked in a *giant* pot of water, enough for four pasta-size bowls of soup, with liberal sprinklings of oregano and garlic powder and equally liberal splashes of olive oil, plus four or five Herb Ox chicken bouillon cubes, some chopped baby carrots, and one package of Lipton chicken noodle soup—all brought to a boil. And then I add my signature ingredient, which Aunt Connie taught me to put in *all* my soup—one cup of Acini di Pepe. After ten minutes of stirring and simmering, the little balls swell, and the soup thickens to oatmeal-like consistency. With parmesan or romano cheese grated on top, it makes for a very hearty and cheery meal— particularly on a cold day—and is even heartier and cheerier warmed up the next day.

I told Abigail I was making soup for her, but she stayed at her desk and didn't see me make it. She did yell down once, "Something smells *really* good!" I brought her a tray with my favorite green-and-white-checked pasta bowl steaming to the brim with a frosted mug of Michelob and a small dish of oyster crackers.

"What is *this*, old guy? It's so *thick* the spoon is standing up in the bowl."

"My special soup, beauty. Matt and Dan call it 'Dad Soup'

and even try to make it themselves. I hope you like it. I brought salt and pepper in case you need to adjust the flavor, but *I* happen to think it's *perfect*. Don't say anything right away. Give it some time to warm you up and grow on you. I'll go down and make some fresh coffee, and then you can tell me what you think."

Before the coffee had finished dripping Abigail appeared in the kitchen doorway with the bowl in her hands and a sheepish grin on her face. "More, sir, *please*?"

"*Oliver Twist*, eh, you sassy girl! I'll bet *my* soup is *way* better than Oliver's gruel."

"*Your* soup is *delicious*! But stop talking, Mr. Bumble, and give me more, *please*?"

We enjoyed my soup, coffee, Oreos and milk at the kitchen table, and dropped a few oyster crackers for Jock and Maggie. After supper, we took the doggies for a walk, I built a fire in the fireplace, and Abigail and I settled in front of the fire with the dogs and mused about our second week together.

"If we're living *weeks*, Matt, tomorrow is our second anniversary."

"I have a feeling, Abby, that you and I are going to live *more* weeks in our first year together than any man and woman have ever done before. And this will be a fast and busy one."

"You remember that I'm working noon to eight on Tuesday and Thursday, right?"

"Yep. Danny has booked us at The Crimson Yard bed and breakfast in Cambridge for Friday and Saturday nights."

"The Crimson Yard? I might have seen that place; I used to *love* walking around the Harvard campus when I needed a quiet place to think."

"Me too; that and the MTA, which is hardly a quiet place, for sure, but was always a good ride for me to think . . . the Boston College/Commonwealth Green Line. I think when I started riding it the fare was only twenty cents, and the Kingston Trio song about 'poor Charley on the MTA' was very popular. I still know all the words."

"I mostly rode the Riverside train to Newton, and the fare was almost *two bucks*. Mom asked me if I would come over after school tomorrow and go with her to pick out her Christmas cards and buy some new decorations and lights. Is that okay?"

"Sure. I have meetings most of the day tomorrow and I can easily shuffle papers with the dogs after I get home. We'll have a working supper together."

"Well, then, maybe I'll take Mom to the UNO in Webster for dinner."

"I'm going to phone Joe Steger tomorrow and see if he and Margie will be able to meet us in Pittsburgh on the third weekend in January, January 19 and 20. It's a three-day weekend because of Martin Luther King."

Abigail's eyes sparkled when she said mischievously, "We can do a practice announcement on them. They can be the *first* people we tell that we're going to get married."

"Well, if *anybody* is the guy, it should be Joe, who could have been my brother-in-law if his sister had had as much faith in me as *you* do."

"Or as much *love*, old guy."

I kissed Abigail on the top of her head as she sat in my lap facing the fire.

"Or as much *love*, beauty."

"Matt, I picked out my first drawing to show you after the fire winds down. We can sit at the kitchen table where the light will be better and sip our coffee. Then tomorrow night can be *your* turn with a poem."

"I like that plan, Abby; it's very ergonomic," I teased.

"Sorry, sometimes I *am* too organized, huh?"

"No, I think it complements my general manana outlook on life. Speaking of manana, I will get to Gennaro for a haircut either Tuesday or Wednesday. When the gray is gone, love, you may think I'm too young for you."

"Just as long as you don't lose your power like Samson. Speaking of Wednesday, what should we bring to your mom and dad's, or should I make something?"

"I thought we'd bring a bottle of Ruffino Chianti and pick up cannoli and eclairs from Lucia's Bake Shop. Mom wouldn't expect us to cook anything until we invite them over to *our* house."

When the last small chunks of charred logs crumbled through the fireplace grate, Abigail and I took Jock and Maggie around the circle. Then I made fresh coffee while she brought down her first drawing, wrapped in white tissue for a grand unveiling.

It was a beach. Looking longwise, the water is on the right, and steep, wooded banks on the left, with old trees hanging over or falling down the banks. Driftwood is at the water's edge, and two fat boulders are in the foreground, each with a fat seagull—

161

one pale gray with a white breast, and one tan with a speckled breast—preening itself. No people are in sight.

"It's *beautiful*, Abby. Is it a real spot?"

"Yep. Would you like to guess where it is?"

"Believe it or not, it actually looks familiar. Is it Durand Beach?"

"How did you *know*?"

"In my early lawyering days I used to go there occasionally in the summer for lunch and a walk along the shore. But more than that, I used to go to Durand all the time in the summer when I was growing up, right through high school. The beach, the golf course and the whole park are special places for me. Before your time, there was even a zoo in the park. When I was studying non-stop for the New York Bar Exam in June and July 1976, I did most of it in Durand Eastman Park. I think I even know both of those seagulls."

Abigail laughed and whacked me playfully on the arm.

"I worked on this drawing for a *week* during the summer after I graduated from Fatima, so there were *way* more than two seagulls posing."

"How do you *know*?" I teased. "Maybe the same two gulls hustled back to those rocks every day as soon as they saw you climbing down the bank to the beach. *I* would."

"Wise guy."

"Your drawing is *perfect*, Abby. I know that beach as well as anybody, and you captured its essence better than even a professional photographer could—and not just the images but also the mood, the atmosphere. The closer I get to Durand the more the summer boy in me comes out."

"Well then, summer boy, you and I will have to take some long walks at Durand as soon as it warms up in the spring."

"But *I've* been doing too much talking, beauty. Tell me what *you* were thinking about when you sat on the beach every day. Why is *this* scene in your life?"

"I think I was a little scared, Matt, and a little sad, too. Scared about going away to college, and sad about splitting up with Jeff, who had been my steady boyfriend for more than two years. We didn't talk about it and we never officially broke up, but I could sense the end was coming when Jeff left for a basketball camp in Pennsylvania the week after graduation and only called me two or three times all summer. We had been a very comfortable and popular couple—we were the envy of all our friends, the king

162

and queen of Jeff's homecoming dance—but I eventually realized after two years of parties, dances and hanging out with good friends that I was not going to miss Jeff as much as the parties, dances and hanging out. When we kissed good night after his senior ball— our last kiss as it turned out—I wasn't sad because we were going our separate ways; I was sad because I had spent two years and a lot of emotions on a guy who never got to know the heart of me, and a guy I never desperately wanted to touch every day. Mary Kay had Josh, and most of my girlfriends seemed to have the guys they wanted, so I felt as if I'd wasted two years without *my* love story.

"It turned out we were *way* wrong. We were just learning. With Mary Kay and Josh all done, only one of my good friends from Fatima is still together with her senior prom date, and they are going to be married at the beginning of June. So I was spending a lot of time in the summer of 1999—in the middle of all the scary stories about what was going to happen on December 31—by myself, thinking, drawing and wondering which way was mine. My only consolation was that Mary Kay would be going off with me to Newton.

"But when I sat with the seagulls on the beach, I realized that life didn't have to be as complicated as we make it. God gave the seagulls what they needed and made the beach and the lake beautiful, and He could do the same for me. He introduced me to a new friend on the beach . . . patience . . . who would show me how to find my way and hopefully meet the man who would find my heart. And here you are, Matt—eight years later—the man of my heart. I can't help but wonder, though, what would have happened if I had met *you* on *that* beach in *that* summer."

"I might have been there on one of those days you were sketching, love."

"Not a chance, Matt, unless you were so far down the shore that I couldn't see you. If I had even *once* looked into your baby blue eyes on that beach, there would be a summer boy on one of the rocks in this picture, and I might have saved myself eight years of patience."

"*Then* wasn't our moment, Abby; *now* is our moment. Eight years ago, only two years after Sarah died, I might have been too gloomy and tentative—although looking into your *green* eyes could have changed that—and you might have been too sad and afraid of new feelings."

"Although looking into your *blue* eyes could have changed

that."

"*Maybe*, beauty. Our eyes don't lie to us and they can't hide us. But the Abby I met in Kitty's coffee shop two weeks ago was confident and optimistic; and the Matt you met was not gloomy any more but mellow. We were not *especially* happy, but we weren't especially *unhappy* either. We weren't *hopeless*, but we *both* needed to be in love—we *wanted* to be in love—and we needed each other to do that. *Now* is our perfect moment in time."

"*Our* time . . . it will be forever, Matt. And yet two weeks ago, the only things I thought about were school projects and the big snowstorm that was supposed to be coming in. Have you picked out a poem for tomorrow night?"

"Not yet. I thought I'd wait to see your first drawing, and maybe that would help me choose."

"Do the doggies need to go out again?"

"No, they're good. They probably want to take us up to bed."

"Okay, baby dogs, take me to bed. I want to pretend it's the beach and make love to Daddy."

In the bedroom, Abigail lit a candle with the fragrance of lilies of the valley.

"It's the closest candle I could find with the flavor of spring and the beach. Matt, what beach shall we be on tonight?"

"I'll tell you some of my favorites, and then *you* choose: Old Orchard Beach, Maine; Durand, of course; Gloucester, Massachusetts; Fort Lauderdale, Florida; Isle of Palms, South Carolina; all the South Jersey shore, from Ship Bottom to Atlantic City to Wildwood to Cape May; Horseshoe Bay, Bermuda; Dawn Beach, Sint Maarten; and I know there are a few I've missed and *way* more that I still want to get to."

"Okay, summer boy, let's start tonight with one I've been to also: Cape May. Then we'll play our way through the rest of *your* list, and then my *own* list, and then we'll go to the beaches that are still on our *wish* list. That should be at least five or ten years of fun in bed and fun in the sun. Did you ever actually make love on a beach?"

"Not quite. Ellen and I were going after it under a blanket in what we thought was a secluded nook of beach in Horseshoe Bay when we heard a voice—in the Queen's English—above our heads: '*Eh*! You two down there, show your faces.' We poked our heads out and saw a bobby in black boots, Bermuda shorts and a safari hat. 'Sorry, miss, you too, lad, but whether you were doing it on *top* of the blanket or *under* the blanket, *what* you were doing is not permitted on the beach at Horseshoe Bay or anywhere in Bermuda in public. Pack yourselves up, then, and be off.'

"And that was as close as I ever came to either making love on a beach or making love to Ellen. I flew back to Boston on BOAC the next day, and before I reported to OTS at the end of July, Ellen had a new boyfriend, the rich neighbor 'lad' who lived in the large estate next to her 'Mum.' I have often wondered—how *many* of those moments do we have in our lives?—whether Ellen would have loved me forever if we had had time to come together under that blanket. She is the *one* old girlfriend I have completely lost track of."

Abigail was as much amused as she was curious.

"Did you save the blanket for sentimental value?"

"It wasn't *my* blanket, and after we left the beach Ellen never said a *single* word about our few hot minutes before the law uncovered us. She seemed merely embarrassed, while I was *crushed* at having to leave Bermuda on such a low note. Ellen wrote a few times over the summer but all she talked about was the weather and what her family was doing. I wasn't surprised two months later when she told me about the new boyfriend."

"Do *all* of your beaches have an old girlfriend attached to them?"

"Let me think . . . no, but except for Cathy from Fatima all of my old girlfriends have a beach attached to *them*. Bonnie goes with Durand for a couple of summers after high school; Bermuda you know about; Missy Steger I met on the Isle of Palms where Joe lived for three months when he was temporarily assigned to the Joint Services Language School at Charleston Air Force Base before he joined me at the Army Medical Language School at Fort Sam Houston; and Sarah and I honeymooned in Wildwood and Atlantic City and loved *all* the Jersey beaches. Now you and I can make all *my* favorite beaches *our* favorite beaches."

"That's my plan, old guy, starting next summer. But for *now*, right here on Cape May, hush up and let me brush all the sand off of you. You must have been *rolling* in it. It's in your hair and all over your belly and your back, it's all the way down your legs and between your toes, it's even in your bathing suit. *Ssh!* You just lie still and let me blow it off and brush it away with my lips.

"Good night, baby dogs."

165

In the morning, I kissed Abigail as she left for Kitty's at six-thirty. Jock and Maggie and I had our breakfast and a walk. I stopped at Kitty's for kisses and Italian roast—on the house—and I was at my desk at eight. I had clients in the office in the morning and afternoon, sandwiched around an annuity seminar at the Monroe County Bar Association and lunch with a third client. I left a message for Gennaro—who never worked on Monday—that I would be in his shop at eight-thirty the next morning for my haircut. Abigail called just before she left Kitty's to let me know that it took four cups of coffee to rinse all of the sand from Cape May out of her mouth. I could see the grin on her face as I heard the mischief in her voice. Danny called from "The Cottons" to tell me that he and Emma had picked out a lovely Italian ristorante for dinner Friday night.

While Jock and Maggie and I were having supper, Abigail called again to tell me that she was looking through beach books at Barnes & Noble while her mom was picking out Christmas cards.

"I found every beach on your list except Horseshoe Bay."

"*Ha*! You have to live in Bermuda to know where *that* one is—it's not on any maps. Are you and your mom having fun?"

"Yeah, Mom is happy to have me along. I'll be home by seven-thirty. Love you, old guy."

I had my poem, "Thirty Years Later," lying on the kitchen table when Abigail came in. After she chased Jock and Maggie for a few minutes and changed into her flannel Tinker Bell pajamas, she sat next to me at the table and sipped some Earl Grey tea.

"Matt, before you read me your poem, tell me why you picked *this* one out."

"Well, beauty, your seagull drawing was at an emotional time in your life—and transitional, too. You found patience and perspective on the beach, and they helped you move on to college and the rest of your life. It was your transition from schoolgirl at home to real life on your own. For me, going into the Army after college, meeting Joe Steger, serving in Vietnam, falling in love with his sister Missy and having her break my heart—that was *my* transition to real life. Before the Army I was Peter Pan himself: whimsical, idealistic and optimistic. After Missy, I became cynical, bitter and lonely, which helped me grind through law school, but it would be *four* years before I opened my heart again. I would never want to relive those years—I lost *four* loves in the space of *nine* years—but they turned me into a grown-up and enabled me to be a good husband and father, and a good advisor to my clients. In dealing with rejection and failure and changed dreams, I learned even *more* than patience. I believe I learned grit. So this poem sums up the impact of that period of my life—the end of my extended childhood. As you may guess from the title, I started it thirty years after I fell in love with Missy, and it took me almost a year to finish."

Abigail tangled her fingers between mine and kissed me on the cheek.

"Matt, you are my Peter Pan, and not just because I'm wearing these pajamas. You are the boy in the painting, lying on his back in the summer sunshine. Don't ever change. It's hard to believe you were ever bitter."

"One of my Dominic Savio friends used to call me Mopey Matt when we were in college."

"That will never happen again as long as *I'm* around, summer boy. Read me your poem."

All the blue cornflowers in July
along the dry shoulders of cracked county roads,
with the locusts buzzing in the brown grass,
remind me of summers long gone,
when we thought we had forever to be young.

I haven't spent much time wishing
for the chance to go back
and do my life over,
because I have two splendid sons,
and my life hasn't been a disgrace.

So it's not regret, exactly,
but it is lament for that season of my youth,
for that moment in northern Wisconsin
thirty years ago,
on a steamy day in July,
when the tornado ended,
and the rainbow began,
in the shade of the doorway,
outside the wedding dance,
and there was Missy.

It's not regret, but hunger
for that first astonishing kiss,
the last to make my bones and memory ache,
a kiss at once so light and deep,
that while it scarred my soul forever,
I wondered if it really happened.

It is hunger for Missy.
She was nineteen years old in that doorway,
with a glow of butterscotch and gold,
fresh, eager, trusting, startling,
with the softest hair I ever touched
and the prettiest legs I ever saw.
And the way she kissed me back
was the promise of melting together
into the next generation.

Then the summer and the cornflowers died,
and before they came back,
she was gone.
And now it's been thirty years
of having her on my mind every day,
and wanting to start that year again
and do it over.

Thirty years later,
it never matters who was right or wrong.
It's only the kiss that matters—
the kind of kiss that stuns all your senses—
the kind you live and breathe once in your life,
if you're lucky,
and if you're hungry,
and if you recognize it when it comes.

Thirty years later,
I see myself looking in her eyes
in the shade in the doorway,
with only a thin, hot breeze
between her and me,
and then my whole self
crossed through the breeze to Missy,

168

and I was completely lost.

It never happened again.
I haven't been lost since.
I know who I am,
and I can explain my life,
but I can't explain that kiss.
It lives by itself,
in a world of its own,
as a prayer and a dream,
a poem, in the words of Hamlet,
'a consummation devoutly to be wished.'

So it's not regret, exactly,
but I'd give back all of my fame and fortune
to do that year over,
cross through that breeze one more time
to Missy
and love her better.
I could never have loved her more,
but I could have loved her better."

By the time I finished, Abigail was sobbing, with her arms around my waist and her face on my chest. "Matt, it's so *beautiful*, and so *sad*. How could she *do* that to you? How could *anybody* do that? Wasn't she ever sorry?"

"We wrote to each other almost every day—I still have all her letters—through the fall and winter of 1972-73. I went to visit her twice in Oshkosh, and she and Joe and Margie came to visit me in Rochester. We even went to Niagara Falls together. Then *the letter* came, just before spring, and hit me in the face like a fist: she had found another guy, an Oshkosh guy, a successful chiropractor named Herb, and would I please stop writing? I wrote her one more letter, pleading. She wrote back that she and Herb were very upset that I had written again, and if I ever cared for her I had to stop. After that I *never* spoke with Missy again. All I ever knew—from Joe—was that she had two children, and she told Joe—did I tell you this already?—that I frightened her because I was too 'romantic and passionate,' and Herb was more solid, comfortable and steady."

"You feel comfortable and steady to *me*, old guy, but that's not why I'm here with you in my pajamas. I'm here for the romance and the passion. Missy made a *big* mistake, and *thank God* for me she did. Want to know what my favorite line is in your poem?"

"Of *course* I want to know, love."

"'*It's only the kiss that matters*'—I have to read the rest of that verse again—'*the kind of kiss that stuns all your senses—the kind you live and breathe once in your life, if you're lucky, and if you're hungry, and if you recognize it when it comes.*' That's what you did to *me* standing in the living room of my apartment, and I *knew* it was that 'kind of kiss' when it happened. I *knew* I could never walk away from you after that. But was it *true*, Matt, when you wrote that 'it never happened again' and you haven't been 'lost' since? You wrote the poem *way* after you married Sarah, and *even* after she *died*."

"You're right, Abby, and it *was* true. I wasn't lost with Sarah the way I was with Missy, and I couldn't understand *why* right up 'til the day she died. I thought I loved Sarah as much as I ever loved *any* woman, but I realized after she died—and even more when I wrote this poem—that there was a part of me I never let Sarah find, a part she never knew, a place in my heart I kept secret and safe. With Missy I *risked* everything and *lost* everything. With Sarah—and it wasn't a conscious decision— my heart had learned hard lessons and held back a little."

"Matt, you *know* the next question . . . "

"I *do,* beauty, and I'm *sure* the answer is that *you* have opened up my *whole* heart. Whatever there is inside me is *yours*. I will be loving you *all* the time with *no* secrets and *no* net."

"No *net*? You mean like tightrope walkers?"

"Love with no net. Showing you my poems will be showing you all the nooks and corners of my life and all the Matts I grew up with. I never did that with Sarah. She never asked to see *any* of my poems and, surprisingly, I never wrote any poems *about* her. I wrote poems about Cathy and Bonnie and Ellen and Missy—and other girls, too—but none about Sarah. By the way, all my poems are in the gray metal box on the floor in the corner of the office."

"I'm never going to look at your poems *without* you, Matt."

"I know, Abby, but you should still know where they *are*, same as my bank statements, IRAs, investments, insurance policies, the deed to the house, *all* that stuff."

"I don't have *any* of those things, old guy."

"Well, those are the things that *make* you old, beauty: forms,

170

statements, contracts, paperwork. But *your* day is coming. If you go ahead with your fantastic plan to *marry* me, everything I *have* will be yours, including what's in the gray box."

"So you're saying I should *reconsider*?"

"Definitely; otherwise you're in for trouble."

"But when I graduate and get my super Mangrums job I'll need a financial planner, right?"

"It would be a good idea."

"If we get married, will the financial planner come with the ring?"

"I think we can work something out. Standard rates will apply, of course."

"Standard rates?"

"You will have to sleep with me every night and kiss me every morning when you wake up and whenever you see me during the day—my standard husband-and-financial-guy package."

"It doesn't sound like *that* bad a deal. I'll review the fine print and let you know before we go to Pittsburgh and meet the Stegers. Let's go upstairs so I can trade these snuggly pajamas in for snuggly *you*. I have to be at Mangrums by noon tomorrow. Will you be home in the morning?"

"I'm going to Gennaro at eight-thirty, then I'll be right back."

"If I'm still in bed will you come and play with me?"

"Are you *kidding*, beauty? Is the Pope Catholic?"

"Matt, because I'm working until eight tomorrow and Thursday and we're going to your mom and dad's on Wednesday, can we put off my second drawing until we get back from Boston?"

"Sure, Abby. This will be a crowded and quick week, and then we start counting off the days until Christmas. We don't have to have a schedule for your drawings and my poems. They'll come on the right days. On the other hand, we *do* have to guard our time together. Even though our friends and family mean well, they will try to *eat* us up—we *are* the hot couple— especially between now and New Year's. So let's put everything from *your* daily planner and *my* daily planner on the kitchen calendar so there will be no surprises. How's my snuggling?"

Abigail didn't answer, and we hugged and stroked each other to sleep without another word. We were wrapped together so snugly that we fell asleep on the same pillow.

16

My wristwatch on the nightstand woke me with twenty dings at seven-thirty, but Abigail didn't stir. She was sleeping behind me spoon-style. Her left arm was stretched out under my cheek, her face touching my neck so I could feel her breath; her breasts and belly were pressing my back, her right arm over my chest; and her legs—bent at the knees—curled against mine.

This is nuts, I thought, slowly separating myself from Abigail and getting out of bed. She hadn't moved at all. *She's so soft and warm and lovely, and you're leaving her for a haircut*! I kissed her forehead, pulled the covers up to her shoulders and went downstairs with the doggies.

My haircuts seldom take more than fifteen minutes, and I was back from Gennaro's at nine. I came in through the front door rather than the garage to avoid stirring up Jock and Maggie.

It worked; I didn't hear a sound. When I peeked into the bedroom, the doggies were on both sides of Abigail on the quilt, but she hadn't moved much in the hour since I'd left her. I decided to take a quick shower to rinse Gennaro's clippings from my head and shoulders before I woke her up. Then I enticed Jock and Maggie into the hallway with cookies, pulled *Pooh* and *Piglet* to the foot of the bed and curled up behind my beautiful girl.

It is impossible to verbalize how wonderful it was to touch and kiss Abigail until she started to stir and make wake-up noises. After two or three minutes she rolled over and reached her arms around my back, but she still had her eyes closed. When she opened them—*God*, they were more stunning than the sun in the morning!—she looked at me slowly and laughed.

"Who are *you*? I don't recognize this young guy with short brown hair. You look *hot*, mister, and I want to make love with you but I don't think I should cheat on my boyfriend—my *fiancé*."

"The *hell* with him, beauty, if he was so *dumb* that he left you in bed by yourself."

We played until almost eleven when Abby had to get dressed

and gather her Mangrums folders together to make it to headquarters by noon. I invited the doggies back into bed, and we dozed and daydreamed for another hour.

Abigail called in the middle of the afternoon to let me know that she was *dazzling* everybody in the office, and they all wanted to know what had her *so* charged up. "I told them it must have been the extra hour's sleep this morning." Once again I could imagine a big grin on her face as I listened to the mischief in her voice. Abigail also said her boss was taking all the interns out for a working dinner down the street at Applebee's, so I shouldn't wait for her for supper.

That inspired me to revert to one of my favorite bachelor staples: a thick, creamy peanut butter and butter sandwich on whole wheat, washed down with several mugs of dark chocolate milk with extra Hershey's syrup. Only the bread—because it's supposed to be *healthy* for old guys like me—had changed since I was a kid. Mom always made my peanut butter sandwiches— cut in half diagonally—on soft, squishy, white Wonder Bread.

When Abigail pulled in to the garage at eight-fifteen, I had two frosted mugs of Killian's and a movie—*Sweet Home Alabama*—ready in case she just wanted to put up her feet, snuggle on the sofa and not have to think too much.

"You got it just right, Matt," she said as she curled between me and the dogs on the sofa. "It's like that great Shania Twain song that always makes me sing along:
'Honey, I'm home . . . I had a hard day . . . pour me a cold beer . . . rub my feet . . . I want to crash and watch TV . . . fix me up my favorite treat . . . turn off the phone . . . give the dogs a bone . . . hey, hey, honey, I'm home.'

"You and the baby dogs are my special treat, old guy."

"Do you really want me to rub your feet, Abby?"

"No, Matt, my feet are very happy tucked under my butt and Maggie's too. It's *so* comfortable and warm to come home to you and the doggies every night. It is hard to remember how *alone* I was before you came into Kitty's. I went back to my silent, drafty apartment every day. Many days I would go *all* day without ever being touched by *anybody*. Today, Joe Christopher, the director of advertising, told me I was 'dazzling'—*his* word. He said to me as we walked out of our second group session that my comments and observations about our recent ad campaign were spot-on and—even *more*—the energy I brought to the group sessions was infectious. He

173

thought there must be something going on outside the office that was making me so happy.

"I told him he was right. 'Usually it's a guy,' he said. I told him he was right again. He kidded, '*Thank* him for me because he's making a *real* contribution to Mangrums.' I said, 'You mean on *top* of all the long-stemmed red roses he buys me almost every day at Mangrums?' He laughed, 'I have to *meet* this guy! Will you bring him to the Christmas party?' I told him I would."

Abigail lifted her face from my shoulder, leaned her whole body in to me and covered *my* face with ferocious, devouring kisses. I thought she might be about to take my hand and lead me from the sofa to the bedroom—but she suddenly stopped and took a deep breath.

"I'm so hot, Matt; more beer!"

I exchanged the empty mugs for two fresh, frosted ones from the freezer.

"Start the movie, Matt. This will be the first one we've both seen. I remember the first time I saw it I couldn't decide which guy I liked better, Josh Lucas or Patrick Dempsey."

"And I remember thinking that Patrick Dempsey had to be the nicest, most handsome guy ever to get dumped at the altar. I actually think his character, Andrew Hemmings, is nicer all around than Jake Perry, who has some rough edges, but no one could replace the lightning spark of *young* love—*first* love—between Melanie and Jake."

"Matt, you did that to *me*, you know, *first* love—except for the lightning, of course—the first day you came in to Kitty's. Not quite love at first sight—even though I noticed you when you walked through the door—but when you looked into my eyes. I thought I was in love two or three times after high school and was surprised to find that when I broke up with each of those boyfriends, it didn't hurt that much. I didn't know what to feel. But *you* looked into my eyes as if I was the prettiest girl you'd *ever* met, and you *never* looked away. Not when you *talked,* not when you stirred in the two Splenda, not even when you reached into your coat for your wallet. Most people look away. And you didn't talk much; you *listened* much. You made me feel comfortable talking because I sensed that you *wanted* me to . . . you wanted to hear *whatever* I said. And when you left for your office I was surprised at how sad I was to watch you walk out the door because I didn't believe that you'd come back the next day."

"I didn't either, beauty."

"So was it love the *first* morning when you left or love the *next* morning when you came back, and we talked and talked while it snowed and snowed. Or was it love when you lifted me off the sofa and kissed me in my apartment? I don't know. Maybe all three, maybe *better* than lightning. Melanie and Jake had all that history that we don't have, all those years together from childhood. Even if she had chosen Patrick Dempsey, all that history and all those years with Jake would have stayed in her mind and heart forever. Just like your poem about Missy. But Melanie and Jake were so young when the lightning struck that they didn't have perspective; they only had innocence and love. You and I, Matt . . . we have *perspective* and love. Which is better?"

"Sweet Abby, my love, your mind is as beautiful as the glow in your eyes, as the music in your voice, as the flavors and the curves of your body. Which is *better*? What's better is *now*. Now is *everything*, beauty. I'm coming off ten years of lonely perspective, and you've had plenty of your *own* perspective in the last ten years. We don't need any more of that. We have lightning and we have love. We have *all* we need. For you and me, it could not have happened any other way."

We turned the movie off right after Melanie got drunk and threw up in Jake's truck, and he had to carry her to bed at her mom and dad's. Then we stretched out on the sofa in a full body hug, with the doggies lying on our feet, closed our eyes and listened to each other's thoughts until I felt Jock jump to the floor and lick my hand to let me know that we both had fallen asleep and it was time for the whole family to go up to bed.

"Can we switch sides, old guy?" Abigail grinned as she lay down on *my* side of the bed. "I want to see if I love you as much from the left as I do from the right."

"Don't blame *me*, beauty, if I *bop* you in the middle of the night."

"You have a free pass; if you bop me it's *my* fault, same if I bop *you*. Did you have a side with Sarah?"

"Same side. We never talked about it, it just happened."

We were tangled together under the popcorn clouds, with a lilac candle flickering on Grandma McKay's night stand and the doggies in their beds on the floor. In between kisses Abigail asked, "Do you miss Sarah a lot, Matt?"

"Not *consciously*, love. I talk with her almost every day: in the car, in the shower, when I walk the dogs—when I'm alone. But *missing* doesn't always make sense. What I miss most in my life are the things I *wanted* but didn't have—*ever*—rather than what I did have *once* but lost. Does that make sense?

"Sarah and I had a full and wonderful life together for twenty-one years. I wouldn't have changed *one* day or done a *thing* differently. So my only regret is that Sarah died so young and didn't get to enjoy our sons as husbands and fathers, and enjoy their wives and our grandkids. On the other hand—and you know some of this already—with the old girlfriends I miss what *never happened*: the young romance that was never allowed to grow; the passion that was never kindled; the love that was never fulfilled; the memories that were never created. That's what I miss. Those are my regrets. But when I think about them, I know I'm being selfish. I've been blessed all my life with Mom and Dad, with my happy childhood, my good health, my brains, my education, my safe return from Vietnam, Sarah, my sons and grandchildren—and now the love of my *new* life."

"Matt, I love you so much."

"Beauty, you are not only bringing out the best in me, you are kissing away my cares and scars. You are magic. With you I'm twenty years younger—in body and spirit—which makes me still much too old for you, by the way."

"You keep touching me the way you are *now*, old guy, and I'll keep touching you like *this*, and maybe we can narrow the gap."

In the morning we felt as if we were on vacation. Abigail didn't have to be at RIT until eleven, and I didn't have any appointments or meetings. This time we imagined we were on the beach on a cloudy, windy day at Gloucester. We were huddled together inside a giant New York Yankees blanket to hide from the gusts and stinging sand. It was the week after our schools let out and the week before our summer jobs started. Our only care in the world was to keep that blue blanket so tightly wrapped around us that the blowing sand would not get between our naked bodies. There were no bobbies.

Our reverie was interrupted at about nine o'clock when Jock and Maggie lost patience with us and jumped on top of us on the beach and poked and whimpered until we reluctantly agreed to get their breakfast. As we went downstairs, Abigail said with a grin that the next time we made love on a *pretend* beach we should *pretend* that it was a balmy, sunny beach in North Carolina rather than a brisk New England beach.

There was a cold rain, and Jock and Maggie—who hate rain as much as they love snow and who are smarter than half the people I know—did their business quickly so that we all could get back in the house to our dry towels, hot coffee and showers. Jock sat at the top of the stairs and guarded against any squirrels and crows while Maggie groomed Abigail and me after our shower. It was only our *fifteenth* morning together, but every morning felt like the next day of our honeymoon. I made Abigail a bacon-and-provolone omelet for breakfast and sent her off to RIT with a McIntosh apple, two mozzarella sticks and a box of Barnum's animal crackers in her Tinker Bell lunch box.

I called Mom at eleven to check on the time for dinner and remind her that we were bringing Chianti and dessert. She asked if Abigail liked both Italian sausage and meatballs, and I said she did and ". . . those are just *restaurant* meatballs, Mom. Wait until she gets a taste of yours."

"Matthew, Abigail's a very nice girl. How are you gonna *keep* her?" We both laughed.

"Mom, you'll have to ask Abigail that one yourself, but *watch* out. She might surprise you. We will be over at six. Call me later if you need us to bring anything else."

I drove to Lucia's on Bay Road and picked up six eclairs— Dad's favorite—and six cannoli—Mom's favorite—three with ricotta cheese and three with vanilla custard. I bought two bottles of Ruffino Chianti at the liquor store next to Lucia's, and then drove across the street to Mangrums for a six-pack of Heineken for Dad and two long-stemmed red roses for Mom and Abigail. While driving home I mused on all the ways that Mom and Abigail were different from each other—two generations apart with me in the middle. I tried to explain it to Jock and Maggie on our wet walk around the circle, but they were only interested in getting out of the rain, getting their rubdowns and getting their naps. I let them join me in the bedroom, and we all crashed for at least an hour before Abigail woke us up when she drove into the garage.

At Mom and Dad's, Abigail stayed in the kitchen to help Mom get everything ready, and Dad and I sipped on our beers in the living room.

"So you're going to see Danny this weekend, son?"

"Right, Dad. I thought Danny and Emma should meet Abigail before Christmas."

"How's Abby doing with all of our family so far?"

"She's a natural Flynn, Dad. She already has a Christmas shopping date with Diane, Stephanie and Barbara, and we're going to dinner at Debbie's a week from Friday. And Terry Ruggeri *loves* Abigail, and she invited us to her house on the tenth for dinner with her whole family."

"*Terry Ruggeri?*"

"I see Terry every Sunday at the eight-thirty Mass at Holy Innocents, so Terry has talked with Abigail a couple of times already, and they hit it right off."

"So Abby is living at your house?"

"For two weeks now. You know how girls can do it, Dad. It doesn't take them long to turn *any* house into *their* house. I've already lost most of my closet and shelf space."

"Abby's very young, son; why does she want an old guy like you?"

"You'll have to ask her that one yourself, Dad. I told Mom the same thing. I'm not sure I know myself, but Abigail tells me I'm young enough."

"How long has Sarah been gone, Matt?"

"It was ten years in October, Dad."

"So you have a new, young girl, but you're *ten years older* than when you lost Sarah."

"And Abigail is *twenty years younger* than Sarah was when she died—I know what you mean, Dad. It's a mystery to me, too, but you and Mom have told me since I was a kid that these things don't just *happen*, they happen for a *reason*. So I'm not afraid to take my chances with Abigail."

My roots are Sicilian, and after a lifetime of pasta and sauce—and too much thin marinara in too many gourmet restaurants—I have *never* tasted anything better than Mom's smooth, thick, Sicilian red sauce. As Mom lovingly set the giant green-and-red bowl of pasta in the center of the dining room table she said that Abigail picked the rotini rather than spaghetti.

"Abby told me that your favorites are rotini, ziti and rigatoni, and this is the only one I had."

"It's *perfect*, Mom. Abby knows me too well after only two weeks."

Abigail laughed and put her hand on my knee.

"Matt is the first old Italian guy in my life—I had to learn

178

fast."

I watched Abigail's face as she tasted each spoonful of rotini and each piece of meatball—she cut them in quarters— sometimes closing her eyes as she savored the flavors. Mom's meatballs are soft and crumble in your mouth, and that surprised Abigail and made her smile. She had the same expression on her face that she had almost every morning when she started to stretch and wake up, with the doggies licking her face and the sun coming in the windows. She even took a couple of spoonfuls of sauce without any pasta or meatball and sipped them like soup, and then she poured a little sauce into a small ice cream dish, cut up some sausage and dunked the pieces in the sauce.

"*Mmm*. Mrs. Flynn, I have *never* eaten any food this good! I don't want it to stop. I would stay with Matt forever *just* for your sauce." And then she whispered in my ear, "Matt—and I'm *not* joking—tasting your mom's sauce is like having a slow orgasm."

I grinned and kissed her on her forehead.

Dad couldn't resist. "Son, what sweet nothings is Abby whispering in your ear?"

"Something I can't repeat, Dad, except to tell you that Abby really means it when she says she likes Mom's sauce more than she likes me."

"*Mangia*," said Mom with a glow on her face. "There's plenty more, and I'll send you home with enough for supper tomorrow night."

"Mrs. Flynn, maybe for a Christmas present you can show me how you make your sauce."

"Honey, you pick a day after you come back from Boston, and we'll make sauce and meatballs together from scratch. I'll turn you into a good Italian cook." We all laughed.

Abigail ate so many meatballs and sausage and helpings of rotini that she had no more room for dessert. I saved just enough room to split an eclair with Dad and a ricotta cannoli with Mom. We all sipped Galliano and coffee and talked for another hour before Mom packed us on our way with the green-and-red bowl filled to the brim with rotini, meatballs and sausage. The lingering hugs that both Mom and Dad gave Abigail as we said good night in the kitchen made most of my bones tingle.

In the Jeep on the way home Abigail poked me and said, "Matt, that was *so* lovely. I *like* being Italian. Your mom said

I'm so young and pretty that she wanted to know 'how's Matt gonna *keep* you?' She said she asked *you* but you told her she had to ask *me* that one and she should watch out for my answer."

"What *was* your answer, love?"

"I'm not telling, old guy. It's a secret between your mom and me. But she was so happy with my answer that she kissed me on both cheeks, just like your cousin Theresa."

Abigail had the green-and-red bowl cradled in her lap. She lifted it up, peeled back the clear Saran wrap and breathed in the aroma two or three times.

"Matt, thank you for making me Italian. I love you so much, but I might just eat this whole bowl myself."

The sky was black and clear, and the half-moon was brilliant when we took Jock and Maggie around the circle. Then we settled on the sofa with our mugs of Prince of Wales tea and watched the rest of *Sweet Home Alabama*.

"Matt, I have never seen lightning actually *hit* the ground, have you?"

"Sort of, on my trip across the country with Matt and Danny in 1995."

"One more thing to put on my list of 'stories that Matt has to tell me'—hopefully soon."

"We are heading into a lot of cold winter days, beauty, when there will be nothing we want to do—nothing we *can* do—but cuddle and tell stories. I'm sure you have plenty for me, too."

"I'll come up with some even if I have to make them up. Now tell me about the lightning."

"We were just past halfway on our trip, in the middle of July, heading back through Colorado on our way to Denver. We spent one night in Durango in the foothills of the San Juan Mountains, and that night we had one of the most spectacular thunderstorms I ever saw. The mountains were right across the highway from our motel, and the storm came while we were watching a baseball game on television right after dinner. The rain was so heavy that the motel parking lot was under two feet of water in *ten* minutes.

"Fortunately we were on the second floor, so I could watch it all safely from our balcony. Lightning bolts as thick as telephone poles pounded straight down into the mountain across the street—one after another like a picket fence. I called the boys out to watch, and Matt brought the video camera. While he was focusing on the rain and the flood, an enormous bolt hit across the road. It was so loud, bright and *immediate* that Matt dropped the camera, which fortunately survived to record the second half of our trip. Both boys quickly retreated to our room, closed the door and left me on the balcony enthralled by the power of nature. I was still smoking cigarettes in those days, and watching that storm necessitated a couple of Chesterfields."

"I've never been on a trip out west. Maybe we could plan one over the summer, depending on when I get a job."

"I would like that a lot. Except for one weekend with Sarah in Las Vegas, I haven't been west of Chicago since my trip with the boys."

"What will we be doing in Boston with Danny and Emma? Should I take a nice dress or two?"

"How about *one*. We'll probably do a fancy dinner at a nice Italian ristorante on Friday and a casual dinner at a pub or sports bar on Saturday. Danny and Emma also know a lot of great spots for breakfast. We'll be walking a lot—if the weather permits—and riding the MTA, so the dress code will be comfortable and warm. I'm sure you'll *love* the bed and breakfast Danny picked out. It is a vintage New England postcard, charming and cozy. We'll probably have a four-poster bed and a fireplace in our room, with a kitchen full of finger food, homemade pastry and great tea."

"It sounds delicious. Maybe I can get some ideas for Kitty."

"What's she going to do without you when you get a full-time job?"

"I don't know; I *am* her favorite," Abigail said with a grin. "Maybe we can stop in every day on the way to work for coffee and a Danish."

"And get *fat* together from our ears to our toes," I laughed.

"Speaking of toes, old guy, today was a long day, and tomorrow will be even longer. Do you love me enough to rub my feet?"

"I love you enough to eat your toes, beauty. Put your head on the Scottie pillow at the end, and let me have your legs in my lap. Move over a little bit, baby dogs. Close your eyes, love, and dream about a warm beach in July."

I took off Abigail's socks and massaged both of her feet slowly, with a kiss mixed in here and there. She murmured blissfully at first, but fell asleep after a few minutes. Her right hand slipped off her hip and over the edge of the couch, her lips parted and she started to snore softly. Her belly rose and fell in a one-two-three, one-two-three rhythm.

Here I am, I thought, *with my baby dogs sleeping on one side and my beautiful girl sleeping on the other side. If my life could be distilled into one photograph, I could live happily forever in this one.*

"*Mmm,* Matt, how long was I asleep? What you did to my feet was *heavenly,* and then I was in our bedroom in Boston with a fire blazing. You and I were wrapped in our popcorn clouds in front of the fireplace. You were reading a poem to me by candlelight. I think it was a poem about the sun rising in the morning over a small lake in the mountains. You'll have to explain *that* one to me. Let's go up to our four-poster, old guy. I want some more massaging."

Abigail lit two bayberry candles in opposite corners of the bedroom.

"Matt, do you suppose that John and Abigail were passionate lovers, or did they just fulfill their matrimonial duty, Puritan-style? Do you think Mrs. Adams was ever on top?" *My* Abigail grinned in the dark.

"From what I've read about Abigail and John—which is a *lot*—I'm sure they were both passionate *and* tender lovers all their lives. From the first time that they were together on their wedding night, they were in awe of being 'one flesh.' They couldn't believe how much bliss and ecstasy they shared when they gave themselves to each other. It was much more than both of them ever anticipated after their strict Puritan upbringing.

"I like to picture Abigail and John by candlelight wrapped together naked in a thick goose down quilt—maybe with a pattern of white clouds on a blue sky—sitting and making love in front of the fire. How many presidents and first ladies do you think have done *that* in their lives? Maybe Abigail and John were the last, but I wouldn't be surprised if George and Laura Bush are still making love in front of *their* fireplace at the Crawford ranch."

"Do you think Abigail loved to touch John as much as I love to touch *you*?"

"I'm sure of it, and the same for John. They both marveled at their nuptial bliss and the wonders of the flesh that were opened to them—and in which they could *revel*—because they were husband and wife, Mr. and Mrs. John Adams. People laugh—or even sneer—at such an old-fashioned concept in the twenty-first century, but it meant the whole world to Abigail and John to be married to each other and at the same time to remain each other's dearest friend all their lives. And they were separated from each other—doing their patriotic duty to our new country—*so* many times and for *so* many months and years that when they reunited they were ravenously hungry for each other in every way conceivable."

"Well, Mr. Adams, I don't want to *ever* be separated from you; and tonight in our four-poster bed I am ravenously hungry for *your* body, sir."

Abigail made love to me slowly, quietly, deliberately. Her touches and kisses seemed almost more thoughtful than fervent. By the time we blew out the candles, curled together under *Pooh* and *Piglet* and drifted off to sleep, I knew I was enveloped in the same *wonder* that had enveloped John Adams.

When Jock and Maggie woke me at eight, Abigail—who already had shown an instinct for never losing contact with me no matter how she slept—was sleeping on her belly with her head turned away but her right arm across my chest. I had to wake her with kisses from the back of her neck to the small of her back. She rolled over and stretched.

"*Mmm*, Matt, I see the four posts are gone, so we must be back in modern times. I had a dream I was sleeping in a flannel nightgown, and you were in a flannel nightshirt, and both of us were wearing those old nightcaps. I'm glad we don't live in colonial days; I prefer skin on skin."

We made love lazily, stretching and yawning in between kisses. When we jumped into the shower Jock and Maggie took their posts on the bathmat, Jock prone and facing the door to guard against cats and chipmunks and Maggie on all fours facing the tub and ready to groom. Abigail slid back the shower curtain and laughed.

"Old guy, there's no room for *us* on the mat."

"Jock, you have to move for Mommy. Maggie, you can stay and give us some licks."

We had breakfast and walked the dogs, and then I brought up two suitcases from the basement, the medium-size one I normally use and the large one—which Sarah always used—for Abigail.

"Matt, I don't need *half* that room. Can we just share the big one?" She gave me her most impish smile. "When we go on our honeymoon I'll kick you out of the big one, and you will have to fend for yourself."

"I can fend. I took a course in fending in law school. If you don't mind being on top, beauty," I teased, "I'll pack my stuff while you're at Mangrums and leave you the rest."

I kissed Abigail goodbye and sent her off to work with her Tinker Bell lunch box stuffed to the top with leftover rotini, meatballs and sausage, Then I vacuumed my Jeep, removed Matt and Emily's car seats, washed the windshield and the side door windows and the back and side vinyl flaps of the rag top.

Then I checked the tires. It was a habit that went back to my first car—my 1971 Volkswagen Beetle that I named Alexander from *Winnie-the-Pooh* and the song by Melanie. I looked between the treads for stones, glass and any other nasty contraband. The two times that I found trouble—one screw and one nail—made up for all the other times that I merely got my knees dirty.

I packed lightly, leaving at least two-thirds of the suitcase for Abigail. And then I filled Jock and Maggie's travel bags with food, beds, blankets and toys for their three days at the Happy Tails kennel.

Abigail called at five o'clock to let me know that the advertising director continued to sing her praises, and her fellow interns all got jealous when she warmed up Mom's leftovers in the break room. She said she would be home by eight because Mr. Christopher was letting the interns leave early. She said she couldn't wait to be on top in the suitcase. As usual I could hear the grin in her voice.

Jock and Maggie ran downstairs and waited like statues at the door in the family room as soon as they heard Abigail's car pull in the garage. After many cold noses and warm kisses, we made a pot of Earl Grey tea, then went upstairs and jumped on the bed to watch Mommy pack.

"You certainly left me enough room, Matt. I will have to put in one more sweater to fill it up."

"How about your favorite pillow? That used to always work for me."

"*You* are my favorite pillow, old guy. Most of the time, I throw the other one on the floor."

Abigail flopped on the bed between Jock and Maggie.

"Do you baby dogs like going to Happy Tails?"

"Yeah, they do. All the people who work there love them. They get play time every day with the other dogs, and they bark their heads off so much that they will have almost no bark *left* by the time they come home. They'll have baths Monday morning so they won't be too stinky when we pick them up at four."

Abigail squeezed Jock and Maggie's snouts against her cheeks and kissed their cold noses.

"I'm going to *miss* you puppies. Tomorrow will be the first day you won't be with me since I fell in love with your daddy. Matt, did John and Abigail have dogs?"

"I don't remember any mentioned in the books I've read—certainly not by name—but with their various farms and all the usual farm animals, I would be surprised if they *didn't* have dogs. Did you pack a hair dryer? Sarah always forgot her hair dryer."

"I don't usually need one. My hair tends to ripple and flip all by itself."

"Speaking of hair, Abby, have you packed enough to stop for a break? I want to take off all your clothes and 'un-ripple' all your hair."

We gently nudged the doggies off the bed and made love next to the big suitcase. Abigail actually had at least one foot *in* the suitcase several times.

We were up at six-thirty in the morning, dropped Jock and Maggie at Happy Tails in Fairport at eight, and were on the Thruway heading into the rising sun at nine. Abigail put her fuzzy red socks up on the dashboard immediately and asked me to tell her more about Danny and Emma.

"You know, Miss Abigail, that a state trooper will be able to spot your bright red feet from two hundred yards away, and I think it's a felony offense for a beautiful passenger to put her red feet on the dashboard and distract the driver."

"Well, I know a good attorney, sir."

"I've never handled a felony foot case before."

"I'll take my chances. I'll flirt with the judge and the jury if I have to, or I'll tell the court I was bewitched by the driver. Tell me more about Danny and Emma before I get too comfortable and switch into nap mode."

"Well, they met at Fordham. Danny was a biology major and a year ahead of Emma, who was a business major. She picked him up one Friday night in his senior year—he graduated in three years—in an Irish pub off campus, and joined him the next year in Syracuse where Emma worked on her MBA while Danny went to med school. After they both graduated this May, they

185

moved to Boston, where Danny started as a first-year resident in urology at Tufts and Mather, and Emma was hired as the special groups director at ASAP, All Sports for All People, a new sports marketing company in Boston. Basically she arranges full packages—transportation, tickets, hotels, restaurants—to all major sporting events from the World Series to the Olympic Games."

"I remember Dad mentioning his urologist. Remind me what they do."

"Mostly they work with men of a certain age—like your Dad and me—fifty-something and up. Prostate stuff. The prostate gland generally gets bigger as guys get older, crowds all the complicated plumbing down there, causes a variety of problems, and often develops cancer. So we guys of that certain age have screening tests periodically to increase the chances of detecting cancer early when it is almost completely treatable. Or so my urologist tells me."

"I've heard Dad talk about a PSA test. What's that?"

"Prostate-specific antigen. When the test numbers either make a dramatic jump or simply keep creeping up beyond the normal range, guys either have the tests more often or get a biopsy to see if there are signs of cancer in the prostate."

"How are *you* doing, old guy?"

"So far, so good. Dad had an enlarged prostate and had prostate-reduction surgery when he was sixty-five, so *I* may get there one day, but right now I'm at the high end of the normal range."

Abigail reached her left hand around the gearshift and rubbed the crotch of my jeans.

"Are there any things a sweetheart can do to help, Matt?"

"As *much* sex as possible, beauty," I grinned. "The more sex my prostate has, the more *toned* and happy he will be."

"Sounds like a perfect plan, old guy, because I'm hoping that the more sex *I* have, the better the chance of the magic cubbies inside of me opening up and helping *you* make our baby."

"*Faith* to move mountains, Abby; and a *magical* baby he or she will be."

Abigail shifted her feet to the side window and laid her head in my lap.

"How long will Danny be at Tufts and Mather?"

"The usual residency is four years. After that, Danny will have a variety of options. You know, Dr. Cotton Tufts was both a cousin and an uncle of Abigail Adams."

"How was that?"

"Dr. Tufts was Abigail's uncle by marriage on her mother's side, and her cousin by blood on her father's side. She used to call him 'Uncle Tufts,' and he called her 'Cousin Abigail.' Almost all the families in colonial Boston were related. Have you ever read *Those Who Love* by Irving Stone? It is a biographical novel of Abigail and John Adams. I probably have read it at least six times. I even have a first edition autographed by Irving Stone."

"*Wow*! I want to start reading it as soon as we go back home. I'm getting *way* comfortable here, Matt. Do you know a good lullaby?"

"How about *Charlie on the MTA,* beauty?"

"*Perfect*, old guy," Abigail said, closing her eyes. "Do you know all the words?"

I brushed my fingers through her hair in my lap, and then lightly across her lips.

"I think so. Here goes."

Well, let me tell you of the story of a man named Charlie on a tragic and fateful day.

He put ten cents in his pocket, kissed his wife and family, went to ride on the MTA.

But did he ever return? No he never returned, and his fate is still unlearned.

He may ride forever 'neath the streets of Boston. He's the man who never returned.

Charlie handed in his dime at the Kendall Square station and he changed for Jamaica Plain.

When he got there the conductor told him, One more nickel. Charlie couldn't get off of that train.

Abigail sang the chorus the second time.

Now all night long Charlie rides through the station crying, What will become of me?

How can I afford to see my sister in Chelsea or my cousin in Roxbury?

We sang the chorus together the third time.

Charlie's wife goes down to the Scollay Square station every day at quarter past two, and through the open window she hands Charlie a sandwich as the train comes rumbling through.

I hummed the chorus the fourth time.

Now, you citizens of Boston, don't you think it's a scandal how the people have to pay and pay?

Fight the fare increase! Vote for George O'Brien! Get poor Charlie off the MTA!

I looked down at Abigail, and she was asleep. She was whistling softly through her parted lips. Her fingers had loosened and fallen from the gearshift knob, and her red feet had slipped down the side window to the armrest. I brushed her hair off her forehead and whispered the last chorus:

Or else he'll never return, no he'll never return, and his fate is still unlearned.

He may ride forever 'neath the streets of Boston. He's the man who never returned.

He's the man who never returned.

17

The sun was streaming through the windshield directly on Abigail's face, enhancing the shades and nuances of all her colors. It's hard to explain, but it's like the difference between looking at an American Beauty rose in the sunlight, and looking at a *photograph* of an American Beauty rose in the sunlight.

As I played with her hair around her ears I saw that Abigail's eyebrows and eyelashes were a little more blond than her hair, and there were two freckles on her forehead and a pale pink birthmark about the size of a dime behind her right ear that I hadn't noticed before— things you can almost *never* see in the fading light of late November. It was not easy to drive, considering that I couldn't keep either my eyes *or* my hands off my sleeping beauty.

About halfway to Syracuse, Abigail shifted to her left side with her legs and red socks curled on her seat, her face in my lap and both her arms wrapped around my right thigh like a hugging pillow.

How can she fit me so well? I asked myself. *It's as if I were a tree, and Abigail is the sunlight and the breeze among my branches and leaves. And we've known each other less than three weeks, and we're thirty-five years—a generation—apart. What's Danny going to say about this girl who could be his sister?* Then Abigail stirred and made all the questions go away.

"*Mmm*, Matt, nice *leg*! I love you *so* much. I would love you even if you *couldn't* sing, but you sing a pretty good folk song— although I think I might have missed the last verse or two. Between the rhythm of your voice and the rumble of your Jeep and the warm sun on my face, I was out fast. How long was I asleep? Where *are* we?"

"We're driving through downtown Syracuse, beauty. It's ten-thirty. When would you like to stop for lunch?"

"I'm sure I'll be good until at least noon, old guy. My coffee's still hot, and I can nibble on *you* any time I want. Did I get in the way of your coffee, flopped all around the gearshift here?"

"No. I moved you a little bit, took my sips and moved you a little bit *back*," I smiled. "You're fun to move, beauty, but it was a challenge driving and playing with you at the same time."

"Will you tell me about Vietnam, Matt? Does it bother you to talk about it?"

"No, pretty girl, I'm one of the lucky ones. As far as my friends and family could tell over the past thirty-five years, I didn't come back messed up in any way. I stayed away from drugs, bar girls and the black market. I didn't suffer any permanent wounds or scars, physical or psychological. And most of all, I came home alive and not disabled.

"I'm one of the lucky ones. So is Joe Steger although I'll let *him* tell you about the money he made in the black market. And Vietnam gave me a perspective that has helped me ever since I came home. Once you've been to hell and come back, nothing around you *ever* looks as bad or as hard as it did before."

Abigail rested her head on my shoulder, wrapped both hands around my right arm and whispered, "How did you *get* there, Matt?"

"It wasn't as complicated in September 1964 as it became by the summer of 1968. I signed up for Army ROTC in my first semester at B.C., and everything went well for all four years. It was a natural thing for me to do. All my family always felt—always *knew*—it was both our *duty* and our *privilege* to serve. Dad and both of his brothers, Uncle Bill and Uncle Jim; and four of Mom's five brothers, Uncle Johnny, Uncle Dom, Uncle Sal and Uncle Vinny. They all served in World War II.

"Only Mom's brother Pasquale, Uncle Patsy, was unable to serve. When we were little, Uncle Patsy always seemed like more of a kid than a grown-up. He probably was autistic, but in the fifties I only remember Mom, Aunt Connie and Uncle Vinny saying that Uncle Patsy was slow. And Dad and all my uncles enlisted before they were drafted. That's the way it was in America after Pearl Harbor.

"By the summer of *1968*, on the other hand, much of America had turned against the Vietnam War, against ROTC in colleges, against our troops in general, and against me, too, it seemed.

"Most of my good friends, though, stayed the course. One joined the Teacher Corps and went to teach in inner-city Detroit (which he always claimed *had* to be worse than Vietnam); one joined the Peace Corps and was sent to Nepal; the rest either did what I did—ROTC—or were drafted. I didn't know anybody

190

who dodged the draft or ran off to Canada. Those were hard summer days for guys graduating from college and facing nothing but difficult choices. There were too many sad partings.

"So I was commissioned a second lieutenant in the Army on June 3, 1968—the day of my Boston College commencement— and ordered to report on July 20 to officer training school at Fort Benning, Georgia, where I met Joe Steger. In between I went to Bermuda and was dumped by Ellen—but you already heard that story. I caught a break at the end of OTS because of my language training—Ancient Greek, Latin and German—at both Dominic Savio *and* B.C., and was assigned to the Defense Language Institute Foreign Language Center in Monterey, California. So was Joe.

"A year later, he and I were promoted to captain and sent to Vietnam to run the Army English Language School at Tan Son Nhut Air Force Base in Saigon. And we did that until July 1971, when we were rotated stateside. Joe was first sent to Charleston Air Force Base for three months, and then he joined me in San Antonio, where we directed the Medical Language School at Fort Sam Houston. We both finished our four-year hitches in June 1972 and were discharged."

Abigail squeezed my arm harder, kissed me on the cheek and whispered again, "How did you get your Purple Heart, old guy? I saw your citation on the mantle in the living room."

"One day, two Viet Cong infiltrators driving two little trucks—supposedly delivering our monthly supply of workbooks and language tapes—parked at opposite corners of the school hangar and then ran off and detonated plastic explosives in both trucks. We were lucky in that the two trucks didn't explode at the same time. The first explosion was smaller and only dented the corrugated metal walls of that corner of the hangar. Fortunately it also alerted all of us inside, and we were face-down on the floor when the second blast blew out all the windows and covered us with nails and sharp fragments of wood and glass.

"Several Vietnamese civilians working outside the hangar were killed. I didn't think I was hurt at all, but Joe said to the MP's who arrived immediately, 'Flynnie's hurt; he's got cuts on his head; he should go to the hospital.' And off they took me to the base hospital, where they cleaned all of the glass out of my scalp and hair and slapped on a couple of bandages. I don't think I ever had any scars, but with my hair cut short you can take a closer look later and see what you can see. It was July 22, 1970. Two weeks later, Colonel Ross pinned on my Purple Heart."

"That's your *license* plate! I keep forgetting to ask you about your license plate: 22JUL70."

"That was Matt and Danny's idea when I bought my Jeep."

"Do you think about that day a lot, Matt?"

"Almost never, Abby. Only when someone asks me, or maybe on July 22 every year."

"Do you mind that I asked you?" She took my right hand in hers and played with my fingers. "Does it bother you to talk about it?"

"No, beauty, I'm glad you asked. It's another part of me that you ought to know. It was part of my growing up, part of the person I became over the last thirty-seven years, just like Mom and Dad and my brothers were part of my growing up. And Dominic Savio and Boston College and law school, and all my good friends in between, and all the girls I loved and lost. There were too many painful days—losing Missy hurt more than being bombed in Vietnam—but I wouldn't want to take any of them back. If I did, I might never have met Sarah and I might not have two splendid sons and two beautiful grandchildren and maybe I would never have walked in to Kitty's and looked into your green eyes.

"*Quo fata ferunt.* Wow! I haven't thought of that Latin motto in *years.* I brought back a box of leather coasters from Bermuda when I left Ellen behind, with the coat of arms in gold, and that motto. *Where the fates carry us.* No, pretty girl, I've been fortunate and blessed; I'm thankful for *every* day of my life."

We stopped for coffee, burgers and fries at the Iroquois service area about an hour east of Syracuse. When I opened the Jeep door for Abigail, I wrapped her tightly in my arms and gave her a very warm kiss—which she gave me right back.

"*Yum*, Matt! What was *that* all about?"

"First of all, beautiful girl, *that* was about, *I love you so much.* Second, *that* was about, *Are you ready?*"

"Am I ready for what?"

"It's *your* turn. Tell me what you were like as a little girl; tell me how you grew up to be such a bright, passionate, loving and beautiful woman."

192

I ran both my hands through Abigail's hair and kissed her again. Other travelers in the parking lot were staring at us.

"Take your time, Miss Abby, and don't leave anything out. We still have more than three hours to go to Cambridge."

"Well, first of all *yourself*, Mister Hot Old Jeep Guy, I wish we were some place where no one could see us so I could jump on top of you in the back seat and attack you right now."

"Let's put that on our list with the grass and the beach. I've never made love in any back seat."

"Me neither. Second of all, I can tell you my whole life story in a lot less than three hours— unless you keep touching me and playing with me like that. So keep your hands on the wheel, Peter Pan, and let me get started.

"The first things I remember are my bedroom at Monteroy Road and playing with Patrick in the back yard. My brother Jack told me that we had lived in an apartment on Monroe Avenue near Cobbs Hill Park, but I can't remember that. Our street was nice, and I made friends right away. I think I was four years old. After I started kindergarten at Our Lady of the Assumption, I met so many new girls, and they all lived in that same neighborhood that's tucked in between Elmwood and Highland and Winton. I had a brand-new, lavender blue Schwinn Princess bike, and I didn't need my training wheels very long. I loved to ride my bike to all my girlfriends' houses every day after school and every Saturday. Mary Kay lived three streets down on Ashbourne. Most of us went to Fatima together. I'm sure we were an *obnoxious* clique when we first got there.

"The only sport I was ever into before Fatima was softball. Pat and I played catch on almost every summer day, and Jimmy Keller too. And I always liked to read: *Winnie-the-Pooh* was my favorite, and the Disney stories—*Snow White*, *Cinderella*, *Sleeping Beauty*, *Lady and the Tramp*. Is that how Jock got his name?"

"Exactly right, Abby. I wanted to name our first Scottie Jock, but Sarah and the boys outvoted me and picked Herbie. Our second Scottie was a girlfriend for Herbie, and we named her Lucy. Two years after Sarah died, Herbie died, and I got a boyfriend for Lucy—I finally got my Jock. Maggie joined us four years later after Lucy died. Did you like Fatima? Cathy *loved* Fatima."

"My friends were all *so* smart and pretty. They made me want to do everything better. As I got older and read more, I started to draw. By the time I was twelve or thirteen, I was drawing pictures from every book I read. Most of my girlfriends from those days—all the way through Fatima and *even* Newton—the more they read and experienced the more they wanted to write. *I* wanted to draw. They wanted to *write* about love. I wanted to *draw* it.

"None of my boyfriends are worth talking about. I don't mean that they were losers or bad guys, but none of them took my breath away or stirred me up inside. It didn't hurt to break up with *any* of them. After I came home from college I was starting to wonder if I was *capable* of real, deep love and great passion. Honest to *God*, Matt, until you kissed me the first time, I really thought that stuff only happened in the movies. Even my girlfriends weren't doing much better— look at Mary Kay. For *ten* years, she thought she had the right guy until she saw you and me together and looked in our eyes and realized what she was still missing after all those years.

"Mom and Dad never traveled much, so I haven't been many places. I'm hoping you will change that. I want you to take me away, and then take me away some *more*. I've been to three or four shore places because my girlfriends from Newton asked me to go with them, and one cousin has a nice cottage near Cape May. But overall, for a girl my age, I'm sure I'm *way* behind on the travel curve, and the experiences curve, and probably a lot of other twenty-six-year-old curves. But I'm *not* behind any more on the *love* curve, thanks to my old summer boy. Except for Mary Kay, none of my friends know about you yet. Maybe I'll send a picture of you and me in my Christmas cards."

Abigail laughed and nibbled on my ear.

"How am I doing, old guy? Have you found out what you needed to know?"

"Beauty, I found out *all* I needed to know the first day we were together—probably with that first delicious kiss in your apartment. But tell me more. Tell me more about your brothers and your mom and dad and your grandparents. Tell me more about your best girlfriends. Tell me what people and places you would most like to *draw*. Tell me what kind of guy you were looking for before I walked in to Kitty's."

"I thought I told you that *already*, Matt. I've been looking for *you* all my life, or at least as long as I knew I wanted a lover and a husband and a best friend—all together in one man. I wasn't *sure* it was you when you first walked in; but after you literally knocked me off my feet with that first kiss I wanted *so much* for it to be you that my whole body *ached* for the rest of the day until you picked me up at Mangrums. By the next morning, I knew I could stop looking. It *was* you. And the next 'people and places' I want to draw is *you*—naked."

"*Naked?*" I laughed. "That will *never* sell, beauty."

"Naked, no clothes, in bed. You're a *natural*, summer boy. You'll be an easy sell. By the time I'm through with you, you may be the most famous nude in history," Abigail teased. "I haven't decided whether I want to draw you sleeping or awake; maybe I won't even tell you. And I wonder if I should draw you with your hair really short, like now—or really long, like last week?"

"Do you want history to remember me younger with no gray hair, or shaggy and grizzled?"

"*Silly* boy! I can make you as old or as young as I *want*—the same as you can do with a girl in one of your poems—and with or without gray hair."

"Seriously, Abby, in *real* life, would you like me to look younger when you take me around to meet your twenty-six-year-old friends? I could get me some Grecian Formula 61, or whatever the latest model is."

"Not a *chance*, summer boy. That's not something you would *ever* do if I weren't around, so I *sure* don't want you to do it because I *am* around." Abigail grinned and nibbled some more on my ear. "Besides, Matt, if you were any *hotter* than you already are, I might not risk introducing you to my girlfriends at all."

"Abby, have you ever seen the nude *Olympia*?"

"Sure, Edouard Manet—people always confuse him with *Monet*."

"I never got into Monet; but there's no confusing his fuzzy flowers with *Olympia*, who is the only nude I ever remember with both the fair, dark-haired innocence of *Snow White* and the heat of Ava Gardner. She's my favorite—or at least she *was* before the first morning I woke up and looked at you sleeping in the sunshine. I wish I could have painted *you* then."

"Who do *I* remind you of, Matt?"

"Beauty, I thought about that the first day I saw you at Kitty's. You have the charm, the eyes, the allure, the colors and the best features of Amy Adams and Rachel McAdams—so how could *any* guy resist, right? In the *way* old days, if your hair were more blond, I think people would have compared you to Doris Day. Have you ever drawn *yourself?*"

"Not yet. Maybe I'll draw you and me *together* in bed," she laughed. "*That* would sell."

"You haven't told me much about your Grandma and Grandpa McKay—except that Grandma McKay gave you her St. Patrick table."

"That's kind of a sad story. Grandpa McKay was an alcoholic. I think he was sober by the time I was a little girl, so I never saw it, but Dad has told me several times how hard it was for him, Uncle Barney and Aunt Helen growing up. Grandma is a very timid woman and was never able to stand up to Grandpa and get him to stop.

Grandpa was a Rochester Transit bus driver. Dad used to talk about how much fun it was to ride Grandpa's bus on Saturday mornings, but in the late seventies, he was drunk on the job and crashed his bus on East Avenue near Goodman Street. He lost his driver's license and was forced to retire. At least that finally got him to go to AA, but he and Grandma had to sell their house and move into an apartment to make ends meet.

"He and Grandma don't get out much and they're always very quiet. I think the memories cut deep and hurt. You'll see them at Christmas, and maybe we can even stop over for a surprise visit before then. I can still get Grandma to smile when I ask her to tell me stories about Dad's shenanigans growing up, and how he always got his little brother Barney in trouble with him.

"Dad says that Jack has Grandpa McKay's disposition and temper, but Catherine is *not* timid, so she is able to keep him mostly in line. Patrick, on the other hand, is easygoing, loveable, very funny, and an adventurer—just like Grandpa Dolan. I'm more like Nannie than like Mom. I'm more romantic, artistic and impatient and *much* less practical and *much* more spontaneous—as you know better than anyone from the way I threw myself at you."

Abigail's eyes gleamed as she looked into mine in the rear view mirror.

"Dad always told me—and he's right—that the best way to learn about life and how to *live* it is not from schools and books; it's from meeting more people and seeing more places. I am sure I'm *way* behind in both of those departments, so . . . in addition to the jobs I've already signed you up for—my best

196

friend, my only love and the husband of my dreams—I'm now designating you my travel guide, my cruise director. So as good as you are at carrying me away in *bed*, it won't be enough, old guy; you're going to have to take me to just as many places *outside* of bed. Is that too many hats, Matt? Will you wear them *all* for me?"

"You've seen all the hats in my closets, Abby; I *love* hats." I brushed my fingers across her lips and kissed the top of her head. "I love *you*. I'll wear all the hats you give me. And our first stop on the Abigail Tour will be historic Cambridge—coming up in about forty-five minutes."

We pulled in to Danny and Emma's apartment complex in Cambridge at three-thirty. They had been watching for my Jeep and ran out to greet us. I saw surprise in Emma's eyes and amusement in Danny's as they first scanned and then hugged Abigail. The girls are about the same height, but Emma is more slender. In contrast to Abby's strawberry-blond glow, Emma has the fair skin and dark hair of *Olympia*; she always reminds me of Moira Kelly in *The Cutting Edge*. If anyone was uncomfortable it didn't show. Abigail jumped into Emma's Ford Explorer, and Danny jumped into my Jeep, and they guided us around a few corners to our bed and breakfast.

In the five minutes it took to get to The Crimson Yard, the only thing Danny said to me was, "I still think you're making a big mistake, Dad, but I gotta hand it to you. Abigail sure is a *babe*." On the other hand, by the time Emma and Abigail stepped out of the Explorer, they were already fast friends, as anyone would have seen from the way they hugged and giggled with every step across the parking lot to the back door of the bed and breakfast.

After we checked in, we left my Jeep in the parking lot, and Danny and I drove Emma's Explorer back to their place. The girls insisted on walking back. I couldn't help grinning as I imagined them reviewing the pros and cons of their Flynn boys. At six o'clock we took the Red Line from Harvard Square to Government Center and then walked to the North End—the Italian heart of Boston. Danny and Emma had made reservations for seven o'clock at a lovely ristorante called La Bella Ragazza—"the beautiful girl," said Emma.

"They named it after *you*," I whispered to Abigail.

"*Sure*, as if *I* can pass for an Italian girl," she responded.

"Although," she continued impishly, "I *do* have a little Italian in me now."

We ordered a bottle of Ruffino Chianti, and Danny talked about his urology rotation schedule at Tufts and Mather. "Our biggest week each month is prostate week, and our 'cash crop' is biopsies for guys your age, Dad." The girls immediately changed the subject, and Emma told us about her hottest ticket packages.

"Now that the World Series is over—which was a *zoo* because of all the Red Sox fans who wanted to go to Denver— the Super Bowl in February in Phoenix is the next big deal, especially because the Patriots are still undefeated. And we're starting to get requests for the Olympic Games next summer in Beijing, and those packages will be *huge* moneymakers for ASAP. There are also a whole lot of people interested in some golf tournament in Georgia in the spring."

I laughed. "*Some* golf tournament in Georgia? That would be the Masters in Augusta in April—always the biggest golf tournament of the year. Some day when we win the *big* lottery, Emma, I'll ask you to put together a package for me and Abby to go to the Masters."

"Fifteen thousand dollars—I just priced it for a prestigious local law firm. That includes round-trip airfare, limo service, four-star hotel accommodations for eight days, full grounds passes and clubhouse privileges for all three practice rounds and all four tournament rounds, all gratuities; and a $300 gift card for either the tournament gift shop or the clubhouse sports bar. No food and drink is included except for the gift card, and I doubt that will go very far. But there are *lesser* packages, of course," she teased, "for those who only win *lesser* lotteries."

When I have dinner with Danny and Emma we always share everything, from the appetizers to the entrees, and our dinner at La Bella Ragazza was no different. It was clearly a new experience for Abigail, though, but she loved it. From the bruschetta to the deep-fried mozzarella sticks, to the Italian bread dipped in olive oil, black pepper and romano cheese, to the Caesar salad with anchovy fillets, to our four entrees, we each had several bites of everybody else's. My entree attracted the most attention: bucatini carbonara: bucatini pasta with pancetta—thick Italian bacon—and peas in a creamy parmigiano-reggiano sauce. We had to draw straws for the last forkful.

We talked about Abigail's MBA program and the new Mangrums that was scheduled to be built in nearby Belmont in 2008, and my diminishing practice, which was becoming more "part" and less "time" with every week. We talked about Emma's trip the following week to Phoenix to scout out restaurants, hotels, transportation services and local entertainment for the Super Bowl. She would also be on the ground in Phoenix for the entire week leading up to the game. Emma shook her head "no" in mock sadness when I asked her if I could accompany her on her scouting trip to Augusta in mid-February. And Danny talked about the difficulties of coordinating his schedule— including vacations—with the other eleven first-year residents in the urology department. It was a challenge even for doctors to be at the bottom of the pecking order in a big hospital.

And then, when we were finishing our second bottle of Chianti and starting on coffee, espresso and dessert, Danny took Abigail's hands, grinned and asked her—almost with a wink in his voice, "Abby, *please* forgive me for asking, but I'm a loving and dutiful son and it's my *job*. You are a bright, beautiful, caring and charming woman. Why do you want to hang around with a sixty-year-old guy like my father?"

Abigail, fielding Danny's question in the spirit in which it was intended, responded with her *own* mischievous wink and grin.

"You mean other than the fact that I love your dad more than my own *life* and I can't take my *hands* off him?"

"Right, forget the incidentals. What are the *real* reasons?"

"Your dad can make me start laughing when I don't feel like it, and he can make me stop crying when I didn't think I could. He understands my old drawings, and he explains his poems to me. He would rather listen to me than talk, but he can see in my eyes when I don't want to talk any more. He knows when to *hug* me, when to *tickle* me, when to just *hold* me. And he knows when a simple *touch* is enough. He doesn't push and he doesn't pull. He's just *there*, whichever way I'm going, even if I don't know where I'm going. He doesn't have any agenda except *me*. And he's let me take over his house, fill up his closets and become Maggie and Jock's mommy. How am I doing so far? Am I missing anything?"

Abigail squeezed Danny's hands and laughed. And Emma hugged them *both* and laughed. Then she poked Danny in the ribs and gibed, "I *told* you, you would be no match for Abby. And I don't think you do all those things for me!"

Danny clapped me on the arm and laughed sheepishly, "You *win*, Dad. You have my blessing."

Those two or three cups of coffee after dinner, with Abby and Danny and Emma, were two or three of the *best* of my life. All three "kids" gabbed and laughed on and on as if they'd known each other all their lives. Part of the time they considered the pros and cons of *me*—as a father, and as a boyfriend; and part of the time they compared brothers—Emma didn't have any sisters either—and growing up, and going off to college. Each time one of them poked fun at "the old guy," Abigail brushed my thigh affectionately under the table.

When Danny and Emma took us back to The Crimson Yard, we agreed that we would meet at their apartment at nine o'clock the next morning and take the T to one of their favorite breakfast places, The Golden Egg, near Faneuil Hall. Then Abby and I settled in to our cozy colonial room.

We turned on the gas fireplace, and the blue-and-yellow flames danced on the walls and drapes around the four-poster bed. We had brought *Pooh* and *Piglet* with us so we wrapped ourselves up at the foot of the bed in front of the fire. Abigail was sitting sideways in my lap, with her head on my chest and her hands playing across my belly.

"Matt, Danny and Emma are *wonderful*! I would have known that you were a *sure* winner just by meeting your *sensational* sons. And you know what *else* you have done for me, besides bringing me to life and lighting fires everywhere in my body? You have given me *sisters*. I never had sisters. I was always sorry I didn't have a sister. First Stephanie and Barbara, and now Emma, and maybe Claire in time.

"I love them all already, and it's different than with girlfriends. I love Mary Kay for sure, but there's something *inside* that ties Patrick and me together, and I never had that with a sister. I love you *so much*, old guy . . . Mister Adams . . . make love to me right *here*, right in front of our colonial fire, just like John did with *his* Abigail every time he came home from being a Founding Father."

After we made love in front of the fire, we made love again in the shadows of the flames in the four-poster. And again. Abigail was on fire *herself* for hours. She didn't want to stop. When we finally drifted away into sleep—so warm that we kicked all the covers to the floor—our colonial fire was still flashing blue and yellow around the bed.

18

Riding the MTA—which the current generation of Bostonians calls the T—in the morning with Danny, Emma and Abigail brought back a lot of memories from my college and law school days. Besides being a relaxing change of pace from classrooms, books and papers, the MTA was a great place to observe people: to look into their eyes, listen to their conversations, see their body language. I even wrote some poems about it back in those days.

And now I enjoyed being the *observed*. Most MTA riders pay little attention to other riders, but Abigail and I made an unusual couple and drew lots of sideways glances. I even sniffed her hair and nibbled on her ears a few extra times to enhance the effect. Danny and Emma pretended to be astounded by our behavior.

The sun came out at The Golden Egg, and after breakfast we started walking: the Freedom Trail, the Commons, the stores on Newbury and Boylston Streets, then around Copley Square, and the old and new Boston Public Library buildings, the old and new John Hancock buildings, and all the historic churches.

In the middle of Copley Square, as Danny and Emma were walking arm-in-arm ahead of Abby and me, Emma stopped, said "Switch!" and stepped back to take my arm and nudge Abigail up to take Danny's. "Dad," she whispered, only half kidding, "Abby is *perfect*, so *don't* screw it up!"

"Screw it *up*?"

"She could be the sister I always wanted, Dad, so *don't* screw it up. Are you two just playing around, or are you *forever*?"

"Emma, have you asked *Abby* that question?"

"Yes. She said, and I quote: 'A lifetime with Matt wouldn't be *nearly* long enough, Emma.' But *I* think it's up to you. What do *you* say, Dad?"

"You're wrong, Emma: it's *completely* up to Abby. No guy from age sixteen to sixty would *ever* let go of a girl like her, so unless she changes her mind we are *forever*."

"That will *never* happen, Dad. Abby is so crazy in love with you—I see tears of joy in her eyes when she talks about you—that she would give up *everything*—friends, family, *everything*—rather than lose you. I've never seen any woman so much in love."

"Well then, Emma, I guess you have a sister," I laughed, and hugged her around the waist.

"Dad, are you and Abby going to get married? She said, 'Matt and I are going to talk about that next year,' when I asked her."

"That's our official position until after Christmas and New Year's," I grinned. "Speaking of the holidays, Emma, when are you and Danny coming home?"

"We think on Friday the twenty-first. Will there still be room for us to stay at your house, Dad? I mean now that you have a boy *and* a girl and two dogs," she teased.

"We have *so* much room that you and Danny can have separate bedrooms if you want."

"Funny guy. What do Abby's parents think about her living with a guy *their* age?"

"Abigail's dad was on board right away; so was *my* dad—as you can imagine—as soon as he saw Abby. The mothers needed more convincing. Mom, Grandma . . . the first time she met Abby she said she was '*adorable* . . . and *so* pretty . . . but isn't she too young? You have two grandchildren.' But on Wednesday we went to Mom and Dad's for dinner. Mom made her special dish: pasta with meatballs and sausage. Abigail got to choose the pasta—rotini—and she loved Mom's sauce *so* much that by the middle of dinner she was eating it by the tablespoon out of the silver sauce boat. By the time we got to dessert, Mom and Abby were practically mother and daughter and were going to pick a day for Abby to go over so Mom could teach her how to make sauce and meatballs."

"She's a natural, Dad. Abby gets everybody to like her so *fast* they hardly have a chance to catch their breath at how *pretty* she is. That's what she did to *me,* anyway. I have to admit I've been selling you short since I met you; I didn't see this in you; you've been hiding the *real* you. Now I know where Danny gets it from." Emma poked me squarely in the breastbone and smiled, "Don't screw it up! But I interrupted, Dad, I'm sorry . . . what about *Abby's* mother?"

"Abigail's mother gave her a hard time from the moment Abby introduced me, for the obvious reasons: *I'm* too old, and her daughter's too *young*. That lecture lasted only as long as it took Abby to ask Mrs. McKay if she could remember just how crazy she was about Mr. McKay when *she* was twenty-six; and to firmly inform her mother that her *daughter* was now *also* twenty-six and that she knew from our first kiss that I was the man she had been looking for *all her life*. And although I'm not sure Mrs. McKay has come around to happy about Abby and me, I *am* sure she remembered the romance of her youth, and respects the fact that her daughter is a grown woman, full of fire. What do you think Abby and Danny are talking about up in front of us?"

"The same things we are," Emma laughed. "I told Danny to ask Abby all the same questions, and then we can compare notes later."

Danny and Emma took us for dinner to Abigail and John, the best-known pub and sports bar in Cambridge. It was called The Adams Tavern when I was in law school, but after the enormous popularity of David McCullough's biography of John Adams in 2001, Abigail's star rose as high as John's, and the owners of the Tavern decided to capitalize by changing its name.

On the colonial blue walls—between the giant, flat-screen televisions flashing tales of the Bruins and Celtics—were reproductions of many of the famous portraits of Abigail and John. There were also miniatures on the covers of the menus, and one quote from each:

> *"Life is for those who love."*
> -   Abigail to John

> *"Oh, my dear girl, I thank heaven that another fortnight will restore you to me–after so long a separation. My soul and body have both been thrown into disorder by your absence . . . But you who have always softened and warmed my heart, shall restore my benevolence as well as my health and tranquility of mind."*
> -   John to Abigail

Over dinner we talked about Danny and Emma's Thanksgiving with Emma's family on Long Island. Emma's father and mother, Jackson and Jane Swift, and her two brothers, Jackson, Jr., and Heath, all live in Huntington. Jackson and Heath operate their own HVAC business; Jane is an emergency room nurse at the Glen Cove Hospital; and Jackson, Jr., drives a FedEx truck. He is thirty-one, Heath twenty-four, and they are both still single. I hadn't seen any of them since Danny and Emma got married. Emma said everybody was doing well, and her mother and dad had just gotten a new puppy, a golden retriever. She couldn't wait to tell them about Abigail.

We agreed to meet for an early breakfast at the Greek diner just around the corner from our bed and breakfast, so that Abigail and I could go to Mass at ten o'clock at St. Ignatius Church at Boston College—St. Iggy's we always called it—and then head out of town. We wanted to get home before the predicted snowstorm from Ohio and Lake Erie made it to Rochester.

Curled at my side that night in our four-poster bed, with the firelight dancing around her head, Abby was pensive as she played with my fingers.

"Matt, it's *December* now. We have thirty more days in December. Every new day, every new thing we do, every new person I meet, seems more exciting than the day before. All of our days in November have been so *intense*, so *full*. I hope I can handle a whole *month* of days like those."

"Abigail Elizabeth, beauty, I think you can handle any*thing* and any*body*. You have dazzled my friends and family non-stop for three weeks, and I have enjoyed watching *every* minute."

"What about my dream poem, old guy? Will you explain that to me in the car tomorrow?"

"I hope I can, love. I wrote a poem like that decades ago when Mom almost died of a stroke."

"Oh my *God*, Matt! What happened?"

"Not tonight, Abby. Tomorrow. No more talking tonight—just you holding me, and me holding you. How many times can we kiss each other before the firelight puts us to sleep?"

We were so tired from walking all day, fully bundled against the frigid downtown Boston winds, that we didn't stay awake long in the shadows of the fire. I don't think we moved all night. We woke with both our heads on the fat pillow we brought from home, tangled together just the way we were when we fell asleep.

It was very cold but sunny the next morning. Abigail and I loaded the Jeep, checked out of The Crimson Yard and walked to the diner to meet Danny and Emma. We shared a lovely breakfast and talked about the week of Christmas. Danny and Emma would be coming in to town on Friday night the twenty-first and would have to go back to Boston on the twenty-sixth. We hugged and kissed each other goodbye, and then Abigail and I went to the ten o'clock Mass at Saint Ignatius. During the sermon she whispered, "Matt, where did you and Sarah get married?"

"Saint Joseph's in Penfield."

"If you were to meet the right babe now," Abigail teased, "where would you get married?"

"I would probably choose Holy Innocents, but the right *babe* might be able to talk me into an old church like Holy Eucharist. Normally, the wedding takes place at the girl's church."

"Well, I sort of left Saint Thomas Acquinas behind when I went to college, so it won't be there."

After Mass we headed out Commonwealth Avenue to the turnpike, and Abigail reminded me that I had promised to tell her about her dream and my poem and Mom's stroke.

"We have lots of time now, old guy."

"Abby, your dream sounded like the poem I wrote twenty-five years ago when Mom had her stroke. It was in July, and Sarah and the kids and I—Danny was just a baby—were spending a week with Tom and Diane and their kids at the cottage they rented for two weeks every summer on Raven Lake near Old Forge in the Adirondacks."

"Why was it named Raven Lake, Matt?"

"Because it was small and surrounded by mountains and tall pine trees. It was almost always in shadows, and the water almost always looked black—except at dawn on a sunny morning.

"A dream about Mom and Dad woke me at five o'clock on a Friday morning, but I didn't remember much of the dream. No one else was stirring, of course, and it was still dark outside. I walked down to the lake and out on the dock. The moon was still bright, but a hint of daylight was starting to creep over the mountains to the east—and the poem just came to me. It was all in my head, and I went back in to the cottage to make myself a cup of coffee and write it down. And then the phone rang. It was Dad, who said, 'Your mom had a stroke about an hour ago and fell down the stairs.' She was in intensive care at Highland Hospital, he said, and we should come home. I woke everybody up, and we packed up and drove home immediately.

"Mom had suffered a fractured skull, a broken collarbone and a punctured lung from the fall. It was touch-and-go for a few days, and she was in intensive care for a week, but she received excellent care and completely recovered from the fractures and the punctured lung. The stroke impaired her speech and weakened the muscles on her left side, but Mom was pretty much fully recovered after six months of physical and speech therapy. My aunts—Mom's sisters—called it a *miracolo di Dio*. She has talked more slowly, taken longer to answer questions and walked more carefully ever since, but anyone meeting Mom for the first time would *never* suspect that she ever had a stroke."

"Your mom seems really sharp to me, Matt. I would *never* have guessed."

"Right, and Mom is very proud of that. It's completely behind her, and I doubt if she ever thinks about it any more. She's always been a very positive woman, and Dad's the same."

"Did you ever write the poem down, summer boy?"

"Almost a year later, beauty, on another summer morning when only Herbie and I were home. I was surprised that I remembered it so well. Would you like to hear it and see if any of it matches your dream?"

"Are you *kidding*, Matt? I'm getting into position right now," Abigail laughed as she shifted onto her back, with her feet up on the passenger window and her head in my lap.

"I call it 'Mercy in the Morning.'"

Watching the sunrise this morning
on Raven Lake
I saw the moon floating
between the gray clouds black in the water,
and the pink in the sky in the water,
and the sun floating together with the moon
in the still black water.
I listened to the blue jays,
woodpeckers, cardinals and loons,
and I thought of Mom and Dad
at home asleep in their bed,
and all the mornings they woke us
to a wonderful day of life.
I saw the fish and the bugs
make ripples in the glassy lake,
and the rocks, plants and beer cans

at the bottom of the clear water.
I watched the green hills all around
turn pink in the water
as the sun rose on one at a time.
I watched the mist sweep off the lake
between the small islands to the south.
I saw my breath in the air
and lit a cigarette.
It was God's gift of time to think.
Not a leaf moved; there was no breeze,
only the chatter of the birds,
the splash of an early fish,
and the water lapping the dam
at the end of the lake.
It was the gift of a place to sense,
feel and commune with God
about the bruises of life and the meaning of love.
And then a hundred mallard ducks
flew from the shadows through the rising fog;
and the sun bronzed the empty trails
on the mountains to the east,
and the small boats along the shore.
And then I heard a telephone ring.
Behind me in the cottage the phone rang.

"That is *so* beautiful, Matt. I can picture all the images so clearly. I couldn't *draw* them that clearly, but I might have to try. Why did I have the same dream about sunrise on a small lake that I have never seen?"

"I've almost never been able to find any logic in dreams or make any sense out of them, but the romantic poet in me says that you and I are connected in more ways than we will ever know; and we may have been pointing toward each other for a *long*, long time."

"Well, old guy, I keep *telling* you how long I've been looking for you, so where have you been? How did you decide on the name for your poem, Matt?"

"It's from an old prayer I like—one of the Psalms: *It is good to give thanks to the Lord . . . to show forth Thy mercy in the morning, and Thy truth in the night.*"

"Tomorrow will be three weeks since we met. I have to pick out another drawing to show you this week." Abigail yawned in my lap. "The time between now and Christmas is going to go by *so* fast. We have dinner coming up at Debbie and Fred's, and then at Theresa's. I have a shopping day or two with Diane and the girls, Christmas cards with Mom, sauce and meatballs with *your* mom, papers and projects in all three of my courses. Mary Kay will be back home the same day as Emma and Danny, *and* I will be making love with you morning, noon and night every day."

She reached up, traced my lips with her index finger and teased, "I could get to be as old as you are just thinking about it."

I brushed some wavy strands of hair away from her eyes, kissed two fingers of my right hand and pressed them to her lips and countered, "Listen, Miss Abby. The deal when I signed on with a young girl like you was that you were going to make me younger, not the other way around. So you'd best close your eyes and get your rest if you want to keep up with me."

Abigail held my hand against her cheek for a few minutes before she fell asleep. I drove almost two hundred miles with my left hand on the steering wheel and my right hand stroking Abby, until she woke up just west of Albany. We stopped at the Pattersonville rest area for gas and Roy Rogers chicken sandwiches. For the remainder of the drive home Abby was as chatty as she was cuddly.

"Matt, Tuesday and Thursday are my twelve-to-eight days at Mangrums, and Friday is dinner at Debbie and Fred's. Can we do Phil Green's either Monday or Wednesday?"

"Sure. You never have to twist my arm to go to Phil Green's."

"What nights does Jinks work? I want to talk with her for a couple of minutes."

"I think she works Tuesday through Friday, so we should go in on Wednesday. What do you want to talk with her about?"

"I want to see if she has a plan—a goal, you know?—for the rest of her life. Mangrums has a new entry-level store manager training program that might be just right for Jinks."

"That would be really great, beauty. Jinks is very bright, and I would not want to see her working a counter ten years from now. She needs to expand her horizon, and you might be the right person to get her to take the first step."

"I think I'll go shopping with Diane, Stephanie and Barbara this coming weekend. What would you like for Christmas, old guy?"

"All I want for Christmas for the next twenty or thirty years is you, Abby. And maybe another two or three grandchildren before I get too old to have them climb on me on the floor."

"Speaking of babies on the floor, I made an appointment to see my gynecologist, Dr. Robert Hansen, on January 3. It will be a fresh new year—with fresh new hopes and dreams for Abby—and I want my doctor to take a fresh look at my baby kit."

"Would you like me to go with you, beauty?"

"I would *love* that, Matt." She grinned. "I would like Dr. Hansen to see the secret weapon in my fight against infertility."

We pulled in to the garage at about seven o'clock, just as some heavy flurries were arriving from the west. I hadn't thought about it, but it was the first time that Abigail walked in to the house when Jock and Maggie were not there to greet her. She stopped in the doorway, listened for a few seconds and gave me a hard hug.

"I'm not used to the quiet, Matt. I don't like it without Maggie and Jock."

"I don't either, Abby. Believe it or not, I can probably count on the fingers of one hand the times since Sarah died that I've come home to this house with no dogs waiting for me. I just haven't done much traveling. With a new *babe* in my life, however, that is certain to change. Happy Tails is nice enough, but I don't want to bring Jock and Maggie there all the time. We'll have to talk with Matt and Claire and Tom and Diane about taking care of each other's dogs. In the meantime, Miss Abby, would you like a winter evening picnic in front of the fireplace? How about a peanut butter sandwich, or a cheese omelet, or a bowl of chicken noodle soup?"

Abigail laughed as she ran up the stairs. "I'm going to change into my winter evening picnic outfit, old guy. I'll split a peanut butter sandwich *and* a cheese omelet with you, and two beers, and two big glasses of milk with Oreos."

Abigail came down wrapped in my long, red-white-and-green-striped, cotton flannel bathrobe, which almost completely covered her cardinal-red wool socks—the same ones she wore the day we sat on her sofa.

"I feel like an Italian flag, old guy, but this sure is soft and comfortable."

"No flag ever looked as delicious, beauty. Come and sit. Your picnic and your fire are ready."

210

We quietly shared our sandwich and omelet, sipped our beer, and dunked a half-dozen Oreos in my gigantic World's Best Grandpa mug of milk. After we finished our soggy cookies and licked each other's fingers, Abigail moved from the blanket on the floor into my lap and rested her head on my chest. The firelight flickered around the living room and played on Abby's face. The wind beat against the front window, and I could see the snow piling up across the street.

"It sounds wild out there, Matt. What time will you pick up Maggie and Jock at the kennel?"

"Eight or eight-thirty."

"What if it snows enough to shut everything down?"

"Well, Jeep and I will get there, no matter what. How about you and Kitty?"

"Our system is to check the local closings either late the night before or early in the morning. If the city schools are closed, so is Kitty."

"It's a funny thing, beauty, but since we met, you have not only been my hot lover but also my cold snow girl. I have a feeling from looking out the window that tomorrow morning is going to be just like the first morning we woke up together: no Kitty's, no RIT, no office."

"Matt, stay right where you are while I take all of our picnic stuff in the kitchen. And then I have a surprise for you underneath this soft Italian flag."

When Abigail returned from the kitchen, she grinned impishly in the firelight and told me to "lie down on the blanket and close your eyes. Since the doggies aren't here to watch, I'm going to take off your clothes and play with you. *No* peeking until I say so."

Of course I did as I was told—who wouldn't?—and when I was permitted to peek, Abigail was sitting on my thighs, with the bathrobe open and over her shoulders, wearing nothing underneath and walking her fingers everywhere on my chest.

"This cozy bathrobe is big enough to cover both of us, old guy, so let's pretend we're still in our four-poster and hope it snows so hard that we can't see out the windows in the morning."

She was almost right. When we woke up at about six o'clock, the bay window in the living room, the corner windows in the dining room and the double window over the kitchen sink were all caked with snow. All the rooms downstairs and the yard outside were that shade of yellow you see in those old sepia photographs mounted on heavy card stock. Abigail wrapped herself in the robe, wrapped me in the blanket on the floor, and went in to the kitchen to turn on the television and check all the closings. I heard her yell *"Yes!"* when they said the city schools and all colleges would be closed. Then she curled back down with me in the robe and the blanket.

Two hours later it was *my* turn to get up, tuck Abby in, and call Happy Tails. Shelby answered and told me she had slept at the kennel overnight, just in case, and would be there all day. She also said the parking lot had not been plowed, so it might be tough getting in and out. I told her I would try to be there at nine o'clock and asked if I could bring her anything.

"How about a double-egg-and-cheese sandwich and a regular coffee with cream and sugar from Phil Green's?" she responded. "That would be really nice, Mister Flynn."

I nibbled on Abigail until she woke up; and then we threw on our blizzard clothes, brewed fresh coffee, hopped in the Jeep, and crawled through the deep streets to Phil Green's to pick up Shelby's breakfast on the way to Happy Tails.

We carried Jock and Maggie from the kennel to Jeep so they wouldn't get the back seat full of snow. As soon as we got home we took them for a walk around the circle so they could get their fill of snow. Then they settled in front of the fireplace on their pile of chewed-up fleece blankets for a morning of licking and napping, with an occasional tug of war mixed in. Abby and I took a shower and decided to go back to Phil Green's. The place was almost empty, although *their* parking lot had been plowed. Judith, the manager, looked frazzled when Abigail and I walked up to the counter.

"Hey, Matt, Abby . . . you're back! Would you like to work a shift? Most of my people are having trouble getting in this morning. I called Jinks—even though it's her day off—and she'll be here in a few minutes to pinch-hit. What can I get you?"

"Two red hots and two hot chocolates, Judith."

"And let's split some tater tots, Matt."

"Coming right up. There's Jinks pulling in the back right now."

"How about I help Jinks with some of the set-up, Judith?"

"That would be *great*, Abby. Then I can work the counter, and Todd can handle the kitchen until we get some other people in. Breakfast is on the house."

While Abigail and Jinks took care of everything from the soda and coffee machines to the mustard and ketchup and plastic silverware, I wiped off the Formica tabletops and padded bench seats in the booths and filled the napkin holders. Abby was grinning when we finally sat down to our hot dogs.

"Jinks is excited about the Mangrums idea but she has to talk with Judith before she commits to starting in January. Let me put my feet in your lap. I can get a lot of work done today on my school projects. What about you, old guy? Did you have anything scheduled?"

"Some work on a couple of 401(k) plans. But I think I'll take Mom grocery shopping—Dad does *not* like to drive in the snow any more. I'll go pick her up as soon as we get home, and then you and I will have the rest of this snow day for our paperwork, and the whole evening to relax."

The snow had stopped and the roads were mostly clear by the time I dropped Mom off with her groceries. Abby and I worked at our desks in between walking the dogs and making tea. The sepia glow persisted until almost sunset. I fixed Caesar salads for dinner, with some baby carrots chopped in for color. After dinner Abigail called her mother, and they decided to have dinner on Wednesday after Abby's classes, and go shopping for Christmas cards and wrapping paper. Abby and I settled on the sofa with Jock and Maggie to watch a movie, and laughed when we saw that the Hallmark Monday night movie was *The Christmas Card*. We had both seen it the previous December when it premiered during Hallmark's annual Countdown to Christmas.

John Newton is Cody Cullen, an Army sergeant serving in Afghanistan, who receives a random Christmas card sent by Faith Spelman—Alice Evans—from Nevada City, California, as a part of her church's holiday outreach to American troops overseas. In the midst of brutal fighting Faith's card brings Cody consolation and inspiration—and even good luck—and he resolves, when his commander orders him to go home on leave, to travel to Nevada City and find Faith. Of course it's a movie, so Faith doesn't learn until the end that it was her Christmas card that brought the stranger Cody to Nevada City.

"Would you have waited that long to tell Faith, Matt?"

"No. And Cody started to pull the card out of his pocket and show it to Faith when he was first invited to stay at her house.

Then they were interrupted, and he put the card back in his pocket. I would have taken her hand right there in the bedroom, not let her walk out, showed her the card and said, 'Faith, I'm here because of you, because of this Christmas card you sent. I've come halfway around the world to meet you and thank you. And now that I'm here, that's not enough. Now I want to love you and be with you forever.' What do you think Faith would have said?"

Abigail put both her arms around my neck. She had tears in her eyes.

"She would have melted into a puddle of tears, just like I'm doing right now, but it would have been a much shorter movie. We can probably watch this movie three or four more times between now and Christmas, and I'll probably cry just as much every time. Do you have to go anywhere in the morning?"

"No. I only have a lunch meeting with an older couple who want to get a life insurance policy for their newest grandson."

"That's a *wonderful* thing for grandparents to do! I expect you've done the same thing for Emily and Matthew, right?"

"Right—and Matt and Danny when they were little, too."

"I'll leave for Kitty's at six-thirty unless we get a lot more snow, but I'll be back shortly after nine. Let's have Maggie and Jock in bed with us tonight, okay? I missed them the last few days."

"Probably not as much as they missed *you*, beauty. It will be really snug after having the whole four-poster to ourselves over the weekend."

"I *live* for snug, Matt. I dream of snug all day long."

Abigail and I made love on my side of the bed while the dogs camped on her side. They mostly left us alone, but Maggie roused herself a couple of times to poke us with her cold nose and lick any arms and legs she could find. Jock was content to protect his preferred sleeping place near Abigail's pillow. The last thing I remember before falling asleep was trying to tell Abby's breathing from Jock and Maggie's.

I didn't wake up when Abby left in the morning. I didn't even hear her open the garage door. The dogs woke me at about eight o'clock when they barked at a siren on Atlantic Avenue. We had our breakfast and walked around the circle, and then waited for "Mommy" to come back. When Abigail got home at nine-thirty, she took my hand in the kitchen, pulled me up the stairs and in to the bedroom, and closed the door.

214

"How was the *office,* dear?" I laughed.

"Shut up, Matt! I want you right *now,* before I have to leave for nine hours at Mangrums. Nine hours is too long for a fragile girl like me," she laughed.

"You don't seem all that fragile, dear," I laughed again, as Abigail threw me on the bed and took off my jeans and sweatshirt.

19

And that's how our Tuesday mornings went in December, and our Mondays, Wednesdays and Thursdays, too, except that I occasionally went with Abigail to Kitty's, and sat at a corner table with the morning paper or Shelby Foote's *The Civil War*, and marveled at the strawberry blond beauty behind the counter, the girl in the black-and-white uniform who had become the center of my life. I stopped scheduling morning meetings or appointments for any days other than Fridays, when Abby had to be at Mangrums at eight o'clock.

On Tuesdays and Thursdays I packed dinner for Abigail in her Tinker Bell lunch box. Most of the time, it was peanut butter and butter sandwiches on whole wheat, a McIntosh apple, occasionally hard-boiled eggs, and almost always Oreos for dessert; with her Tinker Bell thermos filled with chocolate milk. On Tuesday and Thursday nights when she got home, Abigail and I would play with Jock and Maggie, go through the mail together, watch a movie on the sofa in the TV room for as long as we could stay awake, and get in bed by eleven.

Rochester, New York, is dominated by darkness from late October through early March, and the earlier it gets dark and the longer each night becomes, the greater is the urge to get in bed and start over in the morning light—especially when you can get in bed with a woman you love. For Abigail and me *every* hour we had together was our favorite time: the hours when we caught up on our days away from each other; the dark hours when we lit candles and went to bed early; the hours in those winter nights curled together under our quilt; the light hours of every brand-new morning; our play hours with Jock and Maggie; and even the "paper" hours working at our two Uncle Vinny desks in the adjacent front bedrooms of the house. Both of us took frequent breaks to bring each other kisses and coffee or tea. And our offices each had beds, so sometimes we stretched out our breaks.

On Friday night, Abigail and I went to Debbie and Fred's for dinner. Their son Billy, who turned six in August, showed us his Lego collection and giggled about his girlfriend in first grade.

Debbie told us that her brother Barry, his wife Eileen and their daughter Jean would be coming in from Pennsylvania for Christmas and would probably stay at her house, but her mom and dad were not coming up this year from North Carolina. They had all been invited to Uncle Tom and Aunt Diane's for Christmas. She had talked with Stephanie and Barbara, and she was going to meet all the girls at the Pittsford Town Mall at noon the next day for Christmas shopping. It was clear by the end of dinner that Abby now had one more sister.

On the way home, she told me that she had picked out her next drawing to show me tomorrow night after dinner.

"Will you give me a hint, beauty?"

"Only that it's a famous person, old guy."

While Abigail and the girls were shopping on Saturday, Jock and Maggie and I dusted off all the Christmas decorations in the basement and plugged in all the strings of indoor and outdoor lights and replaced the burned-out bulbs. The usual plan was to buy a tree—a Douglas fir or Fraser fir—the week before Christmas, to set it up in the front window of the living room and allow the branches to fall into place, and hold the decorating until both of my sons were in town. That plan went back to their college days, but it still worked. This year we would all get together and decorate the tree and put up the lights when Danny and Emma came in on the twenty-first.

Abigail called me from the mall at about five o'clock, said she was walking to her car, and she felt like pasta for dinner. Could we go to Palermo's? I told her I would make reservations for six.

Over our baked ziti, Chianti, Caesar salad and garlic bread sticks, Abby enthused about her busy day with the girls.

"I got presents for everybody in *my* family—except for Betsy—and some good ideas for you and your mom and dad. Debbie and I were shopping together most of the time, and she told me what you like and don't like, especially colors and styles. She also told me a whole bunch of stories about you since she was a little girl. My favorite is the one about your trip with both of your brothers and all your wives and children to Toronto, when you were clobbered at an outdoor concert on the lake by high-flying geese. Debbie said they ruined a hat *and* a sweater."

"Woody Herman and his Thundering Herd were performing at Ontario Place right on the lake. They were playing one of my favorites, 'Fanfare for the Common Man,' when the gaggle of geese unloaded. We all stayed at the Sheraton Centre, which had an indoor/outdoor pool. The kids would swim under the glass hotel wall inside and outside. None of us had ever seen that before."

"Debbie said that from the way I was talking—and shopping—it was her guess that you and I were serious, and she couldn't wait to talk with Grandma and Grandpa about 'Uncle Matt's new sweetheart.' We all had so much fun we decided to do it again next Saturday and ask Claire to join us."

"I swear, beauty, by the time we get to January *you'll* be more a part of the Flynn family than *I* am. Are we going to have a double Christmas just like Thanksgiving?"

"Probably. I haven't talked to Mom about it. She probably still hopes you'll go away."

After we got home and walked Jock and Maggie, Abby poured two glasses of Montepulciano in the kitchen and brought down her drawing. It was eleven inches by seventeen, with side-by-side images of George W. Bush at Yankee Stadium on October 30, 2001. The drawing on the left showed the president on the pitcher's mound in his *FDNY* windbreaker which covered his bulletproof vest, with his back to center field looking up into the roaring crowd of more than 57,000. His right hand was raised high over his head in a thumbs-up salute as he held a baseball in his left hand.

The drawing on the right showed the president following through on his pitch thrown from the white pitching rubber, with the ball in flight in a low arc halfway to Yankee backup catcher Todd Greene crouched at home plate. It would be a strike, and the wildly patriotic crowd thundered and shook Yankee Stadium in a way it had *never* seen—and Yankee Stadium had seen just about everything. Those who were present—fans, players, coaches, police, firefighters, Secret Service, television announcers—said they had never experienced anything like it . . . any *time*, any*where*. The energy, excitement, anger and resolve were overwhelming.

"Abby, this is *magnificent*! It's almost as if you were there!"

"I wish I *had* been. I drew it from the newspaper photographs and a You Tube video."

"Did you know that President Bush was wearing a bulletproof vest under his *FDNY* jacket, and one of the umpires in the background was really a Secret Service agent?"

"No, I didn't know that. It's amazing the president could throw a strike wearing one of those big heavy things. I tried one on once, and I could hardly *walk* let alone throw."

"And when the president was practicing under the stands in the Yankees locker area, Derek Jeter came in and told him that he had better throw from the mound and not bounce his pitch or the crowd would boo. The president said that the pressure was enormous, and he never felt anything like what he felt when he walked out of the dugout to the mound."

Abigail squeezed my hands at the butcher block table and whispered, "I was in my American Novel class—it was my senior year at Newton—when we heard the news and were instructed to stay on campus and go to the library and wait for more information. Where were you, Matt?"

"I was at a client's house. When I walked in the door at nine o'clock, Mack had the television on and told me that a plane had just crashed into one of the World Trade Center towers. Mack and his wife and I sat and watched the TV coverage until the second plane hit the second tower, and then I hurried home to call Matt and Danny, who were both away at school. Matt was in graduate school at SUNY Albany, and Danny was an undergrad at Fordham. The phone rang non-stop for the rest of the morning and afternoon. I was home by myself for most of the day, so Lucy and Jock got a lot of hugs.

"Abby, beauty, your drawing is *perfect*. We're going to have to frame your drawings and hang them everywhere in the house in place of most of the junky prints I've collected over the years. You captured the courage and determination in George W. Bush's face and stance on the mound, and the fierce anger and defiance in the cheering crowd behind home plate. And black and white is better than color for that moment in time. Speaking of time, what's on our calendar for next week? You are done with your extra hours on Tuesdays and Thursdays at Mangrums, right?"

"Right. We have dinner with Theresa's family on Monday. Tuesday and Wednesday are regular days, except that since I found *you* there *are* no regular days. On Thursday morning I'm going to your mom's to make sauce and meatballs. On Saturday all of us 'sisters' are going shopping again. And Friday night is our Mangrums office party at The Cedarwood. You're coming *with* me, right, old guy? I have been *dying* to show you off to all the girls I work with."

"I wouldn't miss it for the world, beauty. That's one *hell* of a week, but that's the way it usually is at Christmas. *Our* office party is the following Monday, the seventeenth." I laughed and counted on my fingers. "That will be a whole *five* weeks since I met you, Abby."

"I wish it was five *years*, Matt. I'm going upstairs to light some candles. Why don't you turn off the lights and bring the wine. Come on, baby dogs, it's time to take Daddy to bed."

After we made love twice, we stretched in the bed with Jock and Maggie and sipped our wine. Abigail played with the hair down the back of my neck and around my ears and whispered, "Old guy, sometimes during the day my mind just stops—calls a time out—and I think, *I can't possibly be this happy—nobody can. Something bad will happen to me, and it will all go away—Matt will go away.* Do you ever think like that?"

I took Abigail's face in both of my hands and kissed her over and over, all around her lips, breathing her in with every kiss.

"No, Abby, I don't—not with you. But I've been there and experienced that, so I know what you are feeling. With you, when my mind calls a time out and recollects, I say to myself, 'You don't *have* Abby any more than you have the wind or the lilies of the valley. Nobody *deserves* any*body* or any*thing*. What you *do* have is a gift from God: the ability to love. So love this beautiful girl with all of your mind and senses, and thank God every day for Abigail and *all* of His gifts."

"So you'll still be here in the morning then?" she murmured as she lay down and pulled me close to her under the popcorn clouds.

On Sunday morning after Mass, Abigail said, "Matt, let's go somewhere we've never been for breakfast. Let's take a Sunday drive in the country. How long can we leave Maggie and Jock before they'll get mad at us?"

"It's ten o'clock; we took them for a long walk. As long as we're back by four they'll be okay. They won't *like* it but they'll forgive us. How about breakfast at the Bob Evans near Buffalo, and then we can go up to Niagara Falls for an hour or two? It's supposed to be sunny all afternoon. We won't have time to go across the river, but we can walk the American side."

"That's a *great* idea, old guy. I haven't been to Niagara Falls since I was at Fatima. And I've *never* been there with a boyfriend, and never in the winter."

"Well, as a summer boy I like it better when you can get all wet and wear those yellow slickers and do the Cave of the Winds and the Maid of the Mist, but it is beautiful in the winter too."

We had sunshine and dry roads all morning, and a hearty breakfast at Bob Evans. Their biscuits are my favorites. Niagara Falls was Niagara Falls—a wonder. The sun played on the mountains of ice that obscured most of the river and even the waterfalls themselves. And the mist coated all of the walkways and railings with clear ice, which was challenging for the few hardy visitors. Abigail and I walked *so* slowly and snugly together that we might have been a single lumbering beast. We both wore long johns under our jeans, sweaters under our bench warmers, and knit hats under our hoods. When we stopped to kiss—which was often—we had to really squeeze to reach our arms around each other and bring our faces together. But huddling bundled against the cold can be just as sensual as lounging skin-on-skin in the sunshine on a beach.

Jock and Maggie were practically delirious with happiness to see us when we got home, and we all enjoyed a cozy evening in front of the fireplace cuddling, scratching, nibbling, sipping, napping and dreaming about the ice on our faces and under our feet.

I decided to go with Abigail to Kitty's in the morning, so we were all up at six o'clock. It was a dark walk with Jock and Maggie around the circle. Kitty's was busier than I had ever seen it. Abby scarcely had a second to give me a sideways smile or a wink, let alone take a break. I read Foote's account of the Battle of Kernstown, which was not a fine hour for the legendary Stonewall Jackson. Mostly through his own fault, Jackson's troops were soundly defeated, but he chose to blame Brigadier General Richard Garnett—commander of the "Stonewall" Brigade—a false judgment that would haunt Garnett until his death in Pickett's Charge at Gettysburg fifteen months later.

In Section A of the morning newspaper, the *Democrat and Chronicle*, were stories about the ebb in roadside bombs in Iraq as a result of George W. Bush's Surge; the sadly and grimly routine terrorist attacks by the Taliban in Afghanistan and by al-Qaeda throughout the Middle East; and the early winter ice storms and blizzards from Montana to Minnesota. The banner headline on page one, though, was football star Michael Vick's sentencing to twenty-three months in prison for his part in a dog-fighting ring.

Dinner at Theresa's was at six. Abigail and I brought a bottle of Ruffino Chianti and a raspberry cheesecake from Lucia's. Theresa was as good a cook as Mom. Her homemade sausage ravioli were the best I ever tasted, and her meatballs and sauce were second only to Mom's. Abby lingered over every mouthful—firsts, seconds, thirds—and then started on her spoonfuls of sauce from the boat. My cousins loved *every*thing Abby said and did from the moment we walked in the door. Not only did they accept her as my sweetheart but they also embraced her—literally— as a member of the family. And for the next two hours, they regaled Abby with tales of the Fiorino family that went all the way back to Grandpa Fiorino arriving at Ellis Island with his three sisters in 1901.

When we settled into bed that night, Abigail said, "It's so easy to see why you're such a nice old guy. What a *family*! Makes me wish I had an Italian boyfriend a *long* time ago, but then I probably would have fallen in love with him and never met you."

"I never knew Grandma Fiorino at all because she died two months before I was born. And all I remember about Grandpa is that he had white hair and a handlebar mustache. He sat in a straight-back chair in the living room in the old family house where Aunt Connie and Uncle Vinny lived. He smiled a lot and patted my brothers and me on our heads when we ran around the house, and he did not speak a *word* of English. 'Matteo, Alano, Tomasso' he called us. He died from a stroke when I was nine, and I don't have a single picture of me with him. I wish you could have met some of my aunts and uncles, though, especially my favorites, Aunt Connie and Uncle Vinny. They were like a second mother and father to me and Alan and Tommy. Theresa's father, Mom's oldest brother, Uncle Johnny, was also great to us when we were kids. He had a cottage . . . "

Abigail touched two fingers to my lips. "*Shh* . . . enough talking for tonight, old guy. Wrap your body around me and kiss me until I fall asleep. All your cousins . . . so many family stories. They all make me want to have a little more Italian in me."

The doggies and I slept in the next morning when Abigail left for Kitty's, but we had breakfast waiting when she returned at ten o'clock. After breakfast we got out our Christmas cards and our lists, and set up shop at our desks. Abigail had to leave at one for Mangrums, but I stayed with my cards all afternoon. Jock and Maggie cocked their heads attentively as I verbalized my special messages to my best friends and cousins who did not yet know about Abigail. I wrote this to my best B.C. law school buddy, Jerry Brongo, the legal director of the Michigan State Teachers Retirement System, who lives in Bay City, Michigan:

How the hell are you? How are Cheryl and your two girls? I hope the public school teachers are not picking on you as much as they did last year.

Guess what? Your old fart of a roommate has found himself a girlfriend. I hope: a) that she still wants my old body next summer, and b) that we can get to Michigan so you can meet her.

She is Abigail Elizabeth McKay, a graduate student who will get her MBA next May from RIT. I have known her for all of four weeks. I met her at a downtown coffee shop where she works the counter two mornings a week. I know that you of all people will appreciate the fact that she is young enough to be my daughter.

Much to my amazement, she loves me from head to toe, and she has restored the fire in my bones that I thought died with Sarah. Abigail is not only gorgeous but hotter than any woman I've ever been close enough to touch. I'll send you some pictures on the computer.

I wish you and your girls a wonderful Christmas and a healthy New Year!

It became sort of a template for the rest of my cards. I called Abigail at the office to run it by her for fun. "Pretty girl, I thought I'd read you my 'model' 2007 Christmas card greeting that I'm going to send to all of my good friends who don't know that you exist."

When I finished I could almost see the delight in her face as she laughed.

"That's very good, Matt—not surprising for an old poet—and I appreciate all the compliments; but mine is better. Wait'll you hear what I'm telling my old girlfriends and classmates about you. I'll read it to you later. Thanks for breaking up my monotonous afternoon and making me think about sex. I love you and I want your 'old body' right now, but next summer might be a stretch."

After Abigail got home that night and we settled on the sofa with our Montepulciano to watch *Undercover Christmas*, with Jami Gertz, she tucked her feet under her legs between me and the dogs and read me her Christmas message:

I finally met him: the guy we used to daydream about in study hall at Fatima (or in the library at Newton); the guy we used to compare in our minds to the hunky stars—Brad Pitt, Tom Cruise, Andy Garcia, Denzel, Josh Lucas, Patrick Dempsey, Jude Law—except my guy is Harrison Ford and Sean Connery, with Paul Newman's blue eyes.

He walked in to the coffee shop where I work two mornings a week to help pay my school bills, bought a decaf and struck up a conversation, looked in to my eyes (most customers don't make eye contact), said he had to go to his office but wanted to keep talking, and actually came back at seven the next morning—in a blizzard—to keep talking.

Three or four hours later I asked him to kiss me and, when he did, it was just like in the movies: I melted in his arms. I couldn't stand up, he had to hold me up, I couldn't think. I don't know how many minutes it was, but the instant my mind came back, I knew I loved him. I moved into his house the next day.

Matt, his name is Matt. His wife died ten years ago. He's sixty-one, and I call him "old guy." He comes with two wonderful sons who are both married, two beautiful grandchildren, and two loveable Scottie dogs who are now my best friends.

We make love four or eight times a day, and each time is better than the time before. I realize now that I hardly knew a thing about love or sex before I met Matt.

I hope you will get to meet him in 2008. I hope my dream never ends. Until then, I wish you and your family your best Christmas ever and, if possible, the kind of happiness in the New Year that I'm feeling right now.

"That's beautiful, Abby. I hardly know what to say, except I also hope—and pray—that *our* dream never ends. And we have only made love *two* times today, so . . . "

We lay down on the sofa, squeezing Jock and Maggie off their end, and made love two times, the first time with Abby on the outside, and the second time with Abby on the inside. Then we drifted off to sleep and didn't wake up until the movie was over and the *Lucy* reruns came on. It was after midnight when we tucked the doggies in, blew the candles out, rolled *Pooh* and *Piglet* into a cocoon and touched each other to sleep again.

It was almost eight-thirty when the doggies nudged us into morning. Abigail and I both laughed when we realized that we were still wrapped tightly in the cocoon.

"Old guy, I can't believe that I sleep with you holding me the same way I slept holding my giant, sky blue teddy bear when I was five years old. So comfortable, so *safe*. Mom and Dad could never wake me in the morning until they took Teddy away. How do you *do* that to me?"

"It must be your pixie dust, Tinker Bell. It makes all of our cares fly away. Before your first night here with me, I hadn't slept through the night since Sarah died—and not even *that* many times *with* Sarah. Usually we would roll apart to our sides of the bed. I think we slept better that way. I can't believe how much your touch soothes my body and my mind. I used to think about *everything* when I got in bed. Now I have *no* thoughts; I only feel you next to me. I always made my skeptical face when I heard the 'one flesh' line at weddings, but now I know what it means. This is the way it's supposed to be."

When Abigail left for school I told her that I had another poem to read to her that night. "It's a *little* poem, beauty, kind of a silly summer boy poem, but it's *me*."

"Will you take me to Phil Green's when I get home and read it to me there?" She grinned as she kissed me goodbye. "If it's a summer poem I might need a hot dog."

Jinks was working behind the counter when we got to Phil Green's at five-thirty.

"Hey, Abby, Matt, good to see you guys! What can I get you?"

"Two red hots with extra mustard and two hot chocolates. Abby, how about curly fries?"

"Okay, a *large* curly fries, Jinks."

"Judith said okay, Abby. She said the Mangrums program would be a great opportunity for me; and I could still work part-time here."

"Great! After Christmas we'll get together on one of your days off and do the application."

We sat in our usual corner booth with a west window. It was already completely dark. Abby tucked her left hand between my legs and ate her hot dog and almost all of the fries one-handed.

225

"Okay, old guy, I'm ready. How about getting me some more hot chocolate and reading me your 'little' poem?"

"Yes, ma'am, at your service, but only because you're a *babe*."

"Don't be a wise guy; next time *I'll* sit on the outside and be *your* servant."

"This poem is really too short to have a title, but I wrote it on an unusually balmy day in May so I called it 'summer days in may.'

ignore all that "truth"
you hear on the news
life is more simple
from baby to grandpa
a day without shoes
is the joy of our youth

"Shakespeare would be jealous, right?"

"From what I've read of Shakespeare, Matt, especially from his sonnets, I think he would be nodding his head in agreement. That's one poem I can memorize for our first day at the beach."

Abigail lay on her back on the bench seat, nestled her head in my lap and curled her feet against the inside wall of the booth.

"Will you play with my hair, Matt? I feel like a princess when you play with my hair. You can have the rest of my hot chocolate. If I have an orgasm I'll try to be quiet so nobody knows. *Mmm*, that's *so* nice! I'm going to your mom's tomorrow morning at nine. She's going to cook me breakfast, and then we're going to make sauce and meatballs from scratch. Depending on how long it takes, I might go right from your mom's to Mangrums."

"Do you want me to go with you, beauty?"

"Old guy, you know I would always like to have you close enough to me so that I can touch you whenever I want to, but your mom specifically said '*no* Matt.' She also said she's 'kicking out *old* Matt at eight-thirty. He can go have breakfast and walk around the mall with his cronies. You and me, Abby, we're gonna talk about these Matt Flynns. I can see in your eyes how much you love my son, and I look at his face and I know that he will be yours forever, so we have to talk.' *Mmm . . .* around my ears some more, Matt. I haven't picked out another drawing to show you. Can we wait until next week?"

"Sure, Abby. I've been looking at investment performance charts and Kodak SIP paperwork all afternoon. I don't want to look at any more paper tonight. I just want to look at *you* until it's time for bed. And then I might want to sleep with my head on your belly instead of my pillow."

"*Mmm* . . . that's if you can ever get me out of this booth. Is anybody looking at us?"

"Yeah, they are. One guy about my age has walked by three or four times while pretending to be going for coffee refills. And Jinks has smiled and waved a couple of times from the counter. My big problem is that I am *aching* to kiss you, but it's completely impossible at this angle—even if I tried to kiss you upside down."

"Let me have a five-minute nap, old guy, and then you can take me home and put me to bed and kiss me all night until morning—right side up. I *love* you . . . in case I haven't told you in the last hour or so."

Five minutes stretched into thirty. Abigail murmured a little, and her fingers moved a little as I kept playing with her hair. It brought back those peaceful minutes—sometimes *hours*—when Danny and Matt were infants and toddlers and fell asleep on my chest or stomach. I remember thinking that those serene moments were as close to heaven as any man could have on earth. Much to my delight it was happening again with Emily and little Matt. And now Abby.

My right leg—the pillow—fell asleep. I caught Jinks' eye at the counter and gestured for her to come over. When she got close, I touched my finger to my lips in the *"shh"* sign.

"What a pretty picture!" Jinks whispered. "Phil Green would like to put this on the wall with the local sports teams and Boy Scout troops. *I* could use a lap, Matt. Do you have a brother— maybe a little younger?"

"I have *two* brothers a little younger, Jinks, but both of their laps are taken. If Abigail comes to her senses, though, and dumps me, you can try mine."

"Are you *kidding*, Matt? I've never seen *anybody* as much in love as Abby. What do you need? Can I get you something?"

"Yes, please. Looks like I might be a pillow for a while, so would you be extra nice and get me a refill of hot chocolate?"

"Sure. Let me throw away those cups. I'll get you fresh ones."

A few minutes after Jinks brought the hot chocolate, Abigail stirred, reached up and took my hand from her hair to her lips and kissed my fingers.

"*Mmm* . . . Matt, I dreamed that we were in a little boat on that lake in your poem—with Maggie and Jock hanging their heads over the side—and the sun was shining on my face while you tickled my ears. Are my five minutes up?"

"You can have as many minutes as you want, love; but it *is* almost eight-thirty. We've been here for three hours. Jinks just left for the night."

"*Mmm* . . . you sweetie, you let me lie here and dream."

"Well, beauty, it's heaven on earth to touch you and watch you while you sleep."

"Let's go home, old guy. I want more. And I want my baby dogs, too. Remember our first night: *A giant quilt, and candlelight, and thou*? That's what I want right now."

After we walked Jock and Maggie and pulled our giant quilt over us in bed, Abigail and I made love two times—the first time furiously and the second time softly. Then she poked her finger into my navel several times as if she were counting.

"You know, old guy, I've been keeping track, and that was the 129th time we've made love. The reason I mention it now is that I weighed 129 when I stepped on the scale this morning."

"Isn't that a little chubby for someone who's only five-two?" I teased.

"*Hey*, wise guy," she replied as she poked into my navel harder, "I'm five-*six* and I thought you *liked* my body."

"Abby, I *love* your body; you're *perfect*—but my count is at 131."

"Well, maybe I was sleeping for the other two times. Or was that *your* weight this morning?"

"Aren't you *nice*, miss; but guess again."

"Five-eight, 161, summer boy."

"Good *guess*, beauty! Five-nine, 167; but I promise to *get* to 161 by next summer."

"Well, won't *you* be the *stud* then, Matthew Flynn! I'll be afraid to take you out in public."

"Abby, wherever we go *you* will always be the one who makes people stare and dogs howl."

"*Mmm* . . . enough, sweet boy. Your mom will be waiting at nine, so kiss me to sleep, please. My pillow is waiting for you."

20

After Abigail left for Mom's in the morning I went back to my Christmas cards. She called me when she got to Mangrums.

"Your mom and I talked and cooked for almost *four* hours! She not only taught me her secret recipes for meatballs and sauce, but she explained at length—sometimes in Italian—her recipes for living with Matt Flynns, and not just your dad, but *you* too. 'La giusta quantita di fune'—I liked that one the best; I wrote it down: 'A little rope, but not too much,' your mom said."

"Tell me some more, Abby."

"No *way*, old guy; secrets are secrets. 'Ragazza segreti,' your mom said. It's like a sisterhood: your mom said she had the same conversation with Sarah twenty-five years ago, and later with Lisa and Diane. We agreed to have another girls' morning around Christmas with Claire and Emma and share your mom's survival tips." Abigail laughed.

"Survival? *Whoa*! Can't you tell me just *one*, beauty?"

"Okay, just one, Matt. 'Non credo che le facce,' your mom said. 'Don't be fooled by the faces,' Abby. My Matthew is good with the faces.' I'm trying to remember *just* the way your mom said it. 'You gotta look around the corners of his faces, Abby, to find his thoughts. He can throw on a face as fast as snapping his fingers—from happy to sad to confused to mad—so don't let him fool you. My Matt always knows the score. Just because he has a frown or a laugh on his face doesn't mean that he's sad or happy *inside*. But I see how you look at him, and I think you're on to him already. I think you know his eyes after a *month* better even than I do after *sixty* years.' Don't you *dare* tell your mom I told you anything, Matt."

"*Ouch*," I said, teasing and putting on my "frown" face. "Good thing you didn't know that the first day at Kitty's."

"Maybe I just guessed right, Matt. Like I'm guessing you have your 'frown' face on now."

"Ouch, again. I think my goose is cooked."

"When I get home tonight, let's watch the end of *Undercover Christmas* that we slept through Tuesday night—and then I'll take care of your goose. And your mom invited us to come over for dinner Saturday night so you can taste *my* sauce and meatballs. She's going to ask Tom and Diane, too. Gotta go— my boss is giving me his *own* frown face."

"I'll have to talk with him about that tomorrow night at the party."

Abigail was off to Mangrums at seven-thirty the next morning, and I met Sam and Jennie Morris at Joe's for breakfast because they would be leaving on Saturday for their winter home in Sarasota, Florida. Sam was a very successful plumbing contractor, and not only a good client but also a good friend. He was one of only a handful of clients to ever personally hand me a seven-figure check to invest—and he did it *twice*.

Abigail called in the middle of the afternoon to let me know that the party would be casual— boss's orders. No jackets and ties; only sweaters and slacks. When she came home, however, she stepped into a hot, red satin cocktail dress with matching high heels, then bundled her strawberry blond flip into a Santa Claus hat.

"*Hoo-ah*, Mrs. Santa! You're going to have the guys from your office banging into each other tonight at the Cedarwood while they're checking you out from the corners of their eyes."

"My plan exactly, old guy. But I'm more interested in watching—out of the corners of *my* eyes—the girls checking *you* out."

And that's precisely the way the party went. Abigail clearly had great fun introducing me around the room. Once the curious Mangrums employees got over the fact that I was the oldest person in the room—except for Wally Mangrum himself—the conversations drifted comfortably towards family, friends and football—specifically the Buffalo Bills, who were hoping to make the playoffs for the first time in nine years. Wally stepped up to me at the bar at one point and said, "Merry Christmas, Matt. You know, before Abby met you she was already the brightest of our interns, and the most beautiful, of course. Now she is not only the brightest and the prettiest but also the best *leader*. I have been wanting to thank you for weeks."

They had a good band, and though I'm not much of a dancer—either in ability or inclination— Abigail and I did a slow dance to "I'll Be Seeing You"—one of the *saddest* songs ever written— and a jitterbug to "In the Mood," Mom and Dad's favorite '40s song.

It was almost midnight, and we were pretty tired when we got home. The night was clear and cold, and we walked the dogs under a black sky filled with stars.

"Matt, do you have a favorite constellation?"

"Taurus, Abby, and Cassiopeia."

"Taurus is *my* sign, old guy."

"I know, beauty, and that makes it very special to me again."

"*Again?*"

"Missy Steger's birthday is May 11, so Taurus was also very special to me in my *former* life."

"When's the last time you spoke with her?"

"Spring of 1973 when she broke up with me. I stopped lamenting her when I married Sarah, but I never completely got over her."

"What about *now*, Matt?"

"*Now*, Abby? You make it better. You are *everything* to me. Sarah was, too. But Missy is still *'forever on my mind.'* That's from a Willie Nelson song, 'Forgiving You Is Easy, But Forgetting Seems to Take the Longest Time.' I don't still yearn for Missy, but I think about her on a lot of days. It's not like the lonely years before and after Sarah, though. Those were hard times; Missy was like a bad shadow over my shoulder. Now she's merely a memory that *you* blow away every day. *You* are my sun in the morning and my stars at night."

"Speaking of stars, old guy, you *know* you were the star of the show tonight."

"Are you *kidding*, Abby? Not only did every girl in the room want to *be* you in your red satin, but every guy in the room wanted to *touch* you in your red satin."

We had come all the way around the circle. Abigail crouched and said to Jock and Maggie, "We're all done with our walk, baby dogs. Let's go in. It's finally bedtime, and I want Daddy to make love to me in my red satin."

In the morning Abigail was up first. She went in the bathroom for a few minutes and came back with her hair brushed in waves over her shoulders, in her red satin dress and high heels.

"*Wow*, beauty!"

"Am I your *best* fantasy girl, Matt? I want to be your best fantasy girl *ever*."

"*Abby*," I gasped as I pulled her in to bed with one hand around her bare shoulders and one hand under her red dress,

231

"you are the best girl—fantasy *or* real—the best girl of my life."

The next time we woke up it was nine-thirty, and Jock and Maggie were scratching on the door, agitating for their breakfast.

"Old guy, I would like to put the red dress back on for you right now—I *love* the way you take it off—but I'm meeting all the girls at the mall at eleven."

"Well, miss, let's plan a red-dress day for some dark, cold day in January. I'm thinking that if we skip lunch I can take off your red dress eight or ten times between breakfast and dinner."

After Abigail left for the mall, I checked my e-mail. It was the fifteenth of December. I sent Matt and Danny an e-mail asking them if it was the *ides* of December, which was a long running joke between us—we all had taken four years of Latin in high school. Danny, my perfectionist, responded early in the afternoon that the *ides* of December was on the thirteenth.

Joe Steger sent me a note suggesting the Martin Luther King weekend for our January rendezvous in Pittsburgh. I told him I thought it was a good plan, and I would run it by Abigail. I sent the same response to Ann and Dave Connolly's invitation to a New Year's Eve party at their house. Both gave me pause. It had been ten years since I ran any plans by *any*body.

Abigail was home at three and she made me go down into the TV room while she sneaked her Christmas gifts upstairs to hide in the office. I told her about Joe and Dave as we walked Jock and Maggie, and she liked both ideas. She also mentioned that Mary Kay wanted us to have dinner with her and her new friend on the Friday after Christmas. After we fed the dogs, Abby and I curled under *Pooh* and *Piglet* for a nap before we went to Mom and Dad's.

Everybody raved about Abigail's sauce and meatballs at dinner. Tom—who was still clearly amused by the idea of Abigail and me in general—said that "Abby's sauce is as good as my wife's, and she's been practicing Mom's recipe for thirty years." Diane flicked his right cheek firmly with the middle finger of her left hand—her famous left-finger flick.

We talked about Christmas at Tom and Diane's. It looked as if everybody except Alan and Lisa would be there: Mom and Dad; Tom and Diane; Stephanie, Warren, Jeff and Julie; Abigail and I; Barbara, Chuck and Amy; Trent and Katy; Matt, Claire, little Matthew and Emily; Danny and Emma; Debbie, Fred and Billy; and Barry, Eileen and Jean. I counted them on my fingers.

"Wow, that's *twenty-seven* for dinner! Where are you going

to *put* everybody, Diane?"

"Well, if I put the seven little ones at a small table in the living room, I think we can stretch the dining room table to hold twenty grown-ups. Which reminds me, there will also be twenty-seven people for presents. Matt, did you do the Secret Santa assignments for our kids?"

"I did, Diane; I sent out fourteen *top-secret* e-mails last week."

"Great! Abby, did Matt tell you how our Secret Santas work?"

"*You* tell her, Diane."

"Every year all of us *old* Flynns buy presents for all of the little ones, our grandchildren, of course. But it has always been a family tradition for each of our seven children—Mom and Dad's grandchildren—to buy *one* present for one of their first cousins. Now, of course, with spouses and Trent's girlfriend Katy, seven have become fourteen. It has always been Matt's job, as the senior uncle, to choose the Secret Santas for everybody—secretly, of course. Tell Abby about your special rules, Matt. He likes to make everything more complicated."

I laughed. "Not complicated, Diane—better. None of the cousins can be the Secret Santa for either their own spouse or their own brother or sister. What time are we doing presents?"

"How about we do presents at one o'clock and dinner at four? I'll let Debbie know so she can tell Barry and Jean."

"Mom and Dad, Abby and I will pick you up at about twelve-thirty on Christmas. We will likely do midnight Mass at Holy Innocents in case anybody wants to join us. Danny and Emma probably will, but Matt and Claire and the kids plan on going to the afternoon family Mass on Christmas Eve at Saint Joseph's."

Mom and Dad said that they wanted to go with Tom and Diane's family to the afternoon Mass on Christmas Eve at Our Lady of the Rosary in Webster.

On the way home, Abigail rested her head on my shoulder, put her hands on top of my shift hand and mused, "Matt, we are *so* lucky that our families are full of good people. They're happy, healthy and smart; they have good jobs; the kids are beautiful. Everybody—except maybe my brother Jack—not only gets along but really *cares* about everybody else. What do you think Danny and Matt will say if we are able to add a baby to the Flynn family?"

"I think, beauty, that they are *so* sure by now that you and I

233

are going to get married that they won't be surprised by anything that happens next. I am already smiling inside at the possibility of having a baby son or daughter at the same time as a baby grandson or granddaughter."

When we curled under the popcorn clouds that night, Abigail clasped my hands together and asked, "Old guy, when you were a little boy, what prayer did you say when you went to bed?"

"The old classic: *Now I lay me down to sleep. I pray the Lord my soul to keep. If I should die before I wake, I pray the Lord my soul to take.* And then I 'God blessed' everybody: Mommy and Daddy, Alan and Tommy, Aunt Connie and Uncle Vinny, Grandma and Grandpa Flynn, Grandma and Grandpa Fiorino, and so on. How about you?"

"Grandma Mary taught me an old Irish prayer: *God and Mary and Saint Patrick, bless me through the night, guard me by Thy might, keep me in Thy sight, bring the morning bright, and guide me by Thy light to make each new day Thine. Amen.*

"I still say it in my mind when you're kissing me just before I fall asleep—which I would like you to start doing right now. After church tomorrow, I want to buy you breakfast and take you shopping for presents for the seven little ones. And my niece Betsy, too. You can help me with my whole list. *Mmm,* goodnight, love."

In the morning after Mass, Abigail and I went for breakfast to Paulette's Pantry on East Avenue on our way to the Pittsford Mall. We each had scrambled eggs with whole wheat toast, and we split a bowl of oatmeal with brown sugar.

"Matt, the girls helped me pick out some presents yesterday. We got a couple for you, an Irish wool hat for your dad, tan Italian leather gloves for your mom, dress shirts and ties for Danny and Matt, and cashmere knit hats for Emma and Claire. The girls told me that you and your brothers bought your mom and dad a new chair?"

"*We,* Abby—you're a part now—Tom and Diane, Alan and Lisa and you and I bought Mom and Dad a brown leather recliner for the *parlor.* We will put a picture of it in their Christmas card, and Matt and his pal Jason will bring it to their house on Christmas right after you and I pick up Mom and Dad to take them to Tom and Diane's. Matt and Jason will also haul away the *old* chair, which will *surely* make Dad grumble. He loves that chair, but it's disintegrating."

"And the new chair will be in its place when they get home—

what a nice surprise! So you don't buy presents for your nieces and nephews, or your brothers and sisters-in-law?"

"Right. We decided a lot of years ago—when our kids started getting married and having babies—that there were just *too* many presents. So now it's only Mom and Dad and the Secret Santas and the little ones. But even with that, wait'll you see how deep the wrapping paper will be in Tom and Diane's living room."

"Well, yesterday Diane, Stephanie, Barbara, Debbie and I decided that we are going to talk with the rest of the *big* girls— Lisa, Claire, Emma, Katy, Eileen and, *most of all*, your mom— about having Secret *Girl* Santas next year." Abigail laughed. "We think there's *always* room for more presents, old guy. Now give me a kiss that will make these shoppers turn their heads."

"What about *your* family, beauty? When will we see *them*?"

"I told Mom I wanted to spend Christmas afternoon with *your* family, and I persuaded her to have dinner at six o'clock, so that's when we'll go to Mom and Dad's. That actually makes all the pieces fall in place. Jack and Catherine can go to *her* parents' in the afternoon, and Patrick can be with Laurie's family. Nothing like having an internship in ergonomics, right?" she grinned.

"Family ergonomics, Abby—an intriguing concept. Who should *I* get presents for?"

"I think just Mom and Dad, and Betsy, but all the presents can be from *both* of us, including the ones I already got for my parents. We can do that today—Mom and Dad and the little ones."

"What would *you* like for Christmas, beauty?"

"I already *have* my Christmas present, Matt," Abigail said, with her hand in the back pocket of my jeans as we walked around the fountain in the center of the mall. "Let's go to The Great Toy Store first and get all the presents for the kids."

In The Great Toy Store I always like to walk up and down every single aisle until I see the toys that look *just* right for each of the little ones. I used to do that every year with Matt and Danny— *before* they made their lists for Santa Claus—so they would show me what they really, *really* liked, and know just what to put in their letters to Santa.

And that's what Abigail and I did.

When we got to the Lego aisle, Abby started checking the suggested ages on the boxes.

"Matt, Jeff told me at Thanksgiving that he wants Legos for Christmas. How old is he?"

"Jeffrey's nine, and Billy's six, and they both love Legos."

We picked out a gigantic police station for Jeffrey and an equally gigantic firehouse for Billy. Each came with lots of policemen or firemen, and vehicles of all sizes from a motorcycle to a hook-and-ladder truck.

In the Disney aisle, we bought a two-foot-tall Cinderella doll for Julie, who was seven, which came with Gus and all the other mice and animals, and both Cinderella's ball gown and the rags she wore. We also got an Alice in Wonderland tea set for Amy, who was six, which included miniature statues of Alice, the White Rabbit and the Mad Hatter; a Little Mermaid island for Betsy, who was also six, complete with Ariel, Prince Eric, Scuttle, Flounder and Sebastian; and a lovely princess set for Jean, who just turned four, containing Snow White, Sleeping Beauty, Belle, Cinderella, Rapunzel, Jasmine and Ariel. Abigail and I were pretty pleased with ourselves.

Then we came to the aisle full of giant vehicles—mostly plastic—but featuring those sturdy, bright yellow, metal Tonkas. Abigail crouched in front of the biggest ones and simply said, "Oh, wow! I wish I were a little boy!"

"Matthew is *crazy* for trucks, Abby. Should we get him the bulldozer or the dump truck?"

"Well, the bulldozer has more moving parts, but Matthew can *sit* on the dump truck and drive it all around the house, and the yard too—I say the dump truck."

Last but not least, Abigail found for Emily a sky-blue teddy bear bigger than *she* is..

"Matt, he's just like *my* blue bear, Fozzie, who is still in my closet at Mom and Dad's. Fozzie Bear was my favorite Muppet. I will get him before Christmas and bring him home. Home . . . *my, my,* aren't *I* the grown-up now, talking about getting something from Mom and Dad's and bringing it *home*? Did you have a favorite stuffed animal, old guy?"

"I still do. Soft brown Hug Me bears were popular in the eighties, and Sarah bought me one. His name is Hugh, and he sits up on a shelf in the office at home. But Fozzie Bear was also my favorite Muppet, and I used to have a Fozzie hand puppet and imitate his voice when Matt and Danny and I watched the weekly Muppets show."

At home, Abigail and I walked Jock and Maggie, got a fire

going in the living room and then decided to finish up our Christmas cards together at the dining room table. In between cards we nibbled on Abby's leftover pasta and meatballs in the kitchen and sipped Chianti.

"Beauty, I would like you to add a note to three of my cards: Jerry Brongo from B.C. Law, and Dave and Ann Connolly and Joe and Marge Steger. Jerry and his wife and two daughters live in Michigan, and I hope we'll be able to get there to visit them next summer. I told Dave and Ann that we'll be coming to their New Year's party. And Joe and I made reservations at the Hampton Inn in Green Tree, just south of Pittsburgh, for Saturday and Sunday, January 19 and 20."

"I can't wait to meet them. Anything special you want me to say in my notes, old guy?"

"Just be Abigail. No matter *what* you write, beauty . . . it will be special to Jerry and Dave and Joe. I don't want to know. Just lick 'em shut when you're done."

"Where are we going tomorrow night for your office party, Matt?"

"Gleason Gardens on East Avenue."

"Wow, that's a *very* nice place! Last year the RIT School of Business had its annual Graduate Symposium there. How dressy will it be?"

"Suit and tie for me; I'm thinking red satin dress for you."

"The same dress as for Mangrums? *Why?*"

"Well, two reasons, Abby. One, you are *so* beautiful and sexy in that dress that you could wear it for me any time, every time, day or night. Two, I would like to compare the stares of the boys and girls in *my* office with the boys and girls at Mangrums."

"Okay, handsome," she grinned, "but thanks to you I'll have to hang it in the bathroom when we take our shower tomorrow to steam out the wrinkles from yesterday morning in bed. What will your schedule be like Christmas week? There are no classes at RIT until January 7, and the interns don't have to be back at Mangrums until January 8."

"My last appointment or meeting is this Friday morning. Once Danny and Emma get in to town, I'm all yours, all Dad, all Grandpa until the Tuesday after New Year's, which is the 2008 kickoff meeting at my office."

"It should be such a *lovely* week, Matt. Will you come with me to Kitty's tomorrow?"

"Yep. I can catch up on my *Shelby Foote* and cheese Danish. And then, after you leave for RIT, I'm going to finish *my* Christmas shopping."

Abigail refilled my glass of Chianti and kissed the back of my neck.

"I picked out my next drawing to show you, old guy. I thought Wednesday night after dinner would be a good time. Nobody has ever seen this one."

"I'm a lucky boy, Abby—luckier every day with you."

"Matt, would you like me to wear my hair up or down tomorrow night?"

"You mesmerized the Mangrums crowd with your hair down over your shoulders. Let's try the Old Northeastern Life crowd with your hair up. And right now, love, I would like to take you up to bed and *play* with that pretty hair. How long do you usually let it grow before you cut it?"

"I would have gotten it cut before Thanksgiving, but then there was *you*, and I got the sense that you like it long."

"Abby, your hair is *so* beautiful, even on a dark winter night, and it takes my breath away in the morning light! The longer it is, the more I have to play with."

That night under the quilt, my hands were filled with Abigail's hair for hours. I recalled the lines from my Missy poem, but Abigail had replaced Missy: S*he had the prettiest hair I'd ever seen and the softest hair I'd ever touched.* Abby never said a word the whole time I played with her hair and made love. She simply squeezed and purred until we both fell asleep.

21

After we got back from Kitty's at nine-thirty the next morning, Abigail checked her red dress still hanging in the bathroom and pronounced it "wearable, but I'll have to get it to the cleaner's if you want me to wear it for Christmas or New Year's," and then she left early for RIT to get to the library before her first class.

I went to Harriman Jewelers in the mall to check out engagement rings. Abby hadn't said—or even hinted—a word about a ring, but it was time, especially if we were going to tell all the people in our little world in the next few weeks. I saw a princess cut I liked a lot and many other beautiful styles Abby might like, and decided to find some pretext—maybe a trip to Pet City to buy new toys for Jock and Maggie—to get her to the mall before Friday and take her by the hand to Harriman's.

The cocktail hour at the Gardens began at six o'clock, and Milt Cornelius, the Rochester agency manager, was greeting everybody at the entrance to the grand solarium.

"Abby, this is the boss, Milt Cornelius. Milt, I'd like you to meet Abigail McKay."

"Abigail, it's my pleasure. Merry Christmas! Seeing you explains a lot of things. I've been asking Matt for weeks what's had him so charged up about everything; and the only answer he has given me is a Mona Lisa face."

"Matt is very good at faces, Mr. Cornelius."

"Milt, please call me Milt. Shall we go in and join the crowd at the bar?"

Abigail, as usual, was perfectly at home in a crowd of perfect strangers. She mingled without me just as well as we mingled together, even with the eyes of every person in the solarium on her when they thought she wasn't looking. We sat at a table with three other longtime agents and their wives, and Abby fielded questions with grace and good humor while I volunteered to be the "shuttle" person for our regular rounds of drinks from the bar.

On my second "round" trip, Milt put his hand on my shoulder and said, "How'd you do it, Matt? Abigail would be an unbelievable catch for any guy of any age, so how did a grizzled veteran like yourself pull it off?"

"No clue, Milt. I had no idea I was such a charming guy." I grinned.

Glen Montini—the legendary Rochester bandleader who played at my Dominic Savio senior ball in 1964—and his band were playing, and the dance floor was crowded most of the time. I asked Abby to let me know if she wanted to dance to any favorite songs.

"Pick out one or two you like a lot, old guy; that will be enough for me."

We danced to Elvis' "I Can't Help Falling in Love With You." So did everybody else, and the floor was so full that we didn't have to move much, which was fine with me.

"Wise men say only fools rush in," I whispered to Abby.

"Take my hand, take my whole life, too," she whispered back.

"It reminds me of one of my favorite passages from the Bible, beauty: your old men shall dream dreams, and your young men shall see visions. You are my vision, Abby."

"And you are my dream, Matt."

We kissed through the rest of the song and received some scattered applause from the crowd.

After we settled under Pooh and Piglet shortly after midnight, with Jock and Maggie curled on Abigail's side of the bed, our conversation hopscotched the busyness of December.

"So tell me, old guy, how did the glances tonight compare with my party?"

"They were more straight on, beauty; your crowd was more sideways—maybe an age thing."

"Matt, you know how you say 'you can't get ten pounds in a five-pound bag?' That's how I feel about this week. With my two late evenings at Mangrums, and Emma and Danny coming in to town Friday afternoon, I wanted to save Wednesday night just for you to show you my most special drawing. But Mom called on my cell between classes today and asked me to come over after school Wednesday to help her and Dad decorate the tree. She said she would also ask Pat and Laurie, and Catherine, Jack and Betsy. You're invited too. She said she's going to fix

241

a pot roast—which I know you will love—but I hate to give up my 'just-with-Matt' night."

"It's okay, pretty girl. This time of year is never easy, even if you're crazy in love." I smiled and kissed Abby on her nose. "We can do your drawing—unrushed—after Christmas."

"Will you come with me to Mom and Dad's?"

"Sure I will. First of all, I'm excellent at decorating Christmas trees; and second of all, I think Mom's pot roast—which she calls chuck roast—is the best I've ever had, so I'll enjoy comparing it with your mom's.

"And I have another pound to throw in the five-pound bag. How about going with me to Pet City at the mall either tomorrow after Kitty's or Thursday after breakfast to get some new toys for Jock and Maggie?"

"Let's go tomorrow. Thursday all the marketing interns at Mangrums want to meet for lunch at the Pie Oven and have our own little Christmas celebration."

"Wow! You weren't kidding about the full week. And after Danny and Emma get here we'll have a family of four, plus two dogs, waking up together every morning."

"It sounds like heaven to me, old guy. Mmm . . . Matt, I don't think I can stay awake more than ten more minutes, and I know I'm going to be a zombie at Kitty's in the morning, so I would like you to eat me up as fast as you can before I fall asleep."

"Okay, pretty girl. I'll kiss you up and down, and kiss you all around. The baby dogs and I will keep you snug all night. So sleep tight, love."

Abigail brought a change of clothes with her in the morning, so at nine o'clock, after several warm hugs for both of us from Kitty—who would be closed all of Christmas and New Year's weeks—we went straight to the mall. At Pet City we got a black Kong and a squeaky, stuffed soccer ball for Jock, and a red Kong and a squeaky, stuffed squirrel for Maggie.

"There's one more store I want to check out, beauty," I said, taking her hand. I guided her around the corner and past the fountain to Harriman's.

"Matthew Flynn, what are we doing *here*?"

I put the doggie bags down, wrapped my arms around Abby and nibbled playfully on her lips.

"It's time, pretty girl—time for you to find the ring you've been dreaming of. I came into the store yesterday and scouted out the best ones."

"Oh, my God, this is *really* happening! Did you find one *you* love, old guy?"

"I have a favorite, beauty, but I'm not going to tell you which one it is."

"Oh, my God, Matt . . . it's every girl's dream to pick out her engagement ring." Abby clasped her hands on the back of my head and kissed me tenderly. "I love you so much."

The clerks were both amused and delighted to be assisting a slightly different couple like us. More important, they were lovely and kind to Abby, who was lost in a delicious cloud, something they had surely seen many times before. After almost an hour and more than twenty different rings, Abigail narrowed her choice to two: a traditional round stone and the princess cut *I* liked. The older clerk—clearly an expert on diamonds—congratulated Abby on her two choices.

"These are both very special rings, miss."

"Please call me Abby."

"Abby, the round stone and setting came from Juliette Florean of San Francisco. And the princess ring was designed by Giuseppe DiPasquale, one of the most famous jewelers in Italy. You can see the five square diamonds in the channels on both sides, plus the two medium stones on either side of the main princess diamond, which is 1.6 carats. All of the stones on both sides add up to 1.1 carats."

"Matt, these are *so* beautiful! But are they too expensive? The round stone is $5,375, and the princess cut is $4,695."

"Miss Abigail, nothing is too good for the girl who gave me back the joy of my youth."

"There were so many lovely and spectacular choices, Matt. Is one of these your favorite?"

"Yes."

"But you're not going to tell me?"

"Not yet," I teased.

"This is such a wonderful moment in my life—I don't want it to end. I know Mom and Mary Kay would choose the round stone, which is a little larger and brighter. But I think the princess stone and setting has more personality—maybe *my* personality. May I pick the princess ring, old guy? Will you be my prince?"

"I will, beauty. And guess what? *That* ring is my favorite."

Abigail squealed and jumped off the floor into my arms.

"Oh, my God, I can't *believe* how I feel . . . I'm so *happy*! What do we do now?"

The younger clerk interjected, with a huge smile, "The princess ring is a perfect fit, miss . . . Abby. Would you like to wear it home?"

"Matt, what do you think? Are we ready for people to know before Christmas? Who should see it first? The crew at Mangrums today, my friends at RIT tomorrow, Mom and Dad tomorrow night, *your* mom and dad?"

"Wear it now, Abby. Tell anybody who asks. Tell them even if they *don't* ask."

"People are going to want to know if we've set a date. What are we going to tell them?"

"How fast can we get it together without giving your mother heart failure?"

"Mom will be a hard sell, but Dad will work on her. And now I have so many 'sisters' to help me with wedding plans."

"Miss Abigail, how about we tell everybody it will be some time in between Valentine's Day and Mother's Day?"

"Okay, old guy. I'll call Holy Eucharist today from work and see what our choices are."

The clerks gave Abigail's ring one final sparkling, and we finished the paperwork and walked out into the sunshine in the parking lot.

"Look how it catches the sunlight, Matt! It's *so* beautiful!" Abby took my hands in hers and looked deep in my eyes. "Thank you for my ring, old guy, and for being the man of my dreams."

Then she brushed her fingers across my temples and said, "You know, with the sun shining on your hair and your face like that, you are *way* more summer boy than old guy."

"That's the way I feel whenever you touch me, pretty girl."

"I want to celebrate, Matt. Can we celebrate right *now*?"

"How, Abby?"

"I have just enough time before work to take you home—now that you're my *fiancé*—take your clothes off and move my ring finger all over your body. Then when I get to Mangrums and all my advertising friends are admiring my ring, I will be remembering how beautiful it looked on my summer boy."

Abigail called at five-thirty to tell me that she and "our" ring were the talk of Mangrums. I had a fire going and a glass of

Montepulciano waiting for her at eight-thirty. We curled up on the sofa with Jock and Maggie and watched Henry Winkler in *The Most Wonderful Time of the Year*.

Abby kept holding her left hand up to catch the light from the chandelier over the coffee table, while kissing me on the cheek and stroking the back of my neck with her right hand.

"You know, Matt, I have never had to even *think* about being careful with my hands—until today. Today I was paying attention to where my ring was all the *time*, before I did *any*thing—before I made a phone call, before I opened an envelope, before I typed on my laptop. I suppose I'll get over that although I'm not sure I *want* to. I think I'll ask Mom and Nannie if they're still aware of their rings all the time."

"We have another delightful day ahead of us, Abby, when we pick our matching gold bands."

"Big deal, old guy," she joked. "*All* my days with you are delightful. You have been wearing your Sarah band since the first day I met you, and it's okay with me if you keep wearing it."

"You're very sweet, beauty, but I think you and I should pick out new ones which we design for each other. I thought I would save *my* wedding band for little Matthew, and Sarah's band and engagement ring for Emily. We can go back to Harriman's on one of those dark January days. They will custom-design our bands the way we want them. Are you going to your mom and dad's tomorrow evening right from school, or do you want to come home first?"

"I'll come home first. You're my guy now—*every* day—and I go with *you*. We're too young for separate cars," she kidded. "And besides, there is *no way* I'm going into my mother's kitchen with *this* ring on *this* hand without you on the other hand."

Trying to describe the expression on Mrs. McKay's face when we walked in to her kitchen the next evening and she saw Abigail's ring would be as difficult as trying to describe the alternate shades of pink and blue in a sunset.

"Abigail Elizabeth! Oh, my God!" she shouted, lifting Abby's hand. "When did this happen?"

"In truth, Mom, it happened on November 12, the day I met this old guy; but Matt and I picked out my ring at Harriman's yesterday."

"Harriman's! They're so expensive! You're *engaged* after

245

only a few weeks? *Bless us and save us!* I hardly know what to say."

"You could give me a hug, Mom."

At this point Mr. McKay walked into the kitchen and teased, "What's all this racket? All this for a *ring*? Let me see, Abby. Well, now I understand. That is *some* gorgeous ring for my little girl—just what you deserve, honey. Give your dad a hug. *Hurrah* for you, and you too, Matt!" he cheered, clapping me on the shoulder and shaking my hand. "What do you think, Mother?"

"I think you're worse than the kids, Gerald McKay! And I think I need to sit down. Let's go into the living room. *God and Mary and Saint Patrick, give me strength!*"

And then we talked—in between pot roast, ornaments and tinsel—about the ring, about Christmas and a spring wedding. Patrick, Laurie, Catherine and Betsy joined us later; Jack didn't come. The more we discussed wedding plans, the more Mrs. McKay perked up. Abigail said she had called Holy Eucharist, and we could have any Saturday in March, so we picked March 15, two days before Saint Patrick's Day and Danny's birthday.

"Pretty girl, Dave Connolly's brother Dennis owns the Connolly House in Mendon. I'll call him tomorrow and see if March 15 is available."

In the Jeep on the way home Abigail kept her ring hand on top of my shift hand.

"Matt, if you can confirm the date with Dennis Connolly tomorrow before I go to Mangrums, my friends at the office can help me put together an invitation, and we might be able to get it printed and in the mail to everybody the first week in January. Are we rushing this too much?"

"I don't think so, love, but I'm on *your* schedule. I don't want *you* to feel rushed. I only want our wedding to be just the way you want it. Now that almost everybody in my family has met you, none of them are going to be shocked. And once our friends read their Christmas cards, they're not going to be surprised, either. March 15 is not far away, so we need to let people know ASAP. And besides that, what if our best-case, miracle scenario happens and you get pregnant?"

Abigail squeezed my shift hand and rubbed her cheek on my chest.

"Oh, Matt, could my dream be *that* perfect? Okay, captain, I'm with you—full speed ahead."

When we hooked the leashes on Jock and Maggie to take them out, Abby actually got down on her knees and showed the dogs her ring.

"Look what Daddy bought me, baby dogs! Isn't it pretty!"

Jock barked at the ring, and Maggie licked it.

In bed that night, Abigail was alternately philosophical and on fire.

"Matt, Friday is the first day of winter. We haven't even spent a whole *season* together, and you and I are going to get married. I don't blame Mom for being angry and confused. What's the trendy modern word—*conflicted*?"

She was lying between my legs with her hands under my butt, whispering impishly into my belly and kissing my navel.

"Do you think my mother guesses how much I want to get lost in your blue eyes and worship your body?"

Abby slowly slid up my chest, put her hands under my head and danced her lips on mine.

"Do you think our mothers wanted our fathers—wanted their skin, their sweat, their hair, their bodies together—the way I always want you all over me and in me?"

She stopped talking and guided me inside her. Then she locked her arms and legs around me and rolled us everywhere on the bed. Abigail's cries were so loud that they scared the dogs out of the bedroom. When she quieted down, with both of our heads hanging off the foot of the bed, she said breathlessly, "Matt, can we stay in bed all morning tomorrow? Except for walking Maggie and Jock, of course. I can't believe how much I want you right now. I might not be able to sleep; I might play with you all night. And even if I fall asleep, I might wake up and *eat* you up. I feel as if I have to keep touching you or I will burst. I don't know if I want this feeling to go away or quiet down or not. If it doesn't, it will be a tough afternoon for me tomorrow at Mangrums."

I didn't say a word; Abigail didn't *need* me to say a word. I only needed to be as close as she wanted; or to let her move me *where* she wanted. I don't know how long we made love. The last thing I remember before falling asleep was Abby licking my right ear. I have no idea how long she kept going after that. I woke up to daylight, and Michael Martin Murphey singing "I'm Gonna Miss You, Girl" on WCWM, and Abby putting my fingers into her mouth one at a time.

"*Mmm* . . . pretty girl, good morning. You didn't really stay awake all night, did you?"

"No, handsome; but I did wake up around four o'clock and play with you long enough to get you inside me even though you were sound asleep. I just looked down at you sleeping and had one of the sweetest orgasms ever. Then I fell asleep right on top of you."

"Wow, that's amazing! How could I *miss* all of that, Abby?"

"I think I tired you out pretty well, Matt. But now that you have brought me 'the morning bright' from my prayer, do you think you're recharged enough for a quickie before we get Maggie and Jock their breakfast?" she laughed.

"I hope so, pretty girl. And if I can expect this kind of behavior from you in the future, I think we should get engaged every *week*. Do you want me to just be soft and tasty and open like last night, or can *I* do some licking and nibbling this morning?"

"You're on, old guy; come and get me."

If there were a record book or hall of fame for such things, that December morning would be in the top ten. Before Abigail left for Mangrums at one o'clock, we had made love three more times in bed and once in the shower. When she called me at five on her supper break, she whispered, "Summer boy, I have such a buzz in my belly, and up and down my whole body. It feels as if you are still inside me—a miniature Matt Flynn in my underpants. Beware, old guy. I might want to jump you in the Jeep tonight. And guess what? Mr. Christopher decided to leave on his vacation tomorrow so I don't have to work. We can keep playing, and I can help you get ready for Emma and Danny. And I'd like to do lunch at Phil Green's with my fiancé."

We had a quiet night on the sofa sipping tea and watching the Hallmark movie *Fallen Angel* with Gary Sinise and Joely Richardson.

"That's Vanessa Redgrave's daughter isn't it, Matt?"

"Right, Abby. Vanessa has two beautiful, talented daughters, Natasha and Joely. I have an old DVD of Joely as Lady Chatterley."

"Natasha did *The Parent Trap*, which is one of my favorites. Lindsay Lohan was so cute in those days—before she turned into a bad girl. I think Patrick is still crazy about her."

We blew out the candles and went upstairs right after the movie ended at ten o'clock. Abigail and I were really tired, and the doggies were happy to sleep the whole night in bed with us.

We went to Phil Green's at eleven-thirty for lunch, and Abby spent about twenty minutes giving her left hand to Judith, Jinks, Todd and all the crew for a look. Our hot dogs were on the house, and Judith even brought us a small ice cream cake with one candle.

"Happy Winter!" she smiled. "If you're still together next year, there'll be *two* candles."

Then we went to Mangrums for milk, sandwich fixings and Danny and Emma's favorite fruit and cereals. We spent the afternoon putting up the rest of the Christmas lights and decorations. Emma called at about four and said that they had just passed Syracuse and would be pulling into the driveway in about an hour. We ordered two large mozzarella and pepperoni pizzas from Vitello's, and I called Claire and told her to bring the family over any time after five.

Matt, Claire and the kids came through the door—to the delight of Jock and Maggie—five minutes before Danny and Emma arrived. One of the greatest joys of my life has always been watching my sons together—sometimes playing, sometimes arguing, sometimes sleeping—but *together*. Now, with Danny and Emma in Boston, that didn't happen enough. From the time Danny was four or five, the three-year age difference between my sons meant less and less, and they started to do a lot of things together. Fortunately, they were equally bright, clever, healthy, strong, resourceful, curious and dexterous, so neither was ever seriously overmatched. They both loved sports—baseball, football and basketball, in that order—both to play and to watch; and Legos, and G.I. Joe, and the Hardy Boys, and the Ninja Turtles, and Tudor Electric Football and Monopoly. Danny followed me—from his kindergarten days—as a Yankee fan, but Matt rebelled at the age of seven when the Mets won the '86 World Series, and became a Met fan—which he would regret many times in the next twenty years.

Now, watching these two outstanding young men talk about love and Christmas, work and pizza, politics and football, Santa Claus and kids, was as great a joy as listening to them compare the Hall of Fame plaques of Ted Williams and Lou Gehrig the first time we went to Cooperstown, when Matt was ten and Danny was seven.

And it was equally joyous to see Claire and Emma squeal as soon as they noticed Abigail's ring; and then to watch and listen as the girls compared engagement rings and wedding bands, and fiancés and wedding plans. The conversation hummed between the dining room and the kitchen, and the pizza and the chicken wings, until it was time for Matthew and Emily to go home to bed. We all agreed to meet at ten o'clock the next morning at Wheeler's Farm Market to pick out the tree and then go to Phil Green's for lunch. Danny and Emma were exhausted after their seven-hour drive through blowing and drifting snow, so they crashed early.

Abigail and I buttoned up the house and settled Jock and Maggie on their beds in our bedroom, where they would sleep while Danny and Emma were home. I turned off the lights, folded back the quilt and rolled on my side of the bed. Abby was standing motionless in the west window, her body luminous in the moonlight, her hands together as if in prayer, her fingers touching her lips.

"Matt, my beloved old guy, it's almost a full moon, you know . . . so bright on the snow. Can we sleep with the curtains pulled back to let in the moonlight?"

"Abby, you are *so* beautiful standing there. Open up the north curtains, too, and come here."

"Old guy, I cannot possibly describe how I felt being with your whole family together tonight. Your sons are so *wonderful* together. And Claire and Emma, and Danny and Matt, are so lovely to me, as if I've been your sweetheart for six *years* instead of six weeks. Matthew is calling me Aunt Abby. I almost cried a dozen times I was so happy. I'm crying right now."

She tucked her head under my right arm, reached her fingers up to my face and whispered, "Hold me hard, Matt, but kiss me soft. I love you so much."

Part Two
Abigail

22

My first Christmas with the Flynns, in Matt's words, was "filled with more good tidings of great joy" than any family Christmas he could remember. Even though my beautiful ring was a huge hit, especially with all of my new "sisters" and Matt's mother, it was hardly the lead story. Debbie was pregnant; Katy and Trent would be moving in to their new house in May, just before their June wedding; and Warren had a new training job with Xerox, and he and Stephanie and the kids would be moving to Leesburg, Virginia, in the spring. It was going to be a breathtaking New Year for the Flynns.

After we exchanged presents and covered the living room floor with huge balls of crumpled wrapping paper, we sat down to dinner. The conversation from end to end of the grownup table buzzed with all the news and dates: March 15 for Matt and me; April 6 for Warren and Steph's move to Virginia; May 1 for Katy and Trent's new house, and June 7 for their wedding; July 1 for Mr. and Mrs. Flynn's 65th wedding anniversary; and August 15—more or less—for Debbie's new baby. She said that she and Fred didn't plan on telling anyone whether Billy was going to have a little brother or a sister.

After dinner, the guys and the kids sprawled over the living room, nibbled on cutout cookies, played with all the new toys and watched *National Lampoon's Christmas Vacation*—another Flynn tradition, said Diane. In the kitchen all of us girls—Mrs. Flynn, Diane, Stephanie, Barbara, Debbie, Eileen, Claire, Emma, Katy, me, and even Julie and Amy—did the dishes and enjoyed the most wonderful girl conversation I've ever been a part of.

I knew that my life in the Flynn family would never be dull.

Matt and I hugged and kissed everybody goodbye at five-thirty and left for Mom and Dad's. In contrast to the Flynns, my engagement ring was pretty much the *only* story there, and our second Christmas dinner was much quieter. Mom outdid herself with the baked ham *and* roast beef. Pat, Laurie, Catherine and Betsy sang carols. Dad kept the fire stoked and all the drinks filled. And Jack—after he saw my ring—had little to say the rest

252

of the evening. We were disappointed that Grandma and Grandpa McKay both had colds and didn't think they should come over; and Nannie and Grandpa Dolan had called the day before and said they were having a blizzard in Stockbridge. There was a travel alert, so they decided to wait a few days and then come for New Year's. We called them all after dinner to wish them a Merry Christmas. Grandma McKay made me promise to bring "Matthew" over as soon as their colds were gone. Nannie insisted on speaking with Matt. I could only hear his side of the conversation:

"Abby has told me so much about you . . . I know, I'm a very lucky guy . . . the day after we first met . . . I especially liked the part where you knocked off Sergeant Dolan's hat . . . okay, Grandpa Dolan it is . . . I'll ask my dad if he was ever in Cardiff and if he remembers your mom and dad's store . . . wouldn't that be something . . . Abby says she's a lot like you, so I can't wait. Merry Christmas to you too, and safe travels."

On the way home in Jeep, I played with Matt's shift hand. "Old guy, I've been thinking about the differences between Christmas at the McKay's and Christmas at the Flynn's. The best word I come up with for my family—except Jack—is 'mellow.' And the best word I come up with for your family is 'exhilarating.' I had a *lot* more fun at Tom and Diane's, and every single person in your family was happy—there was no Jack."

"It was one of the best days of my life, Abby. I seem to have had a lot of 'best days' since I met you." Matt kissed the top of my head. "We are *so* fortunate that all of the Flynn boys and girls—of all our generations—and all the boys and girls who have married us Flynns, are happy and healthy. Today was the best Christmas *ever*—at least since I got my NHL Power Play HOCKEY game," he joked, "and you were the biggest part of it.

"But you know what, beauty? Next year could be even better. *Think* of what our family has to look forward to. I haven't been this excited about a New Year since Matt and Danny were mapping out our cross-country trip in 1995." He rested his cheek on my head. "It's all your fault for bringing me back to life."

The next two days we played with Emma and Danny, Claire and Matt, and Matthew and Emily. We had lunch both days at Phil Green's, where Matthew and Emily entertained both the staff and the rest of the patrons. On Thursday we had dinner in our own special family nook in Palermo's. Matthew and Emily *love* Palermo's breadsticks and macaroni and cheese. On Friday we had dinner at Claire and Matt's, and Mr. and Mrs. Flynn came too. I made my now-famous sauce and meatballs, Emma and Danny picked up Chianti and Italian bread—plain and garlic—and Claire baked her special chocolate cream pie. Friday morning Claire, Matt and the kids came for breakfast; and *my* Matt made each of us our favorite omelet. I still can't believe that Matthew and Emily like black olives mixed in with their eggs.

We sent Emma and Danny off to Boston on Saturday with long, huge hugs and "happy kisses," as Matthew calls them. Matt and I waved goodbye to everybody . . . and to the most memorable Christmas of my life. Then we brought Maggie and Jock upstairs, got back in bed, and napped and made love the rest of the afternoon—until it was time to feed the dogs and get ready to meet Mary Kay and her new boyfriend for dinner.

Mary Kay wanted to have dinner at Palermo's again because, she said, "There was so much stress and drama the last time that I couldn't enjoy it." As soon as Mrs. Palermo seated us at our favorite table in the back overlooking the frozen bay, Mary Kay took my hand and fell in love with my ring.

"Oh, *Abby*! You and Matt picked this out *together*? It's the kind of ring *I've* always dreamed about. Will, take note."

Will Fischette, Mary Kay's date, was a couple inches taller than Matt and a few pounds leaner. Handsome, with short, sandy hair and gold skin, he was an Army captain and also in the graduate foreign language program at Georgetown. He seemed very confident and comfortable, and not the least bit surprised by the age difference between Matt and me. His mother and father and two sisters lived in Carlisle, Pennsylvania, but he had a first cousin who was a professor nearby at SUNY Brockport, so he had been to Rochester many times.

Mary Kay lifted my hand to her face so she could really study my ring.

"Wow! There are *five* very pretty diamonds in each channel; and the princess stones on either side of the main stone could be in engagement rings all by themselves. I'm *so* happy for you, Abby—and for you too, Matt. You have great taste in girls *and* rings!" she grinned.

"Mary Kay, would you believe that Abby and I separately— with *no* prompting or hints—picked this ring as our favorite one at Harriman's?"

"Of course I do. Why shouldn't a *ring* at first sight come right after *love* at first sight?"

Over dinner, Will and Matt talked a little Army, while Mary Kay and I talked rings, family and wedding plans. Will said a new captain's pay now was a little more than $4,000 per month compared to $1,500 when Matt completed his four years of service in 1972. He expected to be assigned—as a language analyst and interpreter—to U.S. Command Europe at NATO headquarters in Brussels after graduation in May.

Mary Kay's eyes filled with tears when I asked her to be my maid of honor, and she reminded me of our old bet at Fatima: whoever got married first would be treated to a manicure, pedicure and spa day by the loser.

"I'll have to come home from Georgetown three or four days before the wedding so we can do Samantha's (another Fatima classmate) Spa together. Start making a list of the things you need me to do. I'm going to be the *best* maid of honor you'll *ever* have," she laughed.

The four of us were having such a lovely time we didn't want to leave. With our cappuccino, Italian coffee and espresso, we shared Palermo's deluxe dessert sampler: spumoni, gelato, cannoli, limone and tiramisu. Then we lingered with several rounds of after-dinner liqueurs. Mary Kay and Will even agreed to spend the night at our house; and we took them to breakfast at Joe's the next morning before they had to pack up and head back to D.C.

Mom had called while we were at dinner to let me know that Nannie and Grandpa Dolan were in from Massachusetts, and to invite Matt and me to dinner the next day. "Come early, Abigail, come at five o'clock. Nannie and Grandpa can't wait to see you and meet Matthew, and we will also do their Christmas presents. Patrick and Laurie will be here, too, but Jack and his family are going to come for Sunday dinner instead."

As we drove to Mom and Dad's in Jeep, Matt asked, "Abby, does your grandfather like to talk about his wartime experiences?"

"He won't spontaneously bring them up, but he doesn't mind when people ask—and you're not just *people*. You'll ask Gramps the right way because your dad was there too."

Mom ushered us in to the living room where Nannie and

Grandpa were sitting in the pale green wing chairs by the fireplace. They both got up and hugged me at the same time.

"Nannie, Gramps, I'm so happy you're here! Merry Christmas! I love you so much! Matt, I want you to meet my favorite people in the *whole* world, Elizabeth and Patrick Dolan. Nannie, Gramps, this is the love of my life, Matthew Howard Flynn."

Mom and Dad and Pat and Laurie joined in the hugs and kisses and tears all around. Then Matt, Dad and Pat settled on the sofa with their glasses of Harp; and Laurie and I knelt in between Nannie and Grandpa in their chairs so they could all look at my ring.

Nannie was *dazzled.* "My goodness! Abigail Elizabeth, it's the perfect ring for the *best* girl!

"Mr. Dolan," she said mischievously to Grandpa, "it seems that wedding rings have grown a bit more sparkle since you got down on your knees sixty-two years ago."

"Well, Mother," Grandpa grinned, "from what I've been told, our Abigail picked this beauty out herself; and young Matthew here"—Grandpa winked at Matt—"is a successful businessman who has probably saved his nickels and dimes over the years for this happy day. Yours truly, on the other hand, came to you in 1945 with little more than love, hope and a prayer in his heart."

Nannie reached over and touched Grandpa's cheek.

"And a handsome uniform on his handsome self, Mr. Dolan."

Then she took both my hands in hers.

"Abigail Elizabeth, I can see in your eyes that you know this already, but believe your old Nannie: it's never what's in the *ring* that seals the deal; it's what's in the *touch* and in the *eyes*."

Nannie and Gramps wanted to sit between Matt and me on one side of the dinner table. They both had thick, pure white hair and ruddy faces, and they appeared happy and healthy. Nannie turned to me and patted my leg.

"Abigail Elizabeth, you are *prettier* than ever now that you're in love. I remember the *very* day in Mum and Dad's store when my father said that to *me*. It was the day after Sergeant Dolan here shipped away from me across the Channel to fight. Grandpa and I would *love* for you and Matthew to come and visit us, if you can squeeze it in, some time before your wedding. I have something *old* and something *blue* that I think you might like. And Grandpa has heard that Matthew is interested in swapping World War II stories."

"That would be *lovely*, Nannie." I kissed her cheek. "Matt, can we do that?"

"Yes we *can*, beauty. Maybe the long Presidents' Day weekend in February will work. Any stories I tell you, Mr. Dolan, will be just a preview. I hope at the wedding we can find a couple of hours for you and my dad to sit down over a few Harps and Heinekens and share your stories with *all* of us."

"Please call me Grandpa or Pat. What outfit was your dad in?"

"The 99th Infantry, the Checkerboard Division, in General Courtney Hodges' First Army. When the Battle of the Bulge began, the 99th was deployed on the northern shoulder, Elsenborn Ridge. Dad was right on the front line when the German tanks blew past him. How about you?"

"The 35th Infantry, the Santa Fe Division. General Paul Baade was our commander. Our boys stormed Omaha Beach on D-Day, but I was still in Wales training . . . and courting."

Grandpa gave Nannie a wink.

"We were under Omar Bradley at first but, in September, Ike transferred the 35th to General Patton and his newly activated Third Army. Then we took off. The 35th and the whole Third Army chased the Germans all the way across France and back into Germany. Our boys were almost to the Saar River when I joined them in early November with a whole bunch of replacements.

"At the beginning of December, Patton sent us back to Metz for a rest. When the Krauts attacked the Ardennes on December 16 and broke through, Patton immediately ordered us to turn around and march northwest to Arlon, forty miles away near the Belgium-Luxembourg border. The 35th never moved so fast, and through the worst possible winter weather. We made Arlon in thirty hours, had six hours to eat and sleep, and then headed due north towards Bastogne to help save the 101st Airborne."

"Okay, you two," Mom interjected, "I think that's enough war talk at the dinner table. Dad, how about you save the rest for later or for Stockbridge?"

"Sorry, Peg. When it comes to the Bulge I almost never get to talk with anybody who knows what he's *talking* about."

Nannie put her hand on my leg again and leaned against my shoulder and whispered, "Grandpa really likes your guy. So do I, sweetie."

That night in bed I said to Matt, "Old guy, you were a big hit with Nannie and Gramps. How do you know so much about the Battle of the Bulge?"

He kissed me and pulled me tight against him and ran his hands softly up and down the length of my back and over my "tail."

"Well, beauty, Dad was there—at the same time. His outfit—his division—was in position on the northern edge of the Bulge—they later called it the 'shoulder'—and your grandpa's division was on the southern side. Tomorrow I'll show you a map. For some reason, after Mom almost died, Dad started talking more about his wartime experiences, and especially the Bulge. I'm sure it was the most dramatic and memorable experience of his life.

"And then I found all of his and Mom's letters in the attic and started asking more questions, and Dad's stories snowballed. Then Matt got Dad to record many of his experiences on tape, and used the recordings combined with some of the letters as the basis of his Masters thesis at SUNY Albany. All the while I was reading book after book about World War II and Eisenhower and Patton, and the Battle of the Bulge in particular. The three Matt Flynns all got a lot closer than we had ever been. I can't *wait* for Dad to meet your grandpa."

"And *I* can't remember ever seeing Nannie and Grandpa happier than they were tonight. I would *love* to eavesdrop on their conversation with Mom and Dad over breakfast tomorrow about a certain Matthew Flynn."

"Sweetie, you and your Nannie are so close that I'll bet she tells you all about it."

Lying on my side tucked under Matt's right arm, I suddenly felt an irresistible desire to touch his face—*all* of his face: his soft eyebrows, the slope of his nose, the shape of his earlobes, my fingertips against the grain of his sideburns, the middle of his full lips, the thin lids over his closed eyes, the dimple in his chin.

"Matt, even with my eyes closed, you're *so* beautiful. Even if I were *blind* I know I would love you. Isn't that *something*? I've never had a thought like that. That kind of idea would have been inconceivable to me before you kissed me the first time."

He rolled me on top of him and touched all of my body as if *he* were blind. His hands knew me better than I knew myself. We came together halfway between the images in our minds and the dreams of sleep. The last image in my mind was Matt's fingers and his face deep in my hair.

The next morning we went to the ten o'clock Mass at Holy Eucharist and, in between all the prayers, whispered to each other about how we thought the church would look on March 15. Then we went to Phil Green's for a late breakfast, curled together in our favorite booth, and whispered a little more.

"Old guy, I'm going to show you my drawing tonight. I think it's my best one, and nobody has ever seen it." I took off my boots and put my feet on the bench and my head in Matt's lap. "That means you'll have to dust off another poem next week, or write me a new one." I looked up smiling.

"The first of the new year, pretty girl. I'm so excited about 2008 I feel like a *teenager*."

"Who will be at the Connolly's tomorrow night? What should I wear?"

"I'm sure Dave's brothers Peter and Dennis will be there with their wives, and maybe some of the kids too. We can talk with Dennis about our wedding reception. And Dave's sister Charlene and her husband might be in from Toronto. And Dave said maybe a few of his colleagues from the U of R and some of Ann's teacher friends, too. I haven't been to one of their parties since Sarah died. I saw a dress in the closet you haven't worn for me yet. Forest green, sleeveless, short, kind of pleated and flowing . . . chiffon? It's the color of your eyes, beauty."

"Good choice, Matt. That's one of *my* favorites, too. I put it in the same category as the red satin dress: dresses to be worn on *very* special occasions when I really, *really* want to be noticed. Do you want me to really, *really* be noticed?"

"I sure do, pretty girl. Just for the record, for all of the next 834 events we go to, I want you to really, *really* be noticed. It makes me feel like the king of the mountain. And, my beautiful Abby, I can't imagine you wearing *any* clothes—except for maybe a beekeeper's suit in a room full of beekeepers—where you *wouldn't* be noticed. I was the proudest man in the room at your office party and mine."

"Okay, handsome, the green dress it is. And I have black, patent leather high heels to go with it." I made my "impish girl" face. "Is anybody watching us?"

"No. Jinks knows we're here, but it's pretty empty. Why?"

"Will you touch my breasts? I have this ache—I'm going to close my eyes now—and I need you to make it go away."

I felt Matt touching me and playing with my hair and stroking my cheeks. I had a little orgasm and then I fell asleep. The noise from the football game on the overhead television woke me up.

"*Mmm* . . . that was nice, Matt. How long was I asleep?"

"Long enough for Jinks to bring me two more hot chocolates and for me to read the sports section and the comics, beauty." He smiled down at me and traced my lips with his finger.

"Jinks must think I'm such a *slug*."

"Jinks says she's jealous and wants to know if I have a *younger* brother," he teased.

We spent the rest of the afternoon in front of a cozy fire in the living room, playing with Maggie and Jock and reading. Matt was still wading through his Civil War book, and I had just started *The Bridges of Madison County*. We each had our feet flopping over the arms of the comfortable old chairs in the front window, and a dog in our lap. I waved my little book at Matt's big one.

"How are the battles going, old war guy?"

"I'm up to the Battle of Shiloh."

"I know we have this movie, Matt, but have you read the book?"

"Twice, I think, Abby. The first time I checked it out of the library, the librarian said, 'Make sure you have lots of Kleenex ready,' and she was right. Same for the movie. Let me know when you start getting to the Kleenex parts, and I'll kick Jock out of this chair and make room for *you*."

"And then I can use your shoulder instead," I smiled.

After we finished our soup and sandwiches for supper, I brought my drawing down to the kitchen table. It was my brother Pat in his hospital bed, with bags of fluids and medicine hanging down from a post and dripping into his left arm. He had bandages around both of his hands and his forehead and that amazing machine was registering all the green readings behind his bed. I was sleeping under the tubes and bags of fluids, my feet curled under my legs on the uncomfortable hospital chair, my arms wrapped around Pat's left arm just above the tubes, and my head nodding down his shoulder and chest. I was wearing jeans and a sweater, and my hair almost completely covered my face.

Matt took me in his arms and held my face against his and stroked my hair. Then he kissed my tears and said, "Abby, it's *so* beautiful. Especially the way you have drawn *yourself,* so loving and caring and helping but helpless at the same time. The way you are touching and comforting Patrick would make *any* person want to reach *in* to your drawing to hold and comfort *you,* too. You are so *good*! I hope you will keep drawing, even when you get to be president of Mangrums," he teased.

"I haven't drawn anything in three or four years, Matt, but I know I will *now*—now that I'm in your life. You woke *me* up, too, you know."

"You didn't even have a photograph to work from, Abby. You drew this from the picture in your mind and the feelings in your heart. When you exhibit your drawings some day, you should call this one 'A Sister's Love.' I can't imagine any man or woman who wouldn't wish—or even *pray*—to find someone to love them this much."

Matt sat in one of our high top kitchen chairs. I hopped onto his lap, wrapped my arms around his neck and said, "Old guy, what's the most beautiful thing you've ever seen, the most beautiful place you've ever been?"

"You mean other than waking up on a sunny morning with you asleep next to me, pulling Pooh and Piglet and all the covers to the foot of the bed, opening all the curtains to let the light come in from all directions, and watching the sunshine illumine all your colors?"

"My poet. I'll bet you even *dream* in poetry. Okay," I laughed, "*other* than my dazzling beauty in the morning."

"It was the day the boys and I left Yellowstone Park, Abby, on my fiftieth birthday. We left at the south entrance where the Snake River starts as a little stream that I could have waded across, then drove south for about fifty miles to Jackson, Wyoming, with the Snake twisting along the right side of the interstate all the way, and the Grand Tetons towering over the river—all set against a pure blue sky. It was a perfect day in July, a fifty-mile postcard, and I stopped a dozen times to take pictures. But it wasn't just the scenery. It was the combination of the scenery and having my sons there to share it that made it such a beautiful sequence of moments.

"I'll show you the pictures, but they don't do the moments justice. Same as a centerfold of you could never match seeing you glowing next to me in bed in the morning." Matt grinned and kissed my nose.

"I feel the same way, old guy. Waking up in that hospital room and seeing Pat smile at me and feeling him brush my hair

261

off my face was my most beautiful moment—until I met *you*. Now my beautiful moments follow each other like the notes of a song."

When we went upstairs to bed, I took my green dress out of the closet and hung it in the office to let any wrinkles fall out. I couldn't remember the last time I had worn it; there hadn't been very many special occasions in the five years since my graduation from Newton. As I lay next to Matt and he gazed steadily into my eyes without saying a word, I had a very scary thought. He must have seen it in my eyes.

"What's the matter, pretty girl?"

"What if I had never met you, old guy?"

Just that fast I had tears in my eyes. Matt pulled me tightly against him and kissed my ear.

"Abby, sweetie, we all have a million 'what-ifs' through the years, but they are not a part of *life*; they're a part of *history*. We can't forget them, but we learn to leave them behind. We *have* to. Life is today and tomorrow and March 15, also." He kissed me on both my cheeks. "I love you *so much*, but I had that *same* 'what-if' right after I met you. And I said to myself, 'Don't be an *idiot*, Matt; Abby is right *here*—right *now*—just love her.' That's what I plan to do, beauty."

"You're so *strong*, Matt. Come inside me now; you make me stronger."

"Don't sell yourself short, love. There were plenty of years when I got beat up and felt sorry for myself. And now to have an *amazing* girl like you love me and give yourself to me—when people all around us are making faces and shaking their heads— that's as strong and brave as *any* woman can be. I'm a *big* risk—not exactly a safe bet for a nice girl like you."

He smiled and kissed my hair.

"Never mind the 'risk' stuff, handsome, or the faces either. With you I'm 'all in.' Right now, Matt, *please*, don't let me talk any more. Hold me as tightly as you can and love me way down deep inside. I don't want to feel my own body at all."

23

We woke up late the next morning, and slowly, with Maggie and Jock stretching and licking all over us. *This is our last morning of 2007*, I thought. We touched and made love and talked, and Matt caressed my face with every word.

"We've filled the last seven weeks with a lot of life, hey, beauty?"

"So many things, Matt, that I never thought would *ever* happen to me. Do you know what my mother said to me when she called yesterday afternoon?"

And then I had to stop. My lips were trembling, and my eyes filled with tears. Matt took my head in both of his hands, and licked around the edges of my eyes, and kissed me softly on the lips. He was so *tender* . . . he was *always* so tender, and I felt better whenever he touched me.

"Mom said I could wear her wedding dress if I want to. Can you believe that? Two weeks ago, before she saw my ring for the first time, she was still hoping that you would just go away. I wonder if Nannie helped change her mind?"

"I think it was all *you*, Abby. Your mom can see in your eyes and hear in your voice . . ."

". . . that I'm willing to risk *everything* for you, Matt. No matter *who,* no matter *what.*"

"Your mother can see it all and feel it in her heart. You have become the strong, passionate and loving woman she always hoped and prayed her daughter would be."

"Well, *you've* helped a little, old guy. You've *accelerated my growth curve*, as the marketing techies would babble at Mangrums. I've always been *way* proud of Mom and Dad. I met plenty of parents of my girlfriends at Fatima—almost all attractive, bright, successful and happy—but none I would have traded for Mom and Dad. They had a tough time with Jack, who was usually moody, obsessive and ornery. Pat was always in trouble because he was *completely* the opposite—careless, easygoing, mischievous, never focused. And I was a typical, spoiled, bratty, pouting teen-age girl until the good nuns at

Fatima straightened me out."

I squeezed Matt's arm with both my hands and kissed him from his shoulder to his neck.

"Speaking of my parents, Mom's birthday is coming up on January 11—she'll be sixty-one—and that day is even more special because it's Mom and Dad's thirty-fifth wedding anniversary. Mom will probably have us all over for dinner, maybe even Grandma and Grandpa McKay."

"It's really nice that they got married on your mom's birthday. January 11 was also Uncle Vinny's birthday." Matt counted on his fingers. "He would have been ninety this year, three years older than Mom. I think my poem for you this week will be the one about Uncle Vinny."

"I can't wait, old guy. You told me he was like a second father."

I thought I saw tears in Matt's eyes.

"My brothers and I were the sons Uncle Vinny never had, and he loved us as much as our parents did. I never knew *anyone* who loved kids—and was so *patient* with them—as much as Uncle Vinny. And he and Aunt Connie also told me lots of stories about Grandpa and Grandma Fiorino that Mom couldn't even remember. Speaking of grandparents, pretty girl, would you like to get out of bed for a little bit this afternoon and go see your Grandma and Grandpa McKay? They've never met me."

"That is so thoughtful of you, Matt. How can I say no, even though there is no *way* that I want to get out of this bed. Can we go at about two and stay for maybe an hour? Grandma Mary will be delighted to see you, but I never know what to expect from Grandpa. What are all the Flynns doing tonight?"

"Matt and Claire and the kids usually go to one of their neighbors' houses. The couples with young children take turns hosting the parties. Tom and Diane always go to a party at Diane's girlfriend's house—all couples that they know from college and work. Sarah and I did that with them a few times. I think Danny and Emma will be at the annual big party at the Parker House hotel for all the staff from Tufts and Mather. I usually call Matt and Claire early; and Danny and Emma usually call right after midnight. But this year will be somewhat different, eh, beauty?"

"Somewhat, Matt," I said, rolling on top of him, looking straight in to his eyes, brushing all my fingers through his short hair, and kissing him. "There are so many thoughts I still can't

264

wrap my head around, and I'm sure I have that expression all wrong. I'm also sure my brains will be *mush* until after we see Doctor Hansen on Thursday."

Matt touched both his cheeks to mine and stroked my butt and the back of my thighs.

"I'm not scared exactly, old guy, but I'm almost shaking with anticipation. I have a good feeling about it—thanks to you—and I've been saying extra prayers to Our Lady, but you need to touch and hold me all the time between now and Thursday morning so I don't crumble."

"Yes, ma'am, and I plan to touch and hold you all the time *after* Thursday too . . . forever."

We made love again, more slowly and gently than I could remember, and finally got out of bed, mostly because Maggie and Jock kept poking us with their cold noses. I called Grandma Mary and Grandpa and asked if we could come for a short visit to wish them a happy New Year.

When we got to their apartment, Grandma was all smiles and offered us tea and homemade Irish soda bread. Grandpa eyed Matt suspiciously and didn't say much, even though Matt tried to draw him out by talking about when the first Flynns came to America and how much they all struggled through the Great Depression. Grandma wanted to touch my ring again and again. She even pulled a magnifying glass out of the drawer of her writing desk so she could look more closely.

"Miss Abigail, you and Matthew picked out a lovely ring. And I hear you're going to wear your mother's wedding dress. Your Grandpa and I wish you the very best! *May God hold you both in the palm of His hand!* We know you're going to be the most beautiful bride the McKay family has *ever* seen. I can't believe all the years that have gone by since you were the most beautiful *baby* we had ever seen."

Grandma's eyes glistened, and she held my ring hand against her pale cheek with both of her frail hands. "Your Grandpa doesn't ever say such things, but you know how much we love you, dear. I hope Matthew will take good care of you."

"He will, Grandma. He's the best man I've *ever* known. Now we have to go get gussied up for our party tonight, but we'll see you next week for Mom's birthday and their anniversary."

Matt and I exchanged gentle hugs with Grandma, and Grandpa even got up from his recliner to give me a warm hug and Matt a warm handshake. I didn't see him smile, though.

Back home we gave Maggie and Jock their supper and walked them around the circle. Then we all took a nap until it was time to get dressed for the Connolly's.

The party was kind of strange for me. Many of the guests who either didn't see Matt very often and couldn't remember much about his children or had never met him, assumed that I was his daughter, which amused the heck out of Matt and me and the Connollys. Dave introduced us to his brother Dennis, who had brought us a brochure about the Connolly House. It looked like a perfect place for our reception. Matt said we'd call and drive out so Dennis could show us around.

I met several more Connollys. I especially liked Dave and Ann's son Bobby's girlfriend Amanda, who was my age and would soon finish her Ph.D. in optical engineering at Cornell. She already had a good job lined up with Draper Vision in Rochester, and I could see the two of us getting to be friends.

I never enjoyed any drink more than my flute of Asti Cinzano at midnight, looking straight in to Matt's eyes, with both of his arms tight around my waist, imagining a whole new *year* ahead of me with this man of my dreams.

The first morning of 2008, as I looked out the bedroom windows, was gray and bleak. The wind whipping snow flurries through the empty trees did not appear to be in a holiday mood. *Inside*, on the other hand, as I watched Matt still sleeping and Maggie and Jock looking up at me for their cues, my world could not have been warmer or brighter. *How wonderful it would be*, I thought, *if all my thoughts in this infinitely promising new year could be instantly captured in a magic diary.* I had a feeling strong and deep in both my mind and heart that there would be very few moments in 2008 that I would not want to remember and relive. I scratched Maggie and Jock around their ears and under their chins.

"Stay, babies, it's still early."

The clock read *7:08* when I climbed back into bed and stretched my body the full length of Matt's. I'm three or four inches shorter than he is, so as hard as I try I can't touch all of his body at once. I *love* waking him up. No words can describe the joy and pleasure of waking Matt up: touching, nibbling, rubbing, squeezing, scratching, kissing. That morning, he was sleeping hard. After five minutes of my touching him and playing with him, he started stretching and growling inside, just the way Jock does when you lie down next to him and scratch his tummy. After five *more* minutes, Matt—with his eyes still closed—rolled on his back and reached for my belly.

"*Mmm*, that's good, Abby . . . keep going. Happy New Year, pretty girl. I *love* you."

"Happy New Year, old guy. I love *you*."

"*Mmm*, that's *very* good. I was dreaming about Horseshoe Bay in Bermuda, where Ellen and I got kicked off the beach— except it wasn't Ellen with me, it was *you*. There were no other people on the beach, and no bobby wanting to peek under our blanket. We poked our heads out of the blanket because the seagulls were screeching so loud. They were tiptoeing in a circle around us, maybe wondering if we were food or not. You laughed and tried to shoo them away, without leaving the blanket, of course. 'They're so *pushy*, Matt,' you said, 'they don't *listen* at all! They think they're the *boss* of the beach.' You made a pouty face."

Matt opened his eyes and smiled at me.

"I pulled you back under the blanket and whispered, 'There are no rules for seagulls, pretty girl.' And then you were kissing me everywhere, and I woke up here. From this angle, it doesn't look like a beach day outside."

"Not today, old guy. The back yard looks grim, and the wind is mean—but you'll have to take me to Horseshoe Bay one day."

"How about for a honeymoon, Abby?"

"Oh, sweetie, that sounds lovely, but I will only be able to take a day or two off the week after our wedding, so can we maybe save Horseshoe Bay for the week after I graduate?"

"We can do that, beauty. The weather in Bermuda will be perfect in May. How did you keep the doggies so quiet?"

"I gave them scratches and told them to stay because it was still too early, but I think it was the sound of the wind that made them content to settle back down in their beds. Do we have to go out anywhere today, old guy?"

"Matt and Claire invited us over for pizza later, but the rest of the day—before and after—is for you and me and the doggies, with a big fire in the living room, and our books and wine, and maybe a look at the Cotton Bowl or the Rose Bowl."

"So tell me, handsome," I said, tracing his lips, "how old were we in your dream?"

"Well, you had some gray hair," he teased. "I think you were in your late fifties and I was in my late thirties."

I scowled and poked him several times in his navel.

"You're *bad*, Matt! You're making that up."

"Sorry, sweetie, I couldn't resist. I think we were about right-now old. We weren't wearing bathing suits in my dream, and I was kissing all your freckles under the blanket . . . just like this."

He started kissing me everywhere, from my eyes to my belly to my thighs, and his hands were in my hair and over my breasts and around my hips, and my beach boy carried me away into my first dream of the new year.

Except for a couple of brisk walks with Maggie and Jock, we camped in the living room all day with our blazing fire and our books. In *Bridges*, Francesca was having her first dinner with Robert. Later at Matt and Claire's, the kids told us about *their* party down the street, including a visit from Baloo, the giant bear from *The Jungle Book*. We all called Emma and Danny and put them on speaker phone, and they told us that they were at *their* big party at the Parker House until two in the morning. Everybody except Matt and I had to be back to work the next day, so we went home right after we put Matthew and Emily to bed at seven-thirty.

As hard as Matt and the doggies tried to play with me, love me and distract me, questions for Dr. Hansen filled my mind until we walked into his office at ten o'clock on January 3. I told the nurse at the check-in desk that I wanted Matt—my fiancé— to be with me in the examining room. She smiled, looked at Matt, and smiled again.

Dr. Robert Hansen had been our family OB/GYN for many years: Mom went to him, and Grandma Mary, and Catherine and Laurie, too. I hadn't seen him since I went off to college. I introduced him to Matt, and he asked about Mom and the rest of the family.

"The last time I saw your mother, Abigail, she said you were in an MBA program at RIT. How is that going?"

"Great, doctor. I'll get my Masters in marketing in May."

"Congratulations! I'm sure you will do very well in whatever business you choose. Do you mind if I ask you and Matt some questions before I examine you?"

Dr. Hansen asked how long we'd known each other, were we living together, how often we had intercourse, if we had any problems, how were my periods. Matt held both my hands, and *I* answered all the questions. I only saw one hint of a smile on Dr.

268

Hansen's face, when I told him that Matt and I made love three or four times a day. Matt squeezed my hands on *that* one. While the doctor had me on the examining table, Matt's eyes were on mine the whole time. When Dr. Hansen finished and I got dressed, we moved into his office to talk. Matt had his chair turned towards mine and held both my hands again while we sat across the desk from Dr. Hansen.

"Abigail, I'm guessing that you and Matt have future plans together?"

"We're getting married on March 15 and we want to have a baby. *Can* I have a baby?"

"I think so." Matt squeezed my hands. "I didn't see any growths or obstructions or any signs of trouble. From your level of sexual activity and what you've told me, especially about your periods, I think you've outgrown your post-juvenile mumps diagnosis. We *could* try a fertility drug. I often prescribe clomid—clomiphene—which treats infertility by stimulating an increase in the amount of hormones that support the growth and release of mature eggs. But it sounds as if your ovulation is normal, so I recommend holding off on any medications for a while. Pregnancy is rarely an instantaneous occurrence and never a sure thing, anyway. Continue doing what you're doing. If Matt keeps up the good work for three or four more months," (I saw another hint of a smile) "and nothing happens, we can have his sperm tested."

When we walked out of Dr. Hansen's office I was so elated that I leaped into Matt's arms and wrapped my legs around his thighs.

"I love you so much, old guy. Can I have a hot dog and hot chocolate to celebrate?"

In our favorite booth at Phil Green's I was still shaking, but it was different. I felt certain, in the deepest corners of my body, that Matt was going to give me a baby. After I finished my hot dog, I put my feet up, as usual, and my head in Matt's lap.

"It was so *weird*, Matt, to have Dr. Hansen poking around inside me with you there watching."

"No kidding, Abby! The thought that flashed through my mind was: *This is the only other man in the universe who knows how beautiful Abigail is both inside and out.* And *he* needed a light. *I* know without the light."

"You're too funny, old guy. Are you going to read me your poem tonight?"

269

"Yes."

"And I found an old photograph in the office to show you."

After we got home from Phil Green's, Matt had to drop off some papers with Josie, his paralegal, for a real estate closing in February. I decided to go talk to Mom about our visit with Dr. Hansen. She had been there so long ago to tell her pre-teen daughter what that awful diagnosis meant, so I thought she should be the first person—maybe the *only* person—to hear that, hopefully, it didn't mean *anything* anymore. When I told Mom, she gave me a hesitant hug and one of those careful responses that only mothers can give.

"That's what you've always wanted, Abigail." Those were her *words*; but her tone and her body language both said *I still don't think this Matt is a good idea.* So I gave *her* a heartier hug and replied, "Don't worry, Mom. I know what I'm doing—*we* know what we're doing."

"But it's all happened so *fast*, Abigail."

"It's not fast for *me*, Mom. It's been nine or ten *years* for me. I have been looking for Matt since I was at Fatima."

And then my mother hit me with a question that was so *completely* out of character that I didn't know whether to laugh or cry: "Is your 'old guy' *that* good in bed, Abigail?"

I decided to laugh but give her the answer she deserved.

"Mom, I believe that since the dawn of time there could *never* have been a man as good in bed as Matt. You don't think I'm marrying him just for his Jeep and his Scottie dogs, do you?"

I think Mom realized she had embarrassed herself. "Abigail, you know I mean well?"

"I know, Mom. Listen, I haven't told anybody else except you—and I probably *never* will—about our visit to Dr. Hansen. I gotta go. I'll see you over the weekend. Love you."

Over dinner I told Matt about my conversation with Mom.

"Maybe she *would* like me better if I were twenty-six, Abby, although mothers are notorious for being suspicious of *any* guy who wants to take their daughter away."

"It might be different if you were a young guy, Matt, but honestly, I don't think *I* would like you better. You're Matt Flynn, one of a kind, my 'old guy,' and it couldn't be any other way. Let's go sit in the living room, double up in one chair, and you can read me your poem."

"I wrote this poem for Uncle Vinny's birthday in 1984. He was sixty-six, Matt was almost five, and Danny was almost two.

"As far back as I can remember, Uncle Vinny had always been there: my godfather and my second father. He actually was *way* ahead of Dad most of the time. He—and Uncle Sal, too—showed me how to cut wood, with a big saw and a jigsaw; how to sand it and glue it; how to screw screws and nail nails; how to paint everything from the side of a house to a small toy horse.

"Uncle Vinny bought me my first transistor radio, a Realistic Little-Six in a brown leather case with an earphone that kept me up late at night listening to baseball and rock and roll when Mom and Dad thought I was sleeping. And my first electric shaver, a Sunbeam Shavemaster. And he told me stories about all the Fiorinos, from my grandparents to my mother and all their brothers and sisters.

"From the time I was nine or ten, right through high school, I used to take the bus *every* Saturday morning to the old house—Uncle Sal and Uncle Patsy were still alive then—and wash and wax Uncle Vinny's beautiful red-and-white 1956 Oldsmobile 88, which always sparkled. And I also washed and waxed Aunt Connie's gigantic and gritty kitchen floor, which never—*ever*—looked clean or shiny. They usually paid me a dollar each, and that was my spending money for the week."

I thought I saw tears in Matt's eyes, so I snuggled a little closer in his lap and wrapped my arms tightly around his waist.

"When I turned eighteen, Uncle Vinny helped teach me how to drive. Mom and Dad had a 1962 stick-shift, power-nothing Chevy Bel Air, which drove like a truck. Uncle Vinny had a 1962 Chevy Impala with automatic transmission and power steering, which was a lot more fun. That was the car I drove to pass my road test."

Matt squeezed me with his left arm and kissed the top of my head. "I miss Uncle Vinny more than any person who has ever been in my life. So here goes."

> *Thirty-five years ago*
> *You bounced me on your knee*
> *You made me wooden toys*
> *You told me stories*
> *You showed me pictures of my Mother*
> *As a little girl*
> *You were my Uncle Vinny, my Godfather*
> *And I loved you*
> *Though I didn't know why*

Thirty-five years later
You bounce my sons on your knee
You make them wooden toys
You tell them stories
You show them pictures of their Daddy
As a little boy
And they love you
Though they don't know why

Now I know why
You are my Uncle Vinny, my Godfather
A special man of a thousand
Days of favors and love
A lifelong gift to me and my sons
Thank you, Uncle Vinny

I was in tears by the time he finished reading.

"Oh, Matt, I've never heard any words with more love in them."

We were quiet for a while. I reached down and scratched Maggie and Jock, who were staring at us as if they were trying to figure out how to get up in the chair. Then Matt lifted my face to his and kissed me.

"So what's this picture you found, sweetie?"

I took it out of an envelope I had set on the lamp table.

"Where did you *find* this, Abby?"

"In the beat-up, blue *Webster's* dictionary on the shelf, which is stuffed with a *lot* of pictures and newspaper clippings. I was checking on the spelling of 'carageen' for a school assignment, and there it was, tucked on the *CAR . . .* page."

"My definition of *car*, my first car, my 1971 Beetle."

"Putting aside the *very* shiny car for a second, Matt, who is the handsome, cute, bronzed, toned, solid, muscular, *hunky* guy washing and waxing the Bug?"

It was a twenty-something Matt—with long, curly hair falling over his forehead, long sideburns, wearing old-fashioned, gold wire-rimmed glasses, shirtless and barefoot, dressed only in wet khaki shorts cut off at mid-thigh and tied at the waist with a rope belt. He was rubbing a navy blue Volkswagen with a white towel on a sunny summer day.

"Wow! That was the summer of 1971 when I came home from Vietnam and had six weeks' leave before I went back to Ft.

272

Sam Houston. I was twenty-five, Abby. Do you think you would have liked that guy?"

"You were *gorgeous*, Matt—you still are—but all the body parts in this picture look a little more full and firm: your arms, your legs, your *very* pretty belly. I might not have *liked* you but I would have jumped you for sex."

He laughed and buried his face in the hair on my neck.

"Is that when you were in love with Missy?"

"Yeah. And just two years later Missy would be gone and I would be in law school."

"I still don't understand how that girl could let you go."

"Fortunately, that's one of my scars that you've erased, beauty."

"Let's go up to bed, Matt. After Dr. Hansen and your poem and this picture, I am so hungry for your body that I'm afraid I might *hurt* you."

I don't know how long I ravished Matt—twenty minutes, two hours?—I was practically in a *frenzy* after such an intense day. And ultimately, totally exhausted. I crashed so hard that when I woke up the next morning, it was ten o'clock. Matt and the doggies had already had breakfast and gone for a long walk. I knocked on the bedroom wall and yelled downstairs.

"Coffee, please! And *where* are my doggies?"

Maggie and Jock were up the stairs and in bed with me in ten seconds. Matt walked through the door about a minute later and handed me his white mug with seven black Scottie puppies on it—my favorite.

"Thanks, sweetie. Why didn't you wake me up?"

"We *tried*, beauty. I played with you and touched you and kissed you everywhere, and Jock and Maggie licked your feet and your cheeks. But you didn't move a muscle or make a sound. You were really wiped out from last night."

"Lie down with me, Matt. I wanted you so bad last night. How much did I beat you up?"

"We made love—*you* mostly—three times before you fell asleep lying across my stomach. I had to kind of roll you over and turn you to get your head on the pillow next to me. I started kissing some of the perspiration, or maybe tears, on your face, and then *I* was gone, too."

"I think I remember scratching you. Did I *do* that?"

"Hey, pretty girl, whatever you did, I don't feel any pain this morning. But I wouldn't mind if you check me—*very* closely—

for the rest of the day for scratches or bruises."

I hugged him with all the strength I had.

"Matt, the last two weeks have been so *beautiful*—to be with you almost *all* day, *every* day— the best weeks of my life. The truth is that every day since November 12 has been the best *day* of my life. What a way to start a new year! On Monday, I'll be back at Kitty's and RIT, and then back at Mangrums on Tuesday. But none of it will be the same. Do you know there are seventy-one days, including a Leap Day, until our wedding? I love you *so* much."

As soon as I took off my gloves when Matt and I walked through the back door of Kitty's on Monday morning, she spotted my ring, grabbed my hand and squealed, "Oh, my! Abigail, look what you did when I wasn't there to supervise. What a beautiful ring! Hooray for both of you! I take full credit, you know. If I hadn't hired this pretty girl, none of this would have happened."

She gave Matt and me lusty hugs.

"Kitty, I've been meaning to ask you about that for months. Why *did* you hire me? I saw three or four other girls in here filling out applications the same day I did."

"Honey, I thought maybe you were pretty enough and sassy enough to bring a lot of gentlemen customers back for seconds. I never *dreamed* that one of those gentlemen would become your husband. Matt, go sit with your fat book at your usual table in the front window and see if you can bring in some *women* customers. I want to talk to Abby for a minute."

I was back in the real world again . . . sort of. While Kitty and I were talking about schedules and supplies, I thought *This is the real world . . . but not exactly. I'm back at Kitty's place, and at my Masters program at RIT, and at my internship at Mangrums*—here I smiled inside and out— *but now I'm back with a sweetheart, and with an engagement ring, and with a wedding date. That old saying "back to the real world" is never going to sound gloomy any more.*

274

24

Matt and I had two very crowded weeks ahead of us before our weekend with the Stegers in Pittsburgh. He had several insurance and real estate clients to prepare for, and some home-repair projects with Tom at their mom and dad's house; I had to complete my Masters thesis outline for Prof. Foster's preliminary review. Coffee at Kitty's the next morning would be the last time that Matt and I were together during the day for the rest of the week. And the following week would be pretty much the same.

On Tuesday and Thursday when I came home late from Mangrums, we played with Maggie and Jock, played with each other on the sofa or in front of the fireplace, and went to bed *way* early to catch up on our body talk. On Monday and Wednesday after dinner at Phil Green's or Palermo's or at home, we shared our days, watched the snow through the front windows, made our wedding lists, sipped our red wine and enjoyed our books. Matt was now up to the Battle of Winchester and, in *Bridges*, Francesca's husband and children would soon be coming home from the Illinois State Fair.

I was secretly working on a drawing of Matt, and I suspected he was secretly writing a poem for me. We had a lovely evening celebrating with Mom and Dad and the whole family on January 11. It even appeared to me that Mom was as familiar and comfortable with Matt as she was with Patrick and Jack. Maybe it was just wishful thinking.

On Saturday morning, the sun was shining gloriously on all the overnight snow. The glare was so strong that I had to wear sunglasses when we walked Maggie and Jock. After our oatmeal, toast and Cheerios, Matt asked, "Would you like to go to Holy Sepulchre Cemetery to visit Aunt Connie and the boys on this beautiful morning? We can even take the baby dogs."

On my way out the door, I took the red rose from the milk glass vase to leave at the grave. The wind-swept snow was even *more* brilliant at the cemetery. There was a raised gray image of Our Lady near the top of the black FIORINO headstone, and four names engraved at the bottom:

Pasquale F. 1906-1966
Salvatore J. 1911-1976
Concetta M. 1916-2004
Vincenzo T. 1918-1995

"Matt, what do the middle initials stand for?" I asked with my arm around his waist.

"Francis, *Francesco*; Joseph, *Giuseppe*; Maria; and Thomas, *Tomasso*."

I stood the red rose straight up in the snow in the middle of the stone, between Salvatore and Concetta. We said an Our Father and a Hail Mary, then brushed the snow off Maggie and Jock and drove home. I felt like I needed our thinking booth, so we went to Phil Green's for lunch. After my red hot, I stretched out and put my feet up as usual and asked Matt, "Old guy, do you suppose Uncle Vinny and Aunt Connie and your other aunts and uncles are watching us now?"

"I'm sure they are, Abby. I see their faces in my mind and talk to them almost every day. And they'll be with us when we get married, beauty."

I smiled and reached up from Matt's lap and touched his lips.

"What do you think they say when they see us making love?"

"Probably 'Good for you, Mattie!' though they might be saying it in Italian: Urra per Matteo!"

"Mattie?"

"That's what everybody in the family called me when I was growing up. Listen, pretty girl, I am *absolutely* certain that all the old folks would love you . . . the same as cousin Theresa and all of her family love you."

The days before Pittsburgh went by *so* fast. I handed in the first draft of my thesis outline to Prof. Foster on Wednesday, January 16. On Friday, as soon as I got home from Mangrums, we took Maggie and Jock to Happy Tails, went to Phil Green's for a fish fry, then back home to pack. We planned on meeting the Stegers between one and two at the Hampton Inn, so Matt and I hit the road Saturday at seven-thirty. I kept falling asleep and drooping on Matt between Rochester and Erie—I had been that far on my way to Cleveland a few times—but as soon as we stopped for gas in Erie and turned south, it was all new to me. I enjoyed the hills—even *mountains*—heading into Pittsburgh, and crossing the three rivers through downtown was breathtaking.

"Matt, I can't *believe* I've never been to Pittsburgh—this is spectacular!"

"Yeah, it sure is, Abby. I discovered Pittsburgh when Kevin Flynn, my good friend from B.C., went to the University of Pittsburgh Law School after he got out of the Army. I came down here to visit him a few times while I worked for the Post Office. Now we go up over the hills to a little suburb on the south side called Green Tree. Matt and Danny and I stayed at the same Hampton Inn on the last night of our trip in 1995."

After we checked in, we sat in the lobby and sipped tea while we waited for the Stegers. Matt surprised me by choosing Constant Comment rather than Earl Grey.

"I never saw you drink that before, old guy."

"Missy Steger started me on Constant Comment a million years ago, and I still like it."

Just then the Stegers pulled in and waved to us from their Grand Cherokee. As soon as they walked into the lobby, Matt and Joe gave each other *huge* hugs. I never saw men hug that hard. Margie and I gave each other a small hug. She is an inch or two shorter than I am and much more petite. Then Joe *kind* of hugged me, but mostly he had his hands on the back of my shoulders while he studied my face and stared into my eyes. Then he finished the hug and kissed me on the lips and whispered in my ear, "Good for Matt!"

There was an instant bond between us: we knew right away that we were both Matt's best friend. And we knew right away that we would both be willing to give up *everything* for him. That is an overwhelming realization to share, and Joe and I have been very close ever since our hug in Pittsburgh.

Our two days with the Stegers were delightful: swapping stories in the hotel hot tub; talking about the "kids"—Joe and Margie's sons, Matt and Eddie, were about the same ages as Matt and Danny; all four of us hugging together as we walked briskly across the mustard-colored bridges; the ice forming instantly from the spray of the fountain at the Golden Triangle; our concert at Heinz Hall—the Pittsburgh Symphony performing Beethoven's *Sixth*; the musical rainbow fountains at Bessemer Court in Station Square; our sumptuous family-style Italian dinner at Casa Toscano; and our lovely breakfasts at the hotel.

If we weren't friends and lovers, we could easily have been sisters and brothers. I understood that there is no stronger love than that between two men who have faced death together and saved each other. Margie and I agreed that we had to get our guys together *way* more than once a year.

When we got back home, the "real world" was even busier than before we left. Prof. Foster gave me back my outline with enough red comments to require a week to correct. Claire had to spend Wednesday in Albany with her boss, Senator Kelly. And Matthew IV had a cold and ear infection and couldn't go to child care. Matt III had a full day of classes and testing at MCC, so Matt and I had the kids from breakfast through bedtime.

I couldn't cut any more classes, but Matthew and Emily took their afternoon naps while I was at school, so I didn't miss much. Matt said the only problem was trying to keep Maggie and Jock—typical Scotties who want to watch the street through the front windows and bark at any creature that moves—quiet so the kids could sleep. We took them to Phil Green's for dinner, and they kept everybody laughing. Emily was still eating mostly baby food but she enjoyed a few tater tots, and Matthew gobbled up his grilled cheese sandwich. Then they shared a kiddie cone with vanilla ice cream and rainbow sprinkles. Claire told us that she would have to do an Albany day about once a month— probably the last Wednesday of the month—until the end of the state legislature session in late June, so Matt and I marked our calendars . . . and I started laughing.

"What's so funny, beauty?"

"Well, old guy, I'm not even a wife and a mother yet, and here I am setting up a schedule to take care of the *grandchildren*. How did I get so old so fast?"

Matt smiled and wrapped me in his arms.

On Saturday, we had lunch with Dennis Connolly at his party house and finalized the details for our reception.

"You know that's the Ides of March," Dennis said, smiling ominously.

Matt laughed. "I guess we'll have to ask all our family and friends to check their daggers and togas at the door. And cross cousin Brutus off the invitation list, Abby."

Our guest list had grown to almost two hundred. Our immediate families and close friends mostly evened out, but Matt had all his Fiorino first cousins who would fill his side of the church.

I called Nannie to let her know that Matt and I would come to visit on February 16 and 17. She said that she would have the "bridal suite" ready for us, and she and Grandpa couldn't wait.

No matter how busy we both were, Matt and I had dinner together every evening except for my late nights at Mangrums. We took the baby dogs for walks together every chance we had during the day. And we always made love at least once every night before we went to sleep, and at least once every morning before we got out of bed. It was never part of a mental checklist; it wasn't something we thought about at *all*. To Matt and me, it was as natural and necessary and comforting as pulling the covers over each other and squeezing together at night, and stretching and yawning and rubbing against each other in the morning.

It had been more than two months since the first night we slept together and we hadn't been apart one night since. For all those nights, we shared *one* pillow. No one would have believed that. The only time I ever thought about how amazing it was to be so close to Matt was whenever I suddenly became aware that we *weren't* touching, and then I would touch as much of his body as I could without waking him up. Matt felt the same way. He told me on our first night together when I asked him to undress me, and he had told me every day since.

With the handful of boys—only *one* was older than thirty—I had intercourse with before I met Matt, it had always been a production. I would have a script and expectations in my mind, and I'm sure the guy did, too. We knew our cues and we were careful about what *not* to say. Sometimes it was still fun in spite of all that, but mostly sex was something to be accomplished because we were growing up and it was expected, and we *needed* to compare experiences and results with our best girlfriends.

Even though some of my friends kept telling me how special and wonderful it was, I always thought that they were probably rationalizing or pretending. For me, it was as simple as closing my eyes in the sun. Without a commitment or a bond with a boy, sex was always more complicated than satisfying. But the moment Matt and I became a part of each other, sex became a sixth sense, combining the best of all the senses. Now we could no more do *without* it than we could do without daylight or music.

On Sunday in front of the fire, *Bridges* became too much for me, and I had to take away Matt's Civil War book and cry on his chest. Francesca decided not to leave her husband and children and go away with Robert. Was he her second chance at happiness, and she decided to stay with her *first* chance, her husband and family? Or was Francesca's family merely and forever mundane, and she was giving up her one chance at happiness? Was Matt *my* one chance? My *only* chance? I didn't care. I knew in the depths of my heart and body that he was my *best* chance.

After school on Wednesday while we were walking Maggie and Jock around the circle, Matt said, "I wrote a poem for you, beauty. I just finished it today. I haven't written a poem in *five* years."

"Oh, Matt, I'm so excited! I was hoping you would. Will you take me down to Phil Green's for dinner and read it to me for dessert?"

We both felt like Italian sausage sandwiches for a change, and after we finished and sipped our hot chocolate quietly for a few minutes—leaning in to each other in our booth—I rested my head in Matt's lap and whispered, "When did you start writing my poem, old guy?"

He brushed his fingers through my hair and tucked it behind my ears.

"Last Monday night when we got back from Pittsburgh, Abby, but every time you fell asleep in the car the words were coming together in my mind. I couldn't write them down, so I had to repeat them over and over in my head so I wouldn't forget. Are you ready? Has anyone ever written you a poem before?"

"Only my brother Patrick, but it was one of those silly 'roses are red' things: 'Roses are red, and sisters are gabby; but I have the best one, her name is Abby.' I think Pat was maybe six, and I was eleven, and he wrote it with a red crayon on some light blue construction paper. I still have it at Mom and Dad's. After that, I guess I was never inspiring enough," I shrugged.

"*That* I find pretty impossible to believe," Matt smiled, stroking my cheeks with the back of his fingers. "But it *does* make me a very lucky man. Here goes . . . surprisingly enough, my new poem is titled 'Abigail.'"

> *Almost every night I have some dreams,*
> *and almost every morning when I wake up,*
> *they're all gone . . .*
> *except for one who didn't go away.*
> *I don't think she was just a one-night dream;*

I think she was the dream of months and years.
I think she came together in my sleep,
breath by tasted lips by touch,
colors by musical voice by scent,
night by night, one sense at a time.
I didn't make her up—she came to me:
her dark green eyes, her soft vanilla skin,
her new-penny freckles and new-penny hair.
But I never dreamed how delicious she'd be
in a cherry red satin party dress.
And I never dreamed how she'd look at me
in the sunshine in the morning
when I woke her with a kiss.
And I never dreamed that she'd bring me to life
with the light in her eyes and the love in her hands.
I never dreamed that she'd lie with me
every day . . . an old guy like me.
I never dreamed she'd stay.
I never dreamed she'd say,
'I want to have your baby, Matt.'
I never dreamed she could be you."

I started crying at "dark green eyes" and I couldn't stop.

"Oh, Matt!" I took both of his hands and pressed them against my wet face. "It's *so* beautiful! I love you so much. Please . . . will you wipe away some of my tears? I can't see. Oh, *Matt*, that was worth waiting twenty-six years."

"You won't have to wait that long for the next one, beauty. You inspire me *every* day."

"Will you make me a copy, old guy, that I can keep in my purse? I'll read it *fifty* times a day until I have it memorized . . . unless it makes me cry every time. I'm so tired from the tears. Hold my hands, Matt; they're shaking."

"*Shh.* Close your eyes, pretty girl, take a rest. I'll hold you and keep you warm."

I closed my eyes and tried to think about the poem and where I was, but I couldn't. I felt Matt's hands moving over my body, and after a while I think I dreamed that they were touching my "dark green eyes" and "new-penny freckles." I woke up when I heard a car beep. Matt had his head propped in his left hand on the table and he was looking down at me. He had taken off his Yankee jacket and covered me from my shoulders to my hips,

281

and he was rubbing my hands and my belly through the jacket. I wasn't shaking any more.

"*Mmm*, how long was I sleeping, old guy?"

"About twenty minutes, Abby. Are you okay?"

"I think so. Matt,"—I took a deep breath—"your poem turned me inside out. I can't *believe* you keep opening up emotions I didn't know I had."

"A lot of *feeling* went into your poem, beauty. They're not *all* like that. Some are games, some are jokes, some are stories, some are snapshots. Yours was *all* feeling."

"And I felt it coming out. I wonder if it will be the same when I read it myself."

"Don't be surprised if you discover something new or feel something new every time you read it. One of the beauties of poetry is that different people see meanings and experience feelings that the writer was never trying to put in the poem. That even happens to *me* when I read my own poems long after I've finished them."

I rolled onto my side in the booth and hugged Matt's thighs.

"You would have made a *great* English professor, old guy."

"That was my plan forty-plus years ago, love, but then Vietnam and ROTC and the Army took precedence—and here you are, the girl of my dreams." Matt played with my hair. "If I had been a college professor, I might have met a woman from Nebraska and have three beautiful daughters living somewhere in the Midwest. But then where would *you* be?" he grinned. "No, pretty girl, I could not be happier *anywhere* than I am right here in this booth."

For the next few weeks—right up to our trip to visit Nannie and Grandpa Dolan—I felt like I was living in two dimensions. I called them the "motions" and the "emotions." The "motions" was the routine. At RIT, I turned my revised outline back in to Prof. Foster and worked on the preliminary layout of the advertising supplement for my print media course. At Mangrums, our team finalized the marketing and advertising schedule for the rollout of the first six "Ready-to-Eat Dinners for Two."

The "emotions" was Matt and I, and now my poem. I read it in the morning when Matt wasn't home. I read it on my breaks at Kitty's. I read it in between classes at RIT. I read it when no one was watching at Mangrums. I read it in the car and in the bathroom. I could read it now without crying, but when I read it to Mary Kay on the phone, I heard *her* crying. I guess I had given up on the fairy-tale notion of being somebody's "dream girl," but now I loved that idea and that feeling more every day and every time I read my poem. I believed *every* word in the poem, but I knew I would have to ask Matt one burning question.

Saturday night at home was the right time. It was Groundhog Day, and Matt and I were on the sofa with Maggie and Jock watching Bill Murray and Andie MacDowell fall in love day after day.

"Matt, I've read your poem so many times that the lines keep flashing across my mind all day. One question keeps coming up. I'm probably going to say this wrong, but . . . when you walked in to Kitty's the first day, was it *love* at first sight or *dream* at first sight? I mean, did you dream about the girl in your poem for so long that you fell for me because I looked like your dream girl? Or did you walk in to Kitty's and look in my eyes and fall in love, and I just *happened* to match up closely with your dream girl? Am I making any sense? Do you know what I mean?"

Matt wrapped me in his arms and nibbled through the hair around my ears.

"Beauty, I *do* know what you mean, and I think the answer is 'none of the above.' I'm sure I didn't *think* about it at all that first morning. There you were, and I looked into your eyes and listened to your voice—and I *felt* you, I *sensed* you. Over the next three or four days when I *did* think about it, I *realized* that *you* were the girl I had been yearning for.

"Dreams are mostly fleeting glimpses and outlines, and when I worked backwards from you and tried to flesh mine out, I realized that they *were* you. That is not only an incredible realization but an incredible blessing. I doubt if it happens to many people. Most husbands and wives probably spend their whole lives reconciling their *ideal* sweetheart with their *real* spouse. So, I don't think it was so much that I found my dream in you, as that you *became* my dream. That's what I tried to say—in about a third as many words—in my poem. Does *that* make any sense?"

"Your dream girl and I became the *same* girl?"

"More than that, Abby. You changed my dream girl into *you*."

25

It was hard to believe that all the cliches I had heard and read about love were turning out to be true. The more I learned about Matt, the more I loved him. And the more I loved him, the more I wanted to know about him. And he said exactly that about *me* as we talked in the car on the way to Stockbridge on February 16.

"Abigail, every day with you there's something new. Nothing you do surprises me anymore. You *did* the first couple of days. That first morning at Kitty's when you said, 'Can you come in tomorrow?' And the next day in your apartment when you said, 'I want you.' Since then, I've seen one more layer of your personality come to the surface almost every day, or one more secret place in your heart come to light. Or you've told me about one more wish that's been growing in your mind for years. All of those things make me love you more every day.

"I have known a lot of twenty-plus women—including my daughters-in-law, my nieces and all my old girlfriends—very well. But I've never known a young woman with your depth of heart, or the intuitive flashes of your mind, or the sensual nuances of your love. It will take me the rest of my life to try to take you all in, and I expect I will run out of years before I can do it."

The persistent snow flurries and swirling wind made the driving dicey, so I kept touching Matt and playing with him to keep both of us alert.

"We're missing two birthdays tomorrow, old guy. I sent Jack a card from both of us, which is all we usually do, but what about Matt III?"

"Sorry, beauty, I forgot to tell you. Claire invited us for pizza and cake Monday night when we get back. Matt will be twenty-nine tomorrow. How about Jack?"

"Thirty-three. Do we have a present for Matt?"

"We *do*. I actually bought it in September when I saw it on sale at Barnes & Noble: the Tenth Edition of *The Baseball Encyclopedia*. My brother Tom gave me the First Edition for

Christmas in 1969, and it's been a family treasure ever since. Matt loves the statistics and the history even more than I do. So we just need to wrap it up and get a card."

I laughed and kissed his cheek. "Matthew Flynn, I've never met any guys who love baseball as much as you and Danny and Matt do."

"Changing the subject, pretty girl, I heard your Nannie say she had 'something borrowed' and 'something blue' for you for our wedding. Do you know what they are?"

"I have no idea, Matt. And *don't* be playing with my leg— keep that hand on the wheel. Mom already told me that she bought me a 'new' red garter, and the 'something old,' of course, is her wedding dress. Which reminds me, we have to line up our wedding party, like *yesterday*. Who's going to be your best man?"

"Matt *and* Danny. I called them both yesterday. And Matthew will be our ring bearer."

"Oh, that will be *so* special, sweetie."

"How many bridesmaids were you thinking of besides Mary Kay?"

"If we stay small, I would ask my new sisters, Claire and Emma. And then you would need one more groomsman. But what about our brothers? Will your brothers be upset if we don't ask them? Patrick will be okay, no matter what, and Jack probably doesn't even want to *come*."

"Well, our four brothers would require four more girls, and then we'd have a *giant* wedding. But, Abby, I want you to have the wedding *you* want. Don't worry about Alan and Tom; they'll be fine either way."

"Then I say *small*. Who will you ask to match up with Mary Kay?"

"Joe Steger, and hope that none of my other really good friends will be upset."

"I'm going to call Claire and Emma right now and ask them. We'll have to go pick out dresses next week."

We pulled in to Nannie and Grandpa's at one o'clock, and Nannie had lunch ready for us. Ike, their loveable golden doodle, was jumping all over us, and undoubtedly smelled Maggie and Jock. After lunch, Matt helped Grandpa get a fire going in the family room, and then Gramps cleared off the coffee table and opened his two scrapbooks from The War. Nannie and I knew that our boys would be completely absorbed for hours, so we went upstairs to her bedroom.

Nannie opened the mahogany jewelry box on her long bureau and gently took out a red, white and blue ribbon that was about eight inches long. She took my hand, sat with me on the edge of her bed, opened my fingers and laid the ribbon in my palm, smoothing it flat, over and over, reverently.

"Abigail, until today, I have worn this ribbon *every* day since your grandpa gave it to me on the day we arrived in New York from Wales, right after he proposed."

Nannie smiled mischievously.

"Don't tell anybody, honey, but when I was younger, some days I tied it to my garter and some days I tied it to the strap of my bra. When I got to be a grandma, I started putting it in one of the pockets of whatever I was wearing."

"What kind of ribbon is it, Nannie?"

"It's the ribbon that came with your grandpa's Silver Star, honey. He was awarded the Silver Star during the Battle of the Bulge, but even after sixty-two years together, he has *never* told me what he did to receive it. I wouldn't be surprised, though, if he tells your Matthew.

"This is your 'something borrowed,' Abigail. It could also be 'something blue,' I guess, but this time it's not. I have a different 'something blue' for you. This ribbon has brought your grandpa and me good luck *every* day, and I want you to keep it and wear it on your wedding day and *every* day after that until you have your baby." Her eyes glistened with childish delight.

"*Baby*, Nannie? How do you know . . ."

"*Shush*, sweetie. I know what your mother said about the mumps when you were a young girl, but I think it's a bunch of hooey. I can see it in your eyes and in the way you and Matthew touch each other. I know you want to have his baby, and I'm certain you will. When your baby is born and Grandpa and I come to visit you, you can give me back the ribbon. And don't tell Grandpa; he doesn't know a thing about it."

I hugged Nannie and began crying—sobbing really—and she started to stroke my back and my hair, my eighty-four-year-old grandmother comforting me.

"It's all good, honey; it's all good. He's the right man, honey. It's all good."

When I stopped crying, Nannie went back to the jewelry box and took out something else and brought it over to me on the bed. It was a silver brooch in the shape of a butterfly, with one large, blue oval stone in the body of the butterfly and lots of smaller stones in the wings.

"It's beautiful, Nannie!"

"It's sterling silver, Abigail, with blue topaz stones. There are ten in each wing. Grandmother Connor gave this to me when I was eleven, just before she died. She said that *her* grandmother had given it to her in 1890 on her wedding day. Can you imagine that, dear? And *her* grandmother Connor—I think her name was Gwendolyn—told *my* grandmother Connor that she had received the brooch as a gift on *her* wedding day in 1837, when she was seventeen. Apparently London jewelers made many of these in honor of the young Queen Victoria, who loved butterflies, and whose favorite color was blue. Isn't that something? I don't know how many grandmothers that is, Abigail—I'll let *you* count them up—but this butterfly goes back to Queen Victoria when she was a teenager. This is yours to keep, and maybe give to *your* granddaughter one day."

"Nannie, I'm going to cry again."

"Never you mind, honey. It's all good. That's what life *is:* mothers to daughters, and grandmothers to granddaughters. It's all good."

We had a lovely two days with Nannie and Grandpa. Nannie showed me dozens of photographs of Mom as a little girl in Rochester, and herself as a little girl in Swansea. She made a delicious Irish stew on Saturday night, and scalloped potatoes and ham on Sunday night. Gramps entertained Matt with his World War II scrapbooks, and Matt showed him how to pull up maps of the European battlefields on their old desktop computer. And we all went to the giant, indoor Stockbridge Mall to shop for gifts for the members of our wedding party. They were two *perfect* days for Matt and me.

In the Jeep heading west Monday morning—with dry roads in front of us and a brilliant sun behind us—he couldn't wait to ask. "You are positively *glowing* with happiness, but what about 'something borrowed' and 'something blue,' Abby? You haven't breathed a *word*."

"Matt, I can't believe that I get happier every day. It doesn't seem possible. But then Nannie gives you her seal of *highest* approval—'He's the right man,' she said—and she gives us her blessing, and gives me two of her treasures . . . and great days and great plans become perfect."

"Tell me about the treasures, pretty girl."

"I can't, old guy. I have to *show* them to you. You'll have to wait until we get home. They are too wonderful for words, and Nannie didn't want me to show you in front of Grandpa.

"Speaking of Grandpa, Nannie said he was awarded a Silver Star for the Battle of the Bulge, but he has never told her what he did. She thought he might tell *you*. Did he?"

"He did, Abby, but he made me promise to tell you that you *can't* tell Nannie."

"But Gramps doesn't mind if you tell *me*?"

"Nope. Even though he's never told anybody in the family, he said he's wanted to tell *you*— just *you*—for a long time. When we get home, I'll show you on a map where it all happened, but this is what your grandpa said. And I'm going to try to go slow and remember his *exact* words.

My outfit, the 137th Infantry, was moving up the road from Arlon to Bastogne, which was about twenty miles, right along the border between Belgium and Luxembourg. I was in Company K, a rifle company in the Third Battalion, and we were pretty close to the front of the column.

It was the morning before Christmas. We were more than halfway to Bastogne, near the village of Warnach, when Lt. Col. Wilton, the battalion commander, pulled Capt. O'Hara, my company commander, aside and told him that our lead units were taking some heavy fire—he thought it might be one or two Panzers—from some high ground east of the road. Would O'Hara send a couple of men to check it out? The captain asked for two volunteers, and Corporal Walter Jablonski and I said we'd go.

We headed north and east away from the road and over some small hills—and there she was: a giant Panzer, one of the new ones, a Tiger II. We didn't spot any infantry support, so Walt and I circled around from the right, out of sight of the Panzer's front slits. I climbed up on the tank while Walt covered the crest of the hill behind us. I pulled the pins on two grenades and dropped them down the hatch.

At that exact moment, some infantry came over the crest of the hill and started firing at us. Walt took two or three of them out as I jumped off the Panzer and we headed down toward the road. The sound of the two grenades blowing the inside of that tank behind us was the sweetest sound of my life—at least until Betsy said "yes" when I proposed to her on the floor of her mom

288

and dad's store. Walt and I took a few hits as we scrambled down the hill. Walt took one in his left arm, and they had to send him back to the field hospital outside Metz to patch him up. He was back with us in two weeks.

Walter Jablonski was the strongest and toughest man I ever met. He and his wife live near Milwaukee, and we still send each other Christmas cards.

I took one round in the sleeve of my greatcoat and one in the heel of my boot. I was a lucky guy. All I suffered was a leaky boot for a week until Capt. O'Hara got me a new one. And, Matthew, I don't know if you ever saw anything like this in Vietnam, but it was a beautiful sight to see that big, black-and-yellow Tiger split at the seams and engulfed in flames at the top of that hill.

After the Bulge was over, the 35th moved closer to the Rhine, and sometime in the middle of February the Third Army held an awards ceremony in Trier. "Old Blood and Guts" himself, Lt. Gen. George S. Patton, Jr., pinned the Silver Stars on Walt and me. We were standing shoulder-to-shoulder in front of the whole 137th. The general had clear blue eyes, and I thought I saw tears. He said to both of us, "It's not big shots like me but brave men like you who kicked the Krauts back into Germany and who will win this war. Thank you."

I never told Betsy because there were probably five Germans in that tank, and I didn't want her to know that I killed five men just like that. I would do it again, of course, to protect my buddies, but our girls don't need to know about such things. They just need us to keep them safe.

I think I cried for an hour on Matt's shoulder while he told me Grandpa's story, almost all the way to Syracuse. And when we got home and I showed him the red, white and blue ribbon from the Silver Star and told him Nannie's story, Matt had tears in his eyes, too. And he was as much in awe of my 1837 Queen Victoria butterfly as I was.

We still look at it and touch it in wonder.

We had a happy, belated birthday party with Matt and Claire and the kids. Matthew III loved *The Baseball Encyclopedia*, of course, and the pizza and ice cream cake were delicious. After we finished eating, the kids settled on the sofa for a Scooby-Doo video, the Matts flipped pages in the *Encyclopedia*, and Claire and I talked about dresses. I showed her a picture of Mom's dress, and Claire suggested that she, Emma and Mary Kay wear pastel green dresses to celebrate both spring and St. Patrick's Day. We called Emma and Mary Kay, and they both agreed enthusiastically. And much to my relief, they also both said they would come in to town Friday night, and we could pick out the dresses on Saturday. Claire said she knew Vangie of Evangeline's Wedding Boutique and would call her in the morning to give her an idea of what we would be looking for.

By the time we got into bed with the doggies Monday night, Matt and I were completely wiped out. I was so glad that he would be able to take me to Kitty's in the morning. Even though I was overwhelmed with happiness, I was also overwhelmed with details, and I felt as if I needed every person in my world to hold my hands for the next three weeks. Matt could tell. He always sensed my thoughts and feelings better than I did myself. That night he held me as tightly and touched me as gently as he ever had. *God and Mary and St. Patrick, bless this man,* I thought as Matt came inside me and I drifted toward sleep. *God and Mary and St. Patrick, thank you for his love in the night, and please bring the morning bright. Amen.*

At Kitty's, Matt sat at his usual window table with Shelby Foote. He said he was reading about the fighting at Beaver Dam Creek outside of Richmond. When we had a lull in customers, Kitty and I sketched out the three layers of the traditional wedding cake she was going to make for us. "My wedding gift for you and Matt," she said. The flowers and writing and other highlights would be in shades of green to match the bridesmaids' dresses. (When I woke up that morning, one of the first thoughts—other than the urge for Matt's body—that came into my mind was that Claire's, Emma's and Mary Kay's dresses should be different shades of green.)

Mom called right after lunch and said that the RSVPs had really poured in since Friday, and very few people had said no. I told her I would pick them up the next day after school so Matt and I could start arranging the tables. I had a teenage-girl idea at Mangrums, and it grew on me until I got home at eight-thirty. When Matt and I settled on the sofa with Maggie and Jock and our glasses of Chianti to watch the start of *The Cutting Edge,* one of his favorite movies, I stroked his cheek and said, "Old guy, I wanted to ask you first before I talk with Claire, Emma and Mary Kay, but would it be okay with you if I kicked you out of your house Friday night and invited my wedding 'sisters' over for a pajama party? I haven't done a sleep-over since Fatima but, more important, I haven't spent a *single* night without you since our first night together when I asked you to undress me. It's still exciting for me just to *say* that. Anyway, it's a close call for me, and I really, *really* won't be upset if you say no, sweetie."

Matt paused the movie, took my head in both his hands and kissed me tenderly all around my face. "Of *course* it's okay, beauty. What *fun* for you and the girls! Danny and I can camp out at Matt's and do guy stuff.

"I probably won't be able to sleep without you, though. It's funny how our habits and body rhythms change. Before you came in to my life, I had slept alone for *ten* years. Now that's practically unthinkable, and even if I were able to *think* it, to my body it would be completely traumatic. The fact is, Miss Abigail, you turned a restless, *full*-bed, sprawling guy into half of an inseparable one-*pillow* couple.

"A couple of weeks after you moved in with me, I had a flashback to my early nights in Saigon. When I first got there, it was difficult to fall asleep because the B-52 bombers went out at night to hit targets on what was called the Ho Chi Minh Trail along the border between Vietnam and Cambodia. Every night, there was a steady 'thump, thump, thump' as I lay in bed. But after a few weeks, the only time I thought about it was when the bombers *didn't* go out, and I suddenly became aware that there were no thumps."

"Wow, Matt, I've never been compared to a *bomber* before." We both laughed.

"You know what I mean, pretty girl. Listen, if you all want to have a really *cool* slumber party, I'll put four twin mattresses in the living room, and you can all sleep together. I'll even build a fire for you girls before you kick me out."

After my last class the next day, I stopped at Mom's. She had opened and rubber-banded all the RSVPs in a large Mangrums grocery bag.

"I counted them, Abigail. There are one hundred forty-six coming and only twelve not coming."

"Thanks, Mom. I'll let you know if Matt and I need any help arranging the tables."

"How are all the plans coming?"

"Good, Mom. Kitty's making our cake, and we sketched that

out yesterday at the coffee shop. Matt's brother Tom knows a good DJ, and they are working on a song list that will get everybody dancing. Matt booked the photographer who did Danny and Emma's wedding two years ago. I saw his pictures—they're wonderful!

"Danny and *young* Matt are planning a bachelor party for the thirteenth, and Matt and I booked the party room at Palermo's for the rehearsal dinner on Friday the fourteenth. Claire and Emma and Laurie and Mary Kay have been helping me with everything and keeping me on track. And guess *what*? Emma and Mary Kay are coming in to town Friday night, and the four of us—I call us 'the wedding sisters'—are going to pick out the bridesmaids dresses on Saturday. Will you join us, Mom? We might need your expert opinion."

"I would *love* to, honey."

When I got home, I found Matt working at the dining room table, which we had started to call "wedding central."

"Here they are, old guy. So far, one hundred forty-six are 'yes' and only *twelve* are 'no.' I looked through them quickly and put all your best friends on top—they're *all* coming: Joe and Margie, of course; Tony and Maria Lenzi; Jerry and Cheryl Brongo; Dave and Ann; Ken and Melanie Bauman; and Kevin Flynn and his mother Agnes. He's bringing his *mother*? Is he any relation?"

Matt laughed, stood up and gave me a huge hug, and then clasped his arms under my fanny and lifted me off my feet and over his head. I *squealed.* He kept murmuring "I love you" with his face buried in my belly, while I held on to his head for dear life.

"Stop that, Matt! Put me down! You'll hurt yourself!"

And then he surprised me *again*, which I didn't think was still possible: he *carried* me upstairs, laid me down on the bed and closed the door.

"How did you *do* that, old guy?"

"*Shh*, Abby."

Matt took off his clothes, then knelt in bed beside me and undressed me . . . gently, with kisses all over my body. When he slowly pulled down my pantyhose and started kissing my toes, I was too hot to wait any more.

"Matt, please, now!"

He came inside me and sparked all my senses into a blaze. I don't remember anything after that. Matt told me when I woke up that I had been more ferocious and screamed louder than I ever had before. He said I even got the doggies barking downstairs.

"I'm going to have to carry you to bed more *often*, pretty girl."

"Matt, you turn me into a wild *animal*. Before I met you, the thought of a man having that kind of power over my body—to make me lose control of myself—was *way* too scary for me. I always held back. I never, *ever* was out of control with any guy. Now I can't *wait* to give it up. I want you to *take* it—I want the frenzy—every day."

We made love again, more softly. And as much as I love the wild frenzy, I love the softness just as much, when Matt lies still beside me—sleeping or awake—and I touch him and kiss him and play with him as long as I want—any way I want—and then bring him inside me.

When we woke up the second time—mostly because Maggie and Jock were barking outside the bedroom door—it was dark. We took the RSVPs down to Phil Green's and looked through them over our Cheddar burgers and Phil's Brown Lager. Matt said that Kevin Flynn was no relation. In the one class—Latin I—they had together, their professor called Matt Discipulus Quintus Unus and Kevin Discipulus Quintus Duo. Matt also said that even though he and Kevin had double-dated at least twenty times at B.C., Kevin had grown into a confirmed bachelor; and that he had brought his mother to Matt's *first* wedding, too.

"Kevin was a day-hop, a commuter. He lived with his large family in Cambridge. I think he has five brothers and one sister. I had a crush on his sister Delora, but she moved to Oregon, and that was the end of that. Agnes treated me like another son, and I had many a 'grand' Irish meal at her kitchen table. She's getting up there in years, and I'm really glad she's coming."

Danny and Emma drove in at six on Friday, and Mary Kay and Will at seven. Mary Kay didn't tell me Will was coming. He planned to spend the night at his cousin's house in Brockport, and then he and Mary Kay would spend Saturday night with her parents. Claire came over at seven-thirty, after she and *young* Matt put the kids to bed. Then *old* Matt built the fire in the living room, as promised, and we 'wedding sisters' kicked the boys out.

One of the nicest things about our pajama party was that we knew from the first minute that it would be practically a twenty-four-hour party. None of us were expected to check in with our boys until we finished shopping Saturday afternoon. Even without my old guy, it would be one of the loveliest days of my life. We were not in a rush to do *anything*. We pigged out on fattening foods—pizza, wings, subs—drank beer instead of wine, and talked until three in the morning about our boys, the wedding, Claire's kids, school, our jobs and jobs-to-come, sex and politics and St. Patrick. We hugged and laughed and cried. It was *perfect*.

We had a blast bumping into each other in our pajamas in the kitchen making breakfast—bacon and eggs, waffles and muffins, and home fries with peppers and onions. We all concurred that if our guys could see us there in the kitchen, they might have second thoughts. We took all morning to get up and get dressed, laughing as each of us took too long in the bathroom. It reminded all of us of our college dorm days. We finally got out the door at noon and picked up Mom on our way to Evangeline's Wedding Boutique.

Vangie's shop was almost downtown, on East Avenue near Union Street. She had a round table ready for us in one corner of her showroom, set up with tea and coffee and Nabisco Sugar Wafers—one of my favorites since I was a little girl. I can still devour *twenty* of them with one big glass of milk. There were two large books on the table: *The Green Book* and *Bridesmaid Gowns*. We had a photo of Mom's dress for Vangie. It was sleeveless, white satin, A-line, with a white lace princess bodice and spaghetti straps. We "sisters" had agreed, sometime in the middle of our pajama party, that we wanted only solid-colored dresses from straps to hemlines. Vangie showed us all the greens, with fabric samples from chiffon to satin to silk. We all preferred the satin, which was probably an easier choice since Mom's dress was satin. Vangie pointed out which of the greens would complement each the best. We chose mint for Emma, lime for Claire and dark shamrock for Mary Kay.

Vangie complimented us: "You girls are the most 'together' wedding party I've ever had in my store. And you're not even sisters, right? Here's a picture of a style which I think will be perfect: dark green satin, A-line, spaghetti straps, sweetheart neckline, and a ruched or pleated bodice. I think the bride's gown should be the only one with lace. What do *you* think?"

We all loved the look, especially Mom. "Abigail, those dresses will be *perfect* with yours. You girls will be *so* beautiful together with your bare shoulders, tiny straps and pretty necklines." Her eyes glistened. "The boys will want to *eat* you up right in church."

Vangie took all the measurements and said she'd have the dresses ready by Friday, March 7. That would allow a week for the girls to try them on, and to make any alterations. We left Vangie's and drove out Monroe Avenue to The Pie Tin for a late lunch celebration. Claire and Mom and Mary Kay ordered sandwiches, but Emma and I decided to just have pie for lunch. Emma had the Strawberry Peppermint Meringue pie, and I had the pie of the week, which seemed appropriate after our bridesmaid dress choices—the Dark Chocolate Emerald pie, which had an Oreo crust and layers of dark chocolate mousse and lime mousse separated by a layer of white butter cream frosting, topped with whipped cream, thin lime slices and dark chocolate shavings. (*Tomorrow I start my wedding diet*, I mused.)

When we were all finished and sipping our coffee, we decided to do a group, shotgun cell phone call to all our boys. It was four o'clock. With five phones going at once, all on speaker, we had fun confusing the guys. Emma and Claire, Danny and Matt and the grandkids were going to Grandma and Grandpa Flynn's for dinner. Mom and Dad were taking Grandma and Grandpa McKay to the annual Knights of Columbus banquet. And Mary Kay and Will were having dinner with Mary Kay's mother and father. *My* Matt said we were also invited to his mom and dad's, but we would do whatever I wanted to do.

"It's your special 'sisters' weekend, Abby, so I told Mom and Dad we would play it by ear."

"Let's go to your mom and dad's, old guy. We haven't all been together since Christmas. I'll play with your ears later."

Everybody gobbled up Grandma's spaghetti and meatballs, of course, especially little Matthew and Emily. Mrs. Flynn loved both the design and the colors of the bridesmaid dresses. "I already told Mr. Flynn that he has to buy me a fancy new dress," she grinned.

Mary Kay called after dinner to ask if she and Will could take Matt and me to breakfast in the morning before they hit the road for D.C.

"We can do that, MK, because Emma and Danny said they want to just have oatmeal and fruit at our house and leave for Boston by eight-thirty. Danny has an early presentation to prepare for Monday. And Claire and Matt and the kids will be driving down near Dansville to meet Claire's brother and his three children for buckwheat pancakes at a family restaurant called The Sugar Maple. How about we meet you guys at ten o'clock at the IHOP on Elmwood?"

That night, Matt and I curled up on the sofa with Maggie and Jock to watch *The Cutting Edge*. He told me he enjoyed his camp-out with Matt and Danny on Matt's living room floor.

"Danny brought his air mattress from Boston, and Matt and I had our sleeping bags from his Boy Scout days. We all had lots of beer and pizza and watched a DVD of the 2001 Yankees-Diamondbacks World Series. We conked out by midnight."

I wrapped my arms all the way around his waist and squeezed.

"Matt, except for *every* night with you since our first one in November, last night was the *best* night of my life. We were up *way* later than you, talking and laughing and crying. I missed all that growing up without sisters. So even though the love and sex has been pretty good, I think the best thing you've given me is sisters," I teased.

Matt stroked my "tail" with his left hand and my hair with his right, and I fell asleep. I guess he did too, and we both woke up when the movie ended. I was still half-dreaming, and Matt had to put his arm around my waist and take my hand and guide me up the stairs.

"You've had quite a day, my pretty girl. You lie still, and I will kiss you to sleep. And God and Mary and St. Patrick will bring us a bright morning. I love you."

Matt kissed me awake at seven-thirty, and we walked the dogs and made coffee for Emma and Danny. It was a cold but sunny morning for their six hours on the road. When Danny gave me a goodbye hug, he whispered, "Only twenty days until the wedding, Abby, and then I can start calling you 'Mom,' right?"

"*Wrong*, Danny, unless you want me to start calling you 'son' from now on."

We both laughed. I missed Emma and Danny a lot as soon as they got in the car and drove away. Son or brother or friend—I knew my relationship with Danny (and Matt III to a lesser degree) would always be unusual, but it would never again be awkward. It was hard to believe how close we had become since our first, tentative conversation on the phone in November. Danny had come full circle from scolding his father for permitting me to happen, to thanking me again and again for bringing Matt back to life.

At breakfast, Mary Kay and Will said that for their wedding gift they wanted to treat us to a week at Will's family beach house—right after *my* commencement and Georgetown's commencement, both on May 17—in Duck, North Carolina, near the northern end of the Outer Banks. It would be just the four of us. Will's parents usually went down at Memorial Day and stayed until Labor Day. If Matt and I could drive to D.C. on May 18, we would all drive together to Duck the next day, Monday. It sounded *fantastic* to me.

"What do you think, Matt? Can we *do* it?"

"Yeah, sure we can, Abby. I've heard of Duck. I have a couple of good friends and clients in Virginia who go there every spring. They even brought me back a funny Duck T-shirt one year— I still have it. I've never been to the Outer Banks, and that should be a great place for you and me to start our beach life together, beauty."

"Mom and Dad have had the place for fifteen years," said Will. "It's *perfect* there in May."

Mary Kay said she would be back home the Wednesday before the wedding and she wanted to have a little bachelorette party for the "sisters" at her house—and maybe her mom and my

mom and Mrs. Flynn, too. What a week it was going to be.
Mary Kay's party on Wednesday, a stag party for Matt on
Thursday, and the rehearsal dinner on Friday! And I would have
to go to my classes, too. Happily, Wally Mangrum had already
told me, "You had better not come in on Tuesday, Thursday and
Friday" of my wedding week—for which I gave him a huge hug.

In Jeep on the way home, I suddenly remembered Horseshoe
Bay in Bermuda. That was going to be our first beach together
after graduation—sort of a delayed honeymoon. I leaned my
head on Matt's shoulder and touched his lips.

"Old guy, I forgot about Bermuda after graduation."

"It's okay, pretty girl. We'll do Bermuda. As soon as you
know for sure about your new job at Mangrums, we'll schedule
Bermuda for some time before October. It's still summer in
Bermuda in September, and less expensive because sensible
people worry about the hurricane season."

"Should we be sensible, Matt? Or is it too late for us?"

"It's too late, beauty. We are Peter Pan and Tinker Bell,
Jonathan and Sara, Noah and Allie, and Robert and Francesca.
Is that okay with you?"

"I'm okay with lovers and best friends and beaches together,
summer boy."

The next two weeks were a blur. I remember bits and pieces,
moments and thoughts. My thesis was coming together well,
and so were our group projects at Mangrums. Matt and I had the
tables all set for the reception, along with the flowers, the cake,
the Italian cookies, the limos, the DJ, the photographer, and even
the birthday cake for Danny—everybody was helping *so* much.
It seemed as if I was on my cell phone all the time, and it seemed
as if I didn't get *any* sleep.

But Matt and the doggies tucked me in every night by eleven,
and Matt and I talked a little, kissed a lot, made love, said our
prayers and were sound asleep by midnight. And God and Mary
and St. Patrick made each morning bright.

Kitty brought in her niece to take my place 'til after the
wedding. Mom bought thank you notes, and she and Laurie
addressed all the envelopes ahead of time. They also ordered
more than a thousand Kelly green (in honor of St. Patrick)
Jordan Almonds and put five each into delicate white satin tulle
bags—called bomboniere, said Mrs. Flynn—for every guest at
our wedding.

Mrs. Flynn explained the Italian tradition to me. "Almonds have a bitter taste, which stands for life," she said. "They are coated with sugar in the hope that the life of the bride and the groom will be sweet and not bitter. There are five almonds because they stand for the five wishes for the bride and the groom: good health, happiness, long life, many children and prosperity."

It was hard for me to resist the temptation to tell Mom and Laurie to cheat a little on the tradition and put in one more almond for extra fertility.

Every day it felt more and more like a Walt Disney movie. One night I even dreamed that Matt was waiting for me at the end of the aisle at Holy Eucharist on a white horse, so I started calling him "old prince."

And then it was Tuesday, March 11, and everything was as ready as we could make it. Matt and I spent almost all day with Maggie and Jock on the living room floor in front of the fireplace, naked except for when we took the dogs out, listening to our favorite Beethoven symphonies on his old stereo— especially the lovely *Sixth*—making love and sipping Chianti, and making love some more and nibbling on sourdough pretzels and Genoa salami, and pulling the dogs' fleeces over us and taking naps. If anyone ever asked me to tell them what I thought a day in heaven would be like, March 11 would be it.

Mary Kay called me the next morning just before she left D.C. We had decided that we needed to expand her "little" bachelorette party to include all the girls in the immediate family: Stephanie, Diane, Barbara, Katy, Catherine, Laurie, Debbie and Eileen. Lisa would not be able to make it because she and Alan couldn't fly in from North Carolina until Thursday afternoon. I went right to Mary Kay's after my afternoon classes and helped her and Mrs. Galvin get everything ready.

What I didn't know was that Mary Kay had planned all along that her bachelorette party would really be a bridal shower. I had only thought about a shower once, when Margie Steger mentioned it to me in Pittsburgh. But I remember telling Margie at the time that I didn't think it would be possible to find a day for a shower with so many girls—herself, Emma, Eileen and *especially* my maid of honor—out of town. Apparently Margie wasn't convinced, however, because she telephoned Mary Kay, and they started working on my surprise party.

The cat wasn't out of the bag until Margie sauntered down the Galvin's front staircase and into the living room and gave me a "gotcha" grin. We were still hugging and crying when a woman I had never met came through the front door and introduced herself as Cheryl Brongo, the wife of Matt's best law school friend Jerry.

I found out during the party that all of Matt's buddies—*every single one*—had worked out their schedules to be able to drive or fly to Rochester on Wednesday, take their girls to Mary Kay's, and then surprise Matt with a loud bash at Jerry Kelly's Sports Bar in Fairport. It was their *pre*-stag-party party. They would pretty much repeat it the next night, with the *slight* addition of an exotic dancer who called herself Luciana.

What a *night* we had at Mary Kay's! Everyone who was invited—except Lisa—was there. I made four new friends: Maria Lenzi, Melanie Bauman, Cheryl Brongo, and Kevin Flynn's mother, Agnes. Ann Connolly was there, too. It took half an hour for all the girls to meet and hug all the girls they had never seen before. I couldn't believe it. Of the twenty other girls who were sitting and talking in Mrs. Galvin's large living room, the only ones I had known four months earlier before I met Matt were Mrs. Galvin and Mary Kay, and Mom and Catherine and Laurie. And now they were all such a special part of my life. Maria, Melanie, Cheryl and Agnes all did brief double-takes when they met me, followed almost immediately by bright smiles on their faces and in their eyes; then we all became girlfriends very quickly. *Don't let this ever end*, I remember thinking. *God and Mary and St. Patrick, don't let this ever end.*

Matt and I both got home around midnight. He said he was only supposed to have dinner with Dave Connolly, and he was flabbergasted when he saw Jerry, Tony, Kevin, Ken and Joe walk in to Jerry Kelly's. The *real* stag party the next night was going to be at Dave's house, in his basement den.

"Abby, no matter how many years it has been, for each of the guys tonight, it was just as if we picked up from the last time we were together. I'm blessed to have such good friends."

"And I love all their girls, Matt—even Agnes, who immediately adopted me as either her second daughter or her seventh granddaughter."

We both laughed. And then we touched each other—only *three* days before our wedding—as wonderingly and hungrily as

300

the first night we were together. I remember Matt telling me a few times how much he had learned about women over the years from the girls he'd loved and lost. And now he was *perfect*: the way he touched me, the way he kissed me, the words he said to me. When we were in bed together, I never had to *think* about making love or being sexy. I had no consciousness of growing up Abigail McKay. In Matt's arms I was a beautiful, desirable and sensual woman capable of emotion and passion that Abigail McKay could not have imagined.

The next morning, after Matt and I had breakfast and walked the dogs, I packed a bag and headed for Mary Kay's, where I would spend the next two nights before the wedding. Emma and Claire met us at Joe's Diner for lunch, and then we went to Evangeline's to pick up the dresses. They were perfect except for a loose strap on Emma's which Vangie stitched on the spot. When we split up and all went home for dinner, it was the strangest time of the week for me. Emma went to Matt's house—my house—where she and Danny were staying; Claire went to her house; and I didn't go home. I thought it was ironic that after four months of making a new home with Matt, I now had to wait until *after* I got married to go back home. Mary Kay and I laughed about that after dinner, over several glasses of Moscato d'Asti, as we meandered through our Fatima yearbooks and scrapbooks of all our high school parties and boyfriends and dances.

I had made Patrick promise to call me before midnight and tell me all about the bachelor party, and he came through at eleven-thirty.

"Everyone was there, Abby, except you-know-who."

"Jack?"

"Jack—ornery Jack. Dad kept his distance from Luciana, the stripper—who was a *babe*—but Matt's father had fun playing with her. Matt's brother from North Carolina is nice enough, but quieter than Matt and Tom. Grandpa McKay didn't say much; just sat in his chair next to Dad and drank his beer. I enjoyed talking with Matt's buddies from school and the Army; they had a *ton* of great stories about your sweetie-pie. He could be trouble when he was younger."

"He can *still* be trouble, Pat—he's still Peter Pan—but that's one of the reasons I love him. How did *he* like Luciana?"

"Abby, you know I love you, but you also know the *rule*, right?"

"*What* rule?" I could hear him chuckling.

"What happens at a stag party *stays* at a stag party."

"Come on, Pat!"

"Can't do it, Abby. All of us stag brothers took an oath; and no photographs were allowed either. You'll have to ask Matt. What time is the rehearsal tomorrow?"

"Five o'clock at Holy Eucharist, and six-thirty at Palermo's. Are you going to bring Nannie and Gramps?"

"Yep. And Mom and Dad will bring Grandma and Grandpa McKay."

Mary Kay and I intended to sleep in the two twin beds in the guest room, which used to be her brothers' bedroom. We talked for another hour after I got off the phone with Patrick. Mary Kay said that she and Will had fallen hard and fast for each other and she might be looking for a maid of honor *herself* in 2009. That got us out of our beds for more hugs and tears; and we wrapped ourselves together in a couple of blankets, sitting at the foot of one of the beds, where we fell asleep leaning our heads on each other.

The rehearsal was fun. While Father Skelly and the Holy Eucharist wedding coordinators were walking us through our paces and the parts of the Mass, I kept noticing Grandpa Dolan and Matt's dad having an animated conversation—no doubt about The War. Everybody was smiling, laughing and enjoying the show—mostly joking and teasing the bridal party as we tried to pay attention to our cues for the next day—except for Jack and Grandpa McKay.

And there was an extra added attraction: the *drip*. The temperature had gotten into the low fifties for two days, and the snow was melting fast on the church roof. There was one leak, over Our Lady's altar to the left of the main altar, and a large metal bucket in front of the altar was catching the loud drops. Father Skelly assured Matt and me that the Lord would allow *no* drip during our Mass.

Mr. and Mrs. Palermo served us personally at the rehearsal dinner. We had Gramps and Matt's dad sitting next to each other so that they could continue their private history of The War. It was amusing to watch everybody in my family trying to decide what to order from an Italian menu. It may have been the first time that Grandma and Grandpa McKay had ever had Italian food. Mary Kay's toast was sweet and loving, and there were so

many great toasts from all of Matt's buddies and his brothers.
But the one I loved the best was from Joe Steger:

"Flynnie and I met at Fort Benning, Georgia. It's getting to
be a *really* long time ago: forty years in July. We became best
friends the first time we bumped into each other—literally—at
the coffee machine in the lobby of the officers club. 'Blond and
sweet' . . . that was almost every soldier's coffee choice back in
those days.

"From that first instant we started to watch out for each other.
As they say in the Army, I had Matt's back, and he had mine.
Next we were both assigned to the Foreign Language Center in
Monterey, California, and then to the Army Language School at
Tan Son Nhut Air Force Base in Saigon. We kept each other out
of trouble and got each other through the terrible days, especially
the days the Viet Cong bombed our school. We trusted each
other with our lives and—this is Army talk again—both of us
knew without thinking that we would take a bullet for each other.

"When Sarah died, I grieved with Matt as if it had been my
own wife. I never thought he could be that happy again. But
now he is—Abby has made Matt *that* happy again. I am as
excited as if I were getting married *myself* . . . to Margie, of
course." Joe winked at Margie. "So here's to Abby and Matt:
our brother and sister, our son and daughter, and our best
friends."

I was already in tears at "bullet," and Matt had to wrap me in
his arms at the table to keep me from trembling and sobbing. Joe
came across the room and gave both Matt and me a hug. As
dinner broke up and everybody was leaving, Mom and Dad told
me that it was the best rehearsal dinner—both the people *and* the
food—that they had ever been to.

Mary Kay and I decided that we had better not sleep on the
floor again. We needed to get up at seven, shower and wash our
hair, and meet Emma and Claire at Mae's Salon to get our hair
done. We all agreed on a chignon style, with loosely coiled,
wavy curls in the back rather than a bun, and shamrocks woven
among the curls, and no bangs. Then we went back to Mary
Kay's, where Mrs. Galvin, Mom and Laurie were ready to help
us get dressed, help us with our makeup, and help us keep calm
until the limo arrived. Gramps' ribbon was pinned on my slip.

When we got to Holy Eucharist, Mom made the rounds to see
if every*thing* and every*body* was in the right place. Our ushers,
Patrick, Alan and Tom, were ready at the front doors with the

303

programs. Jack refused to participate. He was present only under protest, basically because Dad threatened to disown him if he shamed the family by not showing up. Mom finished her rounds and said everything was perfect.

"Matt and the boys and Joe are on time and in place, and they look *way* more nervous than you girls. And the bucket and the drip are gone. Father Skelly told me that he climbed up on the roof *himself* with duct tape and fixed the leak."

27

At exactly eleven o'clock, the organist started playing Bach's "Jesu, Joy of Man's Desiring," Dad took my arm, and the doors opened.

Matt and I had decided right away on Bach's "Jesu" for our processional, but then he put on his Peter Pan face and pushed for "Take Me Out to the Ball Game" for the recessional. I was never, *ever*, able to figure out if Matt was kidding or not, but I summoned up my sternest scowl and threatened to "hold my breath until my wedding day" unless he agreed to Clarke's "Trumpet Voluntary," which he did, of course, immediately, with a hug and a kiss. But he and Joe would turn Clarke into a surprise at the end of the wedding.

I looked all the way up the aisle to the altar, but I didn't see Matt in his white tux with black piping ("the same as at my senior ball at Savio," he said). Instead, I saw him coming through the door at Kitty's in his tan cashmere overcoat and wool Yankees hat, brushing off snow. That image made me smile long enough to get me up the aisle without crying. Mary Kay, Emma and Claire were simply breathtaking in their lovely shades of green, and little Matthew, carrying the ring pillow, and Emily, sprinkling rose petals from her basket, charmed everybody in the church.

I didn't see many faces on either side of the aisle—Matt brushing the snow off his overcoat kept flashing before my eyes—but I did notice Margie Steger and cousin Theresa blowing me kisses and, much to my surprise, my brother Jack mouthing the words, "I'm sorry, Abby."

I wish I could remember everything Dad said, but I was in such a delicious haze that all I'm sure I heard was, "Babby girl (that's what he called me when I was little), you are the *greatest* daughter a man could ever have—and the most beautiful—and I never believed you would *ever* find a man I thought was good enough for you. But you did. Matt is the right man for you. He's *your* man. God bless, Babby."

That's where the tears came, at the end of the aisle. Dad dabbed my eyes softly with the handkerchief from his breast pocket, then gave me to Matt, and we knelt on the altar to be married.

May the Lord bless you and keep you . . . I take you to be my husband . . . for better or for worse . . . I promise to love you and honor you . . . all the days of my life . . . Matt, you may kiss your bride.

We turned around—Mr. and Mrs. Matthew Flynn—and then I saw *all* the faces of all the family, all our friends. The first notes of the "Trumpet Voluntary" sounded, but it was *not* the organist. It was glorious, triumphal, vivacious, sensuous. I felt it touch my body. Matt told me later that it was a CD of Wynton Marsalis and the English Chamber Orchestra.

Our walk down the aisle was more wondrous and fulfilling than I had ever imagined. I felt so much strength and pride as Matt's bride that I think I could have picked *him* up and walked out of the church with him over my shoulder. Instead, Matt lifted me in his arms, kissed me, and carried me through the doors out into the sunshine—bathed in cheers and rose petals and the last thrilling notes of the trumpet.

The reception was perfect, just what I would have dreamed of if I had ever dreamed of marrying a sixty-year-old guy. Connolly's party house was beautifully decorated in shades of green that matched my "sisters" in their gowns. Tom and the DJ put together exactly the right mix of songs for dancing by children of all ages. Joe gave pretty much the same toast he had given the night before, and Matt held me when I cried in all the same places. Mary Kay surprised me, though, with a completely different toast:

"Abby and I have been sisters of the heart ever since we were six years old, when we first met in the first grade at Our Lady of the Assumption. Then we were girlfriends, and then *best* girlfriends, through Fatima High School *and* Newton College. And now I'm her maid of honor, and maybe next year she'll be mine. But *way* more than all that—and I've never told you this, Abby gal—she has been my hero since we were at Fatima. When girls were mean—and teenage girls can be the meanest creatures on the face of the earth—Abby always knew the right thing to say to either calm them down or put them in their place. When our parents were *totally* unreasonable—which they always are when you're sixteen—Abby always knew how to either change their minds or fool them and get away with it, anyway. When our classes were difficult and our teachers were insensitive or intimidating—which they always were when we would rather party and talk about boys—Abby helped me get through the courses and the teachers and the tests. And when the boys we thought we loved broke our hearts, Abby was always there to give me as many hugs as I needed, and promise me that there would be another boy.

"Miss Abigail Elizabeth McKay always knew the right thing to do—and *did* it. And I don't mean the right thing as in how to be clever, or how to win, or how to get away with something. I mean the *right thing*. She taught me how to stand up for myself when nobody else would; how to be good when so many people around us were not; and how to appreciate life every day, even when we were mystified and terrified by all the new challenges we faced. Abby gal, you taught me how to grow up and be a woman. You not only *taught* me, you held my hand and helped me *do* it; and no matter where I go or what I do for the rest of my life, I will love you forever. So, here's to my beloved sister and best friend . . . God bless you. Take good care of her, Matt."

I don't know *how* Mary Kay got through that toast. I cried all the way. When she finished and we hugged each other, though, she was crying as hard as I was. Claire and Emma had to grab a couple of linen napkins from the table and surround Mary Kay and me and keep us from getting our makeup all over each other. When we were finally able to stop crying, we looked into each other's eyes and laughed. All of our friends and family were on their feet clapping and cheering. I said to Mary Kay, while Claire was trying to touch up my face, "MK, this has been the happiest week of my life, and I have *never* cried more than I have this week. It's so hard to be a girl."

We did all the traditional reception things. Matt and I had *two* bridal dances: one to Elvis' "I Can't Help Falling in Love With You," and one to the Seekers' "I'll Never Find Another You." When we cut Kitty's beautiful cake, we mushed the pieces into each other's faces for all of the cameras. And then we walked around to all twenty-five tables to thank our family and friends for their love and support. Then Patrick jumped just high enough to take the garter away from Trent and Will; and Mary Kay—to cries of "fix" from the crowd—stepped in front of Laurie and Katy to catch the bouquet. Mary Kay had to slap Patrick's hand several times as he inched the garter up her thigh.

Everybody had fun with the dances: the "Makarena," "YMCA," the "Hokey Pokey," the "Chicken Dance," and, last but not least, the "Tarantella"—which brought almost the whole crowd to the dance floor, including Mom and Dad, Nannie and Gramps, Mr. and Mrs. Flynn, even Kevin Flynn and Agnes, and most of Matt's older cousins.

After the end of the "Tarantella," Matt and I sneaked out of the reception, and the limo drove us to the Hotel Monroe downtown on the river. Only Mary Kay knew where we were spending the night. We planned to surprise all the out-of-towners for breakfast at nine o'clock at Phil Green's—we had reserved the back room—before they had to leave for home.

The bridal suite at the Monroe was lovely. We had a huge round bed that must have been ten feet across. It was the first round bed I had ever seen that wasn't a waterbed. There was also a round Jacuzzi about six feet wide, plush white rugs, and a giant, flat-screen wall television that we never turned on. We took off our clothes, sat on the soft carpet, sipped Ruffino Chianti, and poured our sack of envelopes on the floor. Mary Kay and Joe were taking all the wrapped presents back to her house, where Joe and Margie were spending the night.

Matt and I were both so tired that we almost fell asleep while we were opening the cards and envelopes. But then we decided to play in the Jacuzzi before we went to bed, and we got our second wind. Mary Kay—with another of her many surprises—had tucked two gift bags of bath beads and bubble bath into my suitcase.

"Raspberry or lime, old guy?"

"How about one of each, beauty?"

Making love in the Jacuzzi, with raspberry bubbles and lime beads, was so exhilarating and *different* that we couldn't *stop*. We put on the luxurious hotel robes and rubbed each other dry, and hot, and made love again, in our robes on the white rug. And again without the robes. When we finally lay down in the round bed, time vanished. Matt still smelled of fresh soap, delicious, and I wanted to eat him up.

Between kisses he said, "You know, pretty girl, Mary Kay and Margie and Joe are great at keeping secrets. I knew nothing about your shower, or about my buddies and their wives coming in to town on Wednesday, or even about Luciana."

"So you're on a first-name basis, eh?" I teased.

Matt laughed. "Absolutely! Her phone number is 716-HOT-LEGS."

I poked him a couple of times in soft places, and then we played all the way around the bed at *least* two more times, then finally curled into sleep in the middle. I don't know what I expected from my wedding night, but I dreamed no dreams. I only remember Matt's touch.

We joked at Phil Green's the next morning about the round bed. Maria, who is a mathematics professor at Northeastern University in Boston, called it "circumference sex." And Ken, who is a tensile strength engineer with Boeing, informed us that the formula for how much sex two people can have in an hour in a round bed was "two pie-r-screwed."

Those guys and their ladies . . . I knew almost *none* of them a week before, and now I loved them dearly. It seemed as if Matt and I hugged them all for *hours* before we let them drive away from Phil Green's. Then we went home, took Maggie and Jock up to bed with us, and slept through the entire afternoon.

Monday was our one-day honeymoon, and we only got out of bed long enough to eat and walk the dogs. On Tuesday, we were back to our regular schedule, but my world sure wasn't regular any more. I had a handsome husband who kissed me good night and kissed me good morning, and my dreams continued to unfold every day. After that first Tuesday, I stopped working the counter at Kitty's. She told me that her niece needed the job, and that I should be spending as much time as possible in bed with Matt.

"Abby, you're the best counter girl I've ever had, but now you're married, you're going to be graduating in two months, and then you'll have your new job with Mangrums. But make sure you keep bringing Matt in to read his book, okay? He looks good sitting in the window."

Two weeks later, April Fool's Day, when I walked in to the advertising department at work, Art and Wally Mangrum were waiting for me in the interns' conference room, and Art handed me an envelope addressed to "Mrs. Abigail E. Flynn."

"Abigail, Mangrums, and we personally, are delighted to offer you a position as our first-ever Assistant Director of New Projects. The particulars are in the letter. We want you to know that we and Joe Christopher think that you are the best RIT intern we've ever had in advertising. Can you let us know in the next two weeks or so if you would like the position?"

"Thank you *so* much, Mr. Mangrum! I'm almost certain the answer will be yes, but I will read the letter tonight with Matt and let you and Mr. Christopher know for sure tomorrow."

When I called Matt on my dinner break to tell him, he cheered and shouted to Maggie and Jock, "Guess what, puppies? Mommy has a big surprise for you! Hurrah for you, Abby! Would you like me to put some Asti Spumante on ice for later?"

"How about Pooh and Piglet, a jug of Chianti and thou, old guy?"

We celebrated with Maggie and Jock on the rug in front of the fire. The letter said my salary would be $45,000, and I would have health insurance, four weeks vacation, a 401(k) plan and a lot of other "stuff" that my private financial planner said he would explain to me later.

"I think it's a *terrific* offer, Abby—especially for the Rochester area—for a brand-new MBA. What do *you* think?"

"I *love* it! I love *you*! I can't believe I've gone from single and scrounging to pay my rent to married to the man of my dreams, with a beautiful house and a great new job. I can't *believe* I am such a lucky girl."

"You are a professional woman now, beauty; and Mangrums is the lucky one. They want to know when you would like to start."

"Well, I graduate on May 17, and we're going to Mary Kay and Will's on the 18th and coming back on the 24th or 25th. I thought Monday, June 2, would be good. That will give us Memorial Day week to keep playing after we come back from North Carolina. What do *you* think, Matt?"

"Sounds perfect, pretty girl. I'll keep the week clear, and we'll make it our third honeymoon."

Matt lay on his side, with his head in my lap and his arms around my waist, and kissed my belly again and again. "Abby, it's hard to imagine that anyone could be happier than *I* am right here, right now. But I know *you* could; and that means *I* could, too."

"Talk to my belly, summer boy," I whispered, brushing my fingers over Matt's temples and down his neck.

"Are you ready, belly?" he whispered back, nibbling into my navel. "I know we're going to make a baby, beauty. I'm not sure yet if we will have a boy or a girl."

He continued nuzzling and running his hands over the back of my hips.

I leaned down and kissed the top of his head.

"I want *your* baby, Matt. I don't need to know any more than that."

We both quietly stroked each other for a few minutes.

"Stephanie called this morning, Matt. She and Warren and the kids are moving to Virginia on Sunday, and she would like us all to come over on Saturday to help with the last-minute packing and have a pizza party."

"That will be nice, sweetie. Tom and Diane are going to have a very hard time with Steph and the grandkids gone. We'll have to get out to dinner with them a little more often."

"Speaking of dinner, old guy, can I buy you dinner tomorrow night to celebrate my new job as a junior executive? I thought we'd go to some special, fancy place . . . like Phil Green's."

"Great idea, Abby. And I have a surprise for *you*: I dug out another old poem to read to you over the weekend. I can bring it to Phil Green's if you'd like."

"You know there's nothing I like better," I laughed, "than putting my feet up and closing my eyes while you read to me. But that means I'll have to dig out another drawing next week, huh?"

Matt looked up and smiled. "No rush, pretty girl. We're not on a schedule."

What I didn't tell Matt was that right after we came back from playing with Joe and Margie in Pittsburgh, I had set up an easel in my old room at Mom and Dad's, and had been working on a special drawing every day I could find some time. I swore Mom and Dad to secrecy and asked them to promise not to peek.

I was working mostly from my love for this man and his body—I knew every inch of Matt's body better than I knew my *own*—but also from a picture I had taken with my cell phone one Saturday morning when he was sleeping a little later than usual. He was lying half on his right side and half on his stomach, with his right leg extended to the foot of the bed and his left leg bent at the knee. His face was turned left and his lips were slightly parted, his hair falling over his forehead. His right arm was curled around the top of his head on the pillow, and his left arm was bent at the elbow with his fingertips on the pillow under his cheek. He was *so* beautiful. I had a hard time holding my charcoal pencils steady, *and* keeping my fingers off the canvas.

At two feet by three feet, it was the largest drawing I had ever done and, considering that I had not picked up a pencil in five years, so good that I was stunned. *Love is bringing out all the best I have in me* I thought, over and over. *This beautiful man is fulfilling my life.*

When we walked in to Phil Green's the next night, Jinks was behind the counter and she broke into a *huge* grin. "I had a hunch you guys would be coming in tonight so I kind of saved your booth by having all my people take their breaks there one by one. Go kick out Carrie and Rick and tell them to get back to work. By the way, Abby, I really like my management program at Mangrums. I'm learning a lot. So thank you again."

"I hope it turns into a long-term career that makes you happy, Jinks. Matt and I are actually celebrating *my* new job at Mangrums: Assistant Director of New Projects in the Advertising Department. I start the first week of June, so we will have to find each other on campus."

"Hurrah for you, Abby! The beers are on the house tonight."

When our burgers were gone and we had finished clinking our bottles of Brooklyn Lager, I put my feet in the usual place and my head in the usual lap, and Matt unfolded his poem.

"Beauty, I wrote this a couple of months after Matt was born, so it's twenty-nine years old. No surprise that the title is *Matthew Howard Flynn III.*

> *I give my son my father's name*
> *and the love of my father*
> *who am I without my father*
> *who is my son without me*
> *who is my son without my father*
> *who is my father without me*
> *who am I without my son*
> *who is my father without my son*
> *today, questions*
> *tomorrow, riddles*
> *yesterday, family*
> *in the end*
> *only the sons survive*
> *only the fathers are remembered*
> *in the end*
> *father and son are the same man*

the third night after my son was born
I had a dream:
I was pushing a plain brass bed
across my parents' bedroom
my grandfather was in the bed
he was small under the covers
I could only see his head
I pushed the bed up against a wall
covered with white paper with blue flowers
my grandfather's head was so close to the wall
and so white
I couldn't see his face
then he blinked
I saw his blue eyes flicker amid the flowers
close quickly, and they were gone
the wrinkled face in the bed
had become the face of my sleeping son

from my grandfather to my son
my father and I
pass, in a blur of generations
at birth already grown
this inheritance:
I promise you, my son
as my father promised me
as his father promised
I will love you all the days of your life
as I love my father today
I can give you nothing more and nothing less

Matt had to stop reading three or four times and reach down with one of the gold and tan Phil Green's napkins and wipe away my tears.

"That's *so* beautiful, Matt. I was thinking mostly of Mom and Nannie while you were reading. Where would I be without *them*? I have a place in time because of Mom and Nannie. But I feel as if I'm still floating, as if I need to have a baby to fix my place in time. Is that how you felt when you wrote the poem?"

"That is *exactly* how I felt, beauty, as if I was actually complete as a man because I was now in the family line between my father and my son, just as Dad was when I was born. I remember Dad telling me when Grandpa Flynn died that 'life

313

doesn't feel the same any more, because I'm not in the middle. All of a sudden I'm old.' I saw Grandpa Flynn in the hospital just before he died—I think I was about seven—and it was *his* face in the dream and in the poem."

"So what you're saying, my lovely, handsome old poet, is that it's both our parents *and* our children who keep us young?"

"Yes, miss," he said, playing with my hair, "although wives and lovers turn young into happy."

I opened my eyes and reached my left hand up under Matt's shirt and brushed the soft hair on his stomach. "Let's go home, old guy. I want to read your poem myself, and play with Maggie and Jock, and take you to bed. Talking about a baby makes me want you inside me all the time. When you're not touching me, when we're not making love, I wonder and hope. When you're inside me I have no doubts."

Matt was *so* gentle and sweet making love that night, cradling me and rocking me like a little girl. My orgasms were warm and mellow—not wild—and I was able to stay aware of my body and what I was feeling. I thought we might be making a baby that night, and I had never had that thought before. It turned out I was wrong, but my woman-ness was so overwhelming that I felt the ache of motherhood deep inside anyway. Matt sensed what I was feeling and he didn't say a word. He just kept cradling me and kissing me until we both fell asleep.

We had a lovely Saturday with Warren and Stephanie and all the Flynns. Send-offs are hard, especially for a family as close as Tom and Diane's, but everybody agreed that Virginia was *way* closer than New Mexico or Arkansas and we would visit as soon as we could.

I finished my drawing of Matt the following week and decided to show it to him on Saturday, which was also Emma's birthday. When we called Emma and Danny in the morning, they said they were coming to Rochester the weekend of May 3-4 to bring us a big surprise and celebrate my birthday, which is May 5. Emma said the following weekend—Mother's Day— they would be with *her* mother on Long Island.

When we got off the phone, I said to Matt, "Old guy, Claire and Matt told me that they would spend Mother's Day with *her* mother in Saratoga, which will work out pretty well because *my* mother wants us to come over for a family cookout. We're also going to celebrate my birthday and Grandma Mary's, which is

May 10. And then it's graduation, and then North Carolina. Life with you is taking my breath away, Matt."

He laughed and brushed the hair off my forehead.

"Abby, one of the *zillion* things I love about you is that you love your family as much as I love mine. More than that, I think you love *my* family as much as I do myself. But when it comes to breathtaking, if you and I met a hundred people walking down the street, *none* of them would say that *I'm* the breathtaking one."

"Matt, when Emma and Danny are here, let's have Claire and Matt and the kids and your mom and dad over for a cookout of our own. What do you think their surprise is?"

"Do you think Emma might be pregnant? Danny hasn't said anything to me about the two of them trying to get pregnant."

"Well, they're not trying *not* to—Emma told me that in Boston. That would be *so* exciting, especially on top of Debbie's baby and Katy and Trent getting married. I guess I joined your family at the perfect time."

I leaned my head on Matt's shoulder at the kitchen table.

"Mom said almost the same thing to me a couple of days ago. She said, 'Matthew, ever since you brought Abigail into our family, we've had nothing but good news and parties. We have so many more anniversaries to celebrate, and we could have a lot of babies in the next few years.' With that she winked at me. Mom *never* winks."

We both laughed, and I got up to refill our coffee cups.

"Matt, my summer boy, I have another drawing to show you. I think you should look at it in the afternoon, in the daylight." I smiled. "I don't want you to miss anything."

"How about the table on the back porch, beauty?"

When I uncovered the drawing and laid it on the table, Matt was speechless. I had only seen him speechless twice before: when I asked him to undress me the first night we were together, and in Mom and Dad's living room when I told Mom what I said to Matt when I realized that I loved him. Now I stood behind him and wrapped my arms around his stomach and whispered:

"I did this in secret in my old room at Mom and Dad's. I started right after we came back from Pittsburgh. I swore Mom and Dad to secrecy and made them promise not to take a peek. You're the first person to see it, and maybe nobody else *ever* will. It's the first drawing I've done since I graduated from Newton."

"Abby . . . it's so *good* . . . how did you . . .?"

"*Shh*. Don't say anything, old guy. I know your body by heart. I can close my eyes and see every lovely inch of you. But one bright Saturday morning you were kind enough to sleep late, and I took a few pictures with my cell phone. When I finished the drawing this week, I erased all the pictures; so there's no proof of exactly how you look," I grinned, "but this is the way you look to *me*."

"You made me look better than I ever looked in my *life*. How did you *do* that?"

"You forget, handsome, that I saw an old picture of Captain Matthew Flynn, in his twenties, washing his Beetle. And I happen to think you get better looking every day."

"And I happen to think you are one *hell* of an artist. You did this with just black charcoal?"

"Well, the black family. I used some shades of silver and gray."

"That's *amazing*, Abby, because I see colors. I know they're not there, but I see them anyway. I'm probably dreaming of *you*, you know."

"I thought about that while I was sketching: *Wouldn't it be wonderful if I could draw what Matt's dreaming?*"

Matt turned toward me, wrapped his arms around my waist and kissed me.

"Thank you, pretty girl. Thank you for loving me *this* much . . . enough to make me look almost beautiful. I've always been in awe of great painters more than any other artists. They not only have to have the image, the inspiration, the idea in their minds, but they have to have the magic in their eyes and in their hands. Do you care if other people see this?"

"Not if *you* don't."

"I think your drawings are too good to keep under wraps."

Matt's eyes were glistening as he looked in to mine, and his fingers played around my ears.

"If we write a book about our love story, beauty, this drawing could be our cover picture. We could call it *Visions of Abigail*."

"Or *Dreams of Matt*. Start working on it, Shakespeare," I teased, "*you're* the writer in this family. I'll be the illustrator. Are you hungry? All of a sudden I'm hungry. Let's go down to Phil Green's. I think it's nice enough for us to bring the doggies and sit outside."

I took my drawing to Fantasy Framing on Monday and observed closely for an hour as the two skillful women owners—with broad grins on their faces—carefully "matted" my sleeping summer boy and put his body under glass.

Then Matt hung it next to the bow window on the long wall in the living room.

28

For me, the last two weeks of April were filled with project reports and customer surveys and new product analysis at Mangrums, and oral exams and the final draft of my thesis at RIT. Matt was able to move two real estate transactions up to the last week of April and the second week of May and clear his financial schedule for the last two weeks of May. I put my arms around his neck and told him I would make it worth his while.

On May Day, which was a Thursday, Matt and I made three trips each in *both* of our cars, fully loaded with Katy and Trent's "small stuff," to help them move from their separate apartments into their new home off Baird Road in Fairport. The next evening, Emma and Danny pulled into our driveway about six o'clock. I raced out the door to give both of them a hug, and the first thing Emma said to me was, "I know, I know, Abby, our surprise; but Danny and I are *so* hungry. We've been thinking about hot dogs and French fries for the last hundred miles. Get us down to Phil Green's, and we'll give you your surprise."

It only took Emma three bites of her red hot to tell us that she was pregnant and her due date was December 7. She and I got up from the booth and hugged each other for a long time, and I whispered to her, "How did you know? What did you feel?"

"The first thing I noticed was a pain in my back. I *never* get back pains. No matter how I stretched or exercised or tried to baby it, it didn't go away. Danny rubbed my back a *lot* in the first couple of weeks. Then I started to smell everything better than I have in many years. With my allergies and sinuses, I'm usually stuffed up, but all of a sudden I smelled everything from Danny's stinky socks to my orange juice and oatmeal at breakfast. And when the magnolia and dogwood trees started to blossom—wow! But it never occurred to me that I might be pregnant. And then I went *crazy* for cantaloupe. I've always loved watermelon in the summer, but I never cared much for cantaloupe."

"Cantaloupe *and* Cool Whip," interjected Danny. "I started making regular runs to the local Fastrac for cantaloupe and Cool Whip."

"That's when Danny said, 'Hey, Em, maybe you're pregnant.' But I still didn't give it much thought, even when I started peeing twice as much. I don't know whether I was peeing so much because I was pregnant or because I was eating all that cantaloupe."

We all laughed and sipped our beers.

"And then, of course, I missed my period at the beginning of April, and all the hints and clues came together in my little brain." Emma smiled. "I went to see my OB/GYN, and here we are. I said to Dr. Graham before she even asked me, that Danny and I don't want to know right away if we're going to have a boy or a girl. Maybe later . . . maybe not until December 7."

Saturday was warm but drizzly, so our backyard picnic was mostly on the back porch. Matt and the boys grilled T-bone steaks; Mrs. Flynn made ziti and meatballs; and Claire baked a two-layer, double-fudge cake. We all celebrated Emma's "tummy" and my twenty-seventh birthday, and Mother's Day in advance because none of us were going to be together a week later. I invited everyone to my graduation. Danny and Emma said they were going to be in Queens at her brother Heath's graduation from St. John's the same day.

The next morning after Mass, Matt and Danny went for a long walk and run with Maggie and Jock, and Emma and I had a lovely hour together on the back porch, with the warm sunlight and the aroma of the lilacs and lilies of the valley floating through the open windows.

"You know, Abby, except for the back pain right at the beginning, being pregnant has been so much more pleasant than I ever supposed it would be. I haven't felt sick at *all*. No nausea and no morning sickness. I know I'm probably counting my chickens too soon, and those uncomfortable things may come later but, Abby, I can barely even *think* about physical things because in my mind, in my head, in *here*,"—Emma pressed both of her open hands on top of each other over her heart—"I'm the happiest woman on the face of the earth."

She leaned her head on my shoulder and hugged my arm.

"And Danny is the same. Even though we knew we wanted to have children, if you had asked me at your wedding I would have said that Danny and I were as happy as two people can be.

319

And now we look at each other with tears and smiles at the same time, and we touch each other twice as much—even when people are watching—and we make love twice as much."

Emma pressed her cheek harder against my shoulder and squeezed my arm tighter.

"*Listen* to me going on and trying to describe how I feel being pregnant. Mom told me when I was sixteen that some day, God willing, I would be a mother, and that no matter how hard I tried to explain, no matter what I said, no one would ever understand how I felt . . . except a mother."

And then she tipped her head up and looked into my eyes.

"How about *you*, Abby? Do you and Dad," she laughed, "*Matt* . . . want to have a baby?"

"Yeah, we do, Em, as soon as we can. My old guy wants a baby as much as I do—which is a *lot*. And now I have a sister to share the joyous days and the anxious days."

I took Emma's hands in mine, and we leaned against each other and closed our eyes and dozed for a while before the boys came crashing through the front door with the dogs.

The "kids" pulled out of the driveway a little before noon. As soon as their car disappeared down the street, I wrapped my arms around Matt's waist and stared straight in to his eyes.

"What's that look, *Mona Lisa*? What did you and Emma talk about?"

I touched my fingers to his lips and said, "*Shh*, never you mind, sweetie. Take me to bed."

Nannie and Grandpa Dolan surprised all of us by driving in for Mother's Day weekend, so my whole family was together at Mom and Dad's for our cookout on Sunday. This time *I* made the ziti and meatballs—Mrs. Flynn's recipe, of course. Grandma Mary and Nannie always enjoyed each other's company and catching up on all the family news, but Grandpa McKay never had much to say, no matter how hard Dad and Gramps tried to engage him in conversation.

Just after dinner and before we sang "Happy Birthday," Nannie pulled me aside in the living room and asked, "Abigail Elizabeth, are you still wearing Grandpa's lucky ribbon?"

"Every day, Nannie," I answered, with a conspiratorial grin. "Depending on what I'm wearing for the day, sometimes I pin it to the waistband of my panties and sometimes to different places on my bra. I probably shouldn't tell you this but . . . you know what Matt likes to do?"

"What, honey?"

"When we're going to make love, he takes the ribbon off my panties or bra and weaves it into my hair."

Nannie and I were both grinning like schoolgirls. I was trying to picture her at age twenty-two with her soldier boy, and I'm guessing she was trying to picture Matt playing with the ribbon in my hair. But maybe she was remembering *Grandpa* playing with the ribbon in *her* hair. She patted my cheek and whispered, "Matt knows it's magic, honey. You just keep wearing it, and you'll get your wish."

I don't remember a lot of the bits and pieces of my graduation week. I remember there were papers, and *more* papers, to be signed for RIT and Mangrums. I remember wishing the week would be over and Saturday would come, because that would mean that the *next* day was the start of my honeymoon with Matt. I remember packing for our trip in between planning places for lunch and dinner for my family before and after the RIT ceremonies. I remember scanning the threatening skies at the huge outdoor convocation and hoping that all the sunshine was headed for North Carolina.

Mostly I remember Matt, every day, all week, touching me wherever and whenever I needed to be touched; massaging my shoulders when I was tense, and kissing the back of my neck when I was *really* tense; standing behind me with his arms around my belly and his face nuzzling my hair when I needed to close my eyes and take a deep breath; making love to me whenever I gave him my special look; helping me pack and convincing me that all we really needed were lots of shorts and T-shirts; and saying *absolutely* the right thing every time I fretted or made no sense.

As I waited for Dean Jackson to call "Abigail Elizabeth Flynn, Master of Business Administration," I thought about how different the day was from the way I had envisioned it last September when I started my final year of school. I was determined to work hard and earn my Masters, but I didn't know what I would be doing next, or where I would be going, or why. Especially I didn't know the "why" part. I was completing my plan. It was what everyone expected me to do, and I knew I wanted to be in the business world. It all made sense, but something was missing.

Then I met Matt, and the "why" became clear. "Why" is personal, it's selfless, it's the five almonds in the tulle bag, and it's *always* family. I planned to be successful, but the only *real* success is personal, and the best success is family. Abigail McKay had become Mrs. Abigail Flynn, she had a degree and a brand new job, and her chances were getting better every day.

Patrick and Laurie said they would house-sit for us and take care of Maggie and Jock, so Matt and I hit the road for D.C. after eight-thirty Mass on Sunday and arrived at Mary Kay and Will's place at five o'clock. We had a nice dinner at *their* favorite Italian restaurant in Georgetown, Morante's, but the traditional red sauce wasn't as good as Palermo's. I laughed to myself at the table. *Look at the Irish girl who's now an expert on spaghetti sauce*, I thought.

We compared graduation ceremonies and shared photographs and went through a checklist of things we would need at Will's place in Duck. We were all partied out, and the boys wanted to be beyond the Beltway by eight the next morning, so we were in bed by eleven. But we horsed around for a while, Walton-style: "Good night, Will." "Good night, Matt." "Good night, MK." "Good night, Abby gal." "You kids knock it off and get to sleep!"

I rolled on top of Matt, grinned and pinched both his cheeks.

"Summer boy, I can't wait to kiss you on the beach. I know we've had a million wonderful kisses in a *lot* of places, but every time the thought of kissing you on the beach comes into my head I almost have an orgasm. Like now . . . so I'm wiggling my toes in the sand, and the ocean breeze is making my hair wild, and I can't hear my heartbeat over the squawks of the seagulls. I want you *so* much . . . I want you all the time."

"*Shh*, pretty girl. I can feel your heartbeat, like the first night. I love you."

It took five hours to drive to Duck, but it was a lovely morning. Matt and Will sat in the front and split the driving while Mary Kay and I lounged and napped in the back seat and talked about our boys and our new jobs. Mary Kay and Will would be off to Brussels in mid-June. We knew it would be a lot of months between June and the next time we'd be together.

The first thing Matt noticed when we unpacked in Duck was his old Confederate beach towel.

"Abby, I can't *believe* you sneaked this in to our bags when I wasn't looking."

"Summer boy, my plan is to find a hidden hollow for this towel between two or three friendly dunes, with no bobbies nosing around, and make love to you until either the blowing sand covers our bodies or the tide takes us out to sea."

Will's summer house was beautiful, and *huge*. There were four bedrooms, three on the second floor and a third-floor loft; an eat-in kitchen and modest dining room; and a large family room with floor-to-ceiling glass walls and doors leading out to an equally large redwood deck facing the dunes and the beach. *I could live here forever*, I thought. Matt and I chose the master bedroom—the "bridal suite" we called it—on the second floor, and Mary Kay and Will took the loft.

The first afternoon we unpacked, settled in and walked the beach. It was cloudy and cool, so we needed jeans and windbreakers. There weren't many people around. Will said Memorial Day was when all the "Yankees" started coming down. We had supper at Irving's Beach Shack, the locals' favorite diner on the little boardwalk in town. Then we stopped at the Carolina Cupboard, the only supermarket in Duck, for supplies, mostly junk food and twelve six-packs of our favorite brands of beer. This would be an all-beer, no-wine week.

We built a small fire in the fire pit between the deck and the dunes. Will said only small fires were allowed because of the danger to the dunes. As we sat around the fire, every time Mary Kay and I looked at each other we knew that we were thinking very different thoughts from our guys.

As glorious and romantic and happy as this week promised to be, there would be a thin layer of sadness below the surface. My best friend and I read each other's thoughts: *Our youth is ending this summer. Our years as curious schoolgirls, our years as carefree single girls, our years as the little sisters in our families—they are all ending. We are done growing up. We are going into an exciting but difficult and scary world and, for the first time since we met in kindergarten, we are going to be far away from each other.*

One saving grace that kept Mary Kay and me from hugging and crying more than we did was our comforting belief that Will would take good care of *her* and Matt would take good care of *me*.

That night in the "bridal suite" Matt was stroking my hair and kissing me when I asked him, "Old guy, when we were sitting around the fire, could you tell . . ."

". . . that you and Mary Kay were a little sad?"

"You *did* know. MK said you would, just like you knew about her and Josh the first time you met her. How could you tell?"

"I was *there* once, Abby. When I graduated from B.C. in the summer of 1968, my friends and I were all going off in different directions—which was sad enough—but because of Vietnam most of our options were so *bad* that it was hard not to be depressed. I was already in ROTC, so my path was set. But my friends had to choose: enlist, be drafted, run away to Canada, join the Peace Corps or the Teacher Corps. Thank God none of my friends chose Canada. And thank God you and Mary Kay have better choices ahead of you. And it wasn't as easy for me and my friends to keep in touch. No e-mail, no instant messages, no Facebook. It was the *good* old days."

Matt made his "sad dog" face and needed a big hug.

"I promise, old guy, that I will not be the least bit sad for the rest of our honeymoon. MK and I have already talked, hugged and cried our way through this. We are going to be so happy and hot for the rest of the week that you and Will are going to be very sorry to leave Duck."

"Can we get started on that 'happy and hot' right now, pretty girl, because I've never made love in North Carolina."

Matt was so sweet that first night. He wrapped his arms around me and ran his hands slowly down my backside, from the hair on my neck to the hollows of my knees, lifting my body off the bed as he moved down, and kissing me just as slowly in front, from my lips to my kneecaps. He touched and kissed me so slowly and intensely that I had two orgasms on his first trip down my body and one on his second before I stopped him halfway and brought him inside me. We fell asleep tangled and sweaty, with the smell of the damp salt air coming through the windows from the dunes.

We woke up on Tuesday morning to sunshine on the bed and fresh salt breezes from the beach, and the smell of sourdough toast, bacon and eggs from the kitchen. Mary Kay and Will said they had slept like babies. I replied with a sheepish grin that Matt and I had slept like newlyweds. We all decided to walk in to town after breakfast and check out the shops on the boardwalk, and then spend the afternoon on the beach. It was supposed to be in the eighties and sunny all day.

324

My favorite little store was called Sand Treasures. Mary Kay and I bought matching, plain sky-blue rings made from the same giant seashell—or so the shop clerk told us. The bands were almost a half-inch wide, so there was room for engraving. We wrote *From MK 5/20/08* on my ring and *From Abby 5/20/08* on Mary Kay's. We hugged each other and cried, of course, and swore we would wear them forever—and I have never taken mine off my right ring finger.

Will knew the owners of most of the shops and bought little presents for either his family or Mary Kay in just about every shop. Matt lingered in the old bookstore, The Literary Duck, and found an autographed first edition of Nicholas Sparks' *The Notebook*. Matt and I also purchased matching baseball caps in Bait & Bonnet. They were pale, slate blue with navy blue brims, with the word "Duck" in navy blue script on the front. When we adjusted the caps on each other and I gave Matt a big kiss, I suddenly found myself thinking about Nannie and Grandpa Dolan: *I'll bet they would have done exactly the same thing.*

We shared catfish sandwiches, coleslaw, corn dogs and Corona beer at Ben's on the Boards and walked back to the beach house at two o'clock. Mary Kay and Will wanted to walk south on the beach down to the inlet to check out the tour boats. Matt and I walked *up* the beach until there were no more joggers, no more people walking their dogs, no more sunbathers and no more beach houses.

When the beach narrowed to about a hundred yards, we climbed over the front line of dunes and found a perfect hollow among three of the highest dunes. We had brought a large, powder blue blanket from the house, and Matt's Confederate flag, of course. The blanket was the same color as the sky, which was all we could see from our hollow.

And then we did something I never dreamed I would *ever* do—before I met Matt. We took off *all* of our clothes standing and facing each other in the sunshine, out in the open. We made a pile in the corner of the blue blanket. Then Matt reached in the pile and unpinned Nannie and Grandpa's lucky ribbon from my panties and tangled it delicately in my hair. He pulled me tightly against him, kissed the ribbon and whispered, "This would be a lovely place to make a baby, pretty girl."

We lay down on the blanket and played and kissed and talked . . . for a long time. Matt slowly touched and studied my face as if he were seeing it for the first time. We took off our rings and put them on each other's fingers. Then Matt brushed the sand from my feet and licked in between my toes, while I twirled his hair and tickled his ears and nibbled on the back of his neck. Even after six months, it was still a wonder to me how much Matt adored my body although it was no surprise to me how much I worshipped *his*. If I told any of my best friends—which I never would have—nobody except Mary Kay would have believed that I had Matt inside me *six* times on that afternoon on the blanket in the sand. We were so wrapped in each other and so oblivious of the world beyond the dunes that we didn't realize we had burrowed our *own* body-length hollow way down below sand level. Matt fell asleep first, and then I pulled the Confederate flag over both of us and closed my eyes with my beloved summer boy.

It was almost seven o'clock when Matt woke me up. Our private hollow among the dunes was completely in shadows. Matt said the seagulls woke *him* up. We laughed at the picture of ourselves: two wild college kids on spring break. I could envision my next charcoal drawing.

There were two messages from Mary Kay on Matt's cell phone. I called her as we got dressed and said we had fallen asleep on the beach and were on our way back. I could hear the smile in her voice as she quipped, "Did you sleep like newlyweds again, Abby?"

Mary Kay and Will were waiting for us on the deck and, as we walked up from the dunes, MK made a mischievous face and held up four fingers on her right hand. I gave her the same sheepish grin I gave her at breakfast and held up five fingers on *my* right hand and one on my left. At that she clapped her hands and laughed so hard I thought she was going to slide off her rocking chair.

For dinner the guys grilled burgers, and Mary Kay and I baked cornbread and made a salad with baby spinach and chopped scallions, carrots and hard-boiled eggs. Then we walked in to town and went to the The Igloo at the inlet for ice cream. Mary Kay and Will had stopped there earlier to check out the tour boats, and MK pulled a few brochures out of her Redskins tote bag.

"There are whale watching boats, deep sea fishing boats, scuba diving boats and parasailing boats. What do you think, Abby?"

"I would like a boat ride," I grinned, "preferably any morning after breakfast or any evening after dinner, where I can relax without getting too wet or risking my life or working too hard."

"No scuba diving or parasailing?"

"No scuba diving or parasailing for *me*, but you and Matt and Will can do all of those things, and I'll wave to you with my coffee cup from the boardwalk."

We decided to have breakfast the next morning in town at Irving's and then go on the ten o'clock whale watching boat.

29

Matt and I took a long, cool shower that night—probably the longest and coolest in our six months together—because we kept finding more sand in more spots on our bodies, and we were both pink in places we had never been pink before. When we finally got into bed, I felt so mellow that I might have been Matt's body pillow. I was content to be squeezed and plumped, smoothed and flipped, patted and hugged. There was nothing I could say that would add to the day. Matt understood and was just as quiet. I fell asleep wondering how I could ever be happier.

A spectacular thunderstorm woke us in the middle of the night. The digital clock read *3:23*. There was an old piano bench at the foot of the bed, and Matt and I moved it to the open front window, covered it with a folded bath towel, and sat— naked—with the wind and rain blowing in on us, watching the lightning over the dunes and the beach and the ocean. It was exciting sitting almost in the middle of the storm, and in the dark . . . until the flashes lit up both the bedroom and the beach.

I moved onto Matt's lap, facing him, with my arms around his neck and my back to the open window. I kissed him several times and said, "Summer boy, if it were just the two of us in this house, I would take you by the hand, out the door and over the dunes, and run naked with you across the beach and into the water."

Matt kissed the dripping hair around my ears and ran his hands down my back and over my wet "tail," and I felt his frisky guy moving underneath me on the bench. And then he was inside me, and he rocked me back and forth on that old bench, back and forth, fondled by the wind and rain, with the flashes of lightning punctuating my wild cries. I crashed. The next thing I knew, it was morning and I was tangled in Matt in bed. He said I collapsed like a rag doll on the bench, and he had to close the window and try to sit me up and dry me off, and then carry me to bed. It was stunning to think about the number of times since I had met Matt that I had come to realize how little I knew about love, sex or passion *before* I met him.

I squeezed him as hard as I dared and looked squarely in to his eyes.

"You took me away completely, Matt. I remember the bench rocking back and forth, and the wind and the rain touching my shoulders, and then I was gone. How can you keep *doing* that?" I smiled. "Someday, summer boy, you'll have to tell me how you arranged that thunderstorm."

On our walk to town for breakfast, Mary Kay caught my hand, interlocked her fingers with mine and gave me a sly smile. "That was a *noisy* thunderstorm last night, huh, Abby?"

I played along and didn't take the bait. "When it woke Matt and me up, the clock read *3:23.*"

"Will and I didn't get out of bed. We pretended to be scared and hid under the covers, and listened to the thunder for a long time."

"I wanted to watch so we moved an old piano bench up close to the open front window."

"I *thought* I heard you moving and making noise downstairs."

"We got *really* wet, but the lightning over the beach and the water was *awesome*. We sat there for a long time, I think, and then Matt rocked me to sleep and took me back to bed." I squeezed Mary Kay's fingers and lifted her hand and pressed it to my chest. "MK, is there one time you would pick out as the best time you've ever made love?"

"No, not yet, Abby. I used to think a lot of times with Josh were great, but now I know that most times with Will are *way* better. On the other hand," she grinned, "I get the sense that you and Matt are breaking every record in the book."

"MK, I can't *believe* what he keeps doing to me and where he keeps taking me. Almost every day is not only better than the day before, but it's usually a surprise, too. I mean, you and I didn't have *that* many boyfriends and we didn't sleep around, so I knew I was far from an expert when I met Matt; but I thought I knew a *little* about sex and love. I was wrong. I hope some day, *soon*, you get to where I am right now, and you'll understand what I'm talking about. None of my other friends would believe me if I told them, unless they had already experienced it themselves."

The boat ride was glorious. The sun came out and the waves weren't too rough. Matt and I were incredibly cute in our matching Duck hats, and we took lots of pictures. We only saw two whales: a small pilot, which was common in those waters according to Captain Tidrow; and a large humpback, which was extremely rare at that time of the year off the Outer Banks. We also saw a school of dolphins and one of porpoises—which are smaller and shorter in the beak—and several blue marlin and sailfish. The boat, Maisie's Cracker, had a good assortment of coffee and cookies, and the four of us nibbled, talked, hugged and sang silly camp songs like "Ninety-nine Bottles of Beer on the Wall."

When the guys went up to the bridge with Captain Tidrow, Mary Kay and I found a nook near the back of the boat. She was nervous about spending the whole week after Memorial Day with Will's family, but she and I agreed that it would be a good chance to find out how high she stood in Will's estimation . . . *and* an important step toward going across the ocean together.

"Abby gal, what if it doesn't work out for Will and me? What if living together doesn't work out, and we break up when we're in Brussels?"

"Matt and I have discussed that many times. The conversation usually starts with my asking, 'What if you had walked in to Kitty's on a *Wednesday* instead of a Monday?' The answer is that Matt and I both had lives *before* we met, and we would have continued to have lives even if we had never met. Would we *ever* have been as happy? Only God knows, but it's impossible for me to believe that there could be another man better for me than Matt.

"The answer for *you* is that you are Mary Kay Galvin. You are bright and beautiful, you are accomplished, you have two degrees, and you have a brilliant career ahead of you. Is Will the man who will become your happy place forever? Only God knows, but it's not something you can *make* happen. It's only something you can realize—if you recognize it—*when* it happens."

We all spent the afternoon on the beach in front of Will's house. We had two blankets—navy blue and powder blue—a cooler of Corona, two giant bags of Lay's potato chips and two boxes of Bachman hard sourdough pretzels. We walked, holding hands; we napped and soaked up the sun; we ran in the rolling waves and dug in the sand; we tossed a Frisbee and a beach ball; we breathed in the salty air and felt as if we were eight years old. I always thought that the best place to *really* get to know someone would be a beach. There can't be many physical surprises on a beach, and people are more relaxed, open, friendly, philosophical, thoughtful—even more *equal*. Unless you happen to be John F. Kennedy or Marilyn Monroe, it's hard to have pretensions if you have no clothes on. I always remember the "pockets" scene from *Death of a Salesman*: "Who liked J.P. Morgan? Was he impressive? In a Turkish bath he'd look like a butcher. But with his pockets on he was very well liked."

We had dinner in town at Vitolino's, Duck's best Italian restaurant, and built another bonfire later off Will's deck. It was Wednesday night, which meant that we were halfway through our Duck honeymoon. Matt said that he could always feel the dynamic of a vacation change when it was closer to the end than the beginning. The two of us resolved in whispers at the fire that we were not going to leave any unused minutes behind in Duck. We also resolved that we would be back, with or without Mary Kay and Will. I even bought two oval, black and white OBX bumper stickers to "accessorize" our cars back home.

That night, a gentle rain came in a little after midnight. Matt and I listened and made love for *hours* as the steady showers continued and then got out of bed when the clock read *3:23*.

"We *have* to, Matt," I whispered.

I wrapped the powder blue blanket around both of us, and we softly stepped through the house and onto the deck, and over the sand and among the dunes. We let the blanket drop to our feet and stood—touching, kissing, clinging—naked in the warm rain. My mind shut down in the time it took the blanket to fall to the ground. After six months of such incredible and intense physical passion with Matt, I no longer felt in control of my mind or my body once he started touching me. All my thoughts evaporated, my mind vanished, and my entire being became physical . . . purely sensual. In the sea breeze, in the rain, in the dunes, in the night, we were not Matt and Abigail— we were male and female.

I don't remember going back into the house. I don't remember Matt drying me off and carrying me to bed. I don't remember the rain stopping or the sun coming up. When my mind came back, it was morning, and Matt was sitting beside me in bed playing with my hair. He lifted me off our pillow and kissed me and handed me his coffee mug.

"Be careful, beauty, it's hot."

"Matt, how long were we outside last night? I don't
remember anything after we dropped the blanket on the sand."

"I don't know, sweetie; I lost track of time. We made love
standing up, on the side of a dune. We were very wet, and you
cried out a lot, but I guess nobody heard us in the rain. After that
you were pretty much asleep on your feet. I managed to walk
you back up to the bedroom and lay you down on the rug and
dry you off before I carried you to bed. You don't remember
any of that?"

"Only the blanket falling to the ground, and the rain around
your mouth, and your hands down my back and under my 'tail,'
lifting me up. You took me *away* again . . . off the beach to
another place. I almost can't breathe just *thinking* about it. I
love you so much; *you* are my air. I don't want it to stop, Matt.
I know we have to leave Duck on Sunday, but I don't want it to
stop. Let's go back up the beach today and see if we can find
our special place in the dunes."

We found our dunes, where the beach narrowed to about a
hundred yards, and we found our hollow. We knew they were
the same dunes because Matt had noticed an old, black Converse
sneaker stuck in the long grass halfway up the highest dune, and
it was still there.

"The hollow *we* made is gone, old guy."

"So our secret place is still a secret, pretty girl."

"Let's make another hollow, Matt. I told Mary Kay not to
expect us before dinner," I grinned.

There was a hazy sky rather than bright sunshine, so the sand
wasn't as hot among the dunes. We lay down on the blanket and
then took each other's clothes off. This time I tangled the lucky
ribbon in *Matt's* hair. It suddenly struck me—and surprised
me—that it was as exciting to have Matt undress me there in the
dunes as it was on our first night in bed. I was sure our
lovemaking couldn't *possibly* be as wondrous as two days ago,
but I was wrong.

I didn't underestimate Matt. I knew he could do any *thing*,
any *time*. I underestimated *myself*. Because Matt never needed
to show off or be in charge, he encouraged me—he *enabled*
me—without saying a word, to discover the sensual woman
inside Abigail McKay, to uncover her layers of passion. He
waited—as long as it took me—for me to do *what* I wanted, *if* I
wanted, *when* I wanted. Two days before, Matt touched and
kissed me into oblivion—again and again. This afternoon in the

dunes, I sensed that he wanted *me* to ravish every inch of his body and crush him in the sand. I didn't even pull the Confederate flag over us. I didn't care if the whole world watched me love and devour my man. I don't know how many times I had Matt inside me. I don't know if I carried him away from the beach. I don't remember which of us fell asleep first. I do remember that I *woke up* first. I was completely covering Matt. It was six o'clock, and I started kissing and licking the sand off him until he woke up.

"Wow . . . Abby, you totally wiped me out. You were all over me. Every time you took me inside you I felt my body sink deeper into the sand, way down, until I couldn't see the sky any more. And then I don't remember anything until you were licking me. How long was that?"

"I don't know, summer boy. Two hours, three hours? I fell asleep too. It's six o'clock now."

"So any natives or Yankee tourists who wandered from the beach over our dunes would have found us sound asleep—naked—and oblivious of the Outer Banks. We might be on You Tube."

"Well, *you* won't be, handsome, because I had you completely hidden," I laughed.

"Abby girl, even with that hazy sky you could have a pretty pink 'tail' later. Are the kids looking for us yet?"

"We have one message from Mary Kay. I'll call her as soon as you shake the sand out of my clothes and put them back on me," I grinned. "And give me back my ribbon."

"You really *are* in charge today, eh, beauty?"

"You can't fool *me*, Matthew Flynn. I can read you like one of your poems. You *wanted* me to be on top today."

"You got me there, sweetie; but before we brush off all of this hot, beautiful, romantic sand, let me touch *you* one time. Roll over a little and come down with me in the bottom of my hollow. *I* want to be on You Tube, too."

We walked to town for supper at Ben's, and then sat outside at The Igloo with coffee and hot fudge sundaes and watched fireworks over the inlet. The moon was glorious—it was only a day or two after the full moon—and we all decided to go for a moonlight swim and a walk up the beach. Mary Kay was pensive *and* puckish as she walked next to me and held my hand.

"You broke some more records today, huh, sister?"

"What make you think so, MK?" I teased.

"You're so damned *pink* all over!"

As we walked past our spot, Matt—who was in front of us with Will—turned and made his "guilty boy" face. We continued a few hundred yards farther and then turned around and came back. Mary Kay was still holding my hand.

She whispered, "I have a feeling we just passed your special place."

"How could you tell?"

"I saw Matt give you a funny look, and I felt you squeeze my hand a little harder."

"MK, we love it here *so* much. I'm going to cry when we have to leave on Sunday."

"Me too. What would you guys like to do tomorrow? It's supposed to rain, so you might not be able to go to your favorite spot," she grinned.

"Making love in the rain is fun, too, you know," I grinned back. "My body can probably use a break from the sun. I saw a lot of games on one of the shelves in the living room—let's have an old-fashioned family game day."

It was one o'clock when we got in bed. Matt very gently put lotion on my backside from my neck to my ankles.

"Does it hurt, pretty girl?"

"Nothing hurts when you touch me, old guy, but I hope I don't slide off the bed."

There was no chance of that with Matt holding me tightly all night. I slept like a baby and dreamed of our blanket in the dunes.

We woke to a gray morning and the sound of rain coming through the front windows. It smelled delicious, and I wished I could take Matt outside to make love. I wondered if Mary Kay felt the same urge. We had a lovely breakfast watching the big raindrops bounce on the deck. Mary Kay and Will showed us pictures of Brussels and the flat they would be sharing near NATO headquarters.

Then we broke out the games: Trivial Pursuit, Twister, Monopoly and Clue. Matt was the best at Trivial Pursuit, of course; Mary Kay turned out to be ruthless at Monopoly; I was the most limber at Twister, much to Matt's delight; and Will was the best detective at Clue. We actually thought he was cheating because he won twice in a row by guessing "Miss Scarlett with the revolver in the hall." We laughed, hugged and shared Coronas all afternoon.

When Mary Kay and Will went upstairs for a nap before dinner, Matt and I walked out in the light rain over the dunes to the beach. Only the sandpipers and seagulls were out there with us.

"Want to dance, pretty girl?"

"No gentleman has ever asked me to dance in the rain, sir, but you *did* make love to me in the rain. Don't we need some music?"

Matt took me in his arms and started humming "I Can't Help Falling in Love with You." As we moved in a slow circle, making footprints on the shiny, squishy sand, with the tide rushing in and out over our feet, my summer boy caressed me from the wet hair on my neck to the back of my thighs. We were pressed together so tightly that no rain could get between us. We gave each other "a real kiss, like in the movies," like our first kiss in my apartment . . . with the same result: I couldn't stand up by myself. Matt held me and rocked me back and forth as the rain continued to soak us. I think I fell asleep. Can you believe it? With my mouth on Matt's, standing with my feet in rushing waves, with the rain running down my body . . . I fell asleep. Matt roused me by locking his arms under my "tail" and lifting me off the sand.

"Hey, old guy, put me down before you hurt yourself!"

"It's time to go in, sleepy girl. We have to get dried off and dressed for dinner. We're going to Will's favorite fish place, The Naked Hook. We'll probably have to drive if it keeps raining like this."

The Naked Hook was right next to The Igloo on the north side of the inlet. We decided to order four different fish—none of which I had ever tasted—and share: Spanish mackerel, spot, flounder and striped bass. They all came with family-style bowls of salt potatoes and coleslaw, and a bottomless basket of Cajun breadsticks. We pigged out. All the fish were delicious, but the spot was my favorite. We switched from Corona to a selection of local beers—Blue Carrot, Old Starboard Red, Bell Bottom Blonde and Crocodile Black—and Katy Jo, our buxom and tattooed waitress, kept the pints coming. And the rain kept falling. It was very cozy in our booth looking out at the wind whipping the rain over the boat docks and the waves across the inlet.

We laughed, we sang, we were silly, we reached across the table and held hands, we played footsie *under* the table. Mary Kay and Will were happy, and clearly stronger together than when we had arrived in Duck. Mary Kay was going to stay one more week with Will and his family and then come home to Rochester for about ten days before she and Will flew to Brussells on June 16. We already had a pajama party planned for Friday, June 6. Emma was coming in to town, and she and Claire would be joining us at Mary Kay's.

We didn't leave The Naked Hook until almost ten, and it was still raining. *There will be no campfire off the deck tonight*, I thought sadly. We were all still keyed up, so we decided to make popcorn and watch a movie. We didn't want sad, and we didn't want suspense or violence. We wanted happy, so we watched *Uncle Buck* and gobbled up three tubs of Orville Redenbacher. Matt told us about the first time he saw *Uncle Buck* with his sons and a bunch of cousins. They were all together on vacation on the Jersey shore on a rainy July day, and they rented the VHS tape. Everybody laughed so hard that when the movie was over they rewound the tape and watched the whole movie again.

I think none of us wanted the night to end because that would mean we were on our last whole day together in Duck. The rain had finally stopped when we got into bed at one o'clock. Matt pulled back the drapes on both front windows, and moonlight filled the room. We sat up in bed and said our prayers, with an extra one for Mary Kay and Will.

"Matt, do you think they'll be okay in Brussels? Do you think they'll make it together?"

"I do. Will has talked with me on a couple of our walks about his last girlfriend, another Army officer, a Georgia girl named Libby. I think both Will and Mary Kay learned a lot about themselves in the process of breaking up with Libby and Josh."

"I hope so although I suspect that Mary Kay still loves *you* more than she loves Will." I took Matt's left hand and played with his wedding band. "She kidded me a few times that 'if you and Matt ever split up, I'm going after him.' Except I don't think she's kidding. She hasn't forgotten the way you looked into her eyes the first time you met. *I* haven't forgotten that either . . . across the counter at Kitty's."

336

I pulled Matt down on the bed beside me.

"Touch me in this moonlight, old guy, just like it was the first time."

"Abby, beauty, with you it's *always* the first time."

I fell asleep first, wrapped in Matt's arms in the bright moonlight, and I woke up first at seven-thirty, wrapped in his arms in the bright sunshine. I kissed his cheeks and palms and toes and walked my fingers across his stomach until he woke up.

After breakfast on our deck, we all decided to drive south on North Carolina Route 12 to the Cape Hatteras National Seashore and the famous Cape Hatteras Lighthouse in Buxton. Will said it would take about an hour and a half, but we doubled that by stopping almost everywhere along the way.

We toured the Wright Brothers Memorial in Kitty Hawk; Matt and Will bought coffee in Nags Head; Mary Kay and I took pictures in Whalebone; we got off the main highway to drive around the Pea Island National Wildlife Refuge, but didn't see much wildlife—which reminded me of my one trip to the Montezuma National Wildlife Refuge back home, where I also didn't see much wildlife. We stopped again for coffee in Rodanthe and walked along the beach to the house that the locals said was the inspiration for Nicholas Sparks' novel . . . which was made into one of my favorite Richard Gere movies and one of Matt's favorite Diane Lane movies.

After climbing to the top of the lighthouse, we found a lovely restaurant in town, Armistead's, on Buccaneer Drive overlooking Brigand Bay. It was named for one of North Carolina's most distinguished military families, which included Brigadier General Lewis Armistead who died in Pickett's Charge at the Battle of Gettysburg. There must have been a hundred photographs and paintings of Armistead soldiers—from the War of 1812 through Desert Storm and Operation Iraqi Freedom—hanging on the oak-paneled walls. The placemats showed the family tree of Lewis Armistead from his death in 1863 to the birth of the latest Armistead baby, Crystal, in 2006.

Mary Kay and Will told us their initial assignments at NATO were for fourteen months. They were already trying to talk us into coming to visit them at the end of the year. I kidded Mary Kay that she would have to start planning for an October wedding when she came back. We sat for an hour after lunch sipping our beers and watching the sailboats on the bay. On the quiet ride back I curled up on the back seat with my head in Matt's lap and napped all the way.

It was a lovely evening so the boys grilled burgers and hot dogs by the dunes, and we dined on the deck. We sipped more beers until all the stars appeared, and we talked about how much our lives had changed since last fall. Even though there were thirty years separating them, Matt and Will seemed to be kindred spirits who understood each other completely. I thought to myself, *Matt might just miss Will as much as I'm going to miss Mary Kay. Maybe we really will go visit them in Belgium.*

Matt was *so* sweet in bed that night. The way he touched me, I knew he was telling me it was okay to be sad . . . that being sad was a part of being happy. It was life's ebb and flow. I cried while we made love, and Matt became even more gentle, and rocked me and kissed my tears.

We were packed and finished with breakfast by nine, and in the car for our three-and-a-half-hour drive to the Raleigh-Durham airport. One quick kiss was all the goodbye that Mary Kay and I could handle at the gate, but she gave Matt a lingering hug. I could see that she didn't want to look directly in his eyes.

Our Southwest flight took off at two o'clock, and with a fifty-minute stop at LaGuardia, we were on the ground in Rochester at six-fifteen. I dozed most of the way, or tried to anyway, and cried, too. Matt was a rock. He held me, stroked me, kissed me, wiped my tears. At one point about halfway to New York City, I asked him, "How do you *do* it, old guy? I'm such a mess— you'd think somebody had *died.* Thank God you're so strong."

"More practice, love. I've cried through a lot of separations—and many dear people who *have* died—to get here. One of the most memorable lines, and one of the saddest, in *Death of a Salesman* comes from Willy's wife Linda: 'Well, dear, life is a casting off.'

"Sometimes I handled it well; sometimes I was *way* worse than you. I still wish I could have hung on to everybody I've loved in my life. It tears us up to have to let go . . . but then we come back. We live again in our children and grandchildren, and one morning we wake up and there's an Abigail in our lives."

Matt took my face in both his hands, kissed me softly and whispered, "The next time we see Mary Kay and Will, pretty girl, we'll probably be *twice* as happy as we are now."

Matt III met us at the airport and took us home. He said it had been an uneventful week for his family except for Emily's two-day earache, and he invited us over for dinner the next day.

We picked up Maggie and Jock from Pat and Laurie in the morning and pretty much spent the whole week catching up on the real world, taking long walks with and without the dogs, making love at all hours of the day and night, and shopping for clothes for my new job. On Tuesday it rained all day, and Matt and I went to B. Forman's on Monroe Avenue where he picked out five dresses for me—right off the rack—and they all fit *perfectly*, and we bought all five. *We* bought. After a little more than two months as a wife I still smiled every time I used our joint credit cards or joint checking account. We had dinner at Mom and Dad's on Wednesday, and at Matt's mom and dad's on Thursday. On Friday, we met Ann and Dave Connolly at Palermo's.

Mary Kay called on Wednesday night, and we talked for more than an hour. Will's mother and father were *wonderful*, she said, and all the Fischettes made her feel like one of the family. She and Will would be driving back to D.C. on Saturday, and she said she'd call me on Sunday.

The weather was nice on Saturday and Sunday, and Matt and I spent a lot of time outside. We weeded the daisy garden at the front corner of the house; I planted the marigolds in the window boxes; Matt dug up the dandelions on the front lawn and trimmed the long grass around the trees in the back yard. Maggie and Jock were outside with us for a long time on Saturday morning, until they started digging down into too many chipmunk holes on the front lawn and making a mess.

We took them with us to Phil Green's for lunch on both days, and we all sat outside at the picnic tables. I was so hungry from our yard work that on Saturday I had a Snickers Supreme hot fudge sundae with extra peanuts—in addition to my red hot with mustard and onions. On Sunday, I had *four* of those little paper cups full of dill pickles—in addition to my barbecue fries and cheeseburger with lettuce and tomato. Jinks joined us for a while on Sunday and told us how much she was enjoying the entry store manager program at Mangrums. She said she would stop in to the advertising department and see how my first week was going.

Matt packed my Tinker Bell lunch box on Monday morning: one fat peanut butter sandwich on whole wheat, two mozzarella

339

sticks, one McIntosh apple and one package containing four Oreos. I wore my brand-new mint green dress with white piping on the short sleeves and the scoop neck and the hemline. Mr. Christopher met me in the conference room at the office and escorted me to *my* new office, which had a window overlooking Hawkes Avenue.

It was a perfect morning except for some spotting—a white discharge—in my panties. That didn't happen to me very much.

It was both comfortable and exciting to now be in charge of some of the projects that I had worked on as an intern. The difference, of course, was that I was no longer turning in papers to get grades. I would now be turning in reports to help make Mangrums a better supermarket. But the best thing about my new job was how proud Matt was of me. He couldn't stop telling people about "my wife, the Assistant Director of New Projects at Mangrums."

My whole first week was magical. Because Matt's business was built around meeting clients, his schedule was more flexible than mine, so he packed my Tinker Bell lunch box every morning. He wouldn't let me do it. And he and Maggie and Jock kissed me goodbye when they walked me to my car at seven-thirty, and they were all waiting for me every afternoon when I came home.

The spotting continued every day but it wasn't heavy, so I thought I'd wait a week or so before I called my doctor. And even though Matt packed me bountiful lunches, I couldn't believe how hungry I was every evening after work. We took Monday night off from Phil Green's and fixed Caesar salads at home, but we were back on Tuesday and Wednesday. Matt was amazed by how much I was eating: an Italian sausage sandwich with peppers and onions, and a half-dozen cups of pickles, and curly fries, and a Peanut Butter Cup sundae on Tuesday; and a bacon cheeseburger, more pickles, tater tots, and a Snickers Supreme sundae on Wednesday. Matt watched me eat, sipped his hot chocolate and laughed.

"I've never seen a girl eat this much, beauty. What are the chances you're pregnant?"

"Those would be good chances, old guy, but I don't think so. You'll be the *second* to know."

Our evenings were lovely. The weather was perfect for June. After dinner we walked Maggie and Jock around the circle—which was half a mile—and then Matt and I filled our travel mugs with coffee and walked another two miles up and back on Atlantic Avenue. After dark, we watched a few innings of the Yankee games on television or half an hour of our latest romance, *The Lake House*.

We were almost always in bed by eleven, and we almost always fell asleep right after we made love. Matt said I occasionally didn't last until the "right after" part.

30

Mary Kay phoned when she got in at about nine o'clock on Thursday night. She said Emma called and said she'd be in by seven on Friday, so Claire and I should come over at six-thirty.

"Should we bring anything, MK?"

"Just your pajamas, Abby. I'll have beer and wine and subs from Mangrums."

Mary Kay's mother and father had gone to Toronto for the weekend, so we had the house to ourselves. Emma was now three months pregnant, but if you didn't know, you wouldn't have noticed. She said she was feeling great.

"Except for lots of extra trips to the bathroom and a backache every few days, *I* wouldn't even know I was pregnant," she laughed. "That and my latest cravings. I've switched from cantaloupe and Cool Whip to chocolate-covered bananas and celery sticks with cream cheese. I've gained five pounds, which my doctor says is pretty normal. Dr. Graham will know next month if we have a boy or a girl, but Danny and I won't . . . and we probably won't until he or she is born. We're thinking of painting the nursery sky blue with little puffy clouds and pink balloons."

"Have you decided on any names?" Claire asked. "Matthew was easy for us, of course, but it took a lot more time to settle on Emily."

"Right now we're calling the baby Fozzie Bear. Martin is a possibility from Danny's mom's family name and Rachel for my Grandma. We like a few other names also. Victoria and Nathaniel are two we've talked about."

In between our subs and beers and wine we helped Mary Kay organize her wardrobe for her year in Europe. We also talked about what the three of us—Mary Kay would be on her way back to D.C.—would wear to Katy and Trent's wedding the following Saturday. None of us were in the wedding party, which was going to be small: Trent's three best buddies and Katy's sister and her two best girlfriends. I planned to wear another one of the new dresses Matt had picked out. It was a sleeveless, navy blue satin sheath, ruched on the left, with a high neck. Claire and Emma said they planned on going shopping—except for my wedding, they hadn't bought dresses in a long time—and they would coordinate with each other so that we "sisters" would look dynamite together and dazzle the crowd.

We talked long into the night about Mary Kay's adventure in Europe, and Will; and Claire's state senator and the upcoming election, and the summer plans for little Matthew and Emily; and Emma's baby; and my honeymoon in Duck; and helping Mary Kay with her 2009 wedding plans.

In the morning, we went to Joe's Diner for breakfast, then Mary Kay and I went home, and Emma went to spend the day—and stay overnight—with Claire and Matt III and the kids. She would leave early in the morning to drive back to Boston. Matt tucked me in for a two-hour nap, and then we decided to go to the five o'clock Mass so we could sleep in on Sunday.

During Mass, I started feeling funny. Not dizzy, exactly, but I felt a kind of buzz, like when you're high on adrenalin because something exciting is about to happen. I thought my heart was beating faster, although everything around me in church seemed to be in slow motion. When we walked to the Jeep after Mass, I held on to Matt tighter than usual and made him walk slower.

"Are you okay, Abby?"

"I feel kind of funny, old guy. Not dizzy, exactly; not *bad*—but not *sure* either. It's a little like a caffeine high. I want to take a lot of deep breaths. I think you should call Matt and Claire and tell them I'm a little tired and we're going to pass on the pizza and wings with Emma. I'd like to go home and camp on the sofa in the TV room, have some tea and vanilla Sugar Wafers and watch a little more of *The Lake House*."

I felt better on the sofa, leaning on Matt with my feet up on the coffee table and Maggie and Jock nestled next to me. In the movie we watched Alex—two years in the past—walk Kate to his favorite places in Chicago. Then he meets her in *his* time at a surprise birthday party for her at her boyfriend's house. Then they talk about Kate's favorite book, *Persuasion*. And then they start to dance. But I couldn't keep my eyes open.

"Old guy, I'm *so* tired, and I *love* this scene. Take me to bed, please, and we can start their dance over tomorrow."

When we made love, Matt was as gentle as he could be. My buzz kept coming and going, mostly in my breasts and my belly.

343

But then I lost all thoughts and feelings except Matt inside me and fell asleep.

I slept in late—'til *ten* o'clock. I woke to Matt kissing my breasts, which were tingling like *crazy*.

"Matt, what are you doing? You're making my breasts buzz! Stop for a second, *please*."

"Sorry . . . nothing that I haven't done a hundred times, pretty girl."

"Well, they're still tingling, like electricity is going right through them. I thought they felt a little strange when I took off my bra last night."

"They *are* darker, Abby. Your nipples are darker, like old pennies instead of new ones."

"Well, it's probably all the sunshine from Duck," I smiled mischievously. "Anyway, summer boy, would you mind kissing *around* my old pennies for a couple of days until the buzz is gone?"

Matt had already been outside with the dogs, made coffee and read the paper. Claire called at eleven to see how I was. She said Emma hit the road at eight and was already past Albany. It was a beautiful day, and Claire and Matt III and the kids were going to the zoo.

Old Matt and I decided to have a slow day. For a change we drove to Phil Green's at the *lake* for lunch, and then took our ice cream cones for a long walk on the pier. Then we meandered to the boat launch at the south end of the bay where we counted forty-three beautiful, white swans. We threw crumbs from our hot dog buns to the swans, geese, ducks, seagulls and smaller birds who came squawking, honking and begging.

Then we drove through the park to Durand Beach, took off our sandals and walked about a mile up and down the beach. The water hadn't warmed up yet, but it was clearer than it would be later in the summer. I was feeling okay in general, but every time Matt held me close and kissed me, my breasts still tingled. And when I saw a pregnant woman walking towards us in the sand, holding a little girl's hand, it suddenly occurred to me that my period was late.

For supper, Matt grilled Italian sausage, I made Caesar salads and cherry jello, and we had a picnic on the back porch with Maggie and Jock. Then we took the doggies for a long walk up Clark Road to the ice cream stand at Brophy's Farm Market. Maggie had red raspberry, and Jock had orange sherbet. After we walked back home, Matt and I settled on the sofa to watch the rest of *The Lake House*. The last scene—when Kate discovers why Alex didn't meet her at the fancy restaurant on Valentine's Day two years earlier, then rushes to the lake house in desperation to put a message in the mailbox—is one of my favorite scenes in *any* movie.

"Do you think that could happen, Matt? The two years, the dog, the book, the mailbox?"

"After last November at Kitty's, beauty, I believe *everything* can happen."

I lay sideways with my head in his lap and wrapped my arms around his waist.

"My period is late, old guy. When we were walking on the beach and I saw that pregnant woman, I remembered what Emma said: 'All the hints and clues came together in my little brain.' Maybe you *were* the first to know when I was eating so much at Phil Green's. I think I'll wait until the end of the week and then call Dr. Hansen."

The white discharge was gone on Monday, but my period still didn't come all week, so I called Dr. Hansen Friday morning. He said I could be his last customer of the day if I could make it at four o'clock. I called Matt.

"Old guy, Dr. Hansen is letting me come in at four o'clock. Will you meet me there? I am *so* nervous, Matt."

"I'll be there, pretty girl. Don't worry, sweetie. It's going to be okay. I have a good feeling."

Dr. Hansen was partly solicitous but mostly teasing. He knew how nervous I was, and he was trying to get me to relax.

"So what brings you two here? You both are glowing. Have you ramped up the sex lately?"

Matt and I talked about our sand dunes in Duck, and then I told Dr. Hansen about the spotting and the buzz and the tingling and my voracious appetite. He laughed.

"When my wife and I had our first baby, she couldn't get enough pepperoni—which she had never liked before. And I couldn't just buy sticks of pepperoni and cut them up; Beth had to have hot pepperoni off the top of a pizza. Our German shepherd had a lot of pizza crust for a few months."

Dr. Hansen started with a urine test and—while we were waiting for the results—had Matt and me go in to the examining room to get ready for the sonogram, just in case. When Dr. Bob came in smiling, I started shaking and buried my face in Matt's shoulder.

"The pregnancy hormone, hCG, is present in your urine, Abigail. You and Matt are going to have a baby."

I couldn't see or hear anything for the next few minutes because I was crying so hard. Matt wrapped himself around me and rocked me and stroked my hair and kissed me on the top of my head and finally got me to stop shaking and sobbing. Dr. Bob had waited patiently.

"Congratulations, Abigail! Congratulations, Matt! Abby, if you're okay, would you lie down on the examining table and let me do the sonogram—the ultrasound—so we can see about how far along you are? Later on, after about seventeen or eighteen weeks, the ultrasound can tell us if you're going to have a boy or a girl—if you want to know. This is called a transvaginal ultrasound. Just relax while I look around a little bit inside your vagina."

Matt and I had had the "if you want to know" conversation twice already—when Debbie and Fred announced that they were having a baby but they weren't going to tell anybody whether it was a boy or a girl; and when Emma told us that she and Danny didn't want to know until the baby was born. But we were sure that we *would* want to know. Or at least *I* would want to know. Sweetheart that he is, Matt said—*all* the time, *every* time—that he wanted whatever I wanted. He said Sarah didn't want to know for Matt III but changed her mind for Danny.

Dr. Bob patted me twice on the navel to let me know that the ultrasound was finished, and then took both of my hands in his.

"It's early, Abby, probably no more than five weeks. When did your last period start?"

"May 6, I think."

"The start of your last period is usually considered the beginning of your pregnancy. And then conception occurs about two weeks after the beginning of your last period and two weeks before your next period is expected. That would have been about May 20 for you and Matt. Was that a dune day?" Dr. Bob teased.

Matt and I looked at each other and grinned from ear to ear, and Dr. Bob could see that he had it exactly right.

"Wow! You two are *amazing*. I'll be telling the tale of delivering my *dune* baby—without any names, of course—for a *hundred* years to come. So . . . nine months—forty weeks—

346

from May 6 will be February 6, 2009. How does that sound for a birthday?"

He smiled. His voice was gentle and kind. I started crying again. Matt stood behind me and softly caressed my shoulders, while Dr. Bob still held my hands and continued.

"Later on, after a couple more ultrasounds, we can fine-tune the dates, but Mother Nature is never one hundred percent predictable, even with the best scientific tests. Look here at the screen. Can you see that black spot? That's the gestational sac—where your baby starts. And see the small white circle in the upper left of the spot? That's the yolk sac—where your baby's food starts. The presence of the yolk sac tells us that you're going to have a normal, intrauterine pregnancy. I would like you to come back in on July 3—same time as today. That will be about eight weeks, and we should be able to see the embryo and a heartbeat."

I squeezed his hands. "Thank you *so* much, doctor! Is there anything I should be doing? *Start* doing? Other than jumping for joy?"

"That's my advice *exactly*. Jump for joy, play, eat and drink hearty, celebrate the wonder, have lots of sex, cry and laugh as much as you can *every* day, be the happiest woman on the face of the earth. Read a good pregnancy book. I recommend *I'm Having a Baby? I'm Having a Baby!* by Francine Toscano. You are an incredible woman in the full strength of her womanhood. Don't let anybody dampen your spirits. Here's the first lollipop for you and your baby. You couldn't be in better hands than Matt's. See you *all* in three weeks."

Out in the parking lot, Matt and I stood between our cars and hugged quietly for a long time. Then I took his cheeks in my hands and looked in his eyes and kissed him.

"Old guy, I love you more every day—I have since November—but how can I possibly love you more than I do today? You gave me a *baby*, Matt! Day after day you are making all of my dreams come true."

He laughed and—for only the second time since we met—clasped his arms under my "tail" and lifted me straight up off the ground. Then he buried his face in my belly. When I squealed, Matt put me down and made his "pleased-as-punch" face: a closed-mouth grin with scrunched, sparkling eyes.

"You can't *do* that any more, old guy. I'm in a 'delicate condition' now."

347

"I had to do it at least once, beauty—while I still can—before you turn into a baby balloon."

"You think you're such a hot dog—Daddy! I'll race you to Phil Green's. I'm feeling extra hungry just now."

We were in our usual booth, Matt with his Italian sausage sandwich and hot chocolate, and me with my red hot and cheeseburger and dill pickles and curly fries and vanilla milkshake. Jinks came over to say hello and gasped at the food on my tray. Then she laughed.

"Abby, are you going to eat all that? Are you pregnant or something?"

I touched my index finger to my lips and whispered, "*Shh.* We just found out today, and nobody knows. Don't tell the crew yet. Maybe in a week or two, after we tell the family."

Jinks grinned and nodded and went back to work, and I went back to my tray.

"Matt, I don't want to tell anybody tomorrow at the wedding. I don't want to take anything away from Katy and Trent's day. What time are Emma and Danny coming in tonight? I still have to make up their bed."

"Danny said about eight-thirty. I'll help you get the room ready."

"I figured we'd have breakfast with Claire and Matt and Emma and Danny and the kids on Sunday before Emma and Danny drive back to Boston. Can we wait until then to tell them?"

"I can wait as long as you want me to, pretty girl—Mommy."

"Tonight and tomorrow will be hard enough, old guy. I want to tell my 'sisters' on Sunday and call Mary Kay, too. Then next week we can tell your mom and dad and mine and the rest of the family. Matt, before I put my feet up and take a nap in your lap, will you get me a dish of vanilla ice cream with chocolate jimmies?"

I finally ran out of room halfway through the ice cream, and Matt finished it while I curled up on the bench seat. I closed my eyes thinking about the wonder of the day—as Dr. Bob said—with Matt's hand on my belly. I was asleep in a minute. Matt said Jinks brought him two more cups of hot chocolate before I woke up.

"*Mmm*, old guy." I stretched. "*Mmm* . . . I don't know any words to tell you how good I feel, but you know without my telling you. We haven't even seen a *picture* of our dune baby yet, and she's already a regular customer of Phil Green's. Boy or girl, I hope she likes Texas hots, pickles and tater tots. Let's go home and get ready for Emma and Danny. I think I need to practice my 'So, what's new?' face."

We had a lovely evening with Emma and Danny. After our sleep-over the week before, Emma and I didn't have much to catch up on, so we compared our dresses for the wedding and discussed the upcoming sixty-fifth anniversary party on July 5 for Matt's mom and dad. Matt and Danny watched the Yankees game in the kitchen and talked about politics in the urology department at The Cottons. Claire's mother was in town for the weekend to watch the kids during the wedding, so Claire was coming over in the morning to get dressed with Emma and me. I had to fight the urge to grin every time I thought of Emma being only two months ahead of me with her baby. We would soon have a lot to share.

Matt seemed a little reluctant to touch me—intimately—when we got into bed, so I had to play with him and convince him that I was still the same hungry girl who wanted his hands all over me before we got pregnant.

"Old guy, don't you be giving me the delicate treatment. I want you . . . I want your body more than ever. Dr. Bob's advice was 'lots of sex,' and I intend to follow my doctor's advice. I'll let you know when I'm not up for it, which probably won't be until I'm in the birthing room."

31

Claire came over at nine and, for the three of us, it was as if
we were just waking up from last week's pajama party. We
were as silly as teenagers, and we loved each other's dresses:
Emma's was a white sleeveless sheath, with a V-neckline and an
illusion panel in front, a V-back, a tulip hem, and crisscrossed
ruched panels throughout the whole dress; Claire's was a
burgundy lace sheath with cap sleeves and a straight neckline,
floral lace throughout, and a scalloped hem.

The wedding was at noon at St. Ignatius Church in Fairport—
not far from Katy and Trent's new house—followed by a picnic
lunch at Tom and Diane's. The reception was at six o'clock at
the River Falls Hotel in Rochester. The ballroom was beautiful,
the dinner was wonderful, the band was great, the wedding cake
and the desserts were spectacular, and—except for Katy and
Trent—we three Flynn "sisters" stole the show. Claire in
burgundy, Emma in white, and Abby in navy blue—we had our
arms around each other all night. We danced together, sang
together and posed together for a hundred photographs. My old
guy, Matt III and Danny mostly watched us all night, half in awe
and half in amusement.

Right after dinner, before the cutting of the cake, the three of
us excused ourselves and went to the ladies room to call Mary
Kay. She said her plane to London and Brussels was leaving at
ten o'clock the next night. Will would be following her on
Monday. We sent her cell phone pictures of the three of us and
asked her what color *she* would have worn.

"If I'd known you girls wanted to wear red, white and blue, I
would probably have gone for gold. I have a favorite gold
cocktail dress that I only wear for really special occasions—I'll
wear it when any of you come to party with me in Brussels: it's a
nylon soutache dress with a boat neck and an illusion neckline,
long sleeves, and with sequins, beading and embroidery all
over."

"It sounds *gorgeous*," said Claire. "We wish you were here
with us right now."

"Claire, you and Emma have been my 'sisters' for only a few months, but I am going to miss you *so* much."

I told Mary Kay I would call her the next day before she went to the airport, and the three of us went back to the cake and the dancing.

When we went up to bed that night, I asked Matt to undress me—"doctor's orders"—and the night was transformed into our first night. Matt sat me on the edge of the bed and kneeled down. He lifted my left foot and then my right, took off my white satin heels and kissed my feet all over.

Then he stood me up, unzipped my dress and helped me step out of it. I was just a little wobbly after all the champagne and red wine at the wedding. Matt steadied me and slid my panty hose from my hips to my knees to the floor—while his fingertips played down the back of my "tail" and my thighs—and kissed the front of my legs from my belly to my ankles. Then he nibbled on the hair around my ears as he unhooked my bra and caressed my nipples as he laid me gently on the bed. I had one orgasm before Matt could slip my panties off, and it was hard not to scream—with Emma and Danny in the next room—when Matt came inside me. He stayed inside me for a long time—and I came again and again—while he held me, lifting my head and shoulders off our pillow, and kissing my face slowly for many minutes without stopping. I believe I fell asleep in his arms while he was still inside me before he laid my head back down on the pillow.

When I woke at eight o'clock, lying on my back with the sunlight trickling around the edges of the shades, Matt was still sleeping, lying on his right side with his left leg over mine. I felt his breath on my shoulder. I looked at his face in wonder; I touched his lips, his hands, the hair on his stomach, his soft penis . . . all in wonder. It was the same as the first time I woke up with Matt at my side—the wonder. And now there was the new wonder of a baby. *God and Mary and St. Patrick*, I prayed in my heart, *thank you for this man. Thank you for the wonder. Please don't let this ever change.*

Emma and Danny were already in the kitchen making coffee when Matt and I went down at nine, and Claire and Matt III and the kids walked through the door ten minutes later. I could only wait as long as it took me to pour orange juice for the kids and coffee for Claire and Matt III before I burst out, "Everybody,

351

family, *my* family, I've been holding this inside for two days—Matt and I are going to have a *baby*!"

After squeals of excitement from the girls and hugs all around, we sat down, we held hands, we cried—over omelets and pancakes and bacon and coffee—and we talked. Mostly *I* talked. "We found out Friday. Dr. Hansen said it's early. My due date is about February 6. We'll go back to see Dr. Bob in three weeks. I was eating enough food for *three* people, and then I missed my period. I'm two months behind you, Emma. Claire, you're going to have to be the big sister and help us through *everything*. Names? Old Matt and I will talk about names in three or four months when we know whether it's a boy or a girl. Matthew and Emily, you are going to have two new baby cousins!"

It was eleven o'clock when Emma and Danny left for Boston and Claire and Matt III and the kids went home. Then I called Mary Kay.

"Oh, my God, Abby, oh, my God! So soon! How do you feel? Just the spotting? And the tingling. Was it that day in the dunes? You and Matt are unbelievable! February 6, huh. Maybe I'll be able to come home for a few days. Who else have you told? You and Emma will have *so* much to share. Call me at the end of the week after you tell the rest of the family. I wish I could be there with you right now. I know. You will have to tell me *everything*. I'll call you every week. Wait until I tell Will! I love you, sister."

It was a balmy afternoon, and Matt and I settled on the back porch with Maggie and Jock and our books. He was still working on the first volume of Shelby Foote—"I just finished The Seven Days battle," he said—and I was reading a funny romantic novel, *Lucky Jim* by Kingsley Amis, which Matt said was one of his old favorites. The main character, Jim Dixon, is a junior history professor at a small English college, always in trouble—with his job or his girlfriend—always having to suck up to his senior professor, and always making creative and contorted faces whenever his tormentors aren't looking. It was easy to see where Matt got the ideas for some of his faces.

The phone rang, and Matt picked it up.

"It's Tom and Diane, and they're both on the line so I'm switching to the speakerphone. Hey, Tom, Diane, great wedding! Have you two recovered yet?"

"Diane just talked with Trent and Katy at the airport, and they're about to board their flight to JFK and Bermuda. Abby, I'm one hundred percent positive that you and Claire and Emma had a terrific time last night. How about you and the boys, Matt?"

"You know me, Tom—I always enjoy watching the girls party. Same for Matt and Danny. I had an old girlfriend from Bermuda, Diane. Where are the kids staying?"

"The Reefs Resort on the south shore."

"I remember that place. It's just down the road from Horseshoe Bay."

"It looks spectacular from the brochures. Guess what Tom and I have been doing for the last two hours? Going through pictures from the wedding and the reception. The photographer sent us an online file this morning. Abby, I've been laughing every time I come to another picture of you and Claire and Emma. You girls must have *bewitched* the photographer. The file has almost *five* hundred photos, and you three girls are in about *fifty*!"

"Sorry, Diane, we weren't trying to hog the photographer. We were having such a good time we hardly even noticed him moving around."

Tom laughed. "You were being *babes*. Did you wear red, white and blue on purpose because it was Flag Day?"

"*Flag Day*?" It was *my* turn to laugh. "Tom, I swear, the thought of Flag Day never crossed our minds when we were getting dressed yesterday morning."

"Well, the three of you looked *really* hot last night."

"Abby, you'll have to forgive Tom. He picked me up at a wedding reception thirty-three years ago and he still thinks he can check out babes at weddings."

"Well, thanks, because I still like being checked out. But speaking of hot, old Matt and I have some hot news. We found out Friday, but I didn't want to say anything yesterday—we're going to have a *baby*!"

"Abby, big brother, that's wonderful! Yahoo for both of you! We couldn't be happier. When are you due, Abby?"

"February 6. Would you tell Steph and Warren and Barbara and Chuck, and Katy and Trent when they come back?"

"Of course we will. I'll call the girls later today, and Tom can call Trent and Katy later in the week. Everybody will be *so* excited. And Emma is only two months ahead of you!"

"Diane and I were talking about that this morning—what a year for the family! You two and Trent and Katy getting married, three new babies coming, new jobs, new houses, and Mom and Dad's sixty-fifth in three weeks! Did you tell Mom and Dad yet, Matt? Or Alan and Lisa?"

"Not yet. You guys are the first. We'll go to Mom and Dad's tomorrow night after dinner and tell them, and maybe call Alan and Lisa from there. How are we doing with RSVPs for Mom and Dad's party? Palermo's would like a count by Friday the 27th."

"With the immediate family and Abby's family, aunts and uncles and first cousins, and Mom and Dad's best friends, we're just over a hundred, not counting all the kids. That includes your grandparents, Abby."

"Nannie and Grandpa Dolan come and visit every chance they get, but Grandma and Grandpa McKay almost always avoid parties. I know Gramps wants to keep talking with your dad about World War II."

Matt and I told his mother and father on Monday, and mine on Tuesday, and we were on the phone and online all week telling the rest of the family and all of our friends. My colleagues at Mangrums took me out for a two-hour lunch on Wednesday; Art and Maureen sent me two dozen red roses; and Wally gave me a $100 gift certificate to Phil Green's.

When I talked with each of the family girls, though—Stephanie, Barbara, Eileen, Lisa, Diane, Emma and Claire—and Debbie's best friend Meredith, we also planned Debbie's baby shower for Saturday, July 19. It was going to be at Meredith's house in Mendon because she had a beautiful family room leading to a huge deck leading to their above-ground pool.

On July 3, Matt and I went back to see Dr. Hansen.

"How are you feeling, Abby? Any problems?"

"Not really, Dr. Bob. Extra trips to the bathroom, extra hot dogs and pickles, a little earlier to bed, still some tingling—nothing major."

"That's all pretty routine. Don't be surprised if you get more tired, or if you have headaches or back pains, or cramps or nausea. Those are all routine, also. I don't want you to worry about any of those things, but I *do* want you to tell me about them. And Matt—how is old Matt doing?"

"Good, Dr. Bob. Any routine things *I* should be watching for?"

"Well, let's see . . . if Abby gets grumpy, pretend not to notice. If she doesn't want you to touch her, persuade her that she really does."

I laughed at *that* advice. "There's not much chance of that, doc. I think I've been attacking Matt even more than *before* we got pregnant."

"Well, Abby, just don't be surprised at how many times you may change your mind on any new day. Shall we do another vaginal ultrasound and see what we can see? I don't usually do two ultrasounds this early in what looks like a normal, healthy pregnancy, but I'm part of a national study to compare what we can see in early pregnancy with transvaginal ultrasounds as opposed to transabdominal. There . . . there's the embryo . . . there's your baby."

Matt and I could see the shape of the embryo, which appeared to be floating sideways. We could make out the head and an elbow, and a fluttering that Dr. Bob said was the heartbeat.

"About 150 beats a minute right now. And what looks like a hole in the baby's head is the brain cavity. Everything looks perfectly normal for this stage of development. Would you like a picture, Abby?"

"Not yet, Dr. Bob. Matt and I want to wait for that first picture until we know if we are having a boy or a girl."

"Okay. Then unless you're having problems or not feeling well, your next regular visits will be at about fourteen weeks and eighteen weeks, or August 15 and September 12. In September, I will do another routine ultrasound to check you and your baby, and we will know if you have a boy or a girl. The eighteen-week visit is also when some women want to have amniocentesis to check for genetic disorders or a chromosomal abnormality, such as Down syndrome—especially where there are high-risk indicators for the couple. There do not appear to be any of those risk factors for you and Matt, though."

"I don't think Matt and I will want to do that, Dr. Bob."

"Well, let's schedule you for Friday, August 15, same time. Until then, enjoy the best summer of your lives! Have a great Fourth of July! And call me if either of you has *any* questions about *any*thing that's happening."

Matt marched with Chapter 4320 of the Vietnam Vets in the Penfield Fourth of July parade at eleven in the morning; and I watched from in front of the Dunkin Donuts on Five Mile Line Road. Then we went to Claire and Matt III's house for a cookout. Emma and Danny drove from Boston and joined us at five o'clock. Hugging Emma was becoming a very special moment for both of us. When the four of us went home that night and squeezed together on the sofa to watch the fireworks at the National Mall in Washington, Emma and I sat together at one end and held hands and whispered to each other a lot.

I *had* to talk with Matt about it when we got in bed. It was a very warm night—a classic July night—and we had the windows open, no covers on the bed, and the ceiling fan on high. Neither of us ever preferred to cover up and button up the house and turn on the air conditioning. If our lovemaking got really wild and hot, we both liked sweat.

"Old guy, it's too bad that you can't know how nice—sweet, really—it is to be pregnant at the same time as Emma. Not only do I have 'sisters' that I always wanted and never had, but I can share both the awesome emotions *and* the little tiny feelings of being pregnant with my 'sister.' All because you walked in to Kitty's."

Matt kissed my navel and ran his hands all over my belly.

"Beauty, I wish I *could* share your emotions and feelings. Husbands, fathers, have to settle for pride and love, but we can't feel the life and the growth."

I clasped my hands behind his neck and pressed his face into my belly.

"Are you still counting, summer boy?"

"Counting what, sweetie?"

"My freckles, the times we've made love."

"Sure. I guess I should have been giving you the running totals: 944 times making love and 644 freckles. Give or take a freckle or a kiss."

"How did you come up with those numbers?"

"Well, believe it or not, pretty girl, when I was marching in the parade I actually counted up in my head the number of days we've been together since our first night—236—and multiplied that by making love four times a day on average."

"I'm sure you have *that* number right, old guy, but how did you come up with the freckles?"

"I count them one by one as I travel down your body," he grinned, "but I could be off by a few because I occasionally get lost in my travels and lose count. And when you roll over, I have to start over."

"Sorry, Matt," I laughed, "but it's hard for me to lie still while you're counting."

I traced his lips with my finger and nibbled on his ear.

"Summer boy, I have another drawing to show you next week. We've been so busy, we haven't done that since *way* before our honeymoon."

"That's *way* too long, love. I'll find another poem for you, too."

"Let's pick up the count, Matt," I teased as I brushed the soft hair on his stomach, "I'd like to get to 950 by Mass on Sunday. And don't be counting freckles in your *head*; count with your lips and your fingers, please."

The next evening at Palermo's, we not only celebrated Angie and Matt's sixty-fifth anniversary, but also *old* Matt's eighty-eighth birthday (both on July 1) and *my* Matt's sixty-second birthday coming up on July 9, which would also have been Matt and Sarah's thirty-first anniversary. I knew all eyes were on me when we raised our glasses for Sarah, but Matt had me wrapped in his arms, and it was good. And then we cheered the three babies that were coming. There were tears at every table.

Matt's mother was absolutely glowing all night, surrounded by the love of her growing family. She couldn't stop talking about her *three* great-grandbabies-to-be. (Angie has always considered me more of a granddaughter than a daughter-in-law.)

Old Matt and Gramps spent a lot of time—over a lot of beers—talking about The War.

"Look at the two of them," Matt laughed. "They are as animated as Matt and Danny used to be arguing about who was the best hitter in baseball—Tony Gwynn or Edgar Martinez."

The tears and the stories and the hugs and the toasts continued for hours. Tom brought copies of Angie and Matt's wedding photographs, with Matt in his Army uniform. Many of the cousins brought their *own* old pictures of all the aunts and uncles when they were young. It was such a lovely evening. And now I was part of this wonderful family . . . and growing with them.

Two weeks later, most of the girls were back together at Debbie's baby shower. I had never met Debbie's friend Meredith, and I had never seen Lisa in charge, but they both did a beautiful job. It was hot and sunny, and most of us brought our bathing suits and spent some time in the pool. None of us thought Emma was showing yet, but *she* said she could see changes in the mirror in the morning. In contrast, Debbie was *huge*; she said she had put on thirty-eight pounds and felt *every* one of them. She still wouldn't let on as to whether she was having a boy or a girl, but she was so happy that I was guessing girl to go with big brother Billy. Her doctor said that August 15 still looked to be about right.

We decided to do a lottery. The thirty girls at the shower each chipped in $10 and picked the day they thought Debbie would have her baby. The girls who got the day right—or came closest if nobody got it right—would split $150, and the other $150 would go to Debbie for her baby. I picked *really* early, August 6, because it was Nannie's birthday.

On Monday I experienced a day filled with abdominal cramps—which felt a lot like menstrual cramps—and I told Matt after I got home from Mangrums that my antidotes were more sex, and more dill pickles and red hots from Phil Green's. That seemed to work Monday night, and I felt better the rest of the week. Matt had fun in bed when he kept touching me and playing with me for "medicinal purposes."

On Tuesday, we called Nannie and Grandpa Dolan to wish Gramps a happy birthday. He was eighty-six. We said we'd try to come and visit them over Labor Day weekend.

Matt grilled chicken, and we had Caesar salads on the back porch on Wednesday evening, and then I brought down the drawing I had promised to show him.

"This is one of the few drawings I ever did with some colors because I didn't think I could do an October drawing just in black and white."

As soon as I unrolled it on the table, Matt started laughing.

"What's so *funny*, old guy? You're not laughing at my drawing?"

"No, beauty, of course not; you'll understand when you see my poem."

My drawing went back six years, to the year Betsy was born. Dad and Grandpa McKay were sitting on the old redwood bench in our back yard, and Dad was holding Betsy, wrapped snugly in one of those familiar, white hospital receiving blankets with alternating, thin, pastel pink and blue stripes. Dad and Grandpa were both wearing Irish wool caps with the McKay plaid—a pattern of deep blues and greens and black—and Irish wool fisherman sweaters. Grandpa's was tan, Dad's forest green. There were red and yellow leaves—from two of our maple trees—next to them on the bench and all around on the grass. I watched them falling even as Catherine took the picture. Dad was tickling Betsy's chin, and Grandpa was brushing her hair with his fingers.

"We don't have many photographs of Dad and Grandpa together. Grandpa doesn't like getting his picture taken. I thought I would finally get this framed and give it to Dad next month for his sixty-fifth birthday."

"It's *so* beautiful, Abby. It's *better* than beautiful—it's *magic*. You can almost see the leaves falling and your grandpa and your dad moving their fingers. Your colors are perfect. You have captured the best part of October, which is *far* from my favorite time of the year, as you'll see in my poem. But *way* more than that, you have caught a very special family moment— once-in-a-lifetime, really. Have your dad and grandpa seen it?"

"Once, right after I finished it. Grandpa glanced at it quickly and simply said, 'It's very nice, Abigail.' Dad studied it for a long time, with his arm around my waist. He didn't say anything, but he had tears in his eyes. After that I rolled it up and put it away until today."

Matt took my face in his hands, looked in my eyes and said, "Pretty girl, we have to *un*roll everything you've done, for all the world to see. You are *so* good!"

I kissed him and pulled him down on the porch carpet, slid off his cargo shorts and T-shirt and made love to him while Maggie and Jock stood watch at the west windows as the sun set in the blue and pink sky.

Friday after work, Matt and I went to Phil Green's for the "Spectacular Scrod Special" with tater tots and coleslaw, and a couple of pints of amber ale, and Matt brought another poem for me. When I saw the title, "october," I laughed.

"I see what you meant when you saw my drawing, old guy." I put my feet up on the bench and laid my head in Matt's lap. "Will you read it to me, sweetie?"

> *chestnuts are down*
> *sleek horse chestnuts*
> *scattered over the cracked sidewalks*
> *rolling into broken bottles*

and huddled leaves
the air is a whirl of october spice
you see it all around
but mostly you breathe it
each quick breeze
pricks a part of your brain
october
more than any other time
flashes
hints of how you were
faces you can't quite name
voices you can't quite hear
perfume you could never find
corners of your boyhood
card games on a crotchety yellow bus
football on an opal saturday in boston
an awkward hand, a park by the lake
windblown hair
and a plaid blanket

ten years, six years, two years
so many colored leaves you kicked
and you still don't know one tree from another
you just can't put your finger
on where and when it happened
people became pictures
touch became a wish
now flushed october
flits through your soul
laughs in your belly and your eyes
with a chance
but her gaudy leaves and half memories
always fade
into gray november daydreams

"That's kind of sad, Matt." I reached up and brushed my fingers on his cheeks.

"Yeah, it sure is. That was a black time for me. Missy had just thrown me over for the guy from Oshkosh, law school was a lot harder than I expected, and I hadn't met Sarah yet. I dated a few women in law school—all law students—but none of them got to me. I never felt as if any of them were special enough to

360

keep me from moving on to someone else. I was pretty much alone in law school. I worked hard and didn't have much fun. I realized years later that I had probably been wrong about some of those girls. They *were* special, but I never spent enough time with them to find out. Regret became the mood of my days and the theme of my poems."

Matt reached down and twirled the hair on my forehead with his left hand and played with my breasts with his right.

"Sarah saved me from all that and gave me twenty years of happiness. Then came ten years of loneliness and going through the motions, then *you* saved me from all *that*. I am a lucky man."

I grabbed both of his hands and pressed them against my belly.

"Don't give me so much credit, old guy. When you first looked into my eyes, I knew I *wanted* you, but I didn't know anything about *saving* you. I'm sure I needed you as much as you needed me. And even without Sarah you were doing a pretty good job as a dad and grandpa. I think we were *exactly* right for each other at exactly the right time. And I'll bet some of those law school girls are sorry they never got to you. Now, sir, how would you like to split a Peanut Butter Cup sundae with me?"

We stayed for another hour in our booth. Jinks came over to say hello and bring us some hot chocolate. I read Matt's poem myself, and what struck me the most were two lines near the end: "people became pictures" and "touch became a wish." I knew that would never happen with us.

I would never stop touching Matthew Flynn.

32

July moved quickly into August. Every day was a good day for Matt and me. Even the days with back pains and sore nipples and stomachaches couldn't keep me from smiling at the wonder of a baby growing inside me. I called Emma, Claire and Mary Kay just about every day: Claire for advice, Emma to share, and Mary Kay for long-distance hugs.

Emma was at the beginning of her sixth month and was "starting to show above my navel," she said. She had gained thirteen pounds and "just bought my first batch of maternity clothes." She was definitely eating for two: loaded, deep-dish pizzas and loaded omelets were at the top of her list. The baby was moving and kicking and "waking me up sometimes at night." She felt pretty good in general, except for some heartburn and pains in her legs and her breasts and her back.

"*Tums* take care of the heartburn, and Danny massages and soothes all my other pains every day. I'm sure you know, Abby, how good the Flynn boys are at taking care of their girls. We're going to the Parker House for dinner and an overnight on August 7 for our second anniversary. I hope we'll be able to see you guys in September or October—I will need some 'sister' hugs."

Mary Kay was thoroughly enjoying her first months in Brussels.

"Abby gal, it's so *pretty* here, and everything is so *old—way* older than Boston! Will and I have a lovely little flat—four small rooms: living room, kitchen, bedroom and our *own* bathroom, thank God!—on the second floor of a converted grammar school on Saint Catherine Place, right across the street from Eglise Sainte-Catherine, which is French for Saint Catherine Church, one of the oldest churches in Brussels. In Flemish—or Belgian Dutch, as they say around here—it's Sint-Katelijnekerk. They have both Catholic and Orthodox Masses. Parts of the church and the grounds have been turned into a vegetable and fruit market. It's like having our own park across the street.

"Will and I walk everywhere. We don't have a car although Will can get the use of a tiny U.S. Army Opel on weekends. We take the Metro every morning from the Sainte-Catherine station, right through downtown and then three miles northeast to NATO. We have to get on the 7:15 morning train, so we're in bed every night by ten-thirty. Our workday is usually eight-thirty to five, so we don't get home until about six every night. It's a grueling schedule, but Will and I go to work and come home together, and we love it at NATO. Our weekends are generally free—unless some prime minister from a foreign country is in town—and we take road trips in the Opel.

"The best day trip so far was to Dunkirk, just across the border in France. Will and I walked along the Boulevard du 8 Mai 1945 and the shore of the North Sea, watching the ships navigating the Strait of Dover. Unfortunately, it was too cloudy to see 'the cliffs of England' from Matthew Arnold's poem. The World War II museum was close by, on one of the many canals leading into the English Channel. We also walked to town to see the British Expeditionary Force cemetery.

"I thought of you the whole time, and Grandpa Dolan and Matt's dad. I know with your new job and the baby coming you and Matt probably won't be able to visit us in Belgium, but we would have *so* much fun together. I am saving my Euros so that I can fly home when the baby is born."

Matt and I called Nannie on August 6 to wish her a happy birthday—she was eighty-five—but Debbie did not have her baby on that day, so I did not win the baby pot. However, she had a baby girl—Alicia Marie (after Fred's mother)—the *next* day: 7 pounds, 9 ounces, 21 inches, and no hair. Mother and baby were doing fine. Katy picked August 7 and won the baby pot.

So many things were happening, but I tried to slow my days down—slow my hours, slow my minutes—and sense my body and my baby. Claire told me to do that.

"Try real hard, Abby. It was the first advice my mom gave me when I told her I was pregnant with little Matt. I didn't do so well the first time, but I did much better with Emily."

I started closing my eyes and counting to seven or twelve whenever I felt a pain or a twinge or a tingle that was different. Whenever I felt the baby moving I walked all of my fingertips over my belly like a spider, and closed my eyes and counted to seven or twelve. If I was driving and couldn't close my eyes, I played with my ear lobes and counted. It always worked. I always saw Matt when I counted, and our baby all bundled up in his arms.

August 10 was Sarah's birthday, and Matt and I took a red rose to her grave and prayed for her help for the two of us and the baby. Matt said Sarah talked to him almost every week, and he was sure she would be the guardian angel of our new family.

Matt didn't schedule any clients or meetings for Friday, August 15, and I took a personal day from Mangrums, and we basically kissed and cuddled and played with Maggie and Jock from the time we got up until we went to Dr. Hansen's office at four o'clock. Laura, his assistant, took my weight and blood pressure and a urine sample, and got us set up in the examining room. Dr. Bob joined us in fifteen minutes.

"How are you feeling, Miss Abigail? And how's the old guy doing?"

"Matt and I are having a lovely summer, Dr. Bob. There are babies *every*where: Matt's niece had a baby girl on August 7, and his son Danny's wife is due in December."

"Well, that probably means that you are sharing a lot of stories and advice." Dr. Bob gave us a *huge* grin. "It also means that you are in the rare circumstance of having both a baby and a grandbaby in the same year. Get as comfortable as you can on the table, Abby, and let me take a look. Your urine sample is normal; your blood pressure is 119/79, which is ideal; the fetal heart rate is good; and you've gained six pounds since your first visit in June, which is about average. You can expect to start gaining a pound or two a week. My guess is that you'll probably gain twenty-five to thirty pounds by the time your baby is born. Right now, your baby is about the size of a lemon. How are you feeling? Are you having any problems?"

"Not really, Dr. Bob. Cramps once in a while, constipation once in a while—but almost never two days in a row. Back pains and achy breasts occasionally, but Matt makes the aches go away. My top ten cravings include red hots, dill pickles, tater tots and vanilla milkshakes. I actually seem to have much more energy than I did at the beginning of the summer."

"Are you still jumping for joy?"

"Twice every four hours, Dr. Bob, and every other chance I get in between," I grinned.

"And how about my other prescriptions, Abby: supplemental sex and extra doses of laughing and crying?"

364

Matt jumped in on that one.

"I can attest to all of those, Dr. Bob. Abigail is the heartiest laugher and crier I have ever known. I have carried a handkerchief ever since my mother put one in my pocket on my first day of kindergarten. Now I carry three. And I can't even get up from the kitchen table for a second cup of coffee without your *patient* trying to get me up the stairs and into bed."

"Well, sometimes it's tea or wine, Dr. Bob," I laughed. "And Francine Toscano's book is *so* good. *No matter what's going on in the world*, she says, *no matter who's pouting in your family, no matter who screwed up at the office, no matter how jealous or negative or catty people you think are your friends may get— don't forget what you are doing: you are growing a baby who is going to make the world a better place.*

"My daughter-in-law Claire, who is more of a sister because of our ages, says some of the same things that Francine says. *Slow your days down, turn down the volume around you and listen to yourself. Close your eyes and look at yourself in your mind. Sense yourself, touch yourself, stroke yourself—even tickle yourself—as much as you can. Talk to your baby.* This old guy"—I poked Matt in the stomach and laughed—"helps me with all of that just by holding me and listening . . . except when I hit him up for huge quantities of sex or food."

"You two could be my poster couple for how to have a happy pregnancy," Dr. Bob smiled, "if Matt weren't so damned *old*. Unless you have any problems or concerns, Abby, I'll see you on Friday, September 12, same time, for your eighteen-week visit and your next ultrasound."

We took a ride to Skaneateles Lake the next day and walked around the lovely village for three hours. Then we had a breezy, summer dinner on the front porch of the Sherwood Inn, and I dozed on Matt's shoulder all the way home.

The following Friday we brought pizza and chicken wings to Debbie and Fred's and played with Billy and tiny Alicia. They were all fine, and Billy appeared to be a very caring big brother.

The Friday after that, August 29, was Dad's sixty-fifth birthday, and we had a cookout at Mom and Dad's. Patrick and Laurie surprised all of us when they announced that they were engaged and were shooting for June 13 next year for their wedding. Laurie's ring was beautiful.

In the morning, we bundled Maggie and Jock into the back of the Jeep and drove to Stockbridge to spend two days with

Nannie and Grandpa Dolan and Ike. Nannie made her famous Irish stew for dinner, and Gramps roasted corn on the cob on the grill. After dinner, Matt and Gramps took their coffee to the den to watch the Yankees and Red Sox at Fenway Park; Maggie and Jock and Ike chased each other in the back yard; and Nannie and I cleaned up the dishes in the kitchen. I showed Nannie Grandpa's Silver Star ribbon pinned in the pocket of my jeans.

"I've worn it every day since the wedding, Nannie, even on the beach on our honeymoon in North Carolina," I grinned and squeezed her hand, "where I think we got pregnant."

Nannie hugged me and kissed my cheek.

"Oh, honey, I knew the ribbon would be good for you. And on the beach, my goodness! Your grandpa and I did that on the beach once—in the dunes on the Cape, way out near Dennis Port, I think it was. We were so bad! It was the most exciting moment of my life, except for that day in Wales when your grandpa proposed to me on the floor of Mother and Father's store." She patted my pocket. "You keep wearing it every day until your baby is born, honey, and then we'll let your grandpa in on our little secret. When will you know if your baby is a boy or a girl?"

"A week from this coming Friday, Nannie—it's my eighteen-week visit and ultrasound. I'm getting so excited!"

"In my time, dear, nobody ever knew until the baby was born, but I would have liked to know. Have you talked with Matthew about any names?"

"Not really, Nannie. Matthew IV is already taken, but I've been thinking about naming a girl Mary Elizabeth after you and Grandma McKay. I haven't said anything to Matt yet."

"That would be lovely, honey. Mary and I would be very proud."

On Sunday, we went to the Norman Rockwell Museum in Stockbridge. Surprisingly, in spite of all our trips back and forth between Rochester and Boston College and Newton, Matt and I had never been to the Rockwell. We bought two prints, our favorites.

Matt's favorite is called "Homecoming G.I.," and was the cover of the May 26, 1945, *Saturday Evening Post*, which cost ten cents. A young redheaded soldier carrying his duffel bag is home from The War, standing outside the back door of his family's ground-floor apartment in a brick tenement house in the big city. His whole family is rushing out over the stoop to greet him: his mother, two younger sisters and little brother—all redheads—and the family beagle. His father, pipe in hand and grinning, is standing in the doorway. The soldier's strawberry blond girlfriend, in a green dress, white bobby socks and penny loafers, is leaning against the corner of the red brick building gazing lovingly at her sweetheart. The neighbors are looking out their windows, sitting in two trees and coming out the door—all waving and cheering. The family laundry is drying on a clothesline. There is a Blue Star banner with one star in the soldier's window, one with two smaller stars in the neighbor's window, and another with three blue stars in the upstairs neighbor's window. It is a picture of pure pride and joy.

My favorite is titled "Girl at the Mirror," and is dated March 6, 1954. A young girl, maybe twelve or thirteen, is sitting on a stool in front of a large mirror. I think she's in the attic of her house, her very secret place. She's wearing a white summer dress, she's barefoot, and her long chestnut hair is up in a bun. Her doll is on the floor next to the mirror. She has a magazine in her lap, opened to a picture of Jane Russell. On the floor next to her feet are her comb and hairbrush, a simple round compact— probably with a powder puff inside—and an open tube of red lipstick. She is wistfully studying her face in the mirror, and I think she's saying in her mind, *Will I grow up to be pretty?*

Matt made omelets for everybody on Monday morning, and we left for home at eleven. I think Maggie and Jock enjoyed our visit even more than Matt and I did because Nannie and Grandpa's yard is fenced in, and Maggie and Jock were able to play outside with Ike for two days. They slept in the back all the way home—except for one pit stop near Utica—and I did the same in the front, with my head curled around the gearshift on a small pillow in Matt's lap. I fell asleep with my fingers on Grandpa's ribbon in my pocket.

Matt and I worked on house and yard projects every evening, including cleaning the garage and trimming around all the trees in the backyard. On Saturday evening, we brought pepperoni pizza and sub sandwiches to Matt and Claire's to celebrate their fifth anniversary. The following Wednesday, we took Pat and Laurie to dinner at Palermo's for Pat's twenty-second birthday. Laurie was twirling her engagement ring and glowing all evening. When we went to the ladies room, she hugged me and thanked me.

"Abby, you and Matt fell in love so fast, and you went ahead with your plans so fast . . . and so positive and sure of each other, that you speeded up the marriage idea in Patrick's head. We've been going out since high school and living together for a *year*, and we knew we wanted to get married, but Patrick thought we were too young . . . until Matt came along and you showed us that age doesn't matter." She hugged me again. "We're going to *really* be sisters now."

"It's so amazing, Laurie! Ten months ago I had two brothers and *no* sisters. Now I have you and Emma and Claire, and even Stephanie and Barbara and Katy, and Debbie and Eileen. And so many young children and babies! So much to *share* . . . so *much* in one year."

And then it was September 12. Mr. Christopher told me not to come in, and that the vote in the advertising department was thirteen to five that I would have a girl. Matt stayed home with me just as he did on August 15, and we left the bedroom only for breakfast and lunch, and to take Maggie and Jock for two short walks—because it was raining. I remember reading in *Cosmopolitan* and other women's magazines—and even in freshman biology at Newton—that pregnant women frequently experience an increased sex drive. But I never quite believed it until it was me, and I couldn't keep my hands off Matt. I fondled him against me and helped him inside me all day— except for two or three catnaps—until it was time to go to Dr. Hansen's.

Laura, whose hands were always kind, took my temperature, weight, pulse, blood pressure and a urine sample, and then got us settled in the examining room. Dr. Bob joined us in ten minutes.

"Abby, Matt, you both look great. I'm guessing that you have been faithfully following all the prescriptions, and, Miss Abigail, from the sparkle in your cheeks I'm thinking that you had some extra doses today."

I'm sure I must have blushed, and Dr. Bob grinned.

"Well, it's *all* working. All your numbers are normal and healthy: pulse 80, temperature 98.8, blood pressure 117/77, urine sample good, weight 139—up three pounds from August and nine from your first visit in June. Let's get this ultrasound going. I know you're so excited you could burst, but try to lie still and breathe normally."

368

He smoothed the cold gel on me and gently passed the plastic transducer across my belly.

"Because your baby has grown dramatically and we can see so much, we call this eighteen-week ultrasound an 'anatomy scan.' Look up at the screen. See the arms and legs moving? They look just right. The heartbeat is excellent. The placenta appears good, and the amniotic fluid level is where it should be. The vital organs—heart, brain, liver, kidneys, lungs—all the organs appear to be growing normally. Look at your baby doing a cartwheel! And last, but not least—Matt, you had better take Abby in your arms—I counted twice, and *she* has ten fingers and ten toes. You are having a baby girl."

I don't remember anything that happened for the next ten minutes. Matt said he held me as tightly as he dared without hurting me; that I cried and shook the whole time; that the only words he could make out from me were 'I love you'; that he helped Dr. Bob clean the gel off my belly; that he put my clothes on and wiped the tears from my face four times; and that Dr. Bob gave him three photographs from the sonogram, and a giant grape lollipop "for Abigail, when she regains consciousness."

The rain had stopped, and Matt walked me slowly to the parking lot and hugged and stroked me in the sunshine until I finally came out of my joyful delirium.

"Matt, I love you! Oh, Matt, a baby girl! Where's Dr. Bob?"

"We're out in the parking lot, sweetie. Here's a lollipop from Dr. Bob."

"I don't remember getting dressed."

"You know me, beauty; I'm pretty good with your clothes."

"Oh, Matt, you gave me a baby girl!"

"After two brothers and two sons, Abby, I was thinking it was the other way around. Would you like to celebrate with red hots and beer at Phil Green's?"

"You read my mind, old guy. By the way, when is our next appointment with Dr. Bob?"

"Four weeks from today, Friday, October 10, same time, same prescriptions," Matt grinned.

When we told Jinks, she shrieked and told all the staff behind the counter and in the kitchen. Our first beers were on the house. After we finished eating and started on our second beers, I put my feet up on the bench and my head in Matt's lap and asked him, "Have you thought about any little girl names, sweetie?"

"Well, beauty, I like *your* name a *whole* lot. So how about a name with Abigail or Elizabeth? How about with your *mom's* name? How about Margaret Abigail Flynn?"

"That's funny, old guy, because I was thinking about Mary Elizabeth, after both of my grandmothers, and Mom's middle name also is Mary."

"That will be a beautiful name for our beautiful baby girl, Abby."

I was on cloud nine all weekend. I baked cupcakes to take to the office on Monday, and Matt whipped up his mom's butter cream frosting. We put pink frosting on thirteen cupcakes for those in my office who guessed girl, and blue frosting on five more for those who guessed boy.

Matt and I got into a routine by the end of the summer. We had dinner with my mom and dad on Monday, and Matt's mom and dad on Tuesday. On Wednesday and Friday we usually went to Phil Green's. Thursday we cooked at home. Saturday was our *date* night—sometimes dinner, sometimes a movie, sometimes with friends. Sunday we either had a cookout or brought pizza to Matt and Claire's. And almost every Saturday morning, Matt and I were up before eight, I made coffee, and while Matt walked Maggie and Jock, I called Mary Kay. Because of the six-hour time difference, it was two in the afternoon in Brussels.

"Oh, Abby, a baby girl! Mary Elizabeth Flynn. Are you going to call her Mary Elizabeth, or Mary, or Mary Beth? Only if she's a bad girl? That will never happen. I'm glad you're feeling so well. It would have been nice to help you pick out your maternity clothes. How does Matt like your extra nine pounds? Dr. Hansen sounds like a wonderful guy.

"Will and I are having so much fun here! I meet the most interesting people from countries all over the world. On Tuesday, George and Laura Bush were here with both of their daughters at a reception to celebrate the sixtieth anniversary of the storming of the Brandenburg Gate by 500,000 West Berliners during the Berlin Airlift. Will and I and all the American NATO staff got to shake their hands. Jenna and Barbara are so *pretty* up close.

"Next week, maybe you can call me late Friday night, my time, because Will and I are going to England next Saturday morning. We're going to drive to Calais, which is just west of Dunkirk on the Channel, and take the ten o'clock Chunnel to

Folkestone in Kent, which is just southwest of Dover. Then we take a train to Canterbury and check in to a small hotel where we'll spend the night, and then take another train to London. *London*, Abby gal! I'm *so* excited!"

I started working on a new drawing in the last week of September, but I didn't tell Matt. Mom was the only one who knew because my bedroom at Mom and Dad's had become my studio. I drew whenever I could squeeze in an hour or two without actually lying to Matt about where I was going or what I was doing. I didn't have any photographs to work from—only the images in my mind of those two afternoons with Matt in the dunes. I covered the drawing every day when I finished working—and I didn't let Mom in the bedroom *while* I was sketching—but I told her she could peek as long as she didn't comment or criticize.

All my extra time at Mom and Dad's got Mom and me into an extended conversation that continued and expanded with every visit. It was a dialogue that could only take place between a mother-to-be and *her* mother. Usually we talked in my bedroom over a cup of Irish tea.

"Abigail Elizabeth, you know I wasn't pleased when you first brought Matt into our family. But every day I've seen you since, you seem happier than the day before, so I know I was wrong. Matthew is *your* man, the *right* man, *your special* man. *I* remember being as happy as you are right now; *my* special man did that for *me*. How does Matt feel about having a baby girl?"

"Mom, when Dr. Bob told us, I thanked Matt again and again until he finally said that after having two brothers and two sons, *he* should be thanking *me* for a baby girl."

"Your dad was a little different; he was absolutely *crazy* to have a boy. It was only six years later, right after you were born, that he surprised me when he said as he rocked you to sleep in his arms that 'sometimes life doesn't turn out the way you expect, Peg; it turns out better.' You were the apple of his eye from the moment the nurse handed you to him in the delivery room."

"Mom, how did you feel halfway through when you were having me?"

"Well, it was quite different than halfway through Jack. With Jack, I wasn't nervous or scared at all. I was confident, comfortable, even cocky. Nannie had told me that her three babies had all been easy, and my sister Roberta had already had two easy pregnancies before Jack came along. I realized years later that I was almost nonchalant with Jack; I was all business. I didn't stop—or even slow down—enough to *enjoy* being pregnant." Mom made a sheepish face. "I've scolded myself a few times over the years, wondering if my detached attitude caused Jack to grow up to be the hard-as-nails businessman he is.

"With you, I felt different right away. I was older and wiser for sure, but it was a lot more than that. Even though I didn't know I was having a girl, I felt softer—in my mind *and* in my body. I *handled* my first pregnancy just fine, but I never *felt* it, I never *loved* it. Somewhere in my first or second month with you I began to *love* being pregnant. And once the love came, my life changed. I started touching my belly and talking to you. I started listening for you and waiting for you to move. I slowed down; I became quiet. Can you imagine that? Your father had to tell me things two or three times because I wasn't listening to him. I was so much in love with you nine months before you were born. I don't ever remember ever feeling that way with Jack.

"And then when you were born—my sweet girl—all the love poured out of all my senses. Your father said I cried for two whole days in the hospital, and I wouldn't let anyone else hold you until we went home."

Mom smiled and took both my hands in hers and caressed them with her fingers. "And one other thing—your drawing made me think of this: the whole time I was carrying you I wanted to touch your dad all the time. I was so grateful to him for all the love filling my body. We never had better sex than when I was pregnant with you."

"Mom, that's how I feel right now, *every day*, with Matt."

"I can tell, honey. I can see it in your eyes and hear it in your voice. I can see it in your drawing. Is that when you got pregnant, on the beach?"

"Yes, I think so. Mom, we had two *whole* afternoons on the beach—two indescribable, *unimaginable* afternoons—tangled together, burrowed down deep in the sand, in a hollow we made ourselves while making love, hidden from the world by the high dunes. I wasn't thinking very much, I was *feeling* everything; but I do remember thinking as I woke up gradually both afternoons, *Only God is watching us.*"

372

"You were conceived on the beach, too, Abigail, but your dad and I were not quite as naughty as you and Matt. Aunt Roberta and Uncle Whit rented a beach house in August in Gloucester for two weeks every year. That summer of 1980 we were all there together: Roberta and Whit, Uncle Jimmy and Aunt Caroline, your four cousins, and Dad and I and Jack. All five kids slept together in the living room in sleeping bags and on the sofas, and we three grown-up couples each had our own bedroom on the second floor.

"Your dad wanted me *every* night; he said it was the salt air. He could be quite romantic when he wanted to—he still can. In truth, it *was* lovely to have the sea breeze coming in the windows at night, and to see the moon shining on the waves. The only slight problem for me was trying to keep from yelling too loud. As hard as I tried, I still got some knowing grins from Roberta every morning.

"Jack, of course, was not quite as romantic. It was some time in May in 1974, and your father and I were at home. Same for Patrick, although I believe he was conceived in the living room in front of the fireplace, on the Friday after Thanksgiving in 1985, when you and Jack were having an overnight with your cousins at Uncle Jimmy and Aunt Caroline's."

On the last Saturday of September, I called Mary Kay, and she talked for almost two hours about her trip to London.

"It was magical, Abby gal, like in the movies. We had a beautiful, sunny day, and Will and I walked and walked. We went to the Tower of London, and the Victoria and Albert Museum, and Trafalgar Square and the National Gallery, and the Changing of the Guard at Buckingham Palace, and Big Ben and the Tower Bridge and London Bridge, and the Princess Diana Memorial in Hyde Park, and Abbey Road.

"Our hotel in Canterbury, Thomas Becket's Inn—right out of T.S. Eliot—was lovely. We had a fireplace in our room, complete with a real stack of wood to burn, and a four-poster bed. In the morning after breakfast at the inn, we went to St. Augustine's Abbey and Canterbury Cathedral, and—get ready for this, Abby gal—Will *proposed* to me in Becket's Crown, a memorial chapel in the east wing of the cathedral. After that, I didn't remember much of the Chunnel ride or the drive back to Brussels from Calais."

"MK, I'm so happy for you and Will! Do you have a date in mind yet?"

"It could change, but we're kind of looking at Thanksgiving or Christmas next year."

"Let me know if you'll be needing a *matron* of honor," I joked.

"Are you kidding me, best friend? You're the one who made this all happen—you and Matt. If you hadn't gotten me to take a hard look at Josh, I might have hung on with him *way* too long and missed my chance with Will. I *so* much wish you were here! It just doesn't seem right that you are expecting and I am engaged—and we're *not* together."

"I know, but the time will go by fast, MK. Pretty soon it will be a year since I met Matt."

The following Wednesday, October 1, was the eleventh anniversary of the day Sarah died, and Matt and I went to the cemetery with Matt and Claire and the kids—and eleven red roses—and then to Phil Green's for supper. When we got home, Matt called Sarah's sisters, Rebeccah and Norah, and introduced me on the phone, and then the three of them shared some favorite stories and caught up on what all the kids and grandkids were doing.

On Saturday when I called Mary Kay, she wanted lots more details about my baby, so I did most of the talking.

"Next Friday is my twenty-two-week visit with Dr. Hansen, and I'm starting to feel very *large*. Every part of my body is expanding, from my belly to my boobs to my butt. I think I've gained twelve or thirteen pounds. I feel great, but a little more bulky moving around. People I meet outside the office— neighbors, women grocery shopping, people at Mass—are starting to ask how far along I am. Everybody at my office wants to touch my belly."

"Do you *like* that, sister? Lots of women I know don't *like* that."

"Actually, I *do*, MK. They all care and they mean well, so I encourage them when they touch me to say hello to Mary Elizabeth. Matt says I have a *glow* that I didn't have a month ago. And my baby girl is moving all the time. I *swear* she's going to be a gymnast. Sometimes I feel two or three hands and feet at the same time. Matt and I will be starting our nine weeks of childbirth classes—in the gym at Fatima, coincidentally—on October 15."

Our twenty-two-week visit with Dr. Bob was a lot less dramatic than the eighteen-week.

"Abby, Matt, how are you and your little girl doing?"

"Dr. Bob, I apologize for losing all control at our last visit."

"Don't give it another thought, Abby. I would be surprised—even disappointed—if a brand new mother didn't get crazy when she found out she was having a baby girl *or* a baby boy. You look great. You have that special pregnancy glow, and your blood and urine are fine. You have gained thirteen pounds, which is just about average for twenty-two weeks; you can expect to gain about a pound a week until your baby is born. Have you and this old guy decided on a name for your little girl?"

"Mary Elizabeth, for both of my grandmothers."

"That's beautiful! Is Mary Elizabeth moving around much?"

"I feel her hands and feet *all the time*, Dr. Bob—sometimes all of them at once!"

"She's exploring your womb, and discovering her own body, floating in her amniotic world. She's about the length of a football, but much thinner right now—doing flips and somersaults, punching and kicking. Are you having any problems at all?"

"Not really, other than getting used to lumbering rather than walking," I laughed.

"Have you two scheduled a childbirth class?"

"We're starting next Wednesday for nine weeks at Fatima."

"That's a good choice. I know the nurse, Margo Belton, who conducts the classes. Have fun with it. Bring something thick to kneel on, Matt. Margo provides comfortable pads for the moms, but the gym floor can get a little hard on the coaches. Margo sometimes invites me to come to one of her classes as a 'guest kneeler.'

"Your twenty-six-week visit will be on November 7—same time. After that, I'd like you to come every two weeks until your thirty-sixth week, and then every week until Mary Elizabeth is born. As usual, call me if anything seems strange or if you feel any pain. See you in four weeks."

33

Matt and I went home and bundled Maggie and Jock into the Jeep. Then we stopped to get two pizzas at Giovanni's and took them to Tom and Diane's for supper. Tom said that Brownie and Oreo wanted Maggie and Jock to spend the weekend while Matt and I went to Boston to see Emma and Danny. We left at seven the next morning, and we had a mild, sunny day for a drive.

The fall colors throughout the hills in New York and the Berkshires in western Massachusetts were spectacular all the way. It was much harder for me to put my feet up on the dashboard than the last time we went to Boston, but it was *not* harder for me to take naps with my head in Matt's lap.

I needed two bathroom stops in New York. When we stopped for gas and coffee at Lee, the first rest area on the Mass Pike, I told Matt that I had finished a new drawing, which I would show him next week. We checked in at The Crimson Yard at two o'clock, then walked around the block to Danny and Emma's. It was still sunny and balmy, so Emma and I decided to go out for a slow walk along the Charles River. We left the boys sipping their beers and watching the big game, undefeated Texas against undefeated Oklahoma.

"My twenty-two-week visit was yesterday, Emma."

"And my thirty-week visit was on Wednesday."

"Tell me, sister," I grinned, "what can I expect at thirty weeks?"

"Well, the most exciting thing Dr. Graham told me was that 'your baby could be born today and be happy and healthy.' Tigger—that's what Danny calls the baby because of how much he bounces—weighs about three pounds and is about sixteen inches long. His hair is growing, and his eyes are open. When I shine a flashlight on my belly, I think Tigger turns toward the light. I had the glucose screening test on Wednesday to check for gestational diabetes, and my results are normal. I'm starting to feel some of the Braxton Hicks contractions, and my breasts are starting to leak a little fluid—'colostrum,' Dr. Graham called it. All normal stuff, the doctor says. I'm making lots more trips to pee, I'm more tired, sleeping is harder, I'm hungry all the time, and my back aches every day until Danny rubs me down after dinner. All in all, I'm great!" she laughed.

"Abby, I'm *so* happy you and Claire will be able to come to my baby shower on November 1. It's going to be at my girlfriend Nicky's house, but Mom and I would like you and Claire to stay at *our* house for the weekend."

"That will be really nice. Claire and I have reservations on a United flight leaving Rochester at 5:15 Friday afternoon—'Trick or treat!'—and arriving at La Guardia at 6:45. Will somebody be able to pick us up? We'll let you know what costumes we'll be wearing."

We walked, talked, laughed, cried—and stopped to hug frequently—for *two* hours. When we got back, the boys were on their third beers, Texas had just beaten Oklahoma in what Matt called "one of the best games I've ever seen," and we were all *really* hungry. Emma and I freshened up a little, and then we went to Abigail and John for dinner.

We talked about the delights and dreams of becoming new mothers—and, in Danny's case, a new father—and the challenges of being a total of fifty-two weeks pregnant, and the incredibly crowded calendar between October and my due date in February. And we talked about names.

"Danny and I agreed almost from day one that if we have a boy, he will be Daniel Martin Flynn, Jr. But girls' names are another story: Sarah, Olivia, Claudia, Constance—we've talked about a lot of names. My Grandma Heath's name is Olivia, and Grandma Swift's was Constance. Maybe we can do both grandmothers like you guys. When are you going to have *your* shower?"

"January 3, the Saturday after New Year's, I think. I hope people will be able to make it from out of town. Winter weather and the holiday season are difficult."

Matt and I were able to book the same room we had on our first stay at The Crimson Yard, complete with four-poster bed and gas fireplace. I had brought *Pooh* and *Piglet* with us, and we sat for about an hour on the floor in front of the fireplace, making love and not saying a word. When we got into bed, we left the fire going, opened the windows a little and listened to the rain pattering steadily on the tile roof. It was perfectly cozy in the room, and we slept without any covers. The sound of the rain was so peaceful and soothing that I didn't feel Mary Elizabeth move all night.

It was still raining the next morning so, after Mass at St. Iggy's and breakfast at the Central Square Diner, we decided to just hang out at Danny and Emma's and watch the football games. We saw the St. Louis Rams upset Mary Kay's beloved Redskins, and the Patriots—without Tom Brady, who had suffered a serious knee injury in the first game of the season—get clobbered by San Diego.

Danny ordered pizzas at halftime of the Patriots game—one with sausage for him and Emma, and one with anchovies for Matt and me—and the boys ate on the floor in front of the TV while Emma and I nested together on the sofa. We compared Mary Elizabeth's somersaults with Tigger's bounces, and I felt some of Emma's Braxton Hicks contractions. We napped together before and after the pizza, and I helped Emma pre-address thank-you notes for the girls she was sure were coming to her shower. Then we watched *Sweet Home Alabama* for as long as Emma and I could stay awake.

Back in our room at the Yard, Matt and I sat in front of the fire wrapped in *Pooh* and *Piglet*, sipping Constant Comment tea. Matt played with my hair and caressed my belly.

"You know, beauty, Danny and I had a long, heartfelt—and surprising—conversation while you girls were out walking yesterday. He told me that after all the things I had taught him over the years, he's learned more from me in the past year— 'since you met Abby'—than he ever had before. Even after you charmed him on our first visit to Boston last December, Danny didn't think you and I would last past New Year's Day.

"He said he knew how much of a challenge it was to please Emma emotionally and physically on a daily basis, and he didn't think I had it in me any more to satisfy a young woman, in his words, 'as beautiful and passionate as Abigail.' Even when we got married, Danny thought we only made it that far because we got caught up in the romance and surprise—and the fun of raising eyebrows—of being such an unlikely couple.

"He didn't really get it until Emma told him for the 'elebenteenth' time (as Dennis the Menace says) that 'Your dad and Abby don't *know* how old they are. They are *so* in love they could be either sixteen in high school or grandparents celebrating their fiftieth wedding anniversary. Listen to how they talk to each other. Watch their eyes. Look at how they touch each other. You are a very loving and tender guy, Daniel, but you don't touch me like that. I don't know *one* couple— married or not—who look inside each other and talk and touch like your dad and Abby.' Danny said you and I have helped him and Emma 'learn more and learn better' about each other."

I kissed Matt on the cheek and put my hand over his on my belly.

"Emma told me on our walk that Danny has been a better lover since she became pregnant— 'and he was pretty good before.' By the way, old guy," I laughed, "I *do* remember how old you are although I have no idea about myself anymore."

We made love again on the floor, on *Pooh* and *Piglet*, in front of the fire, which required more imagination and patience now than our first stay at the Yard, but the romance of the flames *easily* made up for the hardness of the floor. Back in the soft comfort of the four-poster, we made love a second time in the shadows of the fire and fell asleep going for three.

We hit the road early after pancakes and eggs with Danny and Emma—we promised that we would be back when the baby was born—and were home by four o'clock. The next week was incredibly busy. We celebrated Mrs. Flynn's and little Matt's birthdays on Tuesday—Angie was eighty-seven, and Matty four. Wednesday was our first childbirth class, and Thursday we went to Mom and Dad's for Grandpa McKay's eighty-seventh birthday.

Our series of classes at Fatima was called The Smithers System of Natural Childbirth. There were twelve couples, and we all sat—Indian style—in a circle on our mats on a thin area rug in one corner of the gym. The guys sat snugly behind us girls, supporting our backs. Vivaldi's *Four Seasons* was playing softly on the sound system.

Margo Belton introduced herself and told us about her background and the development of the Smithers System over the years. Then we all introduced ourselves. There was one other lawyer Matt knew and two women from Mangrums I *didn't* know. All of the coaches were husbands except for the boyfriend of one of the Mangrums women. All of us were due in either January or February, and we shared our experiences through the first five or six months of pregnancy. Three of the women were having their second baby, and one was having her third.

Margo asked us about our cravings, which ranged from the legendary pickles and ice cream to *my* red hots and tater tots to jumbo shrimp dipped in ketchup. Then she discussed some basic changes we should make to improve the nutritional value of our diets for the remainder of our pregnancies. She described how we could set up and maintain a healthy daily routine, including exercises, and explained ways we could handle and minimize pain without medications.

We all talked about the challenges of having sex—some of the women wanted no part of it—and the guys were encouraged to contribute their observations and tips. The funniest was the lawyer who described how he "merged my wife's craving for pumpkin ice cream with sex."

Margo concluded our session by announcing that Dr. Hansen would probably be our guest at the fourth class, which would cover the two stages of labor.

On Friday after work, I stopped at Mom and Dad's and picked up my drawing. It was raining hard, so I had to wrap the drawing in a giant black leaf bag. Matt was waiting at home with two large sub sandwiches—one Genoa salami and provolone and one ham and Swiss—from Triassi's Salumeria. We made a picnic in front of the fireplace and shared with Maggie and Jock.

I asked Matt to wait in the living room while I laid my drawing on the kitchen table. It had occurred to me while I was sketching that I had come a long way since my first beach drawing— the seagulls on the rocks—nine years before, but the "long way" had all happened in the eleven months I'd known Matt. *From naked gulls on empty rocks to naked lovers full of sand*, I thought with a smile.

"Come on in, old guy," I called into the living room. "Come and see how we made our baby."

Matt was lying on his back on the blue blanket at the bottom of our burrow in the sand. He was asleep, with his head tilted to the left and Grandpa Dolan's ribbon tangled in his hair. His left leg was bent at the knee, and his left hand was on my "tail." There was sand on his cheek and his chest and all the way down his left arm and leg. I was stretched on top, propped a little on my left elbow, covering most of Matt's body and touching my shadow on his face with my fingers. There was another shadow almost touching Matt's face, coming from a fat, gray and white gull perched high on the dune above our heads. *The only witness*, I thought. My hair was blown everywhere on my face and neck, and you couldn't see my eyes. My backside was sprinkled with sand from my neck to my ankles and had a warm amber glow. Our clothes were almost covered with sand on the Confederate flag towel at the foot of our burrow. Halfway up the dune to my left was the decrepit, black Converse sneaker stuck in the dune grass.

Back in our kitchen, Matt was standing behind me at the table, with his arms around my belly, looking over my shoulder and nibbling on my ear.

"Wow . . . pretty girl, this is *so* good! If I went into a gallery, totally at random, and saw this drawing, I would buy it because I would want that guy to be *me*. Those two people, that man and that woman, look so hot and delicious on so many levels that it's hard to believe you didn't make it all up." He laughed and kissed me. "It's been almost a year now, beauty, and everything *about* you has been hard to believe. Let's go up to bed. Come on, puppies. I have this huge urge to be on the *bottom* of Mommy's drawing."

"Well, that's very convenient, old guy, because it's getting harder for *me* to be there. You will probably be stuck on the bottom until our little girl is born."

Our second childbirth class the following Wednesday was about pregnancy in general. What happens in our bodies; what's normal and what isn't; what to watch out for—what are the red flags; and what kind of choices we will have for our labor and delivery.

Our third class, on October 29, was all about the *guy*—the husband, father and coach. How could he/should he bond with the baby and bring the three of us closer; how would his coaching job change from month to month; how should he help with our plan for natural childbirth; what should he expect in the birthing room; and how important would he be with breastfeeding.

On that Friday—Halloween—Claire and I landed at La Guardia at seven o'clock, in costume: Claire was Ariel from *The Little Mermaid*, and I was Belle from *Beauty and the Beast*. We received applause and cheers at both the Rochester and New York airports. Emma and her mother Jane met us at La Guardia and drove us to their beautiful home in Huntington.

We had a lovely dinner with Emma's mother, her father Jackson, brothers Jack Jr. and Heath, Grandma Olivia Heath, and Emma's best friend Nicky. After dinner the men all left to spend two nights at Heath's apartment, and the six of us girls camped out in the family room in front of the fireplace, nibbled on chips and cookies and talked about the shower and having babies. Claire and I had the boys' old bedroom—with bunk beds; I got the bottom, of course. After all of our baby talk, we actually *slept* like babies and didn't wake up until Emma called us for breakfast.

The shower at Nicky's was wonderful. All of Emma's aunts and cousins were there, and two of her best friends from college. I made some mental notes for *my* shower, and Claire and Nicky helped Emma with the gifts and wrote a list of who gave what. The delicious lunch was catered by De Simone's, which Jane said was the best deli on Long Island. It was a sunny, mild day with the trees still half-full of bright colors.

When the guests left, the six of us plus Jane's sister Alice went back to the Swift house and spent the evening again in the family room, with beer and cheddar popcorn, laughing and crying, snuggling and dozing, and watching *Waitress* with Keri Russell and her incredible pies.

Nicky and Emma drove us to La Guardia on Sunday at noon, and we landed in Rochester at four o'clock. All three Matts and Emily met us at the airport. The next day was Emily's second birthday, and Matt and I brought pizza for dinner, and I made a giant Elmo cake with lots of red frosting.

After we sang "Happy Birthday" and Emily blew out her candles, Claire had to head downtown to Republican Party headquarters to coordinate get-out-the-vote phone calls for her boss, State Sen. Mary Kelly, and several other state and congressional candidates. Sen. Kelly was elected handily the next day to her fourth term, and most of the local Republicans also did well, even though Sen. John McCain and Gov. Sarah Palin lost nationally.

Wednesday, November 5, was our fourth childbirth class, and Dr. Bob and Margo did a "good cop-bad cop" routine walking us through the stages of labor. There were slides showing us the anatomy and physiology of labor, and videos of coaching techniques, practice methods, breathing patterns and exercises and, of course, pushing. It would have been *way* scarier for a rookie like me if Matt hadn't been kissing my hair and my neck and stroking my belly the whole time.

We went around the circle and tried various breathing patterns and words. My favorite words from the beginning were "*who*-t, *how*-t," and I stayed with them all the way through the birth of Mary Elizabeth. Dr. Bob told us to "pick whatever words you like. Practice them—especially when you feel any stress or anxiety or pain—but don't get crazy about the words or the patterns.

"Don't force them or ever get yourselves out of breath," he said. "Stay slow and steady. Find a pace or a rhythm that makes you comfortable and helps you relax. Husbands and coaches, practice all the breathing *with* your sweetheart and get in sync with her rhythm. Touch her while you breathe together and feel your baby. Imagine that your breathing rhythm is making your *baby* feel better too—because it *is*. Try adding soft music to the mix whenever you can."

Margo reminded us that, after our fifth and sixth classes on November 12 and 19, we would not have a class on the Wednesday before Thanksgiving, and our last class would be December 17. Dr. Bob wished all the couples well and said he'd see the five of us who were his patients soon.

Friday was my twenty-six-week visit. Dr. Bob said everything looked fine. "Your little girl is about the size of a head of lettuce and weighs about two pounds and is about ten inches long," he said. "She has eyelashes and is starting to open her eyes. Has your belly occasionally been tightening up on you?"

"Yes, a couple of times a day, usually for less than a minute. It even woke me up last night."

"Those are early contractions—Braxton Hicks—your uterus is practicing. Are you having any serious pains or problems?"

"Not really, other than lumbering instead of walking," I joked. "Some bloating and gas, some cramps in my legs, some heartburn. But Matt touches and rubs me in the right places and makes all that stuff go away."

"Well, the heartburn might be a result of all those red hots and tater tots," Dr. Hansen teased. "Just kidding, Abby. Everything you're talking about is perfectly normal. You're doing *so* well as a first-time mother. You've gained sixteen pounds, which is the low end of the normal range for twenty-six weeks. Has anyone told you about shining a flashlight on your belly?"

"Yes, my daughter-in-law Emma, who is two months ahead of me. I've tried it three or four times and felt my baby girl move each time."

"It's so amazing, isn't it? I wish I could have felt that with *my* children, and I expect that Matt feels the same way. We'll go to two-week visits now, so your next visits will be on November 21 and December 5 and 19. You two are the *best*—just keep doing what you're doing."

Matt and I had been working on Mary Elizabeth's room—mostly on weekends—since we got home from Boston in October. We cleaned out the back bedroom next to ours, which had been Danny's. We removed the wall-to-wall carpet and refinished the hardwood floor. We painted the ceiling and the door and the wood trim very light pink. We papered the walls with Disney princesses: Snow White, Cinderella, Tinker Bell, Sleeping Beauty, Belle and Ariel. And we bought a large, soft area rug with pastel pink and blue swirls, the colors of sunrise. The room looked so *delicious* I wanted to sleep in there myself.

Mom had carefully stored my little girl dresser and changing table in her attic, and Matt and I bought a new, matching oak crib with pink bumpers. I cleaned and polished the black Hitchcock rocking chair on the back porch, bought new pink cushions for the back and seat, and moved it to the nursery. And then I started to spend a few minutes every day sitting in the rocker and reading.

On Saturday November 8, I called Mary Kay to see how my best girlfriend was doing. She and Will were happy, working hard and enjoying every minute of their European adventure. Next week, on Veterans Day, they were going to meet Secretary of State Condoleeza Rice, who would be laying a wreath at the Ardennes American Cemetery just outside of Liege, in celebration of the sixtieth anniversary of the dedication of the cemetery. And the following Friday, November 21, they both had the day off and would be driving the little Opel to Paris for the weekend.

"Sister, I am so excited! Paris! We are going to stay two nights at the Marquis de Lafayette Hotel unless Will can reserve the special NATO suite at the Villa Montmartre. Paris, Abby!"

Mary Kay suggested—and I agreed—that it would be better for her to come home at the end of December for New Year's and my shower than to try to plan a trip for when my baby was born. She wished me and Matt a happy anniversary in advance.

"Abby gal, this has been the most crowded and eventful year of my life; and I'm sure that goes *double* for you. We were mentally and physically in a different world a year ago, and I have you and Matt to thank for a *lot* of things. I'll call you next Saturday and tell you all about our day at the Ardennes Cemetery. Love you."

Our actual anniversary was November 12, but we had a childbirth class that day so we decided to celebrate with a night at the Sherwood Inn on November 10. We dropped the doggies at Tom and Diane's after breakfast and drove to Skaneateles. We had light flurries on and off, but not enough to stick to the roads. Our room at the Sherwood was charming and cozy, with a gas fireplace in the sitting room next to our bedroom, and a bay window looking across West Genesee Street to the lake.

We had lunch at the Gull's Perch, right next to the long pier where the seagulls *did* perch to squawk at and amuse both the natives and tourists who strolled out to the gazebo at the end for photographs or a beautiful view of the lake.

Then Matt and I took several, bite-sized walks— *meanders* was more like it—a mile or so up the street, in and out of the little shops, then back to the lobby of the Sherwood for a hot cup of mulled cider on the soft sofa in front of the *real* fireplace; then a mile or so in the other direction, and more shops, and back to the Sherwood; then a shorter walk around the block to the bakery and the bookstore; and back to the lobby and the sofa and the cider. What a lovely afternoon! With almost every step I closed my eyes, took a deep breath and drifted back to our first days from last November, our first Thanksgiving and Christmas, and *all* the *first* days of our wondrous year together.

Every morning Matt and I woke up *so much* in love; and every night we went to bed even *more* in love.

We had dinner on the front porch overlooking the lake as the sun set on Skaneateles, and then sat for an hour sipping Earl Grey tea in front of the lobby fire. I dozed a few times on the sofa but got my second wind when we went to our room. We brought bayberry candles—the same as we burned on our first night together—and the first movie we watched, *Serendipity*. We laughed at all the little things we missed the first time through the movie, and we paused it here and there to make love. I played on top all the time now and, even though Matt wouldn't say it, I *knew* I was squashing him. He *did* say when he was inside me that he could feel Mary Elizabeth moving, and that made my orgasms almost miraculous. We lost consciousness of everything except our bodies together. When we woke in the morning, the candles were still burning, the fire was still going, and the movie was paused at Jonathan lying on the skating rink with one glove in his hand.

On Wednesday, Matt and I went to Kitty's to celebrate our actual anniversary. After hugs all around, Kitty treated us to two Italian roast coffees and a giant cheese Danish with one candle. She laughed and said she wanted me back after my baby was born.

"Come in part-time, Abby, while you're on maternity leave. You will bring Mary Elizabeth with you, of course. We'll take good care of her. You're still the best counter girl I've ever had. I'll pay you *twice* what Mangrums is paying you," she kidded. "With you back in your little black uniform and your baby on the counter, I'll double my coffee and pastry sales."

I promised to come in more often and told Kitty we could set up my work schedule later.

That night was our fifth childbirth class. We discussed making a birth plan: talking with our doctor about our choices and priorities, visiting the hospital maternity ward and meeting the staff, reviewing the procedures and rules for visitors, and getting a tour of the maternity floor, including the delivery room and birthing room.

Mary Kay called on Saturday and we talked for an hour about her day with Condoleeza Rice.

"She is *such* a strong but gentle woman, Abby: bright, considerate, sincere, *classy*. She treated each of us as if we were her valued confidantes at the State Department. She even asked me to let her know when Will and I were getting married."

As soon as I hung up from Mary Kay and went to the bathroom, the phone rang. Matt picked it up in the kitchen, and I could hear his side of the conversation:

"Joe, how *are* you? Sorry, Abby was on the phone with Mary Kay in Brussels. Oh my God! *When*? How *is* she? Joe, I'm *so* sorry! *That* bad? She wants to see *me*? I'll talk with Abby and call you right back."

I hurried downstairs.

"What is it, Matt?"

"That was Joe Steger. He said Missy had a heart attack."

"Oh, Matt! How *is* she?"

"Not good. She needs multiple coronary artery bypass surgery, which they have tentatively scheduled for November 25, the Tuesday before Thanksgiving. Joe said Missy asked him to ask *me* if I can come to see her before her surgery. He said, 'Missy wants to talk with you before the operation *just in case*—her words.' Joe understands it won't be easy for us, considering where we are right now, so he'll tell Missy whatever we want him to say."

I took Matt's hands and looked in his eyes.

"What do you want to do, Matt? You know *I* want to do whatever *you* want to do."

"Well, I certainly don't *owe* Missy anything, but I don't want to be cruel, either. I guess I'd like to go, but I don't want to go without *you,* and I'm not sure you and our little girl should be making the trip in your seventh month."

"I think your girls will be okay, old guy, but I'll call Dr. Bob right now and see what he says."

I put Dr. Bob on speaker phone: "You and Mary Elizabeth will be fine. Just stay with your daily routine, Abby: a good night's sleep, a walk and fresh air, a warm sweater, a couple of naps, frequent hugs, and not too much bratwurst. I'll see you next Friday."

Matt laid the big kitchen calendar on the table.

"When will we go, Matt?"

"We can't miss our class next Wednesday or our twenty-eight-week visit with Dr. Bob on Friday, so I'm thinking we'll have to fly to Milwaukee on Saturday morning and hope that someone will pick us up. Then we can fly back the Monday before Thanksgiving. I'll call Joe right now."

I made chicken salad sandwiches and cut up cantaloupe for lunch while Matt talked with Joe.

"Joe said that he and Margie will be driving to Oshkosh next Friday to spend Thanksgiving week with the family. He said they will pick us up in Milwaukee, and we can stay the weekend with them at his mom and dad's house. He promised that we will have our own room with a comfortable, king-sized bed. I told him I'd call him tonight with our flight times."

When we walked Maggie and Jock later in the afternoon, I asked Matt, "Do you think she still loves you, old guy?"

"I don't know, pretty girl. I haven't heard a word from Missy in thirty-five years, and I even sent her a birthday card a year or two after Sarah died—just to see if there was still a spark. I know from Joe that her husband is a successful chiropractor, and they have a son and a daughter, and maybe a grandchild or two. Going back to Oshkosh will be like going into a time capsule, with as much pain and sadness as pleasure. Except . . ." and Matt looked in my eyes.

"Except what, old guy?"

"Except you'll be with me, Miss Abigail," he said with a big hug, "and you are everything to me now, so Oshkosh won't matter much."

At our class on Wednesday, Margo spent the first hour discussing problems and complications that might arise during childbirth, including a breech birth or a Caesarean section. We talked about what we could do to minimize the risk of problems, and how we and our doctors and the maternity team would deal with any medical emergencies. It all sounded extremely scary, but Margo said that breech births only occurred in about one of every twenty-five deliveries, and C-sections in about five percent of healthy women. I believed her when she said not to worry.

During the second hour, we talked about how we mothers should take care of *ourselves* after our babies were born—and how our husbands should make *sure* that we did. What bleeding or pain or discharge was normal? What were the red flags? What were the symptoms of depression, and how should we deal with it?

I pressed Matt's hands against my belly and whispered, "It must be so difficult, old guy, for a woman to go through childbirth without a sweetheart like you. I love you *so* much."

Our twenty-eight-week visit with Dr. Bob was as good as *all* of our visits. It was the start of my third trimester. My blood, urine and blood pressure were fine. Dr. Bob examined me and said he was pleased with everything he felt and heard.

"Abby and Matt, your little girl sure is busy. Her heart rate is about 140 beats per minute, and that's great! She's facing down towards the 'door' now. She weighs about two and a half pounds and is about sixteen inches long. She's blinking her eyes and coughing. You might even *feel* that. You've gained nineteen pounds, Abby, so you're on track for about thirty when Mary Elizabeth is born. How are you feeling?"

"Dr. Bob, I'm almost embarrassed to tell you how *good* I feel because I hear some of the other women in our childbirth class talking about how many problems they're having. I'm tired most of the time, for sure, and I have *way* more gas, and I get those sciatica pains from my fanny down the back of my legs a dozen times a day. But none of it really bothers me because I'm so *happy*.

"Margo calls it 'the magic of motherhood' and says all pain is relative and a matter of perspective. Like . . . if you're waiting for the dentist to start drilling, that's *bad* perspective, but if your back pains are caused by your *baby*, that's *good* perspective. I can't believe there's a better place for a woman to be than where I am right now."

"Abby, if more of my patients had your attitude—your 'perspective'—my practice would be a lot easier. Have a safe trip to Wisconsin. I'll see you in two weeks."

After we left Dr. Bob's office, we went to Phil Green's for supper. I was getting to be quite a sight lumbering in on a regular basis. When we called ahead, Jinks or Judith held our favorite booth for us with a handmade sign that said, "Saved for the Pregnant Lady," with a smiley face.

Matt and I split a fish fry with rolls, tater tots and coleslaw, and we shared a bowl of New England clam chowder and a bowl of Italian wedding soup. We also split a peanut butter sundae and sipped hot chocolate and French vanilla cappuccino. It was too hard for me now to lie down on the bench seat with my head in Matt's lap, so I had to lean on him and put my feet up on the seat on the opposite side of the booth.

When we went home, I lay in bed with Maggie and Jock and pretty much directed Matt what to pack. Then he took the doggies to Tom and Diane's to spend the weekend. When he came home, we went to bed early, and I had my best night's sleep in a month.

I don't remember Mary Elizabeth waking me up once.

34

We were at the airport at seven o'clock the next morning for our 8:35 Midwestern flight to Milwaukee, and we landed at nine o'clock Central time. Margie and Joe were waiting for us, and it took about an hour and forty minutes to drive to the Steger house in Oshkosh. Joe's mother and father, Amelia and Gerhard, "Molly" and "Jerry," were about the same age as Matt's mom and dad. They welcomed us with open arms.

"My goodness, Abigail," Mrs. Steger exclaimed, "you're so young and pretty! Jerry, look how young and pretty she is! When are you due, honey?"

"February 6, Mrs. Steger."

Mr. Steger shook Matt's hand, grinned and mused, "Flynn, the handsome soldier boy and poet my daughter let get away. And look at you now, with a child bride and a baby coming."

Mrs. Steger took my hand and led me into the kitchen.

"Come, boys, everybody sit down at the table. Have some strudel and coffee and tell us what you've been doing since the last time you were here. How long ago was that, Jerry?"

"I'd guess about thirty-five years, right, Flynn?"

"Pretty close, Mr. Steger—late fall, 1972. I'll try to keep it short, no more than two pieces of strudel. After Missy sent me packing, I went to law school—Boston College—and right after I graduated I met Sarah, my first wife. We had two sons. Matt is twenty-nine, and Dan is twenty-one. Both are married. Matt has a son and a daughter; and Danny and his wife are expecting their first baby in a few weeks. Sarah died suddenly from an aneurysm in 1997, and I was an aging bachelor for ten years until Abigail came into my life a year ago."

Matt kissed and nuzzled my cheek.

Mrs. Steger patted my hand on the table.

"Was it love at first sight, dear?"

"Almost, Mrs. Steger. Maybe. The first time I saw this old guy we only had about twenty minutes to talk, but it was surely love the *next* day. I moved in with Matt by the end of that week, we got married in March, and here we are."

"She calls you 'old guy,' Flynn?" Mr. Steger interjected with a grin.

"Abby promises it's a term of endearment, Mr. Steger. Joe told us about Missy's condition in the car. How's she doing mentally?"

"She's sad, Flynn. I think she's on the verge of giving up. Are you surprised that Missy wants to see you?"

"Not really, Mr. Steger. Not as surprised as I was thirty-six years ago when she told me to stop writing and calling. Except for Abigail, not too *much* has surprised me in the last twenty or thirty years. When should I go see Missy?"

Mrs. Steger smiled and answered the question.

"Early in the afternoon right after her lunch would be best, Matthew. And my daughter told me *specifically* that she wants to meet your wife if you're up to it, honey."

"Whatever Matt wants, Mrs. Steger."

"That's very nice of you, honey. Why don't you and Matthew rest up from your trip, get your Wisconsin legs under you, and have a nice dinner with us this evening. Jerry and I will go to the hospital later this afternoon and tell Missy that you'll be coming in tomorrow."

As soon as we settled into our room—which Joe said was *his* room growing up—I stretched out next to Matt on the bed and called Mary Kay. It was *way* later than our usual Saturday time, but I was lucky enough to find her home having dinner.

"MK, I'm *so* sorry I'm calling so late, and I know you want to tell me all about Paris, but let me go first. Guess where I am? In Oshkosh, Wisconsin. Last Saturday, right after you and I got off the phone, Joe Steger called and said his sister, Matt's old girlfriend, had a heart attack and wanted Matt to come and see her. You know Matt . . . even for a girl who dumped him, but he said it was up to me. We flew from Rochester to Milwaukee this morning, and Margie and Joe drove us to Oshkosh. We're going to the hospital tomorrow. I guess she's in pretty bad shape; they're doing multiple bypass surgery on Tuesday. Yeah, she said she wants to meet me.

"I'm doing great, sister! My twenty-eight-week visit with Dr. Bob was yesterday. He said Mary Elizabeth is just fine and is 'pointing down toward the door' and ready to go. But she and I really need a nap right now, MK, so can we hold Paris until I get back to Rochester on Monday?"

We agreed that Mary Kay would call me at eleven o'clock her time on Tuesday night and tell me about Paris. Matt was already asleep next to me, with his right arm under my neck. I rolled on my left side, with my head on Matt's shoulder and my belly on his, stroked Mary Elizabeth to calm her down and fell asleep immediately.

That evening, Mrs. Steger cooked what she called a genuine German supper for Matt and me. It was my first genuine German food: German stew, with a thin broth instead of gravy, carrots, peas, kale, boiled potatoes and pork; spaetzle topped with Swiss cheese; and for dessert more apple strudel with pecans and cinnamon.

After supper, we sipped mulled cider and peppermint schnapps in the family room with Lawrence Welk reruns on the TV. We talked about Missy and Mr. and Mrs. Steger's four grandchildren and my baby. I remember thinking that Mrs. Steger was much more hopeful than Mr. Steger about their daughter's chances—before I fell asleep in Matt's lap.

When Matt woke me up and took me to bed, he told me that Joe's mother and father couldn't stop talking about how "sweet and pretty" I am.

"They both said they would have loved to have you as a daughter. They also said they thought Missy would have been much happier if she had married me instead of 'her chiropractor'—Mr. Steger's words. They said he was a good provider, and Missy's son and daughter were fine children, but their son-in-law was *way* too organized and stern—'even for a German.' We all laughed at that one. Mrs. Steger said that we would meet her grandchildren the next day at the hospital, but that Missy had told her husband to not be there when you and I came to visit."

On Sunday morning, we went to the nine-thirty Mass at St. Benedict's—Joe's family church—and then back home for a bounteous breakfast of scrambled eggs, a variety of German sausages, fried spaetzle and pineapple cheese kuchen. It was easy to understand why no one in the Steger family was thin.

At one o'clock, Margie and Joe drove us to the Winnebago County Hospital. Missy's son and daughter, Grant and Evelyn, met us in the lobby. They were about the same ages as Matt III and Danny, and they were both cordial and curious about this mystery man from their mother's past.

They were very nice to me, especially Evelyn, who was engaged to be married in the spring and who told me later—when we had a few minutes to ourselves—that her mother had talked with her many times about Matt. They had already spent a couple of hours with their mother, and they said she was waiting for us. Matt suggested to Margie and Joe that they go see Missy first.

While Margie and Joe were with Missy, Matt and I had about twenty minutes to talk to Grant and Evelyn. He was also a chiropractor, practicing with his father, and married with a daughter and a son. Evelyn's story was bittersweet. She had married her sweetheart Mark right out of Oshkosh High—against the wishes of her mother and father—and had a baby girl, Clarissa, two years later. Mark joined the Army the day after 9/11 and volunteered for the 10th Mountain Division based in Watertown, New York, and fighting in Afghanistan.

When Mark was deployed overseas, Evelyn enrolled in a nursing program at Winnebago County College. Tragically, Mark was killed in Operation Enduring Freedom nine months later.

Evelyn finished her nursing degree after two years at Winnebago and two more at the University of Wisconsin in Madison. She met an assistant professor of history a year ago at the university, and they were going to be married on Memorial Day weekend in 2009. I had a feeling from what Evelyn told me—actually the *way* she told me—that she wanted me to be her friend.

Margie and Joe rejoined us and escorted us to Missy's room. As Margie held my arm in the hallway, she whispered, "Missy wants to see both of you first, and then I think she wants a few minutes alone with Matt."

Nobody looks good hooked up to tubes in a hospital bed, but Missy had her long brown hair brushed, and had put on some makeup and lipstick. It was easy to see why Matt fell in love with her. I'm sure she was breathtaking when she was eighteen. Missy reached her hands out to Matt and me, looked into my eyes and smiled. Matt took her right hand, and I took her left.

"Missy, this is my wife Abigail; Abby, my old friend Missy."

"Abigail, congratulations: first, for marrying this great guy and second, for your baby! Matt, she's so pretty! Abigail, I was eighteen and Matt was twenty-five when we met, and I thought *that* was a big age difference! Thank you both for coming, especially *you*, Abigail. I'm not sure I would have done that for *my* husband when I was twenty-eight weeks pregnant. Has your pregnancy been going well?"

"Considering the stories other women have told me, Missy, I can't imagine it could be better."

"That's the way it was for me with Evelyn; Grant was a different story, but I also think I mellowed quite a bit in the three years between babies. Have you talked with Grant and Evelyn?"

"Yes, especially Evelyn. She's a lovely girl, and I admire her a lot for the way she bounced back after losing her husband."

"Evelyn is my free spirit, my hero-girl. She knows what she wants and she fights for it. Grant, bless his heart, is my organized and predictable German son. You can always *count* on him, but he'll never surprise you or make you cry. He's like his father. Matt, on the other hand, surprised me all the *time . . . and* made me cry. Speaking of which, Abigail, I need to cry a little with Matt right now. Would you mind leaving us for a few minutes, please? I hope everything goes well for you and your baby girl. I will pray for you," she smiled, squeezing my hand.

"Thank you, Missy; that's very kind. You'll be in my prayers on Tuesday."

I joined Margie and Joe in the hallway, and we went to the snack bar for coffee. Joe picked out a table in the corner, and Margie brought me some Constant Comment tea.

"Joe and I have never seen Missy this nervous, and we don't think it's because of her surgery. We think it's because of Matt. What did she have to say?"

"She was very nice, Margie. Polite. She congratulated me on my baby and thanked me for letting Matt come. We talked about Grant and Evelyn for a few minutes, and then she said she needed to 'cry a little with Matt' and asked me to leave."

"My baby sister," Joe said, rubbing his square chin, "has never forgotten what she gave up with Matt. Herb is a good man, a hard worker, and a dutiful father and husband. But he's not romantic. He doesn't make Missy laugh, and he doesn't make her cry."

"Joe and I have had dinner with Missy and Herb fifty times over the years, and I have never heard him tell *one* joke, or seen him become emotional or touch Missy the way Matt touches you every five *minutes*. What do you think they're saying to each other right now, Abby?"

"From what Matt has told me about Missy, I'm guessing that he is mostly listening. I don't think there's anything he wanted to tell her."

Matt rejoined us about fifteen minutes later. His expression was not sad, but there was no hint of a smile, either. He said, "Joe, Missy would like you and Margie to go in for a minute."

When they walked off, Matt kissed me and whispered, "Missy wanted me to thank you again for letting this happen. It meant a lot to her." That was the only thing he ever told me about his conversation in the hospital room, and I never asked for more.

That night, Margie and Joe took us to their favorite Oshkosh restaurant, the Proud Badger Pub, for dinner. The walls were filled with photographs of famous Wisconsin sports stars and historic moments. On our wall I only recognized Vince Lombardi, Warren Spahn and Henry Aaron. Matt and Joe knew everybody, of course. Joe said he actually met Vince Lombardi in the Badger once.

Margie said their steaks were the best in Wisconsin, so Matt ordered a porterhouse, and I ordered a filet mignon. The boys tried several of the local beers, Margie drank pinot noir, and I had one of the pub's signature drinks, hot raspberry cider. I had decided a few weeks earlier to cut out all alcohol in my third trimester.

It was cozy in the pub, with a large fireplace in the main dining room. We talked family and growing up in Wisconsin and New York. Margie and Joe told us how they met in Madison at the university. Matt and Joe reminisced about some of their better times in the Army, like their R&R in Sydney, Australia, and their last year together at the Army medical center at Fort Sam Houston. I fell asleep in the car on the way home and needed a lot of help getting up the stairs to bed. Matt tucked me in and went downstairs to have a nightcap with Joe. The next thing I knew it was eight o'clock in the morning, and Matt was kissing me from my belly to my nose.

"Rise and shine, my pretty girls! It's time to *get* up, *pack* up and have another hearty German breakfast. Joe and Margie said we should leave by ten to get to Milwaukee by noon."

At breakfast, while Mr. Steger was pouring coffee for all of us, he stopped and put one hand on Matt's shoulder and one hand on mine.

"Abigail, Flynn, Molly and I want to thank you both for coming. Our daughter was *so* much better when we went to see her last night, and she said it was because of you. She knows just how dangerous the operation will be, but I don't think she's afraid anymore. I'm sure Joe and Margie will let you know how the surgery goes, but Molly and I want you both to know you are always welcome here—an old friend and a new friend. And we'd love to see your baby girl one day."

"I've always enjoyed being here, Mr. Steger; and Abby and I loved your delicious German food, Molly. We'll be back."

On the way to the airport, Margie and Joe told us they would call Tuesday night or Wednesday and let us know how the surgery went. They also said they'd try to come to Rochester when our baby was born. And Margie whispered to me as we walked through the Milwaukee terminal to our gate, "Missy still loves Matt, you know. She gets tears in her eyes every time she talks about him, and I never saw her get emotional talking about anybody else except her old dog Carolina. But she likes you so much! She called you 'the lucky one' and said you and Matt are just right for each other."

I slept all the way on the plane. When we landed at four o'clock Rochester time, we went straight to Diane and Tom's to get Maggie and Jock, and then home. Matt got a fire going in the living room, and I made spinach and Swiss omelets for supper. We cuddled quietly in front of the fire with the doggies until I started to fall asleep. The next day was a workday for both of us so we were in bed by ten o'clock, although Mary Elizabeth and I needed to play with our old guy for a while before we closed our eyes.

On Tuesday at the office, our entire department met in the large conference room to review the initial success of the expanded and enhanced bulk foods sections in all of our Western New York stores. Joe Christopher said that Art and Wally were delighted with both the presentation of the bulk foods and the sales numbers.

"Wally and Art told me you have all done such a great job they are closing the office at noon tomorrow so you can start celebrating Thanksgiving. We are also happy that our two department members who are in a family way are doing so well. As I'm sure you know, Abigail is due on February 6, and my indispensable Luanne is due on March 4. Would either of you mothers-to-be like to give us a report?"

Luanne said her back ached all the time, and her husband was tired of running out every other day for Buffalo chicken pizza, but mostly they were doing fine. I told the group that I was feeling *so* good I went with Matt over the weekend to Oshkosh, Wisconsin, to cheer up his ex-girlfriend before her heart surgery today. That got me some puzzled looks. When Joe asked what Missy was like, I replied that she was nice, and "as pretty as a woman can be in a hospital bed. Wally would have flirted with her," I added, and laughs replaced the puzzled looks.

Mary Kay called that evening at five-thirty Rochester time, and before she told me about Paris she wanted to hear all about my trip to Wisconsin.

"Why did Matt want to go, Abby gal? Do you think they still love each other?"

"Well, Missy asked Matt to come—by way of Joe—and you know what a nice guy I have. When I asked him how he felt, he sang me a line from a Willie Nelson song: 'Forgiving her is easy, but forgetting seems to take the longest time.' Matt said he didn't 'owe' Missy *anything* but he didn't want to be cruel, either. He left it up to me . . . and Dr. Hansen. Margie and Joe both think that Missy is still in love with Matt, though. And everybody in her family said that seeing Matt improved her spirits. Her operation was scheduled for this afternoon, so we should hear something tonight or tomorrow. Now tell me about you and Will in Paris."

"Oh, sister, what a weekend! We checked in to the Villa Montmartre early Friday afternoon; it's only a quarter-mile from Sacre Coeur Cathedral at the top of the hill. And then we started walking. And walking. It was cool, but there was no rain. We took breaks at sidewalk cafes and restaurants, but I don't actually remember eating or drinking anything—except for one lunch at Moulin Rouge, where the food and service were terrible, and one Bordeaux rouge I took a fancy to at dinner Saturday night.

"We just wanted to keep going and feel as much of Paris as we could. The Eiffel Tower. The Louvre. The Mona Lisa, Abby! Versailles. Notre Dame. The Arc de Triomphe. Champs-Elysees. Napoleon's Tomb at the Hotel des Invalides. The bridges on the Seine. I'm breathless just talking about it! Will was not only a good sport taking me everywhere I wanted to go, but a good sweetheart giving me wonderful kisses at every romantic spot. It would be lovely to retrace our steps one day with you and Matt."

"That's a thought that takes *my* breath away every day, MK—how many steps I have ahead of me with Matt. Where will you do Thanksgiving?"

"All American NATO personnel are invited to Thanksgiving dinner at the American Embassy. It should be fun, but I will miss you and all my family. I can't wait to see you at the shower!"

"Me too, sister. It's seven o'clock, and I hear call waiting beeps on the phone, so maybe it's Margie and Joe calling about the surgery. I'll call you on Saturday around three your time, okay? Okay. Give Will a big hug for me. Matt's taking the doggies out for a walk, but he just blew you a kiss. I'll tell him. Love you."

As soon as I hung up from Mary Kay, the phone rang again. It was a Wisconsin number, but it wasn't Margie and Joe.

"Hello?"

"Hello, Abby? This is Evelyn, Missy's daughter. I asked Uncle Joe and Aunt Marge if I could call you with the news—Mom wanted me to."

"How is she, Evelyn?"

"She's good, thank God! Call me Evie, okay? It was a triple-bypass and it went well. Mom has a good chance for a full recovery and a normal life ahead of her. She might have to cut down on the cheese *kuchens*, though. Abby, Mom wanted me to thank you again for letting Matt come. She thinks he saved her life."

"Evelyn . . . Evie, tell your mom I'm so happy for her. I'm sure the surgeons had a lot more to do with the results than Matt."

"Maybe, Abby. The doctors and the nurses were incredible, of course. But the chief surgeon, Dr. Ryan, said the difference between Mom's attitude last Thursday when they first spoke and late this morning when they prepped her for surgery was 'night and day'—in *his* words. He said that, after twenty years of heart surgery, he is certain that 'a patient who is fighting to live has a fifty percent better chance of doing just that.'

"Dr. Ryan asked Mom what boosted her spirits so much, and she told him about Matt. He said, 'This is the first time I ever heard of an ex-boyfriend riding in on a white horse to save the damsel in distress. I think I'll tell this to some of my other patients to cheer them up.' He said to thank Matt for *him*, too."

"I will, Evie. I'll relay this whole conversation to him as soon as he comes back from walking our Scotties."

"And one more thing, Abby. I'm not sure whether you want to tell Matt or not, but I thought *you* should know. I was in the recovery room alone with Mom when she woke up. My father and my brother had gone back to the office for an hour to return some patient calls. Before Mom even knew I was there, when she was first coming out of the anesthesia, she squeezed my hand and said, 'Matt, is that you? I'm *so* glad you're here. I love you *so much*. Is Abigail here, too?'

"And then she opened her eyes and saw me, and we had a short conversation.

'Evie, honey, how *am* I?'

'You did great, Mom! You're going to be fine.'

'Where are your father and Grant?'

'They went to the office for an hour to check on some patients.'

'Sure, of course they did. Honey, you know I love your father but, just between you and me, Matt would *never* have left me to go to the office.'

"And then she closed her eyes and let go of my hand and dozed off. Abby," Evelyn paused at the other end of the line, "can we be friends? I would like that."

"Evie, we *are* friends. Margie and Joe and your mom told me a lot about you. You have faced *way* more adversity in your life than I have, and you refused to let it beat you. You're a great girl, and I would like to meet your new husband and your daughter Clarissa one day."

"Okay, we can do that. I'll let you know how it's going with Mom and how we're all doing, and maybe you can send me some pictures when your baby girl is born."

"I will. It's a funny thing, Evie—like you, I never had a sister to grow up with. But since I met Matt, I have been gaining a *lot* of sisters, and some from *very* unexpected places—like Oshkosh. Where will you have Thanksgiving?"

"We'll be at Grandma and Grandpa's on Thanksgiving Day, and we'll all go visit Mom in the hospital. She has to stay through the weekend. And then Clarissa, Wayne and I will go on Friday to his mom and dad's in Sheboygan."

"Well, tell your mom that Matt and I send our best wishes and prayers. Evie . . . I'm *so* glad it was *you* who called instead of

Margie and Joe. Stay well and have a good Thanksgiving with all the family. I'll talk with you soon."

When Matt came in with the dogs, I sat him down at the kitchen table and recounted the phone call from Evelyn—all except for the part where Missy woke up. That would forever be between Evie and me. Matt said he would call Joe and Margie the next day to wish them a happy Thanksgiving and get their take on the surgery and Missy's condition.

When we went to bed that night, Matt stroked me more delicately than usual and lingered on all his kisses as he gently made love. Everything was silent and in slow motion until he clasped both his hands under my head, lifted my face close to his and looked in my eyes.

"Pretty girl, you need to know that I thought a lot over the weekend about my old days with Missy. I didn't know it thirty-five years ago—I didn't know a *lot* of things about women then— but I realize it now: she was holding back. Our lovemaking was great, the best I had ever had up to that point in my life. But we didn't get lost in it, you know? I always had to do *way* too much talking. I thought maybe Missy was nervous. She was young, and it was a lot to handle so fast. I believed she loved me—I still *do*—but now I understand that she was afraid to risk everything on me. She might have already met Herb and she was keeping score between the two of us. Who was the better bet?

"I had two *huge* surprises over the weekend. First, I was *amazed* that I didn't feel anything for Missy at *all*. Second, I have always believed I *lost* thirty-five years ago, but I was wrong. Sarah risked everything for me . . . and so have *you*, beauty, and that's why we're here with our baby girl coming. You and I are not even separate *people* anymore."

35

Thanksgiving was going to be at Mr. and Mrs. Flynn's, and I spent a lovely Wednesday afternoon with Mrs. Flynn—I called her "Mama" now—helping her prepare her famous giblet stuffing and bake apple and coconut cream pies. Matt stayed home and cooked his special dark chocolate pudding, and called his brother Alan in North Carolina, and Margie and Joe.

When I got home, Matt called Jinks at Phil Green's, and she had my special sign waiting for us in our booth at five-thirty.

"How was your adventure in Wisconsin, Abby? Did you get to meet this guy's ex-girlfriend?" She winked at Matt.

"I sure did, and I *even* offered her a chance to take him back, but she refused—so you and I are stuck with him," I laughed.

"What would you two like? You get special table service tonight."

"I'll have a Yankee Lager, Jinks, and hot chocolate for my girls. And we'll both have Italian sausage with peppers and onions and a side order of mozzarella sticks."

After Jinks brought our drinks and dinner, I asked Matt, "Old guy, do you remember the first time you brought me here?"

"Are you kidding, beauty? After all that snow. After our first night together. And our first morning. We were the only ones here. It was the best *meal* of my life, after the best *night* of my life. I have been the happiest guy in history ever since. We were so young then."

Matt smiled and kissed me all around my lips and my eyes and my ears.

"Happy guy," I laughed, "the average age of our family is about to get a *lot* younger. Would you like to trade your peppers for my onions?"

"Will you still sleep with me tonight if I eat all these onions?"

"I won't sleep with you if you *don't*. One bed, one pillow, old guy, *always*. It's just that I like the smell of onions better than the taste."

"Want to share a dish of chocolate chip cookie dough ice cream?"

"No, I want my own. I'm already sharing with Mary Elizabeth."

"Okay, *Miss Piggy*. I would rather *watch* you eat ice cream than eat it any day."

When we went home we walked Maggie and Jock and then settled on the sofa with our tea to watch *Serendipity* again because we missed so much on our night at the Sherwood.

"You know, old guy, we didn't reach for the same gloves at Bloomingdale's, but I believe our first meeting at Kitty's was serendipity, too. Think about it. I worked two days a week, and you came in once or twice a week. What were the *odds*— especially on a snowy day in November?"

"Pretty girl, if anyone had predicted a year ago that I would meet a girl like you, marry her and be expecting a baby a year later, I would have said that I had a better chance of winning the New York lottery three *times* during those twelve months."

"It's nice that your mom moved Thanksgiving dinner up an hour and my mom moved dinner back an hour. We won't have to rush, and I'll be able to eat more of Mama's stuffing. She let me add a special ingredient."

"Are you going to tell me, beauty?"

"Nope. I'll let you guess for a while. Can we go to bed? It's the elevator scene, where I think we went to bed last year . . . or fell asleep at the Sherwood."

When I lay in bed, I asked Matt to light our favorite bayberry candles. "And would you mind, sweetie, giving my feet a rub? They've been aching all day. I can put on clean socks?"

"Not to worry, pretty girl. I'll take your feet and piggies naked and sweet. You lie back, close your eyes, enjoy the bayberry and touch Mary Elizabeth for me while I'm here on my knees."

"*Mmm* . . . that's *so* good. Mary Elizabeth can feel it, too. *Oh, Matt* . . . your thumbs are in *just* the right place. *Mmm* . . . I didn't even *ask* for kissing and licking. What are you doing with my *toes*? You're making me all wet and tingly. *Oh, Matt* . . . you'd better get up off your knees, please, and climb on the bed and come inside me. Your girls need to exhale and go to sleep."

Matt let me sleep late Thanksgiving morning while he walked Maggie and Jock, made coffee and read some of his World War II book. He had finished Shelby Foote at the end of the summer and started Volume IV of Winston Churchill's *The Second*

World War. Matt said it was the kind of book you could only read when it's very quiet—"small print and lots of footnotes."

He brought me breakfast at ten-thirty: two poached eggs on English muffins, soft bacon and a bowl of oatmeal with maple syrup. The doggies joined us in bed and watched me hopefully. They each got a bite of bacon for their efforts. When Matt and I got in the shower together—which was becoming a crowded and amusing exercise—he joked about how much more soap he needed on his hands to cover my "blooming body."

After we finished and dressed for dinner, we took Maggie and Jock for a long, slow walk. All my walks were slow now. It was mild and sunny, a rare Thanksgiving day for Rochester. At Matt's mom and dad's, I joined Mama and all of the big girls in the kitchen. Mary Elizabeth got a lot of hugs and kisses. It was one year since I had first met Tom and Diane's family—and they were all home for Thanksgiving—and what a year it had been!

Stephanie, Warren, Jeff and Julie; Tom and Diane; Barbara, Chuck and Amy; Trent and Katy; Matt and I; Mama and Grandpa Matt—we filled the two dining room tables which stretched into the middle of the "parlor" where Brownie and Oreo were camped. (Matt and I had left Maggie and Jock home because we thought four dogs would be too much for Mama.)

Debbie, Fred, Billy and Alicia, and Barry, Eileen and Jean, were in North Carolina for the weekend with Alan and Lisa. Matt, Claire and the kids were in Saratoga, and Danny and Emma were on Long Island.

After we sat down and said Grace, Barbara and Chuck announced that they were expecting a baby sister for Amy in May. That was the *best* news. The only bad news was that Grandpa Matt needed to have his left knee replaced, and that was scheduled for right after New Year's.

About halfway through dinner, Jeffrey—who was now ten— said to Mama, "Great Grandma, your stuffing is more delicious than ever!"

"Thank you, Jeffie," Mama replied. "Maybe it's the secret ingredient that Aunt Abigail added when she helped me make it."

"What was it, Aunt Abby?"

"I'll tell you after dinner, Jeffie—when it's just you and me. Then it will be *our* secret."

It was a treat to be able to relax after dinner, to sample the pies I helped bake, to catch up with my "sisters" and watch

Uncle Buck with the kids, and to play with Brownie and Oreo.
I'm sure I dozed off a few times on the sofa, but not for long; it
was busy in the family room.

We went to Mom and Dad's at five-thirty. Everybody was
happy and healthy. Even Jack was cheerful. He had been
promoted to "senior copier supervisor" at Xerox. Cathy, on the
other hand, was not looking forward to the next day—Black
Friday at Barnes & Noble would be busy.

"Would you believe we're opening at *five* o'clock? It's going
to be a *really* long day in the children's book department."

Betsy told me all about her first grade at the Oak Lane
School. Her teacher was Mrs. Winston, and every day had a
"different color. If we were in school today, Aunt Abby, it
would be a *red* day for PE. Tomorrow would be an *orange* day
for art."

Patrick and Laurie were buzzing about their short-range
plans for the coming weekend in Cleveland, November 29-30—
including the Rock and Roll Hall of Fame on Saturday and the
game between the Colts and the Browns on Sunday—and the
long-range plans for their wedding. They wanted Matt and me to
be in their wedding party.

Everyone in my family was happier than I had seen them in a
long time. Even Grandma and Grandpa McKay were animated
and wanted to hear all the family news and plans. Nannie and
Grandpa Dolan couldn't make it because they both had colds,
but they promised that they were getting better and would come
for Christmas.

Mom and Dad's was *way* quieter than the Flynn's: no dogs,
no *Uncle Buck,* a dull Dallas football game on TV, and nobody
for Betsy to play with, so she sat on the floor of the living room
and brushed and styled Strawberry Shortcake's hair.

Matt and I were home by eight-thirty. While he walked
Maggie and Jock, I brewed a pot of Prince of Wales tea and got
into my pajamas. We watched *Serendipity* until the scene in
which Jonathan decides he's not going to look for Sara any
more, and then we all went up to bed.

It was surprising how well I could still sleep—in my "delicate
condition"—touching Matt. I was able to lie on my left side
with my head on his shoulder or his chest, and his right arm
under my neck, sometimes stretched out straight and sometimes
hugging my back. Matt said he was amazed that his arm never
fell asleep on him. He was now used to sleeping on his back,

which he told me he had never done before he met me. In addition, I was snoring more now than before I was pregnant, "but it's a sweet snore that lulls me to sleep."

On some nights, I would roll over and sleep on my right side, and when I woke in the morning Matt's belly would be against my back and his legs curled against mine—spoon style—and his left arm over *my* belly. He said no matter which way I was sleeping, he could always feel Mary Elizabeth moving throughout the night.

During my whole pregnancy, during my whole *year* with Matt, I never—not even *one* morning—woke up when he and I weren't touching. I don't know if it was sensors or magnets in our skin, or the pure magic of being "one flesh," but it made our bed a sacred place. I was so gloriously happy being pregnant that I even thought about asking Matt whether or not we could do it again—have another baby—but I decided to hold that question until after Mary Elizabeth was born.

I was spending more time in the rocking chair in the nursery soaking up the pink, thinking, napping and reading. I was halfway through *Dear John* by Nicholas Sparks and halfway through *Winnie-the-Pooh*. I was taking turns between the books and trying to get in an hour every day in the rocker. Matt often brought in his desk chair and his Churchill book and sat with me. When I closed my eyes, I could see myself reading *Winnie-the-Pooh* to Mary Elizabeth in her crib.

Matt and Danny called Friday afternoon to tell us about their Thanksgivings in Saratoga and Huntington, and Emma said she was starting to dilate and her doctor told her the baby should be right on time.

"Matt and I will hop in Jeep and head east as soon as you go into labor, Emma. God bless."

Mary Kay called Saturday at noon my time. We talked about Thanksgiving, Mary Elizabeth and our boys. She said it had been cool, rainy and foggy all week. She and Will were going to take a Rhine cruise the following Saturday. They would drive through Liege to Cologne and take Das Flussboot up the river to Koblenz and back. Will was excited that the boat would stop for a break at Remagen, where there is a Ludendorff Bridge and World War II memorial and museum. They would be staying Saturday night in a castle in Rodenkirchen, outside of Cologne. Mary Kay also said she had made reservations for her trip home for my shower.

"Sister, I'll be flying from London to New York and Rochester on December 30, which is a Tuesday, and flying back on Monday, January 5. I want to help out as much as I can with your shower, and spend New Year's Eve with you and Matt. And, I hope, have a pajama party with you and all the girls."

"That all sounds *wonderful*, MK. And we can celebrate a late Christmas together, too. I miss you *so* much. The next time I get pregnant," I kidded, "I want you on *this* side of the ocean."

"The *next* time, Abby? Have you told Matt?"

"*Asked* him, you mean? No. I'll wait until Mary Elizabeth is here, and then the three of us can talk about it. But in my heart, I know our baby girl will be so *wondrous* that Matt will ask *me*."

Margie called later in the afternoon and said that Missy was doing well and would be going home on Monday. She and Joe had made reservations to fly to Rochester on December 31. They would be staying at the Pittsford Hilton, "and we want to party with you New Year's Eve."

"That's a sure thing, Margie, but I probably won't be able to travel any farther than my living room and my kitchen. Mary Kay will be in town, too, and she wants to have a pajama party at her house either the night before or the night of the shower."

"I'm in for the works, Abby. I'm *all* yours while I'm there. Joe and I just need to be dropped at the airport by two on Sunday. It's *so* exciting . . . I can hardly wait!"

"It's only a month away, Margie. You and Joe stay well. We'll talk with you soon."

On Wednesday, we had our seventh childbirth class but, as I said to Matt, after the emotion and busyness of Oshkosh and Thanksgiving, it felt like my first. I even forgot a couple of the mothers' names. Margo, of course, knew that was going to happen, so she had all of us take turns in our circle reintroducing ourselves and talking about Thanksgiving and how we were doing. By and large we were a fortunate group. Only Doria, who had high blood pressure before she became pregnant, was admitted to the hospital for one day because of a spike in her blood pressure. She was diagnosed with mild preeclampsia and would have to be monitored more closely for the rest of her pregnancy.

Our group was also *way* off the national average because we were having seven boys and four girls; only Melinda and Ryan didn't want to know. Remarkably, all the names were different:

Sean, Andrew, Charles, Morris, Christian, Dominic, Jeremy, Veronica, Bethany, Susannah and Mary Elizabeth.

The subject of our class was the first and second stages of labor. In the first stage, the early contractions come slowly and sporadically, with the cervix gradually thinning and opening—effacing and dilating. Then the cervix starts to dilate more rapidly, and the contractions become longer, stronger and closer together. That's the transition to the second stage.

Margo was calm and reassuring.

"When your cervix starts to dilate, your 'bloody show' will come along. Don't be frightened. It's perfectly normal—just the passage of the loosened mucus plug from your cervix through your vagina. If you think it's *too* bloody or if more bleeding follows, call your doctor. And, of course, you'll call your doctor when your water breaks or when your contractions are five minutes apart for about an hour. After that, your doctor will tell you what to do.

"When you are settled in your delivery or birthing room, your cervix will likely be fully dilated, your contractions will be *really* close together and really *strong*, and your nurse will tell you when to bear down and start pushing. By then, you'll be using your favorite breathing pattern and yelling at your coach.

"Your uterus will be naturally contracting and moving your baby down the birth canal. We've seen two movies already and we'll see one more. You'll probably want to try different positions for pushing. Be ready to push more gently or slow down. Follow the guidance of your nurse and doctor. You and your baby will be working one hundred percent together at that point. Talk to your baby as you're pushing. Use whatever four-letter words you need with your doctor or your husband, but talk nice to your baby.

"Finally, and I know this may sound weird or demented, enjoy every second of your delivery. Try to feel the seconds, one at a time. Not enough women truly understand and fully appreciate the miracle they are working. I've had three babies, and only with my third did I really 'get it.' I believe that what you are doing when you give birth is the most remarkable thing a woman can do in her whole life. I've heard—and I'm convinced it's true—that Shakespeare said he would have traded all his plays, and Edison said he would have traded all his inventions, for the ability to give birth. Don't let anyone tell you anything different."

The next evening we went to Phil Green's for supper, and Judith had our booth waiting.

"Good to see you, Abby, Matt. Jinks and Todd worked all Thanksgiving weekend, so they have this week off. What can I get for my favorite pregnant girl, the usual?"

"Not tonight, Judith. I'm trying to cut down on the fatty and fried stuff because I'm getting a lot more heartburn."

"I remember that when I had Jinks."

"Let me have the grilled chicken sandwich and a side of macaroni salad, and a medium Pepsi, please. How about you, old guy?"

"I'll have the Italian sausage with peppers, a side of mozzarella sticks and a Black Lager."

After Judith brought our food, I pressed Matt's right hand on my belly and whispered, "It's hard to believe, sweetie, but it's only a year—almost to the day—since you took me to Boston to meet Danny and Emma."

"Yeah, we've had kind of a full year, eh, pretty girl? When Mary Elizabeth is born we'll start our 'new normal' life—using today's lingo. Are you scared, Abby, excited, not sure?"

"I'm *sure*, old guy, *and* excited. Since our first night together, with not *one* exception, I couldn't wait to wake up with you in the morning, be with you all day, go back to bed with you at night, and do it all over again—every day. Mary Elizabeth is simply going to make all our days better. 'Normal' is the wrong word for us. I think the new 'blissful' is the right word."

The next afternoon was our thirty-week visit with Dr. Hansen, who practically skipped into the examining room with a huge grin on his face.

"Good to see you, Abby, Matt. You both look gloriously happy. What would you like for Christmas?" he kidded as he started to examine me. "How are you feeling, Abby?"

"*Gloriously happy*, Dr. Bob! Ooh, that tickles!"

"All your numbers and tests—blood, blood pressure, urine, weight—are just right. You have gained twenty pounds. Are you having any problems?"

"More backaches, more trips to the bathroom, more gas, more heartburn, an itchy belly— nothing major, nothing to dampen my glow. Ooh, that really tingles!"

"Everything in your baby girl's world feels fine to me. She's about sixteen inches long and weighs a little more than three pounds. Her heartbeat is great. For *your* heartburn and gas, you should cut back on the red hots and tater tots . . ."

"Already done, Dr. Bob, and chocolate, too."

" . . . drink more water—even though that will increase your toilet time—and don't hesitate to take a couple of Tums here and there. The extra calcium won't hurt you and Mary Elizabeth. The best things for your itchy belly are probably Matt's magic fingers and one of those good Vaseline lotions. And for your backaches I recommend that you double down on the pre-natal sex. Don't laugh, Matt. It's no surprise that Abby felt 'tickles' and 'tingles' while I was examining her. She is more sensitive than ever in all of your favorite places."

We all laughed as I got dressed, and Dr. Bob gave us some sample tubes of Vaseline Intensive Care and Total Moisture lotions.

"How long are you going to work, Abby?"

"My boss and I just talked about that today. If I keep feeling this well, I plan to work through Friday, January 9. That will give me about four weeks of lumbering leisure before my due date."

"I think that's a good plan. I'll see you in two weeks—the Friday before Christmas. Enjoy all the good cheer of the season . . . and no aggressive shopping."

We brought pizza and garlic breadsticks to Claire and Matt's for supper and played with the kids and watched a Dora the Explorer movie. We were home in bed by ten-thirty. Matt covered my belly with lots of kisses first, then lots of lotion, and then played with my hair until I was fast asleep. I didn't hear the phone ring at four o'clock, but Matt kissed me awake and whispered, "Danny just called. Emma's water broke, and they're on their way to the hospital."

"Well, don't just sit there kissing me, old guy. Help me out of bed, help me pack, let's get in the Jeep. What about Maggie and Jock," I yawned.

"As soon as we're packed, I'll feed the doggies and take them out, and you can call Tom and Diane. They said they'd come and get Jock and Maggie as soon as we had to leave for Boston. My heart is really pounding! How do you feel, Grandma?" he teased.

"Stop it, sweetie! You know Emma is really my *sister*. I'll make peanut butter sandwiches and cut up apples for the car."

36

We were on the road at seven. It was a cold, gray day, but the Thruway was dry. I slept for an hour in New York between Syracuse and Albany, and an hour in Massachusetts after we stopped for lunch at the Lee plaza—on our long pillow which overlapped the console and Matt's legs. I had become surprisingly adept at inventing positions in which Mary Elizabeth and I could both relax. Before Matt, I had never envisioned even *becoming* pregnant, let alone being *good* at it.

Matt pushed his speed all the way. "The troopers will give you up to seventy-five before they stop you," he said. Even with two bathroom stops for me, we arrived at The Crimson Yard at two o'clock. I was on the cell phone with Danny every hour. There was no baby yet, but Emma was fully dilated and in what I now knew was second-stage labor.

Matt made it to The Cottons in twenty minutes, and Emma's mother and father were waiting for us in the family lounge on the maternity floor.

Jane took my hands. "Danny just came out two minutes ago and told us the doctor said we'll have a baby within the hour. How are you feeling yourself, sweetie?"

"Good, Jane. *Great* actually. Two months to go for me. Have you seen Emma since she and Danny got here? How is she doing?"

"I've been here all morning. I came into town last night, on a mother's hunch. Jack got here about noon from Long Island. Emma's labor has been slow but steady. She's doing beautifully for a first baby, much better than *I* did with Jack Junior."

At that point Danny burst through the DO NOT ENTER doors in his blue paper cap and gown, with tears in his eyes, and barely managed to get out, "It's a girl! She's beautiful! She's perfect! Emma is fine. Give us a few minutes to get cleaned up, and for the placenta to do its thing, and you can all come in. I'm *so* glad you made it, Dad, Abby," Danny added, giving us warm hugs. And then he rushed back through the DO NOT ENTER doors.

Twenty minutes later, the delivery nurse, Marietta, came out and escorted us into the birthing room. Emma was sitting up in bed at a forty-five-degree angle with her baby resting on her chest. Only the baby's head poked out of the pink sheet and blanket covering Emma. Danny was sitting next to her at the head of the bed. Emma gave all of us a radiant smile.

"I'm so happy you're here! Mom, Daddy, Dad, Abby, meet Sarah Jane Flynn."

Jane burst into tears, and Jack had to give her a long hug. Matt and I sat on opposite sides of the foot of the bed. I tickled Emma's big toe through the blanket and whispered, "You two girls are *so* beautiful."

"Skin on skin, Abby," Emma replied. "It's supposed to be the best thing for baby girls. But I think it's the best thing for *big* girls, too," she added as she squeezed Danny's hand. "Honey boy, will you tell everybody the whole story while I rest my eyes for a minute?"

Danny continued to hold Emma's hand with his right hand while he stroked Sarah Jane's thick black hair with his left.

"Sarah Jane was born at 3:02 p.m. She is twenty-one inches long and weighs seven pounds, eleven ounces. Obviously we named her after Mom and you, Jane. After debating girls names for three months, 'Sarah Jane' just came together naturally three days ago."

Emma had dropped off to sleep and was making squeaking noises with her open lips against Sarah Jane's forehead.

"Marietta and Dr. Graham said it was an 'average labor'— eight and a half hours—for a first baby, but it seemed *way* long to Emma and me, especially starting in the middle of the night. Dad, don't underestimate the job of coach," Danny grinned. "Dr. Graham also said it was as simple and uncomplicated as any delivery she's ever had. No medication, no episiotomy, no problems. It means the *world* to Emma and me that you all are here. Listen, she might sleep for a while, in case you want to take a break and come back later. As soon as Emma wakes up, Marietta is going to try to get her milk started."

I walked over to Danny and gave him a kiss on the cheek.

"Why don't *you* take a break? Go with your dad and Jack. Have a beer. Matt brought cigars; take a walk and have a cigar. Stretch out on the sofa in the lounge and take a nap yourself. Jane and I will sit with your girls."

When the guys left, I sat on one side of the bed holding Emma's hand, and Jane sat on the other side stroking her granddaughter's hair.

"Abby, I hope you don't mind my asking, but I know Emma thinks of you as her sister. How do you feel about being sort of a grandmother and an aunt at the same time?"

"I don't mind a bit, Jane. Matt and I and all the Flynns—almost since we first met—have been fine with the novel family tree branch we started. It means that we will love Sarah Jane twice as much as both a granddaughter and a niece. And I'm already smiling in my mind when I see Sarah Jane and Mary Elizabeth," I added, patting my belly, "growing up together as cousins *and* sisters, even though Mary Elizabeth will officially be an aunt on the family flow chart. I hope they will be best friends forever."

Emma squeezed my hand, opened her eyes and smiled.

"Is that you, Abby? Sarah Jane, it's your Grandma Abigail. Mom, are you there, too?"

"I'm here, honey," Jane replied, curling Emma's hair around her ears. "How are you feeling?"

"Wonderful, Mom. Amazed. Happy. Dreamy. I have a beautiful baby girl, Mom! Where are all the dads?"

"When you fell asleep, Abby and I sent them off to have a beer or a cigar, and maybe a nap for Danny. But now we want the whole story of your very special day."

"And," I added, "don't leave anything out, sister, because my turn is coming."

Emma sat up higher in bed, and Jane and I helped her wrap Sarah Jane tightly in one of those classic, pastel-striped hospital receiving blankets. I held the baby for the first time while Emma took a sip of tea and wiped away some tears.

"I woke up a little before four when my water broke. We had our hospital bag packed, so we left for The Cottons right after Danny called you. My contractions were coming about every five minutes and lasting about thirty seconds.

"After we were admitted and settled in the birthing room—about five-thirty, I think—the contractions were a little closer to four minutes apart and forty-five seconds long, and I was dilated four centimeters. The worst contractions sometimes felt like strong menstrual cramps, and sometimes hurt like the really bad stomachaches that used to make me cry when I was a little girl. But Danny said I never cried *once* during my labor.

"The only good part I remember is that when the contractions hurt the most I could feel Sarah moving. And once—it's crazy what comes into your head at the strangest times—I thought of Matt's kidney stone. Danny had told me that his dad had a kidney stone when Danny was a baby, and Matt said that when the pain was sharpest it was a good sign because it meant the stone was moving in the right direction—and the sooner the better.

"All of this took hours, of course. I did my breathing, and Danny held my hands, and Marietta was always there with a cool washcloth and ice chips. But I don't remember much else. Danny said I didn't scream or swear but I grunted a lot— especially when Sarah was crowning. That hurt big time: it burned, it stung like when you put antiseptic or soap on a deep cut." Emma laughed.

"I was talking to Sarah non-stop then, when she was turning and crowning. 'Come on, little girl, we can do this. And Mama wants to give you your first kiss.' I might have also said some not-so-nice things—Danny won't tell me—but luckily Sarah probably won't remember.

"She cried as soon as she came out. It was the most beautiful sound I've ever heard." Emma's eyes filled up again. "In ten minutes Marietta and Dr. Graham had her cleaned up, foot-printed, weighed and measured, and snuggling on my chest—all before the placenta came out.

"Dr. Graham asked me about pain medication several times, but I kept saying, 'Let's wait a little longer,' until Sarah appeared and changed the subject. Same for the episiotomy. Just when I thought I couldn't stand any more stinging, Sarah's head was out, and Mama could coast the rest of the way. She has already made me all these little promises that she's going to be nice to me for my *whole* life."

Emma took a deep breath, still with tears in her eyes.

"Abby, may I have my little girl? And would you mind finding Marietta? I think my breasts need a baby, and probably vice versa."

Marietta was very gentle with Emma and Sarah Jane. She felt Emma's breasts and said they were "quite full of colostrum"— pre-milk, she called it—and helped Sarah Jane latch on to a nipple and begin to suck.

"Sarah Jane is doing really well for a brand-new baby, Emma. I think the two of you will have a great time nursing. How does it feel?"

"Wonderful, Marietta. Dreamy. How do I know when to switch sides?"

"*You'll* know . . . every few minutes . . . you'll *feel* it. *You* will need to switch more than Sarah Jane will. And when she's done—which you'll usually know when she falls asleep—and you still feel full, you can start expressing your milk with one of these pumps and fill bottles so Danny can take the middle-of-the-night shift and let you catch up on some sleep.

"You and Sarah Jane will find your own balance between how much milk she drinks and how much you need to express so that your breasts don't feel too full and uncomfortable. It's different for all women: how much milk you produce; how much your baby drinks; how much time in between feedings; how you fit your job and baby schedule together; how much your husband can pinch-hit. You'll find your own rhythm. Don't let any other woman tell you that *their* way is the right way.

"The pump is a great way to increase your milk supply, and it imitates the sucking action of your baby so it helps stimulate your milk to keep coming. You should pump on one side until the milk slows, then switch to the other side until it slows, then switch back and finish the first side, and then finish the second.

"It's better to refrigerate your milk rather than freeze it; freezing takes away some of the nutrients. And you should try to use all your refrigerated milk within five days, otherwise the same thing happens. And don't warm any milk in the microwave, otherwise it will lose *all* its nutrients."

At 4:30, the fathers came back in the room just as Marietta finished her breastfeeding tutorial. I had made *many* mental notes. Emma greeted them playfully, "Dad, Danny, Daddy, what have you boys been up to while we girls were grinding through our breastfeeding class? Beer and cigars?"

Danny kissed both of his girls and laughed, "These old gentlemen *did* get me out for a cigar, but there's no smoking on the hospital campus so we had to walk half a mile down Beacon to a little park. No beers, though. We had coffee in the hospital cafeteria, and then I got a half-hour nap in the lounge. I think all you grandmas, grandpas and expectant mothers should go do the same thing: get a bite to eat and a nap.

"Come back for dessert. They have great ice cream here in maternity—all you can eat. Emma needs to fill me in on all my breastfeeding jobs."

Matt and I went back to the Yard for a forty-five-minute nap, and then we walked around the corner to the Athena Diner for grilled cheese sandwiches and chicken noodle soup. We were back at The Cottons at seven o'clock. Jane and Jack were already in the room and, much to our surprise, so were Claire and Matt III. When I called them in the morning just before we left, they weren't sure they'd be able to make it to Boston.

After hugs and tears all around, Claire said, "We were able to juggle the schedule, and we stopped in Saratoga on the way and left the kids with Mom and Dad. We'll pick them up at about noon tomorrow. They'll be having such a good time with grandma and grandpa that they won't want to go home. Isn't Sarah beautiful! Look at all her black hair! Abby, you and Dad have had a long day—especially you, mommy. How are you doing?"

"We're okay. I slept a couple hours in the car, and we just had a nap at our bed and breakfast. Oh! Claire, put your hand right here—Mary Elizabeth just gave me a one-two punch."

"Me too," Emma said as she slid to one side of her bed, with Sarah Jane bundled in her lap. "Sit here next to me, Abby. I want to introduce Sarah to Mary Elizabeth. Do you mind pulling up your top for a minute?"

After I did, everybody could see Mary Elizabeth moving inside me. Emma unbundled Sarah and lay her face down on my belly, skin on skin, and we all watched in awe as Sarah moved her hands and feet outside, while Mary Elizabeth tumbled and kicked inside. Emma and I, with tears in our eyes, were both stroking Sarah and my belly at the same time. Claire took a picture.

"Sisters and best friends forever," Emma whispered in my ear.

We wrapped Sarah Jane back up and all had Beverly's Famous ice cream in those little Dixie cups with wooden spoons. I had one vanilla and one orange sherbet. Danny said they would be spending Sarah Jane's first Christmas in Boston, and Jane and Jack would be in town—staying at the Yard—from Christmas Eve until December 28.

"But," Emma added, "we'll be driving to Rochester the day after New Year's for your shower, Abby. Sarah can't wait to meet the whole family."

Matt and I said good night to everyone at eight-thirty and went back to the Yard. We got the fireplace going and found a good movie—*Air Force One* with Harrison Ford—on the flat screen TV on the colonial sideboard.

"Old guy, wouldn't it be great if all of our presidents were as brave and handsome as President James Marshall?"

"Well, I hope the new president will surprise us, but I think life in America is going to be a lot different after our eight years with George Bush. I *do* wish *all* of our presidents would memorize Harrison Ford's speech to the Russians warning terrorists that it was *their* turn to be afraid. Are you comfortable, pretty girl?"

"I think I'm too tired to be comfortable, Matt. Would you just sit behind me and rub my neck and play with my hair?"

I must have fallen asleep even before the terrorists took over the plane. When Mary Elizabeth woke me up to go to the bathroom, the digital clock read *3:14*, Matt was sleeping peacefully with his right arm under my head, and the fireplace was still going. I looked out the front window and saw that it was snowing. I stroked Mary Elizabeth in little circles and whispered, "I hope it stops before morning, baby girl."

Matt woke me at seven-thirty. "Rise and shine, girls! We had some snow overnight, but it has stopped. Danny called and said that before we leave and he goes to the hospital, he wants to meet us all for breakfast at the Athena. Matt and Claire will be checking out of the Hampton soon and joining us. So we're shooting for eight-thirty."

"Well," I teased, "don't just stand there looking hunky, old guy. Assist your girls into the shower, make us a cup of strong coffee, please, and start packing."

Everybody was yawning at breakfast. Danny was clearly anxious to get to The Cottons as soon as he could. We talked about babies, Christmas, New Year's, my shower and hash browns. Danny was going to take off all of next week and maybe the following week, too, depending on how Emma and Sarah were doing. He said he would call us from the maternity room after dinner. He was anticipating that Emma and Sarah Jane would be going home in the morning.

"Are you going to call her Sarah Jane or Sarah?" Claire asked as we left the diner.

"Just Sarah," Danny laughed, "at least until she's old enough to be bad."

We were all on the road by ten, and Matt and I were home by five. He went straight to Tom and Diane's to retrieve Maggie and Jock while I unpacked, threw in a load of white clothes and made our lunches for Monday. I knew it was going to be an early night for me.

Matt came home with the dogs *and* a three-cheese pizza from Vincenzo's, and we all nibbled—Maggie and Jock *love* the crust—and watched the Jets play the 49ers in Candlestick Park. We were just finishing cutting the last of the crust into bite-size pieces to mix with the doggies' food for the week, when Danny called. Emma and Sarah were fine; Sarah was "sucking like an Olympic champion." Jack and Jane had gone, but Jack Jr. and Heath had come up from Long Island for the evening. We said hello to everybody and told Emma that we would call tomorrow night after work.

Matt had several client files to review for a morning conference, but when he tucked me into bed at ten, I asked him to lie with me and play with me until I fell asleep. I tried to kiss him and make love, but I was too tired. I think I fell asleep just as Matt came inside me.

37

The radio woke us at seven to the lilt of Dolly Parton singing "Coat of Many Colors." Matt walked Maggie and Jock in a cold rain while I made oatmeal for breakfast. We were both out of the house by eight and back to the real world. *But*, I thought as I drove to Mangrums, *now there is a new little girl in the real world, and the real world is so much better.*

Matt and I called Emma and Danny every evening that week. Emma said she and Sarah were very happy to be home. Sarah was nursing just fine, and the refrigerator was already well stocked with milk. Sarah woke up twice during her first two nights—around midnight and four o'clock both nights. Because Danny was taking the week off, he and Emma decided to alternate feedings and naps, and eventually errands and shopping too. It was easy to hear in their voices the excitement and anticipation surrounding all the days leading up to their first Christmas with Sarah.

Matt and I had our eighth childbirth class on Wednesday, and the main topic of discussion was the challenges faced by coaches, including best practices. Just about every couple had something to share, either from their own family history, or ideas and stories they had heard. Matt added a few fresh suggestions from Danny's recent coaching experience. Margo also gave each of us an envelope containing the name of one of the other mothers, so we could all be Secret Santas—with a $25 limit—at our final class the following week.

We spent the next week catching up on our families. We had supper with Matt's mother and father on Thursday, and Mr. Flynn told us about his knee replacement surgery that was scheduled for the week after my shower. We went to Mom and Dad's on Friday, and I found my old stuffed Fozzie Bear in my closet and brought him home and laid him in Mary Elizabeth's crib. Tom and Diane met us for dinner at Palermo's on Saturday; and Matt, Claire and the kids joined us at Phil Green's on Sunday.

It was Gaudete Sunday, the third Sunday of Advent. The Gospel told of the Blessed Virgin Mary, with Jesus in her womb, traveling to visit her cousin Elizabeth, with John the Baptist in *her* womb—the same Gospel story as my first Mass with Matt a year ago—*Mary and Elizabeth*, I closed my eyes and mused throughout the Mass, *so much more than cousins.*

We did our Secret Santa shopping Saturday morning and also went to The Great Toy Store for all the kids, trying to remember *not* to buy them the same presents we got last year. Harriman's had a special collection of hand-painted cedar, classic rock-and-roll music boxes, and I purchased three: one for Crystal in my childbirth class, which played "You Baby" by The Turtles; one for Sarah, which played "Puff, The Magic Dragon" by Peter, Paul and Mary; and one for Mary Kay, which played "The Old Crowd" by Lesley Gore.

Five minutes after we pulled in the garage and brought all our bags into the house, Mary Kay called from Brussels. She sounded terrible.

"I have had a cold since we cruised up the Rhine last Saturday. I took two sick days this week, and the weather has been dismal—every day damp and drizzly. Abby gal, Brussels has turned into a long London Fog commercial. But the Z-Pak has finally kicked in, and I feel slightly more human. Congratulations, Grandma!" she kidded. "Mom called me Wednesday and told me the good news about Emma's baby."

"Knock off the 'grandma' stuff, sister. Don't forget you're two months *older* than I am. MK, when are you coming home? We need hours and hours to talk."

"I'll be flying in very late on December 30, which is a Tuesday. I want to spend New Year's Eve with you and Matt, and then as much time as we can right through the weekend. I go back on a nine a.m. flight to New York and London on Monday. I'm hoping we can do a pajama party at my house on Thursday or Friday night."

"We *will*, MK. I'll tell all of our other 'sisters' to plan on it."

"Gotta go, Abby. Will is giving me the high sign for our lunch date. Love you."

"Feel better, sister. Love you."

Matt and I decided to hold off on gifts for each other until Mary Elizabeth was born. We also decided to do a joint message for all of our Christmas cards, and we composed it together at

Phil Green's the evening before our last childbirth class. It went like this:

We probably astonished/appalled/amused (pick one) you with our Christmas card last year. This year we want to thank all of you who were with us during the year, and reassure any of you we haven't seen that love has conquered all. We are happier waking up together every morning than we were going to bed together the night before. And, God willing, we will be blessed with a baby girl in February. We hope to be able to play with you in the New Year, but until we see you, stay well, be joyful and love fearlessly. (P.S. We will send you pictures after Mary Elizabeth is born.)

Our last childbirth class was only partly class and mostly party. We watched a slide show of a normal, healthy labor and delivery, and Margo talked about infant care and breastfeeding when we got home. Most of what she said echoed what Marietta told Emma after Sarah was born. Then we cut the colorful sheet cake—with white frosting and pink and blue balloons—which I had brought from Mangrums, toasted each other with milk, coffee and non-alcoholic eggnog, and exchanged our Secret Santa gifts. Meghan got me a box of fine linen, pale pink notepapers and envelopes, with *Abigail* embossed in pale blue at the top of the papers.

We all agreed to share stories and photographs after our babies were born, and Margo asked us to let her know when we were going to the hospital so she could try to visit us and "see if I taught you right." She also wrapped up a piece of cake for me to give to Dr. Hansen on Friday.

My thirty-two-week visit was enjoyable, but not much had changed in the two weeks since my last visit. My blood and urine readings were fine; my blood pressure was 122/79; and I had gained one pound.

"Mary Elizabeth is not moving quite as much as the last time, Dr. Bob. Is that okay?"

"Good observation, Abby, and it's *perfectly* okay. The two biggest reasons why you're feeling less movement are because your little girl is growing fast and because she's sleeping more. She's up to about four pounds and nineteen inches, so she's squeezed for space. She's probably poking you more and squirming around, rather than swimming and doing cartwheels. And she's sleeping twenty or thirty minutes at a time. You should try to join her in some of those catnaps. She's lying head-down at the bottom of your uterus, getting ready for the big day. How are you feeling?"

"Okay, Dr. Bob. Slow. I have more leg cramps, more leaking from my breasts. I get an extra nap here and there. Most nights, I'm in bed around ten, and Matt plays with me until I fall asleep. Mary Elizabeth usually wakes me up once during the night to pee, but I've been able to get back to sleep pretty well. I'm not as hungry all the time. I've been drinking more milk and eating a lot of Honey Nut Cheerios and cashews and cantaloupe and Nabisco graham crackers. By the way, Margo sent you this cake from our final childbirth class."

"Thank you, Abby. I'll call and thank Margo later. Matt, your wife wears a non-stop smile every time I see her—is she like this at home?"

"Every day, Dr. Bob, and every night until she falls asleep. And every day at the office, too, according to her boss. Some of the happy thoughts came from Margo, and a few from Francine Toscano's book, but mostly it's just Abby being herself. I picked her out for a *reason*, you know. She even quotes Lou Gehrig. Sweetie, tell Dr. Bob what you say to the doggies every morning."

"Puppies, today I consider myself the luckiest woman on the face of the earth." I smiled and squeezed Matt's hand.

"Well, that makes Matt the luckiest guy and Mary Elizabeth the luckiest baby. You all have a wonderful Christmas and New Year's. I'll see you for your next visit on January 2."

We went to Phil Green's for supper and split a large fish fry with sides of macaroni salad and coleslaw, and cups of tomato tortellini soup and New England clam chowder. Then Judith came over with a small ice cream cake with two candles.

"Happy Second Winter to my favorite customers! If you guys are still together next year, and you bring in your baby girl," she smiled, "there will be *three* candles, one for each of you."

After we finished the cake, I put my feet up on the bench seat on the other side of our booth and leaned against Matt and closed my eyes.

"Old guy, Claire called me at the office and said that the kids want to go to Wheeler's in the morning to pick out 'our tree first and then Grandpa and Grandma Abby's tree.'"

"Matt called me, too. We're going to their house at nine for waffles, and then to Wheeler's. We figured we'd set up their tree first and then set up ours. Do you think you'll be *up* for all that excitement, beauty?"

"Sweetie, I expect to play with Claire and the kids and supervise while you and Matt do all the heavy lifting. And right now I'm going to take a short booth nap before we go home and finish our Christmas cards."

It was blustery and cold in the morning, so little Matt and Emily didn't take very long to find *just* the right trees for their family room and our living room. The kids couldn't wait to get back inside and have hot chocolate. Once we had both trees home and solidly in their stands—but still empty—little Matt said we should all take naps "in our own beds" before we started decorating. After Matt, Claire and the kids left, my Matt and I did *exactly* that for a couple of hours before it was time to get ready for my office Christmas party.

The party this year was in Port Sullivan at the Anna Maggiore Winery, set on a beautiful bluff overlooking Lake Ontario. The ballroom faced the water, and there were real fireplaces in all four corners, which made the big room surprisingly cozy in spite of the snow whipping high over the waves and against the picture windows.

Even though Matt teasingly asked me to "give it a try," my red satin dress from last Christmas had *no* chance. I *was* able to find a cherry red, wool maternity dress that hugged all of my round places—front and back—and kept me warm without being too tight, and matching red high heels. The heels only lasted through dinner, and then I went barefoot for dancing and dessert. Matt kept telling me how beautiful I was, especially when we were dancing to the slow songs.

"You're even more beautiful than last year, Abby. Your breasts are more bountiful, and your belly, of course. Your 'tail' is rounder, your legs are perfect, and, most especially, above all else, your face is absolutely radiant. Everyone in the room is watching you all the time—whether you are looking or not— because you're so hot. And I'll bet," he kidded, kissing me, "that every man in the room wishes he was the guy who got you knocked up."

"I think you're wrong there, handsome. I'm guessing that it's all the *girls* who wish they were in *my* place. *Oh . . . Matt*, put your hand right here. Mary Elizabeth is dancing with us."

422

Joe Christopher and Art and Wally Mangrum made short speeches after dinner, and then Art called me up to the podium for a special announcement.

"So far, Abigail—our favorite girl in the red dress—all of us in advertising have bought sixty-five chances, at $10 per chance, to guess the day when your baby girl will be born. February 8 is in first place right now. The winners will split $400, and the rest will go toward a gift card for you and Matt at Belhurst Castle."

"Thank you so much, Art, and Wally and Joe, and *all* of you here. You're like family to me, and I can't imagine a better place to work than Mangrums. Matt and I wish you all a wonderful Christmas and a New Year full of happiness."

I dozed on Matt's shoulder during the drive home, but he told me when we went upstairs with the doggies that there was so much blowing and drifting snow on the roads that the ride would have been a lot more fun in a one-horse open sleigh.

"Old guy, would you help me out of this snuggly dress, please, and hang it on the white satin hanger in my office? I want it to look nice for your party on Monday. Puppies, jump up on your side of the bed so you can warm up Mommy's backside. Daddy will kiss me and touch me and warm up my front side."

Matt lit a bayberry candle and wrapped his arms and legs around me under *Pooh* and *Piglet.* I'm sure I was asleep in five minutes.

We awoke to a sparkling Sunday morning, and Maggie and Jock couldn't wait to bound in the bright new snow. After Mass we went to Claire and Matt's for pancakes and scrambled eggs for breakfast, and finished decorating their tree. Then we drove back to our house for peanut butter sandwiches and apples for lunch, and finished decorating *our* tree. Little Matt and Emily wanted to talk to "Beeba Sary," so we called Emma and Danny. "Beeba Sary" was all Emily could say, but little Matt was able to add, "My name is Matty, and yer my coezen."

Emma said they were all doing great. "Sarah's sleeping about two hours at a time, night and day, and nursing about every two hours, night and day, so we have a pretty good routine. Danny took off eight days from work and just went back to the hospital Wednesday and Thursday to take care of paperwork. He'll be off now 'til we come back from your shower.

"Sarah is a good baby. She doesn't cry for more than twenty or thirty minutes, she has gained back the weight she lost the first week, so she's almost eight pounds, she likes the rocking chair and looking out the window. Friday was our two-week visit with the pediatrician, and Sarah had her Hepatitis B vaccination and a repeat of her newborn screening test. She is so *tiny* in her infant seat in the car. Abby, we can't wait to bring her to see everybody."

"Emma, I'm so happy for you. Can you hear Mary Elizabeth and me smiling? We're going to have a pajama party for all the girls—sisters, mothers, cousins, best friends, grandmas, aunts and babies—at Mary Kay's the night before the shower. We can turn the big bedroom into a nursery, and Mary Kay and I will spend the night with you and take turns helping you with Sarah."

"What fun—Sarah's first sleepover! Oh, sister, we are *so* lucky—and our little girls will be, too—to have each other. We'll call you all at Tom and Diane's on Christmas. Love you."

"Love you too, Emma."

Matt's office party Monday evening was at Gleason Gardens again. Old Northeastern Life gave us gift cards to Palermo's and Phil Green's. Matt thanked everyone, and I rubbed my belly through my red dress and got big laughs when I joked that Mary Elizabeth would soon be enjoying Palermo's red sauce and Phil Green's red hots.

The next morning on the way to work, Matt and I stopped in at Kitty's to wish her a Merry Christmas. She was really surprised and almost in tears and speechless—almost, but not quite.

"Abigail, I did such a *great* job hooking you up with this handsome guy. When your baby girl is born, I want you to bring her in for her first cheese Danish. She'll need an Aunt Kitty."

Joe and Wally donned Mangrums Christmas aprons and served lunch in the large conference room to all of us in advertising, and then they sent us home at one o'clock with gift bags full of gourmet chocolates.

As I wrapped some Christmas gifts in the kitchen while watching *Catch a Christmas Star* on Hallmark, an image began to flash through my mind. Maggie, Jock and I went to the nursery, and I set up my easel in the corner between the crib and the windows. I could see the outline of our crib on the blank paper, or maybe just the shadow, and I traced it in black. I knew Matt would be behind the crib. I pictured him through the wooden slats, fast asleep in the rocking chair with an open book face down on his chest and Mary Elizabeth bundled in the crib

424

with her eyes open, looking straight at me; with my old Fozzie Bear sitting in the corner watching over her. *This will be your best drawing ever, Abigail*, I thought with a smile, *but put the pencils away for now. Wait until your baby girl is born, and she'll help you with the rest of the picture.*

Matt made a pot of his special chicken and spinach soup for supper, and then we sipped Prince of Wales tea in the comfortable living room chairs next to our beautiful blue spruce tree with little Matt and Emily's handmade cardboard stars, stockings and Santas hanging on the front branches. Matt had finished reading Churchill and had just started U.S. Grant's *Personal Memoirs*. I was reading *Past Forgetting* by Kay Summersby, General Eisenhower's sweetheart in World War II.

I closed my eyes and saw Kay and Ike in Telegraph Cottage, with their arms around each other and kissing and holding hands whenever no one was watching; and Ike seated at his desk covered with maps, and Kay standing behind him stroking his temples to take away some of the pressures of war; chain-smoking cigarettes together; sitting on the cottage steps smiling and tickling Telek, their Scottish terrier, under his beard . . . and the image in my mind became Nannie and Grandpa Dolan, kissing and holding hands, taking long walks in the fog, sharing fish and chips and going to the movies. But Gramps got to go back for Nannie, and Ike had to leave Kay behind.

Did Kay and Ike make love? I *hope* they did. They *should* have. They *needed* to: for each other, for my grandparents, for Mom and Dad, for Matt's family, to win the war. Was it wrong for Captain Summersby and General Eisenhower to be in love? How can it be wrong for a man and woman to be in love in war, when they are years from home and they might die any day?

Nannie and Gramps called at eight to let us know that they had just come in from Stockbridge and "can't wait to see you tomorrow." My whole family would be together at Mom and Dad's; even Grandma and Grandpa McKay were coming for dinner.

Christmas Eve day was lazy and slow. There was a snowstorm most of the morning, so our walks with Maggie and Jock were short. Matt had a fire going all day, and we wrapped gifts on the living room floor, with the doggies sniffing every box and trying to eat the scraps of paper. Mary Kay called at nine, and we talked for more than an hour. She and Will were going to the NATO Christmas Eve Ball at seven and spending

Christmas Day with Karl and Trudi, a Belgian couple they had met at Saint Catherine Church. Mary Kay sounded a little sad.

"I can't wait to see you, sister—Matt, too. It's only six days. Have a wonderful day tomorrow, and tonight at your mom's. Love you."

"Love you too, MK. Give Will a big hug for me. Merry Christmas!"

Margie and Joe called after lunch on their way to Oshkosh. They would be going to *her* mom and dad's for Christmas Eve dinner and to the Steger's tomorrow.

"Missy is doing really well, Abby, and she and Evelyn send their best wishes. We'll be flying in to Rochester at noon on December 31. I am *so* excited about the pajama party at Mary Kay's, and New Year's Eve. Joe says he's coming to the shower because he thinks 'the old guy' is going to need help. I told him that *he* ought to know. Our boys will *never* grow up, Abby."

"That's why we love them so, Margie. See you soon."

I made cinnamon apple crisp to take to Mom's, and Matt got garlic bread and four six packs of Murphy's Irish Red and Guinness Black at Mangrums. We were thirteen for dinner, and Mom's Irish beef stew and roast pork have never been better. Grandma Mary and Nannie wanted me to sit between them so they could "play with our new great-granddaughter." Several times during dinner they both had their hands on my belly at the same time. I showed Nannie Gramps' ribbon pinned inside the pocket of my green frock.

"It has been with me all the way, Nannie—at my wedding, on the beach when I got pregnant and now—ever since you gave it to me; and it will be with me in the birthing room."

After dinner we opened our gifts in the living room. Dad and Patrick had a great fire going, and everybody sat on the floor in front of the tree except for Nannie and Gramps, Grandma Mary and Grandpa McKay and me. My favorite present was from Pat and Laurie to Matt *and* me: Clint Eastwood's *35 Years 35 Films* collection. Matt's favorite gift was from Nannie and Gramps: the two-volume biography *Eisenhower* by Stephen Ambrose. He was as excited as a young boy who just saw his new bike under the tree.

"I promise you, Nannie and Grandpa, that I will savor every last page in both of these beautiful books, and then share them with my dad. Abby can tell you how lost I get in my history books."

Matt and I went to midnight Mass with Pat and Laurie, and I cried—as I always do—when the choir led the congregation in "Silent Night." It was different this year, though. This year *I* was a young mother-to-be on a cold winter night; and I thought of Mom and Nannie and Grandma Mary and all the mothers who were a part of Mary Elizabeth and me.

Even though I couldn't keep my eyes open through most of the Mass and the rest of the songs, after we got home and Matt had walked the dogs, I waited for him on his side of the bed and started taking his clothes off as soon as he came into the room.

"Pretty girl, I thought you'd be asleep by the time I got back with the doggies. Are pregnant girls supposed to be this hot?"

"There's room for you in the inn tonight, shepherd boy, and that's where I want you . . . inside. *Mmm* . . . let me help you . . . I know it's cramped in there. *Mmm* . . . old guy, I can feel you and Mary Elizabeth playing with me at the same time. *Mmm* . . . oh . . . that's so good."

When Matt and Mary Elizabeth were both still, I whispered, "Sweetie, nobody—not even my mother—ever said it could be like this, and I never read it in any books. Maybe the feeling would be impossible to describe. Do you think Mary ever felt like this before Jesus was born? I mean, I know she was a virgin before and always, but do you think she ever wanted Joseph?"

"I think she did. She was a young woman with normal desires and real passion. That's what made it so special for her to say 'yes' to the angel." Matt wrapped his arms and legs around me as much as he could. "I'll bet she wanted Joseph to hold her and keep her warm and rock her to sleep just like this."

Maggie and Jock woke us Christmas morning bounding on and off the bed. It was as if they were saying, "It's Christmas, Mommy, Daddy! Let's go downstairs and look under the tree!" I was so cozy wrapped in Matt under *Pooh* and *Piglet* that Maggie and Jock both had to come and lick my face before I stirred.

"Old guy, will you start the coffee and feed the doggies while I roll into the bathroom?"

Although Matt and I had agreed to hold on presents until Mary Elizabeth was born, there were a few wrapped boxes under the tree. Matt had bought us matching Phil Green's baseball caps. His was royal blue, and mine cardinal red. And he got me a gold charm bracelet with two round charms: a picture of us at our wedding and a picture of our dune in Duck. I got Matt the 2008 version of the APBA Professional Baseball Game, a board game he had fallen in love with in Vietnam and taught his sons to play; and a personalized mug with my sketch of us in our burrow among the dunes on one side and the date—May 20, 2008—on the other.

"Wow! I can't believe how clearly the details of your sketch came through on the ceramic. I can even see the *sand* all over us. It will be my new favorite mug, of course," Matt laughed, "but I don't think I'll be able to bring it out at family birthday parties."

We also got the doggies presents and let them tear off the wrapping paper themselves: giant rope bones, blue for Jock and red for Maggie; and stuffed squeaky toys, a gold giraffe for Maggie and green elephant for Jock.

Matt cooked a double batch—eight dishes—of his special dark chocolate pudding, and I made deviled eggs to bring to our Christmas feast. We walked the doggies at one-thirty, loaded up the Jeep and went to Tom and Diane's. Everybody was there— except for Emma, Danny and Sarah— including Alan and Lisa from North Carolina and Matt, Claire and the kids. That made twenty-eight for dinner—not counting Mary Elizabeth and Amy's baby sister who was due in May—at three tables in the living room, dining room and kitchen. Plus four dogs, of course. What a glorious and delicious madhouse!

Emma and Danny called at four, just before we sat down to eat, and the whole family basically lined up to wish Sarah a Merry Christmas. I hardly remember dinner at all. It was a buzz of good stories about jobs, houses, safe travels, healthy babies and the kids in school. After dinner, all of us big girls filled up the kitchen, laughed and cried, cleared away the dishes and brought out the desserts, while the guys stoked the fire, played with the kids and their toys and walked the four doggies. I remember thinking as I waddled through the three rooms, *I hope heaven is like this*.

The next morning, the day after Christmas when we always played with all of our new toys, Matt and I slept in and played with our *favorite* toys: each other and Maggie and Jock. Even after more than a year of seeing it every day, I loved to watch Matt's morning hugs with the doggies. He would get down on the floor in the hallway, naked, and Maggie and Jock would come to him one at a time. Maggie always lay flat, close to a wall, and Matt got down just as low and rubbed his cheeks on both sides of her head while he scratched her hindquarters and played with her tail. Jock, on the other hand, always came to Matt standing on all fours, and Matt knelt and rubbed his cheeks on both sides of Jock's head while he scratched him under his belly and his chin. Maggie never made a sound while she was being hugged and scratched, but Jock usually moaned.

After Matt made us leftover frittatas for breakfast—with turkey, stuffing, mashed potatoes and carrots from Christmas—I told him I wanted to take the doggies for a walk "all by myself."

"Are you sure, beauty? It will be slippery out there, especially in your delicate condition."

"I feel pretty solid after that frittata, old guy. I *promise* I'll be careful. I want to have a talk with the babies, just the *four* of us," I smiled. "You can watch out the window if you're worried."

When I was all bundled up, I looked in the mirror and thought, *Abigail Elizabeth, you're about as wide as you are tall.* Even the doggies had their heads cocked in amusement. Our driveway had been plowed an hour earlier, but there was an inch of fresh snow so I had to be careful on the downhill slope. The challenge on snow and ice *always* is to get the dogs to walk at *your* speed rather than let them rush you to *their* speed.

"We're going to go slow, babies. You can sniff and eat as much snow as you want—except for the *yellow* snow—as long as you don't pull me and Mary Elizabeth. Can you remember what your life was like before I came to live with you? I can't. Let's walk up Uncle Ralph's driveway and let the cars go by.

"I know there was a time when I was in school, and I wasn't in love, and I didn't have any doggies, and I lived by myself—I have books and pictures and letters to prove it. But I can't remember what those days were like. I can't remember what *I* was like. Mom tells me—and I *believe* her—but I can't remember. You have changed me. Daddy has changed me. And now Mary Elizabeth is going to change *all* of us.

"Did you like it better when you had Daddy's bed all to yourselves? I wouldn't want it all to myself without you babies. Don't eat that salt! I wouldn't want to walk around the house and not be able to talk with you. You make Mary Elizabeth listen and laugh—I feel it all the time right here. Do you know what's happening? Do you remember when little Matthew and Emily were babies? Pretty soon there will be lots more noise, and we'll be spending more time on the floor together, and taking walks with my old baby buggy, and waking up in the middle of the night, and singing and crying.

"Are you ready? You'll have to help me—I'm a little bit scared. I would be a *lot* scared— even with Mom's advice and Margo's classes—if it weren't for your daddy, who is the most wonderful man on the face of the earth. He not only made me a *mother*; he made me a *woman*.

"Do you babies remember your mothers? Daddy showed me pictures; they were cuties. They made lots of pretty babies like you. I would like to make more pretty babies, too. Here we are—all the way around the circle—Maggie's house and Jock's house. Let's go in and get you on your fleeces in the living room and dry you off. Daddy's going to make a fire."

We spent the weekend relaxing, reading and adding some finishing touches to the nursery. I was up to D-Day in Kay Summersby's book, with Ike agonizing about the dismal weather over the English Channel in early June and hoping for a narrow window—*one* clear day—to launch the massive invasion. Kay calmed the General as much as humanly possible—*womanly* possible—and the rest, as they say, is history. I wondered if she knew—in those gloomy and desperate but exhilarating days—or sensed, or even feared, that when The War was over, her beloved General would return home and leave her behind.

Matt hung a Winnie-the-Pooh mobile over the crib—with Pooh, Eeyore, Tigger, Christopher Robin and Piglet—and I closed my eyes and saw it in my sketch. We also put sun-catchers on the windows—four Disney princesses: Snow White, Belle, Cinderella and Jasmine.

Mary Kay called on Saturday at three o'clock my time and sounded happier than on Christmas Eve. She told me about Christmas Day with her Belgian friends and said that her Christmas gift from Will was a huge surprise: a week's leave to come home with her. We agreed that Will, Matt, Joe Steger, Danny, Matt III and any other guys who wanted to, could have a stag night at *my* house on Friday while all the girls "pajama-partied" at *her* house.

Emma and Danny called after dinner. They were "deliciously happy on Cloud 9," Emma said. "Sarah is sleeping almost four hours at a time, Abby, and drinking me dry in between. We just started her on a formula, Gerber Good Start Gentle, which

Danny gives her during the night and in between my nursing, or just when I need a nap."

Danny said he was "absolutely in" on the stag party. "It'll be my first night without changing a diaper since Sarah was born," he laughed.

We had pizza at Claire and Matt's Sunday afternoon, played with little Matt and Emily on the Batman rug in the family room, and watched the Steelers crush the Browns 31-0 in Pittsburgh.

38

Monday and Tuesday were very quiet days at Mangrums—
half the office was on vacation— and Wally sent us home early
both days. Wednesday, New Year's Eve, the office was closed,
and I had a lovely morning with Mom preparing party favors and
surprises for the shower. I could not remember ever seeing my
mother happier. Mary Kay called at eleven and joined me and
Mom at noon for lunch. She and Will had gotten in from
London and New York City at midnight. We cried a lot and
hugged for a long time. I hadn't seen her since June.

"I missed you *so* much, MK. You look wonderful."

"Lots of love and sex, Abby gal, and long walks and bike
rides. I've put on about five pounds and I never felt better or
happier in my life—except maybe in Duck. What time would
you like Will and me to come over tonight? What can we
bring?"

"Come about seven. We're just having pizza and beer. Joe
and Margie will be joining us, and Dave and Ann Connolly, I
think. I'm asking everybody to bring their favorite dessert and
wine."

At two o'clock, Dad drove Mom to get her hair done for their
New Year's Eve party at Uncle Jimmy's house, and Mary Kay
and I talked for an hour at the kitchen table over four cups of tea.

"Abby gal, remember how worried I was in June about
whether Will and I would be happy living together? Well, I'm
not worried anymore. Will is strong, smart, considerate,
passionate and devoted to me. He's a young Matt," Mary Kay
laughed. "He always thinks of *me* first. He would marry me
yesterday, in Belgium, if I wanted, but we're staying with
October in Rochester. Maybe October 17. Our wedding needs
to be a full family day, just like yours. I mean, Will's mom and
dad and his family haven't even *met* mine yet. I'm going to need
a lot of help, sister."

I reached across the table and took both her hands.

"MK, starting in March—maybe around my first wedding
anniversary—when we are up to full speed," I said, patting my

belly, "Mary Elizabeth and I will be on call around the clock for brainstorming, consultation, bitching—whatever you need."

I made my "loving BFF face" and squeezed her hands.

"Me too, sister. Will and I will be home around the middle of August and we'll probably live at Mom and Dad's until the wedding and our next assignments. We're hoping for Washington, but it could be New York or even Dallas."

When I got home, Matt said that Margie and Joe had just checked in at the Pittsford Hilton and would be over at seven. The pizza from Palermo's was coming at the same time. And Ann and Dave were bringing their Trivial Pursuit game.

"I fed and walked the doggies, pretty girl, so why don't we take a nap for about an hour before we get ready for the party?"

"*Mmm* . . . that sounds delicious. Will you make love to me, Matt—for the last time in the old year? Are you still counting, sweetie? I kind of lost track after we got pregnant."

Matt laughed as he helped me out of the baggy sweatsuit—one of his—I had worn to Mom's.

"Believe it or not, beauty, I still think about that every morning—mostly in the shower. You and I have been together for *415* days. We've slowed down some since about your sixth month, but I haven't stopped counting. This will be number *1,481*," he smiled, "and that includes about twenty times in the past two months when you seemed to fall asleep on me."

I laughed as I rolled on my left side and started playing with him.

"Old guy, 'seemed' is the right word because I remember *every one* of those times. I may have closed my eyes and drifted some, but I stayed awake—inside, anyway—until you felt just right inside me."

Matt was soft and sweet, and I didn't fall asleep—inside or out—until I felt him dropping off first. We woke at five and showered together—which was more amusing every day because our bathtub was *not* pregnant—and I put on the red wool dress I wore to both of our office Christmas parties. Before we went downstairs, Matt hugged me for a long time in the hallway and touched me everywhere, from my back to my "tail" to my belly to my neck.

"You are *so* beautiful, Abby, and the more of you for me to touch, the more beautiful you are. I don't mean this to sound like a joke," he grinned, "but I can't believe how much we've grown together—in *415* days. Matt and Danny, Joe and Dave, everybody at the office—they all say I'm a different person. If we didn't have our best friends coming over, I would take this hot dress off right now and take *you* back to bed."

I held his head in my hands and kissed him hard.

"Keep that thought until after midnight, old guy, and you might get lucky in the New Year."

Our party was cozy and intimate: plenty of hugs, teasing, tears and telling of secrets. We held hands, kissed and rambled around in the dining room, kitchen and "parlor"—sharing pizza and beer, tales of the old year and dreams of the new.

The boys talked some Army. Dave had served at the same time as Matt and Joe, but he hadn't been an officer. When he got drafted in 1968, he took his chances and ended up with a good two-year hitch as a sergeant in the Army dental dispensary in Manila.

We girls talked about the kids, babies, Mary Kay's wedding and the pajama party and shower. Mary Kay said her parents were leaving Friday morning to spend the weekend with her aunt and uncle in Cleveland, so we would have their house to ourselves. Margie astonished the girls with her colorful version of our visit to Wisconsin to "save Matt's old sweetheart, Joe's sister."

We also played three games of Trivial Pursuit Genus III, and Matt and I won twice. I didn't contribute much—maybe two or three movie stars—but nobody could match Matt at geography, sports, literature and history. He knew every capital of every country and every *vice* president. We didn't turn on the television until eleven-fifty to watch the countdown in Times Square.

This was my second Asti Spumante toast and New Year's kiss with Matt, but it could easily have been the first. It felt exactly the same. I loved him as much as womanly possible on New Year's Eve 2007, and I loved him as much as womanly possible now. I felt as if I were in one of those old Thomas Edison Kinetoscopes, where you watched each picture change a little as they all went around in a circle, and then you ended up back at the beginning. My private Kinetoscope of love with Matt changed a little every day, but always returned to the breathtaking discovery and pure ecstasy of his first kiss. The "urge" he talked about that first day in my apartment . . . I felt it each morning when I woke up and touched him lying next to me, and every evening when I came home from work and saw him

434

waiting to kiss me at the door, and every night when we went to bed and laid our heads on the same pillow.

Claire and Matt and Emma and Danny called shortly after midnight to wish us a Happy New Year. Matt invited us to come for pizza in the afternoon, and to bring Margie and Joe. Danny said he and Emma and Sarah would be driving in around two o'clock on Friday. Our beloved friends all left around one. I heard Joe mention breakfast, but I was too tired to pay attention.

Matt tucked me under *Pooh* and *Piglet* and took Maggie and Jock for a quick walk. When he came back into the bedroom, tiptoeing and expecting to find me asleep, I whispered from the end of our pillow, "Get under the covers, handsome, and let me warm you up. You know I love you more than my life, but you haven't been inside me since last year. I need squeezes and kisses all over my body and way down deep," I smiled. "This will be *1,482*, right?"

We were still sleeping—even the doggies—when the phone woke us at nine. It was Joe.

"Sorry, Abby. I didn't mean to wake you. Tell my old pal that he should have been up with the dogs before now. Margie and I want to take you guys to breakfast."

"Joe Steger, you're in big trouble," I kidded. "Only my mother gets to call me this early. And not only that, but you woke me from an amazing dream."

I made my "pouty girl" face and gave the phone to Matt, who was petting Maggie and Jock.

"It's okay, Joe. Abby will forgive you. I'm surprised the doggies let us sleep so late. There won't be many places to go on New Year's Day, but come over about ten, and we'll call around and see who's open."

We ended up at the IHOP in Webster. Matt said he had been going to IHOPs since his early days at Boston College. He even has one of the old, round, orange plastic menus with the map of the world on the reverse side—when OLD FASHIONED BUTTERMILK PANCAKES were sixty-five cents, and coffee (regular only) was fifteen cents. Mary Kay called during breakfast to let us know that she would be hanging out with her family all day, but that Will had left at eight to drive to Carlisle and spend a day with his mother and father and sisters. He planned to be back in plenty of time for the bachelor party tomorrow night.

Margie and Joe came back to the house with us after breakfast, and we had four very special, quiet hours together before we went to Claire and Matt's. Margie loved all of the colors and what she called "the accessorizing" in the nursery: the drapes, the wallpaper, the carpet, the crib, the mobile and suncatchers, and even my empty canvas.

"I didn't know you drew. What's going on the canvas?"

I described the image in my mind.

"Wow. If you're good, Abby, that drawing could sell a million prints. How good *are* you?"

"Matt says I'm *very* good."

"I hear him say that all the time," Margie teased, "but I thought he was talking about *sex*. May I see a couple of your sketches before we leave?"

I showed her the drawings of George Bush at Yankee Stadium and our hollow in the dunes.

"Oh, my! These are staggeringly good! This one of George Bush could be either on the front page of *The New York Times* or the cover of the annual Yankees yearbook. And this one of you two hot bodies in the sand could be the centerfold in *Cosmopolitan*."

"Thanks, Margie. So far, nobody else has seen these except you, my mother and Matt. One of his New Year's resolutions is to have all of my drawings framed and see about publishing them in a book, maybe with some of his poems."

While Margie and I were upstairs, Matt had dusted off his Army scrapbooks, and he and Joe were sipping beers and flipping pages on the floor in the living room in front of the fireplace. We heard them roaring with laughter while we were in the nursery, but when we joined them in the living room they had tears in their eyes.

Margie's and my favorite Army photograph was of Joe and Matt on the shore of the South China Sea, wearing tight gray T-shirts, jungle fatigue pants and black combat boots, holding their M-16 rifles in one hand and cigars in the other. Margie traced all four sides of the photo with her index finger.

"Joe has this one framed on the mantel over our fireplace," she smiled, "right next to our wedding photograph. I'm never sure which picture he likes better."

We all went to Claire and Matt's at four. Margie and Joe had fun playing with little Matthew and Emily, and we all enjoyed the Sicilian-style pizza from Cappellino's while we watched both the Rose Bowl game at the kitchen table and *Lady and the Tramp* in the family room. Claire and I put the kids to bed at seven-thirty, and when the game was over Margie and Joe drove us home through a couple inches of fresh snow. They asked us to join them for a nightcap at a sports bar near their hotel (where Joe wanted to watch the Orange Bowl game), but I was in dire need of bed after a very busy day. Mary Elizabeth had been punching and kicking all through our pizza party, and we were both quite tired.

Matt walked the doggies—who had to stay downstairs because they were so wet—and joined me in the bedroom. He lit a pine forest candle, turned off the lights, lay next to me under the blue and popcorn sky and played on my lips and my eyelids with his fingertips.

"Pretty girl, would you like to tell me about your amazing dream before you crash?"

"If you rub my feet, Matt, and rub my back, and kiss my neck and keep me awake for twenty minutes . . . I'll try."

"Okay, beauty, I'll do my best."

"Keep touching me and kissing me, sweetie, and don't let me close my eyes. I was walking in a parade . . . pushing a stroller. Was it Mary Elizabeth? I don't know . . . I couldn't see the baby. It was hot and sunny. You were way up ahead carrying a flag . . . you kept turning around and waving. Emma and Claire and the kids were sitting on a curb under a blue umbrella. Claire was holding Sarah, and Emma was giving juice drinks to Matthew and Emily. I didn't see Danny or Matt anywhere.

"Everyone looked about the same age as we are now. And then my mother came alongside of me, and she was pushing a stroller, too. And when I looked into her stroller, I saw myself. The baby was me. I reached in to Mom's stroller to pick up myself, and she reached in to my stroller to pick up my baby— and the phone rang, and it was Joe. *Mmm* . . . that feels so lovely on my neck. I think I want to ask Dr. Hansen tomorrow if pregnant women have different dreams from other women."

"I'm sure they do, Abby. Wow, what a dream! We can talk about it when you're not so tired. Now close your eyes while I tuck myself next to you and rock my girls to sleep."

Mary Elizabeth woke me around eight with four or five robust kicks. I smiled at Matt who was stirring and stretching.

"Put your hands right here, old guy. It feels as if Mary Elizabeth is all knees and elbows this morning, and she's riding a bike. *Ow!* Do you think she's going to be a wild girl?"

Matt laid his cheek on my belly and grinned sideways at me.

"I think, I *hope*, she's going to be just like her mommy. You girls stay right here while I give Jock and Maggie their breakfast and take them for a walk."

While Matt and the doggies were out in the snow, Emma and Danny called and said they'd slept late and were moving slowly, and they'd be in between three and four.

"Take your time. It's snowing here and it's probably heading your way, so be careful. We'll be leaving at three-thirty for my thirty-four-week visit with Dr. Hansen. If we miss you, make yourselves comfortable in both of the front bedrooms, and see how Sarah likes the crib and the nursery. We thought we would all meet Claire and Matt and the kids at Phil Green's for dinner, and then come home and pack our sleepover bags for Mary Kay's."

Matt and I also moved slowly all morning. We sat in the living room with a fire and our books until noon, and then took short rides to his mom and dad's and mine to wish them all a good New Year. At three-thirty, we went directly from Mom and Dad's to the doctor's office.

Dr. Hansen looked a little tired when he came in to the examining room.

"I had two deliveries yesterday—two New Year's babies—and both were difficult: one breach and one Caesarean. Both mothers and babies are fine."

Dr. Hansen must have seen the distress on my face.

"Don't worry, Abby. Both of my mothers yesterday had had difficult deliveries with their first children, so we were anticipating the challenges. You have no medical conditions and no family history, in short, no indications to suggest that your childbirth will be anything other than smooth and normal.

"You are doing *so* well. Your blood and urine are fine; your blood pressure is 121/80; you have gained two pounds since your last visit, for a total of twenty-three since the beginning of your pregnancy. Your baby girl is seventeen or eighteen inches long and almost five pounds. She is adding body fat and filling out—about the size of a cantaloupe," he smiled.

438

"Mary Elizabeth feels more like a *watermelon*, Dr. Bob, and her pokes and kicks are *way* more frequent and sharp. Ow! Like right now."

He and Matt laughed as I rubbed my belly with both hands.

"Part of the reason for that is because Mary Elizabeth is getting bigger, and part is because the amniotic fluid surrounding your baby is decreasing, so there is less padding between you and her elbows and knees. How are you feeling generally, Abby? Do you have any questions?"

"I'm okay. More tired. But okay. More backaches. More swelling. More leaking. But okay. I seem to sleep better on my left side, but that's where this old guy sleeps, so how could it be any other way?"

"Are you still following my prescription for as much sex as possible?" Dr. Hansen kidded.

Matt laughed and jumped in before I could answer *that* one.

"Dr. Bob, you have *no* idea—Abigail is relentless."

Dr. Hansen clapped his hands and grinned.

"Well, whatever you're doing is working wonderfully. You two are, after all, my 'Carolina dunes' couple. And, Abby, you have as beautiful a pregnancy 'glow' as I've ever seen on my patients. You don't even have any stretch marks."

"I thank Mom for that, Dr. Bob. She said she never had any either—after *three* babies. I just remembered, I *do* have a question for you. The night before last—New Year's Eve—I had a very strange dream. Do you hear that from many of your patients? Do pregnant women have *more* dreams, or really *different* ones?"

"They *do*, actually. Several of my patients have told me about dreams which they said were very different from any they had ever had before. And I even read a book on the subject when I was in medical school: *Mommy's Dreams* was the title, and the author, Dr. Raylene Wheeler, has become a friend over the years. She's always interested in new dreams to add to her research on the subject. Did your dream upset you in any way?"

"Not really, except that the phone woke me up before the dream ended," I pouted and poked Matt, "so I didn't get to see my baby in the stroller."

"Well, I'm sure Ray would like to hear as much of your dream—anonymously, of course—as you can remember. If you'd like to send me an e-mail with no names, I'll forward it to her. Your dream might end up in her next book."

439

"I can do that, Dr. Bob, and thank you for always listening to my crazy stuff. It's not my fault, right? Because . . . I'm pregnant."

Dr. Hansen laughed and took my hands.

"Abby, that is almost *exactly* the title of another book I read for my obstetrics fellowship after medical school: *I'm Not Crazy, I'm Pregnant!* So you just keep talking, okay? And unless you and Matt have any problems, I will see you in two weeks, on January 16. After that, we'll meet every week. Be careful out there in the snow."

Emma and Danny were in the nursery when we got home, and Sarah was lying on her back in the crib looking up at her daddy twirling the Pooh mobile. Emma was singing "Bibbidi-Bobbidi-Boo" from *Cinderella*.

"I sing it when she's crying," Emma said, "and so far it works better than any other song."

We met Claire, Matt and the kids at Phil Green's at six. It was even busier than it usually is on a Friday night because it was almost the end of two weeks of Christmas vacation for all the school kids. We grown-ups all ordered haddock fish fries, and little Matt and Emily split a pizza logs kids meal. Matt ate most of the logs, and Emily ate most of the curly fries and fruit cup.

Claire and Matt came in separate cars. Claire had everything she and Emily needed—including Emily's "pack and play"—for our sleepover; and Matt and little Matt had their sleeping bags and snacks for the "daddies" party. After dinner, the boys went to our house, and we girls to Mary Kay's.

All the other girls who were able to do the pajama party were already at Mary Kay's when we arrived: Margie, Mary Kay, Ann Connolly, Diane and Katy, Laurie, Catherine and Betsy, and Debbie and Alicia. Sixteen girls at our sleepover, counting Mary Elizabeth, and there would be sixteen more at the shower the next day.

What a night we had! I don't know who made all the sleeping arrangements, but Mary Kay and I, Claire and Emily, and Emma and Sarah would have the master bedroom. The rest of the girls would share the other three bedrooms and the sofas in the living room and the family room.

After we put Alicia, Sarah and Emily to bed, we turned the whole first floor into our playroom. We pigged out on junk food: potato chips to popsicles. Most of the girls were drinking a variety of white wines—Moscato, Sauvignon Blanc, Chardonnay—or lemon or peach cosmos. Betsy and I shared cherry Kool-Aid. We asked each girl to bring her favorite CD, so we enjoyed a great mix of mood music that ranged from my Shania Twain to Ann's Tony Bennett to Betsy's Lady Gaga. Betsy was "*way*" excited to be spending so much time with so many "grown-up girls."

We all agreed at the beginning of the evening that none of us would call our guys, and we had instructed the guys not to call *us* unless it was life or death. Much to my surprise, not only did *I* not crash early, but neither did anybody else. In addition to all the family news and gossip, and the boxes of Puffs, there was an ocean of hormones flowing through our playroom. We finally decided at one o'clock that we simply had too much to do in the morning to stay up any later.

But even after we all went to our bedrooms and sofas, Mary Kay, Claire, Emma and I talked, cried and laughed for another hour. Mary Kay and I shared the king-size master bed; Emily and Sarah were in their "pack and plays" (Sarah's had an infant insert); and Claire and Emma had separate twin beds. I think I fell asleep holding Mary Kay. It was only the third night since Matt first kissed me that I didn't fall asleep holding *him*.

On Saturday morning, everybody treated me as if I were a princess. I was not allowed to do a thing except take a bath, do my hair and get dressed—and Mary Kay and Margie even helped me with those lovely chores. Betsy brought my breakfast. I gloried in my "sisters" and my friends.

Mom came at noon with Grandma Mary to help with the food, and—much to my delight—Nannie was with them. She and Gramps had surprised even Mom and Dad by driving in Friday evening. All of the other girls—aunts, cousins and nieces—came around one-thirty. Stephanie had driven in from Virginia, and she and Barbara brought Mama. Lisa couldn't make it from North Carolina, and Eileen was home with the flu. Matt, Joe and Will arrived at two, and they were the only boys allowed on the premises—on the strict conditions that they would do *none* of the talking and *all* of the heavy lifting.

I've been to fifty baby showers, so there were no surprises in the assortment of gifts, but they were still all beautiful, thoughtful and generous: the pretty clothes and blankets; the bottles, toys, and Disney princesses diapers; three stuffed

animals—Tigger, Lady and Daisy Duck; the cradle swing from
Nannie and Grandma Mary; the stroller from Diane, Stephanie,
Barbara and Katy; the baby bag with a billion pockets from
Claire and Emma; the handmade rainbow quilt from Margie; the
crystal Belgian music box from Mary Kay, which played all the
songs from *Snow White*; the Fisher-Price high chair with every
bell and whistle from Mom and Laurie; and Mama's white lace
christening dress and bonnet—which looked brand new—that
her mother made for her in Sicily in 1921.

I was too overwhelmed to keep track. Margie and Claire
wrote it all down, and the boys loaded everything into Jeep,
Danny and Emma's SUV and Mom and Dad's van, which Will
had driven to Pennsylvania.

After the shower, Emma and Danny went to Claire and Matt's
for pizza and ice cream. Danny said they watched *Finding Nemo*
and made sundaes with the kids. Mary Kay and Will, Joe and
Margie, and Matt and I had dinner at Phil Green's. The boys
squeezed on one side of our booth, and I sat between Margie and
Mary Kay on the other side. The guys had not stayed up nearly
as late as the girls. We were almost falling asleep in our ice
cream—and it was barely eight o'clock. I reached an arm
around Mary Kay and an arm around Margie and hugged them to
me.

"Sisters of my heart, Matt has to take me home and put me to
bed. I'll call you both in the morning after Mass. We'll
probably have breakfast at home with Emma and Danny before
they head back to Boston. Sleep tight, girls. Thank you for my
wonderful day. I love you."

I was in bed and sound asleep by nine. I didn't even hear
Jock and Maggie bark when Emma and Danny came home with
Sarah. I woke up for no more than a minute when Matt got in
bed, but long enough—he said in the morning—for me to
whisper, "Come inside me, old guy."

When Matt woke me slowly with kisses in the morning, the
clock radio read *9:00*, and snow was pelting the windows.

"*Mmm* . . . what happened to the eight-thirty Mass, old guy?"

"You looked so blissful sleeping, pretty girl, even with Mary
Elizabeth poking your belly, that I called the bishop and got us
the special baby-shower dispensation. And besides, Matt and
Claire and the kids will be here in fifteen minutes for breakfast
because Emma and Danny want to get an early start back to
Boston. The forecast is for snow on and off all day."

"Well, give your girls six or ten kisses and get us downstairs. I'll take a bath and *really* get up after the kids are gone. And thank you, sweetie—I desperately needed the extra sleep after Friday night. The girls had such a lovely time, and I want you to tell me later all about 'daddies' night."

We shared waffles, scrambled eggs, cantaloupe and Lucky Charms for breakfast. And Emily and little Matt couldn't take their eyes off Emma breast-feeding Sarah. It was what used to be called a Kodak moment before Kodak self-destructed, and the boys took some pictures with their cell phones.

The kids were all gone by ten-thirty. Danny said he would call when they got to Cambridge, and they'd be back when "Mary Elizabeth makes her grand entrance." Matt took the doggies for a walk in the snow, and I called Mary Kay and Margie. Mary Kay and I decided to have a good-bye dinner with the guys at six o'clock at Palermo's because she and Will had to be at the airport at five-thirty the next morning.

I told Margie we'd meet them about noon, go with them to return their rental car, and have lunch at Sully's Sports Pub on the way to the airport. We tried to keep the hugs and tears short at the departure gate. Joe and Matt were worse than Margie and I. Just as with love, sex and so many other things, before I met Matt I didn't know much about goodbyes. There had not been many of them that made me sad or made me cry. I had no idea that life could be so full of difficult goodbyes.

Margie wiped away some of my tears and whispered, "When your water breaks, Abby, make me your second call, and we'll be on the road right away. We love you guys."

39

Matt and I had a couple of lovely, quiet hours back at the house before meeting Mary Kay and Will, and I enjoyed them in the nursery with Earl Grey tea and my new book, *Jane Eyre*. I had finished Kay Summersby's book and I wanted to introduce Mary Elizabeth—even before she was born—to my favorite woman in literature.

I had not read *Jane Eyre* since my freshman English class at Newton, and my idea was to read every page out loud to my baby girl—and only her—in the nursery. Just the two of us . . . and Jane. Courageous, passionate, brave, spirited, admirable, loving, faithful, resolute, sincere, caring, *indomitable*—Jane was *all* of those. And humble. And she knew her God and knew herself. I wanted Mary Elizabeth to *feel* Jane before she would ever be old enough to know her. I asked Matt if he thought any other characters—men *or* women—in literature were greater, more inspiring or nobler than Jane Eyre.

"That's a really good question, beauty. Let me play with it for a little while."

After forty minutes and three cups of coffee in the kitchen, Matt came back up to the nursery and said, "I wrote down a handful of names, and crossed them out, and wrote down a few more, and crossed *them* out. There are none. Jane has no equal. She is flawless. All of the other good, strong, noble or honorable characters I came up with—Atticus Finch, Tom Joad from *The Grapes of Wrath*, Elizabeth Bennett from *Pride and Prejudice*, Augustus McCrae from *Lonesome Dove*— either had flaws or had close family and friends to help them through the struggles of their stories.

"But Jane had no one like that to help *her* grow into the woman she was—not even when she was hired at Thornfield and proved to herself that no person was her master, or when Mr. Rochester fell in love with her—because long before Thornfield, Jane's womanhood was already fully formed. She is to be admired above all women," Matt concluded, kissing me, "and you will be the best mother of all because you know the reasons why and will share them with our little girl."

"Thank you, love of my life. Now leave us while we read for half an hour, and then I will be ready to go to dinner."

At our favorite table in our favorite nook in Palermo's we talked about the pajama party, the "daddies" party, Mary Elizabeth, Will and Mary Kay's trip back to Europe and their wedding in October. We were trying to squeeze a lot into one dinner because we knew it would be a long time before the four of us were together again.

There were nine boys at the "daddies" party: the three Matts, Danny, Joe, Will, my brother Pat, Dave Connolly and Matt's brother Tom. Dave, Pat and Tom didn't sleep over, and everybody was in bed by one. After little Matt was tucked into Mary Elizabeth's crib, the eight big boys played pinochle and euchre while they watched *The Godfather*. Matt said he and Dave were the pinochle champs and Will and Patrick won big at euchre. In the morning all the boys met at Joe's diner for a noisy breakfast.

Just before our dessert, Will surprised Matt and me when he asked Matt to be his best man.

"Mary Kay told me on our first date that if it weren't for Matt we would never have *had* a first date. She said, in these *exact* words, 'Matt opened my eyes and my heart' when the three of you had dinner here with her old boyfriend. And it will be perfect with Abby as the matron of honor."

We shared—slowly—tiramisu, limone gelato and cannoli for dessert, and sipped—slowly— Palermo's special liquore sampler: Strega, limoncello, Frangelico and Galliano. We lingered quietly for almost an hour . . . delaying another difficult goodbye.

From *way* deep in our last hug in the parking lot, Mary Kay whispered, "Abby gal, you and I have been best friends forever, since before anybody ever made that up, and I think about you every day in Brussels. My next government job will be on *this* side of the ocean, I promise. I haven't told Will this yet—I may *never* tell him—but I hope I can get pregnant on our wedding night . . . or as soon as I can. Then our babies will be less than two years apart, and I want *them* to be best friends forever, too. Is that foolish of me? Am I a silly girl?"

"MK, you and I have been silly girls together ever since our first summer bicycle rides. Best girlfriends are harder to find—

and keep—than good husbands. If you and I can do both, we will be the happiest 'silly girls' ever. Have a safe trip. Call me when you get to Brussels. Love you."

"I will. Matt, I hope your dad's surgery goes well tomorrow. We love you both so much."

When we came home, Matt walked the doggies, and I went up to the nursery with a cup of tea to read Chapter 2 of *Jane Eyre*.

"Baby girl, remember when we read the last time, the evil Mrs. Reed's mean son John threw a book at Jane and hit her in the head, and then ran into her and knocked her down. When Jane fought back, Mrs. Reed ordered Bessie and Miss Abbott to lock her in the 'red-room.'

I resisted all the way: a new thing for me, and a circumstance which greatly strengthened the bad opinion Bessie and Miss Abbott were disposed to entertain of me. The fact is, I was a trifle beside myself; or rather out of myself, as the French would say: I was conscious that a moment's mutiny had already rendered me liable to strange penalties, and, like any other rebel slave, I felt resolved, in my desperation, to go all lengths.

"Hold her arms, Miss Abbott: she's like a mad cat."

"For shame! for shame!" cried the lady's-maid. "What shocking conduct, Miss Eyre, to strike a young gentleman, your benefactress's son! Your young master."

"Master! How is he my master? Am I a servant?"

Jane only quieted down when Bessie and Miss Abbott were about to tie her in a chair."

I fell asleep in the rocker when Jane was alone in the 'red-room.' Matt woke me at ten and got me into bed. It was going to be an early morning and a long day for both of us. Matt had to take his mother and father to Highland Hospital at seven o'clock for his dad's left knee replacement. I would be starting my last five days of work before my maternity leave. Before Matt left at six-thirty, he had already fed and walked the dogs and packed my lunch.

He called me at the office at noon and said his dad's surgery went well. He was awake, sipping juice and complaining that he was hungry, and the nurses would try to get him out of bed and start him on a walker in a few hours. Matt was going to stay at the hospital until dinnertime and then take his mother home. Tom planned to stay with his dad until lights (and visitors) out, and Katy and Trent were going to spend the night with Mama.

When Matt got home at seven, he found me nodding in the rocker in the middle of Chapter 3.

"How was your day, pretty girl?"

"*Mmm* . . . just fine. Everybody at Mangrums is babying both of us. But you didn't pack me a big enough lunch—I'm hungry! Can we do Phil Green's? Then you can tell me about your dad."

Phil Green's was almost empty. Jinks wasn't working. Todd was the assistant manager for the night, and pretty Louisa was on the counter.

"Hey, Abby, good to see you. You too, Matt. Abby, you are looking so wonderfully pregnant. When are you due?"

"February 6, but Mary Elizabeth may have other ideas—can you *see* those kicks?"

"Wow! What do they feel like *inside*? Do they hurt?"

"There's no feeling to compare them with, and, surprisingly, I don't always notice the kicks in between the cramps and contractions. But they don't *ever* hurt—not the kicks *or* the contractions *or* the cramps—because it's our baby girl. They actually make me smile so big and so often that the women in my office think I'm just pretending to be brave. Even *Mom* scratches her head. But Margo, my childbirth-class instructor, was one hundred percent correct when she told me to enjoy every second of my pregnancy."

"Well, I don't know what's wrong with the women at work, but I can see in your eyes that you *are* as happy as you *say* you are. Some day, God willing, I hope I can feel what you are feeling. You guys go sit in your favorite booth, and I'll bring your burgers and onion rings in a minute."

As soon as we settled in the booth with our hot chocolate, I asked Matt about his dad.

"The orthopedic surgeon said Dad tolerated the operation as well as any eighty-eight-year-old could. He will stay in the surgical rehab unit for three to five days to be sure the incision is healing properly and there's no infection, and until he's steady getting in and out of bed and the bathroom and able to use a walker without assistance. Dad may be a grumbling patient—although he'll flirt with the nurses—but he'll work hard, as he says, 'to get the hell out of here' as soon as he can."

"I'm sure he will. Your dad is even tougher than *you* are. But what about Mama? How is she going to manage at home?"

"Tom and I and the kids will set up a schedule and take turns stopping in at the house. And an orthopedic rehab specialist from the Highland Therapy Group will come every day for six weeks, from ten o'clock to noon, to help Dad with strengthening exercises for his muscles, and practice walking and transferring and getting up and down the stairs. Mom will be okay. She'll probably even enjoy the extra buzz around the house."

Matt curled his right arm around me, rested his left hand gently on my belly and kissed my whole face playfully.

"Tom and the kids know to call me only as a last resort because I have my two girls to take care of, but if it's okay with you, I'd like to do Wednesday this week at suppertime."

"Sure, old guy. I'll call Mom and Dad and invite myself for dinner. Mom has been after me constantly to come over and talk about the baby. I think I'll ask her to call Catherine and Laurie and invite them, too. We can have a girls' gathering. Matt," I whispered into his ear, licking and kissing it at the same time, with my hand caressing his on my belly, "do you know how happy I am? Do you *really* know?"

"Probably not, pretty girl. Right or wrong, I concluded a long time ago that a man who is as happy as he can *possibly* be will always fall short of a woman who's as happy as *she* can possibly be. I think the same goes for *sad,* too."

"You're right, my love. I'm not just *full* of happiness, I'm *overflowing*. I can't even think bad thoughts. This is not in any books I've read. I'm probably driving everybody crazy because I'm not complaining about *anything*. I don't even want to be *tired*, but it seems I don't have a choice. That's why you keep finding me nodding in the rocking chair: Mary Elizabeth is getting me up more often to pee during the night. Do I wake you up all the time?"

"Some . . . some of the time, but only because I lose your touch. I don't *like* that; my *body* doesn't like that. Your touch has become my essence because it not only brings me life and gives me energy, but it also brings me rest and gives me peace. So don't worry about waking me up."

"Okay, old guy, so I will try to touch as much of you as I can every time I get back in bed. I'll call your mom and dad tomorrow and let them know that as soon as my maternity leave starts on Monday, I'll be able to come over in the afternoon for a few weeks—at least until Mary Elizabeth says otherwise—to help out, help Mama cook and do other girl stuff."

"Mom and Dad will like that just fine. They know you can't do any heavy lifting these days. Shall we go home and settle in with the doggies for the night?"

"*Mmm* . . . that sounds lovely. I would like to read Mary Elizabeth a little more of Chapter 4 before you tuck us in."

Jane was no longer being punished in the "red-room," but she *was* being isolated by Mrs. Reed from everybody else in the house. She was alone, it was the gloom of winter, and she had no one to love—except her doll. As I glanced at my old Fozzie Bear in the crib, I read:

"I then sat with my doll on my knee, till the fire got low . . . and when the embers sank to a dull red, I undressed hastily, tugging at knots and strings as I best might, and sought shelter from cold and darkness in my crib. To this crib I always took my doll; human beings must love something, and in the dearth of worthier objects of affection, I contrived to find a pleasure in loving and cherishing a faded graven image, shabby as a miniature scarecrow. It puzzles me now to remember with what absurd sincerity I doted on this little toy, half fancying it alive and capable of sensation. I could not sleep unless it was folded in my nightgown; and when it lay there safe and warm, I was comparatively happy, believing it to be happy likewise.

"*Ooh*, what did you just do, baby girl? You *are* listening. That was a pretty sharp poke, not like the long kicks you used to make. You don't have enough room any more to roll and tumble, huh, but I feel you squirming and stretching. I would like to see the expression on your face when you poke me. I want to see you *so* much. *Mmm* . . . let's close our eyes, baby girl."

The next day at Mangrums I worked on four memoranda—with action plans, goals and timelines—for Wally and Joe and my colleagues in advertising, one each for the four campaigns we would be developing in 2009: elimination of all tobacco products; regular food sample stations in all stores; home-brewing beer aisles in three trial stores; and an increased selection of cut flowers. I was pretty proud of myself for finishing first drafts of all four.

For supper, Matt made a pot of his special chicken spinach soup with acini di pepe. After two full bowls and a dish of fudge ripple ice cream, I lumbered into the living room with a mug of tea and called Mama, Emma and Margie.

I told Mama and old Matt that I would come over Monday afternoon, and they should make a list of chores for a fat, pregnant girl to do. It was good to hear them laugh after two difficult days.

Emma and Danny sounded great. Sarah was a month old. She was looking around all the time, making more happy noises than crying, and sleeping just enough to allow both Emma and Danny to get their rest, too.

"Danny has been able to get back on his regular hospital schedule. Sarah had her first month, well-baby visit today and her second hepatitis B shot. Everything is perfect. She is a very sweet baby, Abby. How is Mary Elizabeth treating you?"

"Well, her head has settled *way* down—Margo called that 'lightening'—so I've been breathing easier and have less heartburn; but I need to pee *way* more."

Emma said, laughing, "I remember *all* of that. My belly was *so* tight in the last month. Sarah was pushing down, pushing down. I was getting up *five* times every night."

"That's about right. Matt has been *so* good about it. He says as long as I get back into bed and touch him all over, he goes back to sleep right away. Thankfully, I do, too. And I've been catching up on my sleep reading to Mary Elizabeth in the rocker in the nursery."

"For me it was Danny's recliner in the den. Gotta go, sister. Danny just got called, and Sarah is hungry. Talk with you soon. Love you."

"Love you too, Em."

Margie had some bad news. Joe's dad had fallen on some ice and suffered a concussion and a crack in his left ulna about two inches from the elbow. He insisted he was fine—another warrior like Matt's dad—but his arm was in a cast, he was in a lot of pain and he was going to be in the hospital for at least one more day for observation.

"Jerry's a tough old bird, Abby—as you probably remember—and stubborn. Joe seems to be laughing it off, and I'm sure we'll still be able to come when your baby is born. How are *you*?"

"Great . . . *really*. I mean, my back aches all the time, and *you* know what's going on inside me. Everything is so fat and tight. Mary Elizabeth doesn't have much room to kick anymore, so she pokes. Instead of a baby rolling, I feel bumps. But I also feel hiccups and burps, and they all make me smile and laugh."

450

"Here's something that worked for my backaches, sister: sweeping. Even if nothing needs to be swept, and no matter what kind of floor—hardwood, tiles, rugs—walking around the room and sweeping will make your back feel better. Believe it or not, Joe's mother taught me that."

"Thanks, Margie. I'll try it as soon as we hang up. Tell Joe's mom and dad that we send our love, and say hello to Evelyn for me also."

"She *asked* about you. She would like your e-mail address. Is it okay for me to give it to her?"

"Sure. I want to keep in touch with Evelyn. Gotta go, sister—bathroom time. Love you."

"Love you too, Abby. See you soon."

Before I adjourned to the nursery and Jane, I sent an e-mail to Mary Kay and told her I would call her on Saturday morning at ten o'clock my time. Then I grabbed the broom from the hallway closet, carried it up to the nursery and swept the immaculately clean, blue-and-pink area rug, and around the rocker and the crib and the dresser and the changing table and my easel.

I smiled and laughed the whole time because first, I wasn't sweeping *anything*; I was merely brushing the nap of the rug the same way I brush the nap of my suede high heels; and second, it *did* make me feel better. When I put the broom in the corner and sat in the chair, I didn't notice my back at *all*; but Mary Elizabeth was pummeling the bottom of my belly as I began rocking.

"Hey, little girl, let's relax and read Chapter 5. Jane is going to school."

Mary Elizabeth stopped punching when I started reading, and I think we both fell asleep about as fast as Jane did on her first night at Lowood. When Matt woke me up and took me to bed, as tired as I was, his touch kindled such an urge, such pregnant heat that I played with him until he came inside me and rocked me back to sleep. As many times as Matt's touch had done that, the suddenness and power of the desire was always breathtaking.

The next morning at the office I finished my four memos and passed them around. Joe said he and Wally wanted to have lunch with me on Thursday. Matt called at noon and told me he would feed and walk the doggies at four and then go to his mother and father's; he promised to be home by eight. I stopped at Mangrums on the way to Mom and Dad's and picked up a Dutch apple pie and vanilla ice cream for all the girls.

Mom, Laurie, Catherine and Betsy were waiting for me at the kitchen table. Dad and Patrick had gone to the Beer Factory for burgers, fries and basketball games on the twenty-one big-screen televisions. Mom baked scalloped potatoes and ham—always a favorite of mine—and macaroni and cheese for Betsy. We set up tray tables in the "parlor," with pitchers of beer and Kool-Aid, and made girl talk. Catherine and Mom shared their memories of the last month of pregnancy, and we joked about contractions, countdowns, and breaking water. Catherine's didn't break until she was in the hospital in labor; but Mom's broke with Jack in the old Chevy on the way.

"I always blamed your father for taking the worst possible roads to Highland," Mom grinned. "Have you been feeling the Braxton Hicks contractions?"

"A little more, Mom, maybe once or twice an hour, and a little stronger; but not every hour and not for very long. They go away if I get up and take a walk or lie down and take a rest."

Betsy was all ears and full of questions.

"Aunt Abby, what's a contraction? Do they hurt?"

"Betsy, put your hand right here on my belly. Can you feel how hard it is? And *there*, Mary Elizabeth is poking me. It's very crowded for her inside because she's so big and almost ready to come out. She's been growing in the womb inside my belly for eight months. The closer we get to the day Mary Elizabeth is born, the more my womb will get tight and squeeze—the same way you squeeze your hand. Those squeezes are the contractions. When they come fast enough and last long enough, I will go to the hospital to have my baby girl—just like your mommy did with you. But they don't hurt . . . you know why?"

"Why? Aunt Abby, are you *crying*?"

"Because, sweetie, it's my baby girl," I said, taking Betsy's hands, "and I can't wait to see her. Nothing she does hurts because I love her so much."

I got home just before Matt pulled in the driveway at eight. He walked Maggie and Jock and then joined me for coffee in the kitchen.

"How was your dinner, beauty?"

"Nice. Mom made scalloped potatoes, and we talked the whole time about the wonders of the ninth month, and finished with apple pie and ice cream. Betsy learned a lot," I laughed. "How are your mom and dad doing?"

"Pretty good. Dad says he likes his 'therapy girl' and they are working hard. Mom smiles and shakes her head. Katy and Debbie have been over the last two afternoons, and Tom and Trent in the evening before bedtime. Mom and Dad will need rides for a while, but I expect Dad to break the rules in a few weeks and start driving. How about you, love? Are you ready for bed, or will you read for a little?"

"I want to *try* to finish reading Mary Elizabeth Chapter 10—Jane is off to Thornfield to be a governess—but I bet I won't make it. Will you scoop me out of the rocker in twenty minutes?"

In the morning, it was snowing lightly when Matt walked Maggie and Jock, but the wind was whipping, and the temperature was two above. The doggies came in and went right to the rug in front of the heat vent below the kitchen sink.

"Pretty girl, it's icy and nasty out there. I'm going to drive you to work and pick you up later, but how about we stop at Kitty's for a sweet breakfast?"

"How about I lick all over your sweet *body* for being my Prince Charming?"

"I'll hold you to that as soon as we get home from work tonight."

Kitty was delighted to see us.

"Abby, Matt, give me hugs! Happy New Year! How are my favorite pregnant friends? This is just about as mean a day as when you met. Come and get warm. Breakfast is *my* treat."

We sat at our special table and shared a cheese Danish and a large wedge of sour cream coffee cake. Matt rubbed my thighs and my back in between sips of coffee.

"These are your last two days of work, beauty. Will Wally and Joe take you out for lunch?"

"Probably not with the weather this bad, but that will give us more time in the executive dining room to talk. Lunch *tomorrow* will be a party for me in the cafeteria. That reminds me, Nannie and Gramps are coming in tomorrow because we are all invited to dinner at Mom and Dad's on Saturday to celebrate her birthday and their anniversary, which are both on Sunday. Did I tell you that already, old guy? It's been harder and harder for me lately to separate my remembering from my forgetting. *Mmm . . . that's the perfect spot on my back. Now scratch."

453

"You *did* tell me, sweetie, and it's Uncle Vinny's birthday too—he would have been ninety-one. I thought I might go to the cemetery on Sunday if the weather isn't like this."

"I want to go with you, love, if it's not too awful and slippery. *Mmm* . . . rub a little higher."

As soon as Matt dropped me at my office, I asked Charley, the security guard on the marketing and advertising floor, if there was a broom closet around.

"Do you need something cleaned up, Abby?"

"No, Charley, but I need a broom for a few minutes," I laughed, "it's a pregnant girl thing."

"Sweeping helps with the backaches, right? I remember my wife doing the same thing with our kids. You go settle in your office, Abby, and I'll bring you a broom."

After I fluffed up the carpet in all four corners of my office, I leaned the broom against the fax machine. *Nobody will miss it for one more day*, I thought.

Wally, Joe and I had a lovely lunch. They insisted that I take as much leave as I needed after my baby girl was born. They would follow the timelines in my memos and run all "broad-brush strategy questions" by me, but I was not to be concerned about any details.

Wally complimented me on organizing the new projects staff, "into a dynamic and intuitive team. You have chosen capable assistants and delegated well, Abby."

"Thank you, Wally. You and Joe are both very kind and completely supportive. I know it's only been seven months, but I can't imagine working in a more satisfying job or with more outstanding people. My assistants know they can call me for anything really important.

"Matt and I have discussed my leave. We're thinking eight to ten weeks, depending on what Mary Elizabeth has to say. I wouldn't be surprised if she wants to come *with* me for my first few weeks back."

Just then Art Mangrum walked through the door and laughed.

"Abigail, that is a first-class idea. Not only would you be back with us sooner, but we could put your baby girl to work, too. What do you think about some beautiful mother-and-daughter photographs in special locations around our stores? Bradley is the best photographer around."

"That sounds nice, Art. I'll mention it to Matt later. Have you ever done that before with employees and their babies?"

"A handful of times. We never put names on the photos, so very few customers know the mother and her baby, and not many employees even recognize them as Mangrums family. But *everybody* likes the photographs; they make people feel good."

"Maybe Mary Elizabeth can help sell more flowers, Art," I kidded.

"You read my mind, Abigail," he laughed, "although I thought we might try her photograph in the beer aisles also."

When Matt picked me up at five, he had a red rose in my milk glass vase—with a red ribbon around the neck—standing in the cup holder of Jeep. After I kissed him six or ten times, I asked, "What's the occasion, love?"

"You mean other than the minor fact that you girls are my life?"

"Right, old guy, other than that," I whispered, hugging his shift arm.

"Well, I got a surprise call from Jerry Brongo about an hour ago. He and Cheryl were on their way to Albany for a teachers' retirement conference and they decided at the last minute—mostly because of the weather—to spend the night in Rochester and take us out to dinner. So I booked our favorite table at Palermo's."

"That is a really nice surprise, Matt. We haven't seen Cheryl and Jerry since our wedding."

Catching up with the Brongos at Palermo's was a special treat on a winter night. The New York State Teachers' Retirement System was hosting a national conference of state retirement directors and senior officials at the Desmond Hotel in Albany. Cheryl and Jerry were very happy to relax after driving through snow all the way from their home in Bay City, Michigan.

"Cheryl and I took turns," Jerry sighed, "but we never dreamed the weather would be this bad and the drive would take so long. I am *extremely* happy to be done for the night—and to spend some time with you guys. This Montepulciano is warming me right up. We're only driving one way; we have a rental car. After the conference, we're going to fly to Raleigh, North Carolina, to visit our daughter Laramie, who is the assistant director of continuing education with the North Carolina Department of Insurance."

"How old are your daughters, Cheryl?" I asked.

"Laramie is thirty-one and she lives with her boyfriend Warner, who is an associate professor of history at the University of North Carolina in Chapel Hill. Libby is twenty-seven and teaches fourth grade back home in Bay City. She's engaged to be married to Doug, also an elementary school teacher, in June."

"Jerry, I showed Abby a few pictures of your vintage violins. How many do you have now?"

"Eleven that are at least a hundred years old and pretty valuable. My number one is a 1707 Antonio Russi which would sell in the high six-figures, and which is on loan to the concertmaster of the Chicago Symphony Orchestra. I have three others on loan to principal violinists in Dallas, New York and Baltimore. I also have a 1959 Sunburst Les Paul Standard that Roy Orbison used on tour. I know Matt has *no* musical ability whatsoever," Jerry smiled, "but have *you* ever played the violin or guitar, Abby?"

"No, I've never been very adept with my fingers, Jerry, except with chalk. I tried a flute for a few years at Fatima, but lost interest after high school. How long have you been collecting?"

"I bought my first old Italian fiddle a couple years after law school when I got my first good job, and then I made a plan to buy one old fiddle each year for ten years. It has been the greatest passion of my life, after my family, and very rewarding—more personally than financially—but Cheryl and I have decided to start selling some of my fiddles."

He gave me a curious look, like a little boy who wants you to tell him it will be okay. I sensed something was wrong from the expression on Cheryl's face as she poked him.

"You'd better tell Matt and Abby *now*, honey."

"Well, I'll be fifty-seven on August 6 and I plan to retire next year when I have thirty years in the state system. And," Jerry hesitated and looked at Cheryl, "I have been diagnosed with a heart valve problem which will probably require surgery within the next year."

"What!" Matt was visibly upset. "When were you going to tell your best friend?"

"Sorry, buddy. I just found out around Thanksgiving, and Cheryl said I should tell you right away, but I thought I would wait until after your baby is born."

"What can Abby and I do? How are you feeling?"

"Good most of the time, but I seem to get tired faster. I don't *feel* anything; I have no pains."

I placed my hands on top of Jerry's on the table.

"How bad is it? Will the surgery fix you up?"

"Abby, I *hope* so. My cardiac surgeon in Detroit *thinks* so. It's a condition called mitral valve stenosis. Calcium deposits have formed on the ring around my mitral valve and they make it more narrow and stiff. It screws up my blood flow and creates a risk of clots.

"It was probably caused by the rheumatic fever I had as a boy. The surgery is called a commisurotomy. It's supposed to clean up the calcium deposits so the valve can work normally. Let's change the subject and get another bottle of this red wine. Cheryl is going to be my designated driver back to the hotel."

Jerry grinned and took my hands in his.

"Abby, what are you going to do with all your leisure time starting next week?"

"I don't know. I don't know what to expect of myself. I'm guessing I'll get up with Matt on the mornings he goes off to work and sleep in with him on the mornings he doesn't. Maybe I'll go to Kitty's—that's the coffee shop where we met—some days for coffee and a Danish; maybe to Mama and Matt's or Mom and Dad's some afternoons. Maybe I won't feel like driving much longer, and I'll spend more time with my doggies in front of the fireplace or in the rocking chair in the nursery.

"I've been reading *Jane Eyre* out loud to Mary Elizabeth; I'm up to Chapter 15 and Jane is starting to notice—and trying desperately to control—her feelings for Mr. Rochester. I have my easel set up next to the crib in the nursery, and I'll be ready to start the best drawing of my life as soon as Mary Elizabeth is born.

"I'm sure I'll take more naps, especially if I'm hanging out in the armchair by the fireplace or in the rocker. Matt *always* finds me asleep in the rocker. How was it for you, Cheryl?"

"I had a ton of energy with Laramie—I played tennis into my seventh month; I went out all the time with my girlfriends and my sisters—but Jerry said I was grouchy too much of the time. With Libby four years later, and Laramie and our chocolate Lab puppy Cookie going full speed all the time, I was one hundred percent the opposite. I wanted to stay home, cuddle and nest for the last four months.

"And even though I can laugh about it now, it amazed me then that my daughters grew up with those opposite personalities. Laramie wants to be out in the world—and *travel* the world—and take on all comers. Libby loves Bay City and her fourth-graders and their families, and all the people and dogs in her neighborhood where everybody knows everybody. Laramie is a *Cosmo* girl, and Libby is the corner coffee shop girl.

"*Hey*, it's getting late. We'd better get back to the hotel; tomorrow will be a long day."

"Would you guys like to have breakfast with Matt and me tomorrow before we go to work and you leave for Albany?"

"We'd love to, but Jerry is chairing an eleven-thirty legal committee meeting, so we want to be on the road at six o'clock."

"Call us when you get to Albany; we want to know you're safe."

"We will, Abby. And you take very good care of yourself and your baby girl. We'll call you after she's born, and we'll see you in the spring. We love you guys."

Matt drove me to Mangrums in the morning, and my party started as soon as I walked onto the marketing and advertising floor. My office was festooned with pink and white crepe paper, and Joe had even wrapped a pink satin ribbon around "my" broom. Joe said I could take the broom home, "compliments of Charley."

"Even though Wally had sent a secret (to me) memo around the department stating "No Gifts," I received a dozen gift cards for Mangrums and Phil Green's. We partied, sang and took turns sweeping through lunch and into the middle of the afternoon—when Joe told me to go home "and start getting your baby girl ready for the *next* party."

Matt picked me up at three, and we went home for a nap before supper at Phil Green's. Jinks saw us coming in from the parking lot and held the door for me and escorted us to our booth.

"Do you feel as good as you look, Abby?"

"Actually *better*, Jinks, thanks. Today was my last day at Mangrums, and my department gave me a wonderful party. I hope Lou Gehrig doesn't mind my saying this, but I'm *the luckiest girl on the face of the earth*. Only twenty-eight days until my due date! Joe Christopher says you are doing *great* in your internship."

458

"I *love* it, Abby. Everybody treats me as one of the team. I am *so* grateful to you for pointing me in the right direction."

"You'd best thank Matt here; but for him I might never have come into your restaurant."

"Thank you, Matt," Jinks laughed, shaking his hand.

"Go ahead, Jinks, give my old guy a big kiss."

Matt stood up, and Jinks wrapped her arms around his back and kissed him on the lips. Matt blushed while I smiled and teased, "That's a terrific incentive, Jinks, for generating new customer referrals. Matt, would you buy a cheeseburger from this girl?"

It was pitch black and snowing when we got home. Matt took Maggie and Jock out, and I took my Earl Grey tea and *Jane Eyre* to the nursery. I was reading Chapter 19, and Mr. Rochester had disguised himself as a gypsy fortune teller to play tricks on the young society women who were visiting Thornfield and to try to draw intimate thoughts from Jane.

I fell asleep in the rocker well before Matt returned with the dogs. He carried me out of the nursery, undressed me and snuggled me into bed and lay with me—spoon-style—and stroked me until, as he told me in the morning, "you started to whistle and blow bubbles with your lips, and Mary Elizabeth stopped poking my hand on your belly."

Then he went downstairs, rubbed the doggies dry, turned off the Christmas lights, locked up and came back to bed.

40

I slept in late Saturday morning. I didn't feel Matt get out of bed, and I didn't hear him either take the doggies out or bring them back in. When I finally woke up, it was almost ten o'clock.

"Why didn't you wake me up earlier, old guy? I told Mary Kay I would call her at ten."

"Because, beauty, you looked so pretty and peaceful; Mary Elizabeth too. Just throw on your flannel nightgown and fuzzy slippers. I have a fire going, and I'll pour you a mug of fresh coffee. You can curl up in your favorite armchair and talk with Mary Kay in front of the fire."

Mary Kay and Will were both getting over colds.

"We each missed two days of work this week, Abby gal. It has been rainy and damp for more than a *month*. I'd rather have Rochester cold and snow; and my family doctor, too. I think we'll be back to normal next week. I'm checking off your days on my NATO calendar: twenty-seven days until your due date, sister. How are you and Mary Elizabeth doing?"

"*Wonderful*, MK. I don't think people believe me when I tell them how good I feel. *I* think *they* think I'm trying to be brave. My only constant discomfort has been my back, but Margie tipped me off that sweeping—even when there's nothing to sweep—with a regular broom helps the backache . . . and it works. They even gave me a broom at my office party yesterday, to take home and sweep with. I'll be on maternity leave until sometime in April, depending on my baby girl.

"Mary Elizabeth is very big now, and very crowded, so she doesn't roll or tumble around. She pokes. I read to her every day. I sit in the rocking chair in the nursery, usually with a cup of tea, and read out loud to her from *Jane Eyre*, and she quiets down and listens."

"*Jane Eyre*! Remember when we *had* to study that in freshman English—Great Women in Literature—at Newton? I wrote my final paper for Professor O'Callaghan on Dorothea Brooke from *Middlemarch*, but didn't you do yours on Jane?"

"I did, but it's amazing how much more fun it is to read one of those classic novels when you don't *have* to. I am almost to the part where Jane leaves Mr. Rochester to go see the dying Mrs. Reed. I hope my little girl will grow up to love Jane as much as I do.

"Next Friday is my thirty-six-week checkup. Tonight we have a big dinner at Mom and Dad's to celebrate Mom's birthday and their thirty-sixth wedding anniversary. Do you and Will have any plans?"

"We'll lie low today and tomorrow—maybe bundle up for Mass in the morning—and hope we are back to one hundred percent on Monday. This will be a busy week because the American Embassy is hosting a joint celebration with NATO on Friday for President and Mrs. Bush and Vice President and Mrs. Cheney. There will be a luncheon at NATO, speeches in the afternoon, and a reception and dinner at the Embassy in the evening. This will be President Bush's final overseas trip before the inauguration of President Obama. Will and I will both be on duty for all of the events. I'll tell you all about it when I call next Saturday. Enjoy your first week off, sister. We love you guys."

Matt and I went to Mom and Dad's at five-thirty. Mom roasted pork tenderloins with all the trimmings. We were fourteen for dinner, counting Mary Elizabeth. I brought my broom with the pink ribbon from Mangrums to show everybody, and Betsy spent an hour after dinner sweeping all around the house. Nannie wanted to see Grandpa's ribbon, which I had pinned in the pocket of my crimson maternity frock. And she became very animated when I told her I was reading *Jane Eyre* to Mary Elizabeth in the nursery every day.

"Oh, my goodness, honey, *Jane Eyre*! 'You come by that honestly,' as Mr. Dolan says. We read *Jane Eyre* when I was in lower sixth form in Swansea—I was sixteen, and I *loved* Jane. We memorized many passages. My favorite part, of course, is in the garden, just before Edward asks Jane to be his wife, when she sobs and says:

Do you think I can stay and become nothing to you? Do you think I am an automaton? Do you think I am without feelings? Do you think I can bear to have my morsel of bread snatched from my lips, and my drop of water dashed from my cup? Do you think, because I am poor, plain and little, I am soulless and heartless? You think wrong! I have as much soul as you, and

*full as much heart! And if God had gifted me with some beauty
and much wealth, I should have made it as hard for you to leave
me, as it is now for me to leave you. I am not talking to you now
through the medium of custom, conventionalities, or even mortal
flesh. It is my spirit that addresses your spirit, just as if both had
passed through the grave, and we stood at God's feet, equal—as
we are.*

"My goodness, dear. *Jane Eyre.* We were so young."

Nannie had tears in her eyes, and I gave her a long, warm
hug. Everybody in the living room had stopped to listen.
Gramps broke the silence with a laugh.

"Listen to you, Betsy Connor-Jones! Sarah Bernhardt in the
flesh!"

Shortly after Nannie's "soliloquy," while we were all in the
living room talking about Pat and Laurie's wedding plans,
Catherine surprised everyone (except Jack) by announcing that
"Betsy is going to have a baby brother or sister."

Betsy stopped sweeping and squealed with delight. The
whole family crowded around Cathy and Jack for hugs, kisses
and claps on the back. When everybody sat down again, Laurie
and I squeezed next to Cathy on the sofa and each took one of
her hands.

Nannie asked, "When are you due, dear?"

"The end of August, maybe August 30."

"God bless you, honey," said Grandma McKay.

I stayed on the sofa with Catherine and Laurie for the next
hour, while Betsy helped Mom and Nannie and Grandma McKay
in the kitchen, and the boys watched the end of the
Ravens/Titans playoff game. Shortly before we all got ready to
leave, Catherine put one arm around my waist and one hand on
my belly and whispered in my ear, "Thank you, Abby."

"Why, Cathy?"

"Jack told me a few years ago—on one of his grumpier
days—that he didn't want any more children. I tried hard to
change his mind but . . . well, you know Jack. Then you found
Matt and turned our family inside out; and as much as Jack
wanted to grind his teeth and confirm his belief that you two
were completely stupid, he couldn't help but see how *happy* you
were, and how your happiness grew geometrically after you got
pregnant, and how happy you made the whole family feel—*even*
Grandma and Grandpa McKay, and *especially* Mom and Dad.
So one evening around Thanksgiving, Jack did something he has

never done: he lit a couple of candles in the living room, poured frosted mugs of beer for him and me and said,

"'Sweetheart, I'm sorry if sometimes I'm too serious and grumpy. I want you to be as happy as all the other women in the family. You deserve it, without a doubt. So if *you* still want to have another baby, Cathy, then *I* want to have another baby.' And here we are. Will you thank Matt for me?" she finished, with tears on her cheeks.

On Sunday after Mass and breakfast at Joe's, Matt and I got three blue spruce wreaths trimmed with white pine cones and red sashes at Wheeler's and took them to the cemetery to Grandma and Grandpa Fiorino's grave, Grandma and Grandpa Flynn's, and Uncle Vinny, Uncle Patsy, Uncle Sal and Aunt Connie's. It was difficult to find Grandma and Grandpa Flynn's grave because it is marked by a flat stone in the old German/Irish section of Holy Sepulchre, and every stone in that section was covered with snow.

Then we bought a coconut cream pie at Mangrums and brought it to Matt and Mama's. They both were doing very well. Mama was in her usual great spirits, including cracking jokes about her "grouchy old patient"; and Matt's father had been "buckling down" and exercising faithfully, both with his physical therapist and on his own time. It was remarkable how well he was getting around with only his wooden cane. He had, as he said, "canned the tin walker."

Claire called on my cell phone while we were having coffee with Matt and Mama and invited us to come over for pizza and wings and watch the Steelers against San Diego in the playoffs.

"Hang on a second, Claire; let me ask Matt."

I put the phone down and said quietly to Matt, "Claire wants us to come over for pizza and the football game. I'd like to go and see the kids, but I need a rest first. How about I tell Claire five o'clock? That will give us two hours at home so you can take care of Maggie and Jock and I can have some nursery and nap time."

"That's a good plan, pretty girl."

When we got home, I took *Jane Eyre* to the nursery, and Matt brewed me a mug of Constant Comment tea. Mrs. Reed had just given Jane the letter from her uncle—which she had kept from Jane for three years—but Jane forgave her: for the letter, for treating her cruelly and sending her away, for *everything*. And then Mrs. Reed died, and I fell asleep. Matt brought *Pooh* and

Piglet from our bed and covered me in the chair, but Mary Elizabeth woke me a few minutes later with the hiccups, so I asked Matt to help me in to bed. However, as soon as I lay on my left side—which had become my comfortable side—and tucked a pillow between my legs, I felt *way* more sensual than sleepy. When Matt retrieved the quilt from the nursery to cover me again, I grasped his right hand and gave him my "I want to play" grin.

"Old guy, I wouldn't mind very much if you took off all of my stretchy clothes and pretended that we were alone under a blue sky surrounded by sand dunes."

He made love to me gently, slowly, considerate of Mary Elizabeth, but I was immediately on fire. With Matt *and* my baby moving inside me, my mind and my body melted in flames. Matt said I made new noises, kicked his back with my heels and pulled on his ears, but I was aware of nothing until he woke me at four-thirty and said it was time to get dressed for Claire and Matt's.

"*Mmm* . . . old guy, what did I *do*? I was crazy on fire and then I wiped out."

Matt made his "you are my whole world" face—my favorite—brushed my damp hair from my forehead and kissed the tears on my cheeks.

"I tried to play nice, but you and our little girl were both *wild*. When we visit Dr. Hansen on Friday, I'm going to ask him if that's normal or if you are some kind of sexual superwoman."

"Matt . . . my dune boy, I hope you're still keeping count. Whatever we just did, I want to do it again as many times as we can before Mary Elizabeth is born. You *make* me wild."

I had a lovely evening reading and coloring with Claire and the kids while the Matts watched Pittsburgh beat the Chargers, but my mind kept drifting back to our bed in the afternoon.

Some time in the middle of the night—maybe the second time I got up to pee—I felt the same urge for Matt. He was sleeping soundly, but I played with him and straddled him and eased him inside me. *Who are you?* I thought, just before I came and crashed. *You are not the nice girl I grew up with.* When I woke up the next time to go to the bathroom, I was still straddling Matt with my face on his chest. *Abigail Elizabeth, you are a wild creature*, I mused as I waddled from the bathroom and rolled back into bed. I curled on my left side with my head on Matt's shoulder and his legs between mine. I fell asleep wondering if he would remember in the morning.

I was slow to wake up, lying on my back, slow to become aware of the daylight. First I felt Jock stretched across my ankles; then Maggie licking my right ear; then I opened my eyes and gazed up into Matt's. He was twirling my hair around my left ear and kissing my nose; the look in his eyes was one I didn't recognize. Then I remembered the middle of the night and smiled.

"Morning, old guy. I love you. What time is it?"

"Eight-thirty. Happy maternity leave, beauty. How did you sleep?" He still had that look.

"*Mmm* . . . I had a *great* night, sweetie. Our baby girl was quiet from the middle of the night until morning. How about you?"

"I had this dream—but it felt so *real*. We were making love on the top of a dune, but it was night. There was only moonlight. Then I rolled off the top and all the way down to a hollow at the bottom, and you rolled down on top of me with cries and a crash and a cloud of cool sand. Then the moonlight was gone and it was black." Matt laughed. "I actually looked for sand in the bed this morning when I woke up."

"I can't believe you didn't wake up last *night*, old guy, with all those fireworks."

"Well, I was way down in the hollow, and it was black, and you covered me like a blanket."

"Was I heavy, Matt?"

"I don't remember that; I don't remember if you were pregnant. But you were moving all over me. I hope you had a good time in the dream." He smiled.

"I did, love, but it wasn't in your dream. It was right here in this bed. You have to add one to your count: I woke up with an urge I couldn't fight—I didn't *want* to—in the middle of the night, so I climbed on top of you. I'm amazed you didn't wake up, but"—I brushed Matt's soft penis—my best friend down here sleepwalked just fine."

It didn't take me long to find my new rhythm. Matt tried to keep at least two mornings a week free from meetings, and on those days we usually went to Kitty's for breakfast. Then Matt drove me home and went to his office. On the other days, I was always up by nine and in the nursery by ten. I kept Nannie's

Union Jack in the nursery to cover myself in the rocker. I generally spent an hour or so reading to Mary Elizabeth and napping. Jane was back at Thornfield, after spending a month at Mrs. Reed's house assisting her daughters after she died. Jane was saddened by the talk of Mr. Rochester's expected marriage to Miss Ingram for she knew she would have to advertise for a new situation and leave the Thornfield she loved.

The rest of the morning each day, and through lunch, I called the special girls in my life: Mom, Emma, Laurie, Claire, Margie, Diane, Mama, Margo, Nannie, Catherine and Grandma Mary. I always saved Mary Kay for Saturday morning. I savored all of the love in every conversation. It was still unbelievable that fourteen months ago I had no sisters except for Mary Kay, and I didn't know any women who were either getting married or having babies. Since then, my world had been filled with babies, weddings and sisters-of-the-heart.

Nannie, Emma and Margie all said they would come to town as soon as my little girl was born. Emma said that she, Danny and Sarah were "great. Sarah is drinking as much milk as I can make, Abby, and she looks around and smiles all the time. Danny and I are so excited about seeing our little girls together. We'll be on our way as soon as you go into labor."

Margo was starting a new childbirth class on Wednesday with eight women. "This has never happened to me before, Abby, but all the women in this class already have at least one baby, so it won't be as stimulating as your class with so many new mothers. Please ask Matt to call when your baby girl is born. I want to debrief you and maybe pick up a happy story for my class."

Margie said Joe's dad was completely over his concussion, and his broken arm was healing nicely. "Mrs. Steger has had enough of Jerry just hanging around. Missy is also fine, and Evelyn gave me a present to bring for your baby girl when we come to visit."

About every other afternoon, depending on the weather, I ventured out in my Taurus to visit, run errands and shop. When I was at Mom's, we usually called Catherine and Laurie to see how the first trimester and wedding plans were going. Mom and I talked and laughed as we each took a broom and swept our way around the house. Mama and I usually talked in the kitchen while we made sauce or meatballs or cookies: cutouts, oatmeal chocolate chip or peanut butter. Old Matt was proud of his rehab progress and determined "to be dancing a jig by St. Patrick's Day."

I tried to be home every afternoon before it got dark at five o'clock. Matt did the same thing, and we always sat down to supper or went to Phil Green's by five-thirty. Except for wanting a nap every hour of the day and waddling in first gear everywhere, I felt wonderful. Between the rocker and the sweeping, my back hardly bothered me. The Braxton Hicks contractions came harder and more often, but they went away just as quickly when I changed positions.

My baby girl's constant pushing down and out didn't hurt as much as it made me smile. Friends, family and even total strangers asked me about the smiles almost every day. I told them all the simple truth. "I'm happy being pregnant." And every time I said that I thought, *I know I'm going to be infinitely happier when Mary Elizabeth is born, but it's hard to believe that's possible.*

On my second day of leave, Matt came home in the late morning—quietly to surprise me—found me sleeping in the rocking chair and lovingly brushed my hair. As I slowly became aware of his hands and the brush, I felt liquid warmth—urgent and breathtaking pleasure—flowing into my limbs and waking my senses. I reached up and stroked Matt's hands in my hair.

"Old guy," I whispered, "take me to bed. If you *ever*, any *time*, any *day*, *forever*, want to light my mind and my body on fire, play with my hair like that."

Matt and I had a delightful visit with Dr. Hansen on January 16.

"Thirty-six weeks, Abby, Matt—the home stretch. Your numbers are great: blood pressure 122/79, pulse, your baby's heart rate, your weight. You have gained one pound in the last two weeks, and twenty-four during your pregnancy. Your baby girl weighs about six pounds and is about eighteen inches long. Her head is down and is dropping further into your pelvis every day: 'lightening'—as I'm sure Margo explained to you. How are you feeling?"

"Wonderful, Dr. Bob! With my baby girl dropping down, there's a little more pain and a lot more peeing. Warm baths help, and I also lie flat on my back in bed and pedal with my feet in the air. And I don't have as much heartburn, and breathing is easier. Eating, too. And between my rocking chair and sweeping around the house, my back has been *way* better. I feel good most of the time although I *do* fall asleep fast."

"Well, you haven't lost any of your pregnancy 'glow.' Your belly looks especially beautiful. Are you having any skin problems or itching?"

"Not much. My old guy here massages lotion on my belly every morning and plays with Mary Elizabeth while he's doing it."

"How about contractions? Are the Braxton Hicks picking up?"

"They come and go quickly—one or two an hour, but not even every hour. Usually all I need to do is change my position or have a glass of water."

"That sounds about right. When your contractions start to come four or five an hour and last more than a minute, then you'll know they're the real thing. That could happen any time, but it also might not happen for two more weeks. Are you talking to your baby?"

"All the time, Dr. Bob: when I'm waddling around the house, taking a bath, in the car, eating, and especially in the nursery when I sit in the rocker and read to her from *Jane Eyre*."

"*Jane Eyre*—*great* choice, great role model for a young girl. When my wife was pregnant with our older son, I used to sit with her in our family room—sometimes while she was taking a nap—and read to my baby son from *The Boys of Summer* by Roger Kahn, about the Brooklyn Dodgers of the 1950s."

Matt smiled and nodded. "The best baseball book *ever* written. *I* have one question, Dr. Bob. Will Abby keep ravishing my body, even when I'm *asleep*, all the way up to the delivery room?"

Dr. Hansen laughed so hard I thought he would fall off his stool.

"Matt, that's not a complaint I hear very often from couples near the end of the third trimester. The first and most immutable law of obstetrics that we memorized in med school was: *Whatever mommy wants, mommy gets.* So my prescription remains the same, Abby—*go* for it."

It was my turn to laugh, and tease. "I can't help it, Dr. Bob. Matt lights me on fire. Do you know that he even brushes my hair and plays with it while I'm sleeping? And then he wonders why I can't keep my hands off him."

"My *dune* couple," Dr. Hansen laughed again. "I should retire after your baby is born—who could ever top *you* two? If you have no other *serious* problems, I'll see you next week."

Mary Kay called at the usual time on Saturday, and we talked for almost two hours. I told her about my first week on maternity leave, and we caught up on all the family news. She and Will were back to one hundred percent after their colds, and she was still excited from the NATO reception for the Bushes and Cheneys the evening before.

"Abby gal, the entire day, from the embassy luncheon through the evening reception, was not only spectacular, but also sad. In addition to President and Mrs. Bush and Vice President and Mrs. Cheney, and Condi Rice and Bob Gates, the NATO Great Hall was filled with presidents, prime ministers and generals: Angela Merkel and her husband; Gordon Brown; Nicholas Sarkozy, who is *very* handsome, and his beautiful wife; Mr. Van Rompuy of Belgium, whom I have met many times; NATO Secretary General Scheffer of the Netherlands; Silvio Berlusconi; Chairman Putin and his wife; General Craddock, the Supreme Allied Commander; and lots more important people I can't remember.

"Will said the entire military contingent, 'from the top brass all the way down to the sergeants,' is grim about their new commander-in-chief, who has the reputation of being very anti-military. There are hints of American budget and staff cuts at NATO which could affect both Will *and* me.

"I'm sorry I can't be there when your baby girl is born, Abby. Best friends should *be* there at times like those. You know I'll be thinking of you every minute and praying for an easy delivery and a healthy baby."

"It's okay, sister. You're always with me in spirit. We'll make up for it when you get home."

After I got off the phone, Matt and I had Italian wedding soup and tuna salad for lunch, and then I settled into the nursery with *Jane Eyre* and Maggie and Jock at my feet. Jane's "month of courtship had wasted," and her "bridal day" had come. "But," I whispered to Mary Elizabeth, "the happiest day of Jane's life is going to become the saddest. I hope you never lose a love, my little girl."

When Matt came upstairs and saw me asleep in the chair—before he brushed my hair to wake me up—with Maggie and Jock sleeping with their heads on my thick red socks, he snapped

469

a few pictures, which he showed me later when we went to Phil Green's for supper.

"I should have taken a video too, beauty, because you were making some *sweet* sounds, and even the doggies were snoring. This Norman Rockwell scene could be a lovely poem or sketch."

"I'll start working on it, old guy, right after I finish my soon-to-be-famous crib drawing."

41

My second week of leave and thirty-seventh week of pregnancy was quiet and buried in snow. Eighteen inches fell from late Sunday night through dawn on Monday. Ed came around seven o'clock to plow our driveway and woke all of us up. I watched from the front window as Matt walked Maggie and Jock through the huge ruts in the street.

It's January 19, I thought, *and there they are: my husband, whom I love more than my life, and my doggies, knee-deep in snow; and eighteen days to go until my baby girl is born. Why am I the luckiest woman I know? God and Mary and St. Patrick,* I prayed, *please don't let this end.*

Matt had a luncheon appointment, but I never left the house. The doggies and I sipped tea in the nursery and napped and read all day. On her wedding day, Jane discovered to her horror that Mr. Rochester had a wife secretly locked up at Thornfield. She left the next morning, alone and desolate, with no friends or family and no place to go.

Mary Elizabeth seemed to sense both the sadness of the story and the silence of deep winter. She slept when I slept, and she started to push and poke every time I got up and walked around the house, especially when I was sweeping.

My first venture into the snow was on Wednesday afternoon, when I picked up Mama and took her grocery shopping. I'm sure we were the most amusing pair in Mangrums: a very old woman and a very pregnant girl, each with one hand on the same shopping cart, shuffling down the aisles. Mama was delighted to be out of the house.

"I need to get away from my 'rehab guy' every few days," she said, rolling her eyes.

Matt and I brought pizza and ice cream to Claire and the kids on Thursday night while Matt III was having parent-teacher conferences at MCC. On Friday morning we woke to six more inches of snow. When Matt took the doggies out for their walk, I decided to fill the tub and soak with *Jane Eyre*. Jane was wandering alone—despondent, miserable, cold, wet—on the bleak moors of northern England.

Suddenly I felt a wiggle or a tickle between my legs—maybe gas or one of those pregnancy leaks I was getting accustomed to—and there it was: my mucous plug, slimy, translucent reddish-brown, floating in my bath. *Yuck!* was my first thought. *It's as gross as Margo said it would be.* But then I laughed. Francine Toscano wrote in her book that for both of her children the mucous plugs looked like "half of a jellyfish with a bad sunburn." They made her smile, she said, because they meant that her cervix was opening up and her babies would be coming in a couple of weeks. I smiled, too. *No need to call Dr. Hansen,* I thought. *I'll be seeing him at four o'clock today.*

When Matt came in with our snow-coated Scotties, I told him. He hugged me for a long time in the living room and then shuffled behind me, with both hands on my butt, up to bed and made love to me.

"Does it feel any different inside me, old guy?"

"Not one bit, pretty girl. It's *heaven* inside you. It has been heaven since the first time. The only difference is that I can't lift your 'tail' as high off the bed, and when you come you whisper more than cry out."

"What do I say?"

"You say you love me. You say *God* loves me. And you pray for our little girl."

When we walked into Dr. Hansen's office at four, I whispered to Matt, "I want to play with Dr. Bob for a few minutes, so I'm not going to tell him about the plug right away."

As he always had since our first visit, Dr. Hansen stepped in to the examining room with a giant grin on his face.

"Abby, Matt, how are my dune parents doing in week thirty-seven? Abby, you have a Mona Lisa smile, which makes me believe you and Matt made out in the car on the way here. And now you're blushing, so I'm guessing I'm right. Your numbers are *great*, as they have been since you first came in last June. Your baby girl is probably a little bit over six pounds and about nineteen inches long. You weigh 154, exactly what you weighed last week. Any changes for you? Pains? Contractions? Problems?"

"Not really, Dr. Bob. The Braxton Hicks contractions come and go quickly two or three times an hour, and"—I couldn't resist—"we didn't make out in the car; we made out in bed before we left the house."

"Well, let me take a look," he said, laughing, "and see if there's still any smoke." He poked and peeked around with his little flashlight, and glanced up at me once from between my thighs and caught my eye with his own amused twinkle.

"Miss Abigail, you seem to have lost something. Where did you find it?"

"In the bathtub this morning, Dr. Bob," I grinned.

"So you have been *testing* me?"

"Not really, Dr. Bob; just playing with you a little."

"Well, good for you. That explains the Mona Lisa smile. You are two centimeters dilated. It is still most likely that your baby girl will arrive on schedule in two weeks, but that could change tomorrow—as you know. Unless your water breaks or you start having longer contractions every five minutes, I'll see you next Friday. But call me immediately if you're worried about anything or if something just doesn't feel right."

We celebrated week thirty-seven at Phil Green's, the same as we had celebrated every visit to Dr. Hansen. I could barely fit into our booth now, but I was very hungry. I devoured a ham-and-Swiss burger, curly fries and a peanut butter sundae—and I didn't share with Matt.

"Beauty, it looks as if you mean to move the needle on Dr. Hansen's scale next week."

"Well, this has been a great week, right? I don't want Dr. Bob to think I'm always good."

"Are you kidding? He knows you're a mischievous *minx*, especially after today."

Emma called just after we returned home from supper. She and Danny and Sarah were great.

"My little girl will be seven weeks old tomorrow, Abby, and we're having a blast. Sarah loves our voices, and she smiles and turns her head and looks around the room when she hears us. She is nursing well and weighs almost eleven pounds. I can't *wait* for you to see her, and for Sarah to see your baby. I just know they're going to be best friends, even if Mary Elizabeth will officially be Sarah's aunt."

That made me laugh because of how much Matt and I had messed up the family flow chart.

"I'm sure you're right, Em, whether our little girls consider themselves cousins, sisters, friends or aunt and niece. Give Danny a hug for me. Soon, Em, see you soon. We love you."

Mary Kay and I didn't talk as long as usual on Saturday morning. They had freezing rain in Brussels, and she and Will planned to watch old movies and bake cookies all day.

"Will and I each picked two. He picked *The Hunt for Red October* and *Field of Dreams*; and I picked *The Mask of Zorro* and *Moonstruck*."

She was excited when I told her about my plug and doctor visit.

"Sister, you're so *close*. I still can't believe everything happened so *fast* for you. Your doctor sounds like a dream; maybe I can start seeing him when I get home. When *my* time comes to be pregnant, God willing, you know I'm going to be looking to you for the answers to every one of my questions. Like . . . how do you feel carrying around 154 pounds?"

"Slow and clumsy," I laughed, "but *so* happy, MK. For me, being pregnant is better than anything I read in any book and better than everything everybody told me, including Mom. The little things—the leaks, the cramps, the contractions and the backache—are *so* little that I usually don't even notice them. Matt and I are still making love every day. I can't tell my *mom* things like that because she would make her famous 'appalled Irish mother' face and say, 'Abigail, really, enough is enough, don't you think?' So *you* get to be the lucky girl who hears all."

"Sister, you are amazing, my hero. If I knew you were going to go and get yourself pregnant so fast, I would have asked for a stateside assignment."

"No way, MK. You and Will needed to be together. Look how *happy* you are. And you and I can share our *future* babies, God willing."

"*Future* babies?"—I could hear the smile on her face—"what does Matt think about that?"

"We haven't talked about it exactly, but I have discovered over the past fourteen months that, almost all of the time, Matt and I think the same. I expect I'll ask him soon after Mary Elizabeth is born. Hey, enjoy your movies. Remember when we went to see *Moonstruck* at the Prudential Center? Was it in our sophomore year?"

"I think it was around Valentine's Day in our freshman year. Wasn't that when we met those guys from B.C., and you ended up dating one of them for a few months?"

"Warren Reilly III, whose father was a rich publisher, and who dumped me for the society girl from Wellesley. I wonder if they stayed together? MK, I'm really tired all of a sudden, so before I fall asleep holding the phone—which I did with Mom last week—I'll say goodbye. Love you."

"Love you too, Abby gal. I'll call you next week . . . unless you call first."

During the last two weeks of my pregnancy, all the days were almost the same. Except for going to Mass on Sunday and to Phil Green's every other night for supper, I didn't leave the house. The last time I drove myself—the week before when I took Mama shopping—I actually dozed off for a few seconds at a traffic light.

As soon as I got home and put my Taurus in the garage, I thought, *That's it. The next time I drive I'll have my baby girl in her car seat in the back.* I also didn't do much *in* the house. Matt did everything: he walked the dogs; he shoveled the front steps; he got the mail; he made coffee and tea; he did all the shopping, cooking and cleaning; he massaged one bottle of lotion after another on my enormous belly; and he made love to me whenever I cried.

I spent most of my time when I wasn't falling asleep checking and counting: checking the nursery, every drawer and shelf; counting the newborn diapers and onesies; opening and closing my hospital bag; counting the stack of Matt's jockey shorts that I intended to wear over the pads I would need for my postpartum bleeding and leaking; and my stack of thick, fuzzy red socks; and my drawer full of wool breast pads (which Margo said were better than disposables).

Sometimes I laughed at what I was doing—over and over— and sometimes I heard Francine Toscano remind me from her book, as *she* laughed, "Whatever you're doing, whatever you *need* to do—during the last week to ten days—whatever your personal checklist or countdown is to baby day, it's okay; it's all good. You're pregnant, your baby is almost here, and it's all good. I only have one thing to add: whatever you're doing— whether you're counting or checking—talk to your baby about it. Count your newborn diapers out loud with your little girl.

475

Describe to your baby boy what's in your hospital bag. Not only will it make your routine more fun, but your baby will also hear you and be even more anxious to see the face that goes with the loving voice."

I needed an extra pillow behind my back wherever I sat down—or sometimes I just clenched my fists behind my back—to relieve the discomfort, especially on my left side. But no matter how much discomfort, no matter the cramps and contractions, no matter my constant urge to pee, whenever I either sat down or simply stopped moving, I wanted to put my head down and sleep.

I read to Mary Elizabeth for as long as I could stay awake in the rocker. Jane had been rescued from near death on the moors and nursed back to health by St. John Rivers and his two sisters. She was comfortable and moderately content teaching "only poor girls—cottagers' children—at the best, farmers' daughters" in her small "village-school," but she reflected and wondered about Mr. Rochester every day.

About half of my days in the rocker I awoke to Matt brushing my hair, which he did more than once every day, even when I was awake, often after breakfast or lunch. If I was awake when he started, I invariably fell asleep *while* Matt brushed my hair. And so did our little girl. Those moments are some of the sweetest memories of my pregnancy.

Mom came over for lunch on Tuesday and Thursday in my thirty-eighth week. Actually, she *brought* lunch: mulligan stew on Tuesday and broccoli-and-cheese soup on Thursday. We sat at the dining room table, with Maggie and Jock between our feet—much to Mom's chagrin—and we talked and remembered. After our soup on Thursday, Mom took both my hands on the table.

"Abigail, when I was carrying you, near the end, my hips were *so* sore that I kind of walked crooked to ease the pain, and that threw off my balance. Your father had to stay with me almost everywhere in the house so I didn't fall down. Your due date was May 9, but my water broke on May 4, in the middle of a beautiful sunny afternoon. We went to Highland right away, but you had your own ideas, as usual, and you didn't come out until seven the next morning. You almost tiptoed out; you were quieter than either Jack or Patrick. You took to my nipples faster than the boys, and you liked to cuddle more. But that was the last time that you were less trouble to your father and me."

Mom reached across the table and stroked my cheek and brushed her fingers through my hair.

"You always knew how to spark my wick and—unlike your brothers—you were never afraid of your father. Also, unlike your brother Jack, you never got spanked. Dad always said that you had such a twinkle in your eyes—he called you his 'leprechaun lass'—that it was impossible to scold you. And you *knew* it; you knew you had him wrapped around your little finger. Which is undoubtedly how you bewitched Matthew. God and Mary and St. Patrick, my beautiful Abigail, I wish, I hope, I pray that your little girl will be just like you. You are the loveliest daughter that God could *ever* give a mother."

We both were crying, but Mom was quicker with her napkin and she wiped my eyes and then her own. I could hardly move, so Mom cleared the table and poured coffee for both of us. After a few sips, I smiled and laid my head on the table. Mom patted my cheek and laughed.

"Sweetie, I'm taking you up to bed. I'll clean up the kitchen before I leave. Call me tomorrow night and let me know how your visit went with Dr. Hansen. Come on, baby, take my arm."

I didn't wake up until Matt came home around four o'clock and curled up next to me in bed.

"*Mmm* . . . old guy, what time is it?"

"Four o'clock. Your mom called me at two and said she'd put you to bed, and I got out of the office as fast as I could. How do you feel?"

"Okay. The usual . . . fat, happy, hungry. *Hot*, too. Play with me before we get out of bed."

We made love, and then Matt wrapped me in *Pooh* and *Piglet* and I fell asleep instantlywhile he fed and walked Maggie and Jock.

We went to Phil Green's through a snow squall for cheeseburgers and black cherry ice cream, then back home where we camped on the sofa and watched *The Americanization of Emily*. With my head in Matt's lap and the doggies warming my feet, I didn't last very long, but Matt watched about half of the movie before he took all of us up to bed.

The next morning I had more energy than I'd felt the entire week. I even threw on leggings, boots and the Browns bench warmer, and waddled around our circle with Matt and the doggies. And I was able to stay awake and read longer in the rocking chair.

St. John learned from "one Mr. Briggs, a solicitor," of Jane's real identity and history, and that her Uncle John had died in Madeira and left Jane "all his property" in the sum of 20,000 pounds. After Jane also learned that she and St. John and his two sisters were cousins, she was so glad to suddenly have "relations . . . fraternal and sisterly love," that she decided immediately to split her new-found fortune into four equal parts for herself and her cousins.

I tickled my belly where Mary Elizabeth was poking the most, and whispered, "Little girl, *you* would do that, wouldn't you? Family comes *way* ahead of fortune. You are going to be luckier than Jane; you'll have beautiful and loving families around you from your very first day."

I felt so bouncy—"Tiggerish," I told Matt—and excited about my thirty-eighth week that I suggested we stop to visit Mama and Old Matt on the way to Dr. Hansen's office. When we got there, we were surprised and delighted to see Debbie and Alicia, who was almost six months old. She was lying on her lavender blanket in the middle of the living room, rolling over, chattering away and playing with a stuffed pink hippo. Mama especially enjoyed listening to Alicia, and she responded in Italian to her baby talk. It was the latest of a thousand Kodak moments I had experienced since I became a part of Matt's family.

Dr. Hansen was even more exuberant than usual when he bounded in to the examining room.

"Abby, Matt, is it countdown-to-baby time? Your lab numbers are as good as ever. You have gained one more pound since last week, and twenty-five for your pregnancy. Let's take a look," he said as he took his flashlight out of his white coat pocket.

"Your little girl is *busy* down here. I think she's almost ready for her grand entrance. Your cervix is about 40 percent effaced and three centimeters dilated. I am still betting on your due date. How are you feeling—any big changes since last Friday?"

"Not really, Dr. Bob. More trips to the bathroom, of course, and some diarrhea. More leaking everywhere, especially the colostrum from these giant boobs. More quick contractions, but none of them last a minute. Not enough problems to dampen my life of Riley," I smiled.

Dr. Hansen laughed as he pocketed his thin flashlight and wheeled his chair from between my thighs to his desk.

"Some pregnant women get *crazy* about this, but I'm pretty sure *you* won't. Start timing your contractions, or maybe every second or third one. When you have at least two in a row that last longer than a minute, start timing them *all*. In general, when your contractions start coming every five minutes and lasting longer than a minute, for an hour, it's time to call me and go to Highland. But if that doesn't happen and your water doesn't break, I'll see you next Friday, your due date."

"Thanks, Dr. Bob. Is there anything special or different I should be doing?"

"Nope. You're the one who will know best now. Sleep when you can, eat when you can, make love when you want to, talk with your baby. Savor your feelings and sensations. Slow down the hours and minutes and listen to your baby."

At Phil Green's, I had a grilled chicken breast sandwich and a cup of tomato basil ravioli soup, while Matt had Italian sausage and mozzarella sticks. I was actually able to stay awake later and watch the rest of *Emily* with Matt; I call it the "James Garner effect." It made me think of Nannie and Grandpa Dolan during their days together after D-Day. *How would you have coped with the love of your life fighting at the front?* I wondered and I made a mental note to ask Nannie the next time I saw her.

On Saturday morning, I was able to read in the nursery for almost two hours before Mary Kay called at eleven o'clock my time. Jane was excited to "*clean down* Moor House from chamber to cellar" in preparation for the arrival of St. John's sisters, her beloved cousins, Diana and Mary. St. John was pressing Jane to "learn Hindostanee" as a prelude to urging her to accompany him as his missionary wife to India, but Jane was sad in spite of the company of her cousins. She had not "forgotten Mr. Rochester . . . The craving to know what had become of him followed me everywhere; when I was at Morton, I re-entered my cottage every evening to think of that; and now at Moor House, I sought my bedroom each night to brood over it."

Mary Kay and I talked mostly about my last week of what she called "pregnanthood." She made me promise to write some of it down—my feelings, sensations, good days and bad days— "so I will have a primer when *my* 'pregnanthood' comes." It was quiet at NATO, "tentative, Abby gal, until we know who Obama intends to appoint as the new Supreme Allied Commander. Both the military and civilian staff have great regard and respect for General Craddock. We hear that Biden will be coming at the end of February. Don't forget, sister, *promise* . . . whatever time of day or night, have Matt call me when you go to the hospital. I told Mom I'd let her know, and she can be my eyes and ears on the ground at Highland. Love you, Abby."

"I promise. Love you, sister."

Even though everybody from Dr. Hansen to Margo to Mom told me that my due date was just a target—only five percent of babies are born on their due date—I was sure my baby girl would be born at the end of the week. I was almost too happy to remember what I should be doing next, so when I wasn't reading in the rocker, I sometimes grabbed my broom and sang and danced around the house. Mom said I had a screw loose. She *never* spent the last week of *any* of her pregnancies dancing with a broom.

But not even Mom could dampen my spirits. I felt like the princess at the end of every Disney movie—except no Disney princess ever had a baby—and whenever I wasn't kissing Matt, which I did any time he was within reach, I imagined with each contraction that I was kissing Prince Charming at the end of our magical waltz at the palace ball.

Matt only took me out three times: to Mass on Sunday and to Phil Green's on Monday and Wednesday. At Phil Green's on Wednesday evening, while I was slurping my chicken noodle soup, I timed two contractions six minutes apart and both lasting longer than a minute. At home I began timing them all. Although most of them lasted longer than a minute, and they were five or six minutes apart, they only continued for fifteen or twenty minutes and then went away completely for half an hour. So I decided to try to sleep on it and not get "crazy" and call Dr. Hansen until at least the next morning.

I slept pretty well that night. I woke up only twice to go to the bathroom, and both times when I got back in bed I curled up next to Matt and touched and played with him—even though he was asleep—until *I* fell asleep. In the morning my contractions followed the same pattern: every five or six minutes, lasting longer than a minute, but only continuing for fifteen or twenty minutes out of each hour. I called Dr. Hansen at eleven o'clock, and he said that if the pattern didn't change, I should come in as scheduled at four o'clock on Friday, "but bring along your hospital bag. You and Matt might be going right to Highland from my office."

I was more keyed up than tired the entire day. I was able to read to Mary Elizabeth for most of the afternoon. *Are you going to hear the end of Jane's story from inside me, little girl, or from your crib?* I wondered. More than six months had passed since Jane had learned of her uncle's death and divided her inheritance among herself, St. John and his sisters. St. John was pressing Jane every day—in truth, browbeating her—to accompany him as his missionary wife to India. Jane agreed to go with him as his equal, his "sister," his assistant, his "curate"—but not as his wife because St. John did not love her and she did not love him. He actually considered love an impediment to his work.

As Jane said in pain and distress, "the very name of love is an apple of discord between us . . . If I were to marry you, you would kill me. You are killing me now." But St. John was relentless, even to the point of preaching damnation for Jane's "lawless and unconsecrated interest" in "going to seek Mr. Rochester." If she followed that path, St. John warned, she would "become a castaway" and have her "part in the lake which burneth with fire and brimstone, which is the second death."

Jane was completely worn down, on the verge of submission, when late one evening with St. John urging her to "decide now," she "heard a voice somewhere cry—'Jane! Jane! Jane!' nothing more. . . . And it was the voice of a human being—a known, loved, well-remembered voice—that of Edward Fairfax Rochester," and Jane knew in her mind and in her heart that she must go and "find out what is become of him." She departed the next afternoon on her journey "to distant Thornfield," only a few hours after St. John left to begin his missionary journey.

Matt made peanut butter sandwiches for supper—on squishy, white Wonder Bread instead of whole wheat—and chocolate milk with Hershey's Syrup, and we had Creamsicles for dessert. Mary Elizabeth was very pushy all through supper, and I had a feeling that my contractions would pick up overnight. From the moment Matt shuffled me from the nursery to the kitchen and for the rest of the evening, he didn't let me take a step without his hands on me.

After supper he walked me down to the family room, and I lay with my head in his lap, with Maggie and Jock at my feet and with a bayberry candle burning. I asked Matt to read from *Jane*

481

Eyre to Mary Elizabeth and me. The last words I remember hearing before I fell asleep were Jane's when she caught sight of Thornfield again: "I saw a blackened ruin. . . . and there was the silence of death about it . . . grim blackness . . . Had life been wrecked, as well as property?"

I didn't remember Matt taking me to bed, taking off my clothes and tucking me under *Pooh* and *Piglet*. When I woke up at two to go to the bathroom, I smiled at the realization that I had slept through his undressing me. From our first night together, almost nothing had been as erotic and sensual as Matt's taking off my clothes. Mary Elizabeth woke me two more times during the night, once from a dream in which Emma and I—both holding our babies—were walking on Durand Beach, near the boulders of my old sketch. It was summer. Amazingly, we saw James Garner in his Navy dress uniform walking towards us. We sat on the boulders, and he stopped to say hello. We introduced ourselves and our little girls, and he said he was Jim Garner (as if anybody wouldn't know!), and he was coming from D-Day and on his way to Australia.

When Matt and the doggies kissed me awake at nine o'clock, my contractions—much to my surprise—were about the same as when I fell asleep on the sofa after supper. I told Matt over breakfast about my dream, and he laughed and said that the "Australia" line was from another famous Garner movie, *Support Your Local Sheriff.*

I laughed, too, because I was dumbfounded.

"Old guy, I've never *seen* that movie. How could I know that line about Australia?"

"*Who* can figure out dreams, beauty? I have that movie on VHS, and that can be the first one we watch next week with our baby girl."

42

After breakfast and for most of the morning, Matt and I timed my contractions out loud—there was no change from the night before—with Beethoven's *Sixth Symphony* on the stereo in the living room. We unpacked, rechecked and repacked my hospital bag four times, smiling all the way. After *two* bowls of Cheerios and an ice cream sandwich for lunch, Mary Elizabeth and I finished *Jane Eyre.* Jane found Mr. Rochester blind and depressed after the horrible fire at Thornfield, but she restored him—resurrected him, in fact—to the man who had been her equal in heart and soul before she had left. They were married and had children, and Mr. Rochester even recovered most of his vision in one eye.

I laid the book lovingly in my lap, closed my eyes, spread all my fingers lightly over my belly and whispered, "Little girl, your daddy and I are going to take good care of you and help you to grow up to be like Jane."

In the car on the way to Dr. Hansen's, my contractions became sharper and faster.

"All of a sudden they're high-definition, Matt. I think Dr. Hansen might be right about going straight to Highland."

And that's exactly what my favorite doctor said with a big smile ten minutes after he wheeled his chair between my thighs and explored with his flashlight.

"Miss Abigail, you are five centimeters dilated. Your last three contractions were each longer than a minute and only about four minutes apart. We'll time a few more, but your active labor is well underway. How would you describe your contractions compared to last week?"

"Sharper, Dr. Bob. Last week I would have said they were dull. Now they have an edge—high-definition, I told Matt in the car on the way here. They're making me catch my breath."

"That's about right. The last two contractions were also longer than a minute and about five minutes apart. I'm surprised your water hasn't broken yet, but it could happen any moment. Do you have towels in the car, Matt?"

"Yes."

"Sit on the towels, Abby, on your way to Highland. Take Maplewood, Matt; Harrison is too bumpy. I'll call ahead so you'll be admitted immediately. Start with your breathing exercises in the car. I will be up to see you at about eight unless I get a call that Mary Elizabeth is in a hurry.

"Don't worry about a thing, Abby. You look great; your cervix looks great; all your numbers are optimal; you haven't gained any more weight, and you are about to lose a *lot*. You and Matt have had a practically perfect pregnancy. When I conduct my next seminar for would-be parents or would-be obstetricians, I'm going to prescribe sand dunes in the spring."

Matt and I were admitted to Highland at five-thirty, and escorted to room 317 on the maternity floor by Louise, our nurse. She showed and explained to us everything at our disposal, from the walls to the drawers to the shelves to the bathroom, which were all full of baby stuff.

"I'll be with you until your baby is born. No question is unimportant, so ask away. I'll get you both dinner in fifteen minutes. Dr. Hansen said he'd be here about eight. In the meantime, we'll chart your contractions, keep an eye on your cervix and practice your breathing. You took Margo's classes," Louise grinned, " so this should be a piece of cake, right?"

The hospital food trays didn't look very appetizing, but I drank all my water, milk and apple juice, and ate my tomato soup and both Matt's and my dishes of orange sherbet. My water broke at eight-fifteen, and Louise finished replacing my bed linens just before Dr. Hansen walked in. My contractions were hurting a lot by then, and they were constant. Matt was spooning me ice chips and wiping the perspiration from my forehead and my temples. Dr. Hansen said I was seven centimeters dilated.

"You're almost in transition labor, Abby. Try to time your breath pattern with the sharpest point of each contraction. There's a rhythm to your contractions—try to feel it. No pushing yet. Let your body—your uterus, your baby—lead the way. You're doing great, and so is Matt. It's all right out of Margo's textbook."

Matt and I thought we'd try to be funny with our breathing: we planned to alternate "boo hoo" with "tee hee." It worked well enough for an hour or so—although I wasn't laughing or smiling much—and distracted me from the sharpest pains. But

Matt's kissing me around my eyes and ears and licking my sweat at the same time, with every second or third contraction, distracted me *way* better. I don't remember a lot of talking. Matt said I didn't yell at him much, although his hands were sore from my squeezing. I do remember Louise's very soothing voice telling me over and over, "You're doing great, sweetie. You're getting really close." I lost all track of time until I heard Dr. Hansen say it was midnight.

"It's now February 7, Abby, and you are eight centimeters dilated. It's transition time, from eight centimeters to ten, the end of your active labor stage. We should see your baby girl within a couple of hours. Your contractions are coming every two and a half to three minutes. You can start pushing, but don't strain; give me a medium push with every other contraction. Try to time your pushes with the peaks of your contractions, just as Margo taught you.

"Give Matt's hands the crushing squeezes for now, and your uterus gentler ones . . . until you are fully dilated. Nice and easy. That's right. Don't think about it too much. Let your body— your uterus, your abdomen, all those muscles—do the work. Keep making those sweet noises. Close your eyes and see how your baby starts and wriggles every time your uterus contracts and you push. Feel the power in your belly when you push."

With my mind completely caught up in my contractions and the constant pressure I felt from my belly down, I wasn't aware of the busyness in the room, and how my body was moving, and what sounds I was making. Matt said I didn't grunt when I pushed—I hummed, but he could not make out any melodies. And he said I rolled a little from left to right and back again with every few contractions. I felt his hands most of the time, and I saw Louise's face some of the time, and heard them both cheering me and comforting me with each contraction, but I totally forgot about Dr. Hansen until he said, "It's one-forty, Abby, and you are ten centimeters dilated. We're there. Mary Elizabeth is ready. Give me a hearty push with your next contraction, then rest for one, and give me a strong push with every other contraction after that."

I remember closing my eyes with my first hearty push, and I could see my baby girl moving toward the light. Two pushes later I opened my eyes and got my first glimpse of the top of Mary Elizabeth's head reflected in the mirror between my thighs. I saw reddish brown hair. My pains were all gone. Matt cradled my head in his left hand and held my hands with his right. He said I started crying as soon as our baby's head appeared and didn't stop until *she* started crying herself.

With each push I saw more: first Mary Elizabeth's head, then her head turning and her shoulders rotating to come out, then her hands and her feet. Then she cried, and Louise wiped her off and suctioned her mouth and her nose. She measured and weighed her, and then laid her on my belly, skin on skin, covered with a striped receiving blanket and wearing her tiny, pink knit hat.

After that I was oblivious of everything except the touch of my baby girl and the touch of my old guy. As exhausted as I was, I couldn't take my eyes off Mary Elizabeth—my *daughter*—and I couldn't wrap my mind around the miracle of my life since I met Matt Flynn. He was stroking my cheek, and I took his hand and placed it on top of mine on the blanket covering our baby girl.

Matt said Louise clamped the umbilical cord and showed him how to cut it. A few minutes later Dr. Hansen asked me to give him one more push, and out wooshed my placenta. My belly felt tingly around my navel, and Louise said it was my uterus getting harder.

"It's just the way it should be, Abby; it cuts off most of the bleeding from where the placenta was attached. You're doing fine."

She cleaned me up and replaced the bed linens, and stepped aside for Dr. Hansen, who laid his hand gently on top of Matt's and mine on our little girl.

"Miss Abigail, you did *so* well, and old Matt wasn't bad either. Your baby girl is beautiful. She is twenty-one inches long and weighs seven pounds, ten ounces. Her hair is reddish brown, and she has a *lot* of it. In keeping with your 'practically perfect' pregnancy, today is February 7, and Mary Elizabeth was born at 2:07 a.m."

I laughed, and cried, and squeezed his hand.

"Thank you *so much*, Dr. Bob . . . from the beginning, from *way* back, for all the smiles and lollipops, from the bottom of my heart! Matt and I think you're the *best* there is!"

"You're very welcome, Abby, Matt. Believe me, it has been my pleasure. I have jotted down so many notes after all of your visits that I could almost write a book about your 'dune baby.' I will now turn you over to Louise and go home and go to bed.

She will keep a close watch on you and Mary Elizabeth for the rest of the night and let me know if there are any difficulties. I don't anticipate a single one. I would like you to bring your baby girl in to my office next Friday, at our usual time, for her first well-baby visit—unless you need me before then. Good night."

After Dr. Hansen left, Louise delicately lifted Mary Elizabeth from my belly to my chest and turned her head so her lips touched my right nipple.

"Let's see what she does, Abby. I know you're exhausted, and you should close your eyes and sleep—Matt and I will take good care of Mary Elizabeth—but it's really beneficial for a number of reasons, as I'm sure you know from Margo's class, for a new baby to start nursing as soon as possible. It helps your milk come in faster; it gives your little girl protection against infectious diseases; it helps you and Mary Elizabeth bond together; it stimulates greater production of oxytocin, which gets your uterus back to normal and shuts down your bleeding; and last but not least," Louise grinned, "it helps you lose weight."

I felt Mary Elizabeth touching my nipple with her lips, then licking a little around the nipple. Then her whole mouth was over my nipple, and I felt her sucking. And then I was gone. Matt said Louise switched Mary Elizabeth from my right breast to my left, and back and forth a few times—and helped *him* do it, too—and our baby licked and sucked on and off, for no more than a minute at a time, on both sides, until *she* fell asleep, too. Matt and Louise bundled her up and laid her in her Plexiglas sleeping tray on her maternity cart.

Louise woke me up at five, helped me to the bathroom, and then brought Mary Elizabeth for me to hold and nurse. Matt was sleeping in the recliner next to the bed.

"She was starting to catch on well, Abby, when you fell asleep, and she seems to have the right idea now. You two will get better at this each time. I'm done for the day; Kelsey takes over for me at five-thirty. How do you feel?"

"Okay. A little sore, very tired . . . but too happy to care."

"You go back to sleep now. I'll bundle your baby girl up, and I'll tell Kelsey to wake you at eight for your next nursing session, and for breakfast for you and Matt, too. Then you'll probably want Matt to help you take a shower. After that, you'll undoubtedly be bombarded with visitors. Make sure that you and Matt don't hesitate to kick them out when you get tired. You have been a champion all night, Abby. Your little girl is lucky to have you for her mother."

"Thank you, Louise, for everything you've done. You're the best! Will I see you later?"

"I'll be back in at six this evening, so you'll have me for the overnight shift. If you and Mary Elizabeth don't have any problems, they will discharge you at ten o'clock tomorrow morning. I know Margo would say this if she were here: try to slow this day down and enjoy each moment."

When Kelsey woke me at eight, Matt was already awake, with our little girl in his arms in the chair, singing "Take Me Out to the Ball Game." Kelsey walked me to the bathroom and helped me wash my face, and she brushed my hair, which was a *wonderful* sensation. And I felt her untie Nannie's ribbon which I forgot I had asked Matt to tie in my hair before we went to Dr. Hansen's.

"Abby, this red, white and blue ribbon that was in your hair— do you want me to put it back?"

"That's a very special ribbon, Kelsey. I forgot that Matt tied it in my hair. If you can find me a safety pin, I'll pin it inside the sleeve of my gown, thanks."

Then I sat up high in bed, and Matt sat next to me holding Mary Elizabeth between my breasts; and with our four big hands and some guidance from Kelsey, we grown-ups managed to move our tiny baby back and forth from nipple to nipple for about fifteen minutes, until she closed her eyes and stopped sucking. Kelsey helped me bundled her up "right and tight," and I rocked my baby girl against my chest while Kelsey pulled the breakfast menu out of her white apron pocket and informed us we could choose whatever we wanted. "*Two* of everything, if you want. It's the new-mommy-and-daddy, special, maternity ward breakfast."

Matt had a ham and Swiss omelet with Italian toast, hash browns, a dish of peaches and a piece of apple pie with vanilla ice cream. I had eggs Benedict on an English muffin, sourdough toast, a plate of crispy bacon, home fries, a dish of lemon ice and a cheese Danish. Matt and I shared and savored everything, slowly, while Kelsey gave Mary Elizabeth her first sponge bath, with a pastel blue Tinker Bell washcloth.

Was it the *best* breakfast of my life? Maybe . . . but I had already enjoyed a *hundred* "best" breakfasts with Matt. The same was true of the glorious shower we gave each other: one of our hundred "best ever." We dried each other off and helped each other into our hospital gowns and robes with only five minutes to spare before my whole family came through the door.

Mom and Dad, Pat and Laurie, Cathy, Jack and Betsy came at the stroke of ten. After that, the day was a kaleidoscope of family, friends, balloons, tears, flowers, photographs, laughter, hugs and stuffed animals. Matt—God bless him—unobtrusively kept a running list of who came and brought what, which I delighted in reading again and again for the next week.

We ended up leaving most of the flowers at the hospital, and the kids—little Matthew, Emily, Betsy, Amy and Billy—took home all of the balloons. Matt and I brought home all the stuffed animals. The first was from Betsy—a pink horse with a white mane and white hooves.

My family stayed for almost an hour. Mom said she called Grandma and Grandpa McKay and Nannie and Grandpa Dolan, who all sent love and prayers. Grandma Mary said she and Grandpa would come with Mom and Dad to our house "on Tuesday or Wednesday." Gramps promised he and Nannie would drive to Rochester on Thursday and stay through the weekend. As the family left, Mom gave me and my baby kisses and whispered she'd be back after dinner "by myself."

Mama and Old Matt, Claire, Matt and the kids came in shortly after Mom left.

Claire said, "We saw your mom and dad and all the family getting off the elevator."

Little Matthew and Emily brought a sky blue, stuffed, wind-up donkey with pink feet and ears, which played "Rock-a-Bye Baby" and walked and cocked its head. The kids both reached out to touch Mary Elizabeth's tiny fingers, but they were afraid to get any closer. Claire said Emma had called. She and Danny had left Cambridge at nine and should arrive at the hospital around four.

Tom and Diane and Katy and Trent came around lunchtime. So did Kitty, with a homemade chocolate layer cake that all of our visitors enjoyed for the remainder of the afternoon. I lost all track of time between lunch and dinner. Everyone wanted to hold my baby—*my* baby—and take photos. Mary Elizabeth had her eyes closed most of the time, but it was easy for *me* to smile. *I think I'm going to smile for the rest of my life*, I thought.

Mrs. Galvin brought a giant present from Mary Kay. "My daughter said that you and Matthew would probably enjoy this more than your baby will, at least for now."

It was a large, soft, rectangular pillow covered with beige brushed cotton. On one side was a photograph of our dunes—including the old, black Converse sneaker—and on the reverse side a photograph of me, Matt, Will and MK on the front porch of Will's house in Duck. *That* made me cry more than any other gift of the day.

Barb, Chuck and Amy came after Mrs. Galvin, and they called Steph and Warren in Virginia, so we were all able to talk together on their speaker phone. I dozed off during that conversation.

Art and Wally Mangrum came with Joe Christopher, carrying an enormous Mangrums basket overflowing with gourmet cheeses, crackers, nuts and sausages. Art and Wally each took one of my hands, and Joe said, "Everybody in the office sends their love, Abby. They all wanted to come, but I suggested that they hold their hugs and kisses until you are able to bring your little girl in to the office. If you e-mail them some pictures, they'll be happy until they can see you in person."

I napped and nursed when I could as friends and family kept coming: Dave and Ann Connolly, who called Ken and Mel Bauman on speaker phone; Fred, Billy, Alicia and Debbie, who called Barry and Eileen and Alan and Lisa, who said they would be up to visit around Easter.

Jerry and Cheryl Brongo called and said they would probably come to Rochester in early May before Jerry had his heart surgery. Joe and Margie called about the same time and said they had left Columbus at the crack of dawn, were outside of Buffalo and would be in around five.

Matt had a permanent grin on his face all afternoon as he alternated between adding to his list and helping Kelsey wrap and unwrap Mary Elizabeth for her feedings and naps. I tried as hard as I could—as exhausted as I was—to listen to what each person said, to look into his or her eyes, to freeze mental images of everyone who came or called, to share the love I heard and saw and felt.

Danny, Emma and Sarah, and Joe and Margie all arrived together at suppertime.

"Look who we found in the elevator," Margie laughed.

Margie and Joe took lots of pictures of Mary Elizabeth and Sarah and Emma and me. Danny and Emma were wiped out after their white-knuckle drive through the snow from Boston, and they were getting ready to leave at about six o'clock, when Louise took over for Kelsey and gave Danny a full report on how well his father and I had done during the night.

Danny was impressed. "Louise says you were both champions. Abby, Dad, you were great! We'll go warm up the house for you and take care of the dogs. It looks as if they will be kicking you out in the morning, so we'll see you then. Call us if you need anything. Good night."

When we were alone with Joe and Margie, she took Evelyn's present out of her Packers tote bag and laid it lovingly in my lap. "Evelyn made this herself, Abby . . . every stitch."

It was soft and floppy, in a pale blue gift bag that was at least two feet long, with a pink bow tied around the neck of the bag. I untied the bow and looked inside, and *gasped*.

"Oh, Margie!" I slowly pulled out a Raggedy Ann-style doll about two feet tall, dressed in a full nurse's uniform. "It's amazing . . . *she's* amazing! And Evie made *everything*?"

"Everything. The doll is handmade, and *every* piece of the uniform. Evelyn has been working on this since you and Matt left Oshkosh in November."

The doll's "skin"—the soft cotton fabric—was vanilla, and Evelyn had given her rosy cheeks, with two copper freckles on each, and wavy, strawberry blond hair. She had dark green button eyes, but all of the other features on her face were stitched: her pink nose, strawberry blond eyebrows and ruby lips. She also had stitched ruby fingernails. I couldn't believe the detail and the skill . . . and the labor of love.

My doll was dressed in nurse's white from head to toe: a classic, stiff nurse's cap with a blue stripe across the front; a starched, long-sleeved, knee-length uniform coat which buttoned down the front and had huge pockets on each hip and a left breast pocket—complete with a small pen—with the name "Abigail" monogrammed in red above the pocket; and white stockings and white leather shoes with white laces and white soles.

"She's so wonderful, Margie! Nurse Abigail . . . so pretty and so perfect! She will be with Mary Elizabeth in her crib as soon as we get home tomorrow. I can't *believe* Evie did all this for me. I would like to call her now, but I'm so tired that I wouldn't be able to talk for long. Would you call her tonight for me? Thank her a million times and tell her I'll call her from home as soon as I can save up enough energy for a long conversation. Old guy, what do *you* think? Shouldn't this doll be for *you*? *You're* the one who was the hero in Oshkosh."

"Pretty girl, *you* made it happen, and Evelyn knew that. And besides, every man at some time envisions his sweetheart in a white nurse's uniform."

"Anyway," Joe added, "Flynnie would look disgusting in white shoes and stockings."

Matt held Nurse Abigail up in his hands and studied her. "She's *perfect*," he grinned, "and she gives me a great idea for our first wedding anniversary, sweetie."

"You're *such* a bad boy, Matthew Flynn . . . which is why I *love* you so much."

Joe laughed as he and Margie put their coats on. "It's time for me to take *my* girl to bed. We have had a very long day. Your baby girl is beautiful! Abby, *you* are beautiful! Matt, old buddy, you are just plain lucky. Give me a hug. We'll send some pictures of you and Mary Elizabeth to Mom and Dad and Evelyn, and we'll stop by your house tomorrow afternoon, if that's okay. We don't plan to drive back to Columbus until Monday morning."

I reached for Joe's hand.

"For sure we want you to spend the day with us. I don't know what kind of company I'll be, but Danny and Emma will be with us, and you are family now, so it will be nice. Thank you *so* much for driving all the way. Get a good night's sleep. We love you—all *three* of us."

I fondled my baby girl, all bundled and sleeping, while Matt sat next to me in bed playing with Nurse Abigail. I must have dozed off for a few minutes, and I woke up to the happy chatter of my mother and Margo as they walked into our room together.

"Hi, Matt. Hi, honey. Did we wake you? I brought somebody special. Margo called me this afternoon and asked how you were doing, so I suggested that she come in and see for herself."

"Margo, it's so lovely of you to come. Here, would you like to hold my little girl? Louise, our nurse, who was with us from start to finish, said Matt and I did pretty well. I don't remember a lot of what she said in the middle of all the action, but she did mention your name once or twice."

"Mary Elizabeth is *beautiful*, Abigail! And *you* look beautiful, too! I'm *so* happy your mom asked me to come. I talked with Louise—she's an old friend—and she told me that you and Matt both were champions and made her job easy."

"Thanks, Margo. I'm *so* glad you're here. How have the other girls been doing?"

"Great . . . a work in progress: six of the girls had their babies in the last two weeks of January; Mary Elizabeth is baby number seven. Remember Melinda and Ryan were the only couple who didn't want to know the sex of their baby? Well, she had a boy, so there will end up being eight boys and four girls from our class. Three boys and two girls are yet to come in February.

"All of the mothers and babies are doing well. Two of the boys were jaundiced and had to go back to the hospital for a day of the light treatment, but they're fine now. So far, all of the moms have said they would like to get together for a spring reunion. What do you think?"

"I love it! Let's pray that the last five deliveries go well this month, and then we can all start planning a spring party."

Mom interrupted our conversation. "I can't wait another minute. Matthew, you are playing with a very pretty nurse doll. It says 'Abigail' on her uniform. Where did she come from?"

"Mom, remember when Matt and I went to Wisconsin in November to see his ex-girlfriend?"

"How could I forget?" she replied, scowling at Matt. "That was so strange."

"Well, strange or not, it was good for Missy, and her daughter Evelyn and I became friends. Evie made me this doll—Nurse Abigail, I call her—she made it completely herself, from cap to shoes. Joe and Margie brought it all the way from Wisconsin. When we get home"—I smiled at Matt—"I'm taking Nurse Abigail away from my old guy, and she's going into our baby's crib."

Everybody laughed, including Louise who had been listening in the doorway. "I'm going to try on my old cap when I get home and see if it still fits."

Margo handed Mary Elizabeth to Mom and took a package wrapped in silver and pink from her large handbag and gave it to me.

"This is for you, Abby. I don't usually give presents to my students, so don't say anything to the other girls, but I couldn't resist this one for you."

It was an old hardbound edition of *Jane Eyre*, with a wood engraving on the cover showing a double line of young women walking in their dark capes and bonnets outside of Lowood. I turned it over, looked at Margo and opened it carefully. It was a 1943 Random House edition with wood engravings throughout by Fritz Eichenberg. The pages, surprisingly, were not brittle or torn, and the drawings were magnificent.

"Margo, it's wonderful! Thank you so much! It's beautiful! Where did you *find* it?"

"I've been hunting in antique bookstores ever since you told me you were reading *Jane Eyre* to Mary Elizabeth. I finally found this when I went at Christmas to visit my daughter in Pittsburgh."

The seven of us—counting Louise and Nurse Abigail—spent a delightful hour sharing delivery and nurse stories and remembrances of girls growing up; helping Mary Elizabeth and me with our breastfeeding; marveling at the heart and skill that created Nurse Abigail; and mellowing in what could only be described as heaven on earth.

No person—from your mother to your best friend to your favorite teacher—could ever anticipate or predict or promise for a young girl such an hour in her life—*ever*. I don't believe it happens to many people. I was so much in awe of the moment and stimulated by the laughter and love in the room, that I was more energized than I had been all day—even though my mind knew that my body should be exhausted. My mind actually seemed to be disconnected from my body, as if I were looking down over myself and every other person in the room—the very same sensation I had the first night Matt and I made love.

Louise broke the exhilarating spell when she had to leave for a doctor's call. Mary Elizabeth was making soft little noises in Mom's arms; Margo was playing with Nurse Abigail's uniform; and Matt was on his cell phone with Claire and Emma. *I'm going to get really tired really fast*, I thought. *It's time for Matt and me and Mary Elizabeth*. I gave *Jane Eyre* to Matt.

"Mom, may I have my baby girl back?"

"Here's your sweet bundle, honey. Will you need my help tomorrow?"

"I don't think so, Mom. Claire and Matt are coming in the morning to help bring everything home, and Danny and Emma will have the house ready for us, so we should be fine. I'll probably need the whole day to crash and sleep as much as Mary

Elizabeth will let me. I think Tuesday or Wednesday should be good for Grandma and Grandpa to visit."

"We'll plan on that, Abby. And you'll call if you need anything, right?"

"For sure, Mom."

My mother kissed the top of her granddaughter's head and kissed me on my forehead.

"Abigail Elizabeth, your father and I are very proud of you."

"Thank you, Mom, and thanks again for bringing Margo. Hey, *teach*," I teased, "are you done playing with my doll?"

Margo laughed. "*Shush*, Abigail. I'm having fun. Nobody ever made *me* one of these. I'll call you in a couple of weeks and let you know about the rest of the February girls. You can call me, too, if you need anything."

"You've already helped me *so* much, Margo. And Mom, you have been my rock. I love you both," I yawned, "but I'm fading fast. Would you mind leaving us now . . . please?" I put on my cutest "mischievous girl" face. "Mary Elizabeth wants to have a heart-to-heart conversation with her daddy and me."

After they left, laughing as they closed the door, I unbundled my baby girl and laid her on my belly under the pink sheet. Matt was standing at the head of the bed in his sky blue paper robe and matching slippers, sipping coffee from his old blue Yellowstone mug.

"Matt . . . Matthew Howard Flynn, stop grinning like the Cheshire Cat. What are you wearing under that sexy gown, sweetie?"

"Just a T-shirt and my checked boxer shorts from Duck."

"Well, take them off, summer boy. Take off that gown and those silly slippers. Get in bed. Put your head on our pillow, Daddy, and lie with me and your little girl."

When Matt was under the sheet next to me, I laid Mary Elizabeth on his chest and rolled on my right side and curled my left leg over his. I stretched my right arm under Matt's head and stroked our baby with my left hand while he looked at her in awe.

"Old guy, I love you so much. I love you more every day— every single day—ever since the first day. And now I love our baby girl so much. And I know I'm going to love her more and more every day—every single day—until the last day. I can't believe I have all this love inside me. *You* did it. You opened me up and uncovered the woman and all the love inside me. Matt, sometimes I feel so much love that I can't breathe."

Mary Elizabeth was asleep now on his chest. Matt was looking at me with his "little boy on Christmas morning" face. I kissed his cheek and played with his hair and touched his lips with my fingers.

"Old guy," I whispered, "let's do it again."

The author with his nine-year-old Scottie, Jennie

Robert Quinn was born in Rochester, New York, in July 1946, and claims to be the first post-World War II Baby Boom baby. He was raised in a nurturing blue-collar family and won every spelling bee he ever entered. He graduated with a B.A. in English Lit from Boston College in 1968 when all hell was breaking loose in America. He joined the Air Force and was sent to Vietnam where he avoided the bar girls and the STDs, the black market and the drugs, and where he was bombed only once (for which he was awarded a Purple Heart). He came home happy, healthy and craving a *Big Mac.*

Bob worked as a mailman for two years to save money for law school, then worked in the usual law firms, got into politics, married a redhead and had two sons. Ten years later, he changed course to the insurance and investment business, married his second (and final) redhead, had four beautiful grandchildren, and learned to cherish, admire and imitate Scottish terriers.

* * *

For additional copies of *Abby* or to arrange a book signing, contact Bob at abbyandtheoldguy@gmail.com. The book is also available at Amazon.com.

19669343R00298

Made in the USA
Middletown, DE
06 December 2018